W9-CGU-376

Hammond Innes:

THREE
- IN -
ONE

Hammond Innes:

THREE
- IN -
ONE

The Land God Gave to Cain

The Doomed Oasis

Atlantic Fury

Alfred · A · Knopf   NEW YORK   1970

THIS IS A BORZOI BOOK
PUBLISHED BY ALFRED A. KNOPF, INC.

Copyright © 1958, 1962, 1970 by Hammond Innes
Copyright © 1960 by William Hammond Innes
All rights reserved under International and Pan-American Copyright
Conventions. Published in the United States by Alfred A. Knopf, Inc.,
New York. Distributed by Random House, Inc., New York.

Library of Congress Catalog Card Number: 77–118710

Manufactured in the United States of America

The Land God Gave to Cain, published 1958.
The Doomed Oasis, published 1960.
Atlantic Fury, published 1962.
FIRST COLLECTED EDITION

Contents

THE LAND
GOD GAVE TO
CAIN

A Novel of Labrador

THIS BOOK IS DEDICATED TO THE MEMORY OF

My Mother

Who died whilst I was in Canada

Foreword

THE LAND GOD GAVE TO CAIN *is the result of two journeys
I made into Labrador. The first was in 1953, just before the big freeze-up. At that time the "Iron Ore Railway" was still under construction, steel having been laid
only as far north as Mile 250. I saw the whole of it, from
the terminal at Seven Islands on the St. Lawrence to the
geologist's camp of Burnt Creek, four hundred miles into
the interior, living in the construction camps and travelling first by train and track motor, then by truck and
car and on foot, and finally by the bush pilots' floatplanes,
and even by helicopter.*

*That I was able to cover so much ground, and see so
much of a country that hardly a white man had seen
before the railway came, was due in the first place to
Hollinger-Hanna, the Iron Ore Company of Canada, and
the Quebec North Shore and Labrador Railway, and I
am greatly indebted to these companies for the exceptional
facilities they gave me, and for their kindness in insisting
that I should be their guest in the camps.*

*Once having been granted these facilities, it was left
to me to make my own way, and in this I was never without friends—particularly amongst the engineers with
whom I lived. There were the pilots, too, and the radio
operators, and the men themselves; without exception
they put themselves to great trouble and personal inconvenience to give me as complete a picture as possible of*

this astonishing project. They are too numerous to mention individually, but should they read this, I would like them to know that I remember them vividly and with affection, for they were very real people. I would also like to make it clear that, whilst I have had to make use of certain executive titles, the names and characters of the men occupying these positions in the book, and their actions, are purely imaginary.

The second visit was made three years later when the book was half completed. I was on my way up to the Eskimo country to the northwest of Hudson Bay and I stopped off at Goose—primarily to check up on my description of this isolated community, and also to work out a satisfactory basis for the expedition's radio link. Here Mr. Douglas Ritcey of Goose Radio, who is himself a "ham" operator, was most helpful, and I would like to record that he has allowed me to use his own radio set-up as the basis of Ledder's.

Altogether I travelled some fifteen thousand miles in quest of the material for this book—one of the most interesting journeys I have undertaken. I sincerely hope that in the result I have achieved my purpose of conveying a picture of one of the last great railways to be built, the sort of men who built it, and, not least of all, some idea of the bleak and desolate nature of Labrador itself.

Part One

The Radio Message

I

"Your name Ian Ferguson?"

The question was flung at me out of a cloud of dust, and
I straightened up from the theodolite to find one of the
company Land-Rovers had pulled in behind me. The
engine was ticking over and the driver was leaning out so
that his sun-reddened face was clear of the windscreen.
"All right. Hop in, chum. You're wanted down at company office."

"What's it about?"

"I dunno. Said it was urgent and sent me up to get
you. Probably you got your levels wrong and the runway's
on the skew." He grinned. He was always trying to get a
rise out of the younger engineers. I entered the figures in
my notebook, shouted to my rod-holder that I wouldn't
be long, and clambered in, and then we drove off across
the rough ground, trailing a streamer of dust behind us.

The company office was just where the old runway
finished and our new construction began. It was a large
wooden hut with a corrugated iron roof, and as I went in
the place was like an oven, for it was very hot in England
that September.

"Oh, there you are, Ferguson." Mr. Meadows, the chief
engineer, came to meet me. "Afraid I've some bad news
for you." The roar of an aircraft taking off shook the hut,

and through it I heard him say: "Telegram for you. Just came through on the phone." He handed me a sheet of paper.

I took it with a sudden feeling of foreboding. I knew it must be my father. The message was written in pencil. *Please come home at once. Dad taken very bad. Love. Mother.*

"When's the next train to London—do you know, sir?"

He glanced at his watch. "In about half an hour. You might just make it." His voice sounded undecided. "I find you had leave about three months ago on account of your father. You're quite certain it's serious? I mean—"

"I'm sorry, sir. I'll have to go." And then, because he remained silent, I felt I had to explain. "My father was badly shot up on a bombing mission during the war. He was a radio operator, and he got a shell in the back of the neck. His legs are paralysed, and he can't speak. The brain was damaged, too."

"I'm sorry. I didn't know." Mr. Meadows's pale eyes looked hurt. "Of course you must go. I'll have one of the Land-Rovers take you down."

I just caught the train, and three hours later I was in London. All the way up I had been thinking of my father and wishing I could remember him as he had been when I was a kid. But I couldn't. The broken, inarticulate wreck that I had grown up with overshadowed all my early memories, and I was left with the general impression of a big, friendly man. I had only been six when he joined the R.A.F. and went away to the war.

When I was at home I'd go and sit with him sometimes in that upstairs room where he had the radio. But he lived in a world of his own, and though he would converse by passing notes to me, I always had the impression that I was intruding. The neighbours thought him a bit balmy, and so he was in a way, sitting up there day after day in his wheelchair contacting other "ham" radio operators.

It was mostly Canada he contacted, and once when I was curious and wanted to know why, he'd got excited; his shattered larynx had produced queer incoherent noises, and his big, heavy face had reddened with the effort of trying to communicate something to me. I remember I had asked him to write down what he was trying to tell me, but the note he passed me simply said: *Too complicated. It's a long story.* His eyes had gone to the shelf where he kept his Labrador books, and an oddly frustrated look came over his face. And after that I had always been conscious when I was up there of the books and the big map of Labrador that hung on the wall above the transmitter. It wasn't a printed map. He'd drawn it himself whilst in hospital.

I was thinking of this as I hurried down the familiar street, wondering whether there was any solid reason for his interest in Labrador or whether it was something to do with his mental state. A shell had ripped open his skull, and the doctors had said the brain was permanently injured, though they'd done a good job of patching him up. The sun had set now, and all our side of the street was black in shadow, so that it was like a wall of brick. The uniformity of it all saddened me, and unconsciously I slowed my pace, remembering that room and the Morse key on the table and how he'd insisted on having the station's call sign painted on the door. Mother didn't really understand him. She hadn't his education, and she couldn't see his desperate need of that radio room.

I think I knew I wasn't ever going to see him in that room again. Our house had its gate and door painted red, which was all that distinguished it from its neighbours, and as I approached I saw that the upstairs blinds were drawn.

My mother came to the door and greeted me quietly. "I'm glad you've come, Ian." She wasn't crying. She just looked tired, that was all. "You saw the blinds, didn't you? I would have told you in the telegram, but I wasn't certain. I got Mrs. Wright from next door to send it. I had to wait for the doctor." Her voice was lifeless and without emotion. She had come to the end of a long road.

At the foot of the stairs she said: "You'd like to see him, I expect." She took me straight up to the darkened room and left me there. "Come down when you're ready. I'll make you a pot of tea. You must be tired after the journey."

He was lying stretched out on the bed, and the furrows of his face, that had been so deep-etched by years of pain, seemed to have been miraculously smoothed out. He looked at peace, and in a way I felt glad for him. I stood there a long time, thinking of the fight he'd made of it— seeing him, I think, clearly for the first time as a brave and gallant man. Anger and bitterness stirred in me then at the rotten deal he'd had from life and the unfair way others get through a war scot-free. I was a little confused, and in the end I knelt beside his bed and tried to pray. And then I kissed the cold, smooth forehead and tiptoed out and went down the stairs to join my mother in the parlour.

She was sitting with the tea table in front of her, staring at it without seeing it. She looked old and very frail. It had been a hard life for her. "It's almost a relief, Mother, isn't it?"

She looked at me then. "Yes, dear. I've been expecting it ever since he had that stroke three months ago. If he had been content to just lie in bed . . . but he would get up every day and wheel himself along to that room. And he'd be there till all hours, particularly lately. The last week or so, he couldn't seem to leave the wireless alone." She always called it the wireless.

And then, when she had poured my tea, she told me how it had happened. "It was very strange, and I wouldn't dream of telling the doctor. He'd never believe me, and he'd want to give me pills or something. Even now I'm not sure I didn't imagine it. I was sitting down here, sewing, when I suddenly heard your Dad call out to me. 'Mother!' he called. And then something else. I couldn't say what it was, for he was up in that room and he had the door shut as usual. But I could have sworn he called out 'Mother,' and when I got up to the wireless room I found him standing up. He had forced himself up out of his chair, and his face was all red and mottled with the effort he was making."

"You mean he was standing up on his own?" It was incredible. My father hadn't stood in years.

"Yes. He was leaning on the table and reaching out with his right hand. To the wall, I think. For support," she added quickly. And then she said: "He turned his head and saw me and tried to say something. And then his face became all twisted with pain. He gave a sort of strangled cry, and all his body went suddenly limp and he fell down. I don't know when exactly he died. I laid him on the floor and made him as comfortable as possible." She began to cry quietly.

I went over to her and she clung to me whilst I did my best to comfort her, and all the time the picture of my father's struggle to stand stayed in my mind. "What made him suddenly make such a desperate effort?" I asked.

"Nothing." She looked up at me quickly with such a strange, protective look that I wondered.

"But it must have been something. And to find his voice like that—suddenly after all these years."

"I can't be certain. I may have imagined it. I think I must have."

"But just now you said you were positive he called out to you. Besides, you went up there. He must have called out. And to find him on his feet; there must have been some compelling reason."

"Oh, I don't know. Your dad was like that. He never would give up. The doctor thinks—"

"Had he got his earphones on when you went in?"

"Yes. But . . . Where are you going, Ian?"

I didn't answer, for I was already through the door and running up the stairs. I was thinking of the map of Labrador. She had found my father standing at the table, reaching out to the wall—and that was where the map hung. Or perhaps he had been trying to reach the bookshelf. It was below the map, and it contained nothing but the books on Labrador. He was fascinated by the country. It was an obsession with him.

I turned left at the top of the stairs, and there was the door with STATION G2STO stencilled on it. It was so familiar that, as I pushed it open, I couldn't believe I wouldn't find him seated there in front of the radio. But the wheelchair was empty, swivelled back against the wall, and the desk where he always sat was unnaturally tidy, the usual litter of notebooks, magazines, and newspapers all cleared away and stacked neatly on top of the transmitter. I searched quickly through them, but there was no message, nothing.

I had been so certain I should find a message, or at least some indication of what had happened, that I stood at a loss for a moment, looking round the small den that had been his world for so long. It was all very familiar, and yet it had a strangeness because he was no longer there to give it point. Only that had changed. All the rest remained—the school pictures, the caps, the wartime photographs, and the bits and pieces of planes with the scribbled signatures of the air crews who had been his companions. And over by the door hung the same faded picture of my grandmother, Alexandra Ferguson, her strong face unsmiling and yellowed above the tight-buttoned bodice.

I stared at it, wondering whether she would have known the answer. I had often seen him glance at the picture—or was it at the things that hung below it, the rusted pistol, the sextant, the broken paddle, and the torn canvas case with the moth-eaten fur cap hanging over it? Alexandra Ferguson was his mother. She had brought him up, and somehow I'd always known those relics beneath the photograph belonged to the north of Canada, though I couldn't remember anybody ever telling me so.

I dug back in my memory to the vague impression of a grey, bleak house somewhere in the north of Scotland and a terrifying old woman who had come to me in the night. The photograph didn't recall her to my mind, for all I remembered was a disembodied face hanging over me in the flickering flame of the nightlight, a cold, bitter, desiccated face, and then my mother had come in and they had shouted at each other until I had screamed with fear. We had left next morning, and, as though by common consent, neither my mother nor my father had ever mentioned her to me again.

I turned back to the room, the memory of that scene still vivid. And then I was looking at the radio receiver and the Morse key with the pencil lying beside it, and the memory faded. These were the things that now dominated all the bits and pieces of his life. Together they represented all that had been left to him, and somehow I felt that, as his son, I should have enough understanding of him to wring from them the thing that had driven him to such a superhuman effort.

I think it was the pencil that made me realize something was missing. There should have been a log book. He always kept a radio log. Not a proper one, of course; just a cheap exercise book in which he jotted things down—station frequencies and their times of broadcast-

ing, scraps of weather forecasts or ships' talk or anything
from Canada, all mixed up with little drawings and anything else that came to his mind.

I found several of these exercise books in the drawer
of the table, but they didn't include the current one. The
latest entry in these books was for September 15, a page
of doodling in which it was almost impossible to decipher
anything coherent at all. Drawings of lions seemed to
predominate, and in one place he had written: C_2—
C_2—C_2 . . . *where the hell is that?* The scrawled line of
a song caught my eye—*LOST AND GONE FOR EVER*
—and he had ringed it round with a series of names—
*Winokapau-Tishinakamau-Attikonak-Winokapau-Tishi-
nakamau-Attikonak*—repeated over and over again as a
sort of decoration.

Turning back through the pages of these old log books,
I found they were all like that—a queer mixture of
thoughts and fancies that made me realize how lonely he
had been up there in that room and how desperately
turned in upon himself. But here and there I picked out
dates and times, and gradually a pattern emerged. Every
day there was an entry for 2200 hours, undoubtedly the
same station transmitting, for the entry was nearly always
followed by the call sign VO6AZ, and on one page he had
written *VO6AZ came through as usual.* Later I found the
name Ledder occurring—*Ledder reports* or *Ledder again*,
in place of the call sign. The word *expedition* occurred
several times.

It is difficult to convey the impression these muddled
pages made. They were such an extraordinary mixture
of fact and nonsense, of what he had heard over the air
and the things that came into his mind, all patterned
and half obliterated with childish lines and squiggles
and odd names and little drawings with the shape of a
lion repeated and repeated in page after page. A psychiatrist would probably say that it was all symptomatic of

cerebral damage, and yet most people doodle when they are much alone with their thoughts, and through it all ran the thread of these reports from VO6AZ.

I turned to the bookcase behind me, which housed his technical library, and took down the *Radio Amateur Call Book*. This I knew listed all the world's ham operators under their different countries, together with their call signs and addresses. He had explained the call-sign system to me once. The prefix gave the location. G, for instance, was the prefix for all British hams. I started to look up Canada, but the book fell open almost automatically at Labrador and I saw that VO6 was the prefix for this area. Against the call sign VO6AZ appeared the names Simon & Ethel Ledder, % D.O.T. Communications, Goose Bay.

The knowledge that he had been in regular contact with Labrador drew me again to the map hanging above the transmitter, the names he had written on that last page running through my head—Winokapau-Tishinakamau-Attikonak. It was like the opening of Turner's poem, and, leaning forward across the desk, I saw that he had made some pencil markings on the map. I was certain they hadn't been there when I'd last been in the room with him. A line had been drawn from the Indian settlement of Seven Islands on the St. Lawrence, running north into the middle of Labrador, and against it were pencilled the initials *Q.N.S. & L.R.* To the right of it, about halfway up, an almost blank area of the map had been ringed, and here he had written *Lake of the Lion* with a large question mark after it.

I had just noticed *Attikonak L.* inked in against the outline of a large, sprawling lake when the door behind me opened and there was a little gasp. I turned to find my mother standing there with a frightened look on her face. "What's the matter?" I asked.

She seemed to relax at the sound of my voice. "You

did give me a turn. I thought for a moment—" She
checked herself, and I realized suddenly that this was
how my father had stood, leaning on the table and reaching over towards the map of Labrador.

"It was the map, wasn't it?" I was excited by the sudden certainty that it was the map that had drawn him to
his feet.

A shadow seemed to cross her face. Her gaze had
fastened on the log books strewn on the table. "What are
you doing up here, Ian?"

But I was remembering something a Canadian pilot
had told me at the airfield—something about a party lost
in Labrador and Canadian Air Force planes searching for
them. The references to an expedition in the log books,
the map and my father's obsession with Labrador, and that
sudden frightened look on my mother's face—it was all
coming together in my mind. "Mother," I said. "There
was a message, wasn't there?"

She looked at me then and her face went blank. "I don't
know what you mean, dear. Why don't you come down
and finish your tea? Try to forget about it."

But I shook my head. "You do know what I mean," I
said, and I went over to her and took hold of her hands.
They were cold as ice, "What did you do with his log
book?"

"His log book?" She stared at me, and I could feel her
trembling. "Aren't they all there?"

"You know they aren't. The current one—it's missing.
What have you done with it?"

"Nothing, dear. You don't understand—I was too
busy. It's been a terrible day . . . terrible." She began
to cry gently.

"Please," I said. "All the log books are there except
the current one. It should have been on the table beside
the Morse key. He always kept it there, and now it's
gone."

"He may have thrown it away. Or perhaps he'd forgotten to keep it for a time. You know how your father was. He was like a child." But she wouldn't look at me, and I knew she was hiding something.

"What have you done with it, Mother?" I shook her gently. "He received some sort of a message. Something to do with Labrador."

"Labrador!" The word seemed to explode out of her mouth. Her eyes had widened and she was staring at me. "Not you, too, Ian. Please God. Not you. All my life—" Her voice trailed away. "Now come down and have your tea, there's a good boy. I can't take any more—not today."

I can remember the weariness in her voice, the note of pleading—and how cruel I was. "You never understood him, did you, Mother?" I said that to her, and I believed it. "If you'd understood him, you'd know there was only one thing would drive him to call out, struggling to his feet and reaching out for the map. It was the map he was reaching out to, wasn't it?" And I shook her gently whilst she just stared at me with a sort of fascination. I told her then about the planes searching for a geological party lost in Labrador. "Whatever Dad may have been during these last few years, he was still a first-class radio operator. If he picked up some sort of a message from them . . ." I had to make her see it my way—how important it could be. "Those men's lives might depend on it," I said.

She shook her head slowly. "You don't know," she murmured. "You can't know." And she added: "It was all in his imagination."

"Then he did pick up a message?"

"He imagined things. You've been away so much . . . you don't know what went on in his mind."

"He didn't imagine this," I said. "It made him suddenly find his voice. It forced him to his feet, and the

effort killed him." I was being intentionally brutal. If
my father had killed himself in an effort to save other
men's lives, then I wasn't going to have his effort go for
nothing, whatever my mother's reason for concealing it.
"Look—I'm sorry," I said, "but I must have that log
book." And when she only stared at me with a sort of
dumb misery in her eyes, I said: "He wrote the message
down in it, didn't he? Didn't he, Mother?" I was ex-
asperated by her attitude. "For God's sake! Where is it?
Please, Mother—you must let me see it!"

A defeated look showed in her face, and she gave a
tired little sigh. "Very well, Ian. If you must have it . . ."
She turned then and went slowly out of the room. "I'll
get it for you."

I went with her because I had an instinctive feeling
that if I didn't she might destroy it. I couldn't understand her attitude at all. I could literally feel her reluctance as I followed her down the stairs.

She had hidden it under the table linen in one of the
drawers of the sideboard, and as she handed it to me she
said: "You won't do anything foolish, now, will you?"

But I didn't answer her. I had seized hold of the
exercise book and was already seated at the table, leafing
through the pages. It was much the same as the others,
except that the entries were more factual, with fewer
doodles, and the word *search* caught my eye several times.

And then I was staring at the last entry on a page
clear of all other jottings: *CQ—CQ—CQ—Any 75-metre
phone station—Any 75-metre phone station—Come in
someone please—Come in someone please—K.*

There it was in my father's laboured hand, and the
desperation of that cry called to me through the shaky
pencilled words in that tattered child's exercise book.
And underneath he had written *Briffe—It must be.* And
the date and the time: *September 29, 1355—voice very
faint.* Voice very faint! And below that, with the time

given as 1405: *Calling again. CQ—CQ—CQ etc. Still no
reply.* Then the final entry: *Calling VO6AZ now. Position
not known but within 30 miles radius C2—situation desperate—injured and no fire—Baird very bad—Laroche
gone—CQ—CQ—CQ—Can hardly hear him—Search for
narrow lake (obliterated)—Repeating . . . narrow lake
with rock shaped like . . .* The message ended there in
a straggling line as though the pencil point had slipped
as he made the effort to stand.

Injured and no fire! I sat there, staring at the pencilled
words, a vivid picture in my mind of a narrow desolate
lake and an injured man crouched over a radio set.
Situation desperate. I could imagine it. The nights would
be bitter, and in the daytime they'd be plagued with a
million flies. I'd read about it in those books of my
father's. And the vital part was missing—the bit that had
brought my father to his feet.

"What are you going to do?" My mother's voice
sounded nervous, almost frightened.

"Do?" I hadn't thought about it. I was still wondering
what it was that had so galvanized my father. "Mum.
Do you know why Dad was so interested in Labrador?"

"No."

The denial was so quick, so determined, that I looked
up at her. Her face was very pale, a little haggard in the
gathering dusk. "When did it start?" I asked.

"Oh, a long time ago. Before the war."

"So it wasn't anything to do with his being shot up?"
I got up from the chair I had been sitting in. "Surely you
must know the reason for it. In all these years he must
have told you why—"

But she had turned away. "I'm going to get supper,"
she said, and I watched her go out through the door,
puzzled by her attitude.

Alone, I began thinking again about those men lost in
Labrador. Briffe—that was the name Farrow had talked

about in the Airport Bar. Briffe was the leader of some
sort of geological expedition, and I wondered what one
did in a case like this. Suppose nobody but my father
had picked up that message. But then they were bound
to have heard it in Canada. If Dad had picked it up at
a distance of over two thousand miles . . . But, according to Dad, Goose Bay hadn't replied. And if by some
queer chance he had been the only radio operator in the
world to pick that message up, then I was the thread on
which those men's lives hung.

It was an appalling thought, and I worried about it
all through supper—far more, I think, than about my
father's death, for I couldn't do anything about that.
When we had finished the meal I said to my mother: "I
think I'll just walk as far as the call box."

"Who are you going to phone?"

"I don't know." Who did one ring? There was Canada
House. They were really the people to tell, but they'd be
closed now. "The police, I suppose."

"Do you have to do anything about it?" She was standing there, wringing her hands.

"Well, yes," I said. "I think somebody ought to know."
And then, because I still didn't understand her attitude,
I asked her why she'd tried to hide the message from me.

"I didn't know if you—" She hesitated, and then said
quickly: "I didn't want your father laughed at."

"Laughed at? Really, Mother! Suppose nobody else
picked up this transmission. If these men died, then you'd
have been responsible."

Her face went blank. "I didn't want them laughing at
him," she repeated obstinately. "You know what people
are in a street like this."

"This is more important than what people think." My
tone was impatient. And then, because I knew she was
upset and tired, I kissed her. "We shan't be bothered
about it," I reassured her. "It's just that I feel that I

must report it. It wouldn't be the first time he picked up a transmission that no other operator received," I added, and I went out of the house and back along the street to the Underground.

I had no idea who I should ask for at Scotland Yard, so in the end I dialled 999. It seemed odd to be making an emergency police call when we hadn't been burgled or anything. And when I got through to them I found it wasn't easy to explain what it was all about. It meant telling them about my father and the "ham" radio station he operated. The fact that he had just died because of his excitement over the message only made it more confusing.

However, in the end they said they had got it all clear and would contact the Canadian authorities, and I left the call box feeling that a weight had been lifted from my shoulders. It was their responsibility now. I needn't worry about it any more. And when I got back to the house, I put the log book away in my suitcase and went through into the kitchen, where my mother was washing dishes. Now that the matter of the message was cleared up and the authorities notified, I began to see it from her point of view. After all, why should she worry about two men in a distant part of the world when my father was lying dead upstairs?

That night my mother had the little bedroom, and I slept on the couch in the parlour. And in the morning I woke to the realization that there was a lot to be done— the funeral to arrange, all his things to go through, and the pension people to be notified. I hadn't realized before that death didn't end with sorrow.

After breakfast I sent a wire to Mr. Meadows and then went to arrange things with the undertaker. When I got back it was almost eleven and Mrs. Wright was in from next door having tea with my mother. It was Mrs. Wright who heard the car draw up and went to the window to see. "Why, it's a police car," she said. And then added: "I do believe they're coming here."

It was a police inspector and a Flight Lieutenant Mathers of the Canadian Air Force. They wanted to see the log book, and when I'd got it from my suitcase and handed it to the Inspector, I found myself apologizing for the writing. "I'm afraid it's not very good. You see, my father was paralysed, and—"

"Yes, we know all about that," the Inspector said. "We've made enquiries, naturally." He was no longer looking at the page on which the message had been written, but was leafing back through the log book, the Flight Lieutenant peering over his shoulder. I began to feel uncomfortable then. The pages were such a muddle, and in the Inspector's hands the log looked exactly what it was, a child's exercise book. I remembered my mother's words: *I didn't want your father laughed at.*

When he had examined every page, the Inspector turned back to the one on which the message was written. "I think you said that your father died immediately after writing this?"

I explained to him what had happened—how my mother thought she heard him call out to her and went up to find he had somehow struggled to his feet. And when I had finished, he said: "But you weren't here at the time?"

"No. My job is near Bristol. I wasn't here."

"Who was here? Just your mother?"

"Yes."

He nodded. "Well, I'm afraid I'll have to have a word with her. But first we'd like to have a look at the room where your father had his radio."

I took them up, and the Flight Lieutenant had a look at the radio whilst the Inspector prowled round, looking at the books and the map hanging on the wall. "Well, it's all in working order," the Flight Lieutenant said.

He had switched on the receiver and he had the earphones over his head whilst his fingers played with the tuning dial. But by then the Inspector had found the old log books in the drawer and was glancing through them.

At length he turned to me. "I'm sorry to have to ask you this, Mr. Ferguson, but we've talked to the doctor, and I understand your father had a stroke some three months ago. You were down here then?"

"Yes," I said. "But only for a few days. He made a very quick recovery."

"Have you been here since?"

"No," I told him. "We're on airfield construction at the moment. It's a rush job, and I haven't had another chance—"

"What I'm getting at is this. . . . Can you vouch for your father's mental state? Could he have imagined this?"

"No. Certainly not." I felt suddenly angry. "If you're suggesting that my father . . ." I stopped then, because I realized what must have prompted the question. "Do you mean to say nobody else picked up that transmission?"

"Not as far as we know." He turned to the Flight Lieutenant. "However, there's no doubt he was following the progress of this expedition," he said. "There are dozens of references to it in these notebooks, but . . ." He hesitated, and then gave a little shrug. "Well, take a look for yourself." He passed the books across to the Canadian. I might not have been there as the Air Force officer bent down to examine them and the Inspector watched him, waiting for his reaction.

At length I could stand it no longer. "What's wrong with the message?" I asked.

"Nothing, nothing—except . . ." The Inspector hesitated.

The Flight Lieutenant looked up from the log books. "We're not doubting he was in touch with Ledder, you know." His voice held a note of reservation, and as though

conscious of this he added: "I checked with our people
at Goose right away. Simon Ledder and his wife are both
registered hams operating their own station under the
call sign VO6AZ. They take on outside work, and in this
case they were acting as base station for the McGovern
Mining and Exploration Company, receiving Briffe's reports by R/T and transmitting them to the Company's
offices in Montreal."

"Well, then?" I didn't understand why they were still
doubtful about it. "The fact that nobody else picked up
the transmission—"

"It's not that," he said quickly. And he looked across
at the Inspector, who said: "I'm sorry, Mr. Ferguson.
All this must be very trying for you." He sounded apologetic. "But the fact is that Briffe and the man with him
were reported dead—almost a week ago, didn't you say,
Mathers?" He looked across at the Canadian.

"That's so, Inspector." The Flight Lieutenant nodded.
"On September twenty-fifth, to be exact." He tossed the
log books on to the table. "I don't want to seem un-
appreciative," he said, looking across at me. "Particularly
as you say your father's excitement at receiving the message was the cause of his death. But the fact is that Bert
Laroche, the pilot of the crashed plane, trekked out on
his own. He reached one of the construction camps of
the Iron Ore Railway on the twenty-fifth and reported
that the other two were dead when he left them. He'd
been five days trekking out, so they were dead by September twentieth. Now you come along with the information that your father picked up a radio broadcast from
Briffe yesterday. That's nine whole days after Briffe was
dead." He shook his head. "It just doesn't make sense."

"The pilot might have made a mistake," I murmured.

He stared at me with a sort of shocked look. "I guess
you don't understand the Canadian North, Mr. Ferguson.
Men just don't make that sort of mistake. Certainly not

experienced fliers like Bert Laroche." And he added:
"He crashed his Beaver floatplane into a rock trying to
land on a lake in a snowstorm. Briffe and Baird were
injured. He got them ashore, and the plane sank. That
was on September fourteenth. Baird died almost immediately, Briffe a few days later, and then he started to trek
out."

"But the message," I cried. "How else could my father
have known—"

"It was all in the newscasts," Mathers said. "The whole
story—it was repeated over and over again."

"But not about the lake, surely," I said impatiently.
"How would my father know it was a lake with a rock
in it? And how would he know about Briffe and Baird
being injured and the pilot gone?"

"I tell you, Briffe and Baird were dead by then."

"Are you suggesting he made it all up?"

Mathers shrugged his shoulders and reached for the
last of the log books, turning the pages until he came
to the message. He stared at it for a long time. "It just
isn't possible," he murmured. "If your father picked up
a transmission, why didn't someone else?"

"You've checked, have you?"

"We're checking now. But, believe me, if anybody in
Canada had picked it up, they'd have reported it immediately. The papers were full of the search when it
was on."

"I can't help that," I said. "Maybe nobody else picked
it up. But my father did. The message is there in that
log book to prove it." He made no comment. He was
looking back again through the old log books. "I remember once," I added desperately, "my father picked up a
message from a yacht in the Timor Sea when nobody
else did. And another time he made a contact—"

"But this is R/T. How could he possibly pick up Voice
from an old set like Briffe's?" The Flight Lieutenant

was still riffling through the pages of the logs, but now
he suddenly closed them. "There's only one explanation,
I guess." He said it to the Inspector, who nodded agreement.

I knew what he meant, and I was furious. I'd done
what I thought was right, and here were these two
strangers trying to make out that my father was crazy.
I wished to God I'd never reported the matter. My
mother had been right. How could I possibly make them
understand that a lonely man could scribble a lot of
nonsense all over those log books and yet be reliable
when it came to picking up a transmission? "Surely somebody else must have picked the message up," I said
helplessly. And then, because they didn't say anything
but stood there looking uncomfortable, I let my feelings
run away with me. "You think my father made it all
up, don't you? Just because he had a head wound and
was paralysed and drew little pictures in those books,
you think he isn't to be relied on. But you're wrong.
My father was a first-class radio operator. Whatever the
doctors or anybody else may say, he'd never make a
mistake over a message like that."

"Maybe," the Canadian said. "But we're two thousand
five hundred miles from Labrador, and Briffe wasn't on
Key, he was on Voice transmission—in other words, radio
telephone."

"That's what my father implies. He says it's Briffe's
voice he's hearing."

"Sure. But I've already checked on this, and all Briffe
had was an old wartime forty-eight set. That's the Canadian equivalent of your British Army eighteen set. It
had been modified to operate on the seventy-five-metre
phone band, but he was still using it in conjunction with
a hand generator. Even with a line aerial instead of a
whip, Goose would have been just about at the limit of

his range—that's why he was reporting back to Ledder instead of direct to Montreal."

"I don't know about that," I said. "But I do know this. See all those books up there? They're about Labrador. My father was fascinated by the place. He knew what it would be like for those men lost out there. He knew that message was important. That's why he suddenly found his voice and called out. That's what forced him to his feet when he hadn't stood—"

"Just a minute," the Flight Lieutenant said. "You don't seem to understand what I've been trying to tell you. Those men are dead. They've been dead more than nine days."

"But that message . . ."

"There wasn't any message." He said it quietly, and then added: "See here, Ferguson. I'm sorry about your father. But let's be practical. We had four planes searching for almost a week. Then Laroche came out and reported the other two dead, and we called off the search. Now you want me to advise a resumption of a full-scale search, involving machines and fliers in hours of duty over desolate country, just because your father wrote down a message in an exercise book before he died—a message that, even if it had been transmitted, it was technically impossible for him to pick up."

There wasn't anything I could say to that. "If it's technically impossible . . ."

"He was more than two thousand miles outside of normal range. Of course," he added, "there's always the chance of freak reception, even at that distance, and, just in case, I'm having enquiries made of all ham operators in Canada. I've also asked for a full report from Ledder. I think you can be quite sure that if any transmission was made on the twenty-ninth, then we'll find somebody who picked it up."

The Inspector nodded. "If you don't mind, I'll keep these notebooks for the time being." He picked them up off the table. "I'd like to have them examined by our experts."

"No," I said. "I don't mind." It seemed useless to say anything more. And yet . . . My eyes strayed to the map of Labrador. He'd forced himself to his feet in order to look at it. Why? What had been in his mind?

"I don't think it's necessary for us to trouble Mrs. Ferguson, after all," the Inspector was saying. They went down the stairs then, and I showed them out. "I'll let you have these back in a day or so." The Inspector indicated the exercise books in his hand.

I watched them as they walked out to the police car and drove away. What had he meant by saying he'd like to have them examined by experts? But, of course, I knew, and I felt as though in some way I had let my father down. And yet, if the men were dead . . . I went back into the parlour to be faced with my mother's reproachful gaze and Mrs. Wright's eager questioning.

But there were other, more practical things to think about, and with the funeral the sense of grief pushed everything else into the background of my mind.

It wasn't until the morning I was leaving to return to Bristol that I was reminded of the strange message that had caused my father's death. The postman brought a registered package addressed to me, and inside were the log books. There was also a letter, impersonal and final: *I have to inform you that the Canadian authorities have been unable to obtain any confirmation of the message claimed to have been received by your father, Mr. James Ferguson, on 29th September. Our experts have examined the enclosed, and in view of their report and the statement by the only survivor that the two remaining members of the party are dead, the Canadian authorities do not feel that any useful purpose can be served by resuming the search. However, they wish me to express their appreciation,* etc., etc.

So that was that. The experts—psychiatrists, presumably—had looked at the log books and had decided that my father was mad. I tore the letter savagely across, and then, because I didn't want my mother to find the fragments, I slipped them into my suitcase, together with the log books.

She came to the station to see me off. Since that visit from the police she had never once referred to the cause of my father's death. As though by tacit consent, we had avoided any reference to the message. But now, just as the train was about to leave, she gripped my hand. "You'll let that Labrador business alone, won't you, Ian? I couldn't bear it if you . . ." The whistle blew then, and she kissed me, holding me close the way she hadn't done since I was a kid. Her face was white and tired-looking, and she was crying.

I got in, and the train began to move. For a moment she stood watching, a small, lonely figure in black, and then she turned quickly and walked away down the platform. I often wonder whether she knew in her heart that she wouldn't see me again for a long time.

II

I had forgotten to get anything to read,
and for a time I just sat there, watching the backs of
the houses until London began to thin out and the green
fields showed beyond the factory buildings. I was thinking about my mother and our parting and the way she
had referred again to Labrador. She hadn't mentioned
the message my father had picked up. She wasn't worried
that the lives of those two men might be at stake. It was
Labrador itself that was on her mind, which struck me
as odd. And then I began thinking about my father again,
wishing I had known him better. If I had known him
better, I might have understood what it was about Labrador that had so fascinated him.

And then I got out the log books and looked through
them again. It wasn't difficult to see why the authorities
and the "experts" had decided to disregard the message.
The books were such a mess. And yet, running through
them was this thread of the Labrador expedition.

My training as an engineer had taught me to break
every problem down to its essentials, and before I knew
what I was doing, I had got out pencil and paper and
was jotting down every reference in the log books that
could conceivably have a bearing on Briffe's expedition.
Disentangled from all the jottings and drawings and
scraps of other messages, the thread became stronger and
more lucid. It told a definite story, though it was necessary

to read between the lines to get at it, for it soon became clear to me that my father seldom took down anything verbatim; a single line of comment or a brief note to give him the gist of the transmission was all he bothered about. This was not surprising, since the forming of legible characters had always been a labour to him. Indeed, there were several jottings that it was quite impossible for me to decipher.

In all I found I had isolated seventy-three references. Twelve of these were unintelligible, and seven I finally discarded as having no bearing on the subject. From the remaining fifty-four I was able, with the help of a little guesswork, to build up some sort of picture of what had happened. Briffe had presumably started out on his survey sometime around end-July for the first reference to a location occurred on August 10. The note simply said: *A2—where's that?* Three days later there was a reference to *Minipi River area,* and on August 15 my father had noted: *Moved to A3.* Then followed B1, B2, and B3. Clearly these were code names for the areas under survey, and as A1 would have been the first, my father must have been picking up Ledder's reports almost from the start. There was no indication of the purpose of Briffe's expedition—whether he was prospecting for gold or uranium or just a base metal like iron ore. He might simply be making a general survey, but this seemed unlikely since he was working for a mining company and was coding his areas and reports. The fact that the location code was dropped in later reports suggested negative results. This happened not only in the case of A2, but in several other cases as well. Thus, A3 later became *Mouni Rapids* and B2 *near old H.B. Post.* Against the reference to Mouni Rapids my father had written: *Winokapau! The right direction.*

By September 9 the expedition had reached Area C1. This was later referred to as *Disappointment,* and later still it became obvious that it was the name of a lake. These scraps of information were all apparently gleaned from the same source—VO6AZ. And always at the same time—2200 hours. An entry for August 3 appeared to be the first reference to the expedition. It simply said: *Interesting—some sort of code.* The next day's entry read: *2200. VO6AZ again. Survey report?* And he had scrawled in pencil: EMPLOYED BY THE MCGOVERN MINING AND EXPLORATION COMPANY OF MONTREAL?

And on the top of the next page, again in pencil: KEEP WATCH 20-METRE BAND 10 P.M. Later in August was an entry: *2200—VO6AZ. Code again! Why can't he report in clear?* And a note on the following page: BRIFFE, BRIFFE, BRIFFE. WHO IS BRIFFE? 75-METRE PHONE. NET FREQUENCY *3.780 kcs.* WATCH *2000.* But this was so fantastically scrawled over that I had difficulty in deciphering it. Two pages farther on I found the name Laroche mentioned for the first time. He had written it in capitals, heavily underlining it and putting a question mark at the end, and had added a note: QUERY LEDDER.

Isolated from all the nonsense and doodles which disfigured the pages of his log books, my father's notes confirmed what I already knew—that he had been picking up messages from Simon Ledder at Goose Bay to the McGovern Mining Company in Montreal, and that these were daily reports in some sort of code passing on information received from Briffe at 2000 hours from somewhere in Labrador. I found one half-obliterated entry which appeared to read: *3.780—nothing, nothing, nothing—always nothing;* it suggested that my father was also keeping regular watch on Briffe's transmitting frequency. But I could only pick out for certain the one entry a day at 2200 hours, until September 14. That was the day of the crash, and from then on the pattern changed and the entries became more frequent, the comments fuller.

Two days before that, Briffe appeared to have called for air transport to move the party forward to C2, for on September 13 occurred an entry: *Plane delayed, W bad. B. calling for usual two flights, three in first wave and Baird and himself in second.* IF C2 NORTH OF C1 THEY ARE GETTING V. NEAR.

The move apparently took place on September 14, but the first flight proved difficult, for at 1945 hours he had made this entry: *In luck—Contact VO6AZ. Beaver float-plane not back.* Scrawled across this were the words TROUBLE and KEEP CONSTANT WATCH ON 75-METRE BAND. And then an hour later at 2045: *Fog cleared, but Beaver still missing.* VO6AZ was now apparently transmitting to Montreal every hour at fifteen minutes to the hour, for the next time entry was for 2145. But nothing had been written against it, and the time itself was barely decipherable amongst the mass of little drawings my father had made. In fact, the whole of this last page of the log book was an indescribable mess, and it took me a long time to sort it out. The next entry, however, was only half an hour later—2215: *Advance party safe C2. Beaver back. Hellish W. report. B. going . . .* The last part was completely unreadable. But the comment that followed was clear enough: POOR HOLDING DISAPPOINT-MENT—THAT THE REASON? BARELY AN HOUR. THE FOOL! WHAT'S DRIVING HIM?

After that the entries were back to fifteen minutes to the hour—2245, 2345, 0045, right on to 0345. They were all blank. There was a sort of finality about those blank entries, and though it was the soft, warm English country-side that slid past the windows of the train, I saw only the cold and fog and the desolate misery of Labrador, the night closing in on the little floatplane, and my father sitting up half the night, waiting to find out whether they were safe or not.

The entries in the log book were, of course, for British

Summer Time, which is four and a half hours ahead of Goose Bay. Briffe's report that the plane was back must have been made shortly after five p.m., so that my father's reference to "barely an hour" obviously referred to the fact that Briffe was taking off with little more than an hour to go before nightfall.

The train stopped at Swindon, and I sat staring down at that last page of the log book. I couldn't blame the authorities for regarding him as unbalanced. It had taken me almost a quarter of an hour to decipher that one page. I could see my father sitting in his wheelchair with the earphones clamped to his head, waiting and waiting for the news of Briffe's safety that would never come, and passing the long, slow, silent hours by drawing. He had covered the whole of that page and all the cover of the exercise book with little pencil drawings—lions and fish with faces and canoes, as well as squares and circles, anything that his wandering hand and brain took a fancy to. It was here that he had written: C_2—C_2—C_2 . . . *where the hell is that?* and had scrawled the words: LOST AND GONE FOR EVER and framed them with the names *Winokapau-Tishinakamau-Attikonak*.

As the train started again, I picked up the last log book, the one my mother had tried to hide from me. He could have had little sleep that night, for the first entry was for 0800 hours: *Ledder failed to make contact.* And an hour later: *No contact.* After that there were entries for every hour, but nothing against them. And by midday he was picking up odd scraps of news commentaries and transmissions from other stations. The word GREENWOOD occurred once. This appeared to be some sort of code word, like MAYDAY, for immediately afterwards there was a note: *Air search ordered.* There was a reference to bad weather and then, two days later: *Nova Scotia Air Rescue Base.*

But this book, like the last, was a mass of doodles, on

the front of the cover, inside, and all over that first page, an indication of the long hours he had spent alone, huddled over the receiver. If I hadn't been so familiar with his writing, I don't think I should ever have been able to decipher it.

I rechecked the entries against the notes I had made, and as I turned the pages the men involved in the disaster were revealed. There was Briffe, the leader of the party, and a man called Baird, and then a third man, the pilot. *Ledder keeps calling Laroche.* This was on the second page, and two days later he had written the name LAROCHE again in capitals, and underneath: *No, it can't be. I must be mad.* Nowhere could I find the names of the three men who had gone up to Area C2 on the first flight, though I did find a further reference to them amongst the jottings from news broadcasts: *Advance party evacuated from C2, all three safe.*

There were two other entries I thought might have some bearing on the disaster, one of which I could only partly decipher. On September 23 he had written: *1705— Made contact VO6AZ—Query geologists.* And then two pages farther on: *1719—VO6AZ.* SO THEY HAVEN'T FORGOTTEN ABOUT . . . The rest was completely obliterated, though I could read my father's initials, J. F. F., written for some unknown reason into the middle of the sentence.

Excerpts from news broadcasts referring to the search continued until September 26. But on that date, against the time 1300 hours, he had written the one word: *Finis.* And then later the same day: *1714—Made contact Ledder. Briffe and Baird both dead. L. safe.* And he had added: *L-L-L-L-L—* IMPOSSIBLE.

Reading all this through as the train ran into Bristol, I saw clearly that my father had not only followed the story of the whole expedition with great interest, but he had even made direct contact with VO6AZ to clarify certain points. And, bearing in mind that he was only making very brief notes for his own personal use and not transcribing messages in detail, it seemed to me there was nothing to indicate that there was anything wrong with his mental state. Some of the comments I didn't understand, and of course these, if looked at amongst the jottings and drawings of the muddled pages in which they appeared, would give a different impression. If, however, the so-called experts had bothered to isolate the references to the expedition, as I had done, they would have seen how clear he was about it all.

All the way out to the airport I was thinking about this and how my mother had seen him standing on his two feet and reaching out to the map of Labrador. There must be something in that message. Whether the men were dead or not, I was convinced my father hadn't imagined it. He'd known it was important. And now all his effort was wasted because I hadn't had the sense to isolate the relevant passages for the police as I had done on the train.

It was after six when I reached the airport—too late to report to the company office. I felt sad and depressed, and instead of going to my digs, I turned in at the Airport Bar. The sight of Farrow drinking with a bunch of charter pilots made me think that perhaps there was still something I could do that would convince the authorities. Farrow was the Canadian pilot who had told me about the search for the missing geologists, and I knew that, flying trans-Atlantic charters, he must land sometimes at Goose Bay.

I thought about it whilst I had my drink, and in the end I went over to the group and asked him if I could have a word with him. "It's about that survey party that was lost," I said as he moved down the bar with me.

"The search was called off over a week ago. Briffe was dead. Baird, too. Only the pilot got out."

"Yes, I know." I asked him what he'd have to drink.

"Fruit juice. I'm flying tomorrow." I ordered, and when I turned to him again I saw that he was watching me. He had baby-blue eyes in a round, friendly face. But the eyes were shrewd. "What's biting you?"

"Do you ever land at Goose Bay?"

"Sure. Every time we do the west-bound flight—unless it clamps down."

"Do you know a radio operator called Simon Ledder?"

"Ledder?" He shook his head. "Where's he work—Control?"

"I don't know exactly. His address is care of D.O.T. Communications."

"That's the civilian radio station. D.O.T. stands for Department of Transport. They're over on the American side."

The drinks came and I paid, conscious that he was watching me as he sipped his fruit juice, waiting for me to tell him what it was all about. And now that I had him here alone with me, I didn't know quite how to put it to him. I didn't want to tell him more than I had to. I didn't want to risk the look of disbelief that it would inevitably produce. "You're flying tomorrow, you say. Will you be landing at Goose?"

"Yes. Around twenty-one hundred hours our time."

"Will you have a word with Ledder for me—telephone him perhaps?"

"What about?"

"Well . . ." It was so damned difficult. "He's a ham operator," I explained, "and he was in touch with a British ham on three occasions—Station G2STO. There's a report, too. Could you ask him to let you have a copy of it?"

"What's the report about?"

I hesitated. But he had to know, of course. "It's about Briffe and his party. Ledder was the radio link between the survey party and the mining company they were working for. The authorities have asked him for a report of all his radio contacts with Briffe and also the contacts with G2STO."

"How do you know they've asked him for a report?" His voice was suddenly different, the softness gone out of it.

"Somebody told me," I said vaguely. But he was curious now and it made me nervous. "I'm sorry to bother you with this, but when I saw you in here I thought perhaps if you could have a word with Ledder . . ."

"You could write to him," he said. And then, when I didn't say anything, he added: "Hadn't you better tell me a little more—why you're so interested in this report, for instance?"

He was still watching me curiously, waiting for me to explain. And suddenly I knew it was no good. I'd have to tell him the whole story. "G2STO was my father," I said. And I told him about the wire I had received from my mother and how I'd gone home to find my father dead. I told it all exactly as it had happened to me, but when I came to my discovery of the message from Briffe, he said: "From Briffe? But Briffe was dead days before."

"I know." My voice sounded suddenly weary. "That's what the police told me." And then I got out the notes I'd made in the train and handed them to him. "But if Briffe was dead, how do you explain that?"

He smoothed the sheet of paper out on the bar top and read it through slowly and carefully.

"They're all references from my father's radio log," I said.

He nodded, frowning as he read.

I watched him turn the sheet over. He had reached the final message now. "Does it sound as though he was mad?" I said.

He didn't say anything. He had read through the

notes now, and I watched him turn the sheet over again, staring down at it, still frowning.

"That's what the authorities think," I added. "They're not going to resume the search. I had a letter from them this morning."

He still didn't say anything, and I began to wish I hadn't told him. The men were reported dead. That alone would convince him that my father had imagined it all. And then his blue eyes were looking straight at me. "And you think the search should be resumed—is that it?" he asked.

I nodded.

He stared at me for a moment. "Have you got the log books or do the police still hold them?"

"No, I've got them." I said it reluctantly because I didn't want him to see them. But instead of asking for them, he began putting a lot of questions to me. And when he had got the whole story out of me, he fell silent again, hunched over the sheet of paper, staring at it. I thought he was reading it through again, but maybe he was just considering the situation, for he suddenly looked across at me. "And what you've told me is the absolute truth?" He was leaning slightly forward, watching my face.

"Yes," I said.

"And the log books look crazy unless all the contacts are isolated, the way they are here?" He tapped the sheet of paper.

I nodded. "I thought if I could find out a little more about the three direct contacts my father made with Ledder . . . what Ledder's reaction to my father was . . ."

"The thing that gets me," he muttered, "is how your father could possibly have picked up this transmission." He was frowning, and his tone was puzzled. "As I recollect it, all Briffe had was a forty-eight set. I'm sure

I read that somewhere. Yes, and operated by a hand
generator at that. It just doesn't seem possible."

He was making the same point that the Flight Lieutenant had made. "But surely," I said, "there must be
certain conditions in which he could have picked it up."

"Maybe. I wouldn't know about that. But the old
forty-eight set is a transmitter of very limited range—I
do know that." He gave a slight shrug. "Still, it's just
possible, I suppose. You'd have to check with somebody
like this guy Ledder to make certain."

He had picked up the sheet of paper again, and he
stared at it for so long that I felt sure he wasn't going to
help me and was only trying to think out how to tell
me so. He was my only hope of making effective contact
with Ledder. If he wouldn't help, then there was nobody
else I could go to—and I felt I had to settle this thing,
one way or the other. If my father had made that message
up, well, all right—but I had to know. I had to be absolutely certain, for my own peace of mind, that those two
men really were dead.

And then Farrow put the sheet of paper down and
turned to me. "You know," he said, "I think you ought
to go to Goose and have a word with Ledder yourself."

I stared at him, unable to believe that I'd heard him
correctly. "Go to Goose Bay? You mean fly there—myself?"

He half smiled. "You won't get into Goose any other
way."

It was such an incredible suggestion that for a moment
I couldn't think of anything to say. He couldn't be serious. "All I wanted," I murmured, "was for you to have
a word with him . . . find out what he thought of my
father, whether he considered him sane. You can take
those notes and—"

"Look," he said. "If you're convinced your father was
sane, then these notes—" he tapped the sheet of paper—

"all the messages, everything—including that final message—are fact. They happened. And if that's what you believe, then you must go over there yourself. Apart from the question of whether Briffe's alive or not, you owe it to your father. If I go to this guy Ledder, he'll just answer my questions, and that will be that. You might just as well write him a letter, for all the good it'll do." And then he added: "If you're really convinced that your father did pick up a transmission from Briffe, then there's only one thing for you to do—go over there and check for yourself. It's the only way you'll get the authorities to take it seriously."

I was appalled at the way he was putting the responsibility back on to me. "But I just haven't the money," I murmured.

"I could help you there." He was watching me closely all the time. "I'm checking out on a west-bound flight at oh-seven hundred tomorrow morning. We'll be into Goose around four thirty in the afternoon—their time. I might be able to fix it. You'd have about two hours there, and I could radio ahead to Control for them to have Ledder meet the plane. Well?"

He meant it. That was the incredible thing. He really meant it. "But what about my job?" I was feeling sud- ·denly scared. "I can't just walk out—"

"You'd be back on Friday."

"But . . ." It was all so appallingly sudden, and Canada was like another world to me. I'd never been out of England, except once to Belgium. "But what about the regulations and—and wouldn't the extra weight . . ." I found I was desperately searching for some sort of excuse.

He asked me then whether I had a British passport. I had, of course, for I'd needed one for my holiday in Bruges and Ghent the previous year, and it was at my lodgings, with the rest of my things. And when he told me that my weight wouldn't make any difference to the safety margin and that he was good friends with the Customs and Immigration people both here and at Goose, all I could think of to say was: "I'll have to think it over."

He gripped my arm then, and those baby-blue eyes of his were suddenly hard. "Either you believe what your father wrote, or you don't. Which is it?"

The way he put it was almost offensive, and I answered hotly: "Don't you understand? That message was the cause of my father's death."

"Okay," he said tersely. "Then it's time you faced up to the implications of that message."

"How do you mean?"

He relaxed his grip on my arm. "See here, boy," he said gently, "if Briffe really did transmit on September twenty-ninth, then either there's been some ghastly error or . . . well, the alternative doesn't bear thinking about." His words reminded me of the shocked expression on the Flight Lieutenant's face when I had suggested the pilot might have made a mistake. "Now do you see why you've got to go over and talk to Ledder yourself? What that message says—" and he jabbed his finger at the sheet of paper he had laid on the bar counter— "is that Laroche was wrong when he said Briffe and the other guy were dead. And I'm warning you, it's going to take a lot to persuade the authorities of that." He patted my arm gently, and the blue eyes were no longer hard, but looked at me sympathetically. "Well, it's up to you now. You're the only man who's going to be really convinced about that message—unless they find somebody else picked it up. If you've the courage of your convictions . . ." And then he added: "I just thought you'd better be clear in your mind about what you're up against."

It was odd, but now that he'd put it to me so bluntly, I no longer felt out of my depth. I was suddenly sure of myself and what I should do, and without any hesitation

I heard myself say: "If you can fix it, I'd like to come with you tomorrow."

"Okay, boy. If that's what you'd like." He hesitated. "You really are sure about this?"

In a sudden mental flash I saw my father as he had been last Christmas when I had been home, sitting up there in his room with the headphones on and his long, thin fingers with the burn marks playing so sensitively over the tuning dials. "Yes," I said. "I'm quite sure about it."

He nodded his head slowly. "Queer business," he murmured. A perplexed look had come over his face, and I wondered whether, now that I had agreed to go—wanted to go—he was about to back down on his offer. But all he said was: "Meet me down at our freight office—that's the end of the block, next to Number One hangar—say, about a quarter before six tomorrow morning. Have your passport with you and an overnight bag. Better pack some warm clothes. You may be cold back in the fuselage. Okay?"

I nodded. "But what about the other end?" I murmured. "Surely it isn't as easy as that to fly somebody into another country?" It was an automatic reaction. Now that I'd said I'd go, the difficulties seemed insuperable.

He laughed and patted my shoulder. "Canada isn't the States, you know. It's still a Dominion—no fingerprints, no visa. I'll just have to clear you with Immigration and Customs, that's all." He stared at me a moment as though weighing me up, and then he said: "Don't forget about the warm clothes." He turned then with a quick nod and walked slowly back to join his group at the other end of the bar.

I stood there, the drink I hadn't even started clutched in my hand, and a feeling of intense loneliness crept over me.

III

I didn't sleep much that night,
and I was down at the charter company's freight office
by five thirty. Farrow wasn't there, of course, and I walked
up and down in the grey morning light, feeling cold and
empty inside. The office was locked, the tarmac deserted.
I lit a cigarette and wondered, as I had done all night,
whether I was making a fool of myself. A plane took off
with a thunderous roar, and I watched it disappear into
the low overcast, thinking that in little more than an hour,
if Farrow kept his word, I should be up there, headed
west out into the Atlantic. I was shivering slightly. Nerves!

It was almost six when Farrow drove up in a battered
sports car. "Jump in!" he shouted. "Got to get you vacci-
nated. Otherwise it's all fixed."

We woke up a doctor friend of his, and half an hour
later I had got my certificate of vaccination, had cleared
Customs and Immigration, and was back at the freight
office. I signed the "blood-chit" that absolved the company of responsibility for my death in the event of a
crash, and then Farrow left me there and I hung about
for another twenty minutes, waiting for take-off. There
was no turning back now. I was committed to the flight,
and because of that I no longer felt nervous.

Shortly before seven the crew assembled, and I walked
with them across the tarmac to a big four-engined plane
parked on the apron opposite the office. Inside, it was a

dim-lit steel shell with the freight piled down the centre, strapped down to ring bolts in the floor. "Not very comfortable, I'm afraid," Farrow said, "but we don't cater for passengers." He gave my shoulder a friendly squeeze. "Toilet's aft if you want it." The door of the fuselage slammed shut, and he followed his crew for'ard to the flight deck. I was alone then.

We took off just after seven, and, though I had never flown before, I could sense what was happening—the sound of the engines being run up one by one on test at the runway end, and then the solid roar of all four together and the drag of the airscrews as we began to move, the dim-lit fuselage rocking and vibrating around me. Suddenly it was quieter, and I knew we had left the ground.

The exhilaration of the take-off gradually faded into the monotony of the flight as we drove smoothly on, hour after hour. I dozed a little, and now and then Farrow or one of his crew came aft. Shortly after ten the navigator brought me sandwiches and hot coffee. An hour and a half later we landed at Keflavik in Iceland and I clambered stiffly out, blinking my eyes in the cold sunlight.

The airport was a featureless expanse, the buildings modern utilitarian blocks without character. The whole place had the crisp, cold, lifeless air of outer space. But the cafeteria in the main building yielded eggs and bacon and hot coffee, and the echoing hall was full of transit passengers passing the time by sending postcards and buying Icelandic souvenirs from counters gay with northern colours. We had over an hour there in the warmth whilst the plane was re-fuelled and a quick check made on one of the engines which was running rough. They found nothing wrong with the engine, and by twelve thirty I was back in the hollow roar of the fuselage and we were taking off on the last lap.

We flew high to clear a storm belt off the Greenland

coast, and it was cold. I dozed fitfully, the monotony only broken by an occasional cup of coffee, the lunch pack, and brief talks with the crew as they came aft. It was nine twenty by my watch when the flight engineer finally roused me. "Skipper says if you want to take a look at Labrador from the air, you'd better come up for'ard right away. We'll be landing in fifteen minutes."

I followed him through the door to the flight deck. To my surprise, it was daylight, and because I could see out, the long, cold hours spent huddled amongst the freight in the fuselage were suddenly forgotten. Not that there was anything to see . . . just the grey of cloud through the windshield and Farrow's head outlined against it. The wireless operator gripped my arm as I passed, pulling me down towards him. "I've radioed the tower to have Ledder meet you," he shouted in my ear. "Okay?"

"Thanks."

Farrow half turned his head and indicated the flight engineer's seat beside him. "Going down now." He jerked his thumb downwards. The engines were already throttled back. "We'll come out of the cloud at eight thousand." He tapped the altimeter dial, where the pointer was dropping slowly. And he added: "You'll have plenty of time to talk to Ledder. Another engine check. Port outer packed up a while back." He nodded towards the lefthand wing tip where it wavered gently in the turbulent cloud mist. The outboard engine was lifeless, the propeller feathering slowly. "We'll be there the night. Get away sometime tomorrow—I hope."

I wanted to ask him whether we'd get down all right, but nobody seemed worried that we were flying on only three engines. I sat down and said nothing, staring ahead through the windshield, waiting for the moment when I should get my first glimpse of Labrador. And because there was nothing to see, I found myself thinking of my father. Had his flying duties ever taken him to Labrador, or was I now doing the thing he'd wanted to do all his life? I was thinking of the books and the map, wondering what it was that had fascinated him about this country; and then abruptly the veil was swept away from in front of my eyes, and there was Labrador.

The grimness of it was the thing that struck me—the grimness and the lostness and the emptiness of it. Below us was a great sheet of water running in through a desolate, flat waste, with pale glimpses of sand and a sort of barren, glacier-dredged look about it. But what held my attention was the land ahead where it rose to meet the sky. There were no hills there, no mountain peaks. It rose up from the coastal plain in one black, ruler-straight line, utterly featureless—a remote, bitter plateau that by its very uniformity gave an impression of vastness, of being on the verge of land that stretched away to the Pole.

"There's Goose now!" Farrow was shouting in my ear and pointing. But I didn't see it. My eyes were riveted by the black line of that plateau, and I held my breath, strangely stirred as though by some old challenge.

"Sure is pretty country," Farrow shouted to me. "You can get lost in there just like that." And he snapped his fingers. "Nothing but lakes, and every one the same as the next." He was suddenly grinning. "The land God gave to Cain—that's what Jacques Cartier called it when he first discovered it."

The land God gave to Cain! The words mingled with my thoughts to trickle through my mind in a cold shiver. How often I was to remember later the aptness of that description!

We were coming in now, the water of Goose Bay rising to meet us, the airfield clearly visible. The flight engineer tapped me on the shoulder, and I clambered out of his seat and went back into the dimness of the fuselage. A few moments later we touched down.

When we had come to rest with the engines cut, the

navigator came aft and opened the freight door. Daylight
entered the fuselage, bringing with it warmth and the
smell of rain, and through the open door I looked out
across wet tarmac to a line of green-painted, corrugated-
iron buildings. A man stood waiting on the apron, alone;
a tall, dark-featured man in some sort of plastic raincoat.

I gathered my things together, and then Farrow came
down through the fuselage. "I'll fix you up with a room
at the T.C.A. hotel," he said. "You can get a meal there.
The time, by the way, is—" he glanced at his watch—
"five twenty-two. There's four and a half hours difference
between Goose and England." And he added: "There'll
be transport to run us down as soon as I'm through with
the maintenance people and we've cleared Immigration."
He had moved on to the door by then, and I heard a
voice say: "Captain Farrow? My name's Simon Ledder.
I was told to meet your flight." It was a slow voice, puzzled and a little resentful.

And then I was at the door, and Farrow said: "Well,
here you are. Here's the guy you wanted to talk to." And
as I jumped out on to the tarmac he was already walking
away with a casual lift of his hand.

"Where will I find you?" I called after him. I didn't
want to lose him. The place looked so vast and desolate.

"Don't worry, I won't forget you," he answered over
his shoulder. His crew were waiting for him, and when
he had caught up with them, they all went on together
in a bunch. I heard the flight engineer's rather high-
pitched laugh, and then they disappeared into the hangar.

"What did you want to see me about?" Ledder's voice
was dull and flat, and I turned to find him standing close
beside me, his hands in his pockets and a bored look on
his face.

I'd thought about this meeting all through the monotonous hours of the flight, but now that I was alone
with him, I found myself at a loss for words. The refer-

ences to him in my father's log books had given him an importance in my mind I couldn't reconcile with this morose-looking individual. "Do you recall the name Ferguson?" I asked. "James Finlay Ferguson. He's dead now, but—"

"The expedition of 1900. Is that what you mean?" There was a sudden flicker of interest in the eyes that peered at me through thick, horn-rimmed lenses.

Intuition should have told me that a gap in the past was being bridged for me, but my mind was on Briffe and the things my father had written. "No, Station G2STO," I said. "It's about those radio contacts you had with him." But the momentary flicker of interest had vanished from his eyes, and his face was blank. "Your call sign is VO6AZ, isn't it?" I asked him.

He nodded, waiting.

"G2STO contacted you three times in the past few weeks. Don't you remember?"

"Sure I do. It was six times, to be exact." His voice sounded weary. And then he added: "What are you, police or Air Force?"

I didn't answer that. I thought maybe he'd talk more readily if he believed I had authority to question him. "Can we go somewhere where we can talk?" I said. It was beginning to rain again, and an aircraft had started warming up its engines farther along the apron. "There are one or two questions—"

"Questions?" That seemed to touch him off. "I've had nothing but questions about this darned ham for the past few days. G2STO! I'm sick of him. The crazy bastard claims he picked up a transmission from Paul Briffe. That's what you've come about, isn't it?" His manner was openly hostile. "Well, I spent a whole day making out a report on him. The station commander here has a copy of it, if you want to see it. I've nothing to add. Nothing at all."

I was too angry to say anything. To come all this way and find that Ledder was completely unco-operative . . . It was what I'd feared the moment I had seen him waiting there, sullenly, on the apron.

"Well," he said, "do you want to see the report?"

I nodded, and we began to walk across the tarmac.

"You know about Briffe?" He was looking at me. I think he was puzzled by my silence. "He couldn't have made that transmission."

"How do you know?" I asked.

"How do I know? Why, the man was dead. How the hell can a man who's been dead a week suddenly start sending?"

"You don't *know* he's dead," I said.

He stopped then. "How do you mean?"

"He's been reported dead. That's all."

"That's all, you say." He was peering at me curiously. "What are you getting at?"

"Just that you can't be absolutely certain he didn't transmit," I told him. "Not unless you were listening in for him on his frequency that day." I was facing him then. "Were you listening in for him at two o'clock on the twenty-ninth?"

"The time I was given was nine twenty-five."

"Yes, of course." That was the four-and-a-half-hour difference. "It would have been nine twenty-five here. But you weren't listening for him then, were you?"

He shook his head. "Why should I? The search had been called off three days before, and I'd no reason to think—"

"Then you can't be absolutely certain."

"I tell you, Briffe was dead." I had touched his professional pride, and he said it angrily. "If I thought there'd been a chance of any transmission, I'd have kept constant watch. But there wasn't. He'd been dead since the twentieth."

Perhaps he wasn't so unlike my father when it came to radio. "You've only the pilot's word for that," I said.

He stared at me, and his face had a startled look. "Are you suggesting . . . Look, for Chrissake, Laroche is all right." He was looking at me with sudden suspicion. "You're not the police. You're not Air Force either. Who are you?"

"My name's Ian Ferguson," I said. "The crazy bastard you spoke of was my father, and I happen to believe that he did pick up some sort of a transmission." My words had shocked him, and I didn't give him time to recover, but added quickly: "My father made several contacts with you." I pulled out the sheet of paper with the entries I had isolated. "The first time was on the twenty-third of September, and then again on the twenty-fifth of last month and again on the twenty-sixth. Did he seem crazy to you then?"

"No, but that was before—"

"He was perfectly rational, was he?"

"He asked some odd questions," he answered evasively.

I hesitated. But this wasn't the moment to find out what those questions were. "Forget for the moment that Briffe has been reported dead," I said, "and that my father ever picked up this transmission. Cast your mind back to the first time he contacted you. Can you remember what your reaction was?"

"I tell you, he asked some odd questions," he answered uncomfortably. "Otherwise there was nothing to it, I guess. He was just another ham."

"Look," I said, trying to get my own urgency across to him. "My father was a radio operator, like you." Surely there was some sort of freemasonry between these men whose world was the ether, some sense of brotherhood. "I know he was contacting you on W/T and that all you get is a lot of dots and dashes, but something must come through, some indication—"

"It's not the same as Voice, you know. And he always contacted me on Key—never Voice."

"Of course he did," I said angrily. "How else could he contact you? But even so," I added, "something must come through, surely—some indication of the sort of man he was, his mood, something."

"I tell you, it was all on Key. If I'd had a QSO—a Voice contact—then maybe . . ." He gave a little shrug. "To tell you the truth, I didn't think much about him—not then."

It was raining harder now, but he made no move to take shelter, and I asked him again what he'd thought of my father. "You must have formed some impression." And when he didn't answer, I said impatiently: "Don't the men you contact on the air mean anything to you? Surely you must have got some impression—"

"He was just another ham, that's all." He said it irritably. "I pick up any number of hams."

I felt suddenly tired of the whole thing then. My father had meant nothing to this morose Canadian operator, nothing at all. There seemed to be no point in my having made the trip to Goose. In desperation I said: "At least you didn't think him irrational or irresponsible—at that time."

"I tell you, I didn't think anything about him. I was puzzled by his questions. That was all."

Over two thousand miles, and I was no further forward. I asked him about the questions then, and he said it was all set down in the report he'd written. "All I could remember, anyway." And he added: "If you want to come back to the house, I could show you the report there. I kept a copy."

I hesitated because the invitation had been made so grudgingly, but then he looked at his watch and said: "It's after five thirty now. I guess the station commander will have left anyway."

"All right." I was thinking that perhaps I'd get more out of him at his home, and without a word he turned and led me back across the apron. As we passed the open door of the hangar, Farrow appeared and called to me. "If you come into the office now, we can get the formalities completed." And then to Ledder: "Give you a lift down, if you like. The truck will be here any minute."

"Okay, thanks," Ledder said. "Save me a wetting. That's the worst of this dump," he added, turning to me with the ghost of a smile. "We're not allowed a car of our own. A question of gas, I guess. The bay's frozen half the year, and then supplies have to be flown in."

We went into the office, and whilst my passport was being checked and my suitcase cleared, Farrow inquired about Ledder. "Got what you wanted?" he asked in a whisper.

"No," I said. "Not yet."

"Oh, well, you've plenty of time. Take-off won't be till seven in the morning, and that's presuming they work on that engine all night."

"You're here the night, are you?" Ledder said. And when Farrow nodded, he turned to me. "Then you'd better get some food and come over to my place afterwards. The D.O.T. houses are right across from the hotel."

The truck had already arrived. We piled in, and a moment later we were bumping along a dirt road overlooking the bay. The airport dropped behind us, desolate in the rain, and below us I caught a glimpse of a jetty with a steamer alongside and beyond that some seaplanes anchored close against the shore, small and indistinct in the fading light. Beside the road, bull-dozers had exposed the gravel soil in raw slashes, the clearings littered with uprooted trees, and here and there the yellow wood of a new construction was reared up out of the naked land. The whole place had a lost feel about it, raw and ugly

like a frontier settlement. It was a gauntlet flung in nature's face, the scrub spruce crowding it in so that I was
conscious all the time of the infinite wastes that lay behind
it.

The hotel was a low, sprawling building made up of a
series of wood-frame huts angled out in the form of a
star. Thin dwarf scrub lapped round the sandy clearing.
The rain had slackened, and as we climbed out of the
truck I could see the hills across the bay again, dark and
remote and very blue. It had become suddenly colder.
Ledder pointed out his house, just visible through a screen
of trees. "Come over as soon as you've had your supper,"
he said. And then we left him and went inside to be
greeted with the hot breath of steam heating turned full
on. The place had a bare, barrack air, but, surprisingly,
the rooms were neat and very modern, the food good.

It was almost seven thirty before I'd finished eating,
and I came out into a biting wind. It was dark, and the
stars had a frosty look. A thin, pale curtain of northern
lights wavered across the sky, and the silence was absolute. Through the trees the lights of Ledder's house
had the warm glow of orange curtains.

He came to the door dressed in a vivid, short-sleeved
shirt open at the neck. There was a little girl with him,
and in the room beyond, his wife and another woman sat
chatting through the blare of the radio. He introduced
me, and I stood there, feeling awkward because I wanted
to talk to him alone. The room was overpoweringly hot,
full of very new-looking furniture upholstered in brilliant
colours. "Would you care for some coffee?" Mrs. Ledder
asked.

I shook my head. "I've just had some."

She laughed. She was young and jolly, with broad features and fair hair, rather pretty except that she was a
little too stockily built. But that may have been because
she was going to have a child and was wearing a smock.

"It's easy to see you're not a Canadian, Mr. Ferguson. No Canadian would ever refuse a cup of coffee because he'd just had one, that's for sure. Simon and the boys drink it all the time. Sure you won't change your mind?"

I shook my head, and Ledder said: "Well, if you don't want any coffee, we'll go down below, shall we? It'll be quieter there." He pulled open a door under the stairs and switched on the light. "You must excuse the mess, but I'm just installing some new equipment."

I followed him down steps that led into a sort of cellar that was probably meant to house just the furnace and hot-water boiler. But there was also a desk thrust close against one wall with a mass of radio equipment stacked round it like a barricade. Toys littered the floor, odds and ends of household gear, the remains of a Christmas tree, a pram, and over everything lay a sprinkling of tools and the insides of old radio sets.

"Is this where you work?" I asked.

"Sure. Folk here are always asking me to fix something or other."

"I mean—is this where you send from?"

He nodded and went across to the desk. "I told you it was a mess."

I don't know what I'd expected. Something neat and tidy, I suppose. It seemed incredible that this junk-room of a basement should be VO6AZ and that out of this muddle he could have made contact with my father on the other side of the Atlantic. "It doesn't look much, I know—not all spick and span like the D.O.T. station." He was sitting down and rummaging amongst some papers in a drawer. "But I can tell you this, there's equipment here that Goose Radio hasn't got." He slammed the drawer shut. "Here you are," he said and held out a typed sheet of foolscap.

I took it from him. It was headed: REPORT ON BRITISH AMATEUR RADIO STATION G2STO.

"You must remember that when I wrote that I knew Briffe was dead," he said, his smile half apologetic. "And I didn't know your father's name. If I'd known his name, it might have made some sense."

Seated at his desk, he seemed a different person, more alive, more vital—I suppose because this was his world, as it had been my father's. His hand had strayed automatically to the key, the way my father's always had. It was a different key, an American side-operated pattern known as a bug key. But though the key was different, the gesture was the same. "As far as I was concerned, G2STO was nuts, and that's all there was to it." His voice was easy and natural, all the hostility gone out of it. "I'm sorry," he added. "But I guess I was pretty tired of the whole business by then. I should have checked his name in the book."

I stared down at the report, wondering why the name would have made any difference. He had detailed six contacts, and two of the three that I didn't know about concerned Briffe's sending frequency. "I see my father first contacted you on August the eleventh," I said. "He asked for Briffe's transmitting time, and you gave it to him. The sending frequency, too."

"Sure I did. There was nothing secret about it."

"What was the frequency?"

"Three point seven eight zero."

I got out my sheet of notes. *August 11;* BRIFFE, BRIFFE, BRIFFE. WHO IS BRIFFE? "Is that it?" I asked, showing him the note I had made.

He leaned forward, looking at it. " 'Seventy-five-metre phone band. Net frequency three point seven eight zero.' Yes, that's it."

It explained the half-obliterated entry I had found. "Take a look at that," I said. "I couldn't read the date, but it was somewhere towards the end of August."

" 'Three point seven eight zero—nothing, nothing,

nothing—always nothing.'" He read it out slowly and then looked up at me. "Well?"

"It means my father was watching on Briffe's frequency."

"It means he was curious, sure. But, then, so were several other hams. There were two Canadians, one at Burnt Creek and the other right up in Baffin Island, listening regularly. It doesn't mean anything. They were just interested, that's all."

"Then what about this contact on September twenty-sixth? That was the day the search was called off. According to your report, my father actually contacted you that evening to check Briffe's frequency and ask whether there was any other frequency he might use in an emergency. Doesn't that make it obvious that he was keeping watch for Briffe?"

"Paul Briffe only had an old forty-eight set. It was operated by a hand generator, and a British ham would be more than two thousand miles outside of normal range."

"Outside of normal range, yes," I said impatiently. "Nevertheless, my father was keeping watch. You knew that, and yet down here at the bottom of your report you give it as your opinion that G2STO couldn't possibly have picked up a transmission from Briffe. And you list your reasons—one of them, that, *'granted freak reception and the transmission having actually been made, the odds against G2STO choosing that particular moment to listen in are too great.'* What exactly did you mean by that?"

"Just what I say," he answered sharply. "Take all those points together—Briffe transmitting when he's known to be dead, freak reception, and finally the remote chance that your father should be keeping watch at that precise moment. It just doesn't make sense."

"Why not? The odds are against it, I admit, but it's not impossible."

"Oh, for heaven's sake!" he exclaimed irritably. "The plane crashed on the evening of the fourteenth. We were on constant watch until the twenty-sixth, when the search was abandoned—not only us, but the Air Force, government stations, and a whole bunch of hams. We picked up nothing. And three days after we ceased watch, G2STO reports contact. Suppose Briffe did transmit on the twenty-ninth, as he says. To be certain of picking up that transmission, he'd have had to be listening on net frequency for three whole days, twenty-four hours out of the twenty-four." He shook his head. "It just isn't credible."

"My father was paralysed," I said. "He had nothing else to do."

He stared at me. "I'm sorry," he said tonelessly. "I guess they didn't tell us anything about him."

"They didn't tell you, then, that he died immediately after picking up the transmission?"

"No. I guess that explains it—why you're here, I mean. I'd been wondering about that."

"That transmission killed him."

His eyes widened, looking at me curiously. "How do you mean?"

I told him then about my father calling out, and how he'd somehow struggled to his feet. I told him the whole story, and when I'd finished, he said: "I didn't know about all this." His soft, slow voice was shocked, his tone apologetic. "They didn't give any details, not even his name. I've been thinking about that over my supper. It was those questions he asked that started me thinking he was nuts. If they'd given me his name, I might have understood what he was getting at. As it was, those questions just seemed so God-damned irrelevant." He nodded to the report in my hand. "Read 'em. They're all there. You'll see what I mean then. You'd have thought he was nuts if they'd come at you out of the blue, so to speak—anybody would."

I could see his point, for on the second occasion my father had contacted him he'd asked if Briffe had ever mentioned Lake of the Lion. That was on September 10, and when Ledder had said no and had refused to give him the exact location of Area C1, he had requested details of the reports or at least the code so that he could follow the progress of the expedition for himself. Finally: *He asked me to question Laroche about Lake of the Lion and report his reaction.*

"Why did he want you to question Laroche about the lake?" I asked. "Did he say?"

"No, he didn't say. I tell you, they're damned queer questions, some of them."

On September 15, the day after the geologists had disappeared, my father had asked him a lot of questions about what had happened and why Briffe had been in such a hurry to reach C2. *Had I asked Laroche about Lake of the Lion and what was his reaction? Where was C2? My negative replies seemed to annoy him.* On September 23 my father had made contact again, asking for information about Laroche. *Could I find out for him whether Canadian geologists still remembered the expedition of 1900 into the Attikonak area?* And two days later he had asked about this again. *I told him that it was still talked about and added that if he wanted further details he should contact the Department of Mines in Ottawa.*

And then there was the final contact, in which Ledder had confirmed Briffe's sending frequency.

I folded the report up and put it down on the desk beside him, conscious that he was watching me, waiting for me to tell him what those questions meant. He expected me to know, and the fact that I didn't made me feel uncomfortable, so that my throat felt suddenly constricted and my eyes moist. To gain time, I asked him about C2. "Was it in the Attikonak area?"

He nodded. "Sure. The advance party were camped right on the river bank." And then he added: "What was his interest in the Attikonak River, do you know that? And this Lake of the Lion he asked about?"

I shook my head. "I don't know." It was a confession that I'd never bothered to get very close to my father. "My mother might know," I murmured uncomfortably.

He was puzzled now. "But those questions make sense to you, don't they?"

I didn't know what to say. It came down to this, that Ledder would only be convinced that the message was genuine if I could explain the motive behind my father's questions, and I didn't know the motive. That belonged to the map and the books and the relics of the Canadian North, all the secret world I'd never shared. "It's a long story"—that was the only reference he'd ever made to it. If only I'd persisted then. With a little patience I could have dug it out of him.

Ledder had picked up the report and was staring at it. "I could kick myself," he said, suddenly tossing it down amongst the litter of papers. "I'd only to look him up in the book. But I'd lent my copy to somebody in the D.O.T., and I just didn't bother to go and find him and get it back." He had misunderstood my silence. "It never occurred to me," he added, looking up at me almost apologetically.

"What never occurred to you?" I asked. There was something here that I didn't understand.

"That his name was important," he answered.

"Important? How do you mean?"

"Well, if I'd known it was James Finlay Ferguson . . ." He broke off abruptly, staring at me with a puzzled frown. "He was related, wasn't he?"

"Related?" I didn't know what he was getting at. "Related to whom?"

"Why, to the Ferguson that got killed up in the Attikonak area in 1900."

I stared at him. So that was it. The expedition of 1900. "Was there a Ferguson on that expedition?" I asked.

"Sure there was. James Finlay Ferguson." He was looking at me as though he thought it was I who was crazy now. "You mean you don't know about it?"

I shook my head, my mind busy searching back through my childhood to things I'd half forgotten—my mother's fears, my father's obsession with the country. This was the cause of it all, then.

"But the name?" He said it almost angrily, as though he were being cheated of something that would add interest to the monotony of life in this distant outpost. "And him asking all those questions? You mean it's just coincidence that the names were the same? Was it just because of that your father was interested?"

"No," I said. "No, it wasn't that." And I added hastily: "It's just that my father never talked about it." I, too, felt cheated—cheated because he hadn't shared the past with me when it belonged to me and was my right.

"Never talked about it? Why ever not?" Ledder was leaning forward. "Let's get this straight. Are they related or not—your father and this Ferguson who went into Labrador?"

"Yes, of course they are," I answered. "They must be." There was no other explanation. It explained so much that I'd never understood. It was a pity that my grandmother had died when I was still a child. I would like to have talked to her now.

"What relationship?" Ledder was staring up at me. "Do you know?"

"His father, I think." It must have been his father, for I hadn't any great-uncles.

"Your grandfather, in fact."

I nodded. And it would have been grandmother Alexandra who would have given him the names of James Finlay. I was thinking it was strange that my father had been born in the year 1900.

"But how do you know it's your grandfather?" Ledder asked. "How do you know, when you didn't even know there was an expedition back at the beginning of the century?"

I told him then about the sextant and the paddle and the other relics hanging on the wall, and about my grandmother and the house in Scotland, and how she'd come to me in the night when I was barely old enough to remember. "I think she must have been going to tell me about that expedition." As I talked to him about it, everything seemed to fall into place—my father's obsession, everything. And then I was asking him about the expedition. "Can you give me the details?" I said. "What happened to Ferguson?"

"I don't know," he answered. "In fact, I don't know very much about it—only what the company geologist told me. There were two of them went in, from Davis Inlet. Two white men, no Indians. One was a prospector, the other a trapper, and it ended in tragedy. The trapper only just escaped with his life. The prospector—that was Ferguson—he died. That's all I know." He turned to the desk and picked up his log, searching quickly through it. "Here you are. Here's the geologist's reply: 'Expedition 1900 well known because one of the two men, James Finlay Ferguson, was lost.' "

"And he was a prospector?"

"So Tim Baird said."

"Was he prospecting for gold?" I was remembering that my mother had once said I wasn't to ask about my grandfather . . . an old reprobate, she had called him, who had come to a bad end and wasted his life searching for gold.

"I don't know what he was prospecting for. Tim didn't say."

But it didn't matter. I was quite certain it was gold, just as I was quite certain that this was the past that had bitten so deep into my father in his loneliness. It was just a pity that I'd never bothered to get the story out of him.

"It's odd he never talked to you about it," Ledder said, and I realized that he was still uncertain about it all.

"I told you, he couldn't talk." And I added: "It's so long since he was wounded that now I can't even recall the sound of his voice."

"But he could write."

"It was an effort," I said.

"And he left no record?"

"Not that I know of. At least, I didn't find one when I looked through his things. I suppose it was too complicated or something. That's what he said, anyway. What else did the geologist tell you?"

"Just what I've read out to you—nothing else." He was sitting there, doodling with a pencil on the cover of his log.

"What about this man Tim Baird? Did he tell you anything else—the name of the other man, or where they went, or what they were looking for?"

"No. I guess he didn't know much about it. I've told you all I know." He shook his head, frowning down at the pattern he was tracing. "Damn queer him not telling you anything about it, and the thing an obsession with him."

"That was because of my mother," I said. "I think she must have made him promise. She didn't want me involved. I think she hated Labrador," I added, remembering the scene on the platform as the train was about to leave. And here I was in Labrador.

My mind switched back to the questions my father had

asked, and I picked up the report again. I was thinking of
the map above the transmitter, the name *Lake of the
Lion* pencilled on it. "Did you ask Laroche about Lake
of the Lion?"

"No. I never had the chance." And then Ledder had
stopped doodling and was looking up at me. "You know,
it wasn't so much the strangeness of his questions that
made me think him crazy. It was this obsession with an
old story—"

"My father wasn't crazy," I said sharply. I was still
wondering why he should have been so interested in
Laroche's reaction.

"No, I guess he wasn't." Ledder's voice was slow, almost reluctant. "If I'd known his name was James Finlay
Ferguson, it would have made some sense." He was excusing himself again. But then, after a pause, he said:
"But even so, if he wasn't crazy . . ." He left the sentence
unfinished, staring down at the desk and fiddling with
the Morse key. "Did he keep a log?" he asked at length.

"Yes, of course," I said. And I gave him the sheet of
notes, glad that I'd isolated them from the actual books.
"Those are all the entries that concern Briffe, right from
the time my father first picked up your transmissions until that final message." I tried to explain to him again
that writing had been difficult for him and that my father
usually just jotted down a note to remind him of the
substance of each transmission, but he didn't seem to be
listening. He was going carefully through the notes, sucking at a pencil and occasionally nodding his head as
though at some recollection.

Finally he pushed the sheet away and leaned back, tilting his chair against the wall and staring across the room.
"Queer," he murmured. "They make sense, and then
again in places they don't make sense." And after a moment he leaned forward again. "Take this, for instance."
He pulled the sheet towards him again and pointed to the

entry for September 18 which read: *Laroche. No, it can't be. I must be mad.* What's he mean—do you know?"

I shook my head.

"And this on the twenty-sixth, the day after Laroche reached Menihek: 'L-L-L-L-L—impossible.' " He looked up at me as he read it aloud, but there was nothing I could tell him.

"Was he much alone?" he asked.

"There was my mother." I knew what he was getting at.

"But that room you described, and the hours he spent there every day with his radio. He was alone there?" And when I nodded, he said: "We get men like that up here. The emptiness and the loneliness—they get obsessions. Bushed, we call it." And then he asked me whether I'd brought the log books with me.

It was a request I had been dreading. One glance at them and he'd begin thinking my father was crazy again. But if I were to get him to help me, he'd a right to see them. "They're in my suitcase," I said.

He nodded. "Could I see them, please?" He was reading through the notes again, tapping at the paper with his pencil, his lips pursed, absorbed in his thoughts. He evidently sensed my hesitation, for he said: "Do you want a torch?" He reached up to the high top of the desk and handed me one. "Just walk straight out. Ethel won't mind." And then he was staring down at the notes again.

The two women were still there in the room upstairs. They stopped talking as I came in, and Mrs. Ledder said: "Ready for your coffee yet?" The room looked very gay and cheerful after the bare, untidy basement.

"I'm just going across to get something from the hotel," I explained.

She nodded, smiling at me, and I went out into the night. The stars were misting over, and the cold had a harshness in it that I'd never experienced before.

I got the log books out of my suitcase, and when I returned to the basement room Ledder was hunched over the desk, writing. He had the radio on, and through the crackle of atmospherics a voice was talking in a foreign language. "Brazil," he said, looking up at me. "Never have any difficulty getting South America." He switched the receiver off, and I gave him the log books, trying to tell him that the drawings and doodlings were irrelevant. But he waved my explanations aside, and I stood and watched him work steadily back through the pages. "He was alone a lot, that's for sure," he muttered, and my heart sank.

"He just did it to pass the time," I said.

He nodded. "Sure. It means nothing." He reached out to one of the cubbyholes of the desk. "Look at my pad." And he showed it to me, all covered with doodles. "You got to do something whilst you're waiting to pick up a transmission. It's like telephoning." He smiled at me, and that was when I began to like him.

"What sort of a person is Laroche?" It was the question that had been in my mind ever since Farrow had pointed out to me the implications of that transmission.

"Laroche?" He seemed to have to drag his mind back. "Oh, I don't know. A French Canadian, but a decent guy. Tallish, hair going slightly grey. I've only seen him once. He kept the Beaver down at the seaplane base, and our paths didn't cross. It was Tim Baird I kept in touch with. Bill Baird's brother. He was base manager—looked after stores and all their requirements." He had turned to the page on which the final message had been written, tapping his teeth with the pencil as he stared at it. *"'Search for narrow lake with rock shaped like . . .'"* He read it aloud slowly and looked up at me. "A rock shaped like what?"

I didn't say anything. I wanted to see if his mind would follow the track that mine had followed.

He was looking back through that last log book. "All

these drawings of lions. I wonder if Laroche knows anything about that Lake of the Lion. Could that message
have finished 'rock shaped like a lion'? Here's a drawing
that shows a lion set into a rock. And another here." He
looked up at me. "You said something about a map of
Labrador over his desk. Was Lake of the Lion marked
on it?"

"He'd pencilled it in, yes," I said and explained how
it had been enclosed in a rough circle covering the area
between the Attikonak and the Hamilton.

He nodded. "And C2 was in that area." He was toying
with the bug key, and suddenly he slapped his hand on
the desk. "Hell! No harm in telling them. Where's your
plane going on to?"

"Montreal." I waited now, holding my breath.

"Okay. The company offices are there." He hesitated a
moment longer, frowning and shaking his head. "It's
crazy," he muttered. "But you never know. There's crazy
enough things happen all the time up here in the North."
He pulled the paper on which he had been writing closer
to the key, read it through, and then reached over to the
transmitter. The pilot light glowed red, and there was a
faint hum as the set warmed up. And then he put the earphones on and hitched his chair closer to the desk. A
moment later his thumb was tapping at the key and I
heard the buzz of his Morse signal as he began to send.

I lit a cigarette. I felt suddenly exhausted. But at the
same time I was relaxed. I had achieved something, at
any rate. I had persuaded a man who had been hostile at
first to take action. But it was all to be done over again
at Montreal—the story of how my father had died, the
explanations. All to be told again, over and over again
perhaps. I wondered whether it was worth it, conscious
of the size of the country out there in the darkness beyond
the airport—the wildness and the emptiness of it. They'd
both be dead by now, surely. They couldn't possibly have

survived a whole week. But it was a chance, and because of my father and because of something in my blood, I knew I had to go on with it.

"Well, that's that, I guess." Ledder switched off the transmitter and pulled his earphones off. "That's what I told them." He handed me the slip of paper on which he'd pencilled his message. "It's up to the company now." He seemed relieved.

Possibility G2STO picked up transmission Briffe should not be ignored, I read. *Urgently advise you see Ferguson's son.* . . . I looked across at him. "I can't thank you enough," I said.

He seemed suddenly embarrassed. "I'm only doing what I think right," he murmured. "There's an outside chance, and I think they ought to take it."

"The authorities don't think so. They think my father was mad." And I told him then about the expert's report. I'd nothing to lose now the message was sent.

But he only smiled. "Maybe I can understand him better than they can. They're a queer lot, radio operators," he added, and the smile extended to his eyes.

"And it's technically possible?" I asked. "He could have picked up that message?"

"Sure he could." And he added: "It would be freak reception, of course. But if a message was transmitted, then he could certainly have picked it up. Look." And he drew a little diagram for me, showing that, however faint the signal was, the waves would still rebound from the ionosphere to the earth and back again to the ionosphere. "They'd travel like that all the way round the earth, and if your aerial happened to be set up at one of the points of rebound, then it would be possible to pick up the transmission even if it were six thousand miles away. It's just one of those things."

"And the transmitter was with Briffe in the aircraft when it crashed?"

"Yes. But the plane sank, and they didn't salvage anything. Laroche came out with nothing but the clothes he stood up in. That's what I've heard, anyway."

Possible, but not probable! And always there seemed to be the blank wall of Laroche to block any credence being given to my father's message.

"You'll see I've asked them to meet you at Dorval Airport and I've given them your flight number," he said. "I've also asked them to confirm through D.O.T. Communications. I don't expect we'll get a reply tonight, but it should come through fairly early in the morning.

I nodded. He couldn't have done more. And at that moment his wife called down the stairs to say that Mrs. Karnak had gone and she'd made some fresh coffee for us.

We went up then, and over coffee in the bright warmth of their living-room he gave me the first detailed account of Briffe's disappearance. He told it, of course, from the point of view of a man whose contact with the outside world was exclusively by radio. Like my father, he was confined to scraps of information plucked from the ether, to news broadcasts and messages from planes flying to search. But he was much closer to it. He had even met the men who figured in the disaster—Briffe twice, Laroche once—and he knew a good deal about Bill Baird from talks with his brother Tim, the company's base manager.

On September 12, Briffe had called for an air lift from Area C1, which was Lake Disappointment, up to C2, on the banks of the Attikonak River. This request was made in the course of his usual daily report. He had completed the survey at Disappointment. " 'Aptly named' was how he described it." Ledder smiled. And then he went on to explain that the survey party consisted of five men, and the procedure in making the hop forward to the next area was always the same: three of the five men, Sagon, Hatch, and Blanchard, would go forward as an advance party to establish the new camp, together with as much of the stores as the floatplane would carry and one canoe; Briffe and Baird would move up on the second flight with the transmitter, the other canoe, and the rest of the stores.

This was the procedure adopted on September 14, and Ledder was now more or less amplifying my father's notes for me. The air lift was actually called for September 13, but the weather had been bad and Laroche had decided to wait. However, the following day it was better, and he took off early in the morning. Ledder had actually seen the little Beaver floatplane scudding a broad arrow out across the still waters of the bay, had watched it take off, circle, and disappear into the haze beyond Happy Valley, headed west. He was off duty that day, and after about an hour he tuned in on the 75-metre band. But Briffe didn't come through until 1133. Laroche had arrived, but thick fog had closed in on the camp and was preventing take-off for C2. The delay in transmission had been due to condensation on the terminals of the hand generator.

Ledder immediately reported to Montreal the delay in the flight. It was apparently the normal procedure for either himself or his wife to keep a radio watch and report regularly to Montreal whenever a supply flight was made or the party were being air-lifted to a new location. He reported again at 1230, Briffe having come through with the news that the fog had lifted and the Beaver had taken off with the advance party.

After that he heard nothing from Briffe until 1500 hours when the survey-party leader came through with the information that the Beaver had not returned and the fog had clamped down again. It was Ledder's report of this information to Montreal that my father had picked up. "I began to get worried then," Ledder said. "We had started picking up reports of a storm belt moving in from the Atlantic, and things didn't look so good. I asked Briffe to report every hour."

At 1600 Briffe came through again. The fog had cleared, but the Beaver had still not returned. And then, at 1700, Briffe reported the plane safely back. Laroche had come down on a lake about ten miles short of C2 just before the fog closed in and had taken off again as soon as it had lifted. The advance party were now at C2, and Briffe's only concern was to get himself and Baird and the rest of the equipment up there before nightfall. "I told him," Ledder said, "that I didn't think it a good idea on account of the weather. He then asked me for a met forecast." He was turning over the pages of his log, which he had brought up with him. "Here you are." He passed it across to me. *Weather worsening rapidly. Ceiling 1,000, visibility 500, heavy rain. Expect airfield close down here shortly. Incoming flights already warned and west-bound trans-Atlantic traffic grounded Keflavik. Rain will turn to snow over Labrador plateau. Winds tonight easterly 20 knots plus. Tomorrow reaching 40 knots; rain, sleet or snow on high ground. Visibility nil at times.*

"And he decided to go on?" I asked.

"Yes, it was either that or stay at Disappointment, and the lake had poor holding ground, so that it meant the possible loss of the floatplane. In the end he decided to take a chance on it and make the flight."

I remembered my father's comment. He had called Briffe a fool, and had added: *What's driving him?* Had there been something besides concern for the floatplane? "The pilot has the final word, surely."

"I guess so," Ledder said. "But, by all accounts, Laroche isn't frightened of taking a chance."

"He could have returned to base here."

He shrugged his shoulders. "A twenty-knot head wind and the risk that he'd be short of gas and unable to locate Goose. Maybe he thought going on to C2 the lesser of the two evils." And then he went on to tell me how Briffe had failed to come through as arranged at 2200 and how he and his wife had kept watch all that night. "But he never came through," Ledder said.

And in the morning, conditions had been so bad that nothing could get in to Goose, let alone fly a search over the Labrador plateau. It had been like that for two days, and then one of the floatplanes from the base had flown in to C2 and had come back with confirmation that Briffe and his party were missing. The search was on then, with the R.C.A.F. contributing four Lancasters out of the Nova Scotia Air Rescue Station and the Iron Ore people flying a search out of Menihek.

He was giving me details of the search when his wife reminded him that they had promised to be at the officers' mess at nine. "Perhaps Mr. Ferguson would like to come with us," she suggested. But I hadn't any Canadian money, and anyway I wanted time to myself to think over what he had told me. I excused myself by saying I wanted to turn in early, finished my coffee, and got up.

"I'll get the company's reply to you as soon as it comes through," Ledder said as he saw me to the door. "If there's anything else I can do, let me know."

I thanked him and went down the wooden steps, out into the night. "Good luck!" he called after me, and then the door closed and I was alone in the darkness. The stars were gone now, and it was snowing. It was so still I could almost hear the flakes falling, and without a torch it took me some time to find my way back to the hotel.

Actually I didn't get to bed till almost midnight, for I sat up in the warmth of my room, making notes and thinking about what I should say to the company officials. I suppose I was tired. At any rate, I didn't wake up in the morning until a quarter to seven, and I jumped out of bed in a panic, convinced that I had missed my flight. I hurried into my clothes and went along to Farrow's room. To my relief, he was still there, lying on his bed in his shirt and trousers. "I was afraid I'd missed you," I said as he opened his eyes, regarding me sleepily.

"Relax," he murmured. "I won't go without you." And he added: "Take-off won't be till nine thirty or later. There was no point in waking you." He turned over then and went to sleep again.

The truck called for us at nine, and we hung around on the airfield until almost ten thirty whilst the maintenance crew, who had been working most of the night, finished fixing the engine. The snow had gone, and the air was cool and crisp, the hills across the bay sharply defined under a cold, grey sky streaked with cloud. There was a steely quality about Goose that morning, the menace of winter in the air. The country round was all greys and blacks, the scrub spruce unrelieved by any colour. The harshness of it was almost frightening.

And there was no word from Ledder. I told Farrow how Ledder had reacted when I had shown him my father's log books, and he phoned Communications for me. But Ledder wasn't there, and there was no message for me.

We took off at ten twenty and I had still heard nothing. I stood in the alley of the flight deck, watching Goose drop away from us below the port wing as we made a climbing turn. All ahead of us was a desolate waste of spruce with the thread of the Hamilton River winding through it. Then we were in cloud, and when we came out above it, there was still no sun and the cloud layer below us was flat like a grey mantle of snow.

Later there were rifts in the cloud layer and, watching from the flight engineer's seat, I could see the ground below, looking strangely close, though I knew it couldn't be, for we were flying at six thousand feet. It was all ridged the way sand is when the tide is out, but the ridges were dark and grim-looking, with patches of exposed rock worn smooth by the tread of Ice Age glaciers, and all

between was water, flat like steel and frosted white at
the edges.

We flew on and on, and the country below never
changed. It was the grimmest land I had ever seen. The
land God gave to Cain! It seemed as though it could never
end, but would run on like that for ever, and after a while
the flight engineer tapped me on the shoulder and I went
back into the fuselage and sat down on the freight, feeling cold and depressed.

I had been there about an hour when the radio operator
came aft to say that Farrow wanted a word with me.
"We just got a message from Goose."

Back in the flight-deck alley, Farrow handed me a message slip. On it was written: *Presd. McGovern Mng &*
Ex now at Iron Ore Terminal. Wishes question Ferguson
earliest. Can you land him Seven Islands?

"Well, what do you want me to do?" Farrow shouted
to me.

"Seven Islands? But that's just an Indian fishing village," I said.

"You think so?" He laughed. "Then I guess you're in
for a shock. It's quite a town. The Iron Ore Company of
Canada is building a railway north from there to get at
the ore in the centre of Labrador. Worth seeing, since
you're an engineer. About the biggest project on this
continent right now."

So the line my father had pencilled on his map was a
railway. "But can you land there?" I asked doubtfully.

"Sure. They got a good airstrip. And they need it.
They're supplying their forward camps entirely by air
lift, flying everything in—even cement for the dam at
Menihek and bull-dozers for the Knob Lake ore deposits."
He glanced back at me over his shoulder. "But I won't
be able to wait for you there. You understand that?
You'll be on your own from then on."

I didn't know what to say. The plane was suddenly immensely precious to me, a familiar, friendly oasis in the immensity of Canada that was beginning to roll itself out before me. To abandon it would be like abandoning a ship in mid-Atlantic. "Better make up your mind," Farrow shouted. "We got to alter course right now if we're to drop you off at Seven Islands." He was watching me curiously. I suppose he saw my dilemma, for he added: "It's what you wanted, isn't it? You've stirred 'em up, and you can't go higher than the president of the company."

There was nothing for it. I'd known that as soon as I had read the message. "All right," I said. And then, because that sounded ungrateful, I added: "You're sure it's all right for you to land there?"

"Who's to know?" He grinned and pointed ahead through his side windows to where a pale glimmer like cloud or mist showed along the horizon. "There's the St. Lawrence now. Another hour and we'll be very close to Seven Islands. Okay?"

I nodded.

He called back instructions to the navigator and the radio operator, and then looked at me with a grin and added: "Who knows—I may even get a mention in dispatches if those poor devils are lifted out alive."

A mood of optimism swept over me then, and as I went back into the fuselage I was thinking that some divine providence must be guiding me.

The mood was still with me more than an hour later when we began to descend. I felt the check as the flaps went down, and then the engines were throttled back, and a moment later we touched down. We taxied for a while, bumping heavily over rough ground, and then we stopped, the engines quietly ticking over.

Farrow himself came back down the fuselage and opened the doors for me. "Good luck," he said, "and see they look after you. We'll be in Montreal until midday tomorrow if you want a ride back."

"Of course I want to go back with you," I shouted. I was appalled at the thought that he might return to England without me.

He clapped me on the shoulder, and I jumped out into the backwash of air from the slowly turning props.

"I'll be there," I shouted up to him.

The door slammed shut, and I hurried clear, to stand a little way off, watching, with my suitcase gripped in my hand. Farrow was back at the controls. He waved to me through the windshield. The engines roared, kicking up a great swirl of dust, and then the machine that had brought me across the Atlantic went lumbering away over the hard-baked dirt of the airfield, out to the runway end.

I watched it take off—watched it until it was a speck in the sky. I hated to see Farrow go. I was alone now, and there was nobody here I knew. I stood there for a moment, waiting and turning the loose change over in my pocket. I'd a few pounds in my wallet, but that was all. Nobody came out to meet me.

Part Two

The Labrador
Railway

I

When I could no longer see the plane

I walked slowly towards the line of pre-fabricated huts that were the airport buildings. I felt abandoned, almost lost now, for there was nothing about Seven Islands to give me a sense of ease.

The bull-dozed road, the dust, the maple leaf in the last flush of autumn, and the distant glimpse of new construction and heaped-up stores and equipment—it had a barbaric newness, an alien quality like the supply point for a battlefield. There were open hangar-like sheds piled with crates and sacks of foodstuffs, pieces of machinery, tires, and a fork lift was trundling the stuff out to a battered Dakota, where a group of men stood smoking. They were a wild, mixed lot in strange headgear and gaily coloured bush shirts, and their kit stacked about them included bed-rolls and thick, quilted jackets.

The place had an edge-of-the-wilds smell about it, and in the dispatch office they knew nothing about me. There was nobody to meet me, not even a message, and when I asked for the offices of the McGovern Mining & Exploration Company, they had never heard of it. "You a geologist?" the dispatcher asked.

"No." I didn't want to start explaining myself here.

"Well, what's your job, then?"

"I'm an engineer," I said. "But that's got nothing to do—"

"You better report to Q.N.S. & L., then." He went to
the door and shouted to a truck driver who was just moving off. "He'll take you down. Okay?" He was back at his
desk, checking a dispatch list, and because there seemed
nothing else to do I went out to the truck and got in. An
office would know where I ought to go, or at least I could
phone. "What's Q.N.S. & L. stand for?" I asked the driver
as we lurched out through the wire on to a dirt road. I
was thinking of the pencilled line my father had drawn
on his map.

"Quebec North Shore and Labrador Railway." He
looked at me, his battered, sun-reddened face softened by
a smile. "You from the Old Country?" He wore a scarlet-
patterned woollen bush shirt, and the open neck of it
showed the hair of his chest grey with road dust. He
asked about England. He'd been there with the Canadian Army. And then we crossed the track and he talked
about the railway. "I worked on the Tote Road when we
started two years back. Boy, that was real tough. Now the
Americans are in, and they got all the equipment they
need to build the grade. You going up the line?"

I shook my head. I was looking at the skyline ahead,
staggered by the mushroom growth of buildings. And to
the left of us were acres of piled-up railway equipment—
great stacks of rails and sleepers, and store sheds as big
as hangars, and in between were the solid, powerful
shapes of big diesel electric locomotives, their paintwork
factory-new.

"Guess I wouldn't mind going back up the line again,"
he said. "Drive, drive, drive; but it's good to see a thing
take shape and be a part of it. You oughter go up there,
just to tell 'em back in the Old Country how we built a
railroad slap into the middle of nowhere." And he went
on: "Gee, you oughter see it now the heat's on. Not
more'n a month to go before the big freeze-up, and Head
of Steel pushing forward near on two miles a day." He

shook his big bullet head. "You oughter see it." He jammed his foot on the brake pedal, and the truck stopped with a jerk. "Okay, fellow. There's the office." He jerked his head at a group of wooden buildings, and there was a board with q.n.s. & l.r. on it.

The airport dispatcher must have phoned them, for the man in the office took me for a newly arrived engineer. And when I told him I had just stopped off to see the president of the McGovern Mining & Exploration Company, he said: "Hell! I thought it was too good to be true."

"If you could direct me to the company's offices," I suggested.

He scratched his head. "There's no company of that name here. There's just ourselves and the Iron Ore Company and the construction combine." He tipped his chair back, looking at me. "What's this fellow's name?"

"I don't know," I said. "I was just told to meet him here in Seven Islands."

"There was a guy called McGovern at breakfast this morning. Came in last night from Montreal—big man with a voice like a nutmeg grater. That him?"

"Couldn't you ring somebody and find out for me?" I asked. "The plane landed me here specially. There must be a message for me somewhere."

He sighed and reached for the phone. "Maybe the Iron Ore Company will know something about you. They handle all the mining and exploration side. We're just the railroad, here." He got through to somebody and told him my name and who I'd come to see, and after listening for a bit, he put the receiver down. "Well, McGovern's your man, all right. But he's busy right now. A conference." His chair was tilted back again, and he was looking at me with renewed interest. "That was Bill Lands. He keeps tabs on Burnt Creek and all the geological parties. He'll be right over. I'm Staffen, by the

way. Alex Staffen." He held out his hand to me. "I'm
the personnel manager. Bill said something about your
being here in connection with this survey party that
crashed."

I nodded.

"Bad business." He shook his head, sucking in air between his teeth. "Briffe was a nice guy. Did you ever meet
him?"

"No," I said.

"French Canadian, but a fine guy. A throwback to the
voyageurs." He stared at his desk. "It's tough on his
daughter." He looked up at me suddenly. "You reckon
there's hope?" he asked. And when I didn't answer, he
said: "There's talk about a transmission having been
picked up in England." His eyes were fixed on mine.
"You know anything about that?"

"That's why I'm here," I said.

I suppose he sensed that I didn't want to talk about it,
for he just nodded and looked away towards the window,
which gave on to a drab view of sand and gravel and huts.
"Well, Paule's lucky, I guess, to have one of them come
out alive."

He meant the pilot, presumably, and I asked him if he
knew where Laroche was now.

"Why, here, of course." He seemed surprised.

"You mean he's here in Seven Islands?"

"Sure. He and Paule Briffe . . ." The phone on his
desk rang, and he picked it up. "Harry West? Oh, for
God's sake!" he exclaimed. "A gas car, you say? Hell!"
He made a note on his pad. "Okay, I'll have Ken Burke
take over at Two-two-four. No, I'll arrange for him to be
flown up." He slammed the receiver down. "The damn
fool got his foot crushed by a gas car. You'd think after
six months up the line he'd know how to handle a
speeder."

The door swung open, and a big, hustling man came

in. He had a tanned face, and his calf-length boots were caked with mud. "Here's Bill now." My hand was gripped in a hard fist as Staffen introduced us. "I was telling him how Briffe was a real *voyageur* type."

"Sure was. Knew the North like city folk know their own back yard." Bill Lands was looking at me, mild blue eyes in a dust-streaked face summing me up. "Okay," he said abruptly. "Let's go across to my office, shall we? Mr. McGovern should be about through now, I guess." He gave an off-hand nod to Staffen, and as we went out through the door he said: "I've sent for Bert Laroche, by the way."

"For Laroche? Why?"

He gave me a flat, hard look. "If a man's going to be called a liar, it better be to his face." He left it at that and led me down a concrete path to another hut. "Ever meet McGovern?" He tossed the question at me over his shoulder.

"No," I said. "I'm from England."

He laughed. "You don't have to tell me that." At the door of the hut he paused and faced me. "I think maybe I'd better warn you. Mac's tough. Spent most of his life in the North West Territories. He reckons this about the damnedest thing he ever struck." He strode ahead of me into his office and waved me to a seat across the desk from him. "So do I, if it comes to that. Smoke?" He tossed a pack of American cigarettes into my lap. "Bert's flown me thousands of miles. We've been in on this thing from the start, since back in forty-seven when they decided to establish a permanent survey base at Burnt Creek and really go to work on this iron-ore project." He took the pack from me and lit himself a cigarette. "Bert's a fine guy."

I didn't say anything. It was McGovern I'd come to see.

"And there's Paule, too," he added. "That's Briffe's

daughter. How do you think she's going to feel when she learns why you're here?" He was leaning back, looking at me through eyes half closed against the smoke of the cigarette stuck in the corner of his mouth, and I could feel him holding himself in. "Did Alex tell you about Bert and Paule?"

He didn't wait for me to answer. "They were planning to be married this fall." He stared at me, and I knew he was hating me and wishing I were dead. But whether for the sake of his friend or because of the girl, I didn't know. And then he said: "Paule works right here in this office—has done ever since her father took this job with McGovern and they moved down from Burnt Creek." He took the cigarette out of his mouth and leaned forward. "What happens when she hears about this? Her father was all the world to her. She grew up in the North, camping and trekking and canoeing with him through the bush like a boy. He was her hero. And now he's dead. Why raise false hopes?"

"But supposing he isn't dead?"

"Bert was there. He says he's dead." He was jabbing the cigarette at me. "Leave it at that, why can't you?"

He was against me. And I knew then that they'd all be against me. I was an outsider, and they'd close their ranks. . . .

"Anyway, I just don't believe it," he was saying, leaning back and stubbing out his cigarette. "If Bert says they're dead, then they're dead, and that's all there is to it. It's not his fault he was the only one got out. It happens that way sometimes." And he added: "He's one of the finest bush fliers in the North. I remember one time, back in forty-nine. We were flying out of Fort Chimo, and the weather clamped right down—"

He was interrupted by the slam of a door in the corridor outside and a harsh voice saying: "I agree. No point in hanging on to those concessions."

"That's Mac now." Lands rose from his chair and went to the door. "We're in here, Mac."

"Fine, Bill. I'll be right with you." And then the voice added: "Well, there it is. Sorry it didn't work out."

Bill Lands turned away from the door and came across to where I was sitting. "I've read the reports," he said. "I know what they say about your father." His hand gripped my shoulder. "But he's dead, and nobody can hurt him. These others, they're alive." He was staring at me hard, and then he added: "Don't crucify Paule just to try and prove a point."

It was said very quietly, but grim-faced, so that I caught my breath, staring up at him. And then McGovern's harsh voice came from beyond the door again: "But don't expect too much from us on the northern concessions. There's a bare month before freeze-up—maybe less." And another voice said: "Okay. Do the best you can, Mac. But we've got to know what we hang on to and what we give up." The outer door slammed, and then McGovern was in the room.

He was a broad, chunky man, hard-jawed and tight-lipped, and the battered face was weathered with a thousand wrinkles. Eyes clear as grey stone pebbles looked me over. "You a ham operator, too?" The voice grated on my nerves, the tone hostile. Or was that my imagination?

"No," I said. I had risen to my feet, but he didn't come across to greet me. Instead he went over to the desk, slammed a bulging briefcase on top of it, and sat down in Bill Lands's chair. The briefcase didn't seem to fit the man any more than his city suit. There was something untamed about him—an impression that was enhanced by the mane of white hair that swept back from his low, broad forehead. It was as though a piece of the northern wild had moved into the office, and I think I was scared of him before ever he started to question me.

Bill Lands gave a little cough. "Well, I'll leave you two to—"

"No, no. You stay here, Bill. I'd like you to hear what this young man has to tell us. Has Bert arrived yet?"

"No, but he should be here any minute."

"Well, pull up a chair. Now, then." McGovern fastened his eyes on me. "I take it you've got some new information for us . . . something that proves Briffe's still alive?" He phrased it as a question, his shaggy eyebrows lifted and his flinty eyes boring into me. "Well?"

"Not exactly new information, sir," I said.

"Then what's this guy Ledder all steamed up about? You saw him at Goose and he radioed a message to our office. You wouldn't have come all this way without something new for us to go on. What did you tell him?"

My mouth felt dry. McGovern was a type I'd never met before, and his domineering personality seemed to bear down on me and crush me. "It wasn't exactly anything new," I murmured. "It was just that I convinced him that my father really did pick up a transmission."

"It doesn't say that here." He tugged at the straps of his briefcase and pulled out a message form. "This is how his message reads." He pushed a pair of steel-rimmed glasses on to his blunt nose. " 'Possibility G2STO picked up transmission Briffe should not be ignored. Urgently advise you see Ferguson's son.' Why?" he said. "What did you tell him?" He was looking up at me over the top of his glasses. "What made Ledder advise us to have a talk with you?"

"It wasn't so much what I told him," I said. "It was more the background I gave him to my father's reception of Briffe's message. You see, my father died, virtually as a result of receiving—"

"Yes, we know all about your father's death," he cut in. "What I want to know is what you told Ledder that made him radio this message."

"I merely filled in all the background for him." I felt at a loss how to break through and explain my father to this man. "It's not so much the facts," I said, "as the story behind the reception. If you'd known my father—"

"So there's nothing new?"

What could I say? He was watching me, and it seemed to me that he was challenging me to produce something new. And all the time his eyes remained wide open, not blinking. It disconcerted me, and in the end I said nothing. He seemed to relax then and looked away, glancing down at the papers he had spread out on the desk. "Your name's Ian Ferguson, I believe?"

"Yes." My voice sounded like a stranger to me.

"Well, now, Ferguson, I think I should tell you, before we go any further, that the report of this transmission your father was supposed to have picked up was given immediate and most serious attention, not only by myself but by the Air Force authorities and others. If we could have found one single radio operator anywhere in the world who could confirm it, the search would have been resumed. But we couldn't, and when we got the police reports of the full circumstances . . ." He gave a slight shrug that dismissed my father entirely.

I found my voice then. "If it's facts and nothing else that interest you," I said angrily, "then perhaps you'll appreciate the significance of what I learned at Goose. You say you couldn't get confirmation of Briffe's transmission. Of course you couldn't. Every other operator had given up listening for him. Every operator, that is, except my father. If you'd read Ledder's report, you'd know that my father contacted him again on the twenty-sixth, the day the search was called off, to ask whether there was any other frequency Briffe might use in an emergency. Ledder told him no and repeated Briffe's transmitting frequency. Surely that's proof enough that my father was keeping a constant watch."

"I see. And you expect me to believe that your father was keeping a twenty-four-hour watch for a transmission that he couldn't possibly expect to receive, and from a man who was dead anyway?" He was looking at me as though to say: *If you tell me yes, then I'll know your father was crazy.* "Well, was he?"

"He had Briffe's sending frequency," I said. "He'd nothing else to do, and he was obsessed—"

"Was the receiver tuned to that frequency when you got home the evening of the day he died?"

I should have checked that, but I hadn't. "I don't know." I felt angry and helpless.

And then footsteps sounded in the passage outside and Bill Lands went to the door. "Here's Bert now."

"Tell him to wait," McGovern said. And then he was looking at me again. "So you believe your father really did pick up a transmission from Briffe. And you've come all this way in order to convince us—without a single item of fresh information. Correct?"

"But I've just told you—"

"You've told me nothing. Nothing that I didn't know already." He pulled a stapled sheaf of papers from his briefcase, and after removing two of the pages, he passed the rest across to me. "Now I want you to read these reports through. Read them carefully, and then if there's anything you can add to them or any new light you can throw on the situation, I'll be glad to know about it." He had risen to his feet. "But," he added, "I think you should understand this. The man waiting outside is Bert Laroche, the pilot of the floatplane that crashed—and he says Briffe is dead."

"I'm not interested in what Laroche says." My voice sounded a little wild. "All I know is that my father—"

"You're calling Bert Laroche a liar. You're doing more than that. You're accusing him—"

"I don't care," I cried. "I'm not concerned with La-roche."

"No," he said. "Why should you be? You never met the guy, and you don't understand his world." He was staring at me coldly.

"It's Briffe I'm concerned about," I murmured.

"Yeah?" His tone had contempt in it. "You never met him either, or the other guy—Baird. They mean nothing to you, any of them. All you're concerned about is your father, and for his sake you're prepared to make a lot of trouble and smear a decent man with the mud of your accusations." He had come round the desk and was standing over me, and now his hand reached out and gripped hold of my shoulder, stilling my protest. "You read those reports. Read them carefully. And just remember that afterwards you're going to meet Laroche, and anything you have to say will be said in his presence." He was staring down at me, the eyes stony and unblinking. "Just remember, too, that his story says your father couldn't have picked up a transmission from Briffe on the twenty-ninth. Okay?" He nodded to Bill Lands, and the two of them went out.

His greeting to Laroche outside in the passage was in a softer tone, and then the door closed and I was alone. The voices faded, and the walls of the office closed in around me, unfamiliar and hostile—isolating me. Was it only two days since I'd run into Farrow in the Airport Bar? It seemed so long ago, and England so far away. I was beginning to wish I'd never come to Canada.

Automatically I started to look through the papers. It was all there—a summary of the notes my father had made in his log books, my statement to the police, the description of the room and his radio equipment, techni-cal information about the possibility of R/T reception at that range, Ledder's report, everything. And then I came to the psychiatrists' report: *It is not unusual for physical frustration to lead to mental unbalance, and in those conditions a morbid interest in some disaster or human drama may result in the subject having delusions that attribute to himself an active, even prominent role, in the events that fill his mind. This occurs particularly where the subject is overmuch alone. In certain unusual cases such mental unbalance can give rise to extraordinary physical effort, and in the case under review . . .*

I flung the sheaf of papers on to the desk. How could they be so stupid? But then I realized it wasn't their fault so much as my own. If I could have told them about that earlier expedition, they might have understood my father's obsession with the country. All those questions that had puzzled Ledder . . . I couldn't blame the authorities really. The questions hadn't meant anything to me until Ledder told me what had happened to my grandfather. Even now I didn't understand all the references.

I got out the list of jottings I'd made from his log books and went through them again, and the name Laroche stared me in the face. Why had my father been so interested in Laroche? Why was his reaction important? I picked up the sheaf of papers McGovern had given me and searched through it again. There was a list of all the radio stations—service, civilian, and amateur—that had been contacted, and three solid pages of reports from pilots flying the search. But the one thing I wanted wasn't there, and I guessed that the pages McGovern had detached before giving the rest to me were those containing Laroche's statement.

I sat back then, wondering what Laroche would be like and whether his story would help me to decide what I ought to do now. McGovern wasn't going to do anything—of that I was certain. But if Laroche had been able to satisfy Briffe's daughter that her father was dead

. . . I didn't know what to think. Maybe Lands was right. Maybe I should just leave it at that and go home.

The door behind me opened and McGovern came in. "Well?" he said, shutting the door behind him. "Have you read it all through?"

"Yes," I said. "But I didn't find Laroche's statement."

"No. He'll tell you what happened himself." He came and stood over me. "But before I call him in, I want to know whether there is any material fact that's been omitted from these reports. If there is, then let's have it right now, whilst we're alone."

I looked up at him, and the hard grey eyes were watching me out of the leathery face. His hostility was evident, and I was conscious of the limitations of my background. I hadn't been brought up to deal with men like this. "It depends what you call material facts," I said uncertainly. "That psychiatrists' report—it's based on the supposition that my father was simply a spectator, that he wasn't involved at all. They didn't have all the facts."

"How do you mean?"

"They didn't know his background, and without that the questions he asked Ledder and many of the jottings he made couldn't possibly make sense to them."

"Go on," he said.

I hesitated, wondering how to put it when I knew so little. "Did you know there was an expedition into the Attikonak area in 1900?" I asked.

"Yes." And it seemed to me his tone was suddenly guarded.

"Well, it appears that the leader of that expedition was my grandfather."

"Your grandfather?" He was staring at me, and it was obvious that the revelation meant something to him, had come as a shock.

"Now perhaps you'll understand why my father was so interested in anything to do with Labrador," I said. "It

explains all those questions he asked Ledder—questions
that the psychiatrists couldn't understand. And because
they couldn't understand them, they thought he was
mad."

"So James Finlay Ferguson was your grandfather, eh?"
He nodded his head slowly. "I thought maybe it was that.
As soon as they told me your father's name, I guessed
we'd be back to that expedition. So did Bert. My God!"
he said. "This is the third generation. And it was never
more than gossip. Nothing was proved. Not even that
woman could prove anything. And now you come over
here with a lot of wild accusations that are based on nothing more substantial than this." He stared at me stonily,
the veins of his face corded with anger. "Why the hell
didn't you tell the authorities that your father was living
in a world of the past—or didn't you dare? Did you think
that would make him appear even more crazy?"

"He wasn't crazy!" I almost shouted at him. I didn't
understand half of what he'd been saying. "As for telling
the authorities—I'd never heard about my grandfather's
expedition until last night."

"Never heard about it?" He stared at me with obvious
disbelief.

I told him then how I'd heard of it first from Ledder
and how he'd only got the briefest information about it
over the air from one of the geologists.

"Good God!" he said. "So you don't know the details.
You don't know who was with your grandfather on that
expedition—or where they went or what they were prospecting for?"

"No," I said. "I didn't come here because of that. I
came because my father was a first-rate radio operator
and I'm convinced—"

"Okay," he said. "I admit that puts a different complexion on it. But only as far as your motive in coming
over is concerned," he added quickly. "It doesn't mean

Briffe is alive. You may have known nothing about the Ferguson Expedition, but your father did."

"What's that got to do with it?" I demanded.

"Everything," he said. "In my opinion, everything. His motive is obvious." And he added darkly: "There are more ways than one of being unbalanced."

I didn't understand what he was getting at, and I told him so.

"All right," he said. "Forget it. You're not involved, and I accept that. But I can't accept the rest—that your father really did pick up a transmission." And when I started to protest, he silenced me with an impatient movement of his hand. "Wait till you've heard what Bert Laroche has to say."

He left me then and went out, closing the door behind him. Through the flimsy wood partitioning I heard the whisper of their voices. What was he telling them? Was he briefing Laroche on what to say? But I couldn't believe that. It was something else—something to do with that expedition. If only I knew all the facts! I twisted round in my chair, watching the door, wondering what Laroche would be like. If my father were right, then the man had made a terrible, unbelievable mistake.

The door opened again and McGovern entered. "Come in, both of you," he said, and went over to the desk and sat down. Lands followed, and then a third man, tall and lean with the sort of face I'd never seen before. A gleam of sun threw a dusty shaft across the office, and he walked right into it, his face dark and angular, almost secretive, with high cheekbones and the eyes laced with little lines at the corners so that they seemed constantly screwed up to peer at some distant horizon. A great gash ran from the top of his head down across his forehead to finish above his right eye. It was part-healed now, a black scab of dried blood, and the hair that had been shaved away on either side of it was beginning to grow again like black

fur against the white of the scalp. The eyebrow had also
been shaved away, and this gave his features a strangely
twisted look.

McGovern told him to pull up a chair, and as he sat
down he darted a quick glance at me. His eyes were brown
and deep-sunk in sockets darkened by strain. It was obvious that he'd been under tension for a long time, and
there was a pallor beneath the dark skin that suggested
exhaustion. And then he smiled at me, pulling a pipe
from his pocket and relaxing. His teeth were very white,
and the smile somehow altered the balance of his face,
so that it suddenly had a boyish, almost debonair look;
the same sort of look that I'd seen on the faces of Farrow
and his friends, careless and yet concentrated. He seemed
younger then, though his dark hair was turning to grey
at the temples.

Lands had shut the door, and he pulled a chair up and
sat down. McGovern leaned forward across the desk.
"Now then, let's get this over with," he said to me. "I
gather you still think your father may have picked up
some sort of a message from Briffe?"

I nodded, my mind still concentrated on Laroche. I was
trying to be honest with myself, to see him as he really
was—an experienced bush flier. It didn't seem possible
that he could have made a mistake, not over a thing like
that, and not when he was engaged to Briffe's daughter.

McGovern had been saying something, and he suddenly
hit the desk in front of him. "Don't just sit there, man!"
he shouted at me. "Tell us why you're still convinced."
And then in a quieter tone he added: "You don't seem to
realize that we knew Paul Briffe. He was a friend of
mine, of Bill's, too. Bert was going to be his son-in-law.
We've all of us every reason in the world to wish him
alive." He leaned back in his chair with a little sigh.
"But we don't think he is." And he went on: "When I
had the first report of this alleged transmission, I thought

for a moment Bert had made a mistake. Sometimes in the bush it's difficult to be sure. . . ." He let it go at that. "But then we got the full report, and when it was clear that nobody else had picked up the transmission, I knew it was no good calling for the search to be resumed. Now you come here, and after reading those reports, you say you're still convinced your father did pick up a transmission. Why?"

I stared at him, sitting squat like a rock behind the desk. How could I explain to him how I felt about my father? The sense of helplessness came back to me, stronger than ever. "I'd like to hear what Laroche has to say," I said obstinately.

"Sure. But first you tell us what makes you so damned sure."

"Because I know the sort of man my father was," I answered.

"You read the psychiatrists' report?"

"Do you expect me to agree with it?" I stared at him, anger flaring up inside me. "He wasn't unbalanced. And he didn't suffer from delusions."

"Did you live in the same house with him?"

"No."

"Then how can you be sure about his mental state?"

"Because I'm his son." McGovern's attitude was that of a brick wall. I could feel myself battering against it. "A son should know if his father's mad or not. And Dad wasn't mad. He knew it was Lake of the Lion, and he knew it was Briffe. Why else do you think—"

"What's that you said?" The question was slammed at me by Laroche, and there was a sudden stillness in the room. He was staring at me, and then he glanced across at McGovern, who said quickly: "We'll leave the matter of your father for the moment." He leaned forward, holding my attention with his eyes. "Right now I want you to hear what actually happened. When you've heard it, I think you'll agree with us that there can be no room for doubt." He turned to Laroche. "Go ahead, Bert. Tell him what happened."

Laroche hesitated, glancing at me and running his tongue along the line of his lips. "Okay," he said. "I guess that's best. Then he can sort it out for himself." He shifted his gaze, staring down at his hands. I thought: *He's nervous.* But then he began to talk and I wasn't sure. He had a slight accent, and though he was hesitant at times, it was mostly because he was searching for the word he wanted. His voice was flat and without emotion; he had been through it all many times before.

They had taken off at approximately six thirty on the evening of September 14. They had abandoned part of the stores and one tent and one. canoe, and cleared out of Disappointment in a hell of a hurry, for the storm was already upon them and the waters of the lake were being kicked up by a twenty-knot wind. Area C2 was about half an hour's flying time away, but before they had covered half the distance, the cloud base had come down very low with driving sleet and poor visibility.

"I should have landed whilst I had the chance," Laroche said. He wasn't looking at me. He wasn't looking at anybody. He just sat there, telling what happened in that flat, slightly foreign voice.

He had been forced down until the floats were skimming the tops of the jackpine and he was lake-hopping from one expanse of water to the next. "At that level things come up very fast. And the lakes take on a different shape. It was only the small ones that I could see as a whole. The rest were just scraps of water, blurred in the sleet and the poor light." He thought he might have underestimated the wind strength. When he had come up with the advance party, the fog and his forced landing had made it impossible for him to memorize the ground. Anyway, memory wouldn't have helped, with dusk falling and poor visibility. He flew a compass course, and when he'd flown the estimated time distance, he began to search, flying in widening circles, still held down to tree-top level. He flew like that for almost fifteen minutes, with the light fading all the time and no sign of the Attikonak River or any feature that would give him his bearings. ?

And then the snow came. It came suddenly in a blinding squall that blotted out everything. "I had no choice," he said. "I had been crossing a lake, and I did a tight turn and put the nose down." He had ripped the floats as he crashed through the trees at the water's edge and had hit the surface of the lake hard, bounced twice, and then smashed into a rock that had suddenly loomed up in front of him. He had hit it with the starboard wing, so that the plane had swung round, crashing into it broadside and shattering the fuselage. The impact had flung him head-first against the windshield, and he had blacked out.

When he came to, the plane was half in, half out of the water, with the rock towering above it. Dazed, he crawled back into the fuselage to find Baird unconscious, pinned there by a piece of metal that had injured his right hand and opened up all one side of his face. "Paul was injured, too." Laroche's eyes were half closed as he talked, and I couldn't doubt that this was how it had happened. His voice and the details carried conviction.

He had done what he could for them, which wasn't much, for there was no wood on the rock with which to make a fire. He was there two days, until the storm had passed, and then he hacked one of the floats clear, patched it, and ferried the two injured men ashore. He had got a fire going and had rigged up a shelter of branches, and he had brought some supplies from the plane. Two days later another storm had come up. The wind had been northwesterly, and the following morning the plane had vanished. The wind had killed the fire, too, and he hadn't been able to light another because all the matches were soaked and he had lost his lighter, which was the only one they possessed. Baird had died that night; Briffe the following night. After that he had started trekking westward. "I knew that as long as I kept going west I must arrive at the line of the railway sooner or later." He had kept going for five days and nights with almost no food, and on the afternoon of the 25th he had reached Mile 273, where a construction gang with a grab crane were working on the grade. "I guess that's all," he said, looking at me for the first time. "I was lucky to get out alive."

"Well, there you are," McGovern said, and the finality of his tone made it clear he considered I ought to be satisfied.

"That trip you made out to the plane," I said. "Did you bring the radio ashore?"

"No," he said. "It went down with the aircraft."

"And you're sure Briffe was dead when you left him?"

Laroche looked at me, his eyes wide in his tanned face. And then he glanced quickly at McGovern. It was as though he had turned to him for help. But it was Lands who said: "He's just told you so, hasn't he?" His tone was angry. "What more do you want?"

And then McGovern said: "You'd like to see the bodies, I suppose." He was glaring at me.

"Did you bury them?" I asked Laroche. I thought if I dug hard enough . . .

"For God's sake!" Lands said.

"No," Laroche answered me. "I didn't bury them. I guess I didn't have the energy." His voice was flat. And then he added quickly: "I tried to locate them afterwards. I flew twice with a pilot out of Menihek. But there are thousands of lakes—literally thousands." His voice trailed away.

"Thousands, yes," I said. "But only one Lake of the Lion." And again I was conscious of a tension in the room. It wasn't only Laroche, who was staring at me with a shocked expression on his face. It was McGovern, too. "What the hell's the name of the lake matter if he couldn't locate it again?" he said angrily.

But I was looking at Laroche. "You knew it was Lake of the Lion, didn't you?" I was so sure it was important that I pressed the point. "That rock in the middle—"

"It was snowing," he muttered.

"When you crashed. But later . . . Didn't you see the rock later? It was shaped like a lion, wasn't it?"

"I don't know," he said. "I didn't notice."

"But you've read those reports? You know the message my father picked up?"

He nodded.

"That transmission of Briffe's—it was from Lake of the Lion."

"You don't know that," McGovern cut in.

"Then why did he say 'Search for narrow lake with a rock shaped like . . .'?" I demanded. "There's only those two words, 'a lion,' missing."

"You're just guessing," McGovern said. "And anyway your father was simply inventing on the basis of what he knew of the Ferguson Expedition."

"Do you really believe that?" I cried. "Those were the last words he wrote before he died."

"That doesn't make them true. He couldn't have known he was going to die."

I stared at him, appalled. "I tell you, he struggled to his feet to look at that map. Lake of the Lion was marked on that map; his log books, too—they were littered with drawings of lions. . . ."

"All right," McGovern said heavily. "Suppose Briffe did send and those were the exact words he transmitted. Do you know where this lake is?"

"It's in the Attikonak area," I replied. "East of the river."

"Hell! We know that already. We know to within thirty miles or so where it was Bert crashed, but we still haven't located the lake. But of course if you know the exact location of this lake you keep talking about . . . But your father didn't pin-point it, did he?"

"No." I was still looking at Laroche. He was busy filling his pipe, his head bent.

"Then it doesn't help us very much." Was there a note of relief in McGovern's voice? I glanced at him quickly, but the grey, stony eyes told me nothing. "As Bert says, there are thousands of lakes out there."

"But only one with a rock shaped like a lion," I said obstinately.

And then Laroche said quietly: "You don't know what it was like out there." It was as though he had been following some train of thought of his own. "It was snowing, and later there was fog. And there was so much to do. . . ." His voice trailed off again as though he didn't want to think about it.

"This isn't getting us anywhere." McGovern's voice was suddenly brisk and businesslike. "Lake of the Lion is mentioned in Dumaine's book and in the newspaper reports of—the survivor." He had glanced quickly at Laroche. And then he was looking at me again. "Your father would have read the name they gave to that lake —their last camp. That was the place where your grandfather died, and, as far as I'm concerned, it only proves that your father was living in the past."

I stared at him unbelievingly. "Won't you even try to understand?" I said. "My father was a radio operator. The ether was his whole world. He'd never have invented a transmission that didn't take place—never!" And I went on to explain what it must have cost him in effort to force himself to his feet. But even as I was telling it to him, I knew it was no good. The hard lines of his face didn't soften, the eyes held no sympathy.

He heard me out, and when I'd finished, he glanced at his watch. "I'm sorry," he said. "But all this doesn't really help us. If you'd been able to tell us something new—give us something positive to work on . . ." He got to his feet. "I've got to go now." He came round the desk and stood over me. "Don't think I don't appreciate it that you've come a long way to tell us this. I do. But you must understand that yours is a personal point of view—a very personal one."

"Then you're not going to do anything?" I asked.

"What can I do? Call for a resumption of the search? I'd have to convince the authorities first." He shook his head.

I jumped to my feet then. "But before you were searching blind," I told him. "Now you'd have something to go on. If you searched for this lake . . ." I turned to Laroche. "For God's sake, try to make him see it," I cried. And when he didn't answer, but remained staring down at his pipe, I burst out wildly: "Don't you want them to be found?" And at that his head came up with a jerk and he stared at me with a sort of horror.

"Bert flew in twice," McGovern reminded me quietly. "Twice when he should have been in hospital. And he couldn't find the lake." He paused and then added: "I understand your disappointment. It's natural after coming so far. And I may say I'm disappointed, too. We all are. When I got Ledder's message I had hoped . . ." He turned away with a little shrug that was a gesture of finality. "I gather your aircraft has gone on to Montreal. That correct?" he asked me.

I nodded, feeling suddenly drained of the will to fight them any more.

"I'm told there's a flight going out to Montreal to-night," he said to Lands. "Do you think you could fix him a ride on it, Bill?"

"Sure."

McGovern glanced at his watch again and then turned to Laroche. "You got your car with you? Then perhaps you'd drive me down into town. I'm late as it is." He picked up his briefcase. "I'm grateful to you, Ferguson—very grateful indeed. If there's anything I can do for you, let me know." And with that he strode out of the room. Laroche hesitated, glancing quickly at me as though he were about to say something. And then he hurried after McGovern.

The door slammed behind him, and I stood there, feeling numbed and exhausted. I should have stopped him, made one final effort. But what was the good? Even if he'd known the name of the lake all along, it didn't mean he could find it again. And the world had got used to the idea that the men were dead. That was the thing I was up against—that and the stubbornness of men like Mc-Govern who couldn't see a thing unless it was presented to them as hard fact. "Damn them! Damn them to hell!"

A hand gripped my arm. I'd forgotten Bill Lands was still there. "What did you expect?" he said in a kindly voice. "We don't abandon men easily up here in the North."

I swung round on him. "But don't you see . . ." And then I stopped because I realized that he'd sat through it all and he still believed that Briffe was dead. He wasn't involved. He was outside it, and if I hadn't convinced him, what hope had I of convincing anyone else?

"I'll just go and check this Montreal flight, and then I guess you'd like some food."

He was gone about ten minutes, and when he came back he told me it was all fixed. "Flight leaves at around twenty thirty hours." He took me out into the slanting

evening light, across flat gravel that had the silt look of a
river bed, and in the distance a locomotive hooted an
inexpressibly mournful note. "Supply train going up the
line to Head of Steel," he said. "Going up myself tomorrow." There was pleasure in his voice, and he smiled at
me. He had warmth, this big American with his eyes
screwed up against the westering sun.

We entered a hut similar to the one we had just left,
to be greeted by a murmur of voices, the rattle of crockery,
and the smell of food. It was good, that smell of food, for
I was hungry, and I sat down with Lands at a table full
of strangers, who took no notice of me and ate with concentration. What talk there was centered around the line,
and it carried with it the breath of railway engineering.
They were blasting rock at one point, bearing down on
the muskeg at another, and the rail-laying gang at Head
of Steel were driving forward at the rate of a mile and a
half a day. Dozens of construction camps, thousands of
men, even an air lift to supply them—a whole world in
itself, thinking, dreaming, eating, sleeping nothing but
this railway. I felt myself being sucked into it mentally,
so that it was difficult, whilst I sat there eating with them,
not to feel a part of it.

And then somebody asked me whether I was going up
the line. When I told him no, that I was going back to
England, he stared at me as though I were some creature
from another planet. "Well, well—and we got such a good
climate up here." They laughed, and their laughter made
me less a stranger.

Lands waited for me to finish eating, and then we went
outside and all the western sky was aglow with the setting
sun. "You'll see a sight before you leave tonight, I reckon,"
he said. "The northern lights should be real good." He
glanced at his watch. "It's early for your flight yet, but I
got to go downtown. Don't mind if I drop you off at the
airstrip right away, do you?"

I shook my head, and he went off to change and get his car. I was to pick up my suitcase and meet him at the Q.N.S. & L. Office. I moved out across the flat gravel space, feeling conspicuous and alone. All the purpose seemed to have been drained out of me. Glancing back, I saw that Lands had stopped to chat to a woman down by the farthest hut. I could see them looking at me and I went quickly on towards the office, conscious that others must know by now what had brought me here. Staffen would have told them, and the knowledge made the sense of failure overwhelming. If only I could have convinced Lands. I liked Bill Lands.

I reached the office and found my suitcase, and I went out and stood looking at the western sky, which had flared up into a violent furnace red. And now that J was leaving, I felt again the strange pull of this country.

Footsteps sounded, quick and urgent on the gravel behind me, and a voice that was soft and slightly foreign said: "Are you Mr. Ferguson?"

I turned and found it was the woman who had been talking to Lands. Or, rather, it wasn't a woman, but a girl with black hair cut short like a boy's and a dark, full-lipped face that had no trace of make-up. I remember, even in that first glimpse of her, she made a deep impression on me. It was her vitality, I think, and a sort of wildness, or perhaps it was just that her eyes caught and reflected the strange, wild light in the sky. Whatever it was, I was immediately aware of her in a way that was somehow personal. "Yes," I said. "I'm Ian Ferguson."

She didn't say anything, just stared at me, her nostrils aquiver and her eyes blazing with the reflected glare. Her wrists were very slender, and her hands gripped the edge of her leather jacket so that she seemed to be holding herself in.

And then she said: "I'm Paule Briffe."

I think I'd known that from the first moment, the sense

of emotion dammed up inside her had been strong. "I'm so sorry," I murmured awkwardly. I didn't know what else to say.

"Bill told me your father is dead, that that is why you come." She spoke in a tight, controlled little voice that trembled on the edge of hysteria. "I can understand that. Believe me, I can understand that." And then, suddenly losing the grip she had on herself, she cried out: "But it doesn't help him. It cannot do any good." The words came in a rush. "Please. Go back to England. Leave us alone."

"It was because of your father that I came," I said.

I thought that would steady her, but she didn't seem to hear. "You come here and you hurt people and you do not care. Please, please, leave us alone."

"But your father—" I began.

"My father is dead!" she cried. "He is dead—dead; do you hear?" Her voice was wild, unrestrained, her eyes wide and scared.

"But suppose my father was right," I said gently. "Suppose that transmission—"

"Your father! *Mon Dieu!* You do not care about us— what we feel. You are afraid to admit that your father is mad, so you come here to make trouble." Her small fists were clenched, and her tight breasts heaved against the leather of her Indian jacket. And then, whilst I stared at her, appalled, she reached out her hand with her breath caught and said: "No. That was wrong of me." She was staring at me. "But it is so horrible," she breathed. "So very horrible." She turned away then, her face towards the sunset. "I do not mind so much for myself. My father is dead. There's nothing to do about that. But for Albert—" she pronounced his name in the French way— "it is driving him out of his mind. I have just been talking to him. It is a terrible thing you are saying." This last in a voice scarcely above a whisper.

"But suppose he *has* made a mistake?" I said.

She rounded on me then, her eyes blazing. "You don't seem to understand," she cried. "He is with my father when he died, and it is because of him they stop the search. And now you come here and try to tell us that my father transmit on the radio, not when they crash, but two whole weeks after. That is what is terrible." She was crying now—crying wildly in a flood of feeling. "It isn't true. It can't be true."

What could I say? What did you say when what you'd come to believe tore another human being in half? And because I didn't know, I stood in silence, scared by the sight of a passion that was quite foreign to me.

"You say nothing. Why?" She made a quick movement and caught hold of my arm. "Tell me the truth now. Please. The truth."

The truth! What was the truth? Did I really know it? Was it really what was written on the pencilled page of that log book? "I'm sorry," I murmured. "I don't know the truth." And I added: "I wish I did. All I know is what my father wrote. He believed your father was alive and that he was transmitting from a place called Lake of the Lion."

She caught her breath then. "Lake of the Lion!" She was staring at me, and now there was intelligence as well as passion in her eyes. "You say Lake of the Lion. How do you know?"

"The transmission," I said. "It was implied in the transmission my father picked up."

"It only said a narrow lake with a rock in it." Her voice trembled slightly. "That was all. I read it myself. Albert showed it to me."

"Did he show you Ledder's reports, too?"

She shook her head.

"Lake of the Lion was mentioned in that." I spared her the context and went on to tell her about the map in my father's room and the log books and how my father

had been obsessed with Labrador because of the Ferguson
Expedition. And all the time I was talking she was staring
at me, her eyes wide, almost shocked. "So you see," I
finished, "I felt I had to come."

She didn't say anything for a moment, and her face
had gone quite white. "Lake of the Lion." She murmured
the name to herself as though it were something she'd
dreamed about. "My father talked about it—often . . .
over campfires. He knew the story, and always he thought
he would find it some day—always he was searching. All
my life I hear that name on his lips." She had turned
away from me, staring at the sunset. *"Dieu me secourrait!"*
she breathed. God help me! Her hands were gripped together as she said it, as though she were kneeling before
an altar. She looked at me slowly. "You are honest. At
least you are honest. And I thank God for that." Her
eyes held mine for a long moment, and then she whispered: "I must think. I must pray to God." And she
turned and walked slowly away, and there was something
so forlorn about her, so matching my own mood of
loneliness, that I started after her.

But I stopped, because with a sudden perception that I
scarcely understood, I realized that I could do no good.
This was something that she had to discover for herself.
It was a terrible choice, striking as it did at the roots of
her relationship with Laroche, and I felt her dilemma as
though it were my own. And in some strange way it
strengthened my resolve. It was as though this other human, whom I had never met till now, had reached out
to me for help. I knew then that I couldn't give up, that I
must go on until I'd found the truth.

It was strange, but the past and the present seemed suddenly inextricably mingled, with Lake of the Lion the
focal point, and I turned my face towards the north, feeling the chill of the faint wind that blew from the Labrador
plateau.

This was my mood when Bill Lands drove up in his

mud-spattered station wagon and told me to jump in.

"I'm not going," I said.

He stared at me, still leaning across the passenger seat with his hand on the door he'd thrown open for me. "What do you mean, you're not going?"

"I'm staying here," I told him. "I'm staying here till I've discovered the truth."

"The truth? You've had the truth. You had it from Bert Laroche this afternoon." He was frowning at me. "Did Paule find you? Did you talk to her?"

"Yes."

"What did you say to her?" His voice was trembling with anger, and his fist was clenched as he slid across the passenger seat and out on to the gravel beside me. "Did you try and tell her that her father was still alive out there?" He stood over me, his eyes, narrowed and hard, looking down into my face. "Did you tell her that?" I thought he was going to hit me.

"No," I said.

"What did you tell her, then?"

"She asked for the truth, and I said I didn't know what the truth was."

"And that set her mind at rest, I suppose. Why the hell Bert had to tell her about you, I don't know." He gripped hold of my suitcase, wrenching it from me and tossing it into the back of the wagon. "Okay. Let's go. You've done enough damage for one day." His voice still trembled with anger. "Go on. Get in."

"But I'm not going," I repeated, my voice childishly stubborn.

"You're going, son, whether you want to or not." And he caught hold of my arm and literally flung me into the seat and slammed the door.

There was no point in arguing with him—he was a big man, powerfully built. But as he got in behind the wheel and we drove off, I said: "You can take me down to the airstrip, but you can't make me board the plane."

He looked at me, frowning. "I don't understand you," he said. "Why the hell don't you accept Bert's statement and leave it at that?" And when I didn't say anything, he asked: "How much money you got—Canadian money?"

"None," I said.

He nodded. "That's what I thought." He was smiling. "How the hell do you expect to stay on here? This is a boom town. It costs money to live here."

"Staffen's short of engineers," I said quietly. "And I'm an engineer."

We had swung out on to the dirt road, and he headed east, his foot hard down on the accelerator. "Alex won't give you a job, and nor will anybody else when they know you're just here to make trouble."

"I'm not here to make trouble," I said. "I just want to find out the truth. And if it's the girl you're worrying about," I added, "then don't you think she's entitled to the truth too? She knows I'm here, and she knows why. She knows about that transmission, and if she never learns the truth of it, she'll wonder about it all her life." He didn't say anything, and I went on: "You say her father was a hero to her. Well, she knows there's one person who doesn't believe he's dead, and if it's left at that she'll worry about it till the day she dies."

We had come to the airstrip, and he turned in through the wire and pulled up at the dispatch office. "All the more reason why I should get you out of here tonight." He flung open the door. "You leave tonight and she'll know there was nothing to it. Okay?" He sat there, looking at me, waiting for me to say something. "Well, it doesn't much matter whether you agree with me or not. You're taking this plane out of here tonight, and that's the end of it. And don't try anything clever," he added menacingly. "If I find you still here tonight when I get back from town, Goddammit, I'll half kill you. And don't think I don't mean it. I do." He got out then and went into the dispatch office.

The sky was a darkening splurge of colour, lurid red down by the horizon, but fading to purple as night spread across it from the east. An old Dakota stood in black silhouette, a fork lift trundling supplies out to it and a little knot of men standing waiting. They were all types, men waiting to be flown up the line. I wished I were going with them. I was feeling the need for action. But maybe I could do something down at Montreal, see the authorities, something.

The door beside me was jerked open. "Okay," Lands said. "It's all fixed. That's your plane over there." He nodded towards a small, twin-engined aircraft parked behind us. "Take-off is at twenty thirty hours. If you'll come into the office now, I'll hand you over to the dispatcher."

I got out, feeling suddenly tired—glad to be going, to be getting out of Seven Islands.

"Can you lend me some money?" I asked as he handed me my suitcase.

"Sure. How much do you want?"

"Just enough to see me through till midday tomorrow," I said. "That's when my plane leaves Montreal."

He nodded. "Twenty bucks do you?" He pulled his wallet out of his hip pocket and handed me four fives.

"I'll send you the sterling equivalent as soon as I get home," I said.

"Forget it." He patted my arm. "To be honest, I'd have paid that and more to get you out of here. I guess I'm a sentimental sort of guy. I just don't like to see two people's lives busted up for the sake of something that nobody can do anything about." He took my suitcase and led me across to the dispatch office. The dispatcher was the same man who had been on duty when I arrived. "Ed, this is Mr. Ferguson. Comes from England. Look after him for me, will you? And see he doesn't miss his flight."

"Sure. I'll look after him, Mr. Lands."

"Here's his flight pass." Lands handed over a slip of paper. And then he turned to me. "I've got to go now. Ed will see you on to your plane." He held out his hand. "Glad you saw it my way in the end." He hesitated as though he wasn't sure whether he ought to leave me there on my own. But then he said: "Well, s'long. Have a good flight." And he went out and climbed into his station wagon and drove out through the wire.

"You've got about an hour to wait," the dispatcher said, writing my name on a dispatch sheet. Then he slapped my pass on to a spike with a lot of other papers. "Flight leaves twenty thirty hours. I'll give you a call when they're ready for you."

"Thanks," I said and walked out into the hangar that adjoined the office. It was full of stores, and outside it was dark. The last patch of red had gone from the sky, and the arc lights had been switched on, flooding the apron; and the Dakota was still there, waiting. The last of the freight was being loaded into it by hand, the fork lift standing idle beside the hangar door. A starter motor was wheeled into position under the port engine, and there was a sudden surge amongst the waiting men as they crowded close around the open door of the fuselage.

Maybe the idea had been at the back of my mind all the time. At any rate, I found myself walking out across the apron to mingle with the construction men who were waiting to board the plane. I hadn't thought it out at all. It was just that this plane was going up the line and I was drawn to it by a sort of fascination. "Gonna be cold in that rig, ain't yer?" said the man next to me. He had a dark, wizened face half hidden by a large fur cap with ear flaps. "First time you bin up the line?"

I nodded.

"Thought so." And he spat a stream of tobacco juice out on to the ground. "Where you bound for?"

I hesitated, but he was looking at me, expecting an answer. "Two-two-four," I said, remembering that a replacement engineer was being sent up there.

The little man nodded. "Be snowing up there, I wouldn't wonder." He said it with a grin, as though he relished the thought that I should be cold.

I moved away from him, edging my way in amongst the rest of the men.

"You on this flight?" A man in a long-visored cap standing in the door of the fuselage was staring down at me.

"Yes," I said, and it was only after I'd said it that I realized I'd committed myself to something I was by no means certain I could see through.

"Well, just wait till I call your name." He turned to the others. "Okay, boys. Let's get started." And he began to call their names one by one and tick them off on the list in his hand as they climbed aboard.

I hadn't reckoned on them having a passenger list just like an ordinary airline. The crowd was dwindling fast, and I wondered how I was going to explain that I'd tried to board a plane going up the line when I was booked out on a flight to Montreal. Unless I could bluff my way on to it! I was thinking of Staffen and his need of engineers.

"What's your name?" The last man had climbed up into the plane, and the man with the list was staring down at me.

"Ferguson," I said, and I could hear the tremor in my voice.

He ran his finger down the list. "Your name's not here. What's your job?"

"Engineer."

"This plane's going to One-three-four." He jumped to the ground beside me. "You work there?"

"No," I said. "I'm going on up to Two-two-four." And

I added quickly: "The engineer there had an accident, and I'm replacing him."

"Yeah, that's right." He nodded. "West. They flew him down this evening." He was looking at me, and I could see him trying to make up his mind. "Did you have a flight pass?"

"Yes," I said. "The dispatcher has it. Mr. Lands drove me down and asked him to be sure I didn't miss this plane."

"Ed didn't say anything to me about it." He hesitated, glancing down at the list again. "Okay, let's go over to the office and sort it out. Hold it!" he shouted to the man with the starter motor.

"What's the trouble, Mike?" asked the pilot, who was now standing in the entrance to the fuselage.

"Won't be a minute. Leave your bag here," he said to me. "We got to hurry."

We ran all the way to the dispatch office. There was no turning back now. I'd just got to make the dispatcher believe me. I remember a car drove up just as we reached the office, but I had other things to worry about, and in the office I stood silent whilst my companion explained the situation to the dispatcher.

"You're booked out on the Beechcraft," he told me. "Twenty thirty hours for Montreal."

"There must be some mistake," I said.

"No mistake, mister." He had got hold of my flight pass now. "There you are. See for yourself. Montreal. That's what it says."

I repeated what I'd said before, that I was bound for Two-two-four, and I added: "You were here when I arrived this afternoon. I came to get a job, and I got it."

He nodded. "That's right. I remember. Came in on that freighter and didn't know who you wanted to see." He scratched his head.

"Maybe I got the wrong pass or it was made out incorrectly," I suggested. "Mr. Lands was asked to drive me down specially so that I wouldn't miss this plane." I pulled my passport out of my pocket. "Look, if you don't believe I'm an engineer . . ." I opened it and pointed to where it gave Occupation.

He stared at the word *Engineer.* "Well, I don't know," he said. "On whose instructions was the pass made out?"

"Mr. Staffen's."

"Well, I won't be able to get Mr. Staffen at this time of night. They pack up at six."

"Is there room for me on this flight up to One-three-four?"

"Yeah, there's room, all right."

"Then can't you just alter the flight pass? Look!" I said. "I'm not taking a plane down to Montreal. That's certain. Why would I want to leave when I've only just arrived?"

He laughed. "You got something there."

"And just when I've got the job I came to get. Besides, Mr. Staffen said I was to get up there right away. He's short of engineers."

"Sure. They're having to move them about all the time." He looked at me, and I saw he was making up his mind and said nothing more. "Okay," he said. "I reckon it's a mistake, like you said. After all, I guess you're old enough to know where you're supposed to be going." And he chuckled to himself as he put a line through Montreal on the pass, wrote in *134,* and altered the dispatch sheet. "Okay," he said. "You're on the list now. Lucky you found out in time or you'd have been back in the Old Country before you knew where you were." And he laughed again, good-humouredly, so that I hoped he wouldn't get into too much trouble for altering the pass.

But I didn't have time to think about that, for I was hustled back to the plane. The port motor started up as we ran across the apron, and I was hauled aboard through the cold backwash of air from the turning propeller. My suitcase was tossed up to me, and as I grabbed it I saw a man come out of the dispatch office and stand there, hesitating, staring at the plane. The headlights of a truck swinging in at the gates caught him in their blaze and I recognized Laroche. The starboard motor came to life with a roar, and at the sound of it he began to run out on to the tarmac. "Mind yourself!" A hand pushed me back and the door was swung to with a crash, and after that I could see nothing but the dim-lit interior of the fuselage with the freight heaped down the centre and the construction men seated in two lines on either side of it.

There was still time for the plane to be stopped. If Laroche had checked with the dispatcher and told him I was really bound for Montreal . . . The engines suddenly roared in unison, and the plane began to move, swinging in a wide turn towards the runway end. And then we were moving faster, the fuselage bumping and shaking as the wheels trundled over the rough ground.

I squeezed myself in between two men on the seat line opposite the door and sat with my hands gripped round my knees, waiting. Nobody was talking. The noise of the engines made it impossible, and there was that sense of strain that always seems to precede take-off.

The plane turned at the runway end. Only a few seconds now. I held my knees tight as first one engine and then the other was run up; and then suddenly both engines were roaring and the fuselage shuddered and rattled. The brakes were released. The plane began to move. And in a moment we were airborne and the nerves and muscles of my body slowly relaxed.

It was only then that I had time to realize what I'd done. I was on my way into Labrador.

II

We climbed for what seemed a long time,
and it grew steadily colder. I put my coat on, but it
hardly made any difference. The plane was a relic of the
war, the parachute-jumping wire still streched down the
centre of the fuselage, and a bitter draught of air blew
in through the battered edges of the badly fitting door.
The dim lighting gave to the faces of the men flanked
along the fuselage a ghostly, disembodied look. They were
types of faces that I'd never seen before, faces that seemed
symbolic of the world into which I was flying—old and
weather-beaten, and some that were young and dissolute,
a mixture of racial characteristics that included Chinese
and African.

The battering of the engine noise dropped to a steady
roar as the plane flattened out. The cold was intense.
"We'll be going up the Moisie River now," the man next
to me said. He was a small, squat man with the broad,
flat features of an Indian. "Been up here before?" I
shook my head. "I work on the line two winters now—
all through the Moisie Gorge and up to the height of land."
There was pride in the way he said it.

"How long before we get to One-three-four?" I asked
him.

"One hour, I think." And he added: "Once I do it by
canoe, all up the Moisie and across to the Ashuanipi.
Six weeks. Now, one hour." He nodded and relapsed into

silence, and I sat there, feeling a little scared as we roared on through the night into Labrador.

I had some idea of the country. I'd read about it in my father's books. I knew it was virtually unexplored, a blank on the map which only four thousand years ago had been covered by the glaciers of the last Ice Age. And I got no comfort from the men around me. They were all part of an organization that I was outside. And their hard-bitten, dim-lit features, their clothes, everything about them only served to emphasize the grimness of the country into which I was being flown.

I was unprepared, inexperienced, and yet I think the thing that worried me most was that Laroche would have radioed ahead and that I should be stopped at One-three-four and sent down by the next plane.

But gradually the intense cold numbed all thought, and when the chill ache of my body had so deadened my mind that I didn't care any longer, the sound of the engines died away, and a moment later we touched down.

We scrambled out into another world—a world where the ground was hard with frost and a few shacks stood against a starlit background of jackpines. Away to the left a solitary huddle of lights illuminated a line of heavy wagons. There was the sound of machinery, too. But the sound seemed small and insubstantial against the over-whelming solitude, and overhead the northern lights draped a weird and ghostly curtain across the sky, a cur-tain that wavered and constantly changed its shape with a fascination that was beyond the reach of explanation.

I stood for a moment staring up at it, enthralled by the beauty of it, and at the same time awed. And all about me I was conscious of the iron-hard harshness of the North, the sense of a wild, untamed country, not yet touched by man.

Stiff-jointed and cold, we moved in a body to the wood-frame huts that were the airstrip buildings, crowding into

the dispatch office, where the warmth from the diesel
heater was like a furnace. Names were called, the dispatcher issuing instructions in a harsh, quick voice that
switched from English to French and back again as though
they were the same language. The men began filing out to
a waiting truck. "Ferguson."

The sound of my name came as a shock to me, and I
moved forward uncertainly.

"You're Ferguson, are you? Message for you." The dispatcher held it out to me. "Came in by radio half an hour
back."

My first thought was that this would be from Lands,
that I wouldn't get any farther than this camp. And then
I saw the name Laroche at the end of it. *Urgent we
have talk. Am taking night supply train. E.T.A. 0800.
Do not leave before I have seen you. Laroche.*

As I stared at that message, the only thought in my
mind was that he hadn't stopped me. Why? It would have
been easy for him to persuade the base dispatcher to have
them hold me here. Instead, he was coming after me,
wanting to have a talk with me. Had I forced his hand?
Did this mean . . . And then I was conscious of an un-
mistakably Lancashire voice saying: "Has Ferguson
checked in on that flight, Sid?"

"He's right here," the dispatcher answered, and I
looked up to find a short, rather tired-looking man standing in the doorway to an inner office. He wore a khaki
shirt with the sleeves rolled up, and he had a green eye-
shade on his head, and over his shoulder I caught a
glimpse of radio equipment. "You got the message all
right, then?"

"Yes," I said. "Yes, I got the message, thanks."

"You a friend of Laroche?" I didn't know quite how to
answer that. Fortunately he didn't wait for a reply, but
added: "You're English, aren't you?"

I nodded, and he came towards me, holding out his

hand. "That makes two of us," he said. "My name's Bob Perkins. I'm from Wigan. Lancashire, you know."

"Yes, I guessed that."

"Aye," he said. "Not much fear of your mistaking me for a Canuk." There was a friendly twinkle in his tired blue eyes. "Two years I been up in this bloody country. Emigrated in fifty-one and came straight up here as wireless op. They still think I talk a bit peculiar like." And then he added: "That message—it's from that pilot who crashed, isn't it?"

I nodded.

"Aye, I thought there couldn't be two of 'em with a name like that." He looked at me hesitantly. "Would yer like a cup of tea?" he asked, and, surprised at anything so English up here in the middle of nowhere, I said yes. As he led me into the radio room, he said: "I only been here a week. Five days, to be exact. I was up at Two-ninety before that. I remember when they picked this Laroche up. Proper hullabaloo there was." He went over to a kettle quietly steaming on the diesel heater. "Newspapers—everybody. Hardly had time to deal with the air traffic."

"Who found him, do you know?" I asked. If I could find out something more before I met Laroche . . .

"Oh, some construction gang. By all accounts, he stumbled out of the bush right on top of a grab crane. The fellow that brought him out, though, was Ray Darcy, engineer up at Two-sixty-three. Radioed us to have a plane standing by and then drove him the twenty-odd miles up the old Tote Road in one hour flat. Or that's what he said. It'd be some going on that road. Would you like milk and sugar? Trouble is you never know with a man like Ray Darcy." He handed me a battered tin mug. "Proper character he is and all. Came up to Labrador for a month's fishing an' stayed two years. You a fisherman?"

"No," I said.

"Wonderful fishing up here for them as likes it. Me, I haven't the patience like. You got to have patience. Not that Ray Darcy got much. He's an artist, really—paints pictures. But he's a proper fisherman when it comes to stories. Twenty miles an hour he'd have had to've averaged, and on the Tote Road. Aye, and you should see his jeep. Proper mess—glued together with the mud that's on it, that's what I say. . . ."

And so it went on. I sat there and drank my tea and listened to him talking, basking in the warmth of his friendliness and the knowledge that he was English. That fact alone meant a lot to me. It gave me confidence and drove out the sense of loneliness.

Bob Perkins was the first friend I made on my way up into Labrador. And though he couldn't tell me much about Laroche—he had just seen him that once as they carried him out on a stretcher to the waiting plane—he had given me the name of the man who could.

I gleaned a lot of useful information from him, too. Camp 224 was a big place, highly organized, with a large engineering staff sending daily reports back to the Seven Islands base by teleprinter. Obviously no place for me. They'd know immediately that I'd no business to be up the line. Some twenty miles beyond 224 was Head of Steel. And after that there was nothing but the newly constructed grade gradually petering out into isolated construction units slicing into virgin country with bull-dozer and grab crane. No railway, no telephone link—nothing but the old Tote Road and the airstrips to link the camps with base. Camp 263 he described as growing fast, but still just a clearing in the jackpine forest, primitive and pretty grim. "The only decent camp between Two-two-four and the permanent camp at Menihek Dam is Two-ninety," he said. "It's right on the lake, with a big airstrip on a hill. Mostly C.M.M.K. personnel—that's the construction combine that's building the grade. They even got a helicopter stationed there for the use of the grade superintendent."

"A helicopter!" But even if I could persuade the pilot to take me up in it, I didn't know where Lake of the Lion was. Laroche had said there were thousands of lakes, and, remembering what the country had been like flying down from Goose, I could well believe it. Had my father known where the lake was? And if my father had known, would my mother know?

Perkins was explaining that they'd used the helicopter to try and bring out the bodies of Briffe and Baird. "He had two tries at it. But it wasn't any good. He couldn't find the place."

"Who couldn't—Laroche?" I asked.

"Aye, that's right. Like I said, he came back just two days after he'd been flown out. Proper mess he looked, too—a great gash in his head and his face white as chalk. They shouldn't have let him come, but he said he had to try and locate the place, and Len Holt—he's the pilot— flew him in twice. It didn't do any good, though. He couldn't find it. I saw him when he came back the second time. They had to lift him out, poor chap, he was so done up."

"Did a man called McGovern come up with him?" I asked.

But he shook his head. "No, Laroche was on his own."

I asked him then about Camp 263. But he couldn't tell me anything more than he'd told me already. He'd never been there. He'd just heard men talking about it. "They say it's pretty rough. And the grub's bad. It's a new camp. All new construction camps are rough." And he looked across at me and said: "You're not going there, are you?"

I'd made up my mind by then. I wasn't waiting for Laroche. I wanted to see Darcy first. "Yes," I said. "I've got to get up there as soon as possible." And I asked him whether there was any way of getting north that night. "It's urgent," I added.

"What about Laroche?" He was looking at me curiously. "He says to wait for him."

"Tell him I'll contact him from Two-sixty-three."

"But—"

"Laroche isn't employed by the company," I said quickly. "I've been told to get up there as fast as I can, and I'm sticking to my instructions. West has been injured, and there's been a switch of engineers."

He nodded. "That's right. Got his foot crushed by a gas car." I thought for a moment he was going to pursue the subject. But all he said was: "Aye. Well, you know your business best."

"Is there a flight going up from here tonight?" I asked him.

He shook his head. "North-bound flights don't stop here any more. This camp's pretty well finished now. Another month and it'll close down altogether, I wouldn't wonder." And then he added: "Your best bet is the supply train. You'd see your friend Laroche then and still be up at Head of Steel before dark tomorrow."

So I was stuck here. "You're sure there's nothing else?" And then, because I was afraid he might think I was trying to avoid Laroche, I said: "I'm supposed to be at Two-sixty-three tomorrow."

He shook his head. "No, there's nothing—" He stopped then. "Wait a jiffy. I got an idea the ballast train's been held up tonight." He went out into the dispatch office, and I heard him talking to the dispatcher and then the sound of the phone. After a while he came back and said: "It's okay, if you want to take it. Usually it's left by now, but the ballast got froze going up the line last night, so she was late back, and they're still loading."

"When will it leave?" I asked.

"Not before two. They've still quite a few wagons to load. That's what the foreman told me, anyway."

I asked him how far it would take me, and he told me they were ballasting right up behind Head of Steel. "And it doesn't stop anywhere, like the supply train," he added. "You'll be up there in a matter of four hours." He poured himself another mug of tea. "Well, shall I tell Sid you'll take it?" And he added: "It won't be all that comfortable, mind."

"It doesn't matter," I said. All I wanted was to see Darcy before Laroche caught up with me.

He nodded and went out again, carrying his mug carefully. It was intensely hot in the radio room, and I began to feel drowsy. "Okay," he said when he came back. "You'll ride up in the caboose with Onry Gaspard. He's the train conductor. He'll look after you." He glanced at his watch. "You've got four hours before the train leaves. You'd better hit the hay for a bit. You look proper played out."

I nodded. Now that it was all fixed, I felt very tired. "I was flying all last night," I explained. And then I remembered that Farrow was expecting me at Dorval Airport in the morning. There was Mr. Meadows to notify, too—and my mother. I ought to tell her where I was. "I'll have to write some letters," I said. And I explained that people back home didn't even know I was in Canada.

"Why not cable them, then?" He went over to the radio and tore a sheet off a message pad. "There you are. Write your message down on that, and I'll radio it to base right away."

It was as easy as that, and I remembered how small the world had seemed in that little basement room of Simon Ledder's house. I hesitated. "I suppose you couldn't contact a ham radio operator at Goose for me?"

He looked doubtful. "I could try," he said. "Depends whether he's keeping watch or not. What's his call sign?"

"VO6AZ," I told him. And I gave the frequency.

"VO6AZ!" He was looking at me curiously. "That's the ham who was acting as contact for Briffe's party."

I nodded, afraid that he'd start asking a lot of questions. "Will you try and get him for me?"

He didn't say anything for a moment. He seemed to be thinking it out. "Okay," he said finally. "It may take a little time. And I may not be able to get him at all. Do you want to speak to him personally, or would a message do?"

"A message," I said. "That's all."

"What's his job at Goose? Is he with the Air Force?"

"No," I said. "He's with D.O.T. Communications."

"Goose Radio. Well, suppose I send it to them. I can always get Goose Radio."

"That would do fine," I said.

"Aye, well, you write the message and I'll let you know whether I've been able to send it when I come off watch." He pulled a pencil from behind his ear and handed it to me.

I sat there for a moment, uncertain what to say, conscious that he was standing over me, watching me curiously. Twice I started to write and then crossed it out. My brain was sluggish with lack of sleep, and I wasn't certain how much I dared say. At length I wrote: *Company refuse take seriously. Going north into Labrador to try and find Lake of the Lion. Please notify Farrow. Request him on return Bristol to notify Meadows, Runway Construction Engineer, also my mother, Mrs. Ferguson, 119, Lansdown Grove Road, London, N.W.1. Would he telegraph her and ask her did my father ever tell her exact location of Lake of the Lion. Reply c/o Perkins, radio operator, Camp 134, Q.N.S. & L., Seven Islands.*

Thanks for all your help. Ian Ferguson. I read it through and handed it to him. "I hope you don't mind me using you as a post box," I said.

"That's okay." He stood, reading it through, and then he was looking at me and I knew there were questions he wanted to ask. But in the end he stuffed the message in his pocket. "Well, if you're going to get any sleep tonight, you'd better get down to the camp," he said. "There's a truck outside will take you down. You can have the spare bed in my room."

I thanked him. "I'd appreciate it," I added, "if you'd regard that message as confidential."

"Aye," he said slowly. "I won't talk." He gave me a sidelong glance. "But if you weren't English and I didn't like you, I might act different." And I knew he'd guessed why I was here. He couldn't very well help it, with Laroche radioing for me to wait for him. "Come on," he said. "I'll get the driver to run you down to our bunkhouse. And I'll let you know what luck I've had with this message when I come off duty at midnight."

He took me out to the truck then and told the driver where to take me. "Call him at one thirty," he said. "He's taking the ballast train north."

The northern lights were gone now. The night was black, with just one star low over the jackpines. A bitter wind sifted a light dusting of powdery snow along the ground. "If I don't wake you when I come in, you'll know your message has gone off all right," Bob Perkins called up to me. "And I'll tell Laroche when he gets in that he'll find you up at Two-sixty-three. Okay?" He grinned up at me as the truck lurched forward.

We swung round the end of the airstrip buildings and out on to a dirt road where ruts stood out like furrows in the headlights. It was like that all the way to the camp, the ruts hard like concrete, and then we stopped outside the dim bulk of a wooden hut. "Okay, feller. This-a your bunk'ouse." The driver was Italian. "You want me call you 'alf past one, eh?"

"Half past one," I said. "Don't forget, will you? The train leaves at two."

"Okay. I don't forget."

He gunned the engine, and the truck bumped away over the ruts, the swinging beam of its headlights shining momentarily on the little cluster of huts that was Camp 134. Somewhere in the darkness an electric generator throbbed steadily. There was no other sound. A few lights glimmered. The place had a loneliness and desolation about it that was almost frightening.

I went into the bunkhouse and switched on the light. The naked bulb lit a small passage with a shower and lavatory at the end. The bare floorboards were covered with a black, glacial sand that was gritty underfoot. A diesel stove roared in the corner, giving out a great blast of heat. There were three rooms, two of them with the doors wide open, so that I could see that the beds were occupied. I opened the door nearest the shower. It was cooler there, and both beds were empty. On the table between them stood a leather-framed photograph of my Lancashire friend and a girl holding hands. There was a litter of paperbacks, mostly westerns, and a half-completed model of a square-rigged sailing ship. There was a bedroll parked in one corner, and the cupboard space was full of cold-weather clothing.

Two canvas grips marked with the name Koster lay on top of one of the beds. I put these on the floor beside my own suitcase, switched off the light, and turned in, not bothering to remove anything but my jacket and trousers. There were no sheets, and the blankets were coarse and heavy with sand. Their musty smell stayed in my nostrils a long time, for sleep did not come easily. I had too much to think about. And when I did doze off, it seemed

only a moment before I was dragged back to consciousness
by somebody shaking my shoulder. "Is it time?" I asked,
remembering the ballast train. The light was on, and as I
opened my eyes I saw the empty bed opposite and the
alarm clock hanging on the wall. It wasn't yet midnight.
And then I looked up at the man who had wakened me,
saw the half-healed wound running down through the
shaved hair of the scalp, and sat bolt upright in the bed.
"You!" I was suddenly wide awake, filled with an un-
reasoning panic. "How did you get here?"

"I came by plane." Laroche had let go of my shoulder
and was standing there, staring down at me. "I was
afraid I'd miss you if I waited for the supply train." He
unzipped his parka and sat down on the foot of the bed,
tugging at the silk scarf round his neck. "It's hot in here,"
he said.

The diesel heater in the passage was going full blast,
and the boarded and papered window gave no ventila-
tion. I could feel the sweat clammy on my face and lying
in a hot, uncomfortable pool round my neck. The atmosphere was stifling. But that wasn't the reason why my
heart was pounding.

"Sorry to wake you. Guess you must be pretty tired."

I didn't say anything. I couldn't trust myself to speak.
The truth was, I was scared of the man. I can't really
explain it, even now. I don't think it was the scar, though
it stood out as a livid disfigurement in the white glare of
the naked light bulb; and it certainly wasn't anything to
do with the cast of his features or the expression of his
eyes. There was nothing about him, except the unex-
pectedness of his arrival, to make me afraid of him. But
that was my instinctive reaction, and I can only think that,
in the instant of waking, something of his mental state
was communicated to me.

He had taken off his silk scarf and was wiping his face
with it, and I wondered what he was going to do now

that he'd caught up with me. I watched him remove his parka, and then he was sitting there in a thick woollen bush shirt buttoned at the wrist, staring at nothing. He looked desperately tired, the high cheekbones staring through the sallow, tight-drawn skin and the shadows deep under the eyes.

"Have you told Lands I'm here?" I asked him, and my voice sounded dry and hoarse.

"No." He reached into the pocket of his parka and produced a packet of cigarettes and offered it to me. It was an automatic gesture, and when I shook my head he put a cigarette in his mouth and sat there, staring at the floor, as though too tired to light it. "I wanted to talk to you first," he said. And then after a while he reached into his trouser pocket for a match and struck it with a flick of his thumbnail against the head. The flare of it as he lit the cigarette momentarily softened the contours of his face and showed me the eyes withdrawn into some secret pocket of thought. His hand trembled slightly, and he drew the smoke into his lungs as though his nerves were crying out for it. And then, abruptly, he said: "Why did you jump that plane and come up here? Didn't you believe what I told you?" He was still staring at the floor.

I didn't say anything, and silence hung over the room, so that the metallic ticking of the alarm clock sounded unnaturally loud and I could hear the murmur of breathing from the next room. The stillness of the world outside seemed to creep in through the flimsy wooden walls, and all the time I was wondering why he hadn't told Lands, why he had needed to see me first.

"Why didn't you believe me?" he demanded sharply, as though the silence were getting on his nerves. "You *didn't* believe me, did you?"

"It's not a question of whether I believed you or not," I said.

He nodded. "No, I guess not." His hands gripped the

silk scarf as though he wanted to tear it in shreds. And
then he muttered something that sounded like "Fate" and
shook his head. "I still can't believe it's true," he breathed.
"That old man's son, sitting there at his radio, listening
to the reports, waiting for it to happen."

"Do you mean my father?"

But he didn't seem to hear. "It's like a nightmare,"
he whispered. And then he turned his head, looking
straight at me, and said: "I suppose you think I killed
them or something." He gave a quick, harsh laugh.

It wasn't said jokingly, but with sudden violence, and
the harshness of that laugh shocked me as much as the
words.

"Because my name is Laroche, eh?" he added, and there
was bitterness in his voice. "Oh, you needn't look so
startled," he said. "I knew what your father had been
thinking as soon as I read Ledder's report." He dropped
the scarf, reached forward, and gripped hold of my wrist,
speaking very earnestly. "You must believe this. I'm not
responsible for their death. That's the truth. It's nothing
to do with me." And he repeated it. "I'm not responsible."

"It never occurred to me you were." I was staring at
him, appalled that he'd found it necessary to make such a
declaration.

"No?" He stared at me, his eyes searching my face.
"Then why are you here? Why, when nobody believes
you, do you tell Paule that I'm a liar and that her father
is still alive?" *Mon Dieu!* And then to say you are employed by Staffen and come up the line when you are
booked out to Montreal . . . Do you think I don't know
what's been planted in your mind? *C'est incroyable!*"
he breathed, and he reached out to the table between the
beds and stubbed his cigarette out viciously in the tobacco
tin that served as an ashtray.

He picked up his silk scarf and wiped his face again. I

think he was sweating as much with exhaustion as the heat of the room. "It would have been better if you'd told Mac the truth this afternoon," he said wearily. "Then we could have had it out, there in that office, just the three of us. If you'd told him the reason you were here . . ."

"But I did tell him," I said. Surely he couldn't have sat there in that office and not heard a word I was saying. "I came because my father picked up a message from Briffe, and I—"

"That's not the reason." He said it impatiently, brushing my explanation aside with an angry movement of his hand.

"But it *is* the reason," I insisted.

"Oh, for God's sake!" he cried. "I'm not a fool. You couldn't be that much concerned about a man you'd never met before. How old are you?" he asked abruptly.

"Twenty-three," I told him.

"And I bet you've never been out of England before in your life."

"Yes, I have," I said. "Once. A holiday in Belgium."

"A holiday in Belgium!" He repeated it in a way that made me feel small, remembering that he must have flown thousands of miles over unmapped territory. "And you expect me to believe that you hitched a ride on a trans-Atlantic flight and came all the way over to Canada, where you don't know a soul, just because of a man you'd never met, never even heard of till your father told you about him. You had already reported the matter to the authorities. You'd have left it at that if you hadn't been driven by something more personal."

"But if they're still alive . . ."

"They're dead." He said it harshly.

"Then how could my father have picked up that transmission?"

But he didn't seem interested in the fact that Briffe

had made contact with the outside world. "Why did you lie to him?" he demanded.

"Lie to him?"

"Yes, to McGovern."

"But I didn't lie to him," I cried. "I told him the truth. My father died because—"

"You lied to him!" he almost shouted at me. "You told him you didn't know the name of the man who'd accompanied your grandfather."

"Well, it's true," I said. "I'd never heard of the Ferguson Expedition until I talked to Ledder at Goose."

"You'd never heard of it!" He stared at me as though I'd said the earth was flat. "But that's absurd. You've admitted your father was obsessed by Labrador. You couldn't have grown up not knowing the reason for that obession. And then, when you heard about that transmission—you must have known the reason he invented it. Otherwise you'd never have come all this way. . . ."

"He didn't invent it," I declared hotly.

"Well, imagined it, then."

"He didn't imagine it either." I was suddenly trembling with anger. Couldn't he understand that this was real, so real that it had brought about my father's death? "He picked up a transmission and recorded it in his log. And that transmission was from Briffe. I don't care what you or anybody else says—"

"He couldn't have." His voice was pitched suddenly higher. "The radio was in the aircraft when it sank. I told you that before. He couldn't possibly have transmitted." It was almost as though he were trying to convince himself, and I stared at him, the sweat suddenly cold on my body. He hadn't said because Briffe was dead. He'd simply said that the radio was in the plane when it sank. "And what about Briffe?" I said.

But he only repeated what he'd said already. "He couldn't have transmitted that message." It was said softly

this time, to himself. He was so wrought up that he hadn't
even understood the significance of my question. And then
his mind switched abruptly back to the Ferguson Expedition. It seemed to worry him that I hadn't known about
it. "I don't believe it," he murmured. "You couldn't possibly have grown up not knowing about your grandfather
and what happened to him."

"Well, I did," I said. It seemed so unimportant.
"What difference does it make anyway? All I'm concerned
about—"

"What difference does it make?" He was staring at me,
and the perspiration was gathering on his forehead again.
"It means—" He shook his head. "It's not possible," he
murmured. "It's too much of a coincidence." And then he
looked at me and said: "Why didn't they tell you?" He
seemed unable to leave the subject alone.

And for some reason it seemed to me important at that
moment to convince him. "I think it was my mother," I
said. And I told him how she'd tried to keep the final
log book from me. "She was afraid of Labrador. I think
she didn't want me involved and made my father
promise—"

"But that woman," he said impatiently. "There was
the diary—" He checked himself. "When did your grandmother die?"

"I was ten, I think."

"Then you were old enough—" He stared at me.
"Didn't she ever talk to you about your grandfather? She
must have. A woman so determined, so full of hate . . .
Well, didn't she?"

"Once, when I was very small," I said. "She came to my
room and talked to me. But I was frightened, and my
mother found her there, and after that we never visited
her again."

That seemed to convince him finally, for he said
quietly: "So you came over her without knowing anything

about the expedition." There was a note of weariness in his voice.

"Yes," I said. "The first I heard of it was from Ledder." And I added: "Why is that so important to you?"

But his mind had leapt to something else. "And yet you knew it was Lake of the Lion. How? How could you possibly know unless . . ." He stopped there and brushed his hand over his eyes. "The entry in the log, of course— the map, Ledder's report. You were guessing. Just guessing." His voice had dropped to a murmur; he looked suddenly smaller, his shoulders hunched. *"Mon Dieu!"* he breathed. "So it's true." He wiped his face again, slowly, and his hands were trembling.

"What's true?" I asked.

"About the transmission." He must have answered without thinking, for he added quickly: "That's the reason you are here. I had to be sure," he mumbled. And then he got quickly to his feet. "I must get some sleep," he said. Again that movement of the hand across the eyes. "My head aches." He seemed suddenly to want to escape from the room.

But by then my mind had fastened on the implications of what he had said. "Then it was Lake of the Lion," I said. "You told me you hadn't noticed . . ."

The sudden wild look in his eyes silenced me. He was standing at the foot of the bed, staring down at me. "What difference does it make to you whether it was Lake of the Lion or not?" he asked, his voice trembling. "You say you know nothing of what happened there before. So what difference does it make?"

"None," I said quickly, my skin suddenly chill. And then I added because I had to: "Except that if you knew where Briffe was transmitting from . . ."

"He didn't transmit!" he almost shouted at me. "Nobody transmitted from that place."

"Then how did my father manage to pick up—"

"I tell you there was no transmission!" he cried. His face was quite white. "Your father imagined it. He was mad—obsessed with Labrador—the whole thing locked up too long inside of him. It was what he saw in his mind—nothing more." He was breathing heavily, so wrought up that the words poured out of him. "It must be that. It must be," he reiterated, as though by repetition it would become reality. "Briffe had nothing to transmit with. And that bit about Baird . . . Bill Baird was dead. I'm sure he was dead."

"And Briffe?" I said in a whisper. "Was Briffe dead?"

His eyes focused on me slowly and I saw them dilate as he realized what he'd been saying. He opened his mouth, but no words came, and it was then that I knew for certain that he'd left Briffe alive. He couldn't bring himself to repeat the lie he'd told so glibly in Lands's office, and I sat there, staring at him, unable to hide the feeling of revulsion that had suddenly enveloped me.

"Why are you staring at me like that?" he cried suddenly. And then he got a grip on himself. "That damned scar, of course. Makes me look odd." He laughed uneasily and reached for his parka.

He was leaving, and I sat there, not daring to ask why he hadn't reported my presence up the line or why he was so concerned about the Ferguson Expedition. I just wanted to be rid of him.

"I must get some sleep." He had pulled on the parka and was muttering to himself. "It's sleep I need." He turned blindly towards the door. But then he stopped as though jerked back by the string of some sudden thought. "What are you going to do now?" he asked, turning to face me again. "You should go home. Nobody believes you."

I kept still and didn't say anything, hoping he'd go. But he came back to the foot of the bed. "You're going on. Is that it? Into the bush? To try and find them?" It

was as though he were reading my thoughts, and I
wondered whether that was what I was really going to do,
for I hadn't dared think beyond Darcy and Camp 263.
"You'll never get there," he said. "Never." He swallowed
jerkily. "You don't know what it's like. There's nothing.
Nothing at all. Jackpine and muskeg and reindeer moss
and water—lake after lake. You're crazy to think of it.
You'll die. You don't know what it's like."

I heard the door of the hut open, and footsteps sounded
on the bare boards. And then Bob Perkins was there,
stopped in the doorway by the sight of Laroche. "Sorry,"
he said, looking uncertainly at the two of us. "Thought
you'd be asleep." He hesitated, and then said: "If you
two want to talk . . ."

"No," I said quickly. "No, we've finished." I was intensely relieved to see him.

Laroche hesitated, staring at Perkins. "I must think,"
he murmured. And then he turned to me. "The supply
train doesn't get in till eight tomorrow. I checked. And
there are no planes. I'll see you again in the morning
. . . when I've had some sleep." He was fumbling with
the scarf which he was tying round his neck. "I'll talk to
you again then." And he pushed past Perkins, walking
slowly like a man in a daze, so that his footsteps dragged
on the boards, and then the outer door closed and he
was gone.

I felt the sweat damp on my face then and realized I
was trembling. "That was Laroche, wasn't it?" Perkins
asked.

I nodded, feeling suddenly limp.

"Thought so." He was looking at me curiously. "He
hopped a north-bound flight and persuaded the pilot to
land him here." I thought he was going to question me,
but in the end he went over to his bed and began to undress. "By the way," he said, "I got your message through
to Goose."

"Thanks."

"I couldn't get Ledder. But they'll give it to him."

"Sorry to have been a nuisance."

"Oh, that's all right." He hesitated, unwilling to leave it at that. But when I didn't say anything, he switched off the light and got into bed. "You've another hour and a half before Luigi calls you." And then he added: "You don't want Laroche to know where you've gone, do you?"

"No," I said.

"Okay, I won't tell him. And I won't tell him about the message either."

"Thank you." And I added: "You've been a good friend."

"Aye, well, I like to help anybody from the Old Country. Good night and *bon voyage,* as the French say."

A moment later he was snoring peacefully. But I couldn't sleep, for my mind was too full of Laroche's visit. His manner had been so strange, and the tension in him; there was something there, something I didn't understand, some secret locked away inside him. The way he had said: *"I suppose you think I killed them."* And that interest in the Ferguson Expedition—it was almost pathological. Or was his manner, everything, the result of his injury? All I knew was that he'd left Briffe alive and that I had to get north as fast as I could and talk to Darcy. I had to find somebody who would believe me—or else locate this Lake of the Lion myself.

It seemed an age before the truck came. But at last I heard it draw up outside, and then the light in the passage went on and the driver poked his head round the door. "If you want the ballast train, mister, you better hurry."

Perkins didn't stir. He lay on his back with his mouth open, snoring. I slipped into my clothes and went out to the truck with my suitcase. The night was bitterly cold— no stars now, not a glimmer of light from the sleeping camp. We took the same road with its iron ruts, bumping and lurching out past the airstrip buildings to the ballast pit, where the train stood black in the headlights on the top of an embankment.

The driver set me down right below the caboose. It was an old-fashioned guards van with an iron chimney poking out through the roof, and as the truck drove off, a torch flashed above me. "Who's that?" a voice called out of the night. And when I explained, he shouted: "Henri! Passenger for you."

An oil lamp flickered beside the ballast wagons, and a voice answered: *"Bon, bon."* He was there waiting for me when I reached the track. *"Bon jour, m'sieur."* The lamp was flashed on my face. "Ah, but of course. You are Eenglish, no? I am Henri Gaspard." As he shook my hand, his face showed in the glow of the lamp he held. It was a sad, lined face with a little waxed moustache. Incredibly, he wore an old C.P.R. pill-box hat complete with gold braid. The effect in this desolate place was strangely old-world, as though he had stepped out of a print illustrating the dress of a soldier of the Grande Armée. "You are only just in time, *mon ami*. We are leaving now." He led me to the caboose and waved me in. "My 'ome," he said. *"Entrez, m'sieur."*

He left me then, and I swung myself up into the van. Inside, it was spotlessly clean and surprisingly cosy. There was a cabin with lower and upper berths on either side, and beyond that a sort of saloon with leather-cushioned seats and a table, and right at the end a wood-fired stove as big as a kitchen range. Mahogany panels and the oil lamp swung from the roof completed the Edwardian atmosphere.

I sat down, suddenly exhausted. Lying in that dark room in the bunkhouse, thinking of Laroche, I had been afraid I should never make this next stage, and now I was here.

For a long time nothing happened, and then suddenly there were shouts and a whistle blew. I went out on to the platform at the back. Torches flickered along the line, and the black silence of the night was suddenly broken by the mournful hoot of the locomotive. Couplings clashed in a rising crescendo of sound that culminated in the caboose being jerked into motion. Henri swung himself up on to the platform beside me. *"Alors, n'marchons."*

I stayed there, watching the single lit window that marked the airstrip buildings slide past. After that there was nothing, no glimmer of light, no sign of the camp. The jackpine forest had closed round us and there was only the rattle of the wheels on the rail joints and the cold and the black night. I went back into the warmth of the caboose, where the oil lamp danced on its hook and Henri stood at the stove brewing coffee.

I had a cup of coffee and a cigarette with him, and then excused myself and went to bed in one of the upper bunks. This time I fell asleep at once and lay like a log, only dimly conscious of the stops and the sound of movement and voices. And after a long time there were shouts and the clash of couplings, and I woke up, feeling cold and cramped and sweaty with sleeping in my clothes. And when I rolled over to face the grimy window, I found myself staring out into a cold grey world of Christmas trees all dusted white with snow, and I could hardly believe it.

I clambered slowly down from the bunk and went out to the rear of the caboose. Men were walking along beside the train, winding open the doors of the wagons so that they spilled ballast out on either side of the track as they trundled slowly forward. The rails ran out behind us in two black threads that were finally swallowed up in the white of the jackpine, and when I dropped to the ground so that I could look ahead, it was the same. There was nothing anywhere in that cold, harsh world but the train, a black and lonely intruder.

I climbed back into the caboose, for I wasn't dressed for this sort of cold. There was nobody else there now, and I sat on the lower berth, shivering and looking out through the window. A board with 235 painted on it slid past, and shortly afterwards the train clanked over a switch and stopped. We shunted backwards then, switching on to another track, and finally came to rest. *"Le fin de voyage,"* Henri called to me from the rear platform. "Come. I give you to my friend Georges."

I followed him out of the caboose to find we were on a section of double track. Parked close behind us was a line of old coaches with smoke rising from their iron chimneys. "Bunk'ouse train," Henri said as we trudged through soft snow already more than an inch deep. "You get brekf'st 'ere." He looked down at my shoes. *"Pas bon,"* he said, and shook his head. "You get clothes from store queek, *mon ami*—or you die, eh?" And he smiled at me. *"C'est le mauvais temps.* The snow, she come too soon this year."

We clambered up into the fourth coach. A bare trestle table with wooden benches on either side ran the length of it, and from the far end came the smell of coffee and the sizzle of frying. It was hot like an oven after the cold outside.

"Georges!"

A big man in a dirty white apron emerged. I was introduced, and then Henri shook my hand and left. "Breakfast in quarter of an hour," Georges said and disappeared into the cookhouse.

A little later men began to pile in, a mixed, half-dressed crowd who filled the benches and sat there, still red-eyed with sleep and not talking. A boy heaped food on the table—steaks and bacon and eggs, great piles of bread, pots of coffee and tea, and tin bowls full of corn-

flakes. It was a gargantuan breakfast eaten hurriedly, the
only conversation shouted demands to pass this or that.
And then they were gone as quickly as they had come,
like a plague of locusts, leaving behind a table full of
scraps and the swill bin at the end half full, with their
plates piled and their knives and forks in a tub of hot
water.

What did I do now? I sat there, finishing my coffee,
whilst the boy cleared the debris from the table. Outside,
the snow was thicker than ever, big wet flakes swirling
softly. There was the hoot of a diesel, and then the
empty ballast train went clanking past the windows. And
when it was gone there was nothing but the empty track
and beyond that a dreary view of stunted jackpine growing reluctantly out of flat, swampy ground, and everything white with snow. I hadn't expected the winter to be
so early.

And then Georges came in and I asked him how I
could get up to Head of Steel. "Is anybody going up from
here, do you think?" I asked him.

He shook his head. "The boys 'ere are ballast gang.
They're rail-lifting and packing the ballast you just
brought up. They ain't going to Head of Steel. But I
guess there'll be somebody come through with a gas car
during the day." And he added: "You want some clothes?
It's cold riding them little speeders."

"Can I get some here?" I asked. "I had to leave in a
hurry. . . ."

He nodded. "Guess I can fix you up. The boys are
always leaving stuff behind. But they'll be cast-offs, mind."

He went out and a few minutes later came back with a
sordid-looking bundle. "Sort those over an' take anything
you fancy." He dumped them on the table. "There's a
parka there ain't at all bad, an' there's a pair of boots
look all right." He nodded and left me.

The parka was a padded waterproof jacket, black with

grease and dirt, and its hood was torn. There was an old fur cap with ear flaps and a pair of gloves with the fingers worn through and waterproof trousers stiff with grease. The trousers were tight and the parka too big, but there was a pair of boots that were a reasonable fit. I went into the kitchen and tried to buy them from him with the twenty dollars Lands had given me, but he said they weren't worth anything anyway; and after that I went back to the diner and sat there, staring out of the window, watching the track.

But the track remained empty. Nothing came. And now that I was equipped to withstand the weather, the snow stopped and the sun came out.

I was still there when the ballast gang returned for lunch. Halfway through a large steak I thought I heard the hoot of a locomotive. It was a faint, faraway sound, scarcely audible above the noise of fifty men shovelling energy back into their bodies, but I jumped to my feet and went to the door, peering out along the line of the through track.

At first I thought I must have been mistaken. North and south the track was empty, the black lines running out into the nothingness of Labrador. Then it came again, a sad sound carried by the wind, and far down the track to the south my eyes became focused on a small blob that didn't seem to move but yet grew steadily larger.

I jumped down and stood beside the track, watching it grow until I could see the yellow of the diesel's paintwork against the drab white background of melting snow. It passed the switch on to the double track, and as it came thundering down on me I could feel the weight of it beating at the ground under my feet.

The track in front of me was leaping under the vibration, and then it was on me with a rush of air, pressing me back against the dining-coach. There was a smell of hot oil, a glimpse of huge driving wheels, and behind the diesel clattered a long line of steel-transporters, their specially constructed bogies beating a rapid tattoo. Wagons full of sleepers followed and, behind them, two coaches, and finally the caboose.

I clambered back into the diner and sat down again at the table. "Was that the supply train?" I asked the man next to me.

He nodded, his mouth full, and I finished my steak, wondering whether Laroche had been in one of the coaches.

The men were beginning to drift back to work, and I went with them. Their transport, parked at the tail end of the bunkhouse train, consisted of small rail cars, hitched together in trains of three. With their upright coachwork, they looked like the rolling stock of an old-fashioned mountain railway. "Are you going up towards Head of Steel?" I asked the foreman. But he shook his head. He had a small, open speeder with a perspex windshield, and I stood and watched him as he put it in gear, eased forward the belt-drive clutch, and went trundling down the track behind his gang. He paused just clear of the points to switch them back to the through-track position and then ran on down the line, the fussy putter of the engine dwindling rapidly.

The brief interlude of sun was over. The world was cold and grey, and I went back to the warmth of the diner, wishing now that I'd come up on the supply train. The tables had been cleared, the benches pushed back against the sides of the coach. It was nearly one thirty. Farrow would be headed for home now. But it was difficult to believe in England up here in this wild country. I sat down by one of the windows, staring out across the empty main track to the solid wall of the jackpine beyond. I'd give it until three. If I didn't get a lift by three, I'd start walking. Ten miles . . . say, four hours. I'd be at

Head of Steel about dusk. Nobody would see me then, and I could slip past the supply train and head north.

Time passed slowly, and nobody came up the line. And then, when it was almost three and I was getting ready to leave, voices sounded below the window, and a moment later the door at the end slid back with a crash and two men entered, shouting for Georges and demanding coffee and doughnuts.

"Mr. Lands been through here yet?" the elder of the two asked.

"Sorry, Mr. Steel, I don't see him for two weeks or more," Georges answered.

Steel came on into the diner, pulling off his fur-lined gloves and throwing them on to the table. He was dressed entirely in olive green, with a peaked ski cap, and his thin, lined face looked pinched with cold. "You here about this esker that's been located?" he asked, looking straight at me.

"No," I said. I didn't know what an esker was, and all I wanted was to get out of there before Lands arrived. I picked up my gloves and fur cap.

But his companion stood between me and the door, a big, broad-shouldered youngster in a fur cap and scarlet-lined hunting parka.

"What's your job?" he demanded. He had an Irish accent.

"Engineer," I answered without thinking. And then I checked, for I knew I'd made a mistake. These men were engineers themselves.

"Then you can probably tell us something about it," Steel said. "All we've heard is that there's talk of pushing a spur line in and starting a new ballast pit."

"I'm new here," I said quickly. "I don't know anything about it."

He nodded, his eyes fixed on my face. "Thought I hadn't seen you before. Straight up from base, are you?"

"Yes." I didn't know quite what to do. I felt that if I left now he'd be suspicious. And then Georges came in with the coffee and a heaped plate of doughnuts. "You like coffee, too?" he asked me, and I saw that there were three mugs on the tray.

"You staying here or going on up the line?" Steel asked me, his mouth already full of doughnut.

"Going on," I said, gulping the coffee, though it was scalding-hot. I had to get out of here somehow before Lands arrived.

"We can probably give you a lift as far as Head of Steel. Where are you bound for?"

I hesitated. But it didn't seem to matter. "Two-six, three," I said.

"Crazy Darcy, eh?" His companion gave a loud guffaw. "Jesus Christ! So they haven't rumbled him yet, the old devil."

"What Paddy means," Steel said, dunking his doughnut, "is that Ray is one of the old-timers on this railroad."

"What I mean is that he's an old rogue and you'll do all the work for him whilst he takes the credit—if you're a hard-working, sober, God-fearing engineer, which is what we all are, seeing this is the Wilderness and no Garden of Eden running with the milk of human kindness that comes from my native land."

"There's no liquor allowed up here," Steel said. "That's what he means. It's a subject of conversation that gets kind of boring after you've been up here a while." He was looking at me curiously. "Your name wouldn't be Ferguson, would it?"

I nodded, my body suddenly tense, wondering what was coming.

But all he said was: "Somebody was inquiring for you just as we left Head of Steel."

"Laroche?" The question seemed dragged out of me.

"That's the guy, yes. The pilot of that plane that crashed. You know him?"

I nodded, thinking that now he was between me and Two-six-three.

"Bad business, that crash," Steel said. "Did he ever talk to you about it?"

But all I could think of was the. fact that Laroche had been on the supply train. "What did he want?" I asked. "Did he tell you what he wanted?"

"No. Just asked if we'd seen you. But it seemed urgent." And then he went back to the subject of the crash. "I guess it must've been a hell of a shock to him, both his passengers dead and then struggling out alone like that. Makes you realize what this country's like soon as you get away from the grade." And he added: "I heard he was engaged to Briffe's daughter. Is that true?"

The sound of a speeder came from the track outside, and the Irishman jumped to his feet and went to the window. "Here's Bill now."

Laroche at Head of Steel and now Lands. I felt suddenly trapped. The speeder had stopped outside the diner, the engine ticking over with a gentle putter that was muffled by the thick glass of the windows. Boots sounded on the iron grating at the end of the coach, and then the door slammed back. I only just had time to turn away towards the window before Bill Lands was there.

"You got my message, then, Al." His voice was right behind me as he came down the coach. "And you brought Paddy with you. That's swell."

He was down by the stove now, and I glanced at him quickly. He looked even bigger in his parka, and the fur cap made his face look tougher, a part of the North.

"You want some cawfee, Bill?" Steel was standing to make room for him.

"Sure," Lands said, his hands held out to the hot casing of the stove. "And some doughnuts. You know why I asked you and Paddy to meet me here?"

"There was some talk about an esker—"

"That's it. Williams found it." His voice was muffled

by the doughnut he was wolfing down. "Thought it might solve our problem. That ballast coming up from One-three-four is starting to get froze. But if we could open up a ballast pit here, right behind Head of Steel . . ." He checked suddenly and said: "Hell! My speeder's still on the track. Hey, you!"

I knew he'd turned and was staring at my back. I couldn't ignore him, and at the same time I didn't dare turn to face him. "Can you drive a speeder?" he demanded.

It was the opportunity I'd been wanting, the excuse to get out without raising their suspicions. But I hesitated because the door seemed a long way off and I was afraid my voice might give me away.

"I asked you whether you could drive a speeder." His voice was impatient.

"Sure," I said and started for the door.

Maybe it was my voice, or maybe I moved too quickly. I heard him say: "Who is that guy?" But he didn't wait for an answer. He was already coming down the coach after me. "Just a minute!"

I had almost reached the door where my suitcase stood, and I might have made a dash for it then, but I hadn't had time to think what the use of a speeder could mean to me. I just felt it was hopeless to try and get away from him, and so I turned and faced him.

He had almost caught up with me, but when I turned and he saw my face, he stopped abruptly. "Ferguson!" There was a look of blank astonishment in his eyes as though he couldn't believe it. "How the hell . . . !" And then his big hands clenched and the muscles of his jaw tightened.

It was the knowledge that he was going to hit me that made my brain seize on the one thing that might stop him. "Briffe is alive," I said.

He checked then. "Alive?"

"At least he was when Laroche left him. I'm certain of that now."

"And what makes you so damned certain?" His voice was dangerously calm.

"Laroche," I said. "He came to my room last night and he virtually admitted—"

"What room? Where?"

"At One-three-four."

"One-three-four? That's a lie. Bert's at Seven Islands."

"No," I said. "He's at Head of Steel right now. Ask them." And I nodded at the two engineers.

That seemed to shake him, for he said: "He followed you, did he?"

"Yes," I said. "He's scared, and—"

"So would I be scared. I'd be scared as hell if I knew some crazy fool—"

"It's not me that's crazy!" I cried.

He stared at me. "What do you mean by that?" His voice had suddenly gone quiet again.

"It's Laroche," I said quickly. "For some reason he can't get the Ferguson Expedition out of his mind. He crashed at Lake of the Lion, and something happened there that's driving him . . ." He had taken a step forward and my voice trailed away.

"Go on," he said ominously. "You think something happened there? What do you think happened?"

"I don't know," I murmured. "But it's preying on his mind."

"What is?"

"I don't know," I repeated. "That's what I've got to find out. But he asked me whether I thought he'd killed them, and then he said he was sure Baird was dead. He didn't say—"

"You damned little liar!" He had suddenly lost his temper. "First you say he left Briffe alive. Now you try to suggest he killed Baird. My God!" he cried, and I

backed away from him into the open doorway. I was out
on the steel platform then, and below me was the track
with the speeder standing there, its engine ticking over.
"You slip up the line," he was saying, "and try to make
people believe a lot of wild, lying accusations. Well, you're
not going any further. Goddammit!" he added. "If you
weren't just a kid—"

That was when I slammed the door in his face and
leapt down on to the track and straight on to the speeder.
I let go the brake and thrust it into gear, revving the
engine, the way I'd seen the gang foreman do it, and I
was just easing the belt on to its drive when he hit the
ground beside me. He reached out and grabbed at the
handrail just as I got the speeder moving. He missed it
and I heard him swear, and then his feet were pounding
after me. But by then I was gathering speed, and after
that I couldn't hear anything but the sound of the engine
and the beat of the wheels on the rail joints.

I was clear of him. That was what the wind sang in my
ears. Clear of him, and I had transport. I glanced back
over my shoulder as I ran clear of the bunkhouse train.
He was standing in the middle of the track shouting
something and waving his arms. I didn't know he was
trying to warn me, and I waved back out of sheer bravado,
and then I pushed the throttle wide open, crouched low
and riding the speeder like a motor bike.

The switch to the double track clattered under the
wheels, and beyond there was nothing but the twin rails
streaming out ahead of me to a long curve where the
speeder bucked and swayed. When I looked back again
the double track and the bunkhouse train had vanished.
I was riding alone, with nothing behind or in front but
the track and the snow-spattered jackpine crowding it on
either side.

III

For the first mile or two

I was swept forward on a tide of exhilaration—the sense of speed, the illusion of power. I felt that nothing could stop me from reaching Lake of the Lion and finding Briffe still alive, and I drove the speeder full out, the wheel flanges screaming on the curves and the virgin country streaming past on either side.

But the mood didn't last. My fingers stiffened with cold where the gloves were worn, my feet became deadened lumps inside the chill casing of my boots, and the wind on my face was a biting blast. I hit a bad patch, where the track had recently been ballasted and the steel was half buried in gravel, and I had to throttle down. I became conscious of the country then, the difficulties that faced me; Lands would phone Head of Steel, and the whole organization would be against me.

I must have passed dozens of telegraph poles lying beside the track before it dawned on me that the linesmen hadn't yet reached this section of the track. Lands couldn't phone them. He'd have to get another speeder and come after me. I opened the throttle wide again, and as I did so there came the crack of a rifle and I ducked my head. But when I looked back over my shoulder, the track behind me was empty.

I thought maybe it was a stone then, thrown up from the track. But the rifle cracked again, unmistakeable this time, and suddenly I could hear wild human cries above the noise of the engine. They came from away to my left, where a lake glimmered like pewter through a screen of trees. There was a canoe there, and an Indian stood in the bows, a rifle to his shoulder, and close inshore a head and antlers thrust towards the shallows. There was a crashing in the undergrowth, and the caribou broke cover a hundred yards ahead of me. It hesitated a moment, pawing at the steel of the track, and then with a quick, terrified leap it was across and had vanished into the bush on the other side.

I didn't catch sight of the Indians again, for the track went into a long bend. There were levelling stakes beside the track here, and in the stretch beyond I found the engineers who had put them there. They stood in a little group round their speeder, which had been lifted clear of the track, and as I rattled past them one of them shouted what sounded like *"Attention!"*

He was a French Canadian with a round fur cap like a Russian, and before I had worked out that it was a shout of warning I was into the next bend. It was ballast again, and the speeder bucked violently as the gravel flew, and through the rattle of the stones came the lost hoot of an owl. And then I was round the bend, clear of the gravel, and there was something on the line ahead. I slammed on the brake as the weird owl hoot sounded again, louder and clearer, suddenly unmistakeable.

Before the speeder had jerked to a halt I could see the yellow paintwork of the locomotive, could feel the rails trembling under me. There was no hope of getting the speeder off the track in time, not by myself. I did the only thing I could and flung the gear lever into reverse, opening the throttle wide and tearing back down the track, round the bend to where the little knot of engineers stood waiting.

The instant I stopped they crowded round, the lifting

bars were pulled out, and then they dragged it clear just as the train came rumbling round the curve. The hooter wailed again, loud as a trumpet note between the enclosing walls of the jackpine, and then the heavy locomotive was on top of us, sliding by at walking pace with a smell of hot engine oil and a slow piston-beat of power. The driver leaned out and shouted down: "You want to commit suicide, just jump in the muskeg. Don't pick on me." He spat into the slush at my feet and went back to the controls. The beat increased with a roar like a power station and the diesel gathered way again, clanking a long line of empty rail flats. And behind the flats came two wooden coaches with men looking down at us incuriously from the windows.

That was when I saw Laroche again. He was in the second coach, and for an instant our eyes met. I saw him jump to his feet, and then the coach was past. The caboose followed, and as it rattled by, Laroche swung himself out of the coach doorway. I thought for a moment he was going to jump. But the train was light, gathering speed quickly. He hung there for a moment, and then he thought better of it and disappeared into the coach again.

I watched the train as it dwindled down the track, and the only thought in my mind then was that the way was clear for me to get to Camp 263. Laroche was behind me now, and Lands, too, and as long as I kept ahead of them there'd be nobody who knew me at Head of Steel. I turned to the engineers and asked them to get my speeder back on the track.

The French Canadian with the fur cap was looking at me curiously. "Why don't you check when you enter this section?" he asked.

"I was in a hurry," I said, my voice a little unsteady because I was feeling badly shaken now.

"You might have killed yourself."

"I was in a hurry," I repeated. "I still am."

"Sure. So is everybody else. But Mr. Lands won't thank you if you wreck his speeder."

I thought he was going to ask me why I was riding it then, but after staring at me a moment he turned to his men and told them to get the speeder back on the track. "That's the trouble with this outfit," he grumbled. "Too much dam' hurry."

Three miles farther on I was stopped by a ballast gang. Their gas cars had been dumped beside the track to let the supply train through, but the track-lifting and ballast-tamping machines were already back at work on the track, and there was nothing for it but to abandon my speeder and continue on foot. Head of Steel, they told me, was two miles up the line.

It was all new grade here, a long fill that ran out across a muskeg swamp. The line sagged in shallow waves where the muskeg sucked at the gravel embankment, and the ties were covered with fresh ballast. It was hard walking, and the wind had swung into the north, so that it cut through my borrowed clothing and chilled the sweat on my body. Out across the marsh, where the black line of the scrub joined the iron-grey sky, I caught a glimpse of hills that were long-backed and bare, as though ground down to the bone by ice.

It seemed a long time that I trudged across that desolate area of swamp, but at last I reached the shallow gravel rim that enclosed it, and round a bend I came on a gang of men working with drills and machine-operated spanners, bolting the rails together and driving spikes. The detached chassis and wheels of dismantled rail transporters lay beside the track, and up ahead were more men and machines, and beyond them the steel-laying train. Everywhere about me now there was a sense of movement, of drive and thrust and effort, so that Labrador seemed suddenly crowded and full of life. The track, laid on the bare gravel without ballast, like toy rails in a sandpit, had a newness about it that showed that it hadn't been there yesterday, and walking beside it, through all these gangs of men, I felt conspicuous.

But they took no notice of me, though as I went by them, my gaze fixed self-consciously on the steel or the machines they operated, I felt that each one of them must know I'd no right to be there. I wondered who was in charge at Head of Steel and what Laroche had told him.

It was better when I reached the train itself. There were no gangs working there, just the wagons full of ties and plates and bolts which men threw out beside the track each time the train moved forward. The train was in a steep cut and I was forced to walk close beside it, so that when I reached the bunkhouse section I was conscious of men lounging in the open doorways of the coaches, staring down at me. But nobody stopped me, and I went up past the engine and the rail transporters until at last I could see the steel-laying crane swinging with a length of rail. A whistle blew and the crane swung back, its claw empty. The train hooted and then moved forward a few yards. Another length of track had been laid.

There was something so fascinating about the rhythmic thrusting of this train into the unknown that for the moment I forgot everything else and climbed halfway up the side of the cut to watch it. Each time, before the train had stopped, the crane was already swinging, another length of steel balanced in its claw grip. A man stood signalling with his hands to the crane driver and shouting instructions to the steel-laying gang, and as the rail came down on to the grade, they seized hold of it, thrusting it into place on the ties and spiking it there with the balanced swing of sledge-hammers.

This was Head of Steel, and I stood and watched with a sort of awe. And then I saw the bare grade stretched

out ahead, naked except for the few ties laid at regular
intervals, and my gaze lifted to the black line of the
jackpine. The yellow slash of the bull-dozed grade ran
into it and was abruptly swallowed.

I don't know what I had expected at Head of Steel.
Obviously there could be no railway beyond this point.
But I had travelled more than a hundred miles of the
line, feeling close to the steel all the time, so that in a
sense I had felt it to be an integral part of Labrador.
And now, suddenly, it ended.

Until that moment I don't think I had faced up to the
reality of what I had set out to do. Lake of the Lion lay
somewhere to the north east—fifty, at most a hundred
miles. But as I looked at the slender line of the grade
and the desolate emptiness of the country ahead, it might
have been on another continent, so remote did it seem.
Even to reach Darcy at Camp 263 appeared suddenly
as a journey into the unknown.

"Hey, you!" A man stood looking up at me from beside
the Burro crane, his scarlet bush shirt a splash of colour
in the gathering dusk. "Yeah, you. What the hell do you
think you're doing up there—watching a rodeo or
somep'n?"

His voice and the way he stood there suggested authority, and I scrambled quickly down, conscious that he
was watching me. "If you're not working, just keep clear
of the steel-laying," he shouted. "How many times I
got to tell you guys?"

He was still watching me as I reached the track, and
I turned my back on him and hurried down the train.
Maybe it was imagination, but I felt I had aroused his
curiosity and that he'd come after me and question me
if I didn't get away from there.

Maybe he would have, but at that moment the train
hooted—a different note this time, long and summoning.
A whistle blew. A voice near me called out "Chow!"

And then the steel-laying gang were coming down the cut, walking with the slack drag of men whose muscles are suddenly relaxed. I was swept up in the movement and went with the tide, down past the rail transporters and the locomotive to the bunkhouse coaches. There were other gangs coming up from the rear of the train, all converging on the diner. I waited my turn and clambered up, relieved to feel that I was no longer alone but one of a crowd. Besides, I was hungry. If I was going up beyond Head of Steel, then it would be better to go after dark when nobody would see me, and with a full belly.

The lights were on inside the diner, and there was warmth and the smell of food. Nobody spoke to me as I pushed my way into a vacant place at the trestle table, and I didn't speak to them but just reached out for whatever I wanted. There was soup, steak with fried eggs and potatoes and cabbage, canned fruit and cream, a mountainous heap of food to be shovelled in and washed down with tea and coffee. And when I'd finished I cadged a cigarette off the little Italian next to me and sat over my mug of coffee, smoking and listening to the sudden hubbub of conversation. I felt tired and relaxed now, and I wanted to sleep instead of going out into the cold again.

There was a sudden cessation of sound from the end of the diner, and through the smoke haze I saw the man in the scarlet bush shirt standing in the doorway. The boss of the steel-laying gang was with him, and they were looking down the length of the table.

"Who's that?" I asked the Italian.

"The guy in the red shirt?" he asked. "You don't-a know?" He seemed puzzled. "That's Dave Shelton. He's in charge at Head of Steel."

I glanced quickly at the doorway again. The two men were still standing there, and Shelton was looking straight at me. He turned and asked the other man a question, and I saw the gang foreman shake his head.

"You wanna keep clear of him," the Italian was saying. "He drive all-a the time. Last week he bust a man's jaw because he tell him he drive-a the men too hard."

Shelton glanced in my direction again, and then the two of them were pushing their way down the diner, and I knew I was trapped there, for there was nothing I could do, nowhere I could go, and I sat, staring at my mug, waiting.

"You work here?" The voice was right behind me, and when I didn't answer, a hand gripped my shoulder and swung me round. "I'm talking to you." He was standing right over me, broad-shouldered and slim-hipped, with a sort of thrusting violence that I'd only once met before, in an Irish navvy. "You're the guy I saw gawping at the steel-laying gang, aren't you?"

The men round me had stopped talking, so that I was at the centre of a little oasis of silence.

"Well, do you work here or don't you?"

"No," I said.

"Then what are you doing in this diner?"

"Having a meal," I said, and a ripple of laughter ran down the table. The line of his mouth hardened, for it wasn't the most helpful reply I could have made, and in an effort to appease him I added quickly: "I'm an engineer. It was supper time when I got here, and I just followed the others."

"Where's your card?" he demanded.

"My card?"

"Your card of employment as an engineer on the line. You haven't got one, have you?" He was smiling now, suddenly sure of himself. "What's your name?" And when I didn't answer, he said: "It's Ferguson, isn't it?"

I nodded, knowing it was no use trying to deny it.

"Thought so." And he added: "What do you think you're playing at, pretending you're an engineer? Alex Staffen's mad as hell about it."

"I *am* an engineer," I said.

"Okay, you're an engineer. But not on this railroad." His hand fastened on my shoulder again and he dragged me to my feet. "Come on. Let's get going, feller. I've instructions to send you back to base just as fast as I can." He jerked his head for me to follow him and led the way towards the door.

There was nothing I could do but follow him down the diner, feeling rather like a criminal, with the gang foreman close behind me. Once outside, away from all the men, I could probably get him to listen to my explanation. But I didn't see what good it would do. Staffen had set the machinery of the organization in motion to get me returned to base, and unless I could make this man Shelton understand the urgency of the matter, he'd stick to his instructions. He'd have to.

Halfway down the diner he stopped abruptly. "Your speeder still on the track, Joe?" he asked one of the men.

He was a big fellow with a broken nose who looked as though he'd been a heavy-weight boxer. "Sorry, Mr. Shelton," he said. "I cleared it just before—"

"Well, get it back on the track right away. You're taking this guy down to Two-twenty-four."

"Okay, Mr. Shelton." The man scrambled to his feet, not bothering to finish his coffee.

"He'll have to wait till we've dumped the empty steel wagons," the foreman said. "The train'll be backing up to clear the cut any minute now."

"Well, see if you can get your speeder on the track and parked down the line before they start. Otherwise, you won't get started for an hour or more."

"Okay, Mr. Shelton." The man headed for the door and pushed his way through the group gathered about the swill bin. Shelton stopped to have a word with one or two of the other men seated at the table, and by the time he reached the door the men were leaving the diner in a steady stream. "Could I have a word with you in private?" I asked. "It's important."

He was pushing his way through the men, but he stopped then. "What's it about?"

"I had a reason for coming up here," I said. "If I could explain to you . . ."

"You explain to Alex Staffen. I got other things to worry about."

"It's a matter of life and death," I said urgently.

"So's this railroad. I'm laying steel, and winter's coming on." He forced his way through the doorway. "People like you," he said over his shoulder, "are a Goddammed nuisance."

I didn't have another chance to make him listen to me. We were out on the platform now, and as we reached the door to the track a voice called up: "That you, Dave?" The earth of the cut was yellow in the lights of the train, and there were men moving about below us, dark shapes with here and there the glow of a cigarette. "They want you on the radio," the voice added. "It's urgent."

"Hell!" Shelton said. "Who is it?"

"They didn't say. But it's Two-two-four, and they're asking for the figure for track laid today and a schedule of shifts worked. . . ."

"Okay, I'll come."

"Sounds like the general manager's there," the foreman said. "He was due at Two-two-four today, wasn't he, Dave?"

"That's right. And one of the directors, too. I guess they're going to turn the heat on again." And he added: "Christ Almighty! We're laying more than one and a half miles a day already. What more do they expect?"

"I guess two miles would sound better in their ears," the foreman muttered dryly.

"Two miles! Yeah, that'd be sweet music. But the men can't lay it that fast."

"You could try paying them a bonus."

"It's not me. It's the company. Still, with the freeze-up due . . ." Shelton hesitated. "Yeah, well maybe it's an idea." He turned to me. "You wait here in the diner. And you better wait with him, Pat," he told the foreman. And he jumped out and disappeared up the track.

The men were streaming out of the diner now, and the gang foreman and I stood back to let them pass. I wondered whether it was worth trying to explain to him about Briffe being alive, but one glance at his wooden features told me it wouldn't be any good. He hadn't the authority to help me, anyway.

In fact, at that moment I think I had lost the will to do anything more. Now that instructions about me had been sent up from base, there didn't seem any point. The whole organization had probably been alerted, and in that case there was nothing I could do. And yet I would have liked to talk with Darcy. Perkins had said he knew more about Labrador than anyone else on the line, and there were things I wanted to know, things that perhaps he could have told me.

"Go on back to the diner," the foreman said. "It'll be warmer in there." The stream of men had thinned, and he pushed me forward. I checked to let two men come out, and as they reached the exit door, a voice from the track called up: "Take this, will you?" One of them reached down, grabbed hold of a suitcase, and dropped it on the platform almost at my feet.

I don't know what made me bend down and look at it— something about its shape maybe, or perhaps subconsciously I had recognized the voice. At any rate, I did, and then I just stood there, staring at it stupidly. It was my own suitcase, the one I'd left in the bunkhouse train ten miles down the line when I'd jumped Lands's speeder.

And then I heard Lands's voice outside on the track. "Okay, but we can't do that till we've seen Dave. Any-

way, I want to get a radio message through to Two-sixty-
three. My guess is . . ." The rest was drowned in a pro-
longed hoot from the locomotive. And when it ceased
abruptly I heard somebody say: "Why bring Darcy into
it?" And Lands answered impatiently: "Because they're
all construction men up there. They got a target on that
grade. Ray's the only guy with a vehicle who's got the
time . . ."

I didn't hear any more, and I guessed he'd turned
away. Peering out, I could see his padded bulk moving
off up the train. There was somebody with him, but I
couldn't see who it was, for he was in the shadows, close
under the next coach.

"What are you up to?" The foreman's hand gripped
my arm.

"Nothing," I said. I was wondering whether it was
Laroche I'd seen in the shadow there.

"Well, come on into the diner."

I hesitated. "That was Lands," I said.

"Bill Lands?" He had let go of my arm. "Well, what
if it was? You know him?"

I nodded. I was thinking that I'd nothing to lose. If
I went to Lands now, of my own accord, maybe he'd
listen to me. I might even convince him there was a
chance Briffe was still alive. At least the responsibility
would be his then. I'd have done all I could. And if
Laroche were there, then perhaps Lands would see for
himself that the man was half out of his mind. "I'd
like a word with Lands," I said.

The foreman looked at me with a puzzled frown. He
hadn't expected that, and he said: "Does he know you're
up here?"

"Yes," I said. And I added: "I came up on his
speeder."

That seemed to impress him. "Well, you'll have to

wait till Dave Shelton gets back. Ask him." And he added: "You a newspaperman?"

"No." And because I felt that it would do no harm for him to know why I was here, I said: "I came up the line on account of that plane that crashed. You remember?"

He nodded. "Sure, I remember."

I had aroused his curiosity now, and I said: "Well, Briffe's still alive."

"Still alive?" He stared at me. "How the hell could he be? They searched for a week, and then the pilot came out with the news that the other two were dead. I heard all about it from Darcy when he was down here a few days back, and he said the guy was lucky to be alive."

"Well, Briffe may be alive, too," I said.

"Briffe? You crazy?"

I saw the look of absolute disbelief in his eyes, and I knew it was no good. They were all convinced Briffe was dead—this man, Lands, all of them. Shelton would be the same. And Darcy. What about Darcy? He'd been with Laroche for an hour—all the way up to Two-ninety. Would Darcy think I was crazy, too? "I'd like to talk to Lands," I said again, but without much hope.

And then the locomotive hooted again, two short blasts. "You'll have to wait," the foreman said. "We're gonna back up clear of the cut now."

There was a clash of buffers, and the coach jerked into motion, the yellow sides of the cut sliding past the open door. It came to me in a flash then that this was my chance. If I were going to contact Darcy, I'd have to make the attempt now. But I hesitated, wondering whether it was worth it. And then I looked down at my suitcase, resting there right at my feet. I think it was the suitcase that decided me. Unless Lands or Laroche had removed them, it contained my father's log books. At least I'd have those to show Darcy, and I felt suddenly that I was meant to go on, that that was why the suitcase was there; it was a sign.

I suppose that sounds absurd, but that was the way I felt about it.

The clatter of the wheels over the rail joints was speeding up, the sides of the cut slipping by faster, and I reached for the suitcase.

"What are you doing with that?" The foreman's voice was suspicious.

"It happens to be my suitcase," I said. I saw the look of surprise on his face, and then I jumped. It was a standing jump, but I put all the spring of my leg muscles into it, and it carried me on to the side of the cut where the ground was softer. I hit it with my body slack, my shoulder down, the way I'd been taught in the army during National Service, and though it knocked the breath out of my body and I rolled over twice, I wasn't hurt.

As I scrambled to my feet, I saw the foreman leaning out of the coach door, shouting at me. But he didn't jump. He'd waited too long. The locomotive went by me with a roar, and in the light from the cab I found my suitcase. The rail transporters followed, finally the Burro crane, and after that the track was clear and it was suddenly dark.

I stood quite still for a moment, listening. But all I could hear was the rumble of the train as it ran back out of the cut. No voices came to me out of the night, no glimmer of a cigarette showed in the darkness ahead. All that seething crowd of men seemed to have been spirited away, leaving a black, empty void through which a cold wind blew. But at least it meant I could keep to the track, and I followed it north, breaking into a run as soon as my eyes became accustomed to the darkness.

Behind me the sound of the train faded and died, and when I glanced back over my shoulder, it was stationary on the track, a dull glow of light that glinted on the rails.

Torches flickered, and I thought I heard shouts. But it was half a mile away at least, and I knew I was clear of them.

A few minutes later I reached the end of steel. It was just the empty grade then, no track to guide me, and I stopped running. Behind me the lights of the train had vanished, hidden by the bend of the cut, and with their disappearance the black emptiness of Labrador closed round me. The only sound now was that of the wind whispering dryly through the trees.

The night was overcast, but it didn't matter—not then. The grade rolled out ahead of me, flat like a road and just visible as a pale blur in the surrounding darkness. But it didn't last. It was like that for a mile, maybe two, and then the surface became rougher. There were ruts and soft patches, and a little later I blundered into a heap of fresh-piled gravel.

After that the going was bad. Several times I strayed from the track into the bull-dozed roots of trees piled at its edge. And once the ground dropped from under me and I fell a dozen feet or more to fetch up against the half-buried shovel of a grab crane.

I was more careful after that, moving slower. And then I came to another section of completed grade, and for about a mile the going was easier again. But again it didn't last.

It was not much more than twenty miles from Head of Steel to Camp 263, but to understand what the going was like, particularly at night in those conditions, I should perhaps explain the general method of grade construction employed by the contractors. It was not a continuing thrust into Labrador, as was the case with the steel-laying, but a series of isolated operations, spreading north and south and ultimately linking up.

In the initial stages of the project a pilot road—known as the Tote Road—had been constructed all the way from the base at Seven Islands to the iron-ore deposits in the neighbourhood of Knob Lake almost four hundred miles to the north. This road, which was little more than a track bull-dozed out of the bush, followed the general line of the proposed grade, and though it parallelled it in many places, its course was far from straight, since it followed the line of least resistance offered by the country. It was up this road that the heavy equipment had advanced—the drag cranes, grab cranes, bull-dozers, tumble-bugs, scrapers, "mule" trucks, and fuel tankers.

At the same time that the Tote Road was being constructed, engineers, flown in by floatplane and operating from small tented camps, surveyed and marked out the line of the railway. Airstrips constructed at strategic intervals were then built, and from these focal points construction camps, supplied largely by air lift, were established and gangs of men deployed to build the grade, section by section.

At the time I started north from Head of Steel the over-all plan was to push the steel as far as Menihek Dam, at Mile 329, before winter brought work to a virtual standstill. This dam was a shallow one constructed almost entirely from air-lifted supplies where the waters of the ninety-mile Ashuanipi Lake ran into the great Hamilton River. All it needed now was the generators to make it operational, and the whole weight of the contractors' organization, backed by some hundreds of pieces of heavy equipment, was concentrated on this stretch of the grade.

The effect, so far as I was concerned, was bewildering. A section of completed grade, scraped smooth as a road, would suddenly end in piled heaps of gravel or drop away into the quagmire of an uncompleted fill. The half-finished cuts were full of rock from the day's blasting, and the whole line of the grade was littered with heavy machines that were death traps in the dark.

Somewhere around midnight the wind died away and everything was preternaturally still—a stillness that had a quality of hostility about it. And then it began to snow, a gentle floating down of large flakes that were wet and clinging. The darkness around me slowly changed to a ghostly white, and once again a completed section of grade petered out and I was stumbling through ridged heaps of sand, keeping by instinct rather than sight to the open swathe that had been bull-dozed through the jackpine.

It was shortly after this that the ground abruptly dropped away from me and I slithered down into the mud of a gulley where the corrugated-metal sheets of a half-completed conduit stood like the whitened bones of a huge whale. It was muskeg here, and I knew it was hopeless to try and cross it in the dark. Weary and cold, I paused for a spell, and then I retraced my steps to an opening I had seen in the white wall of the jackpine, and when I found it, I abandoned the grade, dully conscious that I was on some sort of track.

But the track was little better than the grade. The ground became soft under my feet as I descended into the same shallow depression that had called for a conduit in the grade construction. Patches of water showed dark against the snow, and as I splashed through them I could hear the soft crunch of the paper-thin layer of ice that had already formed on the surface. And then it was mud, thick and heavy and black, with deep ruts in it where bull-dozers had wallowed through.

But the ground under the mud was frozen hard, and when I was through the worst of it and the ruts still continued, I knew I had found a section of the old Tote Road. Gradually the surface hardened as the ground rose again; the ruts disappeared, and the country became more open, the trees stunted. I had difficulty in keeping to the track then, and twice within a matter of minutes I found myself blundering through thick scrub, and the snow shaken from the branches of the trees soaked me to the skin. I was very tired by then, my senses dulled. The handle of my suitcase was like the cold edge of a piece of steel cutting into my stiffened fingers, and the boots that were too big for me had raised blisters that burned with the pain of frostbite.

When I lost the track again, I gave it up and made a bed of pine branches and lay down to wait for dawn. I would go on then, I told myself—when I was rested and could see. The sweat was cold on my body, but I didn't care because of the relief I felt at just lying there, making no effort.

The snow fell softly, but it didn't seem cold any more, and the stillness was overwhelming. In all the world there was no sound, so that I thought I could hear the flakes falling.

I hadn't intended to sleep, but once I had relaxed I suppose there was nothing to keep me awake. The snow whispered, and I lay drifting in a white, dark world until consciousness began to slide away from my numbed brain.

Maybe I heard the car and that's what woke me. Or perhaps it was the gleam of the headlights. I opened my eyes suddenly to find myself staring up at a jackpine floodlit like a Christmas tree, and a voice said: "I guess you must be Ferguson."

I sat up then, still dazed with cold and sleep, not quite sure where I was. But then I saw the track and the trees all covered with snow and the man standing over me, black against the lights. He was short and broad, with a gnome-like body swollen by the padding of his parka, and my first thought was that this wasn't either Lands or Laroche. This was a man I'd never seen before. His face was square and craggy, the colour of mahogany, and the snow clung white to tufted eyebrows as he leaned forward, peering down at me through rimless glasses.

"A fine dance you've led me," he growled, and he reached down and dragged me to my feet. "I bin all along the grade as far as Head of Steel searching for you. Came back by the Tote Road, just in case."

I mumbled my thanks. My limbs were so stiff with cold I could hardly stand. Numbness deadened the pain of my blistered feet. "Come on," he said, grabbing hold of my suitcase. "There's a heater in the jeep. It'll hurt like hell, but you'll soon thaw out."

It was a jeep station wagon, a battered wreck of a car with one mudguard torn off and the bodywork all plastered with mud and snow. He helped me in, and a moment later we were bumping and slithering between the trees that lined the track, and the heater was roaring a hot blast that was agony to my frozen limbs. His face showed square and leathery in the reflected glare of the headlights. He wasn't a young man, and the peaked khaki cap was strangely decorated with a cluster of gaudy flies.

"You were searching for me, were you?" I asked. And when he nodded, I knew that Lands must have contacted him. "You're Mr. Darcy, then," I said.

"Ray Darcy," he grunted, not taking his eyes off the road. He was driving fast, the car slithering on the bends that rushed towards us in a blaze of white. "Bill reckoned I'd find you around Mile Two-fifty."

"You saw him, then?" I asked.

"Sure I did."

"And Laroche? Was he there?"

"Laroche?" He glanced at me quickly. "No, I didn't see Laroche."

"But he was up there, wasn't he? He was at Head of Steel?"

"So they told me." And he added: "You just relax now and get some sleep. Guess you're pretty near all in."

But this was the man I'd trekked through the night to see. Circumstances had brought us together, and I wasn't going to waste the opportunity, tired though I was. "Did Lands tell you why I was here?" I asked him. "Did he tell you about the transmission my father picked up?"

"Yeah. He told me."

"And I suppose he told you I was crazy to think Briffe might be still alive."

"No. He didn't exactly say that."

"Then what did he say?" I asked.

Again that quick sidelong glance. "He said you were James Finlay Ferguson's grandson, for one thing." He dragged the car through the mud of a long S bend. "And that, to my way of thinking," he added, "is about as strange as the idea that Briffe should have been able to transmit a message."

"What's so strange about it?" I asked. Why did it always come back to the Ferguson Expedition? "It's just a coincidence." The warmth of the heater was making me drowsy.

"Damned queer coincidence." He said it almost savagely.

"It explains my father's interest in Briffe's party."

"Sure. But it doesn't explain you."

I didn't know what he meant by that, and I was too sleepy to ask. I could hardly keep my eyes open. My mind groped back to the Ferguson Expedition. If I could just find out what had happened. "Perkins said you knew more about Labrador than anybody else on the line." My voice sounded thick and blurred. "That's why I came north . . . to find you and ask . . ."

"You go to sleep," he said. "We'll talk later."

My eyes were closed, waves of tiredness engulfing me. But then we went into a skid, and I was jerked back to consciousness as he pulled the car out of it. "You do know what happened, don't you?" I said thickly. "I must know what happened to my grandfather."

"I've read it up, if that's what you mean." He turned

his head and looked at me. "You mean to say you really don't know the story of that expedition?"

"No," I replied. "That's the reason I wanted to contact you—that and the fact that you brought Laroche out."

He stared at me. "Goddammit!" he said. "If that isn't the queerest thing about the whole business."

"How do you mean?"

"You not knowing." He was still staring at me, and we hit the edge of the road, so that snow-laden branches slashed against the cracked windscreen. He pulled the car back on to the track and said: "Now, you just relax. Plenty of time to talk later."

"But what did happen?" I asked.

"I said relax. We'll talk about it later." And then he added: "I got to think." It was said to himself, not to me. And when I tried to question him further, he turned on me angrily and said: "You're not in a fit state to talk now. And nor am I. I been up all night chasing after you, and I'm tired. Now, go to sleep."

"But—"

"Go to sleep," he almost shouted at me. "Goddammit! How do you expect me to drive with you asking questions all the time?" And then in a gentler voice: "Take my advice and sleep whilst you can. I'll talk when I'm ready to—not before. Okay?"

I nodded, not sure what he meant. I was too tired to argue, anyway. I'd come a long way, and I'd found the man I thought could help me. My eyes closed of their own accord, and consciousness slid away from me. I was adrift then in a sea of ruts, rocking and swaying to the steady roar of the engine. And when I opened my eyes again, dawn was breaking and we were running down into a hutted camp.

"Two-sixty-three," Darcy said, seeing that I was awake. The place looked raw and desolate in the cold morning light, the wooden buildings standing bleak and black against the snow. It was a new camp built on a slope above the grade, the site only recently bull-dozed out of the bush. Great piles of sawn logs stood outside every hut, and all round the edge of the camp was a slash of lopped branches and uprooted trees.

We bumped over rough ground and drew up outside a hut that was set a little apart. "I'm usually better or-ganized than this," Darcy said as he scooped up an armful of logs and pushed open the door. "But I only been here a few weeks." He went over to the iron stove at the back and fed logs into it.

He only had part of the hut, a small bare room with two iron beds, some shelves full of books, several lockers, and a cupboard built of three-ply. It reminded me of an army hut, and the mud on the floor showed what the ground outside would be like when the snow melted. A big refrigerator, gleaming new, stood incongruously against one wall. The room looked drab and cheerless in the dim light that filtered through the dirty windows, but it was warm, and the flames that licked out of the top of the stove as he opened the ash door flickered on the bare wood walls to give it an illusion of cosiness. There were several pictures, too: oil paintings of Labra-dor—a river scene, all blacks and greys, a study of jack-pines in the snow, and one of a little group of men round a campfire that looked so lonely and desolate that it re-minded me of Briffe.

"Yours?" I asked.

He turned and saw I was looking at the picture of the campfire. "Yeah. All my own work." And he added: "Just daubs." But I knew he didn't mean that, for he was staring at the picture with a self-critical intenseness. He was serious about this, and he said slowly: "I guess that's the best I ever did. Like it?"

"I don't know much about painting," I murmured awkwardly. "It looks cold and lost. . . ."

"It's meant to." He said it almost harshly. And then he replaced the lid of the stove with a clang. "Okay, now you get your wet clothes off and hit the sack. You can have that bed." He nodded to the one that wasn't made up. "Sorry I can't give you a shot of liquor, but liquor ain't allowed up the line. Too many alcoholics up here. Anyway, you'll be okay. All you need is warmth and sleep."

Steam was rising from my clothes. I sat down on the bed. I felt suddenly very tired—too tired to take off my clothes or do anything but just sit there. "I've got to talk to you," I said, and my voice sounded blurred.

"Later," he answered.

"No, now," I said with an effort. "Laroche will be here later. Lands, too. If I don't talk to you now, it'll be too late."

"I've told you before, and now I'm telling you again— I'll talk to you when I'm ready, and not before. Okay?" And he turned abruptly away from me and went to the corner beyond the stove. "You don't have to worry about Laroche or anybody else," he said over his shoulder. "Not for several hours yet. There's no airstrip here; they'll have to come by jeep, and they won't start till after breakfast." He came back with a pair of long rubber boots. "You just get your clothes off and turn in. You're dead beat." He reached across me to the shelf above the bed and took down a green tin box. "Go on, get some sleep. I'll be back in an hour or so."

He was moving towards the door, and I jumped to my feet. "Where are you going?" I cried.

"Fishing." He had turned and was staring at me curiously.

It didn't seem possible he could be going fishing, not

after being up all night. I don't know why, but I'd come so far to see him I'd somehow taken it for granted he was on my side, and now I suddenly wasn't sure. There was a radio somewhere in the camp. He could talk to Lands at Head of Steel, probably Staffen down at base. "What instructions did they give you about me?" I asked him.

He reached out to a rack on the wall and took down a fishing-rod swaddled in a green canvas case, and then he came back across the room towards me. "See here, young fellow," he said. "If I say I'm going fishing, I'm going fishing. Understand?" His voice shook, and his eyes glared at me from behind the rimless glasses. "Don't ever try doubting my word. I don't like it."

"I'm sorry," I murmured. "It was just that I thought . . ."

"You thought I was going to report to Lands, is that it?" He was still glaring at me. "Well, I'm not," he said. "I'm going fishing. Okay?"

I nodded and subsided on to the bed. "It seemed so odd," I murmured.

"Odd?" His tone was still belligerent. "What's odd about going fishing?"

"I don't know," I muttered, trying to think of something that would pacify him. "I should have thought you'd need some sleep, too."

"I'm not a kid," he snapped. "I don't need a lot of sleep. And fishing helps me to think," he added. He smiled then, and the gust of anger that had shaken him seemed suddenly swept aside. "You're not a fisherman, are you?"

I shook my head.

"Then you wouldn't know. It's like painting—it helps. You need things like that up here." He stared at me for a moment. "There's a lot of things you don't know yet," he said gently. "About the way life is in a Godforsaken country like Labrador. I been two years up here." He shook his head, as though at some folly of his own. "I came up here for a month's fishing, a sort of convalescence, and I ain't been outside since—not even down to Seven Islands. That's a long time." He turned away. "Christ! It's a long time." He was staring out of the window, at the camp and the country beyond it. "It does things to you." And then, after a moment, he looked at me again, smiling. "Such as making you quick to take offence when a young fool doubts your word." And he added brusquely: "Now, you get some sleep. And don't worry about what I'm up to. I'm just going down the grade as far as the river, and with any luck I'll come back with a *ouananish,* maybe some lake trout. Okay?"

I nodded. "I just wanted you to hear what I had to say before you did anything."

"Sure. I understand. But there's plenty of time." He went to the door and pulled it open. "I'll be back in a couple of hours or so." And then he was gone, the door shut behind him. But though he was no longer there, something of his personality still lingered in the bare room.

I sat there for a long time, wondering about him. But gradually weariness overcame me, and I stripped off my clothes and climbed into the bed. The blankets were rough and warm against my skin. I didn't care that they were musty with the smell of dirt. I didn't care about anything then. I was satisfied that I'd found somebody who felt about Labrador the way my father had, and though he was strange and I was a little scared of him, I knew he would help me—and I closed my eyes and went to sleep with a picture in my mind of a tough little man, knee-deep in a cold river, fishing with long, practised casts.

I woke to find him standing over me, and the sun was shining in through the window. "Do you like salmon?" he said.

I sat up. "Salmon?"

"Sure. I brought you some salmon. Land-locked salmon. The Montagnais call them *ouananish*." He pulled up a chair and set a big dish down on it and a knife and fork and a hunk of bread. "Caught two. The boys and I had one. You got most of the other. Strictly against camp rules. No fish to be cooked. Give you tapeworm if they're not properly cooked. You ever had tapeworm?"

"No."

"You're lucky. You feed like a horse, but it's the worm feeding, not you, so you just go on getting thinner." He was searching in a desk in the corner, and he came up with a sheet of graph paper. There was the sound of voices and the scrape of boots in the other half of the hut beyond the partition. "Lucy!" he shouted. "You boys ready yet?"

"*Oui, oui.* All okay, Ray."

"I got to get the boys started on levelling up a new section of the grade," he said, turning to me. "I'll be about an hour. After that we'll go north as far as the trestle. Maybe I'll fish a bit whilst you tell me your story." The eyes glinted at me from behind their glasses. "Then we'll see. Maybe we'll go and have a word with Mackenzie."

And with that he turned and went out. The door closed, and after a moment I began to eat my first *ouananish*. It was close-fleshed and pink, and there was a lot of it. And whilst I ate I was thinking about Darcy again—about his painting and his mania for fishing. "Crazy Darcy" that young engineer had called him. Two years without a break was certainly a long time, long enough to drive a man round the bend. I remembered something Lands had said and wondered whether Darcy was what they called "bushed."

I ate the whole of that fish, and when I had finished it energy was flowing back into my body so that I no longer felt tired. There was a basin beside Darcy's bed, and a bowl of water steamed on the stove lid. I got up stiffly and had a wash, standing naked over the basin. Bushed or not, the man was closer to the country than anybody else I'd met. I had a shave, and then I sat on the bed and broke the blisters on my heels and covered them with adhesive tape I found in the medical kit on the shelf above the bed. There were books there, too, and the photograph of a young Canadian soldier in a battered leather frame.

My clothes had dried out with the heat of the stove, and I put them on. And then I went back to the shelf and the books, wondering whether they would tell me anything about the man. They were mostly technical, but there was Izaak Walton's *Compleat Angler,* a single leather-bound volume of Shakespeare, the collected poems of Robert Service, several books by Jack London, and then four books that took me right back to the little room where my father had had his radio. They were *Labrador* by W. Cabot, two volumes of *Outlines of the Geography, Life and Customs of Newfoundland-Labrador* by V. Tanner, and a small slim book titled *Labrador —In Search of the Truth* by Henri Dumaine.

Tanner's book I knew. I'd often looked at the pictures in those two volumes when I was a kid. And Cabot's book, too—that had been on my father's shelves. But Henri Dumaine's book was new to me, and I took it down and opened it, casually leafing through the pages. It was a record of a journey into Labrador, not very well written. I glanced at the fly-leaf. It had been published by a Toronto firm in 1905, and, thinking that perhaps it might have a reference to my grandfather's expedition, I started going carefully through the pages from the beginning.

I found a reference to it almost immediately, at the foot of page five. He had written: *Thus it was on June 15,*

1902, that the ship brought me to Davis Inlet and the Hudson's Bay Post there. I was at the starting point of the Ferguson Expedition at last. . . .

I stared at that sentence, hardly able to believe my eyes. Here, in this hut at Camp 263, I had stumbled on a book that could help me. My eyes were devouring the printed words now, and a few lines farther on I read: *Standing there, looking at the Post, so clean and neat in the cold sunlight, the red shingle roofs of the buildings glistening with the rain that had just passed and the planked walls gleaming in their fresh coat of white paint, I was thinking of Pierre. It was to this place that the poor fellow had returned—alone. I was thinking, too, of my wife, Jacqueline, and of all the hopes she entertained of my present journey. She had been at her brother's bedside when he died and had listened to the last strange mutterings of a mind deranged by the tragedy of what had happened and by all the terrible hardships suffered. I turned my back on the Post then and looked across the water to the hills of Labrador. It was then that I first felt the impact of that lonely country, and I stood there in sudden awe of it, for somewhere beyond the black line of that escarpment lay the truth. If I could find it, then maybe I could clear his name of the vile accusations that had so darkened his last hours and contributed so much to his state of mind.*

I turned the pages quickly then, searching for some statement of the accusations, some hint as to what was supposed to have happened to my grandfather. But Henri Dumaine seemed to take it for granted that the reader would know that, for I could find no further reference to it. Page after page was taken up with the rather dreary account of his struggle up the old Indian trail to the Naskopie. He had had two coast half-breeds with him, and it was clear that neither he nor they had much idea of bushcraft. Dogged by misfortunes, which were largely of their own making, they had reached Cabot Lake on July 19. They had then gone south across Lake Michikamau and had finally turned west towards the Ashuanipi.

Here we found a camp of Montagnais Indians waiting for the coming of the caribou, and luck was with us, for two years ago at this very spot a lone white man had passed them, going towards the great lake of Michikamau. He had a canoe, but his supplies must have been getting low, for he had avoided them and they had been scared to go near him for some reason, so that they could tell me little about him except that his clothes were ragged and his feet bound with strips of canvas and he talked to himself as though communing with some unseen spirit. They showed me the place where he had camped beside the river. There were several caribou bones, and close by the place where he had built his fire was a little pile of cartridges, the greased wrapping partly disintegrated.

There was no doubt in my mind then that this was one of the places where my brother-in-law had camped on the way back, and the cartridges so recklessly jettisoned proved that his situation was already desperate. Clearly we were still some distance from the place where death had overtaken Mr. Ferguson, and I asked the Indians if they knew of the Lake I sought. I described it to them as Pierre had described it so often in his delirium. But they did not know it, and of course the name that Pierre had given to the Lake meant nothing to them, and so we left them, giving them two packages of tea and a small bag of flour, which was all we could spare of our supplies. And after that we went south, following the Ashuanipi, and searching all the time. . . .

The door behind me burst open, and I turned to find Darcy standing there. "All set?" he asked impatiently, as though I had kept him waiting. And then he saw the book in my hand. "Oh, so you found that." He came in and shut the door. "I wondered whether you would." He took it out of my hand, leafing idly through the pages. "Dull stuff," he said. "But interesting when you know the country."

"Or when you know what happened," I said.

"To Ferguson?" He looked at me quickly. "Nobody knows that."

"When you know what's supposed to have happened, then," I corrected myself. "On page five . . ." I took the book from his hand and pointed to the line referring to "vile accusations." "What were the accusations?" I asked him. "They were made against the survivor, weren't they? That was Dumaine's brother-in-law. It says so there. Who accused him, and what did they accuse him of?"

"Goldarnit!" he exclaimed, staring at me. "It's the damnedest thing I ever heard. You come all this way, right up here to this camp, where you're not more than fifty miles or so from where your grandfather died, and you say you don't know the story."

"Well, I don't," I said. "I came up here because of Briffe."

"Because of Briffe, or because Laroche crashed his plane in the same area?"

"Because of Briffe," I said. I was watching his face, wondering whether he, too, had guessed where the plane had crashed. I glanced down at the book again. I had only got about two-thirds through it. "Did Dumaine reach Lake of the Lion?" I asked.

"Ah, so you know about Lake of the Lion, do you?"

"Yes, but I don't know what happened there."

"Well, it's like I told you," he said. "Nobody knows for sure. Dumaine never got further than the Ashuanipi." He reached over and took the book from me again. "Some Indians showed him a lone white man's camp on the banks of the river, and after that he found two more. But that was all." His grizzled head was bent over the book, his stubby, wind-cracked fingers leafing through the earlier pages. "The poor devil spent more than a month searching for that lake," he murmured. "And all the time he should have been getting the hell out of the country." He seemed to be trying to check on something in the first few chapters of the book. At length he said: "The big freeze-up was on them long before they'd reached Davis Inlet. If it hadn't been for the half-breeds, he'd never have got out alive." He snapped the book shut and replaced it on the shelf beside the photograph. "The irony of it was," he added, looking at me curiously, "there was a woman came to Davis Inlet that year and strolled across half Labrador as though it were no worse than her own Scots moors. She had three trappers with her who knew the country, and she covered the same area that Dumaine covered, and she went out by way of the Hamilton and the North West River Post as fit as when she started."

But I didn't intend to be sidetracked. "This man who accompanied my grandfather," I said. "Dumaine talks of him as though he were mad. 'A mind deranged by the tragedy of what had happened,' he says. What sent him mad?" I asked.

He gave a quick shrug and turned away towards the stove.

"Can't you give me some idea of what happened?" I persisted. And when he didn't answer, I added: "At least you must know what the accusations were. What was he accused of?"

He was leaning down, staring at the red-hot stove, but he turned to me then and said: "He was accused of murdering your grandfather." And he added quickly: "Nothing was proved. Nobody knows what happened. It was just a wild accusation made out of—"

"Who made it?" I asked.

He hesitated, and then said: "The woman I was talking about—Ferguson's young wife, Alexandra." He was

staring at me with a puzzled frown. "You must know that
part of it at least. Hell, boy, she was your own grandmother." And then, when he realized it was new to me,
he shook his head and turned back to the stove. "The
newspapers got hold of her and printed some pretty wild
things. Not that there was anything new in it. There'd
been a lot of talk when the poor devil had come out alone
raving of gold and a lake with the figure of a lion in
rock. He was half out of his mind then, by all accounts."

"So it was gold my grandfather was after, was it?" I
was remembering what my mother had said about him.

"Sure. You don't imagine a seasoned prospector like
Ferguson went into Labrador for the good of his soul, do
you?" He fell silent then, but after a while he said: "She
must have been a remarkable woman, your grandmother.
Didn't you know her at all?"

I explained how we'd stopped going to the house in
Scotland after my mother had found her talking to me in
my room that night, and he nodded. "Maybe your mother
was right. And yet, in spite of that, you're here. Queer,
isn't it?" And then he went back to my grandmother. "It
would be remarkable even today. You wouldn't understand, of course—not yet. All you've seen of the Labrador
is a railway under construction. But you get away from
the camps and the grade, the country's different then—
a land to be reckoned with."

"In fact, the land God gave to Cain." I said it without
thinking, repeating Farrow's words.

He looked at me, a little surprised. "Yeah, that's right.
The land God gave to Cain." And the way he said it gave
a significance to the words that chilled me.

"Did my grandmother reach Lake of the Lion?" I asked
then.

"God knows," he said. "But if she did, she kept damn
quiet about it, for there's no mention of it in the newspaper reports. But she back-tracked their route in and

got further than Dumaine did, or else she got there first, for she came out with a rusted pistol, a sextant, and an old map case, all things that had belonged to her husband. She had those photographed, but she never published her diary, though she admitted she'd kept one. I guess she'd have published that all right if she'd found her husband's last camp. Is the diary still in existence, do you know?" he asked me.

"I don't know," I replied. "I've seen the pistol and the sextant and the map case. My father had them hanging on the wall of his room. There was part of a paddle, too, and an old fur cap. But I never knew there was a diary."

"Too bad," he murmured. "It would have been interesting to know the basis of her accusations. She was three months up here in the wild and all the time following the route her husband took. I guess those three lonely months gave the iron plenty of time to enter into her soul." He went over to the stove and held his hands close to the iron casing, warming them. "The strange thing is," he said, "that Dumaine never mentions her once in that book. And yet the two parties started out from Davis Inlet within a few days of each other, and they were covering the same ground. I wonder whether they ever met," he murmured. "Even if Dumaine never met her face to face, he must have come across traces of her party. And yet he never mentions her. There's not one reference to Mrs. Ferguson in the whole of the book."

"That's hardly surprising," I said, "considering she'd accused his wife's brother of murder."

"Well, maybe not. But she didn't put it as bluntly as that, you understand. And there'd been all that talk. . . ." He was staring down at the stove again. "It's a queer thing," he murmured, half to himself. "Those two men —I would have thought it would have been the other way about."

"How do you mean?" I asked.

He shrugged his shoulders. "I dunno. A question of character, I guess. I've thought a lot about it since I been up here. Take Ferguson." He was staring down at the stove. "Came over as a kid in an immigrant ship and went out west, apprenticed to one of the Hudson's Bay posts. A few years later he was in the Cariboo. I guess that's where the gold bug got him, for he was all through the Cariboo and then up to Dawson City in the Klondike rush of the middle nineties." He shook his head. "He must have been real tough."

"And the other man?" I asked.

"Pierre?" he said quickly. "Pierre was quite different —a man of the wilderness, a trapper. That's what makes it so odd."

He didn't say anything more, and I asked him then how he knew all this. "It's all in Dumaine's book, is it?"

"No, of course not. Dumaine was a storekeeper in a small town in Ontario. He didn't understand the wild, so he never bothered to assess the nature of the two men's personalities. His book is a dull inventory of the day-to-day tribulations of a man whose wife had talked him into a journey that was beyond his capabilities."

"Then how do you know about my grandfather?" I asked.

He looked up at me. "Newspaper cuttings, chiefly. I had somebody look them up and type them all out for me. There was a lot about it in the Montreal papers, as you can imagine. I'd show them to you, only they're in my trunk, and that's up at Two-ninety still."

"But what made you so interested?" I asked him.

"Interested?" He looked at me in surprise. "How the hell could I fail to be interested?" His craggy face was suddenly smiling. "You don't seem to understand. I'm not up here because I like engineering. I don't even need the dough. I'm fifty-six, and I made enough money to keep me the rest of my life." He turned and reached for his gloves. "No," he added, "I'm up here because I got bitten by the Labrador." He laughed softly to himself as he pulled on the gloves. "Yeah, I guess I'm the only man along the whole stretch of the line that's here because he loves it." He was talking to himself again, and I had a sudden feeling that he often talked to himself. But then he looked across at me. "Know anything at all about the Labrador?" he asked me.

"My father had a lot of books," I said. "I've read some of them."

He nodded. "Then you'll know that all this is virgin country, unmapped and untrodden by white men till the Hollinger outfit got interested in the iron-ore deposits up at Burnt Creek. Hell!" he added. "It's only four thousand years ago that the last Ice Age began to recede. It was all glaciers then. And until floatplanes came into general use for prospecting, only a handful of white men had penetrated into the interior. A few rough maps of the rivers and all the rest blank, a few books like Dumaine's on journeys made by canoe and on foot—that was all anybody knew about the Labrador. It wasn't until 1947 that the government began an aerial survey. And you ask me why I'm interested in the story of the Ferguson Expedition. How the hell could I help being interested, feeling the way I do about the country?" And then he added, almost angrily: "You don't understand. I guess you never will. Nobody I ever met up here feels the way I do—the lonely, cruel, withdrawn beauty of it. Like the sea or the mountains, the emptiness of it is a challenge that cuts a man down to size. See what I mean?" He stared at me belligerently, as though challenging me to laugh at him. "The aircraft and the railway, they don't touch the country, never will, I guess. It's wild here—as wild and lonely as any place on earth. Do you believe in God?"

The abruptness of the question startled me.

"Well, do you?"

"I haven't thought much about it," I murmured.

"No. Men don't till they suddenly discover how big Nature is. You wait till you're out there in the silence of the trees and the bitter cold is freezing all the guts out of you. You'll think about Him then, all right, when there's nothing but the emptiness and the loneliness and that great stillness that remains a stillness in your soul even when the wind is blowing to beat hell." He laughed a little self-consciously. "Okay," he said abruptly. "Let's go." He strode across to the door and pulled it open. "Mackenzie's camped up by the trestle. If we're going to talk to him, we'd better get moving." His voice was suddenly impatient.

I followed him out of the hut and climbed into the jeep. "Who's Mackenzie?" I asked as we drove off.

"Mackenzie, he's an Indian—a Montagnais. One of the best of them." He swung the car on to the camp road. "He acts as guide for the geologists," he added. "But right now he's hunting. He may be willing to help you, he may not."

"Help me—how?" I asked.

"Mackenzie's never seen a lion," he said. "The word means nothing to him. But he's seen that lake." His eyes were suddenly fixed on mine, an ophidian blue that held me rigid. "I take it," he said, "that you haven't come all this way to sit on your fanny in a construction camp or to wait around until you're sent back to base?" And then his gaze was back on the road again. "Anyway, that's what I decided whilst I was fishing this morning—that I'd take you to see Mackenzie. I've sent him word by one of the Indians that hang around here to wait for us at his camp."

IV

What exactly I'd expected from Darcy

I don't know, but it came as a shock to me to find him taking it for granted that I'd want to pursue my objective to its logical conclusion. And as we bumped across the iron-hard ruts, up out of the camp on to the Tote Road, I began to consider the problems it raised, for I couldn't just walk off into the bush with this Indian. I'd need stores, equipment, things that only the construction camp could provide. I started to explain this to Darcy, but all he said was: "We'll discuss that when we've seen Mackenzie. He may not want to leave the hunting. Winter's coming on, and the hunting's important."

We were headed north, and after a while he said: "I suppose you realize you've caused near-panic down at the base. They've never had anybody gate-crash the line before, and one of the directors is on a tour of inspection. There've been messages flying back and forth about you all night. If I weren't something of a rebel in this outfit," he added with a quick grin, "I'd have had nothing to do with you."

I didn't say anything, and he went on: "But since I've got myself involved, I guess it's time I had all the facts. Bill gave me the gist of them, but now I'd like to have the whole story from you."

Once again I found myself explaining about my father's death and that last radio message. But this time it was

different. This time I was explaining it to someone who
could understand how my father had felt. He listened
without saying a word, driving all the time with a furious
concentration, his foot hard down on the accelerator. It
was beginning to thaw, the snow falling in great clods
from the jackpine branches and the track turning to slush,
so that the jeep slithered wildly on the bends, spraying
the mud up in black sheets from the wheels.

I was still talking when the trees thinned and we came
out on to the banks of a river, and there was the trestle, a
girder-like structure built of great pine baulks, striding
across the grey stone flats of the river to the thump of a
pile-driver. He stopped by a little group of huts that huddled close under the towering network of the trestle and
cut the engine, sitting listening to me, his gloved hands
still gripping the wheel.

And when I had finished, he didn't say anything or ask
any questions, but just sat there, quite silent, staring out
across the river. At length he nodded his head as though
he had made up his mind about something. "Okay," he
said, opening the door and getting out. "Let's go scrounge
some coffee." And he took me across to the farthest hut,
where a wisp of smoke trailed from an iron chimney.
"The last time I was here," he said, "was when I brought
Laroche out." He kicked open the wooden door and went
in. "Come in and shut the door. The bull-cook here's a
touchy bastard, but he makes darn good blueberry pie."
This in a loud, bantering voice.

The hut was warm, the benches and table scrubbed
white, and there was a homely smell of baking. A sour-
looking man with a pot belly came out of the cookhouse.
"Saw you drive up," he whispered hoarsely, dumping two
mugs of steaming black coffee on the table. "Help yourselves." He pushed the canned milk and a bowl of sugar
towards us.

"Where's the pie, Sid?" Darcy asked.

"You want pie as well?"

"Sure we want pie."

The cook wiped his hands down his aproned thighs, a gesture that somehow expressed pleasure. And when he had gone back into the cookhouse, Darcy said: "Sid's quite a character. Been in Labrador almost as long as I have—and for the same reason."

His eyes smiled at me over the top of his mug as he gulped noisily at his coffee. And then I asked him about Laroche. "You say you stopped here on your way up to Two-ninety?"

"Yeah, that's right. I thought he could do with some hot coffee. And I wanted blankets, too. His clothes were soaked." The cook came back with the blueberry pie, and Darcy said: "Remember the last time I was through here, Sid?"

"Sure do." The cook's eyes were suddenly alive. "You had that pilot with you, and he sat right there where you're sitting now with that look in his eyes and muttering to himself all the time. And then he went off to sleep, just like that."

"He was in a bad way."

"Sure was. More like a corpse than anything else."

"It was the warmth sent him to sleep," Darcy said. "He hadn't been warm since he'd crashed."

"Yeah, I guess that's what it was. But I reckoned you'd have a corpse on your hands by the time you got him to the aircraft." The cook hesitated. "I ain't seen you since then."

"No, I been busy." Darcy stared at the cook a moment and then said: "What's on your mind, Sid?"

"Nothing. I been thinking, that's all." And he looked at Darcy with a puzzled frown. "It was his eyes. Remember how they kept darting all round the place, never focusing on anything, as though he were scared out of his wits. And every now and then he'd mutter something.

Do you reckon he was bushed?" And when Darcy didn't say anything, the cook added: "I only seen a man bushed once. That was in the early days down at One-thirty-four."

"Mario?" Darcy said.

"Yeah, Mario—that Italian cook. He moved his eyes the same way Laroche did, and he had that same scared look as though he expected to be murdered in his bunk. Queer guy, Mario." He shook his head. "Always muttering to himself. Remember? You were there."

Darcy nodded.

"And then running out naked into the bush that night; and all those crazy things he wrote in the snow—like 'I want to die' and 'Don't follow me. Leave me alone.' As though he was being persecuted."

"Well, he was." Darcy cut the blueberry pie and passed a thick wedge of it across to me. "Those Germans," he added with his mouth full. "They played hell with the poor bastard. Good cook, too."

"Sure was. And then they got another wop for cook and they tried playing hell with him. Remember how he fixed them?" The cook was suddenly laughing. "So you make-a the fool of me, he told them. You wanna have fun at my expense. How you like-a the soup today, eh? Is okay? Well, I urinate in that soup, and every time you make-a the fool of me, I urinate in the soup. That's what he told them, wasn't it? And never another peep out of them." His laughter died away and he fell suddenly silent. And then he came back to the subject of Laroche. "You'd think when a guy's left two men dead in the bush he'd want to tell somebody about it soon as he was picked up. But he wouldn't talk about it, would he?"

"He was pretty badly injured," Darcy said.

"Sure he was. But even so—you'd think he'd want to get it off his mind, wouldn't you? I know I would. I'd have been worried sick about it all the time I was trekking out." He nodded his head as though to emphasize the point. "But you had to try and dig it out of him. What happened? you asked him. What about Briffe and the other guy? But all he said was: Dead. Just like that. Dead—both of them. And when you asked him how it happened, he just shook his head, his eyes darting all round the room. Wouldn't say another word."

So Laroche hadn't been normal even then. "You think he was bushed, do you?" I asked. "Or was it because of his injury?"

The cook's beady eyes were suddenly suspicious. "You're a newcomer, aren't you?" I think he'd forgotten I was there. "An engineer?" he asked Darcy.

But instead of saying yes and leaving it at that, Darcy said: "Ferguson's up here because he believes Briffe may be still alive."

"Is that so?" The cook regarded me with new interest. "You think maybe Laroche made a mistake, saying they were both dead?"

And then, to my surprise, Darcy began explaining to the man the circumstances that had brought me out from England.

"Hadn't we better get moving?" I interrupted him. I was annoyed. It hadn't occurred to me that he'd repeat what I'd told him.

"What's the hurry?" he said. "Nobody will look for you here." And the cook, sensing the tension between us, said: "You like some more cawfee?"

"Sure we'll have some more coffee," Darcy said. And when the man had gone out, he turned to me. "If you think you can keep the reason you're up here a secret, you're dam' mistaken. Anyway, what's the point?"

"But he'll gossip," I said.

"Sure he'll gossip. Cooks are like that—same as barbers. And there's a bush telegraph operates along the grade here faster than you can get from one camp to the next. It'll go all up the line from here to Menihek and beyond, and right down to base, until there isn't a soul doesn't know you've come all the way from the Old Country because you believe Briffe's alive. That's why I brought you in here." And then he got up and thrust his round head forward, his eyes staring at me from behind the glasses. "What are you afraid of? That's the truth you told me, isn't it?"

"Of course it's the truth."

"Well, then, what have you got to lose? The more people know your story, the more chance you've got of getting something done. Okay?"

The cook came back with the coffee-pot this time. "Help yourselves," he said. And then he asked: "What happens now? Do they resume the search?"

"No," I said. "They won't do a thing."

"But suppose you're right and they're alive. . . . They going to be left to die, is that it?"

Darcy was looking at me, and I knew what he was thinking. I'd come all this way. . . . "No," I heard myself say. "No, I'll go in myself if necessary." But even as I said it, I was thinking it was a forlorn hope. So much time had elapsed since Briffe had made that transmission.

And then I saw Darcy nod his head, as though that was what he had expected me to say. He gulped down the rest of his coffee and said: "We got to be going now, Sid." He set his mug down on the table. "Mackenzie still camped in the same place?"

"Yeah, same place—up beyond the trestle."

"Well, thanks for the coffee." Darcy gripped my arm, and as we moved to the door, the cook said: "I wish you luck, Mr. Ferguson."

It made me feel good to have somebody wish me luck. But then we were outside, and I became conscious again of the desolate emptiness of the country crouched along the steel-grey river. I thought I'd probably need some luck then. "You were the first person to question Laroche, weren't you?" I asked Darcy.

We had reached the trestle, and he paused at the foot of a wooden ladder. "Well?"

"If you thought his behaviour odd, why didn't you report it at the time?"

"A man's entitled to a certain oddness of behaviour when he's been through as much as Laroche had," he said slowly. "He was skin and bone, a human skeleton, like something out of a death cell, and covered with sores. There was that head wound, too. How was I to know his brain wasn't injured?"

"All right," I said. "But you and the cook, you both had the same reaction, didn't you?"

He seemed to consider that. "I'll give you this much," he said finally. "I went in there this morning to find out whether Sid's reaction had been the same as mine. Needless to say, we didn't talk about it at the time—we were too busy trying to stop Laroche dying on us." And he started up the ladder.

When I joined him at the top, he added: "You don't have to be half crazy to be bushed, you know. I'm bushed. And there's a lot of other guys who are what the docs would call bushed. It simply means that you've been withdrawn from the outside world for so long that you don't want to be bothered with it. You just want to be left alone to the freedom of your own little world and let the rest go hang. I guess that's the real reason I didn't do anything about Laroche. That's why I went fishing this morning, to get things straight in my own mind. You were the outside world breaking into my comfortable solitude, and I can't say I was pleased to see you." He gave me a wry little smile and then started out across the timbered top of the trestle. "You're an engineer," he said, suddenly changing the subject. "This should interest you." He indicated the girder-like structure with a movement of his hand. "Down in the Rockies the Canadian Pacific are filling in their trestle bridges. The timber lasts about twenty years, and now it's got too costly to rebuild them. But it's still the quickest way of pushing a railway through virgin territory."

We reached the other end of the trestle, and he paused, looking back. The long curve of the timber stood black and gaunt above the river. "This far north it could last for years," he said. "Timber don't rot in this country. There's no termites and no fungi. Queer, isn't it? Up at Burnt Creek they're building houses of raw, unpainted plywood." As he stood there, his squat, heavily clothed body outlined against the stark light of the Labrador sky, he was looking at the trestle with the appreciation of a man who understood the technical achievement it represented, and at the same time his eyes were drinking in the beauty of it in that setting—and it had a strange, arrogant, man-made beauty. He was a queer mixture, part engineer, part artist, and I wasn't certain that he hadn't a touch of the mystic in him as well.

"Maybe I'll try and paint that sometime," he murmured. And then abruptly he tore himself away from the scene. "Okay, let's go find Mackenzie." And he jumped down on to the gravel fill that would carry the steel on to the trestle, and as we scrambled down to the river's edge, the noise of the water came up to meet us, drowning the thump of the pile-driver.

I caught up with him on a grey pebble bank where the waves set up by the current broke with little slaps, and I asked him how long he'd known that the Indian had found the lake. I had to shout to make myself heard above the sound of the water.

"Couple of weeks, that's all," he answered. "It was just after Laroche came out. I was talking to Mackenzie about it, telling him the story of the old expedition—and when

I mentioned Lake of the Lion, he asked what a lion was. He'd never seen one, of course, so I drew him a picture of a lion's head. He recognized it at once and said he knew the lake. He called it Lake of the Rock with a Strange Face." Darcy had stopped and was looking intently at the river, so that I thought he was considering the fishing on that stretch. But then he said: "I was thinking of going in myself. Next spring with a geologist friend. I'm due some time off. Thought maybe I'd find Ferguson's gold and make my fortune." He gave a quick laugh and went on across the pebble bank, up into the thick scrub that edged the river.

There was no track here, and the going was rough, the undergrowth interspersed with patches of reed. And then the scrub opened out into a small clearing, and there was a weather-beaten tent and a canoe and two Indian boys chopping firewood. I stopped then, conscious of an intense awareness. This was the logical outcome of my journey, and I knew there was no turning back from it. The stupidity of it! The probable futility of it! I was suddenly appalled. It was as though Labrador were waiting for me.

And then I remembered what Darcy had said. A challenge, he had called it. Perhaps that was the way I felt about it, too, for I knew I should go on, even if it killed me. I rediscovered in that moment the fascination in a lost cause that was something deep-buried, a part of my Scots heritage, and realized dimly that I had within me the instincts and the courage that had carried my race through countless generations to the distant corners of the globe. I felt I wasn't alone any more, and I walked slowly into the clearing, towards the tent where Darcy was already talking to Mackenzie.

"He thinks he could guide you to the lake all right," Darcy said as I came up. "But he doesn't want to leave now. It's like I said—he's hunting, and he needs the meat for the winter. Also, it's a bad time of the year for travelling."

"Yeah, bad time." The Indian nodded. "Very bad." He was a small, square man dressed in a deerhide jacket and blue jeans, his feet encased in moccasins. His face was broad and flat and weather-beaten, and yet strangely smooth, as though the winds had not touched it. And because he was beardless he might have been any age.

"How many days do you reckon?" Darcy asked him.

The man shrugged his shoulders. "Very bad land. Water and muskeg. Better you wait for freeze-up," he added, looking at me. His eyes, no more than slits in the lashless flesh, were dark and remote, with a touch of the Mongol about them.

"Laroche took five days coming out," Darcy said.

Again a shrug of the shoulders. "Then maybe five days." His face was impassive, his manner obstinate. "Bad time to go."

"He's right, of course," Darcy said, turning to me. "Any moment now you can expect the freeze-up. It's the wrong time."

"Yeah, wrong time." The Indian nodded. "You wait for winter, eh? Then you go on snowshoe, and water all frozen. Two-three day then."

I should have been thankful for the chance to back out of it, but instead I said: "Suppose we left tomorrow? It would only be five days." And I turned to Darcy. "If my father's right, then there's a radio there. We could radio for a plane. Surely the freeze-up won't come in five days."

"I can't answer that," he said. "Nor can Mackenzie. It might be early, it might be late."

"I'll have to chance that," I said.

He stared at me hard for a moment, and then he nodded. "Okay," he said. "Leave it to me. It's the hunting he's worried about. The winter's a long one up here. You take a walk and I'll see what I can do."

A little reluctantly I strolled off along the bank. The sun had come out, the sky fluffy with cold streamers of wind-blown cloud, and the river ran swift and breaking over the shallows. Occasionally a fish jumped, and down by the solitary tent I could see Darcy and the Indian standing on the dark glacier silt where the canoe lay. They stood close together, and sometimes Darcy's hands would move in a gesture of insistence or explanation.

And then at last he turned away and came towards me.

"Well?" I asked. "Will he take me?"

"I don't know," he answered, and his manner was strangely preoccupied. "Maybe he will. But he doesn't like it."

"Surely the weather can't change as suddenly as all that." It was quite warm standing there in the sunshine of the clearing.

"I don't think it's the weather that's bothering him," he said thoughtfully.

"What is it, then?" I was impatient to get the thing settled.

"It's the place he doesn't like. That's what it boiled down to in the end. Bad place he called it and kept on talking about spirits."

"Spirits!" I stared at him. "What sort of spirits?"

He shrugged his shoulders. "He wouldn't say."

But it was obvious what it was. He'd told him about my grandfather. "If you hadn't told him about the Ferguson Expedition . . ." I said.

"Then I wouldn't have known he'd found the lake." He hesitated and then added: "But all I told him was that another expedition had come to grief in that area a long time ago. I told him the leader had died, and I described the lake. But that was all."

"You didn't tell him my grandfather was supposed to have been killed there?"

"No."

It was odd that he should have reacted like that. "When did he find the lake?" I asked. "Was it recently?"

"No. It was on a hunting trip two winters back, he said."

I wished then that I knew more about the Montagnais. "Are they superstitious?"

"Who—the Indians?" He shook his head. "Not particularly. And I certainly wouldn't have thought Mackenzie superstitious. I can't understand it," he added, and his voice sounded puzzled. "Maybe it was just an excuse. They're like that—they don't like to give a direct refusal. Oh, well." He shrugged his shoulders. "I got work to do, I guess." And he started back along the river bank. "You're to come and see him tomorrow. He'll talk to his wife and his sons, and he'll give you his decision then."

"That's too late," I said. Now that we had started back, I was remembering that instructions had been issued for me to be sent down to base.

But he looked back at me and said: "The company doesn't own Labrador, you know. It's only got concessions here. And once you're clear of the line of the grade . . ." There was the suggestion of a smile in his eyes. "What I'm saying is that nobody can stop you—if you've really made up your mind to go."

We returned to the car, and all the way back down the Tote Road Darcy talked, giving me the benefit of his experience, all he'd learned of bushcraft in the two years he'd been up in Labrador. I can't remember now a quarter of what he told me: how to get a fire going from reindeer moss when everything was sodden, how to live off the land—the things you could eat, the fish you could catch—and the way the country had been fashioned by the thrust of glacier ice so that I'd never get lost, even with no compass and the sun hidden by leaden skies. I doubt whether I took it all in at the time, for even then I hadn't quite convinced myself that it was real and that the next day I might be out there in the wild with no-body but the Indian for company.

He set me down where the track to the camp led off the Tote Road. "I'll be back in about an hour," he said. "Then we'll see about kit and decide what's to be done. Somebody ought to go in with you." He drove off then to have a look at his survey team, and I went down towards the camp, wondering whether in the end I'd be able to persuade him to come with me.

A bull-dozer climbing the muddied slope out of the camp checked as it drew level with me, and a face like mahogany under a shapeless hat leaned down. "That Ray Darcy just dropped you off?" And when I nodded, he said: "Guess you must be Ferguson, then." The big diesel throbbed against the stillness of the trees. "Somebody asking for you down at the camp. . . . Waiting for you at Ray's hut." The gears crashed and the monstrous piece of machinery lurched forward, ploughing two deep tracks in the mud.

It could only be Lands—Laroche, too, probably. I stood and watched the water seeping into the tracks left by the bull-dozer, wondering what I should do. But I'd have to face them sooner or later, and in the end I started slowly down towards the camp, wishing that Darcy were still with me. I wasn't altogether convinced that Lands couldn't stop me if he wanted to. The company might not own Labrador, but right now they were in possession of it.

I hesitated a moment at the door of Darcy's hut, re-membering how Lands had been the last time I'd seen him. But he'd had time now to get used to the idea of my being up here, and with a sudden desire to get it over and done with, I lifted the latch and pushed the door open.

My first thought was that the room was empty. There was nobody standing there, waiting for me, and when I went inside everything was just as I'd left it—the stove roaring, the wash-bowl still with dirty water in it and my empty plate beside it, and the cupboard door half open, with Darcy's clothes hanging there.

And then I saw the rucksack and the heavy boots and the figure lying in Darcy's bed, the blankets pulled up round the shoulders and the face turned to the wall so that only the black hair showed. I was so convinced it was Laroche that I was on the point of slipping out again. But at that moment the sleeper stirred and turned over. The eyes blinked at me uncertainly from behind their dark lashes.

It wasn't Laroche. It was Briffe's daughter. And when she saw me standing there, she threw off the blankets and swung her legs out of bed. "I thought perhaps you are gone for the day, so I went to sleep." She pushed her hand up through her close-cropped hair in a gesture that reminded me of Laroche.

I was too surprised to say anything for the moment, but just stood there, staring at her. She was dressed in faded green corduroys and a thick bush shirt with a red check, and her face was still flushed with sleep.

"How did you get here?" I asked, suddenly finding my voice.

"By plane—last night," she answered. "I stopped off at Two-ninety, and from there I hitch a ride in a truck coming south."

"South?" I had forgotten for the moment that there were other camps to the north, a whole string of isolated outposts linked by the thread of the air lift.

"I am here just after you leave with Ray," she added.

Her feet were encased in thick woollen socks. The socks and the heavy boots under the bed had a purposeful look. My gaze shifted to the rucksack. It was the sort of pack a man would take for a week's hike through mountains. A fishing-rod lay beside it and a rawhide belt with hunting-knife and axe, and flung down on top of it was a thick polo-necked sweater and a leather jacket like the one I'd seen her wearing down at Seven Islands, but older. "What made you come here?" I asked, my mind still on that pile of gear.

"What else am I to do?" Her tone was impatient. "Do you expect me to stay down in Seven Islands when you have gone north up the line?"

"Then you came here to see me?"

"But of course."

And she had come straight here. "How did you know where to find me?"

She was staring at me, and there was a hardness in her brown eyes that I had never before associated with that colour. "If you don't believe Albert's story," she said, "then you must come here. It is the nearest camp to where he came out of the bush. Also, Ray Darcy is the man who brought him to the aircraft."

Her eyes hadn't moved from my face. They stared at me, wide and unblinking, and I had a sudden uneasy feeling that she could read my thoughts. But it wasn't only her eyes that unnerved me. There was something about her, a peculiar quality of stillness and tension, as though all of her were coiled up inside her body like a spring. She was half Indian. I don't know how I knew it, but I did, and it scared me because I knew nothing about them.

She got to her feet in one swift, almost cat-like movement. "You still think my father is alive, don't you?" Her voice had a peculiar flatness, so that I knew she had accepted the fact of my belief. And yet, the way she said it, it was an accusation, as though I were guilty of a terrible heresy.

I knew then that she hated me. She hated me for the choice I was forcing on her, and I couldn't blame her. She was torn between love of Laroche and love of her father, and it was my presence that had forced those two loyalties into conflict. I had known what it must do to her ever since that meeting with her down at Seven Islands. But it had never occurred to me that she would follow me up the line.

"You don't answer," she said, frowning.

"How can I?" I said. "I don't know." I couldn't possibly be certain he was still alive.

She got my meaning at once. "Of course not. But he was alive when—when Albert left him. You're certain of that, aren't you? That is why you came north, instead of going back to England."

Half Indian or not, her mind was logical enough. She had thought it out and reached the inevitable conclusion. What it had cost her to do that I didn't dare to think, but the strain was there in her small, tense face. I didn't say anything, just nodded my head.

"And now?" she asked. "What are you going to do now?"

I hesitated. But if I were going to do anything more about it, she'd a right to know. "There's a chance we may be able to locate the lake where they crashed," I said.

"Lake of the Lion?"

"Yes. I'm hoping to start tomorrow."

"You!" Her voice was suddenly incredulous. "But you cannot possibly go in by yourself. Besides, Albert has flown in twice by helicopter, and each time he has failed to find it."

I realized then that she hadn't considered the possibility that he might not want to find it, or if she had, her mind had rejected it.

"I'm not going in alone," I said. And I told her about the Indian and how he'd recognized the lake from Darcy's drawing of a lion. "But I don't know yet whether he'll go. He's worried about the hunting, and he's scared of the place. He's going to talk it over with his family and let me know tomorrow."

"What is the Indian's name?" she asked. "I know some of them who hunt up here." And when I told her, she seized on it eagerly. "Mackenzie! Which Mackenzie? There are so many—a whole tribe."

"I don't know," I replied. "But Darcy said he acted as guide to the geologists."

"Then I know him," she cried. "I was hoping perhaps it is the same one. He was guide to my father three years back." She sat down on the bed and reached for her boots. "Where is he camped?" she demanded as she hurriedly put them on.

I told her. "But he doesn't know anything," I said. "It's two years ago that he found the lake. And even if he does agree to act as a guide for me," I added, "there's no certainty that he'll be able to find it again."

"If he has been there once," she said firmly, "then he will be able to find it again." And then she was staring up at me, frowning. "You were really planning to go in with him alone?" she asked.

"Yes," I said. And because she looked so incredulous, I added: "It's bad country, I know. But at the worst it'll only take five days, and there'll be the radio there—"

"How can you be so stupid?" she cried angrily. "I tell you before it is not possible. Do you think you can walk into Labrador as though you are strolling down a country lane in England? The Montagnais pace would kill you. And it is necessary we move fast," she added.

She had said "we," and I knew then what that pile of gear meant. She intended to come in with us, and my heart sank. It was bad enough to have her up here in this camp, but the thought of her trekking in with us to Lake of the Lion appalled me, for if, when we got there, my fears were confirmed, then its effect on her didn't bear thinking about.

I suppose she misunderstood my reaction, for she jumped up off the bed and, with a quick change of mood, came and put her hand on my arm. "I am sorry," she said. "That was not very kind of me, and maybe I owe you a great deal. I am still half asleep, I think. I don't get any sleep last night. But it is true what I said," she added. "I was brought up in this country. I know what it is like."

"Well, anyway, he probably won't agree to go," I said. And I realized that it was what I was beginning to hope.

"He'll go if I ask him," she said. "But I'll have to hurry." She knelt down and began to lace up her boots.

I watched her then as she pulled on her outer clothes, moving quickly with a sense of urgency. "You're going to see him now, are you?" I asked. And when she nodded, I said: "I'll come with you."

"No. It is better I go alone. Because I am a woman, he will be shamed, and he will do what I ask."

"Well, you'd better wait for Darcy," I told her. "At least he'll drive you as far as the trestle."

But she shook her head. "Ray has his work to do. By the time he returns, it may be too late." She looked like a boy as she stood there facing me in all the bulk of her clothes, except that her face was too small and the large brown eyes burned with a feverish intensity. "You see," she explained, "Mackenzie will not like to say no to a white man. If he does not like the place and decides not to go, then he will simply move his camp, and it will be days before we can find him again."

"I wish you'd wait till Darcy gets back," I said. Darcy would know whether it was right for her to go up to Mackenzie's camp on her own. But probably it was. Bill Lands had said she'd been raised in her father's survey camps.

A car drew up outside and there was the slam of a door. "Here's Darcy now," I said, feeling relieved.

But it wasn't Darcy. The latch clicked, the door was flung back, and Laroche stood there, facing me. He didn't see the girl at first. I think she had stepped back so that I was between her and the door. "I was told I should find you here," he said, and the dark eyes seemed unnaturally bright. "I have something to tell you—something I felt I should tell you myself. We've decided—" He saw her then, and he stopped, his face frozen with the shock of seeing her. "Paule!" He was standing quite still, framed in the rectangle of the door with the muddied clearing of the camp sharp-etched in sunlight behind him, and the surprise on his face turned to an expression that I can only describe as one of horror. It was there on his face for an instant, and then he turned and slammed the door to. The crash of it seemed to release the sense of shock in him, and he strode across the room towards her, suddenly talking in a furious spate of words.

I didn't understand what he said, for he was speaking in French, but I could see the anger blazing in his eyes. And then he was gesturing at me with his hand and Paule Briffe was answering him, standing very still and tense, staring up into his face. The anger in him seemed suddenly to flicker out. *"Mon Dieu!"* he breathed. "It only needed this." And he turned to me and said: "What have you been telling her?"

I hesitated. They were both looking at me, and I could feel their hostility. I was an intruder, and because of that they were drawn together again, both of them hating me for coming between them with facts that couldn't be answered.

"Well?" His voice trembled.

"There's an Indian," I said nervously, "camped up beyond the trestle. He says—"

"Mackenzie. Yes, I know about him. We met Darcy down the Tote Road, and he told us." He loosened the scarf about his neck. It was a slow, deliberate movement to give himself time. "You were thinking of going in with him, weren't you? That's what Darcy told us. You were going in with Mackenzie to try and find Lake of the Lion."

I nodded, wondering what was coming.

He was staring at me, and the anger seemed to have drained out of him. "Well, I guess there's nothing else for it." His breath came out of his mouth in a little sigh as though he were suddenly resigned. "I don't understand you," he murmured—"why you are so determined." He sounded puzzled and pushed his hand up over his scalp as though the wound still worried him. "But it doesn't matter now," he added. "I'm going in with you. That's what I came to tell you."

"You're going in with me?" I couldn't believe it for a moment.

"That's right." He nodded.

I stared at him, feeling no elation, only a sudden, inexplicable sense of fear. "But why?" I murmured. What had made him change his mind?

"You've given me no alternative, have you?" It was said quietly, and I was conscious of a change in him. He was different, more relaxed, as though he had come to terms with something inside himself. "I talked it over with Bill Lands driving up this morning," he went on. "We agreed that I should make one more attempt—try and back-track my route out. And then we met Darcy and heard about this Indian."

"Then you're not going to try and stop me?" I was still bewildered by his change of attitude.

"Why should I?" He smiled, a touch of the boyish charm that I'd noticed down at Seven Islands. Somehow I found that more deadly than his anger, and suddenly I knew I didn't want to go into the bush with him. It was a strange thing, but now that the opposition I had been fighting against ever since my arrival in Canada had

crumbled, all I wanted to do was to get out of this desolate country and go home and forget about the whole
thing. But I couldn't do that—not now; and I heard myself say: "When did you think of starting?"

"First light tomorrow. That is, if Mackenzie agrees to
guide us." And then he had turned to Paule Briffe again
and was talking to her in French. I think he was trying
to dissuade her from coming, for I saw an obstinate look
come into her face. "Excuse us a minute," Laroche said.
"I have to talk to Paule alone." And they went outside,
closing the door behind them.

I could just hear their voices then. They were arguing
in French, and gradually the tone of his voice changed.
He was pleading with her. And then suddenly there was
silence.

I went to the window and saw them standing close together by the car, not talking. He was staring out across
the camp, and she was standing, looking at him, her small
figure stiff and somehow very determined. And then he
gave a shrug and said something to her, and they climbed
into the car and drove off.

I was alone again then, and the sense of fear was still
with me, so that my whole body felt chilled, and I went
over to the stove and piled more wood on and stood
there, warming myself. But the heat of it couldn't drive
out a coldness that came from nerves. It sounds absurd,
writing about it now in cold blood, but I had what I can
only describe as a premonition—a premonition of disaster.

It's not a nice feeling to be scared, particularly when
there's nothing positive to be scared of, and I tried to
reason myself out of it. I hadn't been scared at the thought
of going into the bush with the Indian—nervous, yes, but
not scared. Why should I be scared now? But the answer
was there in the memory of Laroche and Paule Briffe
staring at me. To go in with Mackenzie was one thing,

but it was quite another to go in with those two for company. And the fact that they were foreign to me, both in temperament and race, only added to my sense of uneasiness.

There was something else, too, something that I think had been at the back of my mind ever since that meeting with Laroche at Camp 134, and it sent me hurrying over to the bookshelf to take down Henri Dumaine's book again and search the pages anxiously for any mention of the surname of the man who had accompanied my grandfather. But the only name he gave him was Pierre, and as I searched the pages I was gradually absorbed into the story of his journey. As Darcy had said, it was a trivial day-by-day account of the hardships and appalling travelling conditions he experienced, but now that I was on the brink of a similar journey they had a significance that held me fascinated. Outside the sunlight vanished, and as I read on, the light faded and it began to snow, and I felt again that Briffe couldn't be alive.

It was shortly after this that Darcy returned, and he had Bill Lands with him. They came in stamping the snow off their boots, and when Lands saw me, he said: "Well, I guess Bert told you. We're gonna have one last try at locating them." It was in my mind to tell him that it was too late, that they'd be dead by now, but his next words silenced me. "You may be right," he said in a surprisingly gentle voice, "or you may be wrong. I guess it doesn't much matter either way. You're here, and by to-night there won't be a man up and down the line who doesn't know why you're here. There's talk already. God knows where it started—that fool Pat Milligan down at Head of Steel, I guess." He came across to me, his eyes fixed on my face. "If it's any satisfaction to you, your damn-fool obstinacy has left me no alternative." He stood there, glaring at me. And then abruptly he said: "Where's Paule? We just been talking to the camp superintendent.

He said she got in from Two-ninety this morning. Have you seen her?" And when I told him I'd found her asleep in the hut, he asked me how she was dressed. "Did she have cold-weather clothing and a lot of gear with her?"

I nodded.

"Goddammit!" he cried, and he swung round on Darcy. "I told you, Ray. Soon as I knew she was here. Where is she now?" he asked me.

"I think she's gone up to the trestle," I said. "She was going to talk to Mackenzie."

He nodded angrily. "Yeah, I remember now. He was guide to her father one season. And Bert? Where's Bert?"

"He was here," I said. "They drove off together."

"So he's with her?"

I nodded.

"Well, I suppose that was inevitable." He unzipped his parka.

"You think she intends to go in with them?" Darcy asked.

"Of course."

"But surely you can stop her."

"How? She's as obstinate as the devil. And I don't know that I'd care to try now," he added. "Her hopes have been raised, and she's entitled to see it out to the bitter end, I guess." He swung round on me. "Christ Almighty!" he said. "You'd better be right about this or . . ." He scowled at me, pulled up a chair, and sat down on it heavily. "Well, it can't be helped." His voice was suddenly resigned. "But I don't like it, Ray. It's too late in the season."

"Maybe you could get the use of the helicopter again," Darcy suggested.

But Lands shook his head. "They need it on the grade right now. Besides," he added, "the Indian would never find the lake from the air. It's got to be a ground party." He looked across at Darcy. "Will you do something for me, Ray? Will you go in with them? I'd go in myself, but things are piling up and I got to get that new ballast pit going."

"I don't know how Staffen would take it," Darcy said.

"I think I can square Alex for you. If I can . . ." He hesitated, shaking his head. "Bert's no fool in the bush. But he's been injured, and I'm not certain—how he'll stand up to it. I don't want anything to go wrong, Ray. I know it's asking a lot of you. . . ."

"Okay," Darcy said, his tone flat and matter-of-fact. "So long as you square Staffen."

"Thanks. Thanks a lot, Ray." His tone was relieved. And after a moment he got to his feet. "I'll go down to the radio shack and contact Alex. You'd better start getting organized. You'll need stores for five of you, including the Indian."

"You think he'll agree to act as guide?" Darcy asked.

"Sure he will. Paule will see to that. You'd better leave it to him to decide whether it's worth lumping a canoe along and portaging. Depends how much water you're going to strike between here and the lake. And take one of those lightweight tents and those down sleeping-bags we issue to the smaller survey parties. If they haven't any in store here, get them sent down from Two-ninety. And see that Bert and Ferguson are properly kitted out." He turned to me. "You'll go in with them. Do you good," he added savagely, "to see what it's like, since you're responsible for the whole thing." And he turned and strode out of the hut.

"He's hoping it'll kill me," I said.

"Oh, don't let Bill worry you," Darcy said with a smile. "He's upset on account of the girl."

"Anybody'd think he was in love with her." I said it only because I was annoyed at his attitude, but Darcy took it seriously.

"Maybe you got something there. Maybe he is—in a

fatherly sort of way." And then he came over and looked down at the book I had dropped on the bed. "Did you find anything?"

He seemed afraid that I might have discovered something vital in it, and I remembered how he had searched through the pages when he had found me reading it the first time. "No," I said. "Nothing new." The relief on his face convinced me I was right, and I saw again the name LAROCHE written in capitals in my father's log book.

He nodded. "Well, let's go up to the store and see what we can dig up in the way of clothing. And then we'd better go and talk to the cook about stores." He seemed to take the whole thing very calmly, as though a five-day trek into the bush were all part of the day's work.

I felt very different about it myself, and as we walked down through the camp I had the impression that the country was lying in wait for me. It is difficult to convey my feeling, because nobody who hasn't been there can fully appreciate the latent menace of Labrador. I am told there is no country quite like it anywhere in the world. Maybe it's something to do with the fact that it has so recently—geologically speaking—emerged from the grip of the Ice Age. Whatever the reason, the raw emptiness of it took hold of me that morning in a way it hadn't done before. The camp was deserted, of course—and that made a difference. All the men were at work on the grade, and though I could hear the distant rumble of their machines, it was an isolated sound, tenuous and insubstantial in the virgin vastness of the surrounding country—a vastness that seemed to dominate—and the huts, black against the snow, were solitary outposts without any sense of permanence.

My mind conjured up the picture of Briffe crouched alone by that radio set—the only hope he had of contacting the outside world. "Can you handle a transmitter?" I asked Darcy, for I had a sudden feeling that in the end our own safety, too, might depend on it.

"No. I don't know a dam' thing about radio. Do you?"

"Not enough to transmit."

"Well, Bert Laroche will know."

But I didn't want to be dependent on Laroche. "He might not—" I hesitated. "He might get sick," I said.

"You're thinking of the survey party's radio?" His tone was preoccupied. "Well, yes, I guess it'd help if somebody besides Bert knew about it. We'll have a word with the operator here sometime this evening."

We were at the store then, and for the next hour we were busy kitting up. I came out of the hut completely reclothed right down to string vest, long pants, and bush shirt, and in one corner we left what seemed to me a mountainous pile of things that included axes and cooking utensils. By then it was time for lunch and the camp had filled up again, men streaming in from the grade on foot and in trucks. The big dining-hut was full of the smell of food and the roar of men eating.

"All set?" Lands asked us as we seated ourselves at his table.

"It's coming along," Darcy answered. And Lands nodded and resumed his discussion with a group of contractors' foremen. For him this was just one more project for which he was responsible.

We were halfway through our meal when Laroche and Paule came in, and the set, bleak look on her face as she sat down told me that something had gone wrong. Lands saw it, too. "Did you see Mackenzie?" he asked her.

She nodded. But she didn't say anything—as though she couldn't trust herself to speak. It was Laroche who answered. "Mackenzie wouldn't come."

"Why the hell not?"

"The caribou. He'd got word of a herd on the move to the north."

"Dam' sudden, wasn't it?" Lands was frowning as he stared down the table at Laroche.

And Darcy said: "It's just his way of saying he doesn't want to go."

Paule nodded. "Except for his tent, he was all packed up when we got there. He had one canoe already loaded. In another half-hour we would have missed him."

"And you couldn't get him to change his mind?" Lands asked.

She shook her head. "I did everything I could to persuade him. I offered him money, stores for the winter . . . but no, he must have caribou. Always it was the caribou. They must come first. And when I said men's lives came first, and that it was my father, whom he knew and loved as a brother, he told me it was no good—my father would be dead by now." She was near to tears. "And then he was talking about the caribou again. I don't believe there were any caribou," she cried. "It was just an excuse."

"He said there were caribou," Laroche murmured. "A big herd three days to the north."

"It was just an excuse," she repeated. "I know it was." And then she looked at Darcy. "Why didn't he wish to come? What is he afraid of?"

"Spirits—that's what he told me."

"Spirits! But he is not superstitious. And he was afraid of something—something positive. He would not look at me, not all the time I was talking to him." And then she turned to Laroche. "But he was looking at you. Every now and then he looked at you. I think if you had not been there . . ." Her voice trailed away, and then she gave a hopeless little shrug of her shoulders.

"I only wanted to help." His voice sounded tired, as though they had been through all this before. And he added: "Anyway, you went off into his tent and talked to him alone, but you still didn't get him to change his mind."

"No."

"So we're back where we were before." Laroche glanced

uncertainly round the table. "I suggest a small party—just one other guy and myself. That's what we agreed this morning, Bill." He was looking at Lands now. "A small party, moving fast, and I'll see if I can trace my route out."

"No." Paule's voice was clear and determined. "Whatever is decided, I go with you. You understand? I go, too." Her insistence might have been due solely to a determination to be present when her father was found, but I couldn't help wondering whether it wasn't something more, a feeling of distrust. And then she said: "Anyway, you have to take me. I have something here—" She put her hand to the breast pocket of her jacket. "A map of how to get there."

"A map?" Laroche's tone was sharp with surprise.

And Lands said: "Let's see it, Paule. If it's clear enough—" He held out his hand for it.

She hesitated. "It's very rough," she said. "I got Mackenzie to draw it for me in the tent." She pulled a sheet of paper out and passed it across to Lands. "It is not very good, but I think perhaps we can follow it." She watched nervously as Lands spread it out on the table. "At least it gives the lakes," he said. "Did he put them all in?"

"No. I think just those that have a shape or something by which we can distinguish them. Also, he has marked in some hills and some muskegs and a section of trail that is blazed. It is very rough, but I think it is possible for a party on the ground to follow it."

"I was thinking of an air reconnaissance. Bert, you come and look at it. See what you think."

Laroche got up and peered at it over Lands's shoulder. "Do you reckon you could follow it?"

Laroche hesitated. "Be difficult," he said. "His choice of landmarks is based on ground observation. You'd have to come right down on to the deck to get the same perspective. Even then—"

"Suppose you had the helicopter."

"I don't know." He glanced quickly at Paule and then down at the map again, licking his tongue across his lips. "Worth trying."

"That's what I think." Lands got to his feet. "I'll get on to Two-ninety right away."

"I'll come with you," Laroche said.

Lands nodded, glancing at his watch. "If Len Holt got it down here by two thirty, that'd give you four and a half hours. Okay?"

"For a reconnaissance—yes, I guess so. But the weather's not too good."

"No, but it's going to get worse. The forecast's bad."

They went out, and Paule Briffe watched them go with a tenseness she didn't bother to hide. "Do you think Bill can get them to send the helicopter down here?" she asked Darcy.

"Depends on the grade superintendent. It's his machine. But he's a reasonable guy, and Bill's got a way with him when he's made up his mind to something."

She nodded and got on with her food. She ate like the men, fast and with concentration, and, watching her, covertly, I was amazed that so much vitality and determination could be packed into such a small person, for she did look very small, seated there in that huge dining-hall, surrounded by construction men. And yet she seemed quite at home amongst them, entirely oblivious of the fact that she was the only woman there. And the men themselves seemed to accept her as though she were one of themselves. Glancing round the hut, I saw that, though they were all conscious of her presence and glanced at her curiously once in a while, they were careful not to make their interest obvious. They had been up there, some of them for months, and in all that time this was probably the first white woman they'd seen, and yet even the roughest of them was possessed of innate good manners in this respect. It was a part of their code, and I realized that this was the same code that must have operated in every frontier town since the North American continent began to be opened up.

"Cigarette?"

She was holding out the pack to me in a slim brown hand, and as I took one I was conscious again that there must be some Indian blood in her, the wrist was so thin, the fingers so wiry-looking. If Briffe was really descended from the *voyageurs,* there'd almost certainly be Indian blood. I lit her cigarette, and her dark eyes watched me through the smoke.

"Don't you find it strange that we should be going to this Lake of the Lion?" she said.

"How do you mean?" I asked.

"You will maybe find out the truth about your grandfather and what happened there."

"You know the story, then?"

She nodded, and I remembered then that she'd said her father had always been talking about the lake. "It's not all that important to me," I said.

"But your grandfather is supposed to have been murdered there."

"Yes, I know. But it's past history now."

And then Darcy said: "He'd never heard of the expedition until he came to Canada. All he knows about it is what I've told him." He was leaning towards her, and a quick glance passed between them. It was almost as though he were trying to warn her of something.

"So." She stared at the smoke curling up from her cigarette. "That's very strange." And then, before I had time to explain, her eyes suddenly looked at me with disconcerting directness, and she said: "And you are quite certain that it is Lake of the Lion that my father transmit from?"

"Yes." And I gave her the details of the message,

though I was perfectly well aware that she already knew them. "What I can't understand," I added, "is why your fiancé didn't admit that it was Lake of the Lion in the first place."

"Perhaps he is not sure." Her eyes were suddenly clouded and on the defensive.

"He seems to have accepted the fact now."

"I can understand," she said. And then she stubbed out her cigarette with quick jabs and got to her feet. "I am going to rest now. I think you should get some sleep, too." I started to follow her, but Darcy stopped me. "Sit down a minute." He was watching her as she crossed the big room, a small, lonely figure threading her way between the crowded tables. "Don't ask her that question again," he said.

"What question? About Laroche not admitting it was Lake of the Lion?"

He nodded.

"But why ever not?"

"Just don't ask her, that's all," he said gruffly. And then he, too, got to his feet and I went with him. Outside we found Lands and Laroche standing by a jeep.

"No good," Lands said, in answer to Darcy's query. "The damned thing's in pieces. A scheduled overhaul." He looked up at the sky. A ridge of cloud lay motionless to the west, its blackness emphasized by a fitful gleam of sunlight that flitted across the camp. "Anyway, Len probably couldn't have made it. There's more snow coming, by the look of it." He shrugged his shoulders. "Well, that's that, I guess. I'll see what the chances are tomorrow." He climbed into the jeep. "We'll chew it over again this evening after we've fed. Meantime, better get some rest."

He drove off then, and Darcy said to Laroche: "Better do as he says and get some rest. It looks like we're going to have to make it on foot if we're going in at all."

This was confirmed by Lands that evening. He called

us into Darcy's hut after the evening meal and told us
that the helicopter was definitely out. "The general manager and one of the directors came through here this
afternoon," he said. "They'd just talked to the grade
superintendent, and they told me bluntly that as soon as
the helicopter's in service again it goes back to the work
on the grade." He was sitting on Darcy's bed, and he
turned to Paule with an apologetic little shrug. "I'm
sorry, but there it is. The orders are that it's to be used
for supervision of the grade construction and nothing
else."

"But surely," I said, "if it were explained to them—"

"If what were explained to them?" he demanded
harshly. "They know all there is to know." He hesitated,
and then said awkwardly: "They don't believe Paule's
father is alive. Anyway," he added quickly, "they have a
lot on their plate. There's more than a thousand men
working on the grade north of here, and a hell of a lot of
machinery, and that helicopter is the only means the
superintendent has of keeping them driving." And then
he was staring at me. "Well, you've seen a bit of the
country, you know what it's like now. Do you still insist
your father was sane and that message a genuine transmission?"

They were all staring at me, and I suddenly realized
that this was the moment of decision. I had only to say I
wasn't sure and Lands would veto any further attempt.
His eyes were fixed on me, and I could almost feel him
willing me to say it. Laroche was watching me intently,
too, his long fingers nervously running the zipper of his
parka up and down. Darcy's expression was one of curiosity, an artist watching human behaviour. And Paule—
she was staring at me, too, but I couldn't see what she
was thinking. Her face was a sallow mask, the features
fine-drawn, the mouth a tight line. And then I heard myself saying in a flat, colourless voice: "I'm quite satisfied

my father was sane, and I'm perfectly certain he received that transmission."

What else could I say? If there'd been a way out, then I think I'd have taken it. But there wasn't. I'd gone too far to turn back now.

In the sudden silence I heard the girl's breath expelled in a little hiss of sound, and then Laroche said: "How can you be certain?" The words seemed dragged out of him.

"Because my father had been a radio operator all his life," I told him. "A man doesn't make a mistake like that when his whole life has been given to one thing." I hadn't meant to emphasize the word "mistake," but as I said it, it seemed to hang in the air, and I felt Laroche withdraw into himself.

"Okay," Lands said. "That settles it, I guess." But he sounded uneasy about it. "It's up to you now, Ray," he added, turning to Darcy. "You willing to go in?"

"I guess so." Darcy's voice was flat, matter-of-fact.

"And you, Bert?"

Laroche glanced at Paule Briffe. "If that's what you want?" And when she nodded, he said: "Okay then." But, like Lands, he didn't look happy about it. And the girl, aware of his reluctance, said impatiently: "What else is there to do—if we cannot have the helicopter?" She looked across at Lands, and he shook his head.

"There's no question of that, I'm afraid."

"Then it is agreed?" She was looking round at the rest of us. "We will start at dawn, yes?"

And so it was settled. We came down to the details then, and there was a long discussion as to whether or not we should take a canoe with us. In the end it was decided we should. From what Laroche could tell us of the country, there was as much water as land ahead of us, and though the portaging of a canoe would slow us up on the land stretches, it was felt that we should more than make up for it by avoiding the long detours necessary in skirting lakes and muskeg. It could always be abandoned if it didn't work out as we hoped.

The task of getting together all the things we needed for a bare existence in the bush took us about an hour and a half. We collected them in Darcy's hut—food, cooking utensils, clothing, packs, a gun, axes, fishing-gear: a great pile of equipment that had to be sorted and divided into loads for portaging. We finished shortly after nine, and then I asked Darcy to take me down to the radio shack.

I had already raised with them the question of the transmitter Briffe had used. It seemed essential that we should be able to make use of it if necessary, and I thought Laroche would say he could operate it. But all he said was: "The transmitter went down with the plane. I told you that already." He said it flatly, with an insistence that carried conviction, and though it made nonsense of the whole basis of our expedition, I could see that the others believed him.

Trudging down through the frozen camp, I wondered if I could persuade the operator to keep a regular watch for us on Briffe's frequency. "I suppose the radio operators here are kept pretty busy," I said to Darcy.

"Oh, I wouldn't say that," he answered. "There's not all that traffic. Mostly they're brewing coffee or reading paperbacks."

The dark shape of a hut loomed up behind the blazing eyes of its windows. Darcy went to the far end of it and pushed open the door. The heater was going full blast, the small room oven-hot, and a man in a T-shirt raised his eyes reluctantly from the magazine he was reading. His face looked pale behind a straggling beard, and his body lay slack against the tilted chair. Even when I explained what I wanted and why, his tired eyes showed no flicker of interest. Yes, he knew how a 48 set worked, and when I insisted that he explain it to me in detail, he grudgingly drew it out for me on his pad.

I couldn't help comparing him with Ledder. Simon Ledder had been like my father, an enthusiast. This man was just an employee doing a routine job. As soon as he had finished explaining the workings of the set to us, he tilted his chair back again and picked up the magazine.

I hesitated then, unwilling to commit ourselves to him. Our lives might depend on radio contact, and I thought of Ledder again. "Could you contact a ham radio operator at Goose Bay for me?" I asked. "The call sign is VO6AZ."

He shook his head. "I got to stay tuned to our own frequency."

"You expecting news of world-shaking proportions?" Darcy asked. I think he realized what was in my mind.

The operator stared at him with a puzzled look, not understanding the sarcasm. "My orders are—"

"To hell with your orders!" Darcy exploded. "You're here to operate a radio service. Now get your fat arse off of that seat and see if you can raise this ham. And hurry —it's urgent."

"Okay, Mr. Darcy. If you say so." He hitched his chair forward. "What's the frequency?" he asked me.

I told him, and we stood and watched him as he fiddled with the dial settings. He tried Voice first and then Key, and as the minutes slipped by on the clock above the transmitter I knew it was no good. I'd either have to trust him to get a message through or . . . "Could you get Perkins down at One-three-four?" I asked him, wondering why I hadn't thought of it before.

He lifted one of the earphones. "What was that?"

"Perkins at Camp One-three-four. Could you get him?"

"Sure. If he's on duty." He shifted the dials and began to call: "CQ—CQ—CQ. Two-six-three calling One-three-four. Come in, One-three-four. Over." And then Bob Perkins's voice was there in the room, the solid North

Country accent sounding homely and reliable. The phone
was put in my hand, and when I told him who I was,
he cut in immediately with the information that a cable
had come in for me from Farrow. "Arrived shortly after
midday, but I decided to sit on it. There's been a proper
flap on about you, and I was afraid if I started radioing
messages to you at Two-six-three, it'd give the game away
like. You're at Two-six-three now, are you? Over."

"Yes," I said and flicked the switch back to receive.

"Aye, I thought you'd make it all right. But I suppose
they've caught up with you now. Are they sending you
back to base, or what? Over."

"No," I said. "We're to make one more attempt to locate Briffe. I'm leaving in the morning with Laroche and
Darcy." And I explained then that I hoped to find Briffe's
transmitter still serviceable. "Will you do me a favour
and keep a radio watch for us on Briffe's old frequency?
Any time you like, but I must know that I can rely on
somebody to pick up any message. Over."

"So you're going in with Laroche, eh?" Even the loudspeaker couldn't conceal the surprise in his voice. And
then, after a pause, he said: "Maybe you'd better take
down Farrow's cable and then have a right good think
about it. I'll read it to you slowly." The radio operator
pushed his message pad towards me and reached for the
pencil behind his ear. And then Perkins's voice was saying: "It's a night-letter cable signed Farrow. Message
reads: 'Mother desperate your departure Labrador in
ignorance Alexandra Ferguson's diary stop Diary shows
grandfather killed by partner Lion Lake stop Partner's
name Pierre Laroche stop Fears may be some connection . . .' "

Laroche! So I had been right. There was a connection.
It was as though my father had suddenly called a warning across the ether in Perkins's tin-box voice. No wonder
he had written the name in capitals. And that scribbled
line that had so puzzled me: L-L-L-L-L—IMPOSSIBLE. It

was all clear to me in a blinding flash, and I turned on Darcy. "They're related, aren't they?" I cried. "You knew they were related." I didn't need his nod to confirm it; he'd been so careful not to mention the surname of the man who'd come out raving. "My God!" I breathed. "No wonder my father was so absorbed in Briffe's expedition." And I added: "Does Lands know about this?"

He nodded.

"And Paule Briffe?"

"I don't know. But I guess so."

Everybody but myself! They had all known. "What's the relationship?" I asked. "What's this Laroche to the one that murdered my grandfather?"

"Same as yours to Ferguson," he answered. "He's Pierre Laroche's grandson."

So it was as direct as that. The third generation. No wonder I'd been scared at the thought of his coming with us. And then I became aware again of Perkins's voice. "Have you got it?" His tone was impatient. "I repeat, have you got it? Come in, please. Over."

I pressed the sending switch. "Yes," I said, and I turned again to Darcy, wondering whether he was feeling about it the way I was—the way I knew my father had . . . feeling that history was repeating itself. "Do you think . . ." But I stopped there, unwilling to put it into words.

"It's just a coincidence," he said harshly.

A coincidence—yes, but a damned strange one . . . the two of us up here in Labrador and leaving together in the morning for the scene of that old tragedy.

I was so dazed by it that I had to ask Perkins to repeat the message. Apparently my mother, faced with the fact that I was actually in Labrador, was determined now that I must see the diary before I took any further action. It was being flown out to Montreal on the next flight, and from there it would be posted direct to Perkins.

But it was too late, and anyway it didn't seem to mat-

ter. The one vital fact was in my possession. "We leave
first thing in the morning," I told Perkins, and then went
on to arrange with him that he should keep watch between seven and half past, morning and evening. He said
he would contact Ledder and arrange for him to keep
watch, too.

It was the best I could do. Between the two of them
they ought to pick us up if we were able to transmit. His
last words were: "Well, good luck, and I hope it keeps
fine for you." Banal words, and only a voice out of the
ether, but it was good to know that somebody would be
listening for us the way my father had for Briffe.

And then we were outside the radio shack and it was
snowing; not soft, gentle flakes like those of the night before, but hard little crystals of ice driving almost parallel
to the ground and dusting the edges of the ruts like a white
powder. Darcy took my arm, his gloved fingers pressing
hard against the bone. "It's a coincidence," he repeated.
"Just remember that." And when I didn't say anything,
he added: "Best forget all about it. This isn't going to
be any picnic."

I didn't need him to tell me that! But it was manifestly absurd for him to suggest that I should forget that
Laroche was the grandson of a homicidal maniac. Once a
thing like that is put into your mind, it stays, and all the
time we were discussing the final arrangements for our
departure in the morning, I found myself covertly watching Laroche's face, searching for some definite indication
of the mental instability that I was certain he'd inherited; appalled at the thought of what the next few
days would bring. And later, after we'd turned in, I
couldn't get the past out of my mind, and lay awake for
a long time, watching the red-hot casing of the stove
gradually dull and listening to the howl of the wind
against the thin wood walls of the hut.

Part Three

Lake of the Lion

I

I woke to the shrill of the alarm clock
in that dead hour before the dawn and knew that this
was the day and that there was no turning back. The
light snapped on, and I opened my eyes to see Darcy bent
over the stove in his long woollen underpants. "Is it still
snowing?" I asked him, reluctant to leave the warmth of
the blankets.

"I guess so." He struck a match, and flames licked out
of the top of the stove. "You'd best get moving. Breakfast's in quarter of an hour."

We washed and shaved and then went down through
the white desert of the camp. Paule Briffe was already in
the diner, and the lights blazing on the empty tables made
the place look vast. Laroche came in shortly afterwards.
"Even if the helicopter had been available," he said, "Len
couldn't have flown in this weather." It was still blowing
hard, and the snow was the same mist of drifting, powdery crystals.

We ate in silence, joined by the driver of the truck
we'd been allocated, each of us wrapped in our private
thoughts. And then we loaded the truck and left, and
the wretched little oasis of the camp was swallowed up
by the blizzard before we'd even reached the Tote Road.

The truck bringing the canoe down from Camp 290
was due at the rendezvous at 0700 hours. But when we

finally got there, more than two hours late because of the drifts, there was no sign of it. There were no tire tracks either, and when we reached the trestle, five miles farther on, and there was still no sign of it, we knew it had failed to get through.

There was nothing for it then but to sit in the cook-house hut, drinking Sid's coffee and waiting. We didn't talk much, and there was an atmosphere of strain, for Paule and Laroche were like two strangers, united only in their hostility to me, which they scarcely bothered to conceal. This, I realized, was something I should have to learn to live with.

"I don't think we should wait any more," Paule said finally. "The lakes will be freezing over, and in this cold per'aps it is better without the canoe." Her small, peaked face was pale, and the edge to her voice revealed her impatience.

"There's the tent," Darcy reminded her. "The sleep-ing-bags, too. We can't leave without those."

She nodded and went back to plucking at the frayed edges of her parka. And then she slipped her hunting knife out of its sheath and began trimming the threads. It was an Indian knife with a carved handle and a long, slender blade worn thin by constant whetting. It wasn't the sort of blade you'd expect a girl to have, and to see it in her small, capable hands sent a cold shiver through me, for its thinness was the thinness of constant use, a re-minder that the North was her element. She finished trimming the edges, and after that she sat staring dully at nothing, the knife still in her hands, her fingers toying with the bright steel of the blade. I couldn't help think-ing that I was now in a land where there was no law as I understood it, where justice was something to be meted out on the spot. Looking across at Laroche, I saw that he, too, was watching her play with that knife.

It was shortly after eleven that the truck finally rolled

in. We transferred the canoe and the tightly rolled bundle of tent and sleeping-bags to our own vehicle and went back down the Tote Road, to the point where Laroche had crossed it on his trek out. And then we started into the bush, carrying the big canoe as well as our loads.

For a few paces the sound of the truck's engine stayed with us, but then it was lost in the noise of the wind, and when I looked back, the Tote Road had disappeared and there was nothing but the jackpines drooping under their load of snow. We were alone then, just the four of us, with all Labrador stretched out ahead, and not a living soul between us and the coast, almost three hundred miles away.

We camped that night on the pebble shores of a lake no bigger than a mountain tarn. The blizzard had blown itself out, and in the dusk, under the frosty stars, the trees had a Yuletide stillness, their whitened branches mirrored in the steel-grey water, and all round the edges of the lake was a crusting of new-formed ice that became a pale, almost luminous ring as darkness fell.

It had been a bad day—the late start, and then heavy going through deep snow with several bad patches of muskeg. We had only been able to use the canoe twice, on short stretches of water. The rest of the time we had carried it. We were wet and dirty and tired, and we hadn't even reached the first lake marked on Mackenzie's map.

Darcy fished till the fire was blazing and the coffee made, and he came back empty-handed. "Too cold for them, I guess." He flung his rod down and held his hands to the blaze, his wet feet amongst the embers. "Goldarnit! I could have done with a nice salmon." He grinned at us ruefully, and I found my mouth watering at the memory of the pink-fleshed *ouananish* I had eaten the previous day. Instead, we had to be content with a mixture of dehydrated soup and potatoes mixed with bacon and

beans. After that there was more coffee, black and strong
and sweet, and we sat, smoking, the mugs cupped in our
hands.

"Feel better?" Darcy's hand dropped on to my knee,
gripping it in a friendly gesture.

I nodded. My shoulders still ached, and the rawness remained where the straps of the pack had rubbed; the
blisters on my heels were throbbing, too. But the bone-
weary feeling of exhaustion had gone, and my body was
relaxed. "I'm fine," I said.

"Feel you got the Labrador licked, eh?" He stared at
me hard, smiling, but not with his eyes. "My guess is
we've done no more'n five miles, as the crow flies—one
tenth of the least possible distance. One twentieth, if you
count the trek out as well."

"Is that meant to boost our morale?" Laroche said.

Darcy turned his head and looked across the firelight at
him. "I just figured he'd better know the score, that's all."
And then he added with a grim little smile: "There's one
consolation. As we eat into our supplies, the packs'll get
lighter."

It was a warning. We were starting very late in the
year, and whilst he'd fished, he'd been considering our
chances. They were all three of them thinking about it,
and because I knew what was in their minds I found it
necessary to justify myself. "If it's tough for us," I blurted
out, "it's a lot tougher for Paule's father."

They stared at me, frozen into silence by my words.
And then, with a quick movement, Paule picked up the
cooking-pot and went down to the lake to wash it. Darcy
got to his feet, too. "Okay," he said gruffly. "Just so long
as you're sure." And he picked up his axe and went into
the timber to cut more wood.

Laroche hadn't stirred. He was staring into the fire,
and the flames, flickering on his high cheekbones, gave to
the skin a ruddy, coppery glow that made him look half

Indian. His head was bare, and the wound was a black shadow across his skull. "You shouldn't have said that." He spoke in a tone of mild reproach.

"About her father? Why not?" I said. "She knows perfectly well—"

"Just don't talk about it, that's all I'm asking." He stared at me across the glowing circle of the embers. "It only raises her hopes if you talk like that." His eyes dropped to the fire again, and after a moment he murmured: "You see, for her there isn't any hope—either way." He said it quietly, almost sadly. And then, as though speaking to himself, he added: "He'll be dead anyway by now." And the way he said it, I knew it was what he was hoping.

"But he wasn't when you left him, was he?" The words were out before I could stop myself.

But he didn't seem to notice, or else he didn't care whether I knew or not. He sat, staring down at the embers, lost in thought, and I wished I could see into his mind. What had happened after the crash? What in God's name had induced him to say Briffe was dead when he wasn't? And then I was thinking of his grandfather and what had happened at that lake before, and my gaze fastened on that ugly gash. His head was bent slightly forward, and the wound looked livid in the firelight. He would be marked by it for life. Like Cain, I thought suddenly.

As though conscious of that thought in my mind, he suddenly raised his head and looked at me. For a moment I had the impression he was about to tell me something. But he hesitated, and finally his lips tightened into a thin line and he got abruptly to his feet and walked away.

I was alone by the fire then. Yet my mind still retained a picture of him sitting there with his head bent to the blaze, and the certainty that he wasn't any saner than his grandfather had been took hold of me again. It was a terrifying thought, and I tried to put it out of my mind. But once there it seemed to take root. And later, when the four of us were huddled together for warmth inside the tent, I became convinced of it, for what other possible explanation could there be?

I remember telling myself that it wasn't his fault. He had been badly injured. But insanity is something of which we all have a primitive dread, and though I could pity him, I was still appalled at his presence among us, sleeping peacefully on the far side of the tent. It seemed so much worse out there in the bush, for we were shut in on ourselves, entirely dependent on each other. No doubt I was affected by the unnatural quiet that surrounded us. There wasn't a sound except for Darcy snoring gently beside me, and the cold that came up from the hard ground and seeped in through the thin walls of the tent prevented me from sleeping.

It seemed different in the morning. We were up at first light, busy rebuilding the fire and cooking breakfast. It was a raw morning, a thick mist lying over the water, which was lightly filmed with ice. Seeing the methodical way Laroche went about the job of striking and folding the tent, it was difficult to believe that he wasn't normal. And yet the very normality of his behaviour only served to increase my uneasiness, and the frightening thing was that there was nothing I could do about it. I could only watch him and hope that the strain, as we neared our objective, wouldn't drive him beyond the edge of sanity again.

"What are you thinking?"

I turned to find Paule standing behind me. "Nothing," I said quickly. She was the last person with whom I could share my fears. Darcy, yes—I would have to talk to him about it sometime when we were alone. But not Paule—not yet.

She frowned. "Then perhaps you will help me load the canoe."

The canoe proved its worth that day. We crossed three lakes in it during the early morning, with only short portages between, and just after ten we reached a long, narrow stretch of water. We crossed it diagonally, picked up the old Indian trail, and in no time at all, it seemed, we had reached the second of Mackenzie's lakes. But after that the country changed and became featureless. The lakes weren't buried in deep-scored clefts but lay in flat alluvial country, so that water and land were intermingled, with little change of level. We kept due east as far as possible, but there was nothing to guide us.

The going was good, however, the portages short and mostly easy. As a result, I was never alone with Darcy all that morning. In or out of the canoe, we were all together in a tight little bunch. And the only rest we had was when we were paddling. We ate our lunch of chocolate, biscuits, and cheese on the march, not stopping, and the extraordinary thing was that it was the girl who set the pace.

Darcy, of course, was much older than the rest of us, and as the day progressed and the portages became longer and more difficult, the pace began to tell on him. It told on Laroche, too; the skin of his face became tight-drawn, and all the spring went out of his stride. He had taken charge of Mackenzie's map, and more and more often he stopped to study it; but whenever Paule asked him whether he recognized anything, he only shook his head. And when the next lake, to be identified by a pebble bank in the centre, failed to materialize after ten miles of good going, she began to get worried.

I was up in front with her now, for my body had adjusted itself to the conditions of travel, and though the blisters on my heels still troubled me, I had begun to get

into my stride. We didn't talk much, for she was preoccupied with our direction and I was looking about me
at the country, even enjoying it, for it had an austere
beauty of its own.

And then we came to a small lake and had to wait
for Darcy and Laroche, who were bringing up the canoe.
"Do you think we are per'aps too far south?" She stood
there, staring at the flat surface of the water with a
worried frown, and when I said I didn't know, she
dropped her load and stretched herself out on the coarse
silt of the beach. "Well, anyway, it's nice here." She
closed her eyes in an attempt to relax. The sun had come
out, and though it was already low over the trees behind
us, there was no wind and it was almost warm. "If
only there were a hill," she murmured. "We could get a
view of the country if there were a hill. As it is, we shall
have to waste time scouting for this lake." After that she
was silent for so long that I thought she had fallen asleep.
But then she suddenly sat up. "You're sure it is Lake of
the Lion where they crashed?" she demanded.

The suddenness of the question took me by surprise.
"Yes," I said. "It's quite clear from the message—"

"I know." She made an impatient gesture with her
hand. "But Albert has never admitted it is Lake of the
Lion. He never saw the lion shape in the rock. And now he
says Mackenzie's map is taking us too far south. He wants
us to go further north."

I knew then that Laroche was going to try and turn us
away from the lake, and I asked: "How does he know
we're too far south?"

"Because he has recognized nothing. If it is Lake of the
Lion and the map is correct, then all day we must have
been passing through the same country he came through
on his trek out, but he does not recognize it. That night
before we set out, he warned me he thought Mackenzie's
directions wrong. Now he is convinced of it." She frowned

down at the pebble she had picked up and then tossed it into the water. "I don't know what is best to do—to follow the map or turn north until we find something that he recognizes."

There was a movement in the jackpine behind us and Laroche and Darcy emerged, bent under the cumbersome load of the canoe. "We must stick to the map," I told her urgently. And because she still looked doubtful, I repeated it. "If we abandon the map now and turn north—" I had been going to say that we'd never find her father then, but that meant trying to explain to her why Laroche should want to turn us away from Lake of the Lion, and I let it go at that.

She had got to her feet. "Did you see anything you recognized on that portage, Albert?" Her voice was devoid of any hope, and when he shook his head, she said: "Not even that big rock outcrop?"

"I told you before, my route was north of the one Mackenzie drew you." He was tired, and his voice sounded petulant. "And now we're even south of that."

"How do you know?"

"We've come a long way from the Indian trail and that last lake we identified. We should have reached the next one by now. We're getting pushed south all the time." He said it wearily, and then he turned to Darcy. "What do you think, Ray?"

Darcy nodded. "It's like Bert says," he told Paule. "It's the way the darned country's built. It's edging us south all the time, particularly on the portages."

She hesitated, glancing from one to the other of them. "Then we'd better head northeast for the rest of the day," she said at length. "And if we don't find that lake by nightfall, then we must begin scouting for it."

"Why bother about the lake?" Laroche said. "My view is we should keep going northeast till I pick up my route out."

She was looking at him uncertainly, and at length she said quietly: "But how can you be sure you will recognize it? So far you have recognized nothing—not even when we started in from the Tote Road."

And Darcy said quickly: "Well, anyway, we head northeast till nightfall. We can discuss this later."

And so it was decided. Nobody asked me what I thought, and anyway I couldn't have argued with them. It was perfectly true that the country was forcing us to the south. But I didn't like the thought of turning north, even for the remainder of the day. It was the way Laroche wanted us to go, and north lay the Arctic.

We crossed that lake and two more on the new compass course, and in the early evening we reached a broad sheet of water with a pebble bank in the middle of it. Paule was instantly convinced that this was the lake we were looking for. "You were right," she said to Laroche. "We were a little too far to the south."

He didn't answer her, but stood there, staring out across the water, his face clouded. And then he brought out the map and stared at it, glancing every now and then to compare the drawing with the bank itself. "I think we're still too far south," he said finally.

"But the bank . . ." Paule moved to his side, peering at the map. "You see. He has marked it. Right in the middle."

"The shape isn't the same," he said. "And he's marked some trees. This bank is completely bare." And he added: "He's been remarkably accurate on his detail so far."

I stared at him, certain now that his intention was to confuse us. He'd hoped to lead us astray, and now here we were on the shore of the very lake he'd been trying to avoid. And then Paule said: "I'm sure this is the lake Mackenzie meant. I remember him telling me that the

bank only just showed above the water—an island of
pebble, he called it."

"We're in glacial country here," he said. "Probably
most of the lakes have pebble banks in the middle of
them."

Paule was staring up at him, frowning, and I turned to
Darcy. "How far have we come today?"

He considered for a moment. "All of twenty miles, I
guess. Maybe more."

"Then we're about halfway."

"If it's fifty miles altogether."

And there were three more lakes before we reached the
river that was the last thing marked on the map before
Lake of the Lion. "Then this must be the lake," I said.
"It's in the right position, and—"

Laroche rounded on me then. "Okay—since you know
this country so dam' well, you better lead us from here."

"But he's right," Paule said. "We are about halfway,
and Mackenzie said it would be two days, maybe three."

"And I still say we're too far south. This may be the
lake. But I don't think it is." He gave a little shrug and
began to fold the map. "Staring at it won't help us to
make up our minds."

Paule frowned. "Let me have another look at it. He
didn't say anything about trees. Per'aps what he has
marked . . ."

But Laroche had already turned away. "However much
you look at it," he said, "you'll never be certain whether
it's this lake or the other." And he put the map back in
the breast pocket of his parka.

She stood up and faced him then. "But I want to look
at it again," she said obstinately.

"You can look at it later," he answered, moving away
from her, down towards the canoe. "If we're going to cross
before dark, we'd better get moving."

Whether she had suddenly become suspicious, I don't
know. It was a fact—and I had been conscious of it for
some time—that Laroche had never once let the map
out of his hands since we started. Maybe it was just that
she was tired and in a petulant mood. At any rate, she
ran after him and caught hold of his arm. "Albert. Give
it to me. It's my map." And when he told her it was
quite safe in his pocket, she repeated: "It's my map. I
want it." Her voice was suddenly quite shrill.

"For heaven's sake, Paule." He shrugged her hand off.
"Just because you're not certain this is the right lake—"

"I am certain."

"Then what do you want the map for?"

"Because it's mine." She grabbed hold of his parka.
"Give it to me. Please." She was almost sobbing.

It would have been childish, except that it suddenly
brought the tension between them out into the open. I
remember the shocked expression on Darcy's face. He knew
it was serious, and he moved in quickly. "Steady, Paule."
He caught hold of her arm none too gently and pulled
her away. "The map's okay, and we got to get across. A
lake the size of this could hold us up for days if it
came on to blow."

She hesitated, staring at Laroche as though she wanted
to tear the map out of his pocket. And then abruptly the
violence of her mood vanished. "Yes, of course," she
said. "You are right; we must hurry." And she gave Darcy
a quick smile and went quietly down to the canoe.

The temperature had fallen quite sharply, and it was
cold out on the water. We paddled in silence, and the
only sound was the dip-dip of the paddle blades and the
whisper of water along the skin of the canoe. All the
world seemed hushed with the gathering dusk and so still
that the endless blacks and greys had the static quality of
a photographic print.

And then, from beyond the pebble bank, came the call

of a goose, so clear and perfect in the stillness that it took my breath away. We saw them as we glided round the end of the bank, four birds like white galleons swimming in line astern, and Darcy reached for his gun. He fired as they spread their wings; three birds thrashed the water and became airborne, the fourth keeled over and lay on its side. And when we'd pulled it into the canoe, the quiet returned, so that it was difficult to believe it had ever been disturbed by the shot and the frenzied beat of wings.

Darkness was falling when we reached the farther shore, and we went straight into camp on a little promontory of stunted trees. Whilst Paule plucked and cleaned the goose, we got a roaring fire going, and in no time at all the bird, neatly skewered with slivers of wood, was hanging from a cross-pole supported by two forked stakes and turning slowly before the blaze, the frying-pan set below it to catch the fat. The sight and smell of that roasting bird was something out of this world in that remote wilderness. We sat round the fire, drinking coffee and talking, and eying it with the eager anticipation of children at a feast. The affair of the map seemed to have been entirely forgotten.

It takes a long time to roast a goose in front of a fire, but at last the juices ran at the prick of a knife, and we cut it down and fell on it ravenously, burning our fingers with the hot fat. Paule used the same little thin-bladed Indian knife that she must have used at countless campfires, and the sight of the worn steel winking in the firelight reminded me that it was her father who had done the hunting then. But I was too absorbed in the flavour of that goose to worry about what she might be feeling. It was only afterwards, when my stomach was full, that I noticed the tense, withdrawn look on her face and became conscious of Laroche's moody silence.

After such a meal they should have been relaxed, like

Darcy. But they sat so still and tense that it was impossible not to be aware of the atmosphere of tension between them. And if this were really the lake Mackenzie had meant, then tomorrow or the next day we'd be at Lake of the Lion. Time was running out, and when Darcy got up and strolled off into the darkness of the timber, I followed him. "I've got to talk to you," I said when we were out of earshot of the camp.

He stopped and waited for me to say what I had to say, standing quite still, his bulky figure in silhouette against the glimmer of the water. "It's about Laroche," I said. But it was difficult to put my fear into words, and when I tried, he stopped me almost immediately.

"Now listen, Ian. You got to forget he's the grandson of Pierre Laroche. I told you that before. What happened at that lake between your grandfather and his has nothing whatever to do with the present."

"I think it has," I said. And then, in a rush, I poured out all my fears, not giving him time to interrupt me. And when at last I had finished, he stood there, staring at me in silence with the starlight gleaming frostily on his glasses.

"You realize what you're saying?"

"Yes."

"And you believe that? You think he tried to kill them?" His breath hung like steam in the night air. "Good God!" he breathed, and after that he was silent a long time, thinking it out. "He seems sane enough," he murmured half to himself. "It was Paule I was beginning to worry about." And he shook his head as though he still couldn't believe it. And then his hand gripped hold of my arm, and he said: "Why have you told me this? What do you expect me to do about it?" His voice sounded angry and bewildered.

"Nothing," I replied. "There's nothing either of us can do about it, except watch him."

"Hell! There must be some other explanation."

"What other explanation can there be?" I demanded impatiently. "It's the only possible explanation—the only one that fits all the facts."

He let go of my arm then. "It's bad enough having you along with us, believing a thing like that. But if it's true . . ." His voice was suddenly an old man's voice, tired and angry.

"If it isn't true," I said, "why do you think he's always trying to get us to turn north? He daren't let us reach Lake of the Lion. He daren't even face the sight of it himself. Anyway," I added, "I've warned you."

"Yeah." He stood for a moment longer with the sky behind him full of stars and the northern lights weaving a luminous pattern in the night. "Okay," he said wearily. "Let's go back now. It's cold out here." And he started towards the fire, which showed a red glow through the sticks of the trees. "You haven't said anything to Paule about this, I hope."

"No."

"Well, don't," he said.

But back at the fire I wondered whether she hadn't guessed it already, for they were sitting there just as we'd left them, sitting quite still and not talking, and I could feel the tension between them. Darcy noticed it, too. "It's late," he said gruffly, and as though glad to be released by the sound of his voice, they got up at once and followed him to the tent.

I threw some branches on to the embers of the fire and watched the crackling flare as the needles caught. It was so peaceful, so unbelievably peaceful. And beyond the leap of the flames lay the immensity of Labrador, all still and frozen in the night. I sat down, cross-legged in front of the fire, and lit a cigarette, and let the stillness seep into me. It gave me a strange sense of peace, for it was the stillness of space and great solitude, a stillness that matched the stars and the northern lights. This, I thought, was the beginning of Creation, this utter, frozen stillness, and the fire felt to me then the way it must have felt to the first man who'd experienced it—the warmth of something accomplished in a cold, primitive land.

There was a movement behind me, the snap of a twig, and I turned my head to find Paule there. "You should come to bed," she said. "If you sit here, you will be tired in the morning."

I nodded. "It was the night," I said. "It's so still."

"And there is so much sky—all the stars. I know." She seemed to understand my mood, for she came and sat beside me. "You have never been in country like this before?"

"No."

"Does it worry you?"

"A little," I admitted.

"I understand." She touched my arm, a quick gesture of companionship that surprised me. "It is so empty, eh?" And she withdrew her hand and held it to the blaze. "My father always said it is the land of the Old Testament."

"The Old Testament!" It seemed odd to compare this frozen country, so full of water, with a land of heat and desert sand, and yet I could see his point, for I suppose he'd never known anything but the North. "What was your father like?" I asked.

She didn't answer for a moment, and I was afraid that perhaps I shouldn't have asked her that. But then she said: "When you are very near to a person, then I think per'aps it is difficult to tell what they are really like. Some men thought him hard. He drove them." And she added with a little smile: "He drove me, too. But I didn't mind."

She was silent for a moment, staring into the flames as though she could see him there. "You would like him, I think," she murmured at length. "And you would get on

together. You have guts, and that always appealed to
him." She sighed and shook her head sadly. "But I don't
think you meet him now; I don't think he can still be
alive." She leaned forward and pushed a branch into the
fire, watching it flare up. "It is a little sad if it is Lake
of the Lion where they crash. There is supposed to be
gold there, and that was his dream—to strike it rich and
have a big mine named after him. It wasn't the money so
much, though we never had any and my mother died
when I was a little girl because he could not afford a
sanatorium; it was more the need to justify himself. He
was a prospector," she added. "It was in his blood, and,
like a gambler, he must always try his luck again—one
more expedition, one more attempt to find what he is
searching for."

I nodded. "Like my grandfather. Ray says he was like
that."

She turned her head and stared at me, her eyes very
wide in the firelight. "That was a terrible story," she said
at last, her voice little more than a whisper, and I knew
it wasn't my grandfather she was thinking of, but Pierre
Laroche. "But it has nothing to do with my father," she
declared, her voice trembling with the effort needed to
carry conviction. "Nothing at all."

I would have left it at that, but the train of thought
had made me curious on one point. "You told me your
father often talked about Lake of the Lion," I said.

She nodded. "That and a hidden valley up in the
Nahanni River Country and another lake somewhere
on the edge of the Barren Lands; places he'd heard about
from the old-timers." And she added: "I tell you, he was a
prospector. That was his life, and nothing else mattered."
She was staring into the fire again. "But he was a wonderful man. To see him handling a canoe in the rapids,
or with a gun . . . And always round the fire he would
be telling stories—strange, unbelievable stories of the

Canadian wild. . . ." She stopped there, and I saw she was crying, the tears welling gently from her eyes. And then abruptly she got to her feet, in one quick, graceful movement, and left me without a word.

I watched her crawl into the tent, and after that I sat alone beside the fire for a long time, staring at the star-filled night and thinking about my grandfather, who had died in this country, and about that indomitable woman, my grandmother, who had followed his trail with vengeance in her heart. *The land of the Old Testament:* that phrase stuck in my mind, and the frozen stillness that surrounded me seemed suddenly cruel and menacing. And for the first time in my life I thought about death.

I'd no religion to retreat into in the face of that ultimate enemy, no God to support me, nothing. Science had done that for me. Like all the rest of my generation, I hadn't dared to think too deeply, and as a young engineer my days had been full. I had been content to leave it at that. But here it was different. Here, it seemed, I was faced with the world as it had been in the beginning, when the mind of man first began to grope after a meaning for infinity; and, as Darcy had predicted, I began to think about God.

But in the end the cold drove me to the tent, and I crawled in and lay down in my place beside Darcy. We were on spruce boughs that night, and the soft aroma of them sent me to sleep almost immediately.

When I woke, the stillness was gone, shattered by the crash of waves on the lake shore and the roar of wind in the trees. It was a grey day with a savage wind blowing out of the northwest, and as we started on the portage to the next lake, it began to rain. At first it was no more than a drizzle, a thick curtain of mist driving across the country. But gradually the sky darkened, and soon the rain was sheeting down, slatting against our bodies with a fury that was almost personal.

That portage was the worst we had experienced, the

ground strewn with boulders, slippery and unstable. Darcy and I were carrying the canoe, and all the time the wind threatened to take charge of it and tear it out of our hands. We were wet to the skin long before we reached the next stretch of water, and when we stood on its shores, our backs to the rain and our clothes streaming, we were a sorry sight.

It was a small lake expansion, not more than two hundred yards across, yet the surface of it boiled under the lash of the storm and the waves were two feet high and breaking. "Will the canoe make it?" I asked Darcy, and as I turned to speak to him, the wind drove solid water into my mouth.

It was Paule who answered me. "Of course it will," she said. But I could see Darcy didn't like it. He stood there, wiping his glasses on a sodden handkerchief, staring at the lake and muttering to himself.

We shipped so much water on the crossing that the canoe was half full by the time we reached the other side. And as we stumbled on over the next portage, the country changed again; the timber became thicker, and between the boulder ridges we began to encounter muskeg. At first they were only small patches, which we were able to skirt. But then we came to a big swamp, and though we scouted north and south along its edge, we could see no end to it. There was no alternative then but to cross it, which we succeeded in doing after a long, heart-breaking struggle, in the course of which we were often up to our waists in water.

We came out of it wet and filthy and utterly exhausted, only to be met by more muskeg beyond the next ridge. "Did you meet much of this on your way out?" Darcy asked Laroche as we stood looking at it.

"You saw the condition I was in."

"Yeah." Darcy nodded. "But how much of it is there? That's what I'd like to know."

Laroche hesitated, glancing nervously from one to the

other of us as we stood staring at him. "We'll get into better country soon, I guess."

"How soon?" Paule asked.

"When we're near the lake. We'll be on rock then."

"Well, how near have we got to get before we're out of this damned muskeg country?" Darcy demanded. "Two miles from the lake, five, ten?"

"I don't know." Laroche licked the water from his lips. "About five, I guess."

"And all the rest is muskeg, is that it? Fifteen miles of it, at least."

Laroche shook his head. "I can't seem to remember very clearly. There was muskeg, I know. But not fifteen miles of it. I'm sure it wasn't as much as that." And then he added: "It just bears out what I've been saying— we're still too far south. We should turn north until we strike the route I took coming out."

"No, we'll stick to the map," Paule said.

"But you can't be certain that lake we crossed last night—"

"I am certain." Her voice was suddenly shrill again. "And you admit yourself that you don't remember your route very clearly."

Darcy moved towards the canoe. "No good standing here arguing," he said. "We'll only get cold."

Paule and Laroche stood facing each other a moment longer, and then they shouldered their packs and we started down into the muskeg. It stretched ahead of us as far as our eyes could see through the curtain of the rain, and we waded on and on through country in which sodden tussocks of cotton grass were the nearest approach to dry land, and never a stretch of open water in which we could use the canoe.

We went into camp early that day on a little stretch of gravel where a few morose-looking jackpine grew. It seemed no more than an island in that sea of muskeg, but it was a relief just to stand on something firm, and we were too wet and exhausted to care that we'd only covered a few miles. We managed to get a fire going, but though it enabled us to cook some sort of meal, there was no real heat to it, and the smoke blackened our faces and made our eyes sore. The rain was still teeming down when we crawled into the tent and lay there steaming in our sodden clothing.

All night the wind beat at the tent. Twice we had to go out and weight the walls down with stones, and in the morning it was still blowing. But the rain had stopped, and we saw then that our island was, in fact, a long spit of gravel running out from the shores of a lake that was bigger than any we had so far encountered. It was fortunate that the rain had stopped, for we were on the lee shore, and in poor visibility we might have attempted the crossing, which would have been disastrous. There was a big sea running out in the centre, and there was nothing for it but to camp there on the shore and wait for the wind to drop.

It was here that we lost the map. Laroche had placed the damp sheet of paper on a rock to dry in the wind, and he'd weighted it down with a stone. At least, that was what he said, and certainly the stone was still there. But the map was gone, and though we searched all along the gravel beach, we couldn't find it. "I guess it must have blown into the water," Darcy said, and Laroche nodded. "I didn't realize the wind was so strong here," he murmured, not looking at any of us.

Paule stared at him for a moment, and then she turned quickly away, got a notebook out of her pack, and set to work to re-draw the map from memory. But though we all checked it with her on the basis of what each of us remembered of the original, we knew we could never place the same reliance on it. Our only hope was that we should recognize the river when we came to it. The river had been the last thing marked by Mackenzie on the map, with the falls a guiding mark only a few miles from Lake of the Lion. But, as Darcy pointed out, rivers in Labrador are apt to be lost in lake expansions, and often the current is so slight as to make the lake unidentifiable as part of a river system.

We were pinned there on the shore of that lake until dusk, when the wind suddenly dropped and the temperature with it. We crossed at once on a compass bearing in almost complete darkness. It was the worst crossing we'd had, for though the waves were no longer breaking, they were still big, and the movement was so violent that we were in imminent danger of capsizing, and the water rolled green over the sides of the canoe, so that we had to bail continuously. And when we reached the other side, it took us a long time to get a fire going.

We were all of us at a low ebb that night, and as we sat in the smoke of the fire, cooking our meal, the tension that had been building up all day between Paule and Laroche suddenly exploded. We had been arguing about the lake we had just crossed. It was too big for the Indian to have ignored it when drawing the map, and we were all of us quite sure that this wasn't the next lake he'd marked, the one he'd called Burnt Tree Lake. There were no burnt trees here. "Maybe I was wrong," Paule murmured unhappily. "Maybe that lake with the pebble bank was not the one." She looked across at Darcy. "I guess I was tired."

"We were all tired," he said.

She turned to Laroche then. "Are you sure you don't remember this lake when you are trekking out? It is so big—"

"Exactly," he said. "It's so big it would have meant a detour of several miles."

"But you may have forgotten it. You were injured and—"

"*Mon Dieu!* I'd no canoe. Do you think I'd have forgotten about a lake the size of this?"

"No. No, I suppose not. But then you have recognized nothing—nothing at all." There was a note of exasperation in her voice.

"I've told you before," he said irritably, "I was much further north."

"But not when we started. We started from the same point where Ray picked you up. Yet you recognized nothing."

"Why should I?" he cried angrily. "I was at the end of five days with no shelter and little food. I was in no state to remember the country."

"But you remembered the muskeg."

"Sure. But I was fresher then, and it doesn't mean it was the same muskeg."

"Muskeg's much the same any part of this country," Darcy said soothingly.

But she was looking at Laroche. "If only you hadn't lost the map," she said furiously. "Now we can never be certain . . ."

"Well, I lost it, and that's that. I'm sorry." He waved the smoke away from his face. "But I don't see what difference it makes. We couldn't identify the last lake for certain and we can't identify this one. The map was only a rough one, far too rough to follow in this sort of country." And he added: "I still say we should turn north and try and pick up my route out."

His insistence annoyed me, but as I opened my mouth to make some comment, I caught Darcy's eye and he shook his head urgently. I hesitated, afraid that by constant repetition he'd convince her. But when she didn't say anything, I returned to the consideration of my feet. I had taken off my boots and was attending to my blisters, which had become a suppurating mess under my wet socks. But then she said: "Why are you so insistent that we go north, Albert?" Something in the quietness of her voice made me look up, and after that I forgot about my blisters, for she was staring at him through the smoke and there was a frightened look in her eyes. "You never wanted us to follow the map, did you?"

"I was never convinced we'd crashed at Lake of the Lion," he answered her.

"Then why did you lose the map?" It was such a sudden, direct accusation that I stared at her, aghast.

"It was an accident, I tell you." His eyes darted from her to Darcy. And then he was staring at me, and his face had the wild, trapped look that I'd seen that night at Camp 134; I thought then that if she persisted in her questions, she'd drive him over the edge, and I began to put on my boots.

"Very well. It was an accident." Her voice trembled. "But why did you refuse to let me have it? It was my map. Why did you insist on keeping it yourself?" And then, before I could stop her, she cried out: "What are you afraid of, Albert? You don't want us to get to Lake of the Lion. No, don't deny it, please. I have been feeling this for some time. You are afraid of something. What is it?"

I had got my boots on then, and all my muscles were tense, for I didn't know what he'd do. But all he said was: "You must think what you like, Paule." And he got up wearily and went off into the trees. Darcy glanced quickly at me, and then he got up and went after him.

I was alone with Paule then. She was sitting quite still, as though her body were frozen rigid. But at length she turned to me and said: "What happened there, Ian? Please. Tell me what happened." Her face looked ghastly in the firelight, and there were tears in her eyes. And when I didn't say anything, she caught hold of my arm. "I must know what happened," she insisted. "Please." And then with sudden violence: "Don't you understand? I love him. I love him, and I can't help him if I don't know."

"I don't know what happened," I said awkwardly. What else could I say? I couldn't tell her my fears.

"But something happened. Something terrible happened out there after they crashed. I can feel it." Her voice was distraught, and she was trembling.

Darcy came back then, and she let go of my arm. "I guess we're all pretty tired," he said heavily. "Time we turned in." Laroche came back, too, and asked for more coffee, and Paule gave it to him. The moment of crisis was over. But later, as we were going into the tent, Darcy stopped me. "I think," he whispered in my ear, "that we should see to it those two aren't left alone again."

I nodded. "It's only twenty miles now," I said. "To-morrow or the day after, we should know the truth—if the going's good."

"I hope you're right." He had turned his head towards me, and his craggy, weather-beaten face was set in deep lines. "I sure hope you're right," he reiterated. "Because my guess is that right now we're lost." And then he added: "If we have to go casting about in search of this lake, then our bellies are going to feel the pinch. The last two days we've got no fish. The only game we've had is that one goose. Just remember that when it comes to a decision whether to go on or turn back."

It was cold that night, so cold that I lay shivering on the edge of sleep, and when Laroche stirred and sat up, my eyes were instantly open. There must have been a moon, for the inside of the tent was quite light and I could see him staring at me. And then he crawled quietly out through the flap. I was on the point of following him, but then I realized it was only nature that had called him because of the cold, and a moment later he was back and had lain down in his place on the other side of the tent.

I suppose I slept after that, for the next thing I knew
it was morning and Darcy was coaxing the fire into a blaze,
and when I crawled out, it was to find the world frozen
into stillness and all the lake shore rimmed with new ice.
"And how are you today?" Darcy said.

"Fine," I replied, and it was true; I did feel fine. The
air was so clean and fresh it seemed to sparkle.

"A dandy morning like this, we should make good
progress." He put the coffee on, humming tunelessly to
himself. And when the others emerged, they, too, seemed
affected by the frozen stillness that surrounded our camp.
After two days of being battered by the wind, it had a
quality of peace about it that was balm to our frayed
nerves, and all the tension of the previous night seemed
to have vanished away.

The sky turned to palest blue, and as we started out,
the sun rose. And it wasn't only the weather that had improved; it was the country, too. We seemed to have left the
muskeg behind. Ahead of us, it was all gravel, flat as a
pan and full of water—small, featureless lakes that ran
into one another or were separated only by short portages.

By midday we had covered well over ten miles and all
along the horizon there was a black, jagged line of hills.
They were only small hills, little more than rock outcrops, but they marked the rim of the gravel pan; and
when Darcy asked Laroche whether he remembered this
stretch of country, he nodded. But though he stood for a
long time looking at the line of little hills, he didn't seem
able to recall any particular feature. "All I remember is
that I came out of the rock into this flat country and the
going was easier for a time." His voice sounded flat and
tired in the windless cold.

"But can't you see something you recognize?" Paule
asked.

He shook his head.

"I don't understand," she cried, and the note of exasperation was back in her voice. "Surely you must have marked the spot where you came out into the flat country here."

"You seem to forget I was injured," he said sharply. "Just to keep going was about all I could manage."

"But you knew you would have to go back and look for my father. You knew it was important to have some landmark to guide you."

"I tell you I was too ill and exhausted to care."

She was about to make some comment, but Darcy stopped her. "It doesn't matter," he said. "Bert's already told us we'll be within about five miles of the lake when we get back into rock country. And if Mackenzie's map was accurate, then the river runs right across our line of march. When we reach it, we've only got to scout along it till we find the falls, and then we're almost there. That shouldn't be difficult." And he picked up his end of the canoe again, and we started forward.

Two hours later we reached the hills. They were covered with a dense growth of conifer, and as we started in, we lost the wide Labrador skies, and the going became rough and difficult. It was all rock outcrops, most of them so steep that there was no question of keeping to a compass course, and we went into camp early at the first lake we came upon.

It was a sombre little stretch of water, and though Darcy and Paule both fished it all the time Laroche and I were making camp, they had no luck, and we went to bed very conscious that if we didn't find Lake of the Lion within the next two days, we should be forced to turn back for lack of supplies. There was some talk of abandoning the canoe at this stage, but I don't remember what was decided because I fell asleep in the middle of the discussion.

I had meant to stay awake, for now that we were so close to our objective, I was afraid Laroche might make some desperate attempt to stop us. But though I was too tired to fend off sleep, my senses must have remained alert, for I woke suddenly in the early hours to the certainty that something was wrong and saw that Laroche was no longer in his place beside Paule. I could hear him moving about outside, and for a moment I thought the cold had driven him out as it had the previous night. But his movements were different, and when he didn't immediately return, I leaned forward and peered out through the flap of the tent.

I could see him quite clearly in the moonlight. He was standing over the embers of the fire, shouldering his way into his pack. I opened my mouth to ask him what he was doing, but my voice seemed suddenly to have deserted me. I watched him pick up his axe and fit it into his belt, and then he was gone from my line of vision and I heard his boots on the rocks of the lake shore. The sound gradually faded. I scrambled out of the tent then to see his tall figure moving like a ghost in the moonlight down the far end of the lake.

He was heading south—south, not north—and without stopping to think, I laced up my boots and went after him, moving quickly through the timber. I emerged at the far end of the lake and from the shelter of the trees watched him climb a bare outcrop of rock that stood at its southern end. He paused a moment on the very summit of the outcrop, a lone, black figure against the moon's light, gazing back at our camp and then all round him, as though to get his bearings. Finally he turned and disappeared from sight.

I found my voice then and called to him as I scrambled after him up the steep rock slope of the outcrop. I shouted his name all the time I was climbing, and when I reached the top I hesitated. Clouds were beginning to cover the moon. But I could hear him ploughing his way down through the timber on the far side, and a streak of grey light in the east told me that it would soon be dawn. Without thinking what the clouds might mean in that country, I plunged after him, suddenly determined that he shouldn't escape us, that I'd catch up with him and confront him with the truth, whatever the risk.

It was a stupid thing to do, for I'd no compass, no food, no equipment, nothing but what I was wearing, and the conifer growth was so thick that I could only follow him by ear. This meant pausing every so often to listen, and as a result he gradually drew away from me, until I lost the sound of his movement entirely. I didn't know what to do then, and I stopped, undecided, in a small clearing. It was almost daylight, the sky heavy and overcast and a light sprinkling of snow falling, and suddenly I realized that I didn't know my way back. Travelling by sound only, I had lost all sense of direction.

I had a moment of sheer panic then and stood screaming Laroche's name at the top of my voice. And then, because there was nothing else I could do, I plunged forward again in the desperate hope of catching up with him. Luck was with me, for not more than a hundred yards farther on I came suddenly out of the timber on to the shores of a small lake, and there was Laroche, skirting the far end of it. I could only just see him, for it was snowing heavily now. "Laroche!" I yelled. "Laroche!"

He stopped abruptly and turned, and then he stood, staring back at me in silence.

"Laroche! Wait!" I called. He was on the very edge of visibility, and I knew, as I started towards him, that he'd only to turn and dive into the bush and I should have lost him for ever.

But instead of trying to escape, he stood quite still, waiting for me. It was only when I was a few yards from him that I saw the dull blade-gleam of the axe gripped in his hand, and I halted with my heart in my mouth, for I'd no weapon with which to defend myself.

II

That bleak little lake

with the snow falling softly—it might have been the lake
where he'd tried to kill the others. My knees were trembling as I stood there, facing him; there was only a few
yards between us, and I thought that this was how it had
been before, when he'd had the brainstorm, with him
standing so still and the axe gripped in his hand, and all my
body was tense, waiting for the attack.

But instead his gaze went past me, down along the
edge of the lake. "Where are the others?" he asked. "Are
they following, too?"

I shook my head, not trusting myself to speak.

His dark eyes came back to me. "Just you—alone?" And
when I nodded, he seemed to relax. "I guess you saw me
leave the camp, eh?" He swore softly to himself, using the
Canuk word *"Tabernac!"* "I thought I'd slipped away
without any of you seeing." And then he added: "Well,
you'd better go back to them now."

It was my chance to escape. I started to edge away from
him, and then I stopped. "But I don't know . . ." The
words died in my throat, for I didn't dare admit that I
was lost. Once he knew that . . . My body was suddenly
chill with fear, a fear that was greater than my fear of him.

"Try and persuade Paule and Ray to wait there for
me," he went on, his voice still reasonable, his gaze fixed

now on the far end of the lake. "I'll be about two days," he added.

I stared at him, puzzled by his manner. He seemed so sane. And yet . . . "Where are you going?" I demanded.

"That's my business," he answered sharply.

And then, suddenly reckless, because anything was better than being left to die of cold and starvation: "You ran out on him when he was still alive, scared at what had happened. Isn't that the truth?"

He was staring at me, his dark eyes wide in their shadowed sockets. And then suddenly his gaze shifted to the ground. "You're so damned logical, aren't you?" It was said without any trace of hostility. And then he murmured: "Well, it's true—in a way. I was scared. I was certain Baird was dead, and there seemed nothing else . . ." His voice trailed away as though at some ghastly recollection. And after a moment he lifted his head and looked straight at me again. "If I told you history had repeated itself there at that lake, then you'd think I'd gone mad, wouldn't you?"

"How do you mean?" My throat was suddenly dry.

He stared at me a moment longer, and then he shook his head. "No, it's no good," he murmured. "I guess you can only see it the one way. I knew what you were thinking that first day at Seven Islands. *Mon Dieu!*" His voice was no more than a whisper. "Why did it have to be you? Queer, isn't it?" He gave a little, nervous laugh. "If I told you . . ." But he stopped there and shook his head again. "No, you'd twist it round in your mind. But I'll tell you this much: that Indian was right. It's a bad place."

"Then it *was* Lake of the Lion?"

"Sure it was Lake of the Lion." He was still looking at me, and his lips were drawn back from the even line of his teeth in that same wry little smile. "Yeah," he said. "The place where my grandfather killed yours." And he

added: "The body's still there. A heap of bones—that's
all that's left of James Finlay Ferguson, and there's a hole
drilled in the skull where the bullet struck him. In the
back of the skull. Pierre Laroche must have come up behind him and shot him in cold blood. The forehead's all
splintered." His eyes stared at me unblinkingly a moment, and then: "It's not a pretty thing," he muttered,
"to discover that your grandfather is a murderer." His
tone was suddenly bitter.

The fascination that old tragedy had for him, his bitterness—if I had needed to be convinced, this would have
convinced me. It was the sight of my grandfather's remains, the evidence of his own grandfather's guilt that
had unhinged his mind. "And what happened—afterwards?" I heard myself ask, and my voice shook slightly.
"What happened then between you and Briffe?"

But he shook his head. "Oh, no," he said. "I'm not
telling you that. Or what happened to Baird." He hesitated, and then he added: "But you can come and see it
for yourself, if you want to."

"You mean now?"

He nodded.

"You're going to Lake of the Lion?"

"But of course." He said it impatiently. "Where else did
you think I was going?"

And I stared at him, the skin crawling on my scalp.
It was incredible—quite horrible. He was going back to
the scene of the tragedy. Why? To gloat? Or was it
the murderer's subconscious fascination for his crime?
Whatever it was, I knew now he was mad, and my voice
trembled as I said: "But you're going south." Fact—anything to keep him to facts.

"South—yes." He nodded. "I have to pick up my route
out."

"But you told us that was to the north."

He shrugged his shoulders. "What does it matter what

I told you?" And then he added: "If you come with me, you can see for yourself what happened to Baird. Then maybe you'll believe me."

But I knew I could never believe anything he said, now or in the future, for his mind seemed so confused. Perhaps to him there was no truth any more. "You said Baird was injured in the crash," I whispered. "You told me they were both injured in the crash."

But he shook his head. "No," he said. "Nobody was injured in the crash." And then he suddenly smiled with that touch of boyish charm that I had found so frightening before. "You mustn't think, because I told you they were injured in the crash, that it was so. I had to tell you that, because I didn't want you to pursue your inquiries." It was said with such an appalling candour that I felt almost sick. And then he said: "Well, are you going to come on with me or are you going back to join the others?"

I hesitated—not because I'd any choice, but because I was so horrified at the thought of going on alone with him. My only hope was that Darcy and Paule, by following the Indian's instructions, would reach Lake of the Lion before us. If I were to be the only witness to what had really happened there . . . "Are you sure you can find the lake?" I asked.

"Oh, yes," he replied. "In the early stages I was very careful to memorize my route and even blazed some of the trees."

"But if you're prepared to let me come with you, why not the others? Why didn't you tell them you could guide us in?"

He shook his head and the smile on his lips had become oddly secretive. "I didn't want to. I didn't want anybody to know."

"But Paule—"

"Least of all Paule," he said harshly, the smile suddenly

wiped from his face. And he added, still in the same
harsh voice: "I guess you'd better come with me anyway.
If you go back you'll talk, and the one person who must
never know what happened there is Paule."

It surprised me that in his state of mind he should still
care what Paule thought, and I took the opportunity to
point out that she'd be worried about him. "They'll
wonder what's happened to us," I said.

But he shook his head. "I left a note. They'll guess
you're with me." And he added: "I hope to God she does
what I asked and stays at that camp." He made a gesture
with the axe. "Okay, let's get going. You lead the way."
And he stood back to let me pass.

I barely hesitated, for if he once knew that I was lost,
then it would be so much simpler for him to abandon me
here. Nevertheless, as I went past him the muscles of my
shoulders contracted in anticipation of a blow, even
though my intelligence told me that he was now determined to take me to Lake of the Lion and that anyway,
if he intended to kill me before we got there, he would
have plenty of opportunity. From now on we would live
as close as it is possible for two human beings to live,
for we'd no tent, nothing but our own warmth to protect
us from the cold.

We left the lake behind and the timber closed round
us again, and after that I was conscious all the time of the
sound of the axe close behind me as he blazed the trail
for the return journey—but whether for his return or for
mine I didn't then know, and because of that, the chip
and bite of the axe on wood had a hollow, mocking
sound in the silence of the falling snow.

And then suddenly the timber fell away before us and I
stood looking out over the same flat country that we'd
come through the previous day. But now it was all white,
with the vastness of the sky a dirty curtain of lazily drifting snow. My first thought was that I had been right after

all in thinking he was running out on us. "You're going back," I said. "You're not going to try and reach the lake."

But he shook his head. *"Pas du tout."* He smiled at me almost cheerfully. "I've come back here to pick up my landmark."

However, it was impossible to pick out anything, for it was snowing harder than ever, and we remained in the shelter of the trees and lit a fire to keep ourselves warm. Later, when the snow eased up, we went out along a ridge of sand as far as the first lake, and from there Laroche was able to identify his mark, a lone rock outcrop topped by three ragged-looking firs.

Then began a nightmare journey that lasted two whole days. No sooner had we started back into the rock country than it began to snow again. And even when it finally ceased some time in the late afternoon, the going remained heavy and tiring, an unending struggle through deep, wet snow, with every branch unloading its sodden burden on us. The temperature fell steadily, and with the disappearance of the clouds it dropped below freezing, so that the snow formed a crust through which we broke at every step. And all the time our progress was further slowed by the need for Laroche to search back and forth for the trail he had blazed. In the conditions in which he had marked it, there would have been no difficulty in following it, but now, with the trees all blotched and weighted down with snow, it was a wonder we were able to keep to it at all.

We went into camp at dusk in a little clearing full of snow-covered rocks, and I swear if we'd had a tent, we'd have been too tired to put it up. It was as much as we could do to cut wood for a fire, and when it was lit in an angle of the rocks that would reflect the heat, we lay down in the wet snow and fell into a stupor as we shared a little of the food Laroche had brought with him.

I shall not easily forget that night. The cold was intense. At first the fire kept it at bay. But it melted the
snow, so that we lay in a pool of water with the sharp
edges of rocks sticking into our flesh. And later, as the
fire died down, the cold crept in, numbing our bodies and
turning the water to solid ice.

In these conditions it was impossible to sleep; I simply
lay in a dazed half-world of consciousness, chilled to the
bone and tired beyond belief, with no vestige of hope in
my heart. Denied the blessed balm of sleep, there was
no escape from the fact that the only source of warmth I
had was to lie close against the body of a man I knew to be
a murderer. This, and the circumstances of our journey
—not to mention the conditions—would, I truly believe,
have driven me to a state bordering on madness if it hadn't
been for the fact that in that pitiless country I discovered,
or perhaps I should say rediscovered, something deep-
buried within me that was akin to belief in the Almighty.
I do not intend to dwell on this. The conversion of the
unbelieving and the unthinking into an acceptance of
God is of great moment only to those who have experienced it, and that I should have done so is not much to
my credit, being due more to my wretched circumstances
than to any innate piety, for by then I was convinced I
was going to die—if not by the hand of Laroche, then by
the country. Only one of us could leave Lake of the Lion
alive, and if it should be me, I did not know the way
back to the others and had no hope of getting out of the
country on my own.

Accepting, therefore, the certainty of death, my mind
dwelt again on what that step meant, and in the frozen
quiet of that night I came to terms with it and made my
peace with God, so that before the first dawn-light made
grey ghosts of the trees, I had reached a strange state of
calm that was somehow in tune with the country.

Our breakfast that morning was one biscuit apiece and

a small square of chocolate. That Laroche had taken so little from the general store of our supplies was in itself somewhat surprising, but I don't think I considered it at the time—nor the fact that he was willing to share it with me. In country as bleak and inhuman as Labrador you take it for granted that the essentials of life, things like food and warmth, are shared between you, regardless of the future; and because of that, even if I had been in a condition to think about it, I do not believe I should have reached any other conclusion.

As it was, the pitiful inadequacy of our breakfast did little to comfort us after the wretchedness of the night, and though we built up the fire and got some warmth back into our bones, we were both of us in a wretched state as we started out that morning. Laroche, in particular; he seemed suddenly to have come to the end of his strength. His face was flushed and his eyes unnaturally bright, and there was a slackness in his muscles that made his movements clumsy, so that he was inclined to stumble. But when I asked him whether he was all right, he pulled his stooped body instantly erect and assured me he was. "I'm stiff, that's all," he said. "It's the cold." And after that I didn't comment again on his condition, for I knew by his manner and the tone of his voice that he'd resented it, and I was afraid, as I had been from the time I had caught up with him, of precipitating a showdown.

The cold that morning was very severe. The sky, when we glimpsed it through the trees, was grey with it, like a canopy of frozen lead, and the land itself was held immobile in an iron grip. Because of this, the snow was hard and the going easier.

We skirted two frost-rimmed lakes, following all the time the trail Laroche had blazed on the way out, and shortly after ten we came to a big expanse of water, curved like a bow, with the ends lost in the trees that stood thick along its banks. That was when I suggested turning back. It was going to take us a long time to skirt that lake, and I felt that if we didn't turn back now, neither of us would get out alive. "It's the only sensible thing to do," I urged. "Turn back now, before it's too late."

"Listen!" He was staring northwards, his head cocked on one side. "Do you hear?"

But all I could hear was the whisper of a chill wind in the trees.

"Sounds like the falls," he said. "The water here is a lake expansion of the river Mackenzie marked on his map." He sank down on to his hands and knees and bent his ear close to the water. "Yeah, it's falls, all right." And he got to his feet, and stood staring along the shore. "I guess there's more water now than when I crossed here before." It seemed to worry him. "I didn't hear the falls then."

"What's it matter?" I asked. "We certainly can't cross a river where there are falls." And then, because I was too exhausted to care any more, I said: "I'm turning back now."

I thought that would precipitate a showdown, but all he said was: "You do as you like. It's only two miles from here, and I got to hurry in case . . ." But I didn't hear the rest, for he was already wading into the water.

I couldn't believe it for a moment. He didn't seem to care whether I stayed with him or not. The water was already over his knees. He called to me over his shoulder then. "If you're coming with me, better hurry. I shan't wait for you." And he waded straight on into the lake.

I had moved automatically to the water's edge, and there I hesitated. I could so easily leave him now and go up to those falls and wait for Paule and Darcy; I was sure that Paule, at any rate, would push on as far as the river. But it took more nerve than I possessed to deliberately abandon the company of another human and blaze a lone trail through that sort of country. Moreover, now that I was so near to my objective, I found it exercising an increasing fascination, so that though I had been offered a means of escape, I couldn't bring myself to take it.

I stepped into the water then, and the cold shock of it made me catch my breath at the same moment that Laroche shouted something, so that I didn't hear what he said. I thought for a moment he was in difficulties, for he was now waist deep in the water. But he hadn't been pulled off his feet by the current. In fact, he was standing stock still, staring at the farther bank. He cupped his hands and shouted again. "Paule! Paule!" The name wandered down along the jackpine fringe, a dwindling ghost of a sound swallowed by the empty vastness of sky and water. "Paule!" And then he went plunging forward, driving his body through the water with a sudden, desperate energy.

I didn't hesitate then, but followed him, not caring any longer how cold the water was or how deep. Paule was here, and Darcy would be with her. I shouldn't be alone with him any more.

Fortunately there was a gravel bottom to the lake expansion, for long before I reached the middle I was feeling the tug of the current, and all the time the water got deeper until it covered my genitals and was reaching up to my stomach, freezing all the guts out of me. At the deepest it reached to my lower ribs and my boots were just touching bottom. I saw Laroche scramble out and climb the rocks that fringed the shore. But there was no sign of the others, and he didn't call again. And when I came up out of the water I found him alone, standing over the burnt embers of a fire, staring at the thin wisp of blue smoke that curled up from it. "You saw them," I gasped. "Where are they?"

He shook his head, and his face was deathly pale. "No, I didn't see them."

"But you called out to Paule."

"I saw the smoke. I thought maybe . . ." He shook his head wearily. "They're ahead of us." His teeth were chattering, and the bitter frustration he seemed to feel made his voice sound hollow. He pushed back the hood of his parka and ran a trembling hand up over his head. "I didn't think they could possibly get here ahead of us." He was almost crying. At any rate, there were tears in his eyes, and his whole body shook as though with ague.

"But how do you know?" I cried. "If you didn't see them . . ."

"The fire," he said.

I stared down at it then, seeing it suddenly as the footprint in the sand, the proof that there were other humans besides ourselves in this desolate wilderness. And I knew that he must be right, because there was nobody within five days' march of us except Paule and Darcy.

By then my own teeth were chattering and I could feel my clothes stiffening as they froze. A numbness was creeping through my body. But I didn't care. That wisp of smoke meant that Paule and Darcy had stood here on this lake shore and dried themselves at this fire less than an hour ago. The knowledge that they were so close comforted me. "I'll get the fire going again," I said. "Give me the axe."

But he shook his head. "No. No, I got to get on. I got to catch up with them before they reach the lake." He was looking now at the trees ahead of him, searching for the marks he'd made.

"But we must have a fire," I said. "We've got to dry our clothes."

He shook his head again, impatiently, as he moved in amongst the trees, his body still shaking with the cold. And then he found what he was looking for, and he started forward.

"Laroche! Come back!" I almost screamed his name.

"You damned crazy fool!" I shouted after him. "You'll die of cold if you don't get dry."

He didn't stop, but went straight on, half running, and though I shouted at him again and again, he took no notice. There was nothing for it then but to follow him. I knew it was crazy. We were soaked to the waist, and the temperature was way below freezing. But I'd no alternative.

I thought I'd catch up with him in a moment, for he was in a far worse state than I was. I thought that as soon as he'd got over the first shock of his surprise and began to weaken, I could persuade him to stop and get a fire lit. But in fact I was only just able to keep him in sight. He seemed suddenly possessed of a demoniacal energy. The timber was sparse here, and he was running, not caring that the ground was rocky and treacherously strewn with moss-covered boulders. Twice I saw him fall, but each time he scrambled to his feet and plunged on at the same frantic pace.

We went on like that for a long time, until I, too, was so exhausted I could barely stagger, and then suddenly the ground fell away and through the bare poles of the trees I caught a glimpse of water. A moment later I stumbled out of the timber on to an outcrop, and there was the rock, crouched like a lion, in the middle of the lake.

I stopped then and stared at it, hardly able to believe my eyes. I had reached Lake of the Lion, and the sight of it gave me a sudden chill feeling of despair, for it was a black, sombre place. The lake itself had a white rime of ice round its edge, and all the length of the long, narrow cleft, its surface had the dull, leaden look of water beginning to freeze over. The Lion Rock stood in the very centre of it, the blackness of it emphasized by the ice that ringed it round.

"Paule!" Laroche's despairing cry came up to me

through the trees, and it had the lost quality of the damned in it. "Paule! Wait! Please, Paule!"

He was running down the steep-timbered slope towards the lake, and beyond his bobbing figure I caught the glint of metal. It was the Beaver floatplane, and it wasn't sunk after all. It lay with its wings sprawled along the ice at the water's edge. And to the right of it two figures stood against the black bulk of some up-ended rocks that formed a platform overlooking the lake, a repetition at a lower level of the outcrop on which I stood. They were standing quite still, and like me they were staring down at the plane.

"Paule!" That cry, so full of fear and despair, rose crazily up to me again, and as though the cry had galvanized the two figures into action, one of them detached itself from the other and went scrambling down towards the lake and the half-sunken aircraft. It was Paule. And then Darcy started after her, and he was calling to her, a cry of warning.

No doubt he thought Laroche, in his demented state, might be dangerous. It was my own immediate thought, for the Beaver floatplane was evidence that he'd lied, and I left the outcrop and went racing down the slope, shouting to her to stay with Darcy.

It's a wonder I didn't break my neck on that hillside, for it was a tangle of roots and I went down it regardless of the fact that I was dead weary and all my muscles uncontrollable through weakness. But I was unencumbered by any pack, and I reached the lake shore only a little behind Darcy, who had stopped and was standing with a shocked look on his face. And beyond him, Paule had stopped, too, and so had Laroche—the three of them quite still like a tableau.

They were all of them staring at something down along the lake shore, and as I passed Darcy, I saw it, too: a body lying crumpled in the snow, with the torn canvas of a tent forlornly draped from its slanting pole. I checked then, and I, too, stood momentarily frozen into immobility, for beside the body were two rusted steel containers, and from one of them the thin line of an aerial swept up to the trees that fringed the lake.

So my father had been right. That was my first thought, and I went slowly forward, past Laroche, past Paule—until I stood looking down at the pitiful remains of the man I'd come so far to find. He lay on his side, a stiff-frozen bundle of ragged clothing, and his thin, starved face was turned upwards, staring with sightless eyes at the Labrador skies. One hand still clutched the phone mike of the transmitter; the other, wrapped in a filthy, bloodstained bandage, lay by the handle of the generator. My only thought then was that he had never given up; right to the very end he had been trying to get through, and he had died without knowing he had succeeded. Across all those thousands of miles he had made contact with my father, a disembodied voice on the ether crying for help. And my father had met that call with a super-human effort that had been his death. And now I had failed him.

Behind me I heard Paule echo my thoughts in a whisper so hoarse that I barely recognized her voice. *"Mon Dieu!"* she breathed. "We are too late."

"Yes," I murmured. "We're too late." And then I looked up at the Lion Rock standing there in the middle of the lake. At least I had reached Lake of the Lion. I had done what my grandmother had tried to do—what my father would doubtless have done in the end, if he hadn't been so badly injured in the war. I had reached James Finlay Ferguson's last camp. That at least was something.

I looked down at Briffe's body again, and my eyes, blurred with exhaustion, seemed to see it as that other body that had lain here beside this lake for more than fifty years, and I remembered what Laroche had said: a heap of bones—and a hole drilled in the skull. At least Briffe hadn't died like that. But still a shudder ran through me, for the drawn and sunken features told of a slower death, and close behind me Paule whispered: "He killed him, didn't he?"

I turned then and saw her standing, staring down at her father, with a blank look of misery and despair on her face. I didn't say anything, for she knew the truth now; the body and the transmitter were evidence enough. And then slowly, almost woodenly—like a puppet on a string—she turned and faced Laroche. "You killed him!" The whisper of her words carried down the lake's edge, so clear in the frozen stillness that she might have shouted the accusation aloud, and her face as she said it was contorted with horror. "You left him here to die—alone."

Alone! That one word conjured a vision of what Briffe's end had been. I think Laroche saw it, too, for his face was quite white, and though he tried to speak, he couldn't get the words out. And then Paule repeated her accusation in a rising crescendo of sound that bubbled out of her throat as a scream of loathing and horror. "You killed him! You left him here to die. . . ." Her throat closed on the words, and she turned away from him and went stumbling blindly up through the trees like an animal searching for some dark corner in which to hide.

If Laroche had let her go, it might have been all right; but he couldn't. "Paule—for God's sake!" he cried. And before Darcy or I could do anything to stop him, he had started after her. And he was up with her in a second, for she was sobbing so wildly, so hysterically, that she tottered rather than ran up the slope. He reached out and caught hold of her arm. "Paule—you've got to listen to me." He jerked her round, and then his hand fell from her elbow and he stepped back as though at a blow, for her eyes blazed with hatred and her white face had a trapped look, full of bewilderment and fear.

"Paule!" He held out his hand to her in a pleading gesture.

But in the same instant she cried: "Don't touch me! If you touch me, I'll—"

"Paule, you've got to listen to me."

I heard her cry: "No. Keep away from me." It was said as he reached out and gripped hold of her again, and in the same instant she made a quick movement of her arm, there was the glitter of steel, and then she was stabbing at him with that thin-bladed Indian knife, stabbing at him again and again, screaming something at him in French, or it may have been Indian, until finally his knees sagged under him and he sank groaning to the ground at her feet. He looked up at her then, and for a moment they stared at each other, and then he suddenly collapsed and lay still, and she was left standing, staring with a dazed expression at the knife in her hand. She stared at the reddened blade, and a drop of blood gathered on the point and fell like a piece of red confetti on to the trampled snow.

Suddenly she flung the knife from her and, with a sobbing intake of breath, fell on to the snow beside him. "Darling!" She had seized hold of his head and was staring down into his face, which was paper white and bloodless under the stubble. *"Mon Dieu!"* She looked up then and searched about her blindly as though for aid, and finally her eyes lighted on Darcy and myself, still standing there, helpless spectators of the tragedy. "I think I've killed him," she said in a toneless voice. "Would one of you see, please?" And as Darcy went and knelt beside Laroche's body, she laid the head down and stood up, suddenly quite composed. "I am going to—see to my father now," she said, and she went slowly down through the trees towards the sunken aircraft and the sandy beach below the rocks that had been Briffe's last camping-place, moving slowly like a girl walking in her sleep.

I went over to Darcy then, my knees trembling and weak with the shock of what had happened. "Is he—dead?"

Darcy didn't reply. He had laid Laroche's body out on the snow and was unzipping his parka.

"It all happened so quickly," I murmured.

He nodded. "Things like that always do."

"I was thinking about Briffe and what had happened here."

He had undone Laroche's parka, and the sweater underneath was all soaked in blood, sodden patches that ran into one another, dark red against the dirty white of the wool. He cut it away with his knife, deftly exposing the white flesh beneath the bush shirt and the sweat-grimed undershirt, as though he were skinning an animal. And when he had the whole chest exposed, with the half-dozen knife wounds gaping red and slowly welling blood, he put his head down and listened to the heart. And then he nodded slowly, like a doctor whose diagnosis has been proved correct. "Where's that girl gone?" he demanded, looking up at me.

"She's gone to see to her father."

"Well, she can't do anything for him. Fetch her back here. I want a big fire built, and hot water and bandages."

"He's alive, then?"

"Yeah—just. I guess the thickness of the parka saved him." He looked quickly about him. "Build the fire over there in the shelter of those rocks where Briffe had his camp. And tell Paule to find something clean for bandages." Darcy slipped his axe from his belt. "Here, take this. I want a big fire, and I want it kept going. Now get moving." And as I left him, I heard him say: "This is a hell of a thing to have happened." And I knew he was wondering how we were to get out with a wounded man.

I went back through the trees and down over the rocks to the little beach where Paule knelt on the gravel beside the frozen body of her father. I remember I was surprised to see how small a man he was, and though death had smoothed some of the wrinkles from the weather-beaten skin, the face was the face of an old and bitter man. Starvation had shrunk the flesh of the cheeks and stretched the skin tight across the bones, so that the features looked shrivelled and only the grizzled beard had any virility left in it. His body, with the lower half still encased in his sleeping-bag, was sprinkled with a light dusting of snow. There was snow on the radio set, too, and all the simple necessities with which he had endeavoured to support life lay scattered around him, half-buried in a white, frozen crust.

I told Paule what she had to do, but she didn't seem to take it in. "He's dead," she murmured. "My father's dead."

"I know," I said. "I'm sorry. But there's nothing you can do for him now."

"We were too late." She said it in the same dull, flat voice, and though she wasn't crying, she seemed utterly dazed. "If only I had done something about it when that first report of a transmission came through. Look! He was trying to get through to me. And I agreed with them," she murmured brokenly. "I agreed that the search should be called off."

"It wasn't your fault," I said.

"It *was* my fault. I should have known." She gazed dully round her at the snow-covered camp-site. "There's no sign of a fire," she said. "He hadn't even a fire to keep him warm. Oh, God!" she breathed. And then she was staring up at me, her eyes wide in the pallor of her face. "Why did Albert do it?" she cried. "Why did he leave him here? And then to say he was dead!"

Speaking of Laroche seemed to remind her of what she'd done. "Have I killed him?" she asked.

"No," I said. "He's still alive. But we've got to get a fire going and some bandages." And then, because she was looking down at the corpse of her father again, lost to everything but her own misery, I caught hold of her arm and dragged her roughly to her feet. "Pull yourself together, Paule," I said. "There's nothing you can do here."

"No—nothing." And she seemed suddenly to collapse inside. "It's all so terrible," she cried, and she began to sob, wildly and uncontrollably.

I shook her violently, but she didn't stop, and because I didn't know what else to do, I left her there and went up into the trees and began to hack down branches, building them into a great pile in the shelter of the rocks. And after a while Darcy came and helped me. "I've patched him up as best I can," he said.

"Will he live?" I asked.

"How the hell do I know?" he growled. "Will any of us live, if it comes to that?" And he set a match to some dry twigs he'd gathered and nursed the little flicker of flame to life, kneeling in the snow and blowing on it gently till the branches of the jackpine steamed and finally smouldered into a crackling flame.

It was only then that I looked round to see what had happened to Paule. She had left her father and was kneeling beside Laroche in nothing but her bush shirt. She had used her parka and her sweater to cover him and keep him warm, and the sight of her there reminded me of what she had said to me when we were alone beside that campfire. She had half killed the man, yet she still loved him. Whatever he had done, she still loved him, and the knowledge brought a lump to my throat, for it was such a terrible twist of fate.

As soon as the fire was blazing, we carried Laroche

down to it and laid him on a bed of pine branches and dried moss close against the rocks so that the heat of the fire would be reflected to form a pocket of warmth. At least he wouldn't die of shock through exposure to cold. But when I said this to Darcy, he gave me a hard, calculating look. "That's a matter we've got to decide tonight," he said in an odd voice.

"How do you mean?"

He glanced round quickly to see that Paule wasn't listening. "We can't carry him back, and we've food for only one day. That's all Paule and I brought with us. If we stay here with him, we all die."

"There's the radio," I said.

"Yeah?" He gave a sceptical grunt. "It'd need a skilled operator to get that thing working. It's been out in the open for days. Even when it was under cover, Briffe only managed to get that one message through." And he added: "The chances of being able to raise anyone on that set are about as remote as the chances of a plane happening to fly over and see us here. Still . . ." He hesitated. "It's a pity Paule didn't do the job properly whilst she was about it." And with that he turned abruptly away and went over to where Paule was searching in the snow beside her father's body.

She straightened up just as he reached her, and she had a rusted tin box in her hand. "I found it," she said. "I knew it must be here, because of that bandage round my father's hand."

It was the first-aid box she'd found, and though all the bankages were gone from it and the morphia had been used, there was till some lint and gauze left and a bottle of antiseptic. With these, and strips torn from a clean undershirt, she bandaged Laroche's wounds, whilst Darcy and I brought the radio set up close to the fire. I cranked the handle of the generator whilst he kept his fingers on the leads, but there was no sign of life.

"It's the damp," I said.

"Sure it's the damp."

"It'll be all right when it's had time to dry out."

"Think so?" He stared at me. "It'll dry outside. But it's the inside we got to dry. Shut up in that tin box, the works will just steam like they were in the tropics. Course, if you happen to have a screw-driver on you so that we can open it up . . ."

"No, I haven't got a screw-driver," I said.

He laughed. "I didn't think you had." He peered morosely at the generator. "Looks to me like it needs a whole work bench full of tools, the condition it's got into; certainly we'd need a wrench for those nuts."

"Isn't that water ready yet?" Paule asked.

Darcy lifted the lid of the smoke-blackened kettle he'd filled with snow and hung over the fire. "Just coming up," he said.

"If we could find an old tin or something . . . I want to get him warm." She had got Laroche's boots off and was pulling her own down sleeping-bag up over his legs.

Darcy got to his feet. "I'll see what I can find. There'll be something around here that we can use."

I was on the point of following him, but Paule stopped me. "Help me lift him, please."

Between us we got Laroche into the sleeping-bag, and when it was done, she sat back on her haunches and stared at the white, bloodless face. "Ian—what are we to do?" She was suddenly looking at me, her small face set in a tragic mask. "I couldn't help myself," she murmured. "I didn't know what I was doing."

There was nothing I could say that would help her, and I turned away and stared into the hot heart of the fire. We had warmth, at least—so long as we had the energy to cut wood and keep the fire going. But it wouldn't last. She knew that. Gradually we'd weaken through lack of food the way her father had, and then the end would come in a blizzard of snow or in the cold of the night. I thought of Dumaine then and what he'd gone through. But he'd got out in the end, and so had Pierre Laroche. There wasn't much chance for us. "Maybe we'll get the radio working," I said.

But she didn't believe that either, and she squatted there, quite still, watching Darcy picking over the pitiful remains of her father's last camp like a tramp going over a refuse heap. "I shall stay here," she said at last in a small, tight voice. "Whatever happens, I shall stay with him."

"Even though he left your father to die?" I didn't look at her as I said that.

"Yes—even though he killed him," she breathed. "There is nothing else for me now." And after a moment she asked: "Do you think you and Ray could get back to the Tote Road—just the two of you?"

"We could try." And I knew as I said it that I'd accepted the fact that she wouldn't be coming with us.

"If you started at dawn tomorrow . . . Per'aps, if the weather is good, you will make it in less time." But she said it without conviction. She was thinking of the muskeg and the weight of the canoe which we should have to carry if we were to cross those open stretches of water. "You must help him as much as you can." Her hand touched mine. "Ray is very tired, though he tries to hide it. He is not a young man like you, Ian." And she added: "I am not thinking of myself, or of Albert. For us, this is the end. But I would like to be sure that you two will get out alive. The knowledge that you will both be safe will make it—easier for me."

"I'll do my best," I said.

She gave my hand a little squeeze. "I wish my father had known you." She smiled, a barely perceptible move-

ment of the lips that left her eyes still empty. She let go
my hand then and went to her pack and took out a small
tin of Bovril and a metal flask.

She was mixing the hot drink in her own tin mug when
Darcy returned. "This do you?" he said and placed a
rusted oil can beside her. She nodded, and then she was
bending over Laroche, lifting his head and trying to force
a little of the hot liquid between his teeth.

Darcy dropped wearily on to the ground beside me.
"He buried Baird a little way back amongst the rocks,"
he said quietly, leaning his head close to mine. "I just
seen the grave."

"Where?" I asked.

"Over there." He nodded towards the edge of the beach
where boulders were piled against the rock of the shore.
"I guess he was too weak to dig a hole, or else the ground
was frozen. He just heaped some rocks over the body and
tied two sticks together to form a cross." He hesitated, and
then he opened his hand to show a piece of stone the size
of a pigeon's egg lying in the palm. It was grey with grit,
but where he'd rubbed it clean there was a dull gold gleam
to it. "Know what that is?"

I opened my mouth to answer him, but the word
seemed to stick in my throat, for this surely was evidence
of the cause of that old tragedy. And then I was suddenly
remembering that first meeting with Laroche, when Mc-
Govern had been so taken aback by my certainty that
the plane had crashed at Lake of the Lion. "I found that
oil can on top of the grave. It had been filled with these—
like some pagan offering to the dead." Darcy's voice
trembled slightly, but whether it was anger or fear
I wasn't certain. "Feel the weight of it," he said, and
dropped it into my hand.

The cold touch of that fragment made me shiver, and
I turned without thinking to stare out across the dark
surface of the lake to the towering mass of the Lion Rock.

In my mind I saw the rusted can on the grave more vividly than if I had discovered it there for myself, and I knew then that the Indian had been right. I hated this place and should always hate it.

"I can't get him to swallow any of it," Paule said. She had laid Laroche's head back on the pillow of her sweater and was squatting there, disconsolate, with the steaming mug in her hand.

"Then drink it yourself," Darcy said harshly. And he added under his breath: "The bastard deserves to die anyway."

She heard him, and the shock of his words seemed to stun her.

He took the fragment from my hand and passed it to her. "After all the years you've spent prospecting, I guess you know more about minerals than I do," he said. "Tell me what that is."

She stared at the fragment as it lay in her hand, and then a look came into her eyes that I knew was fear. She was reacting to it the way I had. "It's gold," she said in a small, tight voice.

"Yeah, that's what I thought it was." And he told her how he had found it.

She turned her head slowly and stared towards the boulder-strewn edge of the lake. "Oh, no," she whispered. And then she was staring at us, and the fear that had suddenly taken hold of her was there in her eyes and in the trembling of the hand that held the nugget. "Oh, no," she said again, and she got slowly to her feet and went down to the water's edge, her body stooped as she searched along the frozen margin.

In a few moments she came back with four small nuggets, which she dropped into my lap. "It's true, then," she whispered. "This place is a—" Her voice died away, and she suddenly burst into tears.

"What's true?" Darcy scrambled to his feet. "What's

the matter, Paule? What's got into you?" He had his arm round her shoulders, trying to comfort her. "What is it?"

"I don't know," she sobbed. "I'm frightened."

"We're all frightened," he said soothingly. And because she was sobbing uncontrollably, he shook her quite roughly. "Pull yourself together, girl," he said gruffly. "We're in enough trouble as it is without you going crazy just because we've discovered gold." He pulled her hands away from her eyes. "Is that what's upset you—that your father found what he'd been looking for all his life, and when he'd found it, it wasn't any good to him?"

"It's not the gold," she cried desperately.

"Then what is it?"

"Nothing. Nothing." Her voice was quite wild, and she broke away from him suddenly and went stumbling blindly down towards her father's body.

"What the devil's got into her?" Darcy was staring after her.

I shook my head, for a sudden terrible thought had crossed my mind and I didn't dare put it into words. "I don't know," I muttered, and I watched her as she stood staring down at her father. She was there a long time, and then she came slowly back and sat down beside Laroche, gazing down at his ashen face, and though she didn't say a word, I could feel the turmoil of doubt in her mind.

"You all right, Paule?" Darcy was watching her anxiously.

She nodded dumbly, her face wet with tears. "If only he were conscious," she murmured at length, and her hand went up to Laroche's head, touching the place where the hair was growing up over the wound. "If he could just speak."

"It's better, perhaps, that he can't."

She turned and looked at him then. "You don't understand," she whispered.

"Don't I?" Darcy's voice was thick with the anger he was trying to hide. "This place is a gold mine, and that's explanation enough for me. Ian was right."

"Ian?"

"Yeah. He said all along Bert had gone crazy."

Her gaze went back to Laroche, and then she said to me in a voice so quiet that I barely heard her: "Do you still believe that?" And I knew she was remembering what she had said to me that night beside the campfire when it had been so still.

"Just try to forget about it," Darcy told her gently. "He did what his grandfather did—and for the same reason. You've just got to accept it, that's all there is to it."

But she shook her head. "You don't understand," she said again. And then she turned her stricken gaze on me. "Tell me the truth, Ian," she pleaded. "Tell me what happened." And when I didn't say anything, couldn't even meet the desperate pleading of her eyes, she cried: "For God's sake, I must know the truth." Her voice had risen to a note of hysteria, and Darcy gripped hold of my arm. "Better leave her alone for a while," he whispered in my ear. "She's tired and she's overwrought."

I wasn't certain whether to leave her alone or not, but she was staring down at Laroche again, and in the end I went with Darcy, for I knew there was nothing I could do to help her. "Where did he bury Baird?" I asked him.

"Over there." He nodded to a group of rocks halfway between the camp-site and the sunken aircraft. And when I started towards it, he called to me to wait. "Give me a hand and we'll take Briffe's body up there and bury it beside him."

But I was already moving down along the lake shore.

"Later," I said. I had to see that grave. I had to be certain what had happened now. But when I reached the place, it told me nothing. The grave was just a mound of rocks the length of a man, covered over with grey silt. Two jackpine branches tied with wire served as a cross. "I wonder when he died," I said as Darcy joined me.

"Does it matter?"

"I don't know," I murmured. "But Laroche was convinced he was dead when he left him. I'm quite certain of that."

"Well, he was probably killed in the crash."

But I shook my head. "No. Nobody was even injured when the plane crashed. Laroche admitted that to me." I was thinking of that oil can full of nuggets. It was Briffe who had placed that there. "I—I think we ought to have a look at the body," I said.

"Good God! Why?"

"I don't know," I murmured uncertainly. "It might tell us something." I didn't dare tell him what I expected to find, but, much as I disliked the thought of disturbing the grave, I knew suddenly that I had to see for myself how Baird had died, and I went down on my knees and began pulling the silt and boulders away with my hands.

"Goddammit!" Darcy's hand seized hold of my shoulder. "What's got into you? Can't you let the man rest in peace?"

"Uncovering him won't do him any harm now," I said, tearing myself free of his hand. "He's dead, isn't he?" I added almost savagely to cover my own nervousness, for I didn't like it any more than he did. But there was no other way I could discover what had happened, and for Paule's sake I had to discover that.

My urgency must have communicated itself to Darcy, for he didn't try to stop me after that, and in the end he got down beside me and helped to shift the pile of stones. And when we had finally uncovered the upper part of the body, we stayed for a long time on our knees without moving or saying anything, for the whole side of the man's face had been cut open.

"An axe did that," Darcy said at length, and I nodded. But though it was what I'd feared, I hadn't been prepared for such a ghastly wound. The right ear was gone completely, and the cheek had been laid open to the bone, so that the teeth showed white through the curled flesh. And yet it hadn't killed him outright, for pieces of gauze still adhered to the wound where it had been bandaged, and the face, like Briffe's, was hollowed out by privation and suffering. The beard was still black, almost luxuriant in growth, so that he looked like the wax image of some crucified apostle.

"That settles it," Darcy said thickly. "I've made up my mind. We start back tomorrow, and we leave him here." He meant Laroche, of course, but he couldn't bring himself to mention his name, and I wondered whether to tell him what was in my mind. "Well, say something, can't you?" he cried angrily. "Do you think I'm wrong to leave a man to die—a man who could do a thing like this?"

I had uncovered Baird's right hand then, the wrist all shattered and a gritty bandage covering the wound where some fingers were missing. And below the hand was the top of a canvas bag. "Paule won't go," I said, and I wrenched the bag out from under the stones that covered it. It was an ordinary canvas tool bag, and it was full of those dull grey pebbles that were so heavy and metallic to the touch. The body itself was less terrible to me then than the sight of that canvas bag, and as I stared at it, appalled, I heard Darcy, behind me, say: "How do you know she won't go?" And I knew he hadn't understood its significance.

"She told me—just now. She's staying with Laroche."

I said it impatiently, for my mind was on that bag full
of nuggets so carefully buried with the body—like a
sacrificial offering. And there was that tin can full of
them that Darcy had found on the grave. The man who
had buried Baird had given to the dead all the wealth
he'd picked up; a gesture of abnegation, a madman's
attempt to purchase absolution? "My God!" I thought
to myself. The irony of it, to want it all for himself and
then to die alone in the midst of it!

Darcy plucked at my arm. "I'll go and talk to her,"
he said.

"It won't do any good."

"No? Then I'll bring her here. You think she'll want
to stay with the man when she's seen what he's done?"
He had got to his feet.

"Wait," I said. "You can't show her this." I glanced
down at the dead man's face and then at the bloodied
hand, remembering suddenly that Briffe's hand had been
injured, too. "And if you did," I said, "she still wouldn't
change her mind." I looked up at him then. "Laroche
didn't do this," I said.

"What do you mean?"

"It was Briffe who went berserk."

"Briffe?" He stared at me as though I'd gone crazy.

I nodded, for now that I'd said it, I knew it was true;
I could see how it all fitted in—the wound in Laroche's
head, his decision to trek out on his own. And no wonder
he'd been convinced that Baird was dead. How could
he have expected any man to live with his head cut open
like that? And then his determination that nobody should
find the place, that the search should be abandoned and
Briffe given up for dead. He'd been prepared to go to
almost any lengths to save Paule from the truth.

But even when I'd explained all this to Darcy, he
didn't seem to grasp it. "I just can't believe it," he muttered.

"Then what about this?" I said and thrust the canvas bag at him. "And the can full of them you found on the grave? It was Briffe who buried Baird, not Laroche." And I added: "You know the sort of man he was—you said it to Paule just now. He'd spent all his life prospecting, and this was one of the places he'd always wanted to find. She told me so herself the other night. Well," I said, "he found it." And in my mind I could picture the scene as it must have been when the three of them stood on the lake shore here and Briffe held that first nugget of gold in his hand.

"I still can't believe it—her own father."

"If we ever get out alive," I said, remembering now that first day in Labrador, "you go and talk to McGovern. I think he knows what really happened. I think Laroche told him."

He was silent a long time then. Finally, he said: "Well, see you don't let Paule have any idea what's in your mind. It'd just about kill her." And when I didn't answer, he seized my elbow in an urgent grip. "Do you hear me, Ian? You may be right. You may not. But Laroche is going to die here anyway. She mustn't know."

"She knows already," I told him. "She knew the instant you handed her the nugget."

He looked at me a moment, and then he nodded. "Yeah, I guess so," he murmured unhappily, and he crossed himself. "It's a terrible thing," he breathed. And as I started to cover Baird's body again, he said: "We'll have to bury him—up here beside Baird." And then he added, with sudden decision: "But we leave in the morning. You understand? Whatever Paule decides, we leave in the morning. We got to."

III

That Paule now knew the truth

was obvious as soon as Darcy told her we would be leaving in the morning. "We'll make him as comfortable as possible," he said, nodding to Laroche, "and then the three of us, travelling light—"

But she didn't let him finish. "Do you think I will leave Albert to die here alone?" she cried, staring at him, white-faced and determined. "I couldn't. I couldn't possibly—not now." And then she added softly: "I love him, Ray. I love him, and I shall always love him, and I shan't leave him. So don't ask me again—please." She was past tears, past any show of emotion. She stated it flatly, and I saw that even Darcy accepted her decision as irrevocable. "You and Ian—you leave in the morning. Try to get through. I will keep the fire going as long as I can. If you have good luck, then per'aps you get a plane out to us in time."

Darcy shook his head slowly. "There's ice forming on the lake already. In a few days it'll be impossible for a floatplane to land here. And it'll be too thin for a ski landing."

"Then per'aps you get the helicopter."

"Yeah, maybe the helicopter could make it, though there's not much room." He eyed the narrow beach doubtfully. And then he said: "We're just going to bury your father, Paule. Maybe you'd like to be there."

She didn't say anything for a moment, and then her hand went slowly up to the little gold chain at her neck. "No," she said in a small, dry voice. "Bury him, please. And I will say a prayer for him here—with Albert." There was a little crucifix attached to the chain, and she pulled it out of her shirt and held it, tight-clutched, in her hand.

Darcy hesitated. But when he saw she intended to stay there, he put more wood on the fire and then said to me: "Okay, let's get it over with, and then we'll have some food and decide what we're going to do." I followed him back to the place where we'd left Briffe's body, and as he stood over it, staring down at the emaciated face, he said: "I guess you're right. She knows."

He didn't say anything more, and we carried the body along the shore and laid it out beside Baird's grave. Then we covered it with stones and the black silt from the beach. It was a slow business, for we'd no tools but our hands. And when we'd finished, Darcy got his axe and cut two branches and fixed them over the grave in the form of a cross. "May God be merciful to you, and may you rest in peace." He crossed himself, standing at the foot of the grave, and I murmured "Amen."

"Well, that's that, I guess," he said, and turned abruptly away. "How much food you and Bert got?"

"I don't think we've any."

"Hmm. We got a little coffee, some chocolate and raisins, a few biscuits, and some cheese. Hungry?"

"Yes," I said.

He nodded. "So'm I—Goddamned famished. But we sip a little coffee, and that's all. The rest we leave for Paule. Agreed?"

I nodded, though my mouth was running at the thought of food and there was a dull ache in my belly. "You've decided to leave them here, then?"

"What the hell else can I do?" he demanded angrily.

"She won't leave, I know that now. And another thing," he added. "If we do manage to get out, we don't tell anybody what we know. They were dead, just like Bert said. Okay?" He had stopped and was looking at me, waiting for my answer.

"Yes," I said.

"Good." He patted my arm. "It's a hard thing for you to have to do, considering what it was that brought you out here. But I think you owe it to Bert. He risked a lot to keep that thing a secret—and he'll be dead before we've any chance of getting him out."

When we got back to the fire, we found Paule lying beside Laroche, her head buried in her arms, sobbing convulsively. Darcy stood for a moment, looking down at her. "Poor kid!" he murmured. But he didn't go to her. Instead, he got the empty kettle and started down to the lake to fill it. "Leave her," he said as he passed me. "Just leave her, boy. She'll be better for a good cry." And to my astonishment I saw there were tears running down his cheeks.

Whilst he was seeing to the coffee, I went down to where the remains of Briffe's tent lay and searched about in the snow for the tools that must have been in that empty tool bag. There is no point in giving a list of the things I found there; there were his personal belongings, and Baird's, too—clothes, instruments, some empty tins that had contained emergency rations, an alarm clock, of all things. They had salvaged what they could from the plane. Lying there, scattered about in the snow, rusted and wet and gritty to the touch, it was a pitifully inadequate assortment with which to stand the siege of approaching winter in this bleak spot. I found the axe, too. It lay bedded in the ice at the water's edge, its blade all pitted with rust, but whether he'd just dropped it there or whether he'd tried to fling it into the lake I didn't know.

The tools were scattered about under the snow near where we had found him, and as I retrieved them, I kept on finding nuggets. They were obviously nuggets he'd collected, for there was an empty flour bag that still contained a few and a tin mug full of them. The sight of them sickened me. I could picture him searching frenziedly along the lake edge, with Baird lying in a pool of blood and Laroche fled into the timber on the start of his long trek out, and I couldn't help wondering how he'd felt when the gold lust had left him and sanity had returned. He'd thrown the little useless hoards away in disgust; that much was obvious, for they were strewn all about the camp-site. But how had he felt? Had he thought at all about the future and what his daughter's reaction would be, as he crouched over the set, hour after hour, trying to make contact with the outside world?

I collected the tools and went slowly back with them to the fire. By then Darcy had made the coffee, and we drank it black and scalding hot, and it put new life into us, so that even Paule seemed almost herself again, though she didn't talk and her face still looked unnaturally pale. She ate what Darcy put before her, but automatically, as though the function of eating were something divorced from reality, so that I was surprised when she said: "Aren't you hungry? You're not eating."

Darcy shook his head, avoiding her eyes. "We got work to do," he said awkwardly, and he gulped down the rest of his coffee and got to his feet, glancing at his watch. "There's about two hours of daylight left. We'll leave you with as much wood as we can cut in that time." He picked up his axe and, with a nod to me, started up the rocks into the timber.

I hesitated. I wanted to get to work on the generator. But I couldn't help remembering that message from Briffe. *No fire. Situation desperate.* The radio probably wouldn't work, anyway. Wood seemed more important, and I retrieved Laroche's axe and followed Darcy up into the timber.

It was desperately hard work. We were tired before we started—tired and hungry. Paule helped us for a time, dragging the branches down to the edge of the timber and tipping them over the rocks. But then Laroche cried out, and after that she stayed with him, refilling the oil can with hot water to keep him warm and trying to get him to swallow hot Bovril and brandy.

He hadn't regained consciousness. He was still in a coma, but delirious now, and every time I approached the fire I could hear him babbling.

Sometimes he'd cry out: "Paule! Paule!" as though he were trying to make her listen. At those times he was back at the point where she'd struck at him with the knife. At other times he'd be talking to Briffe or wandering on an endless trek through Labrador. It was just an incoherent jumble of words, with now and then a name cried out—Paule's or Briffe's, my own once—and then as often as not he'd struggle in a feeble attempt to take the action dictated by the wanderings of his mind. And the horrible thing was that, though none of it made sense in a literal way, it was impossible, knowing what we did, not to understand that his mind was trying to unburden itself of a secret too long bottled up.

And Paule sat there with his head on her lap, stroking his brow and murmuring to him as she tried to soothe him, her face all the time set in a frozen mask of wretchedness and despair.

The light went early, fading into a sleet storm that chilled us and covered everything with a fresh, powdery white dust. We went back to the fire then, and when I had recovered a little and my body was no longer ice cold with the sweat of exhaustion, I tried the generator again. But though the casing was hot to the touch, it was still damp inside. At any rate, cranking the handle produced no sign of life. By the light of the fire and to the intermittent babblings of Laroche's delirium, I set to work to dismantle the thing.

It took me more than an hour, for the nuts were all seized solid with rust. But in the end I got the casing off and with a handkerchief wiped the brushes clean. Fortunately, the sleet had passed, and after leaving the generator to toast beside the fire for a time and checking the leads and scratching at the terminals with the blade of a knife, I reassembled it. And then, with Darcy cranking the handle, I held the two points close together. When they were almost touching, a small spark flickered into being. It wasn't much of a spark, but it was there, nevertheless, and when I held the two leads gripped in my hand, the shock was sufficient to make me jump.

"Think it's enough to work the set?" Darcy asked, after he'd held the leads whilst I cranked.

"God knows," I said. It wouldn't be much of a signal. "Anyway, the set's probably out of action by now." It was over two weeks since Briffe had made that transmission.

However, we coupled it up, re-rigged the aerial, and after cleaning the rust from the terminal, I slipped the headphones on, switched the set to receive, and, with Darcy cranking, went slowly round the dial. But I could hear nothing, not even a crackle or the slightest murmur of any static. I checked carefully over the set, trying to remember everything that fool of an operator at Camp 263 had told me. As far as I could see, I'd done everything I should. But when we tried again, there was still nothing.

"It could be the jack of the earphones," Darcy suggested. "Suppose we give it a clean."

But I shook my head. "We could clean the jack, but we'd never clean the socket. Once we disturb the phone-jack, we're done." I switched over to send then. It was

long past the time I'd agreed on with Perkins, but there
was no harm in trying. The transmission might work,
even if the reception didn't. "Crank her up again," I
said. And then I put the mouthpiece to my lips. "CQ—
CQ—CQ," I called, with the tuning dial set at the net
frequency. "This is Ferguson calling from Lake of the
Lion. Any 75-metre phone station. Come in, please. Come
in. Over." I flicked the switch to receive. But there wasn't
a sound.

I tried again and went on trying. And when Darcy
was tired of cranking, he tried whilst I operated the
generator. But we got no response, and when we were
both exhausted we gave it up. "I told you the Goddammed
thing wouldn't work," Darcy said.

"Okay," I said wearily. "If you knew, why did you
bother to go on cranking?" I was tired and angry.

"You'd got the generator going. I thought you might
get the set going, too."

"Well, I haven't." And because I thought this was
probably our only hope, I added: "We'll try again in
the morning."

"There'll be no time in the morning. We're leaving
at first light."

"You can leave if you want to," I said. "I'm not going
till after seven thirty."

"That'll lose us an hour and a half, and we can't
afford—"

"I tell you, I'm not leaving until seven thirty," I said
obstinately. "I told Perkins seven to seven thirty. He'll
be listening in for us then. Ledder, too, probably."

"Oh, for God's sake!" he said angrily. "You know there
isn't a hope in hell of your raising them. The set's out
of action, and that's all there is to it. Apparently Briffe
only managed to make it work once."

"Briffe started with a set that was waterlogged. He had
to crank the thing himself, and he was exhausted and his

hand was injured. If he could get it to work, then so can we."

"I think Ian is right," Paule said suddenly. "Per'aps my father only get the transmission side of it to work. But I think you should try, even if it means delaying your departure."

"That hour and a half could make all the difference," Darcy growled. And then he was looking at me, and the firelight on his glasses gave his eyes a baleful look. "Try if you must. I don't know anything about radio, but I'd say the set was useless after being out in the weather all this time."

So it was agreed, and we heaped more wood on the fire and went to sleep. And every few hours during the night one of us would get up and replenish the fire, so that the hours of sleep alternated between intense heat and intense cold, and all through that endless night I seemed to hear Laroche's voice as in a nightmare.

At last daylight crept back into the sombre cleft of the lake. The Lion Rock lifted its black profile from the mist that lay like a white smoke over the water, and I went stiffly back to the radio set, checking and rechecking it in the forlorn hope that, by fussing over it, I could make the damned thing work.

We had our coffee, and just before seven o'clock I squatted down in front of that malignant, rusted box, put the earphones on, and switched the set to send. And as Darcy cranked I began my fruitless monologue: "CQ— CQ—CQ. Ferguson calling Perkins. Calling Ledder. Camp one-three-four—can you hear me? Goose Bay? Any seventy-five-metre phone station. Come in, please. Anybody, come in. Over." Sometimes I called "Mayday," which I knew to be a distress call. Sometimes just "Perkins" or "Camp one-three-four." But whenever I said "Over" and switched across to receive, there was absolute silence. Nothing. An infinity of nothing, so that I knew the thread was broken, the contact nonexistent. And yet I kept on trying. And when Darcy was tired, I handed over to him and he tried with the same result. And at seven twenty-five, in desperation, I began describing our position—the river, the falls, the bearing and distance from the place where we'd crossed.

And then it was seven thirty, and I put the mouthpiece back in its place. "Well, we tried, anyway," I said. Darcy nodded. He made no comment, but began quietly collecting his things together. Paule had disappeared into the timber. Laroche was asleep, no longer delirious.

"What chance do you think we've got?" I said.

"Of getting back?" Darcy asked.

"Of getting back in time," I said.

He hesitated, staring down at Laroche. "We're in God's hands," he muttered. "But he'll be dead, for sure." And he turned to me and said abruptly: "You afraid of death?"

"I don't know," I said.

He nodded. "No, I guess none of us knows that till we're faced with it. I only faced it once before, like this. I was scared, all right, then. Maybe not this time. I'm getting old." He reached down for his pack, which was barely half full. "All set?" And then he looked up as Paule came hurrying back to us. Her face had a white, frozen look of horror on it, and her eyes were wide as though she'd seen a ghost. "What is it?" Darcy asked.

"Up there by that outcrop." She pointed a trembling hand towards a huddle of rocks that stood amongst the trees. And she sat down suddenly as though her knees had given way beneath her. "Where did you bury him?" she asked.

"I told you, down there where we found Baird's grave," Darcy said.

"Of course. It was silly of me, but I thought for a moment—" A shudder ran through her. And then she was staring at me with her wide eyes, and almost involuntarily, as though she had willed it, I started up over the rocks.

I don't think I was surprised at what I found under that rock outcrop. I think I had known the instant she looked at me that I was being sent to pay my respects to the mortal remains of my grandfather. He lay close under the largest of the rocks, in a sort of gulley—a skeleton, nothing more. No vestige of clothing remained; just a pile of bones, grey with age and weather. Only the cage of the ribs was still intact. The head lay beside it, quite detached from it, smiling a bare-boned, tooth-filled smile at the Labrador sky, and the bone of the forehead was all shattered and broken open as Laroche had said. I turned it over, and there at the base of the skull was the neat-drilled hole where the bullet had entered, and I thought of the pistol that hung in my father's room. Had my grandmother found that pistol at one of Pierre Laroche's camp-sites? Was it the very pistol that had fired the bullet into this poor, bare skull? I stooped and stared in fascination, and then I heard Darcy behind me.

"Funny thing," he murmured, peering down at it over my shoulder, "I'd almost forgotten about that earlier expedition."

"I suppose it is my grandfather?" I said.

"Well, it isn't an Indian, that's for sure. You only got to look at the shape of the skull. No," he added, "it's James Finlay Ferguson, all right, and there's not much doubt what happened."

"No." I was thinking of the man we'd buried the previous day, and I looked at Darcy and then past him, down to the sombre lake and the black rock standing crouched in the middle of it. "No wonder the Indian was scared of the place."

He nodded. "It's a bad place, all right. And this isn't going to make it any easier for Paule."

"Well, we can cover it up," I said. "And she needn't

come up here."

"Sure. But how would you like to be left here alone with the body of the man you love dead by your own hand and those two graves by the shore there and this lying up here? Nothing but tragedy in this place. And she's part Indian, remember."

"Laroche may not die," I murmured. But I wasn't any happier about it than he was.

"He may not die today or tomorrow. But he'll be dead before we get out, and she'll be alone then. There won't be much incentive for her to go on living after that." And then he said almost angrily: "Well, come on, we got to get going."

We covered the bones with handfuls of wet earth and then went back down to the fire. "We're going now, Paule," Darcy said.

She was crouched over Laroche, and she didn't look up. "He's conscious now," she said gently. And when I went nearer, I saw that his eyes were open. A flicker of recognition showed in them as I came into his line of vision, and his throat moved convulsively, as though he were trying to say something, but no words came.

"Don't try to talk," she whispered urgently. "You must save your strength."

And then she got suddenly to her feet and stood facing us. "You've—covered it up?"

Darcy nodded. "Yeah. There's nothing for you to see there now."

She was staring at me. "It must be terrible for you—to have discovered what happened. For both of us," she murmured. And then, pulling herself together, her voice suddenly clear and practical: "You'll go fast, won't you—as fast as you can." It wasn't a question, but a statement. And when Darcy nodded, too affected to speak, she went to him and gripped hold of his hand. "God bless you,

Ray," she said. "I'll pray that you get through in time."

"We'll do our best, Paule. You know that."

"Yes. I know that." She stared at him a moment, and I knew what was in her mind; she was thinking she'd never see him again. And then she leaned suddenly forward and kissed him. "God help us!" she whispered.

"He will," he assured her.

She turned to me then and held out her hand. And when I gripped it, I couldn't help myself—I said: "I'm sorry, Paule. It would have been better for you if I'd never come to Canada."

But she shook her head. "It wasn't your fault," she said softly. "We both wanted the same thing—the truth; and that cannot be hidden for ever." She kissed me then. "Good-bye, Ian. I'm glad I met you." And then she turned back to Laroche, who all the time had been staring at us with his eyes wide open. And as we picked up our things and turned to go, he struggled up on to one elbow. "Good luck!" I didn't hear the words, but only read them through the movement of his lips. And then he fell back and Paule was bending over him.

"Okay," Darcy said thickly. "Let's get going."

We left them then, going straight along the narrow beach, past the two graves and the half-submerged aircraft, and up through the timber, the way we'd come. The knife with which Paule had attacked Laroche still lay where she'd thrown it, and I picked it up and slipped it into my pack. Why, I don't know, unless it was that I didn't want her to find it lying there to remind her of what had happened.

Neither of us looked back, and in a little while we'd climbed the slope above the lake and the wretched place was gone, hidden from view by the timber. It was a bright, clear day, but by the time we'd crossed the river at the lake expansion the wind had risen and was blowing half a gale, with ragged wisps of cloud tearing across the cold blue of the sky.

We were travelling light, and we didn't spare ourselves, for our need of food was urgent.

An hour before nightfall we were back at the lake where Laroche and I had left them, and there was the canoe and the tent and my pack and all the things they'd abandoned to make that final dash to Lake of the Lion. It all looked just as I had left it, except that everything was covered with snow and there were only the two of us now.

Darcy collapsed as soon as we reached the camp. He had let me set the pace, and it had been too much for him. And as I cut the wood and got the fire going, I wondered how we'd make out from there on, with the canoe to carry, as well as the food and the tent and all our gear. But he revived as soon as he'd got some hot coffee inside him, and by the time he'd fed, he seemed as full of life as ever, even managing to crack a few jokes.

As soon as we had fed, we turned in. It was the last night of any comfort, for in the morning we decided to abandon the tent—in fact, everything except food to last the two of us three days, one cooking utensil, our down sleeping-bags, and a change of socks and underwear. We ate a huge breakfast, shovelling all the food we could into ourselves, and then we started up through the jackpine with the canoe and our packs on our shoulders.

It took us six hours to get clear of the timber and back down into the open country of gravel and water, and by then Darcy was stumbling with exhaustion. But he refused to stop, and we went on until we reached the first of the lakes and could launch the canoe. His face was the colour of putty, and his breath wheezed in his throat. And still we went on without a pause, heading well to the south of west in the hope of avoiding the worst of the muskeg. The wind dropped, and it began to snow. Night caught us still in the open, and we lay in our sleeping-bags on a gravel ridge with the canoe on top of us.

It was a grey-white world in the morning—grey skies, grey water, white ridges. And on the lake ahead of us a dozen or more geese sat and called to each other in a little patch of open water they'd made in the new-formed ice. But we'd left the gun behind. We'd nothing but the fishing-rod, and we'd no time to fish.

There is no point in my describing that terrible journey in detail. I doubt, in any case, whether I could, for as we struggled on, my mind as well as my body became frozen into numbness, dazed with exhaustion. How Darcy kept going, I don't know. It was sheer will power, for his body gave out before mine did, and as my own energy diminished, my admiration for him increased. He never complained, never gave up hope. He just kept going doggedly on to the limit of endurance and beyond. It was this more than anything else that enabled me to keep going, for the cold was frightful and we ran out of food long before we reached the Tote Road and the line of the grade.

We were cursed with bad luck. The weather, for one thing. The freeze-up caught us, and ice formed so thick that in the end we couldn't use the canoe. The compass, too, led us astray. The reason was probably a deposit of iron ore. At any rate, the result was that we didn't go far enough south and got into a worse area of muskeg than the one we'd come through on the way in. We were caught in it all one night, and when we finally made it to open water, still carrying the canoe, we found the ice too thick to paddle across and too thin to bear our weight.

A week later and we'd have been able to walk across the top of the muskeg and over all the lakes. As it was, we just had to abandon the canoe and struggle round the lakes on foot. And all the time we were thinking of Paule back there at Lake of the Lion. Twice we thought we heard aircraft away to the south, flying low. On the first occasion we were quite convinced of it. It was on the second day—the only still day we had—and we were sure they must be searching for us. But we were in thick timber at the time, and anyway the sound was a long way off. "I guess it's just one of the airlift boys got a little off course," Darcy said when the sound had dwindled without coming near us. The second time was several days later. I can't remember which day. I'd lost count by then. It sounded like a helicopter, but we couldn't be sure. We were so dazed with cold and exhaustion and lack of food that we couldn't trust ourselves not to have imagined it.

We were eight days on that journey, and the last two days I doubt whether we made more than half a dozen miles. We were both suffering from frostbite then, and fifty yards or so was all we could do without pausing to recover our strength. By then we hadn't eaten anything for three days, and our feet were so frozen and painful that we had difficulty in moving at all.

We reached the Tote Road on the evening of the eighth day only to find it choked with drifts. Nothing had been down it for several days, so that we were forced to spend another night in the open. And in the morning Darcy couldn't go on. He'd come to the end of his strength, and he lay there, staring at me out of his red-rimmed eyes, his cracked and blackened lips drawn back from the teeth and his beard all frozen stiff with ice. He looked much like Briffe had looked when we'd found him. "Can you make it?" he asked, and the words came out through his teeth without any movement of the lips.

I didn't answer, because to answer required an effort, and anyway I didn't know whether I could. All I wanted to do was to go on lying there in the snow beside him, to abandon myself to the dream world that my mind was already groping towards—a lotus-land of perpetual sun and hot food where the warm planks of an imaginary boat bore me gently towards a horizon of infinite ease, without effort, without discomfort. "You've got to make it," he croaked at me urgently, and I knew it was Paule he was thinking of, not himself, and I crawled slowly to my feet.

To make a fire for him would have taken too much energy. "Good-bye!" I stood for a moment, looking down at him, and I remember thinking vaguely that he didn't look like a man any more; just a bundle of old clothes lying in the snow at my feet. "I'll make it, all right," I said.

He nodded, as much as to say "Of course, you will," and then his eyes closed. I left him then and plunged into the timber beyond the Tote Road. It was still snowing. It had snowed on and off for three days now, and even under the cover of the jackpine, snow lay in drifts and hummocks up to three feet deep. It looked pretty as a picture. It was virgin white and as soft and snug as a down bed. It was also as cold as hell, and at every step it dragged at my legs, my thighs, my whole body, until I lay like one drowned in a white sea, unable to go a step farther.

It was then I heard voices. I shouted and they stopped. But then they started again, and I knew it wasn't a dream. I was within earshot of the grade, and I screamed at them. And once I'd started, I couldn't stop, but went on screaming to them for help, even when they'd reached me; which was perhaps just as well, for the sound that issued from my lips was no louder than the squeal of a jack rabbit caught in a trap.

They were two engineers, checking the levels they'd run through a rock outcrop due for blasting the next day. They had a tent half a mile farther up the grade, and between them they got me to it, handed me over to the bull cook, and went straight off again to get Darcy.

My memory of what happened after that is fragmentary and confused. I was in some sort of bed, and there was an oil heater roaring, and faces stared down at me. I kept on asking for Lands, but none of them seemed to have heard of him. It was like a nightmare, for I didn't know who else to ask for, and I kept on drifting off into unconsciousness. And then gradually the pain of my frozen limbs blotted out everything else, and the next thing I remember, they'd brought Darcy in.

He was still alive, but that was about all. They thought there was about a fifty-fifty chance of him pulling through. By then, of course, the two engineers had guessed who we were, and when I asked for Lands again, they told me he was at Camp 290. "He's been there all week, organizing the search for you," one of them said. I was given another hot drink then, and they told me not to worry. We'd struck the grade way to the north of our starting-point, halfway between the trestle and Camp 290. The man who told me this said he was leaving right away for 290 on snowshoes. He reckoned with luck he'd get through by nightfall.

I tried to tell him how they could find Lake of the Lion, but they'd put something in the drink to make me sleep, and before I was halfway through explaining it to them I had drifted back into unconsciousness. And when I woke again to the throb of intense pain in my hands and legs, it was dark. But the entrance of the tent had been pulled back, and through it I saw lights and men moving. There was the throb of an engine, and a tracked vehicle slid into view, backing up close to the tent.

"They're in pretty bad shape, I'm afraid," a voice said. A pressure lamp appeared at the entrance, the hissing white light momentarily blinding me, and another voice said harshly: "What do you expect, after a couple of weeks out in the bush? It ain't exactly picnic weather." That voice, so like a nutmeg-grater, took me right back to the day I'd first arrived in Seven Islands. "Okay," the voice added. "The sooner we get 'em loaded on to the snowmobile, the sooner they'll be in hospital."

The light bobbed closer until its hissing glare was right over me. "Well, young feller—awake, are you?" I could see them then, just their faces picked out by the light—McGovern and Bill Lands, and the man holding the pressure lamp was the engineer who'd left for 290 on snowshoes. "We got an aircraft standing by for you," McGovern said. "Reckon you can stick a ride in a snowmobile, or do you want a shot of something to put you out?"

"I don't want anything," I said angrily. "I just want to talk to Lands." And when he came to the side of the bed, I said: "Did you get my message—about Paule and Laroche?"

"Sure," he said. "But you don't have to worry—"

"Get me some paper," I said. "I'll try and draw you a map."

"Take it easy," he said. "There's nothing to worry about. They're going to be all right." He said it as though he were talking to a child, and it made me angry, for I knew every moment was precious. "You don't understand," I cried, forcing myself up in the bed. "Laroche was injured. He's probably dead by now, and Paule's been there—"

But he gripped hold of my shoulders. "I'm trying to tell you," he said, holding me down in the bed. "It's all right. We got them both out the end of last week."

I stared up at him, barely able to grasp what he'd said. "You got them out?"

"Yeah. Four days ago. You don't believe me, eh?" He laughed and patted my shoulder. "Well, it's true, so you can just relax. They're both safe down at Seven Islands, and I got a report today to say that Bert's going to be all right."

"Then the transmitter was okay? They got my mes-

sage?" I was thinking we could have saved ourselves the
journey. If we'd stayed with Paule . . .

"What message?" Lands asked.

"The morning we left. I was sending for the full half-
hour, from seven until—"

"Well, nobody heard you."

"Then how did you manage to find them?" I was suddenly suspicious, afraid he was trying to make our failure
easier to bear.

I think he realized this, for he told it to me in some
detail. "The first day conditions permitted, Mac here had
his Beaver floatplane fly in. But there was ice on the
lake, and though the pilot was able to drop supplies, he
couldn't land. Then, two days later, though the conditions were bad, Len took a chance on it and flew Mac in
in the helicopter. He got Laroche out that trip, and then
flew right back in again and got Paule and Mac out. After
that the weather closed in and we couldn't fly. Len and
the Beaver pilot have been standing by, ready to fly a
search for you the moment there was a let-up."

So Paule and Laroche were safe. It seemed incredible.
I half closed my eyes against the glare of the pressure
lamp, and clear in my mind was the picture of the lake
and Paule crouched there beside Laroche. We'd been so
certain he'd die. And Paule—after all that lapse of time
we'd come to accept the fact that if we did make it we'd
be too late to save her. Neither I nor Darcy had ever mentioned it, but I knew it was what we'd come to believe.

"But how?" I said again. "How did you manage to locate the lake?"

"It was Mac," Lands answered. "He knew where it was.
He was down in Montreal—"

"Just a minute, Bill." The harsh voice moved nearer.
"Would you take the others outside a moment? There's
something I've got to say to this young man whilst he's
still conscious." I saw his face clearly then—the lined,

hard-bitten features framed in the white hair. The other faces had receded. The tent flap dropped across the entrance. "First," he said, bending down and lowering his voice, "I owe you an apology. And there's not many guys I've said that to. Tell me, did you guess that I knew about Lake of the Lion when we had that little talk down at Seven Islands?"

I nodded, wondering what was coming.

"Yeah, I thought so." He paused as though to collect his thoughts. "I gather from Paule Briffe you know the truth now of what happened out there after the crash. That correct?"

"Yes," I said.

"Okay. Well, this is what I want to tell you. This expedition of yours—it's news. You're headed for hospital, but as soon as the docs give the okay, there'll be a score of newspapermen asking you for your version. You say your father was right and that Briffe made that transmission, you tell them the truth of what happened and you'll ruin two lives. That girl's had about all she can take right now. As for Bert—well, he came to me as soon as he got out and told me the whole thing. In that he acted right. I was his boss. He was employed by me. And because of that he was prepared to abide by my decision. He told me what had happened and what he'd done and why. He was thinking of Paule mainly, but the fact is that if we'd flown back in and found Briffe alive, we were certain he'd have to stand trial for murder. In the circumstances, it seemed to me Bert had acted for the best." He hesitated. "It was rough justice. But it was justice as we saw it. You must remember that Bert was convinced that he'd left Baird dead, killed by that blow from Briffe's axe." And then, after a moment, he added: "I guess you can understand now how we felt when you arrived at Seven Islands!"

"What do you want me to do?" I asked.

"Keep your mouth shut. Leave the world thinking
Briffe and Baird were both dead when Bert left them at
the lakeside. Okay? In return, I'm gonna call that concession the Ferguson Concession and cut you in for a
share of whatever we get out."

I stared at him, remembering that he, too, was an old-
time prospector, like Briffe—like my grandfather. "I don't
need to be bribed," I said hotly.

"No," he said. "No, I guess you don't. But if you're
gonna save those two from a lot more misery, then you're
gonna have to deny your own father. You're gonna have
to say there never was a transmission. And if you do that,
it's only fair that your grandfather's original discovery
should at least be recognized. As for the share of what
we get out, that's your right—a legacy, if you like, from
old James Ferguson. Well?" he added. "What do you
say?"

And when I agreed, too tired to insist that I didn't
want anything more to do with the place, his face broke
into that sudden, transforming smile, and he patted my
arm. "That's swell," he said. And he added: "You don't
have to worry about the transmitter. Neither of the pilots
saw it. It was covered in snow. And whilst I was there I
threw the darn thing into the lake." He turned towards
the entrance of the tent. "Bill!" he shouted. And when
Lands lifted the flap, he said: "Time we got going."

"He's agreed, then?" Lands asked.

"Sure he's agreed. What did you expect?"

I saw the relief on Lands's face as he bent over me in
the circle of light, but all he said was: "Okay, we'll get
you to the airstrip now."

And so, with Darcy unconscious beside me, I started on
the journey back to civilization. I had been only eighteen
days in Labrador—a very short time compared with the
weeks my grandfather had spent in the country. And yet
I, too, had got to Lake of the Lion, and though I hadn't

lost my life, I had come very near to it, had been involved in both tragedies—the past and the present—and had suffered as much hardship as most men who have trekked into the heart of that inhospitable land. And if this account of my journey has been too much taken up with the conditions of travel, I can only plead that it is not my fault, but the fault of Labrador.

Part Four

Endpiece

It is five years now

since I made my journey into Labrador, and this account has been written largely from notes made whilst still in hospital at Seven Islands. These notes were not intended for publication. They were a purely personal record, written in the form of a diary, and were prompted by reading the meticulous day-by-day entries made by my grandmother, her diary having reached me the day after I entered hospital.

However, circumstances alter.

From the moment Laroche was allowed to receive visitors, he was plagued by reporters, and this continued through his convalescence and even after he and Paule were married. And when Ferguson Concessions Ltd. was registered as a private company and the newspapers began running garbled versions of the old Ferguson Expedition, the Laroches could stand it no longer and emigrated, at the same time changing their name.

By then Darcy and I had already made our escape. Darcy had returned to Labrador, minus most of his toes and walking with the aid of two sticks. But, as he said, "A few toes won't make any difference to the way the fish rise; and I can still paint." An indomitable figure. I left him at Seven Islands, for I was bound for South Africa to work for a Canadian engineering company sub-contracting on the construction of a dam.

With the departure of the four people chiefly concerned, interest in the story subsided. But I suppose it was inevitable that sooner or later some enterprising journalist should embark on a full-scale investigation and should arrive at the same conclusion, the same suspicions that had clouded my own judgement of Laroche.

There had been a good deal of talk, of course. But it was a chance meeting in a bar with Perkins that sent this man hot-foot into Labrador. He was the only journalist to visit Lake of the Lion, and he arrived just as the Ferguson Concessions company was dismantling its equipment, having dredged till it became uneconomic and having failed to find the source of gold. Nobody cared then that a stranger was wandering around the concession. He uncovered my grandfather's remains and then dug up the bodies of Briffe and Baird, which McGovern had had properly buried. After that he tracked down and interviewed everybody he could find who had been in any way connected with the affair. He even got hold of the nurses who had attended Laroche and had them describe the nature of his injuries.

The resulting article, which appeared in a Canadian magazine, whilst carefully avoiding any direct accusation, was written from the standpoint of history repeating itself. "Like grandfather, like grandson," was the corny phrase the writer used, and he pointed out that Paule and Bert Laroche had both had shares in Ferguson Concessions. The implication was obvious, an implication that was far worse than anything I had ever thought Laroche guilty of, and it involved them both.

The article was sent to me by Laroche, and in his covering letter he said they had no desire to take legal action, but at the same time they had decided it would be better if the truth were known. He knew I had written what amounted to a journal of my three weeks in Labrador, for I had shared his room in hospital, and now he wanted me to send it to a Canadian newspaper for publication. "It is better that it should come from you," he said at the end of his letter, "than from any of those directly involved —least of all myself. You were throughout the inquiring stranger seeking after the truth."

This I have tried to bear constantly in mind through the long months of writing. And I hope that in the result I have done justice to two people for whom I have a great admiration and whose lives have been bedevilled by a tragedy that was not of their making. And in conclusion I feel I cannot do better than quote the final passage of the diary of that extraordinary woman, Alexandra Ferguson:

And so, with God's help and the courage of the men I took with me, I have returned safe out of Labrador, having been in that forsaken country one hundred and four days. I left my small son and my home in Scotland to search for the truth of my dear husband's death, and now in this I have failed. I shall not go into that land again, but will give this record to my son on the day he comes of age, and may the good Lord guide him to that lake and to the truth, whatever that may be.

THE
DOOMED
OASIS

A Novel of Arabia

Cold voices whisper and say—
"He is crazed with the spell of far Arabia,
They have stolen his wits away."

Walter de la Mare

TO

The Royal Air Force and the Officers
of the Trucial Oman Scouts

With my admiration for the work
they do in circumstances of difficulty,
often of great hardship; and with
my appreciation of their cooperation,
without which this book could not have been written

I would like to express my appreciation of the help I have received from Neil Innes during the actual writing of The Doomed Oasis. *He was Minister of External Affairs to the Sultan of Muscat at the time I was journeying in Arabia; not only did he check the final typescript for me, but at the various stages of the writing I benefited greatly from his knowledge. I should perhaps make it clear, however, that I have ignored his advice on the spelling of two Arab names, in particular believing that my own spelling of Makhmud would be more helpful in conveying the sound of that name than the correct Mahmud. Both the sheikhdom of Saraifa and the emirate of Hadd are, of course, entirely imaginary Arab states.*

Part One

The Court
of First Instance

I

Call Aubrey George Grant!

Aubrey George Grant!

The moment had come. My mouth felt suddenly dry. The Court was waiting and I knew the ordeal ahead of me was a long one. And at the back of my mind was the knowledge that in telling the truth, the whole truth, I might convict an innocent man. I felt the touch of her hand on mine, the quick pressure of her fingers, and I rose to my feet, the sweat sticking the shirt to my back as I followed the attendant. The doors of the courtroom stood open. I checked, a moment's hesitation in the entrance; the place was packed, the atmosphere tense with expectancy.

Quickly I walked down through the Court, the setting familiar to me, a part of my working life; only my role had changed. It was the first time I had entered Court as a witness. I kept my eyes on the Judge, on the pale London face above the tropical suit. He had been specially appointed to try this unusual case, and he looked tired after the long flight, shrunken almost, the suit too large; without the scarlet robes he seemed less awe-inspiring and the Law robbed of some of its majesty. Counsel, too, looked ordinary without wig and gown, and the courtroom itself—all open shirts or pale, loose-fitting jackets, a scattering of Bahrainis in flowing Arab robes. The Code of Criminal Procedure in this Court was based on the Indian Penal Code, yet in essence it was the same Law, and as I moved towards the witness box, the Judge leaned slightly forward, peering at me short-sightedly, his hands clasped together.

Once in the box, I faced the crowded courtroom, no

longer a mass of unidentifiable humanity, but a sea of faces all lifted to stare in silent expectation, waiting for the full story which they now knew I alone could give.

I had been called as a witness, not for the Defence, but for the Prosecution. Every word I uttered would be taken down and rushed out of Bahrain by telephone and radio, and thousands of miles away the metal drums of the presses would pour the story out to waiting millions. Representatives of almost every London newspaper were here and half the world's press, packed so tight in this improvised courtroom that they could hardly breathe. And outside in the broiling, humid heat were the photographers and the newsreel men and the television recording units, and at the airfield across the water on the island of Muharraq, special planes waited to fly the pictures that would be flashed on the screens of television sets in the homes of countless people.

Here and there in that sea of faces below me were people I recognized, people who had taken part in the events I was going to have to describe. There was Sir Philip Gorde, director of Gulfoman Oilfields Development, looking old and battered, his heavy-lidded eyes half closed; and beside him, Erkhard, very neat and cool. Colonel George was there and Captain Berry, easily distinguishable, smart in their uniforms of short-sleeved khaki shirts and well-creased khaki longs. Sue had followed me in, and it came as something of a shock to me to see that she had seated herself next to that strange, half-Arab, half-French girl who called herself Tessa. Captain Griffiths, too, his beard neat and pointed—a reminder of Cardiff and the visit that had started it all.

Raise your right hand.

I did so and my gaze shifted involuntarily to the prisoner in the dock. He was watching me, and for a moment our eyes met. I thought he smiled, but I couldn't be sure. I had a sense of surprise, almost of shock. Perhaps it was the tropical suit, the neatly brushed hair; he looked a different man. There was only the arm still in a sling to remind me that this was the man whose singleness of purpose had captured the world's imagination. The Book thrust into my hand disrupted my thoughts.

Repeat after me. My lips were dry. I had turned away from him, but I knew he was still watching me. *I swear by Almighty God.*

"I swear by Almighty God . . ."

That the evidence I shall give the Court.

"That the evidence I shall give the Court . . ." And as I said it I was wondering how the public at home would react to what I was going to have to tell the Court. Until today they would have had quite a different picture of the prisoner—a mental picture culled from garbled versions of his exploits heard over radio and seen on television, read in newspapers and periodicals, a colourful, larger-than-life picture entirely at odds with the neat figure standing alone there in the dock accused of murder.

Shall be the truth,

"Shall be the truth . . ." They should never have brought the case. He was a national hero and, whatever the verdict of the Court, the public's reaction would be a violent one. But would they be for him or against him?

The whole truth,

"The whole truth . . ."

And nothing but the truth.

"And nothing but the truth."

Your full name, please?

"Aubrey George Grant."

And then Counsel for the Crown, on his feet and facing me: "You are a solicitor by profession, I believe?"

"Yes."

"Were you called upon to act for the prisoner on his arrest?"

"Yes."

"When did you cease to act for him?"

"As soon as I realized I was being regarded as a material witness for the Prosecution."

"You have acted for the prisoner before, I think?"

"Yes."

"When was that?"

"Just over four years ago."

The Judge's voice suddenly interjected: "How long ago?" His hand was cupped to his ear.

"Four years, my Lord."

The Prosecution moved a step nearer, hands hung in the lapels of his jacket, the skin of the face cool as parchment in the humid heat. "I will ask the witness to take his mind back now to the afternoon of March twenty-first four years ago. On that afternoon you received a telephone call from a Mrs. Thomas of Seventeen, Everdale Road, Cardiff. And as a result of that telephone call you went to that address."

"Yes."

"Perhaps you will now tell the Court in your own words what happened. . . ."

Part Two

The Whole Truth

I

Escape to Saraifa

Everdale Road was

in the Grangetown district of Cardiff. It was one of those
terrace streets of grim Victorian brick, roofs hunched
against the wet west wind, windowed eyes peering blindly
for the view of river and sea that was blocked by other similar houses. Two streets away and you could look across
the Taff to the litter of cranes, the glimpse of funnels that
marked the Bute Docks. It always depressed me, this area
of Cardiff; it lacked the squalid colour of Tiger Bay, the
bridge across the Taff seeming to cut it off from the toughness and sense of purpose that gave a lift to the real dock
area. The street was deserted except for one car, a small
black sedan. It stood outside Number Seventeen, and as I
drew in to the curb behind it, I glanced quickly at the
house. There was nothing to distinguish it from the others, except the number. A light was on in one of the down-
stairs rooms. Neat lace curtains were looped back from
the windows.

I got out and rang the bell, wondering what I was going
to find inside. Trouble of some sort; nobody ever called me
to this district unless he was in trouble. And the voice over
the phone—it had been a woman's voice, low and urgent,
near to panic. I glanced at my watch. Four thirty. The
light was already going out of the cloud-filled sky. A slight
drizzle gave a black shine to the surface of the street.

Across the road a curtain moved; hidden eyes watching, something to gossip about. I knew the black sedan parked at the curb. It was Dr. Harvey's. But if there had been death in the house, the curtains would have been drawn. My hand was reaching out to the bell-push again when the latch of the door clicked and voices sounded: ". . . nothing else I could have done, Mrs. Thomas. A case for the police . . . you understand, I hope. And the ambulance will be here any minute now." The door was flung open and Dr. Harvey bustled out, almost cannoning into me. "Oh, it's you, Grant." He checked in mid-flight, black bag gripped in his hand, no overcoat as usual, a young, fair-haired, very serious man in a perpetual hurry. "Well, I suppose you'll be able to make some sort of a case out of it in Court. The boy's certainly going to need legal advice." There was no love lost between us. We'd tangled over medical evidence before. "Got to deliver a baby now. Can't do anything more for that chap." And he almost ran out to his car.

"Mr. Grant?" The woman was staring at me uncertainly.

I nodded. "Of Evans, Jones and Evans, solicitors. You telephoned me a little while back."

"Yes, of course." She held the door open for me, a small, neat-looking person of between forty and fifty with deep-set, shadowed eyes. Her hair was greying, swept straight back from the forehead, the face dead white against the dark background of the passage. "Will you come in, please?" She shut the door behind me. "Dafydd didn't want me to call you. But I thought you wouldn't mind, as your firm it is that handled that little allowance for me."

It was the first I knew we acted for her in any way. I thought she'd phoned me because I'm willing in certain circumstances to take a case without a fee. "What's the trouble, Mrs. Thomas?" I asked her, for she was standing motionless as though unwilling to let me go further into the house.

She hesitated, and then almost in a whisper: "Well, it's

Dafydd really, you see. He came back—and then . . . Oh
dear, it's all so difficult to explain." Now that she had shut
the street door, I could see no more than the outline of her
face, but her voice, trembling to a stop, told me she was
having to fight to keep control of herself. She was frightened, too. "I don't know what he'll do," she whispered.
"And Sue not here. Sue could always manage him when I
couldn't."

"Sue is your daughter, is she?" I knew it would steady
her if I asked questions.

"Yes, that's right. She works at the Infirmary, but I
didn't phone her because she'd never get back here in
time."

"And David—that's your husband?"

"No, Dafydd's my son. He and Sue are twins. She understands him, somehow."

"I see, and he's in some sort of trouble?"

"Yes." And then she added hastily: "He's not a bad boy,
not really." She drew in her breath quickly as though gathering herself together. "If I hadn't written to him like I did,
it wouldn't have happened. But I'd had about all I could
stand, you see, and then he came home and there was a bit
of a row and Mr. Thomas, he said things, you see, that he
shouldn't have done, and suddenly they were hitting out at
each other. It wasn't Dafydd's fault. He'd had a terrible
shock, poor boy. And Mr. Thomas, he'd had a few beers,
and then—" She sucked in her breath again as though gulping for air. "Well, then he had this stroke, you see, and I
called Dr. Harvey right away and then I telephoned you
because I knew it meant trouble for Dafydd." It had all
come out in a rush as though she couldn't contain it any
longer. "My husband looked so bad, you see," she added
lamely, "and I didn't know what would happen. I just
didn't know what to do, Mr. Grant—not for the best, as
you might say. And then Dr. Harvey came and he said
there wasn't much hope for him and he phoned the police,
so it's glad I am that I called you now. You'll know what

to do and what Dafydd should say to them. He's not a bad boy," she repeated in a voice that was suddenly on the defensive. "Just a bit wild, you know." And she added quickly: "Mr. Thomas hit me, you see."

"There was a family row, in other words?"

"Yes. Yes, you could call it that. But I wouldn't like you to think that because Mr. Thomas was a bit of a drinker there was anything wrong between us. He's good at heart, you know."

"And he's had a stroke, you say?"

"Yes, that's right. That's what Dr. Harvey called it." She seemed to have got a grip on herself. "Come in now, won't you, Mr. Grant? He's lying on the couch in the parlour. And Dafydd's there, too. I expect you'd like a word with him. But don't try and rush him, please," she added in a whisper, and I got the impression she was afraid of her son. "He needs a bit of handling, you see. And he's had a shock, as I say—a dreadful shock." She pushed open the door and stood back for me to enter. "This is Mr. Grant, Dafydd—Mr. Grant the lawyer."

The room was lit from the ceiling, a stark, glaring light without compromise. It showed me a couch with the body of a man lying on it. He was in his shirt-sleeves, the brass gleam of a stud showing where his shirtband had been loosened. His eyes were closed and he was breathing with difficulty, his rather heavy, florid features fallen away so that the bone showed through the flesh. The nose had the veined look of a heavy drinker's. Close against the gas fire, one elbow on the mantelpiece, leaned a youth of about twenty. He was rather over-dressed in a jacket with a lot of elaborate pockets and tucks and a pair of tight-fitting trousers. His face was as white as his mother's; the same features, too, except that the nose was more beaky, the jaw stronger. He didn't shift his position as I entered the room, didn't even look up. He was staring down at the gas fire and his immobility was oddly disconcerting.

Close by his feet was a litter of broken glass from the smashed front of one of those over-pretentious china cupboards. The mahogany beading as well as the glass had been broken in the struggle, and the bric-à-brac with which the cabinet had been filled, mostly white china souvenirs from seaside towns, lay in confusion on the worn carpet. A vase, too, lay where it had fallen from the table by the window. It was unbroken, and beside it lay a much-thumbed photograph album spilling press-cuttings. There was something a little macabre about the whole room—nothing cleared up after the struggle, and the father lying there half dead on the couch with a blanket tucked round him, and the mother and son standing, facing each other, absolutely still.

I could feel the tension between them. It wasn't hate, but it was something just as strong, an emotion so violent that the man on the couch, myself, the state of the room didn't exist for them.

"Well, now." I addressed the boy, my tone as matter-of-fact as I could make it in that sort of atmosphere. "Suppose you tell me what happened." But it was like talking to a brick wall. He had a sullen, withdrawn look.

"I've told you what happened," his mother said in a whisper.

"Quite so, Mrs. Thomas, but I'd like to hear it from your son." She looked deathly tired. I turned to the boy again. "You've had a shock," I said gently. "It's natural you should be a bit dazed by what's happened. . . ." But even as I said it I knew the boy wasn't dazed. The knuckles of the hand that gripped the mantelpiece were white with pressure and there was a muscle working at the back of the jaw. He was holding himself in like a boiler under pressure and I wasn't sure how best to handle him. His gaze had shifted now and he was staring at his mother. I felt sorry for the woman. "Listen to me, young man," I said. "I understand Dr. Harvey has called the police. They'll be here any minute now. If you want me to act for you, then you'd better start talking now, before they arrive."

A slight movement of the shoulder, that was all the answer he made. It wasn't a shrug, more a muscular twitch as though he was impatient for me to go.

"Mr. Grant is only trying to help, Dafydd."

"*Dammo di!* What the hell good is a lawyer man now? It's done, and arguing about it won't alter anything." His voice trembled. And then he turned on me, a flash of pale amber eyes, and told me to get out, the words violent, laced with obscenities.

"Dafydd!" But she was frightened; she had no control over him.

"All right," I said, and I moved towards the desk, where I'd left my hat. "I hope for your sake," I added, "that your father's condition isn't serious."

"He's not my father." The words flashed out from between clenched teeth. "I'd have killed him if he'd been my father." I turned to find his pale eyes fixed on his mother. "I mean that, Ma. I swear I'll kill the swine—if I can ever find him." The words had a violence and a bitterness that appalled me.

"He's not himself," his mother murmured. "He doesn't know what he's saying." Her hands were plucking at the apron round her middle, and her brown, doe-like eyes were wide with fear. She knew he'd meant it.

"You'd better get control of yourself," I said. "You've done enough damage for one day without threatening more and frightening your mother."

But now the pressure inside him couldn't contain itself any more. "You get out of here." He said it quietly, and because of that his words had force. "What's happened here is nothing to do with you or any one else. It's between my mother and me." He spoke through clenched teeth as though he were still trying to keep some control over what he was saying. And then suddenly he lashed out wildly, all control gone: "When you're suddenly told you're illegitimate, and your sister's illegitimate, too, you want to know a little more about it, don't you? You want to talk it over with your mother—ask her a few questions, find out who and what the hell you really are."

He flung out an arm, pointing dramatically at the album on the floor. "See that? Uncle Charles's scrap-book. She subscribed to a press-cutting agency. Every story the newspapers published about him—it's all there, pasted in with loving care. My own mother clinging to the worn-out bed of an old love. Jesus Christ! It makes you want to weep. And me and Sue coming up the wrong side of the bloody blanket, and being fooled into calling that poor drunken sot Dada." He stared at me balefully. "Eight years old I was when I first stole a peek at the contents of that book. A relation, that's what she said, an uncle of mine. Started me getting interested in Arabia, it did. I thought he was a bloody hero. Instead, he's just a low-down, dirty heel who left my mother flat. Well, what do you say to that, eh? You're a lawyer. Maybe you can tell me what I ought to do about it?" And he glared at me as though I were in some way responsible.

And then he suddenly moved, a quick step forward that brought him face to face with me. "Now you just get the hell out of here and let me talk to my mother alone, see?" His eyes had a wild look, the sort of look I'd only seen once before on a boy's face, but that had been in the midst of battle.

I'd known how to deal with it then. But this kid was different. It wasn't only that he looked tough; I had a feeling he *was* tough. Well, I'm not exactly soft, but I don't walk into things with my eyes open. But then I glanced at Mrs. Thomas, saw how scared she was of him, and after that there was nothing for it but to stand my ground, not knowing what exactly he'd do, for I could feel the tension building up inside of him again. He was like a spring coiled too tight.

And then the ring of the ambulance bell sounded down

the street and the violence suddenly died out of him. The ambulance drew up outside the house and a moment later two hospital attendants came in with a stretcher.

The attention of the three of us was focused then on the man on the couch. He murmured as they shifted him, an inarticulate sound, and Mrs. Thomas, fussing over him now, spoke his name. The tone of her voice had a quality that is only possible between people who have shared their lives together, and it seemed to reach him, for his eyes flicked briefly open and he murmured her name: "Sarah." It came quickly from his twisted lips, obscured by the effort of moving half-paralysed muscles. "Sarah—I'm sorry." That was all. The eyes closed, the face became clay again, and they took him out.

Mrs. Thomas followed them, sobbing uncontrollably. The door swung to of its own accord and the room was still. "I shouldn't have hit him. It wasn't his fault." The boy had turned away and his shoulders were moving. I realized suddenly that he was crying. "Oh, God!" he sobbed. "I should have known. If I'd any sense, I should have known."

"You couldn't have known he'd have a stroke," I told him.

He turned on me then. "You don't understand." The tears were standing in his eyes. "He and I—we hated each other's guts. I can see why now. But at least he stood by us, poor sod." And he added viciously: "He was a dam' sight better than my real father. If I can ever lay my hands on that bastard . . ." He checked there and gave an odd little laugh. "Bastard! That's funny, isn't it, me calling him a bastard." He turned away then, brushing the back of his hand across his eyes. "I wish I hadn't hit him," he said quietly.

"He'll be all right."

"You think so?" But then he shook his head. "No, he's going to die. That's what the doctor said. He was the only father Sue and I ever knew," he added, "and now I've killed him."

"Don't talk nonsense. It's not as dramatic as that. He's had a stroke and anyway you're entitled to defend your mother when a man hits her."

He looked at me. "Did she say that?" And then he laughed, a little wildly. And after a moment he said: "Yes, that's right—he hit her." And he added: "Christ! What a bloody mess!" The door of the ambulance banged in the street outside and he turned to stare out of the window. The engine started and it drove off. As though its departure had started an entirely new train of thought, he swung round on me. "You're Whitaker's lawyer, aren't you?"

The name meant nothing to me, but then no doubt Mrs. Thomas's allowance had been arranged by Evans years ago and it would be handled by my clerk as a matter of routine. "Whitaker is the name of your father, is it— your natural father?"

"That's right. My *natural* father." He spoke the word slowly, savouring it for the first time. And then he said: "I want his address."

"Why?"

"Why the hell do you think?" He was back at the window again. "A bloke's got a right to know where his father lives, hasn't he?"

"Maybe," I said. "But I'm afraid I don't know his address."

"That's a lie." He came back to me, his eyes searching my face. "Well, you've got it on your files, haven't you? You could look it up."

"If he's a client of mine, then I'm not at liberty to disclose—"

"Not even to his son?"

"No, not even to his son." I hesitated. The boy's temper would cool and, after all, he'd a right to know where his

father was. "If I've got his address," I said, "then I'll write
to him if you like and get his permission—"

"Oh, don't give me that crap. You know bloody well
where he is." He caught hold of my arm. "Come on. Arabia, it is—somewhere in Arabia. Tell me, for Christ's
sake." He saw it was no good then and began to plead:
"Please, I haven't much time and I got to know. Do you
hear? I got to know." There was a desperate urgency in his
voice. And then the grip on my arm tightened. "Let's
have it." I thought he was going to hit out at me and my
muscles tensed, ready for him.

"Dafydd!"

Mrs. Thomas was standing in the doorway, her hands
plucking again at the apron. "I can't stand any more."
There was an edge to her voice that seemed to get through
to him, and he relaxed slowly and stepped back from me.
"I'll come for that address," he muttered. "Sooner or later
I'll come to your office and get it out of you." He was back
at the window again, looking out. "I'd like to talk to my
mother now." He stared at me, waiting for me to go.

I hesitated, glancing at Mrs. Thomas. She was still as
stone, and her eyes, as they stared at her son, were wide
and scared-looking. I heard the slow intake of her breath.
"I'll go and make some tea," she said slowly, and I knew
she wanted to escape into her kitchen. "You'd like a cup
of tea, wouldn't you now, Mr. Grant?"

But before I could reply and give her the excuse she
needed, her son had crossed over to her. "Please, Ma." His
voice was urgent. "There isn't much time, you see, and I
got to talk to you." He was pleading with her—a small boy
now, pleading with his mother, and I saw her weaken at
once. I got my hat from the roll-top desk. "It's all right,
Mrs. Thomas," I said. "I'll leave you now." There was a
phone on the desk, an old-fashioned hook-up instrument
standing amongst a litter of books on greyhounds and racing form. "You can always phone my office if you want
me."

She nodded dumbly. She was trembling slightly and I could see she was dreading the moment when she'd be left alone with him. But there was no point in my staying. This was something that lay between the two of them alone. "Take my advice," I told him. "When the police arrive, be a little more co-operative with them than you have been with me if you want to avoid trouble. And stick to your mother's story."

He didn't say anything. The sullen look was back in his face. Mrs. Thomas showed me to the door. "I'm sorry," she said. "He's upset."

"It's not unnatural." I was remembering how I'd felt when I learned that my parents were divorced. I'd heard it first from a boy at school and I'd called him a liar and half murdered the little swine. And then when I discovered it was true, I'd wanted to kill my father and had had to content myself with a letter, which for sheer brutality had been inexcusable. "It's a pity you didn't tell him before."

"I always meant to," she said. "But somehow . . ." She shrugged, a gesture of hopelessness, and as I went out to my car I was wishing I could have done more to help her.

As I turned out of Everdale Road a squad car passed me. There were four of them in it, including Sergeant Mathieson of the Cardiff CID. It seemed an unnecessarily large force to answer Dr. Harvey's call, but I didn't go back. It was past five already and Andrews would be waiting to clear the day's business.

Andrews was my clerk. He was also secretary, switchboard operator, office boy. Poor devil, he had come to me with the furniture and the two-roomed dingy office, all that remained of the once prosperous business my uncle had left to me in a fit of misplaced optimism, for, though I'd passed my law exams, I'd never practised. There'd been the war and then I had drifted to Tanganyika and tea-planting, a venture which had turned out badly, leaving me virtually broke at the time of his death, so that the legacy of that miserable place seemed like the smile of fortune.

"Know anything about a Mrs. Thomas?" I asked Andrews as he helped me off with my coat. He had drawn the curtains, and with the coal fire burning brightly in the grate, the place looked almost snug, despite the dust and the piles of documents and the black deed-boxes littering the floor by the open strong-room door. "It's a matter of a small allowance she claims we handle for her."

"Mrs. Thomas is it?" I had seated myself at the desk and he stood over me, tall and slightly stooped, the skin stretched taut as vellum across the bones of his long face. "You know, Mr. Grant, almost half our clients are named Thomas." It was part of the game that he must always make the simplest thing appear difficult.

"It's one of your old clients," I said. "Something I have apparently quite unwittingly inherited from the old man."

"From Mr. Evans, you mean."

That, too, was part of the game, and because his position was privileged I had to humour him. "All right, Andrews. From old Mr. Evans." The firelight flickered on the lined, hang-dog face bent obsequiously over me. He'd been with my uncle since before he was articled and had stayed with him right through his long illness until he had died two years ago. God knows how old he was; his scrawny neck, covered by a hard stubble, stuck up out of the soiled stiff collar like the flesh of a plucked fowl. "Well, what about it?" I said impatiently. "I inherited so little in the way of business that it rather narrows the field. Does the name Whitaker ring a bell?"

"Whitaker?" His Adam's apple moved convulsively. "Ah, yes, of course. Colonel Whitaker. A little matter of a settlement. It used to come to us quarterly from Bahrain in the form of a banker's draft, which we cashed and forwarded to an address in Grangetown."

I asked him to get the file. But of course there wasn't any file. However, whilst I was signing the letters, he managed to dig up some record of the arrangement. It was written on the firm's notepaper in my uncle's sloped writing and went back to before the war. In it Charles Stanley Whitaker undertook to pay *to Sarah Davies the sum of twenty-five pounds quarterly for a period of fifteen years* or, in the event of his death, *a lump sum from the estate equivalent to the balance ALWAYS providing that such sum* . . . The clue to what it was all about was contained in the final paragraph, which read: *THIS settlement to be binding on my heirs and assigns and to be accepted by the said Sarah Davies in full settlement of any claims real or imagined.* The signature at the bottom was a barely decipherable scrawl, and below it Sarah Davies had signed her name in a clear, schoolgirl hand.

"If you ask me, Mr. Grant, the Colonel got this young lady into trouble."

The dry snigger with which Andrews accompanied this appraisal of the situation annoyed me. "The young lady, as you call her, is now an unhappy and rather frightened woman of middle age," I told him sharply. "The son, according to this, is nineteen and he's only just discovered that he's illegitimate. There's a twin sister, too. Not a very amusing situation." And Whitaker—was he still in Arabia? I wondered. "Do you think the man has any idea he has a son and daughter here in Cardiff?"

"I couldn't say, sir."

"Have we got his address?"

"The bank in Bahrain. That was the only address we ever had."

And Bahrain was in the Persian Gulf. But it was over three years since the last payment had come through. He might be anywhere now—back in England, retired, probably. "A pity we haven't got his address," I said. I was thinking that the son must take after his father: the beaky nose and strong jaw were both physical characteristics that didn't suit his circumstances. "This is all we've got on Whitaker, is it?"

Andrews nodded.

"Then how the devil do you know he's a colonel? There's no mention of colonel in this settlement."

Apparently Andrews had seen his rank given in some newspaper story. "Something to do with oil concessions, I think. There was a picture, too, with some sheikhs in flowing robes and Colonel Whitaker in the centre dressed in khaki shorts and a military cap."

"How did you know it was the same man?"

"Well, I couldn't be sure. But I don't think there could be two of them out in that area."

He was probably right there. "I'll ask Captain Griffiths about him." A man who spent his life taking his ship in and out of Arabian ports should know, and he was due in the office at five thirty. "Is the conveyance on that property of his ready now?"

Andrews produced it from the bottom of the pile, a bulky package that looked as though it contained enough deeds to cover a twenty-thousand-acre estate instead of a little cottage on the Gower Peninsula. "There's still a map to be inserted in the conveyance. Otherwise it's all there, title deeds, searches, everything."

I told him to get on to the man who was doing the map right away. "Griffiths wants all the documents before he sails tonight." The phone rang. It was Mrs. Thomas and I knew by the tone of her voice that something had happened. "They came just after you left, and I'm so worried, Mr. Grant, I don't know what to do. And now Sue has got back and she said to ring you. I'm very sorry to trouble you when you were so kind and came out here all for nothing, but you did say to telephone you if I needed any help and so I thought perhaps . . ."

"Just tell me what's happened, Mrs. Thomas," I said.

"Well, you see, they've taken Dafydd away and . . ." Her voice broke down then. "I'm so terribly worried about him, Mr. Grant. I don't know what's going to happen. So determined he is, you see. Once he's got an idea into his head . . . Always been like that, he has, ever since he was little, you know. Nothing would ever make him change his mind once he had made it up."

"Never mind about what's in your son's mind. What happened when the police arrived?"

"They just said he was to go with them."

"To the police station?"

"I don't know."

"For questioning, was it?"

"They didn't say. I asked them why they were arresting him, but they wouldn't tell me. Been in trouble he has, you know, and them behaving as though—"

"Did Sergeant Mathieson say he was arresting him?"

"No, he didn't say that exactly. He just said he was to come along with them. But it's the same thing, Mr. Grant, isn't it?"

"Did he charge him?"

"No. No, I don't think so. He just said he was to come along, and he went. He didn't try to resist or anything. They just took him, and now I don't know what is going to happen to him."

"Mrs. Thomas," I said, "there's something I want to ask you. Can you tell me where Colonel Whitaker is now?"

The quick gasp of her breath and then a long pause. "No. No, I don't know. But somewhere in Arabia it will be."

"He's still alive, then?"

"Oh, yes."

"You've heard from him?"

Again the pause. "No. No, I never heard from him. Never." And she added quickly: "Only the allowance. Very good he was about the allowance." She sighed. "Never a penny I took for myself, but spent it on Dafydd. Clever he is, you know—a quick brain and good with his hands. I thought perhaps he would become an engineer." Her quick tongue ran on, about the books she'd bought him and how she'd sent him to night school, and I let her talk because it

seemed to help her. "He couldn't understand it when the
money ceased. It was then he began to run wild, you see;
down in the docks all the time and his heart set on getting
to Arabia. Speaks Arabic, you know." She said it with
pride, and in the same breath added: "I tried to discourage
him, but it was no good. He had books, you see, and all
those Arabs down in the Tiger Bay district. In the blood
it is, I suppose—in the blood and in their stars. And that
book of cuttings. I should never have let him see it." And
then she added: "A pity you weren't here when they came
for him. I know it would never have happened if you'd
been here."

"Well, don't worry about it any more," I said. "I'll phone
them and find out what it's all about. Have you heard how
your husband is?" But she'd received no word from the hospital. "Well, that's good," I said. "They'd have been in
touch with you if they were worried about his condition.
I'll phone you if I've any news about your son." I put the
phone down. "First thing tomorrow, Andrews," I said, "get
on to the newspapers and see if they've anything in their
files about Whitaker. What that boy needs right now is a
father, the sort of father he can look up to."

I hurried through the rest of the business, and as soon
as Andrews had gone I phoned Dr. Harvey's surgery.
"George Grant here," I said when he came on the line.
"Any news of Thomas?"

"Yes," he said, "and it's bad, I'm afraid. I've just had a
call from the matron. He died in the ambulance on the
way to hospital."

"I see."

"Did the police pick that boy up?"

"Yes." It could well mean a charge of manslaughter.
"Has anybody thought of notifying Mrs. Thomas that her
husband is dead?"

"The matron is telephoning her right away."

"About time, too," I said. Incredible how soulless an
institution can be. But, in fact, it was the boy I was worry-

ing about more than the mother. "They've taken David Thomas into custody," I said.

"Good."

His comment angered me. "Why did you consider it your duty to notify the police? Did you know the man was going to die?"

"I thought it likely." And then, after a pause, he added: "He was a bookie, you know. Greyhounds, mostly. Heavy drinker, heavy smoker, immoderate in everything, if you get me. That type goes quick. But I couldn't be certain, of course." And he added: "Frankly, I wouldn't have expected the boy to stay there till the police arrived. I'd have thought he'd clear out. Probably would have done if you hadn't been there."

"I wasn't there," I told him. "I'd left before they arrived."

"Oh, well, doesn't make any odds. He's no good, that boy."

"What makes you think that?"

"Oddly enough," he said on a note of asperity, "I don't hold with boys hitting their fathers. Far too much licence allowed this new generation. He's a street arab, that boy—dock arab, rather." He gave a quick, awkward laugh. "It's the war, of course, but that doesn't excuse them entirely."

I asked him then to tell me what he knew about the boy. But he couldn't tell me much. The Thomases had only been going to him since the start of the National Health Service, and he hadn't set eyes on the boy more than once or twice. He'd grown up with the dock gangs, he said, mixing too much with the Arabs, had been in and out of a number of jobs, and had finally been sentenced for his part in the beating up of a rival gang leader. "I imagine he's only just been released from Borstal," he said. "Dockside toughs like that are the devil in my parish."

"And that's why you called the police?"

"Well, he killed his father, didn't he?" His voice sounded on the defensive.

"You don't make much allowance for human nature," I said.

"No. Not with boys like that. You try stitching a few flick-knife wounds and bicycle-chain gashes; you'd soon see it my way."

"All right," I said, and left it at that. He didn't know Thomas wasn't the boy's father or what had caused the row between them. "Life's not all as straightforward as you chaps see it in your clinics," I said and put the phone down.

By then it was five thirty and Captain Griffiths had arrived. He was a small man with a pointed beard and a high, cackling laugh, and he wore a tweed suit which was a little too large for him. This and his scrawny, wrinkled skin gave him a shrivelled look. But though he was not an impressive figure, long years of command had given him the knack of making his displeasure felt. "You promised me the documents before I sailed, man." He thrust his beard at me accusingly.

"Don't worry," I said. "You'll get them. When are you sailing?"

"Nine thirty on the tide."

"I'll bring them down myself."

That seemed to satisfy him, and since he showed an inclination to chat, I asked him about Whitaker. "Colonel Charles Stanley Whitaker," I said. "Do you know him, by any chance?"

"Yes, indeed. The Bedouin, that's what they call him out there. Or the Bloody Bedouin in the case of those that hate his guts and all his Arab affectations. That's the whites, you know. The Arabs call him *Al Arif*—the Wise One—or *Haji*. Yes, I know Colonel Whitaker. You can't trade in and out of the Gulf ports without meeting him periodically."

"He's still out there, then?"

"Oh, Lord, yes. A man like that would never be happy retiring to a cottage in the Gower." His small blue eyes creased with silent laughter. "He's a Moslem, you know. He's been on the *Haj* to Mecca, and they say he keeps a harem, and when it isn't a harem, there's talk of boys. . . . But there—" He shook his head. "It's just gossip. If I took account of all the gossip I heard on my ship, there wouldn't be any one with a shred of reputation left. Too much time, you see. Everybody's got too much time, and the damned humidity . . ." He gave that high-pitched, cackling laugh. "But, dear me," he went on, "there's a real character for you. You don't find men like Whitaker back here in Britain—not any more. One-eyed and a patch, and a great beak of a nose that makes him look like a bloody bird of prey."

"And you've met him?"

"Yes, indeed. I've had him on board my ship, too—often and often. I've had him on board in all his flowing Bedouin robes, with the silver of his great curved *khanjar* knife gleaming at his girdle and the black *agal* of Arabia round the *kaffyah* that covered his head; yes, and holding court on my own boat deck with the prayer mats out and his bodyguard all round him, armed to the teeth."

"A sort of Lawrence?" I suggested.

"Well . . ." He sounded doubtful. "He hasn't quite that standing with the political crowd. Too much of an Arab. Changing his religion like that, it made a difference, you see. But the oil boys all treat him like God, of course—or used to. But for him, the Gulfoman Oilfields Development Company wouldn't have had a single concession out there. And then there was his theory—the Whitaker Theory, they called it. He believed that the proved oil-bearing country that runs down from Iraq through Kuwait, Dahran, Bahrain and Qattar would be found to continue, swinging southeast along the line of the Jebel Mountains, through Buraimi and into the independent sheikhdom of Saraifa. Well, there's no knowing whether a man's right about a thing like that except by prospecting and drilling. And there was Holmes, you see—he'd had the same sort of bee in his bonnet about Bahrain and he'd been proved right."

"And Whitaker wasn't?" I prompted, for he had paused, his mind engrossed in the past.

"No. It cost the Company a lot of money and nothing but dry wells for their trouble. And now things are changing out there." He shook his head sadly. "There's a new type of man coming to the top of these Middle East oil companies, technical men who understand oil, but not the Arab. Whitaker and the world he represents—it's doomed, you know; finished. You can't lord it in the deserts of Arabia, not now, with the oil flowing and half the world trying to grab a stake in it. And he's the manner of a ruling prince, you know. He might have been descended from the Prophet himself, the way he behaved at times."

It was an extraordinary picture that Griffiths had drawn for me, and when he left to go back to his ship I felt that my drab office was the brighter for the colour his musical tongue had brought into it. I put some more coal on the fire and settled down to finish the day's work.

It was about half an hour later that I was interrupted by the sound of the street-door bell. It startled me, for I very seldom have a caller after office hours except by appointment, and a glance at my diary confirmed that I'd no appointment for that evening.

My visitor proved to be a girl, and as she stood there in the driving sleet, clutching her bicycle, she seemed vaguely familiar. She had the sort of face that comes together around the nose and mouth, a face that was attractive, rather than pretty, its composition based on the essential of bone formation. She smiled, a little nervously, a flash of white teeth, the bright gleam of pale eyes. I remember that it was her eyes that attracted me at the time. She was just a kid and she was brimming over with health and vitality.

"Mr. Grant? I'm Susan Thomas. Can I speak to you a moment, please?" The words came in a quick rush, breathless with hurrying.

"Of course." I held the door open for her. "Come in."

"May I put my b-bike inside?" There was a natural hesitancy in her voice that was oddly attractive. "I had one stolen a few weeks back." She wheeled it in, and as I took her through to my office, she said: "I was so afraid you'd have left, and I didn't know where you lived."

In the hard glare of my office lighting I was able to see her clearly. The beaky nose, the strong jaw—they were both there, recognizable now. But in her these facial characteristics were softened to femininity. Unlike her brother, she had no resemblance to the mother that I could see. "It's about your brother, I suppose?"

She nodded, shaking the sleet from her blond hair whilst her long, quick fingers loosened the old fawn coat she wore. "I only just got back from the Infirmary. Mother's beside herself. I had great difficulty . . ." She hesitated, a moment of uncertainty as her clear wide eyes stared and she made up her mind about me. "She—she's reached an odd age, if you know what I mean. This is just too much for her."

Nineteen years old, and she knew everything about life, all the hard, unpleasant facts. "Are you a nurse?" I asked her.

"Training to be." She said it with a touch of pride. And then: "You've got to do something about him, Mr. Grant . . . find him, stop him from trying to kill his—from killing somebody else."

I stared at her, appalled. "What are you talking about?" I said. She was over-dramatizing, of course. "You've heard about your—" I stopped there, uncertain what to call him. "About Mr. Thomas?"

"Yes." She nodded, her face as withdrawn as her brother's had been, set and white. "Mother told me."

"The hospital phoned her, then?"

"About half an hour ago. He died in the ambulance, they said." There was no emotion in her voice, but then her lip trembled slightly. "It's David I'm worried about."

"I was just going down to the police station," I said. "It was an accident, of course, but there's always the chance that the police may view it differently."

"He's got a bad record, you know. And they never got on together. Of course," she added, "I knew he wasn't my father—my real father, that is."

"Your mother told you, did she?" I was thinking that it was odd she should have told her daughter and not her son.

"Oh, no," she said. "She never told me. But it's something you know by instinct, sort of."

"Then why in heaven's name didn't your brother know?" I said.

"Oh, well, boys are so slow, you know. And it's not something you can just blurt out, is it, Mr. Grant? I mean, it's something you feel, deep inside, and it's sort of secret." And then she said: "What will he do, do you think? Was he serious when he said he'd kill him? I wasn't there, you see. But Mother is convinced he meant it."

"Kill who?" I said.

"His—my father. Colonel Whitaker. He swore he'd kill him, didn't he? That's what Mother says. You were there. Did he say that?"

"Well, yes." I nodded. "But I didn't take it very seriously. It had all come as a bit of a shock to him. Besides," I added, "there's not much he can do about it at the moment, even if he were serious. And by the time he's released, he'll have had a chance to get used to the idea."

She stared at me. "You haven't heard, then?"

"Heard what?"

"David's escaped."

"Escaped?" So that was why she was here. The stupid, crazy young fool! "How do you know he's escaped?"

"The police just phoned. They said he'd escaped from a police car and that it was our duty to inform them if he returned to the house. That's why I came to see you. Mother's almost out of her mind. You see, it isn't only David she's worrying about. It's this Colonel Whitaker—my f-father.

I don't understand after the way he treated her, but I think she's still in love with him . . . always has been, probably. And now she doesn't know what to do for the best." She came closer to me then, touched my arm in a gesture of entreaty. "Please, Mr. Grant, you've got to do something. You've got to help us. I'm scared to death Mother will go to the police and tell them what David said. That's what she wanted to do, right away. She said it was her duty, but I knew it wasn't that. She's just about out of her mind as a result of what David's done already. And he does have a bad record, you know. So I said I'd come to you, and she promised she wouldn't do anything until I got home." And she stood back, drained, her large eyes staring at me expectantly.

I didn't know what to say. There was nothing I could do. No point in my going out and searching the city for him. A filthy night like this the whole police force would have their work cut out to track him down. "Where was it he escaped?"

"Somewhere along the Cowbridge Road, they said."

"And your father—have you any idea how I can get in touch with him?"

Her eyes brightened for a moment. "Oh, if you could!" But then she shook her head. "I've no idea where he is now. Mother doesn't know. Did she show you the book of press-cuttings?"

"No."

"No, of course not, it was still lying there on the floor. The place was an awful mess." And then she said: "I checked myself because I had the same idea. But the last cutting she got was three years ago. I don't know whether he's been in the papers since then. Dad found out, or maybe he knew all the time—anyway, he made her stop them. That last cutting was a picture taken in Basra. But he may have retired by now. He was getting on—over fifty. And if he's retired, then he'd probably be in England somewhere, wouldn't he? That's what all these people who've lived all their lives abroad do when they retire. Do you think perhaps David knows where he is?"

"No," I said. "He tried to get the address out of me." No point in telling her that he might have the same idea that I had and try to check the newspaper files. "In any case," I told her, "he'll have his work cut out to elude the police. I think you can set your mother's mind at rest. The police will pick him up and . . . and time will do the rest. Your mother can see him in prison, talk to him; in no time at all he'll have accepted the situation."

She thought that over for a moment and then nodded. "Yes. That makes sense." And then she said: "Do you think that's why he escaped? . . . I mean, did he really want to kill Colonel Whitaker, do you think? His own father?"

"At the moment, perhaps." There was no telling what the boy had in his mind. He might simply have been jealous of his mother's affection for an old love. But I couldn't tell her that. "In my opinion, it was the shock," I said. "A perfectly natural reaction. When he's had time to think it over, get used to the idea—"

"But why did he escape? He's never done that before. He's been arrested twice, you see, but he never tried to escape." And when I didn't say anything, she gave a little shrug. "Oh, well, it'll all come out in the wash, I expect." She smiled briefly, but the smile didn't extend to her eyes, which were sad and suddenly without lustre. "It was silly of me to come, really." She started for the door, hugging her coat round her. "I should have known there was nothing you could do. It's Mother I'm worried about. David's in enough trouble. . . ." She moved her shoulders as though bracing herself. "I think perhaps I'll go and see Dr. Harvey. Maybe he'd give her a sedative, something to make her sleep so she doesn't keep going over it in her mind and getting silly ideas in her head." She turned and held out her hand. "Goodbye, Mr. Grant. And thank you. I feel a bit better now anyway."

I took her back through the empty office to the street

door, and as she wheeled her bicycle out she asked me to
telephone her if I had any news. "During the day you can
always get me at the Infirmary if it's important. I'd rather
you didn't phone my mother. Promise?"

"Of course," I said.

Shortly after she'd gone Andrews came in with the map.
By the time I had dealt with the conveyance and finished
my other work, it was almost seven thirty. Time enough to
call in at the police station on my way down to the docks.
What the boy needed was to be given some purpose in life.

I was thinking about this as I pulled on my coat, wondering at the chance of birth, how some people are born
to parents happily married, and others . . . My own childhood hadn't been all that happy. I shrugged my shoulders.
Life was a battle anyway. Sex, money, happiness—it was all
a struggle, like trying to build up this decrepit business. It
took all the guts, all the energy you'd got sometimes just
to make some sense out of life, and when things didn't work
out . . . I set the guard carefully in front of the dying fire,
feeling sorry for the boy, sorry for myself.

I suppose I was tired. It had been a frustrating week, and
now it was Friday and the week-end stretching ahead. I was
feeling the need of a drink. There was a pub I went to
sometimes in the dock area, a rowdy place, but virile and
full of masculinity and talk of far places, a seamen's pub
that always gave me the illusion of islands just beyond the
horizon. With a few Scotches, imagination could soar, leaping the tawdry problems of money and piddling lawyer's
briefs.

I went out, closing the door of my office behind me, following the white beam of my torch through the empty
outer office with its clumsy mahogany counter and frosted-
glass panels. I had reached the street door and my hand was
on the latch when I remembered the package for Captain
Griffiths. I had left it propped up on the mantelpiece so
that I shouldn't forget it.

I went back to my office, my footsteps sounding hollow on

the bare boards. He'd never forgive me if I let him sail
without his dream of the future all set down in the mumbo-
jumbo of legal phraseology. A man needed a dream, something to aim at. You couldn't go through life without a
goal. For him it was retirement and that little whitewashed
cottage looking out over the sweep of Rhossilly Bay; for
me it was just a solicitor's office with new paint, new furniture, and clients tumbling over each other for my services.
My hand reached out for the handle of the door, and then,
suddenly, there was the tinkle of glass falling. The sound
came from beyond the door, startlingly loud in the empty
stillness.

I switched off my torch and eased the door open a frac-
tion, every nerve in my body tensed and expectant. I heard
the scrape of the window latch, the scrabble of boots on the
sill, the rustle of the curtains as they were pushed aside. A
burglar? But nobody but a fool would expect to find cash
lying around loose in a solicitor's office. Perhaps he was
after some particular document? But I could think of nothing I was handling at the moment sufficiently important to
warrant breaking and entering. I heard him stumble
against my chair and then I could hear his heavy breathing
coming nearer as he crossed the room to the door. I guessed
he'd be making for the light switch, and I flung the door
wide and at the same time switched on my torch again.

David Thomas stood there, checked in the white beam of
it. His fair hair was plastered down by the rain. His face
was streaked with blood from a gash on his forehead, the
left cheek bruised and filthy with mud. There was mud on
his clothes, too—black, wet patches of it that clung to the
sodden cloth. His jacket was ripped at the shoulder and
one trouser leg was torn so badly that the flesh of his leg
showed through the rent. He was breathing heavily as
though he'd been running.

"What the hell are you doing here?" I said and switched
on the light. His face was ghastly white, his eyes unnaturally wide. He looked scared out of his wits. "Well, I don't

expect they'll think of looking for you in my office." I closed the door and walked past him and put the curtains straight. Then I took the guard from the fire and put some more coal on, poking it till a flame showed. And all the time I was conscious of him standing there, watching me in silence, too surprised, too scared probably, to move. I pushed the old armchair reserved for clients close to the hearth. "All right," I said. "Take your jacket off and come and sit by the fire and dry yourself out." He did as I told him, too startled to have any initiative of his own left. "Now," I said, "just tell me what in God's name made you do such a damn-fool thing."

For a moment I thought he was going to close up on me the way that sort of kid does when things go wrong and people start asking questions. The sullen tough-boy look had come back into his face. "Take your time," I said. "There's no hurry. You've got all evening if you want it." I thought I'd try flattery then. "Not many chaps manage to get away from the police so soon after being taken in charge. How did you do it?"

The tight lips relaxed slightly, a ghost of a smile. "Luck," he said. He was shivering and I poked the fire again, coaxing it into a blaze. "They'd got a car to take me to one of their bloody jails. Said I'd feel more at home in the nick." His tone was a sneer.

"And you made a break for it."

"Yeah. That's right. There was only one of them in the back with me, and I made a dive for it when they were driving down the Cowbridge Road. I hit the pavement and just about knocked myself out. They nearly had me then. But there was a pub I knew, and I dived in there and got away out the back." And he added: "I said I'd see you in your office." There was a touch of bravado in the way he said it.

"Your sister was here a little while back," I told him.

"Sue? What did she want?" He was on the defensive immediately.

"Wanted me to help you."

"Help me?" He gave a derisive laugh. "The only way you can help me is by giving me that address. That's what I came for."

"Your mother's worried sick," I told him.

"So what?"

I lost patience with him then. "Can't you get it into your thick head that your actions affect other people? Stop being so damned irresponsible. The police phoned your mother that you'd escaped, and now she's half out of her mind. . . ."

But he wasn't interested in the heartbreak he was causing other people. "She should have thought of that before she wrote me that letter," he said. "She was half out of her mind then. Did Sue tell you I'd two more months to do in a Borstal Institute?"

"No."

"Well, I had. Two more months and I'd have been out and in the clear. And then I got this letter threatening she's going to commit suicide. Your Da's driving me to it, she said, and I can't stand it any more. And then to come home and find she's been holding out on me all the time, kidding me I was that drunken old fool's son. Christ! And you talk about being irresponsible."

"It isn't an easy thing for a woman to tell her son."

"She'd nineteen years. In nineteen years she ought to have been able to screw up her courage. Instead, she drives the old man to fling it in my face." He stared at the fire, his shoulders hunched, his face bitter. "Does Sue know?" he asked at length. "Does she know she's illegitimate?"

"Yes."

"And what does she feel about it?"

"She said she'd known for a long time—deep down."

"Then why the hell didn't she tell me?"

"I said, deep down. Her mother didn't tell her. She just knew."

He looked sulky then. "We never kept anything from each other before."

"It's not the sort of thing you want to share with anybody else," I said.

"Too right, it isn't." He suddenly beat his fist against the arm of the chair. "Christ! If I'd only known before."

"It wouldn't have helped you," I told him.

He thought about that for a moment and then he nodded. "No, I guess you're right." And he added: "I always wondered why the old man hated my guts." He leaned suddenly forward, picked up the poker, and jabbed at the fire. "Guess I hated his guts, too," he said viciously.

"Well, he's dead now," I said. "Did you know that?"

He nodded and let go of the poker so that it clattered into the grate. "Yep. They told me that. Croaked on the way to hospital, blast him."

His attitude to the man's death shocked me. "For God's sake!" I said. "Haven't you any compassion for the man who was a father to you?"

"He wasn't my father," he cried. "I told you that before."

"He was your father in the eyes of the law."

"Then the law ought to be changed, oughtn't it? You can't make chalk cheese by a legal declaration."

"He supported you all the time you were growing up," I reminded him.

"All right, he supported me. But he hated me all the same. I always knew that. When he took a strap to me, he enjoyed it. He hasn't been able to do that for a long time now. But he'd other ways of getting at me, jeering at me because I read a lot, and at my Arab friends. Do you know what he'd done whilst I'd been in Borstal? I went up to my old room after you'd left. All my books on Arabia, every damn one of them, he'd pulled out and torn to pieces. The only books he hadn't destroyed were the technical ones. I'd a lot of them on oil—geology, seismology, geophysics. He left me those because he didn't think I cared about them."

He stared at me. "Now he's dead, and I'm glad. Glad, do you hear?" His voice had risen, and suddenly the tears were welling up into his eyes and he began to cry. "I didn't mean to kill him," he sobbed. "Honest. I didn't mean to." He broke down completely then, sobbing like a child, and I went over to him and gripped his shoulder.

"It was an accident," I said, trying to steady him.

"They don't believe it."

"Did they prefer a charge?"

"No, but they think I killed him. I know they do." And he burst out: "I haven't a chance with them."

"You certainly haven't made it any better by making a break for it like that." I was wondering whether I could persuade him to come with me to the police station and give himself up. I hesitated and then walked over to the phone, but he was on his feet immediately.

"What you going to do? Ring the police?" There was panic in his voice.

"No," I said. "I'm going to ring your home—get your mother down here, your sister, too."

"What for? What good'll that do?"

"If your mother makes a statement, explaining exactly how it happened . . ."

"It's no good," he said. "She wouldn't do it. She'd rather have me hanged. . . ."

"Oh, don't be childish," I said.

"It's true," he cried. "She told me so herself—after you'd gone." He had followed me to the desk and his voice was intense, very serious. "She thinks I'm going to kill Whitaker if I ever lay my hands on him. And she loves him. After all these years, she still loves the man. I don't understand it, but that's how it is. You'd think after the swine had treated her like that, after he'd left her flat . . ." He pulled a blood-stained handkerchief from his pocket and blew his nose. "When I got back this afternoon the old man was giving her hell. I could hear it out in the street. He was calling her all sorts of names. I suppose he was drunker than usual. He had that book of press-cuttings in his hand, and when I told him to shut his mouth, he taunted me with being a bastard, said he'd had all he could stand of another man's whelps. And then he turned on my mother and added: 'And all I can stand of another man's whore. After all I've done to cover up for you,' he said, 'you creep off as soon as I'm out of the house to mope over your lover's pictures.' And he flung the book at her. That's when I went for him." He paused, staring at me, his eyes over-bright. "That book was full of press-cuttings of him—pictures, some of them. I've grown up with that book, grown up with the man himself. I know him, know his way of life, everything about him. It's like I told you—he was a sort of god to me. I wanted to be like him, tough, independent, an adventurer in far places. I tried to get a job as a seaman on ships going out that way from Cardiff docks, but at first I was too young, and then there was the union. I even tried to stow away once. And now I find he's no more than a rotten, dirty little sham who'd leave a woman to bear her twins alone. I told Ma I'd kill him if I ever laid hands on him. Remember? You were there when I said it."

I nodded.

"Well, she believed me. She's convinced I really will kill him if I ever catch up with him."

"And you didn't mean what you said—is that what you're trying to tell me?"

He walked back to the fire and stood staring at it for a moment. Then he slumped down in the chair again, his body limp. "I don't know," he murmured. "Honest, I don't know. All I do know is that I have to find him."

"And that's why you came here, to search my office for his address?"

He nodded. "I knew you'd have it somewhere in your files."

"Well, I haven't." I hesitated. But, after all, the boy had a right to know where his father was. "Will you promise me something? Will you promise me that if you find him, you'll remember that he's your father and that blood is something you just can't rub out with violence?"

He looked at me and was silent a long time. At length he said: "I can't promise anything. I don't know how I'd act." He was being honest at least. "But I'll try to remember what you've just said. And then on a sudden, urgent note: "I've got to find him. I've just got to find him. Please, please try to understand."

The need of that kid . . . It was the thing that had been lacking for him all his life. It was his mother's need reflected and enlarged. The sins of the fathers . . . Why in God's name should a sense of insecurity lead to violence, in people and in races? "All right," I said. "I accept that." And I passed on to him what Griffiths had told me. "But then you know the sort of man your father is. Anyway, there it is, he's still out there. And if you want to contact him, I imagine a letter to the Gulfoman Oilfields Development Company—"

"A letter's no good. I wrote him already—twice. He never answered." He looked up at me. "This Captain Griffiths, is his ship the *Emerald Isle?* She sails regularly to the Persian Gulf." And when I nodded, he said: "That was the ship I tried to stow away on. I was fourteen then, and a year later I tried to sign on. She's in port now, is she?"

"Yes."

"When is she sailing?"

"Tonight."

"Tonight?" He looked up at me, suddenly eager, like a dog being offered a walk. "Tonight. When? What time?" He had jumped to his feet, all the tiredness falling from him. "For Christsake, what time?"

I hesitated. It was no part of a lawyer's job to get involved in a criminal case. My duty was plain. "The sensible thing would be for you to give yourself up to the police."

He didn't hear me. His eyes had fastened on the envelope I had left propped up on the mantelpiece. "Were you taking this down to the ship tonight?"

I nodded, and his hand reached out for the envelope, clutched at it. "I'll deliver it for you." He held it as though it were a talisman, his eyes bright with the chance it represented. "That's all I need. The excuse to go on board. And they wouldn't catch me this time, not till we were at sea." He glanced at the window, balanced on the balls of his feet, as though about to take off the way he had come. But then I suppose he realized I should only phone the police. "Will you let me take it?" His voice was urgent, his eyes pleading. "Once on board the *Emerald Isle* . . . Please, sir."

That "sir" was a measure of his desperation.

"Please," he said again. "It's the only hope I got."

He was probably right at that. And if I didn't let him take it, what other chance would he ever get in life? He'd escaped from Borstal. He'd escaped from the police. With that sort of record he'd be lucky to get away with three years for manslaughter. After that he'd be case-hardened, a criminal for life. And there was the sister, too. A nice girl, that. I sighed. "I'm supposed to be a lawyer," I reminded him . . . or maybe I was reminding myself. "Not a travel agency for boys who've escaped from the police."

"But you'll let me deliver it, won't you?"

What the hell can you do when faced with youth in all its shining innocence and eagerness. "All right," I said. "You can try it, if you like. But God knows what Griffiths will do."

"All I want is the chance to meet up with my father."

I realized then that his mind had leap-frogged all the obstacles; he was already mentally sailing the coast of Arabia in search of his father. "All I'm giving you," I warned him, "is the excuse to get on board that ship. She sails at nine thirty. And those documents have got to be delivered into Captain Griffiths's hands, understand?"

"I'll give them to him. I promise."

"You know your way about the ship?"

"I knew every corner of her once. It'll come back to me as soon as I get on board."

"Well, kindly remember that I'm a solicitor. When you're caught, as you will be eventually, don't implicate me. Shall we say you walked into my office to get legal advice, saw the envelope I had forgotten, and took it on the spur of the moment? Is that understood?"

"Yes, sir."

"I'll take you down to Bute East Dock now," I said. "After that you're on your own." I hesitated. It wasn't much of a chance I was giving him. He'd no clothes other than what he stood up in, no money probably, nothing, not even a passport. But at least I'd have done what I could for him—what I'd have hoped somebody would do for a son of mine if he'd got himself into a mess like this. But then I hadn't a son; I hadn't anybody. "Better clean the blood off your face," I said and showed him where the wash-place was. "And you'll need something to hide your torn clothes."

I left him in the lavatory and went through the office to the cupboard under the stairs. There was an old overcoat that had been there ever since I'd taken over the place, a black hat, too. He tried them on when he'd finished cleaning himself up. The coat wasn't too bad a fit, and with the sweatband padded with strips from an old conveyance the hat was passable. I wondered what my uncle would have said if he knew to what use these sartorial relics of his were being put. And because I wanted him to realize how slender his chances were, I said: "If you're caught before the ship sails, don't try and bluff it out with Captain Griffiths. Tell him the truth and say you want to give yourself up to the police."

He nodded, his face bloodless, his pale eyes almost fever-bright with the nervous tension that was building up in him. The dark coat and the black hat accentuated his pallor, accentuated, too, his beaky nose and the strong jaw. In the old lawyer's cast-off clothes he looked much older than his nineteen years.

There was a back way out of the office, and I took him out by that. It was still sleeting, and there was nobody in the street where I parked my car. We drove in silence down Park Place and across Castle Street, and then we crossed the railway and were in the maze of little streets that edge the docks. I slowed in a dark gap between street-lights and told him to climb into the back and lie on the floor with the rug I kept for my dog pulled over him.

It was fortunate that I took this precaution, for the police at the dock entrance had been alerted and there was a constable there who recognized me; a fortnight before, he had given evidence in a case I'd defended. I told him my business and he let me through. I hadn't expected the police to be watching the docks already and my hands were sweating as I drove on across the slippery steel of the railway tracks.

The *Emerald Isle* was at the far end of the Bute East Dock, close to the lock. She had completed loading and she had steam up, smoke trailing from her single stack. The cranes along the quay were still, their gaunt steel fingers pointed at the night. I stopped in the shadow of one of the sheds. The sleet had turned to snow and it was beginning to lie, so that the dock looked ghostly white in the ship's lights. "Well, there you are," I said. "That's the ship."

He scrambled out from under the rug. "Couldn't you come with me?" he asked, suddenly scared now that the moment had arrived. "If you were to have a word with Captain Griffiths . . ."

I didn't reply to that, but simply handed him the package. I think he knew it was out of the question, for he didn't ask me again. A moment later the rear door opened and I heard him get out. "I—I'd like to thank you," he stammered. "Whatever happens—I won't let you down."

"Good luck!" I said.

"Thanks." And then he was walking across the dock, not

hesitantly, but with a firm, purposeful tread. I watched him mount the gangway, saw him pause and speak to one of the crew, an Arab; and then he disappeared from sight through a door in the bridge deck.

I lit a cigarette and sat there, wondering what would happen now. I didn't think he'd much of a chance, but you never know; he was a resourceful kid.

I finished my cigarette and lit another. I was thinking about the constable on the gate. I ought to have realized that that would be one of the first things they'd do following his escape. And the man had recognized me. I tried to analyse my motives in doing such a crazy thing, but I couldn't sort them out. The cold crept into the car as I waited, and still nothing happened, except that the snow thickened and the dock turned dazzling white. A tug hooted out in the river, a lost, owl sound in the winter night. It was twenty minutes past nine.

Ten minutes later a whistle sounded from somewhere high up on the *Emerald Isle* and two men came quickly out of a hut at the end of the dock. They manhandled the gangway ashore and then stood by the warps. Another whistle and the for'ard warp went slack, fell with a splash into the dock. Black smoke belched from the funnel, and as the stern warp was let go, a gap opened up between the ship's side and the quay. I switched the engine on then, turned the heater up, and sat there smoking as the *Emerald Isle* locked out into the River Taff. And when her lights had finally disappeared behind the whitened shoulders of the loading-sheds, I drove back to the solitude of my flat, hoping to God I'd done the right thing.

The story of what happened to him after that I got partly from Captain Griffiths on his return and partly from a letter David wrote me. When he left me on the dock there and went on board the *Emerald Isle* there was no clear-cut plan in his mind. He knew the layout, of course. She was the only ship trading regularly out of Cardiff to Arabian

ports, and she had exercised a fatal fascination for him
since he was old enough to wander in the docks. It was the
Somali steward and not a deck hand who met him at the
top of the gangway, and on the spur of the moment, almost
without thinking, he inquired whether the passenger accommodation was fully booked. The steward told him no:
there were six cabins and only three were occupied. Feeling
suddenly more confident, he asked to see the Captain.

Captain Griffiths was in his cabin on the port side of
the bridge-deck housing, and when David was shown in he
was seated at his desk checking the Mate's trim figures. He
took the packet, glanced at it, and then looked up at David.
"You work for Mr. Grant, do you?"

"I—I run errands for him."

"Office boy, eh? Well, you're only just in time. We sail in
quarter of an hour." Griffiths peered up at him from under
his bushy brows. "What's the matter with your face, boy?
Been in a fight?"

"No. No, sir. I—I had a fall."

"Must have been a bad one. You're as white as a sheet."
He bent down, pulled open a drawer of his desk, and came
up with a bottle of whisky. "I'll give you a drink for your
pains." He gave that high-pitched cackling laugh, filled the
glasses half full, and handed one of them to David. "Well,
young fellow, you can wish me luck, for it's a Welsh land-
owner I am now." And he slapped the packet of documents
with unconcealed pride. "There's times, you know," he
confided as he swallowed his drink, "when I feel like the
Wandering Jew himself, doomed to ply from one silt-laden
port to another, right through to Eternity. This," and his
hand touched the packet again, "this may help me to preserve my sanity when the temperature's over the hundred
and the humidity's so thick your lungs feel as though
they're stuffed full of wet cotton wool and will never
breathe clean air again; when conditions are like that, then
I'll take these documents out and read them through just
to convince myself that I really do have a little place on the

Gower Peninsula where rain washes the air clean of dust
and heat and the damned, Godforsaken, everlasting flies."

"That's the Persian Gulf you'll be referring to, isn't it?
Then maybe you'll know where Colonel Whitaker lives
now?" He hadn't intended to ask that question, but the
unaccustomed liquor had overlaid his nervousness.

Griffiths glanced up at him quickly. "Funny thing," he
murmured. "Grant asked me that same question only this
afternoon. Is Colonel Whitaker one of the firm's clients?"

"I—I don't know, sir."

"Then what made you ask about him?"

David hesitated. But if he were to succeed in stowing
away on board, there was no harm in telling Captain Griffiths the truth right now. "He's my father."

"Your father!" The blue eyes stared. "Good God! Didn't
know the Bedouin was married."

"My natural father, sir."

Griffiths's eyes suddenly crinkled at the corners. "Natural father, you say? Well, by God, that's a good one." And
he lay back in his swivel chair, pointed his beard at the
steel deck above, and cackled with laughter. And then he
stopped suddenly. "I'm sorry, boy. You're sensitive about
it, I can see. Have you ever met your father?"

"No, sir."

"Well, if you had, you'd know why I laughed. Bedouin
sons—and daughters. There's gossip enough about him,
but never a whisper of a son in Wales, you see. I'll tell him,
next time he's aboard—I'll say to him casually . . ." But
David was spared the rest, for the bridge communicator
buzzed and a voice said: "Tug coming alongside now, sir."

"Very good, Mr. Evans." Griffiths got to his feet. "I'm
needed on the bridge." He paused in front of David, staring up at his face. "Yes. I can see the likeness now. Any
message you want me to give him?" And when David
shook his head dumbly, he patted him on the arm. "Well,
I'll tell him I saw you when next he comes aboard. And
now you'd better get off the ship quick or you'll find your-

self in Arabia with a deal of explaining to do." And he went off, cackling with laughter, to the bridge above.

David found himself standing alone outside the Captain's cabin. An alleyway ran athwartships. Numbered mahogany doors led off it on either side. He listened, every nerve taut. He could hear voices on the bridge and down below in the saloon, but the deck on which he stood seemed utterly deserted. Treading softly, he walked the length of the alleyway to the starb'd side, as far away from the Captain's cabin as possible. The first door he tried was locked, the second opened to a glimpse of heavily labelled baggage and the startled face of a man lying prone on his bunk with a book. A tug blared so close alongside that he jumped. Cabin Number Four was empty, and he slipped inside and locked the door. And after that he stood for a long time, quite still and breathing heavily, listening to the sounds of the ship, waiting tense for the sudden outcry that would inevitably follow the discovery that he had not gone ashore.

That period of waiting, ten minutes at the most, seemed the longest he had ever known. And then a whistle sounded. It was so like the shrill of a police whistle that he reached for the handle of the door, instinctively seeking escape in movement. But then the engine-room telegraph rang from the bridge overhead and the ship suddenly came to life, a gentle throbbing against the soles of his shoes. He knelt on the unmade bunk then and cautiously pulled back the curtain that covered the porthole. He could see the deck rail and beyond it a flat expanse of water with the snow driving across it. And then the water was swirling to the bite of the screws and he knew the ship was moving.

He took off his hat and coat then and lay down on the bunk under a ship's blanket, listening with his ears attuned to every sound. A gong sounded for the evening meal and there was movement in the next cabin, the gush of a tap, the bang of a suitcase. The shrill of the whistle on the bridge was answered a moment later by the tug's farewell blast on her siren. The beat of the engines increased, and later, after they had slowed to drop the pilot, the ship began to roll.

He slept during the night, rolled from side to side of the narrow bunk. But when daylight came, he lay awake, tense and hungry. Footsteps sounded in the alleyway, cabin doors slammed, somewhere a loose porthole cover rattled back and forth. The hours of daylight seemed endless, but nobody came, nobody even tried the handle of the cabin door. It was as though he didn't exist, and, perversely, he felt deserted, lost and forgotten in this strange world he'd been thrust into by events. He had no watch, so that he'd no idea of the time. The sky was grey with a low wrack of cloud, no sun. The violence of the movement was exhausting, and towards nightfall he was sick, retching emptily into the washbasin. Nobody seemed to hear the sound of his misery, nobody seemed to care. The seas, thudding against the bows of the ship, made her tremble, so that everything rattled, and each time she buried her bows the noise of the impact was followed by a long, shuddering movement that seemed to run through his tired body as though he were himself being exposed to the onslaught of the gale.

Night followed the day at last and he slept; and then it was day again. Darkness and light succeeding each other. He lost count of the days, and when the sun came out and the sea subsided, he knew he was too weak to hold out alone in that cabin any longer. The moment had come to face the future.

Just above his head, within easy reach of his left hand, was a bell-push. He lay half a day, staring at the yellow bone button embedded in its wooden orifice, before he could summon the courage to press it, and when the steward came he told the startled Somali to take him to the Captain.

Griffiths was seated at his desk so that to David's bemused mind it seemed like that first time he'd met him, except that now the cabin was full of sunlight and they were off the coast of Portugal. The Somali was explaining excitedly and Griffiths's small blue eyes were staring up at him. The Captain silenced the man with a movement of his hand. "All right, Ishmail. You can leave us now." And as the steward turned to go, his eyes rolling in his head, Griffiths added: "And see you don't talk about this. The passengers are not to know that a stowaway has been hiding in their accommodation." And when the door closed and they were alone, he turned to David. "Now, young man, perhaps you'd explain why the devil you stowed away on my ship?"

David hesitated. It was difficult to know where to begin, though he'd had four days of solitude to think about it. He was scared, too. The little man in the worn blue jacket with the gold braid on the sleeves was more frightening to him than either of the judges who had sentenced him, for his future was in the Captain's hands. "Well, come on, man, come on." The beard waggled impatiently, the blue eyes bored into him.

I would like to think that he remembered my advice then, but more probably he was too weak and confused to invent a satisfactory story. At any rate, he told it straight, from the receipt of his mother's hysterical letter and his escape from Borstal, right through to the tragedy of his return to the house in Everdale Road. And Griffiths listened without comment, except that halfway through he took pity on David's weakness, for he was leaning on the edge of the desk to support himself, and told him to pull up a chair and sit down. And when finally he was asked to account for his possession of the documents that had been his excuse for boarding the ship, he stuck to the explanation we'd agreed on.

But Griffiths was much too sharp for him. "So you took the packet from Mr. Grant's office and decided to deliver it yourself?"

"Yes, sir."

"You say you found the door of Mr. Grant's office open. That means he'd only gone out for a moment. When he came back and found the packet gone, the natural thing would be for him to come down to the ship and give me some explanation. You're lying, you see."

There was nothing he could do then but tell Captain Griffiths the truth, and the blue eyes, staring into his, began to crease at the corners. By the time he had finished, Griffiths was leaning back in the swivel chair and roaring with laughter, his mouth so wide open that David could see the movement of his uvula in the red hollow of his gullet. "Well, I'll be damned!" Griffiths said, wiping his eyes. "And Grant an accessory . . ." And then he started in on a cross-examination that seemed to go on and on.

Finally he got up and stood for a long time staring out of the porthole at the sunlight dancing on the waves made by the ship's passage through the water, whilst David sat there, numbed and hopeless. "Well, I believe you," Griffiths said, still staring out at the sea. "You could never have made all that up." There was a long silence. "You got Grant to help you—and how you did that I don't know, considering he'd never met your father. He was risking his reputation, everything. You've no passport, of course? That means you can't land in the normal way. And you've never had word from your father, which means he doesn't care to acknowledge your existence—right?"

And when David didn't say anything, Griffiths swung round from the porthole, his beard thrust aggressively forward. "And you stow away on my ship, expecting me to get you into Arabia. How the devil do you think I'm going to do that, eh?"

"I don't know, sir."

"Perhaps Grant suggested something?" But David shook his head unhappily and Griffiths snapped: "A lawyer—he should have had more sense." And he stumped across the cabin and stood peering down at David's face. "Is your father going to acknowledge you now, do you think? How old are you?"

"Nineteen."

"And do you think Colonel Whitaker's going to be pleased to have a bastard he sired nineteen, twenty years ago, suddenly turn up with no passport, nothing—and a jailbird at that?"

David got to his feet then. "I'm sorry, Captain Griffiths," he said stiffly. "I didn't realize . . ." The words didn't come easily, and his mouth felt dry and caked. "I've always dreamed of this, you see—of getting out to Arabia. I suppose it's in my—bastard blood." He said it with bitterness, for he was convinced now that the world was against him, as it always had been—as it always would be. "I'll work my passage," he added wearily, "and when we get to Aden you can hand me over to the authorities."

Griffiths nodded. "That's the first sensible suggestion you've made. And it's exactly what I ought to do." He turned away and stood for a moment lost in thought. "Your father did me a good turn once. I owe him something for that, but the question is would I be doing him a good turn . . ." He gave a quick shrug and subsided into his chair, chuckling to himself. "It has its humorous side, you know." And David watched, fascinated and with a sudden feeling of intense excitement, as Griffiths's hand reached out to the bridge communicator. "Mr. Evans. Come down to my cabin for a moment, will you?" And then, looking at David: "Well, now, for the sake of Mr. Grant, whom I wouldn't have suspected of such lawlessness, and for the sake of your father, who's going to get the shock of his life, I'm going to sign you on as a deck hand. But understand this," he added, "any trouble at Aden and I hand you over to the authorities."

David was too relieved, too dazed to speak. The Mate came in and Griffiths said: "Stowaway for you, Mr. Evans. Have the galley give him some food and then put him to work. I'm signing him on. And see the passengers, at any

rate, don't know how he came aboard. His name is—
Whitaker." David caught the glint of humour in the blue
eyes.

"Thank you, sir," he mumbled, but as he turned away
all he could think about was that name, spoken aloud
for the first time. Whitaker. Somehow it seemed to
fit, as though it had always belonged to him; it was a symbol, too, a declaration that the past was gone, the future
ahead.

All down the Mediterranean and through the Suez
Canal, the life of the ship, the sun's increasing warmth,
the sight of places all dreamed about and now suddenly
come to life absorbed him completely, each day bringing
the promise of Arabia twenty-four steaming hours nearer.
But when they entered the Red Sea, with the water flat
like a mirror and the desert hills of the Hejaz shimmering
to port, he knew they were getting close to Aden. And at
Aden the police might be waiting for him.

It was night when the anchor was let go off Steamer
Point, and as he stood on the foredeck directing a stream
of water on to the hawsehole, he could see the lights of
Crater and the black shape of the volcanic hills behind
towering against the stars. His first Arabian port. It
touched his nostrils with a breath of sun-hot oil waste. But
instead of excitement, all he felt was fear.

Customs and Immigration came aboard. He stood by
the rail, in the shadow of one of the boats, and watched
them climb the side from a launch. His work was done and
he'd nothing to think about now but the possibility of
arrest. A subdued murmur came to him from the town,
strange Arab cries drifting across the water. Another
launch glided to the ship's side. The agent this time. And
later two of the passengers were climbing down into it,
followed by their baggage. The officials were leaving, too,
and he watched the launches curve away from the ship, two
ghostly arrow-tips puttering into the night. He breathed
gently again, savouring the warm, strange-scented air . . .

and then the steward called his name. "Captain want you in cabin."

Slowly he went for'ard to the bridge-deck housing. Captain Griffiths was seated in the leather armchair, his face a little flushed, his eyes bright, a tumbler of whisky at his elbow. "Well, young fellow, it appears that you're in the clear. Nobody is in the least bit interested in you here." And he added: "Doubtless you have Mr. Grant to thank for that. I'm sorry I can't send him a message; the man must be half out of his mind, considering the chance he took."

"I'll write to him as soon as I can," David murmured.

The Captain nodded. "Time enough for that when you're safely ashore. But it's only fair to tell you that if I fail to contact your father, then you'll complete the voyage and be paid off at Cardiff." And having delivered this warning, he went on: "I'll be going ashore in the morning and I'll cable Colonel Whitaker care of GODCO—that's the Gulfoman Oilfields Development Company. It may reach him, it may not. Depends where your father is, you see; he's not an easy man to contact. Meantime, I am instructing Mr. Evans to give you work that will keep you out of sight of the passengers. We have two oil men with us on the voyage up the coast, also an official from the PRPG's office—that's the Political Resident Persian Gulf. See to it that you keep out of their way. If you do get ashore, then I don't want anybody saying afterwards that they saw you on board my ship." And with that David found himself dismissed.

He saw Captain Griffiths go ashore next morning in the agent's launch. All day they were working cargo, the winches clattering as they unloaded Number One hold into the lighter dhows alongside and filled it again with a fresh cargo. In the evening four passengers came aboard, all white, and a dhow-load of Arabs bound for Mukalla who strewed themselves and their belongings about the deck. And then the anchor was hauled up and the ship shifted to the bunkering wharf. The *Emerald Isle* sailed at midnight, steaming east-northeast along the southern coast of Arabia, the coast of myrrh and frankincense, of Mocha coffee and Sheba's queen.

It was a voyage to thrill the heart of any youngster, but David saw little of it, for he was confined to the bowels of the ship, chipping and painting, and all he saw of Mukalla, that gateway to the Hadhramaut, was a glimpse through a scuttle—a huddle of terraced Arab houses, so white in the sunlight that it looked like an ivory chess set laid out at the foot of the arid mountains. Only at night was he allowed on deck, and he spent hours motionless in the bows of the ship, drinking in the beauty and the mystery of the Arabian Sea, for the water was alive with phosphorescence. From his vantage point he could look down at the bow wave, at the water rushing away from the ship in two great swathes as bright as moonlight, and ahead, in the inky blackness of the sea, great whorls of light like nebulae were shattered into a thousand phosphorescent fragments as the ship's passage broke up the shoals of fish—and, like outriders, the sharks flashed torpedo-tracks of light as they ploughed their voracious way through the depths. And every now and then a tanker passed them, decks almost awash with oil from Kuwait, Bahrain, and Dahran.

They passed inside the Kuria Muria Islands at night, and to get a better view of them he ignored his orders and crept up to the boat deck. He was standing there close beside one of the boats when the door of the passenger accommodation opened and two figures emerged, momentarily outlined against the yellow light. They came aft, two voices talking earnestly, as he shrank into the shadow of the boat, bending down as though to adjust the falls.

". . . the last time I was at the Bahrain office. But even in Abu Dhabi we've heard rumours." The accent was North Country.

"Well, that's the situation. Thought I'd warn you. Wouldn't like you to back the wrong horse and find yourself out on your ear just because you didn't know what was going on."

"Aye; well, thanks. But the Great Gorde . . . It takes a bit of getting used to, you must admit. He's been the Company out here for so long."

"I wouldn't know about that, old man. I'm new out here, and, as far as I'm concerned, Erkhard is the man."

The voices were no more than a whisper in the night. The two oil men were leaning over the rail at the other end of the boat, and David was just going to creep away when he heard the name of his father mentioned. "Is it true Colonel Whitaker's the cause of the trouble? That's the rumour." He froze into immobility, listening fascinated as the other man gave a short laugh. "Well, yes, in a way; the Bloody Bedouin's got too big for his boots. And that theory of his, a lot of damned nonsense. He's not thinking of the Company, only of his Arab friends."

"Oh, I don't know. The Company owes him a lot."

"Concessions, yes—and a string of dry wells. The man's a dangerous amateur. I'm warning you, Entwhistle—you talk like that when Erkhard visits you at Abu Dhabi and you'll be out so damn quick—"

"It's Gorde I deal with."

"Okay. But you can take my word for it that it'll be Erkhard who does the next tour of inspection of the development sites. And unless you've got something to show him . . ."

The voices faded as the two men moved away, walking slowly and in step back towards the deck housing. David moved quickly, slipping down the ladder to the main deck, back to his position in the bows. He wanted to be alone, for that brief overheard conversation had given him a strange glimpse of the world on which he had set his heart.

The ship stopped at Masira Island with stores for the RAF, and then on again, rounding Ras al Hadd at night and ploughing northwest into the Gulf of Oman. On the afternoon of the seventh day out from Aden she anchored at Muscat, in a cove so narrow and rocky that David could scarcely believe his eyes; it might have been the Pembroke-shire coast of Wales except that a white, sun-drenched Arab town stood close by the water's edge at the head of the inlet. On either side the rocks bore the names of visiting ships with dates going back to the 1800's, all painted in foot-high letters. Long, double-ended boats of palm wood, their broad planks sewn together with thongs, swarmed round the ship, paddled by Arabs whose faces shone black in the sun.

They were there twenty-four hours, and in the night David thought more than once of diving over the side. The shore was so near. But, once ashore, what hope had he? There was nowhere for him to go. In a halting conversa-tion with one of the crew, a coast Arab from a fishing vil-lage to the north called Khor al Fakhan, he learned that Muscat was backed by volcanic mountains of indescribable brutality. They were almost fifty miles deep, with every route through guarded by watch towers; and beyond the mountains was the desert of the Rub al Khali—the Empty Quarter. He knew it was hopeless, and so he stayed on board, and the next afternoon they sailed.

He was having his evening meal when he was told to re-port to the bridge. Captain Griffiths was there, seated on his wooden stool, staring out over the bows to the starlit sea ahead. The only other man on the bridge was the Arab helmsman, standing immobile, his eyes fixed on the lit compass card in its binnacle, only his hands moving as he made small adjustments of the wheel.

"Ah, there you are." Griffiths had turned his head. "When I went ashore at Muscat last night there was a slave from Saraifa waiting for me with a message from your father. You'll doubtless be relieved to know that he's will-ing to take you off my hands." And as David mumbled his thanks, the lips smiled behind the beard. "I may say I'm just as relieved as you are." And he added brusquely: "There's an Arab *sambuq* waiting now off Ras al Khaima to pick you up. Tonight we shall pass through the Straits of Hormuz into the Persian Gulf. With luck we should sight the *sambuq* about an hour after dawn. Now, you speak Arabic, I'm told."

"A little," David admitted. "But it's not easy to make myself understood—it's the different dialects, I think."

"Well, do you think you can pass yourself off as an Arab?" And without waiting for a reply, Griffiths added: "It's the passengers, you see. They'll talk if they see a white member of my crew being put aboard a dhow." A few words of briefing and then the Captain's hand gripped his arm. "Good luck now, man. And a word of advice before you go—tread warily. It's no ordinary man you've got for a father, indeed it isn't. He's the devil of a temper when he's roused. So go easy and watch your step." And with that he dismissed him and turned again in his seat to stare through the glass at the lights of a ship coming up over the dark horizon.

David left the bridge, dazed and almost reluctant, for now the future was upon him—unknown, a little frightening. At dawn he would leave the ship and the companionship of the men he'd lived with for the past few weeks, and that last link with the home he'd known all his life would steam away, leaving him alone in a strange country, amongst strange people. It surprised him that he felt no excitement, no exhilaration—only loneliness and a sense of desolation. He didn't know it then, but it was in this moment that he said goodbye to his boyhood.

The Mate found him sitting on his bunk, staring vacantly into space. "Here you are, Whitaker." And he tossed a bundle of clothing down beside him. "Ali Mahommed sold them to me—*kaffyah, agal,* robe, sandals, the lot, even to an old brass *khanjar* knife. Three pounds ten, and I've deducted it from your pay." He placed some East African notes and some silver on top of the clothes. "The Old Man told you what to do, did he? Okay, so long as you greet the *naukhuda* with a *salaam alaikum* and a few more words of

Arabic. And get along to the paint-shop and put some stain on your face and hands. Your face is about as pink as a white baby's bottom."

Dressing up as an Arab for the first time in his life helped to pass the time, but still the long hours of the night stretched ahead. He lay awake a long time thinking about what the morrow would bring and about the man he hadn't known was his father till that tragic day. And then suddenly it was light, and almost immediately, it seemed, one of the Arab crew came down to tell him the *sambuq* had been sighted. He listened then, waiting, tense and expectant. And then the pulse of the engines slowed and finally died away. This was it—the moment of irrevocable departure. His hand touched the brass hilt of the great curved, flat-bladed knife at his girdle. He checked the *kaffyah,* made certain that the black *agal* was in its place, circling his head. He went quickly up to the after well-deck and waited in the shelter of the main-deck ladder. The rope ladder was over the side opposite Number Three hatch, one of the crew waiting there to help him over. The faint chug of a diesel sounded in the still morning air, coming slowly nearer. He heard the bump of the dhow as it came alongside, the guttural cry of Arab voices, and then the man by the ladder was beckoning him.

He went out quickly with his head down, hidden by his *kaffyah*. A dark-skinned hand caught his arm, steadied him as he went over the bulwarks. Glancing quickly up, he caught a glimpse of the Captain leaning with his elbows on the rail of the bridge wing and below, on the boat deck, a short, tubby man in a pale dressing-gown standing watching. And after that he could see nothing but the ship's rusty side.

Hands reached up, caught him as he jumped to the worn wood deck of the dhow. He called out a greeting in Arabic as he had been told and at the same moment he heard the distant clang of the engine-room telegraph. The beat of the *Emerald Isle*'s engines increased and the hull plates began to slide past, a gap opening between himself and the ship. He turned away to hide his face and found himself on a long-prowed craft built of battered wood, worn smooth by the years and bleached almost white by the torrid heat of the Persian Gulf. A single patched sail curved above it like the dirty wing of a goose hanging dead in the airless morning. The sea around was still as a mirror and white like molten glass, and then the swirl of the ship's screws shattered it.

There were three men on the *sambuq* and only the *naukhuda*, or captain, wore a turban as well as a loin-cloth. He was an old man with a wisp of a grey moustache and a few grey hairs on his chin, which he stroked constantly. The crew was composed of a smooth-faced boy with a withered arm and a big, barrel-chested man, black as a Negro, with a satin skin that rippled with every movement. The *naukhuda* took David's hand in his and held it for a long time, whilst the other two crowded close, staring at his face, feeling his clothes—six brown eyes gazing at him, full of curiosity. A flood of questions, the old man using the deferential *sahib,* legacy of India. Whenever David said anything, all three listened respectfully. But it was no good. He couldn't seem to make himself understood.

At length he gave it up and, judging that it would be safe now to turn his head to take a last look at the *Emerald Isle*, he was appalled to find that she had vanished utterly, swallowed in the humid haze of the day's beginning. For a time he could still hear the beat of her engines, but finally even that was gone and he was alone with his three Arabs on a flat calm sea that had an oily shimmer to its hard, unbroken surface.

He felt abandoned then, more alone than he'd ever been in his life before. But it was a mood that didn't last, for in less than an hour the haze thinned and away to port the vague outline of a mass of mountains emerged. A few minutes later and the sky was clear, a blue bowl reflected in the sea, and the mountains stood out, magnificent, tumbling down from the sky in sheer red cliffs to disappear in a mirage effect at the water's edge. Ahead, a long dhow stood with limp sail suspended in the air, and beyond it the world seemed to vanish—no mountains, nothing, only the endless sky. For the first time he understood why men talked of the desert as a sea.

Twice the *sambuq*'s aged engine petered out. Each time it was the boy who got it going. The *naukhuda* sat dreamily at the helm, steering with the toes of his right foot curled round the smooth wood of the rudder bar. A charcoal fire had been burning on the low poop ever since David had come on board, and the big cooking-pot above it eventually produced a mess of rice and mutton, which they ate in their fingers. A small wind stirred the surface of the sea, increased until it filled the sail, and the engine was switched off. In the sudden quiet, the sound of the water sliding past the hull seemed almost loud. The mainsheet was eased out and the *sambuq* took wing. "Ras al Khaima." The *naukhuda* pointed across the port bow. At the very foot of the mountains and low on the horizon, David made out the dun-coloured shape of houses, the tufts of palms. And shortly after that the coast ahead showed up, low and flat, a shimmering line of dunes.

The sun was barely halfway up the sky when they closed that dune coast. A line of camels marched sedately along the sand of the foreshore, and close under the low cliffs a Land Rover stood parked, a lone figure in Arab clothes standing beside it. He thought then that this was his father and braced himself for that first meeting, wondering what he would be like. But when the *naukhuda* paddled him ashore in the *sambuq*'s dugout, it was an Arab who waded into the shallow water to meet them.

Again the difficulty of trying to make himself understood. The Arab's name was Yousif and he spoke a little English. "Coll-onell Sahib not here. You come Saraifa now." The word Saraifa was shouted at him several times as though he were deaf.

"How far is Saraifa?"

The man stared at him as though he were mad. He was a very dirty-looking individual, his greasy turban trailing one end over his shoulders, a torn and very filthy European jacket worn over his Arab robes. His dark face was smudged with oil; this and the little black moustache below the curved nose gave him a sinister appearance.

David tried again: "Saraifa . . . ten miles, twenty?" He held up his fingers.

"Saraifa no far in machine of Coll-onell Sahib." The gap-toothed smile was clearly meant to placate. "Me driver to Coll-onell Sahib. Drive very quick." That seemed to exhaust his fund of English, for he turned to the *naukhuda* and launched into a guttural flood of conversation. At length the *naukhuda* stepped forward, kissed his hand, and touched it to his heart with a little bow. David gave him one of the notes the Mate had handed him and found his hand held in the other's horny palm whilst the old man made him a long farewell speech.

Then at last he was in the Land Rover and they were roaring along the sand of the foreshore, the driver bent over the wheel like a rider urging on his horse, with the stray end of his filthy turban streaming out behind him. A mile or two further on they left the sea's edge by a camel track that climbed the shallow cliffs. Looking back, David got a last glimpse of the dhow that had brought him to the Arabian shore, and then they were bouncing past the Bedouin caravan he had seen moving along the sands. The camels stared with supercilious gaze, padding effortlessly through the sand under their mountainous loads. The men, wild and bearded, raised their hands unsmilingly in desert salutation. The silver mountings of their old-fashioned guns winked in the hot sun, and David caught the wicked gleam of *khanjar* knives and the brass of cartridge belts. He was seeing for the first time the desert world that was to be his home.

II

Enquiries of an Executor

The account of
his actual arrival in Arabia was contained in the letter he
dispatched to me almost immediately after he had reached
Saraifa. For that reason, I suppose, it told me little about
the actual meeting between himself and his father. Scribbled in pencil on scraps of paper, it had been written
mostly on board the *Emerald Isle*. Except for the final page,
it had been completed at a water-hole somewhere in the
desert where he and Yousif had spent the night. The final
page was nothing more than a hastily written postscript:
*Saraifa at last, but I arrived at a bad time—my father was
with the Sheikh and an oil director and his pilot, and he
leaves with them in the morning for Bahrain. He seemed
angry at first, but it's all right now, I think. The Sheikh's
son, Khalid, is to look after me whilst he is away, and I
am to go on a hunting expedition with him to get to know
desert ways. My father is a great man here, with a bodyguard and a mud fort or palace where I am writing now.
He has only one eye and a black patch over the other,
which makes him a bit terrifying at first, and everybody
seems afraid of him. Men keep coming into this room for*

one reason and another, but really to stare at me. It is all very strange—but exciting. Thank you again. David.

At the end of the year he sent me a Christmas card. It was a Gulfoman Oilfields Development Company card and was postmarked Basra. He was at an oil school studying geology and seemed happy. That was the last I heard of him until I received the news, three years later, that he was missing in the Rub al Khali desert, the Empty Quarter.

By then I was involved in his father's affairs. It was a strange business and one that was causing me considerable concern—though at the outset it had seemed straightforward enough. In fact, I wasn't in the least surprised when he asked me to act for him. A lawyer's business is a very personal one and tends to grow through personal contact. *What my son has told me about you, and the fact that your firm acted for me for many years in the matter of the settlement to his mother, leads me to place complete confidence in your discretion and in your ability to use your own initiative when required.* He wanted to consolidate his financial affairs, he said, and he sent me power of attorney and gave me authority to collect all monies, meet any accounts that became due, and generally manage his business interests. There was nothing particularly unusual about this, except that I was on no account to attempt to communicate with him in any way once the arrangement was working.

My correspondence with him lasted over several months. His letters were all hand-written, and the only address he gave was his bank in Bahrain. Shortly after it was all agreed, money began to flow in from all over the Middle East, from Arab merchants and bankers, from traders, from a firm of stockbrokers in Cairo, and a large sum from the cashier of the London office of the Gulfoman Oilfields Development Company. This went on for about a year. Some of it was in kind—pearls from a dealer in Bahrain,

even a box full of Maria Theresa dollars and another full
of silver, presumably gifts from the local sheikhs.

Finally the flow had dried up, and, presuming that the
operation was against his retirement, I invested the money
for him, mostly in local industry of which I had personal
knowledge. The market, of course, was a restricted one,
but it never occurred to me that he would almost immediately want large sums in cash. And then in May of the
following year accounts began to come through for settlement—for stores, equipment, vehicles; the largest single
item was almost £5,000 for a second-hand seismological
truck, complete with geophones and all the necessary
equipment for a geophysical survey, and there had been
a shipping agent's account for freighting it down from
Basra to Muscat on the *Emerald Isle.*

It was clear that he was embarking on a program of oil
exploration on his own, expecting it to be financed by the
nominee account, and it worried me, for I'd no means of
knowing where it was going to end. I ignored my instructions then and wrote him several times, care of his bank,
but received no reply. And in the New Year I received another batch of accounts, this time for fuel and stores and
drilling-pipe. I was by then thoroughly alarmed about the
whole situation. He obviously didn't realize that there
were restrictions on bank lending, and I was reluctant to
sell securities on a weak market. I was able to meet the immediate accounts, but I had to know what his future plans
were. On March 5 I received an account for the hire of a
complete drilling-rig. I phoned an oil man I knew in Mil-
ford Haven, and he gave me figures for the probable cost
of drilling, even with a hired rig, that staggered me. I
wrote to Whitaker then, stating that unless he sent me a
statement of his plans and the probable cost by return, I
should have no alternative but to fly out at his expense to
discuss the whole situation.

That was the position on the morning of March 24 when
I came into the office and found an airmail letter with a

Bahrain stamp amongst my post. I thought it was the reply I was expecting, but when I opened it I found it was from Susan Thomas. Apparently she was now working as a nurse at a hospital in Dubai. She enclosed a copy of a cable she had received from the offices of the Gulfoman Oilfields Development Company in Bahrain. I read it through twice before my mind was able to take in and accept what the words meant, so great was my sense of shock.

NURSE SUSAN THOMAS THE HOSPITAL DUBAI FROM GODCO—MARCH 18: REGRET INFORM YOU YOUR BROTHER DAVID WHITAKER MISSING DESERT RUB AL KHALI SINCE FEBRUARY TWENTY-EIGHT STOP TRUCK NOW DISCOVERED ABANDONED SOME FIFTY MILES WEST NORTHWEST OF SARAIFA OASIS STOP EXTENSIVE GROUND SEARCH WITH AIR CO-OPERATION RAF IN DIFFICULT DUNE COUNTRY HAS REVEALED NO TRACE ALSO UNREPORTED NOMAD TRIBESMEN STOP SEARCH NOW RELUCTANTLY CALLED OFF MUST BE PRESUMED DEAD STOP COMPANY OFFERS DEEPEST SYMPATHY YOU AND YOUR MOTHER—ERKHARD.

Presumed dead! It was hard to believe. Dealing as I had been for the last two years with his father's affairs, I had often thought about him, wondered how he was getting on, what he was doing. I had even thought of writing to him to ask him about his father's plans. And now this. My own sense of disbelief was echoed by Susan's letter—a purely intuitive reaction. *We were twins, as you know, yet all this time, whilst they have been searching, I knew nothing, felt nothing. If David is dead, then surely I would have known.* And then, a little further on in the letter: *Early last month he came to see me, very late at night. He was in some sort of trouble. But what it was he wouldn't say. He seemed withdrawn and he had a rather wild look. I felt he was in danger, but I still cannot believe he is dead.* And then the words: *He told me then that if anything were to happen to him I was to write to you at once.* In the final paragraph she apologized for being a nuisance and added: *But please, please contact the London Office of the Company and try to persuade them to have the search resumed.* The letter was signed simply *Susan*, as though I were an old friend.

I was due in Court at ten o'clock and still had the rest of my post to go through; I put the letter aside and didn't get back to it until late that afternoon, when I rang the London office of the Gulfoman Oilfields Development Company. But of course they knew nothing. A thin, cultured voice informed me that all local administration was dealt with by the Bahrain office. "The cable is signed Erkhard, you say? Then I think you may take it that everything possible has already been done and the facts are as stated. Mr. Erkhard is our General Manager out there and in charge of all developments." However, he took my name and address and promised to pass on my observations to Bahrain.

I cleared my desk and then got my car and drove down to Grangetown to break the news to Mrs. Thomas; not a very pleasant task, but one that I couldn't very well avoid, since Susan had written: *This is something I cannot bring myself to do in a letter. It would be so much kinder if you would do it—more personal, and you can explain the circumstances better. Tell her I will write later.*

Mrs. Thomas had aged, of course, but more so than I would have expected. Her hair was completely grey now, no longer drawn back tightly from her forehead, but hanging untidily in wisps. The dress she wore was none too clean, and the eyes looked almost furtive as they flickered from one thing to another, never at rest and never looking directly at me. At the same time, the lines of strain had gone; her face seemed to have filled out, become smoother.

She invited me into the parlour, where the couch was still in the same place, the roll-top desk still littered with books on racing form. She was nervous, and she was talking all the time as we stood there, almost in the same positions, like actors cued to their places, talking about David, about Sue, about her life and how lonely it was now. "But Dafydd is a great comfort to me. He was never much of a letter writer, but since he went to Arabia . . ." Her eyes flicked to my face. "Is it about Dafydd you've come, Mr. Grant?" But then they had fled to another part of the room and she was saying: "I'm expecting a letter from him soon. He doesn't write regularly, of course. He's in such strange places. But such a picture he gives me, I can almost see it, you know . . . the Bedouin men and the camels and the heat; like a dream it is and me twenty again and waiting for letters." She gave a little hurried laugh, almost a titter. "I get confused sometimes. Over two years it is now since Sue went out there. I've been alone ever since, you see, and the mind plays tricks. . . ."

"When did you last hear from David?" I asked her.

"Oh, recently. Quite recently. And I'll have another letter from him soon. Any day now, I expect . . ." And then, sheering away from the subject, she said: "You've never seen his room, have you? All his books. I'd like you to see his room." And without waiting for a reply, she bustled out of the room as though anxious to escape from me. "I've kept it just as it was, you know."

She led me up the ill-lit stairs to a little room at the end of a short landing. The place smelt musty and had the chill of long abandonment. A flick-knife lay on the painted top of a chest of drawers like a warrior's trophy from some forgotten war, and above the bed was a shelf full of books. "He was a great one for reading," she said. "Anything about Arabia. I did my best to get him interested in other things, but there . . . I knew he'd go there sooner or later. It was in the blood, as you might say."

There were about fifty books there, most of them books on Arabia, including expensive volumes like Doughty's *Arabia Deserta*—all damaged, but stuck together with loving care. It was a strange glimpse of a young man's yearning. "I believe Colonel Whitaker once wrote a book about Arabia," I said. "I tried to get a copy, but it was out of print."

She nodded. "It's a long time since anybody could get a copy. It wasn't very successful, you see. But there is one here somewhere." She leaned her weight against the bed and ran a work-coarsened finger along the bookshelf. And then she took down a book and handed it to me. The title was *Wanderings by Camel through the Empty Quarter.* "Signed it is, you see," she said proudly. "He gave it to me before he left." And she added wistfully: "It was the only present he ever gave me."

The book, of course, brought back memories to her. She smiled at me shyly—almost coyly. "You know it was whilst he was home writing that and getting it published that I came to know him. I was in service then at Llanfihangel Hall. That was his family's place." She hesitated. "I suppose he was bored, really." The coy little smile had spread to her eyes, so that her whole face was strangely transfigured. "But we enjoyed ourselves." She said it with a happy little sigh, and then she added: "Ah, well, you only live once, Mr. Grant. That's what I tell myself whenever I'm feeling lonely. You've had your fun, Sarah, I say. You've had your fun and you've paid the price. Are you married, Mr. Grant?"

"No."

"And no illegitimate children?" She gave a queer laugh as I shook my head. "Well, there you are. People like you miss a great deal in life." And she added with surprising perception: "You shouldn't always live at second hand, you know. Rummaging about in other people's lives . . ."

"We do our best to help," I murmured uncomfortably. And then I asked her if I could borrow Whitaker's book for a few days. I thought it might help me to understand the sort of man he was. She looked at me in surprise. "No," she said quickly, her eyes darting to the book. "No, I don't think I'd like any one to borrow that." And she took it from me and put it quickly back in its place. "I'll make you some tea if you like," she said as she took me back down the stairs.

At the bottom, under the light, there was a faded photograph of a pretty girl in a high-necked frock. "That was taken just about the time I met the Major," she said as she saw me looking at it." "He was a major then, you see—from the Kaiser's War. You didn't recognize it as me, I suppose?" She smiled. "I was considered very pretty then, you know—though I didn't look so pretty when he'd finished with me and I was bearing twins; more like a balloon, you know. Now, won't you stay and have a cup of tea, Mr. Grant, and you can tell me how you managed to get Dafydd out to his father. I should have thanked you for doing that, shouldn't I, but at the time I thought it might . . ." She hesitated. "You see, I've always been afraid of what would happen when they met. And then Dafydd started to go wrong—all those Arab friends of his. . . ." We had reached the parlour again, and she said: "I shall never forget that afternoon. Mr. Thomas lying there on the couch, and Dafydd—" She pointed towards the spot where he had stood. "And Dafydd standing there and swearing he'd kill his own Da. But there . . ." She gave me a weak, uneasy smile. "They're together now. And nothing has happened, has it? It was silly of me to take a young boy so seriously." And she added almost violently: "But it scared me at the time. It scared me silly."

"You say they're together *now*?"

"Oh, yes—in a place called Saraifa. That's an oasis—"

"What was the date of that last letter you had?"

"I—I don't remember." Her mouth was suddenly trembling. "It was quite recent, Mr. Grant."

"Could I see it, please?"

She hesitated, her eyes wandering round the room. And then finally she went to the roll-top desk and took a single sheet of paper from the top of a neat little pile of similar sheets. "August it was," she said almost in a whisper. "August the twenty-third."

Seven months ago. "And you haven't heard from him since?"

She shook her head, her hand trembling as she stared down at the letter.

"And he was at Saraifa; does he say what he was doing there?"

"He'd been on a gazelle hunt with Sheikh Makhmud and his son. . . ."

"What sort of work, I mean?"

"No, he doesn't mention work. But it would be something to do with oil. He's a geologist, you see, and works for one of the oil companies." She was reading the letter to herself again, her lips forming the words which I was certain she knew by heart. "He writes beautiful letters, you know—all about the country and the people he meets. He writes so I can almost imagine I'm out there with him." She put the letter back on the pile. "That was my dream once, that I'd go out there to live." She stood there smiling to herself and staring out at the dingy street. "Just a dream," she repeated. "But with the books and the maps I can see it all from his letters. I'm a Welsh woman, you see. I have the gift of imagination." And then with a sudden edge of bitterness to her voice: "You need imagination sometimes in a hole like this."

How could I tell her the boy was dead? "Have you heard from his father at all?"

She shook her head. "No, I've never heard from the Major—not once in all these years." There was a catch in her voice, and she moved quickly away towards the door. "I'll make you some tea."

"Please don't bother," I said. "I have to go now."

But she was between me and the door, her hands fumbling at her dress, her eyes searching my face. She had finally screwed herself up to the pitch of facing the implication of my visit. "What's happened, Mr. Grant?" she asked. "What's happened between them? As soon as I saw you standing there on the doorstep . . ."

"Nothing has happened between them. According to my information—"

But she didn't let me finish, wasn't even listening. "I knew they should never have met," she cried. "They're alike, you see. They've the same nature—obstinate, very obstinate." She was almost sobbing for breath. "I knew what it would mean. It's in their stars. They're both Sagittarius, you see. And he was such a fine man when I knew him. Such a fine man—and lusty, so full of fire and vitality." She was wringing her hands, and a sound came from her lips like the sound of keening. "Known it I have, always. Oh, God!" she whispered. And then, staring straight at me: "How did it happen? Do you know how it happened?"

There was nothing for it then but to let her know the facts, such as they were. And because it was easier I handed her the copy of the cable her daughter had sent me. She read it through slowly, her eyes widening as the shock of it went home until they became fixed, almost vacant. "Dafydd!" She murmured his name.

"He's reported missing, that's all," I said, trying to comfort her, to offer her some hope.

But she didn't seem to take that in. "Dead," she whispered. And then she repeated his name. "Dafydd?" And her tone was one of shocked surprise. "I never thought it would be Dafydd. That's not right at all." The fixed stare was almost trance-like. "It was never Dafydd that was going to die." And a shiver ran through her.

"I'll write to your daughter. No doubt she'll let you have any further information direct." She didn't say anything, and her eyes still had that fixed, trance-like look as I took the copy of the cable from her nerveless hand. Her behaviour was so odd I didn't like to leave it with her. "Don't worry too much. There's still a chance. . . ."

"No." The word seemed to explode out of her mouth. "No, better it is like this, God rest his poor soul."

Appalled, I hurried past her, out into the fresh evening air. The stars—what a thing to be believing in at a time like this. Poor woman!

But as I drove away, it was the father I was thinking about, a sense of uneasiness growing in my mind, fostered by the violence of her strange reaction. Going back to that house, to that poor woman driven half out of her senses by an old love she couldn't discard; it was all suddenly fresh in my memory—her fears and the way he'd sworn to kill his father. What had happened between those two in the intervening years? Or was this just an accident—one of those things that can happen to any young man prospecting out there in the remote deserts of Arabia?

Back at the office I got out the Whitaker file and read that postscript to David's letter again. But there was nothing in it to give me a clue as to how his father had reacted. The words might have been written by any youngster plunged into new and strange surroundings, except that he had described his father as though he were looking at him with the eyes of a complete stranger. But then that was what he was. Right at the bottom of the file was the dossier Andrews had produced from press-cuttings in the library of the Welsh edition of a popular daily, and I read it through again:

Charles Stanley Whitaker, born Llanfihangel Hall near Usk, 1899. Joined the cavalry as a trooper in 1915, served with Allenby in the offensive against the Turks, and rose to the rank of major. After the war, he stayed on in the Middle East. Policeman, trader, dhow-owner; he adopted the Moslem religion, made the pilgrimage to Mecca, has lived with the Bedouin. His book on his crossing of the Rub al Khali desert was published in 1936. By then he had already become something of a legend. Following publication of his book, he went back to the Middle East, and after three years with Gulfoman Oilfields Development, he

joined Wavell's staff on the outbreak of war with
the rank of colonel. Awarded the V.C. for gallantry, wounded twice, served with Wingate and
later with Wilson. Was still a colonel at the end
of the war. He then rejoined Gulfoman Oilfields
Development as political representative.

There was a picture pinned to the dossier which showed
him in Arab dress standing beside a Land Rover on a
desert airstrip. The black patch over the right eye was
plainly visible; so, too, was the prominent, beak-like nose.
He was slightly stooped, as though conscious of his height;
he was a head taller than the other two men in the picture.
This and the beard and the black patch over the eye gave
him a very formidable appearance, and, though the picture wasn't a very clear one, looking at it again, I couldn't
help feeling that he was a man capable of anything, and I
could appreciate the impression he had made on a Welsh
servant girl all those years ago. He would have been thirty-
six then, a good deal younger, and I suppose he had taken
her the way he would have taken a slave girl in a Bedouin
encampment; but for her it had been something different,
an experience so out of the ordinary that she had thought
of nothing else for the last twenty-five years.

I wondered whether she still possessed that album full of
press-cuttings. I would have liked to look through it and
also through the letters from her son, but I couldn't face
the thought of going back to the house. I returned the file
to its place and wrote to Susan advising her to make the
journey to Bahrain and see Erkhard. *Nothing can be done,
it appears, at this end,* I told her. *Erkhard seems to be the
only man who has the authority to order the search to be
resumed.*

Two days later the news of David's death was in *The
Times*—a rather guarded account, it seemed to me. It was
clearly based on a Company handout, but it did include

a brief description by one of the RAF pilots who had flown the search.

> Flight-Lieutenant Hill described the truck as similar to those used by oil companies for seismological work, though no company markings showed on either bonnet or sides. It was halfway up the side of a big sand dune, as though it had stalled or bogged down in an effort to surmount this obstacle. It was hardly surprising, he said, that he had flown several times over the area without seeing it; high winds—the local *shamal*— had piled the sand up on one side of it. He had only sighted the truck because the sun was low and it was casting a shadow.

It was less a news story than a short article, and most of it was about Colonel Whitaker—*that strange, half-Arab figure, so prominent in the search for Gulf oil during the past twenty years.* It was "From Our Own Correspondent," and I had a vague sense as I read it that there was something behind the piece, something that he was not in a position to reveal but that was nevertheless there for those who could read between the lines. Such phrases as: *The fascination of this man who has maintained his theory about oil in the face of persistent failure;* and *Whether he is another Holmes or not, whether the oil company he served for so long will live to regret his departure, only time will tell.* Finally there was this: *It appears there is some foundation for the rumour that his son, though employed by GODCO, was on loan to him for some private purpose, presumably connected with prospecting for oil.*

The suggestion that David had been on loan to his father at the time of his disappearance did nothing to allay the uneasiness that had resulted from my visit to Mrs. Thomas. And then the following morning Captain Griffiths walked into my office and I knew for certain that there was something more to the boy's death than the Company had so far revealed.

Griffiths had docked at first light and was still in uniform, having come straight form his ship. "I promised to deliver this personally into your hands." He put a fat envelope down on the desk in front of me. "Personally, you understand. He wouldn't risk it through the post."

"Who's it from?" I asked. But the address was handwritten, the writing familiar. I knew it was from David before he answered my question. "Young Whitaker," he said and sat himself down in the chair opposite my desk.

I was too startled to say anything for a moment, for the boy had been alive when he'd handed this to Griffiths. I picked it up, staring at the address as though that would give me some clue as to what was inside. "When did he give you this?"

"Well, now . . ." He frowned. "It was Sharjah, and we were anchored about a mile off—"

"Yes, but what was the date?"

"It's the date I'm trying to remember, man." His little beard bristled. "Without my log I can't be sure. But we left Basra on January twenty-third and we called at Kuwait, Bahrain, Doha, Abu Dhabi, and Dubai before we anchored off Sharjah; it would be about the middle of the first week in February."

And David had been reported missing on February 28. Griffiths must have been one of the last people he saw before he went out into the desert—perhaps one of the last of his own race to see him alive.

"Still the same offices, I see." Griffiths had pulled his pipe out and was busy filling it. He didn't know the boy was dead.

"The trouble is the clients don't pay their bills," I said and slit the packet open. The old rogue had never settled my account, though he'd admitted that Whitaker had made him a present of fifty quid for getting the boy out to Arabia. Inside was a hand-written letter folded around another envelope that had GODCO, BAHRAIN, printed on the flap. Across the front of it he had typed: DAVID WHITAKER—TO BE OPENED ONLY IN THE EVENT OF MY DEATH.

Those words—they came as a shock. I stared at them, wondering how he could possibly have known he was going to die. Or was it just a coincidence?

"What's the matter?" Griffiths asked. "What's he been up to?"

I suppose he thought he was in some sort of legal trouble. "You haven't seen *The Times* then?"

"Of course not. I only got in this morning. Why?"

"David Whitaker is dead," I said. And I told him about the truck they'd found abandoned and the description of it given in *The Times*. "You must have been one of the last people to see him alive."

"I see."

His acceptance of it might have surprised me, except that my mind was still on that envelope. "It's almost uncanny," I murmured.

"What is?"

"Your coming here, with this." I turned the envelope round so that he could see what was typed across it. "He must have had some sort of premonition. . . ."

Griffiths nodded his head slowly. "That explains it." And he added: "May his soul rest in peace, the poor devil." He said it quietly, with reverence, as though he were on the deck of his ship and consigning the boy's body to the deep.

"Explains what?" I asked him.

"The circumstances . . ." He hesitated. "Very strange they were." And then he looked at me, his gaze very direct. "I don't think you quite understand, Mr. Grant. That boy risked his life on a filthy night with a *shamal* blowing to get that packet to me without any one knowing."

"Risked his life?" I was reading through the covering letter, only half listening to him.

"Yes, indeed, for he came off in one of those fisherman's dugouts and just an Arab boy with him. It was a damned foolhardy thing to do. There was a wicked sea running. He needed a lawyer, he said, somebody he could trust."

"Why? Did he say why he needed a lawyer?"

"No." Griffiths shook his head. "No, he didn't say why, and it's something I've been asking myself ever since I put that envelope away in the ship's safe. What would a young geophysicist want with a lawyer out there in the middle of Arabia?"

I finished reading the letter and then I put it down on the desk. Griffiths was lighting his pipe, his head cocked on one side. "Well, he's dead now, you say." He was eying the unopened envelope the way a thrush eyes a worm.

"Perhaps you'd tell me just what happened?" I suggested.

"Well . . ." He hesitated, his eyes still on the envelope. "It was night, you see. We had finished unloading and the deck lights had been switched off about an hour when one of my Arab crew reports a dugout alongside and a white man in it called Thomas asking for me. Well, I couldn't recall his name—how should I? I have so many passengers; they come and go along the coast—oil men, Locust Control, Levy officers, Air Force personnel, Government officials. How should I remember his name, even if he was another Welshman? It was four years since he'd used it anyway. And then he came stumbling into my cabin and I recognized him at once, of course."

I thought he was going to stop there, but after a moment's silence he went on: "Only the previous voyage I'd had him on board as a passenger, from Bahrain down to Dubai. He'd changed a great deal in those six months; all the vitality of youth seemed to have been whipped out of him, his skin burned almost black by the sun and the hard, angular bones of the face showing through. But it was the eyes, man. They weren't the eyes of a youngster any more;

they were the eyes of a man who'd looked the world in the face and been badly frightened by it."

"Who was he afraid of?" I was thinking of the father then.

"I didn't say he was afraid of anybody."

"Did he talk to you at all—about himself?"

"Oh, yes, indeed. He was talking all the time. To be honest, Mr. Grant, I thought he might be going round the bend. Some of them do that, you know . . . the heat and the sand, and if it's lonely work—"

"Yes, but what did he say?"

"Nothing very much. Nothing that I can remember, that is. He was talking very fast, you see, the words tumbling over themselves—about his job and where he'd been."

"And where had he been? Had he been to Saraifa?"

But Griffiths shook his head. "I can't remember," he said. "I don't think he mentioned Saraifa. It was talk for the sake of talking, you know—for the sake of hearing the sound of his own voice and having somebody listen to it. He'd been in some wild places, I think, and mostly on his own, nobody with him but Arabs."

I asked about the packet then. "Did he talk about that at all?"

"No. He sat at my desk and wrote that covering letter. And when he'd finished it, he borrowed an envelope from me, sealed the whole thing up, and asked me to put it in my safe and deliver it to you personally the moment I docked."

"Didn't you ask him why it was so urgent?"

"Of course I did. I was damned curious about the whole thing. But his manner was so odd—"

"He didn't say anything about it being political dynamite, then?"

"Political dynamite?" Griffiths's bushy eyebrows lifted. "No, he didn't say anything like that." A wary look had come into his eyes. "Is that what he says in that letter?"

I nodded. "Where's Colonel Whitaker now? Can you tell me that?"

But he didn't know for certain. "Probably in Saraifa," he said. "Why?" His tone was suddenly cautious, as though he were a witness under cross-examination, and since I had no intention of telling him the reason for my interest in Whitaker, I asked him about the previous voyage when he'd had David on board as a passenger. "Was he going to join his father, do you know?"

But he couldn't even tell me that. "All he said was that he was going down into the Rub al Khali." He took out his watch and glanced at it. "It was a hell of a time to be going down into the Empty Quarter," he added as though glad to escape into generalities. "That time of the year the sand is hot enough to burn the tires off a truck and the soles off your boots."

"It was summer?"

He nodded. "Early July it would have been."

And that was the month I'd received the shipping agent's account. "Did you have a seismological truck on board?"

"Yes." He stared at me curiously, surprised that I should know about it. "It was deck cargo, and we shipped it down to Muscat. I remember that because we had a devil of a job getting it ashore; had to lash four of the local boats together and bridge them with planks."

"You don't think it could be the same truck—the one that was found abandoned?"

But of course he couldn't tell me that.

"Did you know he was on loan to his father? Did he say anything about that?"

He shook his head and got to his feet.

"Did he talk about his father at all?"

"No, he didn't mention him." He said it flatly, as though to discourage any further questions. "I must be going now, Mr. Grant. Just docked—a lot of things to see to, you know."

I was reluctant to let him go. "One more question, Cap-

tain Griffiths." I was standing facing him then. "You said
once that you heard all the gossip out there. Have you
heard any rumours about Saraifa?"

"Rumours?"

"That Colonel Whitaker is prospecting for oil there."

He started to say something, but then he seemed to think
better of it and shook his head. "A man like that, you
never know what's true and what isn't. And Saraifa is a
long way from the coast. A trouble spot, too." He glanced
uneasily at his watch again.

I read him the *Times* correspondent's report, the paragraph about David being on loan to his father. But all he
said was: "The Whitaker Theory. It crops up whenever
anybody writes about that man." And then he was moving towards the door. "Well, I've done what I promised,
and that's that." He held out his hand. "Sad about David
Whitaker, very sad. Good boy—lots of character." He
shook my hand briefly, cast a quick glance at the envelope
still lying unopened on my desk, and then went to the
door. His last words to me as I saw him out were: "It's a
tricky business, oil. Lot of money involved; politics, too.
And if he was operating anywhere near the Hadd-Saraifa
border . . . Well, you'd understand if you'd ever been
out there." He said it in a fatherly way, as though he were
giving me some sound advice.

I was reluctant to let him go. That little Welsh sea captain was stuffed full of all the gossip of the Gulf if I could
only have wrung it out of him. But I don't think he wanted
to talk, and anyway I was anxious to find out what that
envelope contained. The covering letter had given me no
real indication.

*You helped me once long ago. Now I'm asking you to
help me again.* He mentioned the envelope then and asked
me to put it in a safe place and only open it in the event
of his death. *You're the only man I feel I can trust with a
thing like this.* And he added: *I should warn you that it's
political dynamite, and if anybody knew it was in your*

possession it might lead to trouble. He concluded with apologies for bothering me with his affairs, and then these words: *Thank you again for helping me to a life that has suited me and that I have enjoyed*. It was signed: *Yours gratefully—David*.

I read it through again, standing at my desk, and there was no escaping the significance of those final words. For some reason he had believed he was going to die. Had he been ill, suffering from some terrible disease? But that didn't fit Griffiths's description of him. Nervous, wrought up, even frightened—yes; but not ill. And why the secrecy anyway?

I picked up the envelope and slit it open. Inside were a typewritten letter, his will, and two envelopes—one addressed to Sir Philip Gorde at the London office of GODCO, the other marked: *Location and Sketch Map.* Location of what? But it wasn't difficult to guess, for what else but the discovery of oil could be described as political dynamite in the deserts of Arabia?

The letter didn't say so in so many words, but it made it pretty clear. And because it gives some indication of his frame of mind—and also because it formed the basis of my subsequent actions—I give it here in full. It was dated December 29 of the previous year, and above the date he had typed: *Somewhere in the Sheikhdom of Saraifa.*

Dear Mr. Grant,

The time has come to put my affairs into the hands of somebody I know and can trust. I am working here on an old survey. It was carried out a long time ago and the man who did it is dead now. If my own results confirm his report—and I shall know very shortly—I shall try and catch Captain Griffiths at Sharjah when the *Emerald Isle* stops there about the end of next month. I cannot explain to you why it is necessary. All I can say is that this is a forbidden zone and that

I am working against time and without authority.
Everything is against me—almost like it was when
I came to you last. I've always been a bit of a
rebel at heart. But outside of the pack, you're on
your own. And whatever happens to me, I'm determined that Saraifa shall have the benefit of my
efforts. The oasis fights a losing battle with the
desert. Without money it is doomed. And I spent
six of the happiest months of my life there.

When you read this I shall be dead. Please then
take the following action: Contact Sir Philip
Gorde, who is on the board of directors of
GODCO, and give him the envelope I have addressed to him. It contains a document which is
correctly phrased and is a copy of other concession agreements. It will also contain my survey
report, but without the locations. The locations
will be contained in a separate envelope, together
with additional copies of my survey report. This
envelope is only to be handed over after Sir Philip
Gorde has signed the concession agreement and
legally bound the Company, to your satisfaction,
to drill *four* test wells at the locations indicated.
[The *four* had been written in in ink, presumably
later.]

In the event that Sir Philip Gorde refuses to
sign, then you will please take whatever action
you think best in the interests of Saraifa. Khalid,
the Sheikh's son, knows what I am doing and you
will find he fully understands what is at stake so
far as the oasis is concerned. It is essential that
somehow you get the concession taken up. Saraifa
needs oil desperately and if you succeed you will
not find Khalid lacking in appreciation, or
Sheikh Makhmud for that matter. You may, of
course, make what use you can of the circumstances of my death, my parentage, and my past to

achieve publicity and so attract the interest of other oil companies.

Enclosed also is my Will. I have appointed you my Executor and after making the necessary arrangements with my bank in Bahrain, you will please draw on the account for fees and expenses. Please understand that I would not again involve you in my affairs if I were not desperate. In the event of my death I have instructed my sister to contact you immediately.

David Whitaker

It was an unusual communication for a solicitor to receive, most unusual; and, reading it through again, I was struck by the fact that he made no mention of his father. In the whole of that document there wasn't one reference to Colonel Whitaker. *Everything is against me.* There were other phrases, too. I was greatly disturbed about the whole thing, particularly as I knew that Whitaker was engaged in an operation that must run counter to the interests of the company he had served and which David was serving at the time of his death.

However, there was no point in speculating. His instructions were clear, and I picked up the phone and rang the London office of GODCO. And whilst I was waiting for the call to come through I had a look at the will. He had typed it himself, but it was a perfectly legal document even though the witnesses to his signature were two Arabs. It appointed me executor and his sister, Susan, sole legatee with instructions to take care of their mother. Again no reference to his father.

This and the letter and the fact that he had made such careful provision against the possibility of death gave a strange quality of isolation to his activities, as though he were operating alone in a hostile world. I think it was then that I seriously considered the possibility that his disappearance was no accident.

My call to GODCO came through and I was put on to
the same thin, cultured voice. No, Sir Philip was not available, would not be for some time. He was on a tour of the
Company's Middle East properties and not expected back
for at least a month. I could contact him through the Bahrain office if the matter were important.

I put the phone down and sat there for a long time, considering. But I don't think there was ever any real doubt in
my mind. I hadn't heard from Whitaker, and, quite apart
from his son's death, the necessity for a meeting with him
was urgent. It was just that the Persian Gulf was a long
way away and I had got out of the habit of travelling.
Fortunately, I now had an arrangement with another firm
of solicitors which enabled me to get away when necessary,
and in the end I put a call through to a local travel agency.
BOAC flights direct to Bahrain were weekly, leaving on
Thursdays at 1000 hours and arriving 0305 hours Friday.
That just gave me time to make all my arrangements, get
visas, and clear my desk of the more urgent matters. I told
them to book me out on the next flight, locked the contents of the envelope in the safe, and went out for a drink.
I needed to think, for I was beginning to realize what it
was he'd landed on my desk. *Political dynamite!* If he was
a good geophysicist, then what I'd locked away in my safe
might well be the location of a new oilfield.

Three days later I flew out of London Airport in a
storm of rain and wind. March going out like a lion; but
at Rome it was hot, and all down the Mediterranean we
had bright sunshine. And I sat in my seat with an empty
feeling inside me, for the day before I'd left Cardiff a man
had come to see me, a tired-looking, hard-faced man with
a skin like leather who'd refused to give Andrews his name
or state his business.

Even when he was alone with me in my office he went
about it in such a tortuous way that it only gradually
dawned on me what he was after. It was cleverly done—a
hint here, a hint there, and the abyss gradually opening

up at my feet. He knew David had boarded the *Emerald Isle* off Sharjah, knew, too, that Griffiths had delivered that packet to me. He'd been down to see him at his cottage in the Gower. He'd been to the police, too; had talked with Sergeant Mathieson and had checked the files. He knew the boy's real name, his whole background, everything, and what he wanted from me was that packet.

He smiled when I told him I couldn't discuss my client's affairs. "Professional etiquette? Your professional etiquette, Mr. Grant, is somewhat elastic, if you follow me." It was a cat-and-mouse game, for he knew I'd helped the boy to get out of the country. "There are several charges outstanding and a warrant."

"The boy is dead," I reminded him.

But it made no difference. He had his instructions, he said. These were to take possession of the packet. "You can hand it to me or forward it to the Company—one or the other." I asked him what authority he had for making such an outrageous proposal, but all he'd say was that it was in the country's interests. One knows, of course, that there are men like that employed by Government and by large companies, but one doesn't expect to come across them. They belong to a half-world that lies outside the experience of ordinary citizens.

"In your own interests, I suggest you hand it to me. Nobody need know anything then."

It was blackmail, and by then I was sweating, for I was beginning to realize what I was up against. Politics and oil—the Middle East; the scope of a provincial lawyer doesn't cover that sort of world. . . . I just hadn't the right sort of pull, the contacts, the friends in high places.

"You can go to the devil," I told him.

He got to his feet then. "I had hoped for your cooperation." And he added: "Think it over, Mr. Grant. The police have an interest in this, and if they began an investigation . . . It could be very unpleasant for you.

A man in your position, a lawyer . . ." He left it at that
and picked up his hat.

I wondered then whether he knew I was leaving for
Bahrain in two days' time. The Foreign Office had my
passport. They could still refuse to grant me the necessary
visas. "All right," I said. "I'll think it over."

And the next day, in London, I found I had been
granted a visa for Bahrain, but not for either Dubai or
Saraifa. A note pinned to my passport stated that for *any
further visas you should apply to the office of the Political
Resident Persian Gulf in Bahrain.*

Darkness fell, the port light showing red. I woke to the
touch of the air hostess's hand on my shoulder and the
sighing sound of the flaps going down. The sliver of a
new moon had risen, reflected with the stars in the still
surface of the sea coming up to meet us, a steel mirror
suddenly patterned with the arrow-heads of fish traps as
we skimmed the shallows. A moment later we touched
down in Bahrain. And at three thirty in the morning the
air was still heavy with the day's heat. It came at us as
soon as the door was opened, suffocating in its humidity.

The squat, white-fronted coral houses of Muharraq were
without life as the airport bus drove us across the long
causeway to the main island and the town of Manama. A
solitary dhow was putting to sea, the curve of its sail a
thing of ghostly beauty against the blackness of the water;
all the others lay dormant in the mud or bare-poled against
the coral hards with sails furled.

Only the BOAC Hotel showed any sign of life at that
hour. It was down an empty side-street, the airline's blue-
bird insignia standing out against the drab of concrete;
lights were burning against our coming. I was given a
room with a balcony that was full of the sounds of a late-
night party, laughter and the clink of glasses. There was a
lot of coming and going in the passage outside, and I went
to sleep to the sound of a girl's voice harsh and loud and
slightly drunk.

Sunlight woke me four hours later, the hard sunlight of a hot country. An Arab boy brought me tea, and I drank it, lying naked on the bed, a stale feeling at the back of the eyeballs and my body hot and without energy. Getting up, shaving, having breakfast—it was all an effort. And this was only April. I wondered what it must be like in mid-summer.

When I enquired at the desk for the offices of the Gulf-oman Oilfields Development Company, I was told that they were several miles out of town on the Awali road. A fat man in a tropical suit of powder blue was asking about a taxi he'd booked for Awali. He was an Italian who had joined the flight at Rome, and I asked him whether he would give me a lift. "*Sì, sì, signore.* Of course."

His name was Ruffini and he was a journalist. "You are in oil?" he asked as we drove past the Customs Quay crowded with dhows. And when I said no, he looked surprised. "But you 'ave an appointment at GODCO, no?"

"A matter of an estate," I told him. "A client of mine has died."

"So!" He sighed. "A lawyer's business—always to concern itself with death. Is depressing for you, no?" He offered me an American cigarette. "Who do you see at this Company? Is none of my business," he added quickly, seeing my hesitation. "But though I am never in Bahrain before, I 'ave contacts—introductions, you say. If I can 'elp you . . ." He left it at that, reaching into his breast pocket for a pair of dark glasses. And because he was being helpful I told him who it was I'd come to see.

"You know anything about this Sir Philip Gorde?" he asked.

"He's a director of the Company in London."

"But not the most important man out here, I think." And he leaned forward and asked the driver, a pock-marked Bahraini with a lot of gold teeth. "Who is the big man at GODCO?"

"Is Meester Erkhard."

Ruffini nodded. "Alexander Erkhard. *Bene.* That is also my information."

"Many years," the driver added, turning to face us. "Many years it is Sir Gorde. Not now." The car touched the road verge, sending up a cloud of dust. "Ten years now I have taxi and am driving down the Awali road, sir, with men from BAPCO, GODCO, ARAMCO. I speak not well Eenglish, but understand plenty, get me? I look after the boys good, very bloody good. They all friends of Mahommed Ali. That my name, sir." He was looking over his shoulder again. "You want something, you find my car outside BOAC Hotel."

"When did Mr. Erkhard come out to Bahrain?" I asked.

"Five, six years ago, sir. Before I get this Buick."

"And Sir Philip Gorde was the big man then?"

"That's right, sir. He is here before Awali, before I am born—a friend of the Ruler, of all Arabs. Very great man, Sir Gorde. But then he is sick and this Mr. Erkhard, he come to Bahrain. Everything different then. Not friend of Ruler, not friend to Arabs." And he spat out of the open window. "Here is GODCO office now."

We turned left with a screech of tires. The dusty date gardens were left behind and a white building stood at the end of a tree-lined road. Beyond it lay the sea, a blue line shimmering on the horizon. "*Ecco!*" Ruffini gripped my arm, pointing away to the right, to a litter of small mounds. "Tumuli. *È molto interessante.* There is a Danish man who dig in those tumuli. The oldest burial ground in Arabia per'aps."

The brakes slammed on and the car stopped with a jerk. I got out. "I will see you at the 'otel. Per'aps we 'ave a drink together, eh?" I thanked him for the lift and he waved a pudgy hand. "*Ciao!*" The taxi swung away and I went in through the double glass doors. It was like walking into a refrigerator, for the place was air-conditioned to the temperature of a London office. Glass and tiled walls, steel furniture, and the girl at the reception desk cool and immaculate. But when I asked for Sir Philip Gorde she frowned. "I don't think Sir Philip is back yet. Have you an appointment?"

"No," I said. "But I've flown out from England specially to see him."

She asked me my name and then got on the phone. A white-faced electric clock ticked the seconds away on the wall above her head. Finally she shook her head. "I'm sorry. It's as I thought. Sir Philip is still in Abu Dhabi."

"When will he be back?" I asked. Abu Dhabi was the first of the Trucial sheikhdoms and at least a hundred and fifty miles from Bahrain.

She started talking on the phone again and I lit a cigarette and waited. At length she said: "Could you tell me the nature of your business with Sir Philip, please?"

"If he's in Abu Dhabi," I said, "there's not much point, is there?"

She cupped her hand over the mouthpiece. "If it's urgent, then I think they'd contact him for you. I told them you'd come out from England specially."

I hesitated. But there was no point in concealing what I'd come about. "It concerns David Whitaker," I said. "I'm a lawyer."

"David Whitaker." She repeated it automatically, and then the name suddenly registered and her eyes widened. "Yes," she said quickly. "Of course. I'll see what I can do."

I leaned on the desk and waited, watching her as she talked into the phone. There was a long pause while she just stood there holding it, and occasionally glancing at me with an expression of curiosity she couldn't conceal. And then I heard her say: "Yes, of course, sir. I'll send him up right away." She put the phone down and came back to the desk. "Mr. Erkhard will see you himself." She said it on a note of surprise. "If you'll go up to the first floor, his secretary will be waiting for you."

I thanked her and went up the stairs. Erkhard's secretary proved to be a man, neat and immaculate with a copy-book smile of greeting. "Mr. Grant? Will you come this way, please?" He took me along a cool corridor and into an office that looked out across the tumuli. "Mr. Erkhard's very busy and you've come unexpectedly without an appointment. If you'd keep it as short as possible."

"I didn't ask to see Mr. Erkhard," I said, and that seemed to upset him.

"No, no, of course. I understand." He paused at the communicating door on the far side, a discreet little pause that gave emphasis and importance to the moment. Then he opened the door. "Mr. Grant, sir."

The room was dove-grey, the furniture black steel. The big window looking out across the tumuli was a single sheet of flawless glass fitted with plastic Venetian blinds. The desk at which Erkhard was seated filled most of the far side of the room, and all the wall behind him was taken up with a relief map of Arabia dotted with flags. He didn't rise to greet me, but simply waved me to the chair opposite his desk.

"You're a lawyer, I understand?"

I nodded and sat down.

"And you're out here on account of young Whitaker's death?"

"I'm his executor."

"Ah, yes." There was a peculiar softness about his manner, a smoothness almost. It was something to do with the roundness of his face and the way the lips were moulded into the suggestion of a smile. He was sitting perfectly still, watching me—waiting, I felt. It was disconcerting, and I found him a difficult man to place, probably because he wasn't a type I had met before. In a weaker man that half-smile might have appeared ingratiating. But there was nothing weak about Erkhard. And the eyes were cold as they stared at me, unblinking. "Have you seen the young man's family?" There was an accent, but so slight it was barely noticeable.

"The mother," I told him. "I haven't seen the sister yet."

"She's out here in Dubai—a nurse."

I nodded. "You cabled her the news. She sent me a copy."

"Yes. A very unfortunate business. It's not often we have a casualty." There was a long pause, and then he said: "Why are you here, Mr. Grant? Are you hoping to persuade us to resume the search? I had a message, something to that effect from London Office." And he added: "I assure you it would be quite useless."

"Perhaps if I had a full account of the circumstances," I suggested.

"Of course. There is a report of the search. I'll see that you're given a copy before you leave." Another long pause. "You were asking for Sir Philip Gorde, I understand. Why?" And when I didn't answer, he added: "I signed that cable to Nurse Thomas and you've been in touch with London. You know perfectly well that I gave the order for the search to be abandoned." He stared at me. "Perhaps you would care to explain?"

"There's nothing to explain," I said. "It happens that I have to see Sir Philip on a private matter."

"Connected with Whitaker?"

"Yes."

He got suddenly to his feet. "I'm the General Manager in Arabia, Mr. Grant. Whitaker was employed by me. His death is my responsibility, not Sir Philip Gorde's."

"I appreciate that."

"Then your correct approach was surely to ask for an interview with me?"

It seemed to worry him, and I wondered why. He was staring down at me, waiting for an answer. Finally he turned away and stood looking out of the window at the brown, dried-up landscape. His light tropical suit was obviously tailored in London and the silk shirt was monogrammed with his initials. "Sir Philip is in Abu Dhabi." He said it quietly as though he were speaking to himself. "Tomorrow, or perhaps the day after, he will be going on to Sharjah. That's another of the Trucial sheikhdoms, further to the east. He will not be back here for at least a week, perhaps a fortnight." He turned then and looked directly at me again. "How do you propose to contact him? Have you thought of that?"

"I only got in this morning," I said.

"Have you visas for the Trucial sheikhdoms?"

"No. I have to apply to the Political Resident's office—"

"Mr. Grant." He was smiling again. "I don't think you understand. It isn't easy to get visas for the Trucial Oman. The PRPG is very naturally extremely reluctant. . . ." He gave a little shrug. "This is Arabia, you know, not Europe. The political situation is far from stable and there is a great deal at stake; enormous sums of capital have been sunk in this area." He paused there to give me time to consider. "Of course, we could help you. Not only in the matter of your application for a visa, but in transport, too. We have flights going east along the coast to our various development projects. In fact, I think there is one going to Abu Dhabi tomorrow. But," he added, "in order to help you we should have to know the exact purpose of your visit."

He was taking a lot of trouble over this. "I'm sorry," I said. "Beyond saying that my business with Sir Philip concerns the estate—a matter of a signature—I cannot disclose . . ."

"You have a document for him to sign?" He sounded puzzled, and when I refused to be drawn, he gave a little shrug and returned to his desk. "Since it is a private matter and not the concern of the Company, I'm afraid I can't help you, Mr. Grant. I'll send Gorde a personal note, of course, to tell him you're here." A fractional hesitation and then with that little smile that never remotely touched his eyes: "And if you'd care to communicate with him direct, then I've no doubt we could arrange for a letter to be delivered to him by tomorrow's plane." His hand reached out to the onyx bell-push on the desk.

"One moment," I said. I wasn't sure how to handle it, but I knew that once I was out of that office, the opportunity to question him would be gone for ever. "I wonder . . . Perhaps you would be good enough to clear up one or two points for me?" I said it tentatively. "Whilst I'm here," I added.

There was a momentary hesitation whilst his hand still hovered on the bell-push.

"I'm a little puzzled about certain aspects of the boy's death," I murmured.

The hand moved back from the bell-push, reluctantly. And then he smiled and leaned back in his chair. "Of course."

"You say he was employed by you at the time of his death?"

"He was employed by the Company, yes."

I hesitated. The devil of it was I didn't know what I was after. Something . . . but what? The map, towering behind him, caught my eye. "Could you show me exactly where it was his truck was found?"

He got up at once, almost with relief, I felt. The position he indicated was well to the southwest of Buraimi Oasis, a position where three dotted lines met. Peering over his shoulder, I saw that these marked the boundaries of Saudi Arabia, the sheikhdom of Saraifa, and the emirate of Hadd. His finger rested on a point inside the Saudi Arabian border. The whole area was shaded with little dots. "The sands of the Rub al Khali," he explained. "Dune country. It's called the Empty Quarter."

"You've no concession in Saudi Arabia, have you?"

"No."

"Then what was he doing there?"

"That's something we should like to know, Mr. Grant."

"He was there without your authority, then?"

"Of course." His nod was very emphatic.

"If he was carrying out a survey, then presumably he had a survey crew. What happened to them?"

He hesitated and the quick glance he gave me suggested that this was something he didn't want to go into. But in the end he said: "He had an Arab crew. They were picked up by askari of the Emir of Hadd. However, the men have been interviewed. It appears they became nervous. Hardly surprising in that area. Anyway, they downed tools, took the Land Rover, and left Whitaker there on his own."

"In Saudi Arabia?"

"No, no."

"Where, then?"

He glanced at me quickly again, his eyes narrowing. "They wouldn't say. At least . . . they couldn't give the exact location."

"Was it somewhere on the Hadd border?" I asked, remembering what Griffiths had said.

He ignored that. "Doubtless they could have led us to the place, but the Emir refused to allow them outside the Wadi Hadd al-Akbar." He gave a little shrug. "The Emir is very difficult." And he added: "But of course this is hardly a matter that concerns you."

"On the contrary," I said sharply, "it's important that I know exactly where the boy was supposed to be operating at the time of his death. Until I know that . . ."

But he shook his head. "Best leave it at that, Mr. Grant."

"Because of the political aspect?" I was convinced now that the locations in my briefcase would show that David had been operating somewhere along the Hadd-Saraifa border.

"Politics come into it, yes. They always do in Arabia."

"And particularly where oil is concerned?"

He nodded agreement, and I asked him then whether he thought there was oil in that area.

He looked at me very tight-lipped and said: "We've no reason to imagine so."

"Then what's the political problem?"

He hesitated, and then half turned to the map again.

"Those borders," he said. "They're all three in dispute. Particularly the border between Hadd and Saraifa."

"Would you describe that as 'political dynamite'?" His eyes narrowed and I pushed it further: "If oil were discovered there?"

"Yes," he said, and turned back to his desk. "I think, Mr. Grant, we are getting a long way from the purpose of your visit."

"I don't think so." He wanted to terminate the interview. Equally, I wanted to continue it. "Did David Whitaker submit a survey report to you at any time during, say, the two months before his death?"

"No."

I stared at him, wondering whether that was the truth. And then I decided to play the thing I'd been holding in reserve. "Suppose I told you that I have in my possession the locations he was working on at the time of his death?"

He affected disbelief. But it lacked something, the quickness of spontaneity, the sharpness of genuine surprise. And suddenly my mind clicked. "Four days ago," I murmured, "in my office in Cardiff . . . I was visited by a gentleman who attempted by threats to get those locations from me." He didn't say anything, and I let the silence drag out. "He didn't get them, of course," I said quietly. I was staring at him, but he kept his eyes on the desk.

"I don't think this concerns me." The silence had forced it out of him. His hand reached for the bell-push.

I waited, and he hesitated. Curiosity had won. He turned to me and said harshly: "David Whitaker was employed by us. We should know the locations he was surveying. We have a right."

"Have you?" I asked.

"Yes. And I'll add this: I find it very difficult to understand why you should have been given this information whilst the Company has been left in the dark."

He was facing me, and after what seemed a long time

his eyes fell away to the desk again. He was puzzled. A little frightened, too. I thought he'd every reason to be both.

"David Whitaker knew he was going to die." I said it slowly and with emphasis. And before he had time to recover from the shock of what I'd said, I shifted my ground. "Does Colonel Whitaker know his son's dead?"

"I really cannot say." He was still considering the implication of what I'd told him, and I was convinced it was something he hadn't known before.

"We regarded the sister as the most suitable person to inform." And he added: "The boy was illegitimate, you know." It was a mistake, for it confirmed something I had come to suspect—that David's background was known to the Company. But he didn't seem conscious of it. Nor did he seem conscious of the drift of my questions. "I think you will agree, when you've read the report of the search, that everything possible was done."

"But they didn't find his body?"

"No. And if you knew the sort of country it is there, that wouldn't surprise you." He seemed anxious to reassure me on this point. "It's big-dune country and the sand is moving all the time. It obliterates everything. Even his truck was half buried when they located it."

"It was a seismological truck, I believe?"

He nodded.

"One of yours?"

He didn't answer immediately and there was a sudden stillness in the room. And when he spoke he chose his words carefully. "I've already told you he was employed by the Company at the time of his death."

"Oil-company trucks are usually marked with the name of the company, aren't they?"

"What are you implying?"

"There were no markings on this particular truck."

"How do you know?"

"There was a report of the search in *The Times*."

"Oh, so you've seen that." He hesitated. "Not every truck, you know, is marked with the Company's name."

"That doesn't answer my question," I said. "Was that truck a Company truck or not?"

I thought he was going to evade the question. But then he said: "No. No, it wasn't one of our trucks."

"Whose truck was it, then?"

But he'd had enough. "I'm not prepared to discuss the Company's affairs. The truck has no bearing on the boy's death."

"I think it has," I said, as his hand reached for the bell-push again. And I added: "One final question. Can you tell me where I'll find Colonel Whitaker?"

"Whitaker? I thought it was Gorde you'd come to see?"

"Whitaker, too," I told him. "David may have been employed by you, but he was on loan to his father at the time of his death."

"Quite untrue. *The Times* is in error." And he pressed the bell. The interview was at an end.

As though he had been waiting for his cue, the secretary came in immediately.

"See that Mr. Grant has a copy of the report on the Whitaker search, will you, Fairweather? He can take it away with him." Erkhard turned to me. "Have you a taxi waiting?" And when I shook my head, he told his secretary to arrange for a Company car to drive me back to Manama.

"You haven't told me where I'll find Colonel Whitaker," I said as I got to my feet.

He couldn't very well refuse to answer me in front of his secretary. "In Saraifa, I imagine." And he added: "But if you're thinking of going there, I should remind you that you will not be granted a visa."

Did that mean he'd use his influence to prevent me getting one? I hesitated, glancing up at the map. The flags had names on them, and because it might be the only opportunity I'd have, I went across to it and had a close look at them. There were only two anywhere near the Saraifa-Hadd border and the names on them were Ogden and Entwhistle.

"That map is confidential, Mr. Grant." It was the secretary, at my side now and quite agitated.

"You needn't worry," I said. "I know nothing about oil, so it doesn't tell me anything. Who did the ground search?" I asked Erkhard.

"Entwhistle," he answered without looking up.

"I'll give you that report now," the secretary said.

Erkhard didn't look up as I left, determined to give me no excuse for further questions. In the outer office I asked if I could write a note to Sir Philip Gorde. The secretary gave me a sheet of Company notepaper and I wrote it at his desk with him more or less standing over me. I marked the envelope *Personal*, but I was careful to say nothing in it that Erkhard didn't know already. The secretary promised to see that it went out by the next plane. "If there is a reply, I'll send it down to your hotel." He gave me a duplicated copy of the report of the search and showed me out.

I read that report in the car driving back to Manama. It told me very little that I didn't already know. The truck had been discovered by nomads of the Rashid tribe, who had passed the news on to some Harasis going down to the Gulf of Masira. The *naukhuda* of a dhow had brought the news across to Masira Island, and the RAF station there had radioed it on to RAF HQ, Aden. A Valetta, landing at Masira on the milk-run up from Kormaksar, had begun the aerial search on March 11, and the abandoned truck had been located after a three-day search. Erkhard had then ordered Entwhistle, who was operating about seventy miles away, to break off his seismological survey work and proceed at speed to the area.

Due to a broken spring, Entwhistle had not reached the abandoned truck until three days later. He had then car-

ried out a systematic search, but had found no trace of
David, and the few nomads he encountered knew nothing
about him. After four days, lack of supplies had forced
him to retire. Meantime, the Valetta, supported by a plane
chartered by GODCO, had carried out an intensive air
search. This had been abandoned on March 16. Everything
had then depended on the ground search, but the rough
going had put Entwhistle's radio out of action and it was
not until he joined up with Ogden's outfit on March 24
that he was able to report his failure to find even the body.

It was obvious that no blame attached to the Company.
As Erkhard had said, everything possible had been done.
I put the report away in my briefcase. The only man who
could tell me anything more was Entwhistle, and, remembering the position of his flag on Erkhard's operations
map, I knew there wasn't much chance of my having a
talk with him.

We were approaching the town now, the twin minarets
of the Suq al-Khamis Mosque standing slender against the
sky, and I told the driver to take me to the Political Resident's office. "The PRPG, sir?" He slowed the car. "Is not
in Manama. Is out at Jufair by the Naval Base." He hesitated. He was a very superior-looking Bahraini. "You wish
me to drive you there?"

"Please."

He turned right and we reached the Jufair road by the
National Cinema. "Have you a pass, sir? Everybody need
a pass to enter Jufair Naval Base." But the native sentry on
the gate knew the car and he let us through without question. We were close to the sea then with a frigate lying
white as a swan on the oily-calm water. The road curved
amongst the trees, the Government blocks standing dis-
creetly back in semblance of a country estate. It was all
manifestly English, and so, too, was the Passport Control
Office with its forms. Purpose of visit . . . what did I put
for that? I handed my passport to the clerk, together with
my application for visas.

"Abu Dhabi, Dubai, Sharjah, and Saraifa. That's quite a tour." He shook his head doubtfully, turning over the pages of my passport. "The first three, they're Trucial sheikhdoms—they may be possible. But Saraifa—that's quite out of the question."

"Isn't that for the Ruler to decide?" I asked. "I understand it's an independent sheikhdom."

The suggestion seemed to strike him as a novel one. "We decide who goes to Saraifa," he said stiffly. And he added: "If you'll come back later . . ."

"This afternoon? I want to leave for Abu Dhabi tomorrow."

"This afternoon?" He sounded doubtful. "Well, perhaps . . ."

I drove to the BOAC office then, only to discover that if I wanted to fly to Abu Dhabi I should have to charter a plane. Gulf Airways ran a service to Sharjah, but not to Abu Dhabi. It was my first experience of the difficulties of communication in the country. Back at the hotel in time for lunch, I was hailed by Ruffini, sitting alone like a pale-blue toad in front of a tall glass. "You like a beer?"

He had seen one of the chief executives of BAPCO—the Bahrain Petroleum Company—out at the oil town of Awali, and then had an interview with Erkhard. "This afternoon I go to Jufair, but I do not think they tell me anything." He leaned towards me across the table. "You puzzle me, Signor Grant," he said. "A lawyer, always with your briefcase. You say you are not interested in oil, yet your business is with two of the most important oil men in the Gulf."

The boy brought my drink. "Salute!" Ruffini raised his glass. "That girl at the reception desk—she is new to GODCO and she talk. This morning when you ask for Sir Philip Gorde and he is not there, Erkhard immediately sees you 'imself. Why?" His eyes were fixed on my face, full of curiosity. "Why are you so important? What is in that briefcase of yours, signore?" He shook his head and gave

a mock sigh. "You will not tell me, of course. Not yet."
His face creased in a smile and he gulped down the rest
of his drink. "Let's go and eat."

Over lunch he told me why he was in Bahrain. He
worked for a newspaper group in Milan and he'd had a
tip-off from one of Italy's leading oil men. "I think he is
right," he said. "There is trouble. But where?" He had
been up since six, talking in the bazaar, to Indians chiefly.
A squadron of bren-gun carriers of the RAF regiment was
rumoured to have been sent to Sharjah, and two RAF
reconnaissance planes had been fitted with long-range
tanks. There was talk, too, of additional transport allocated
to the Trucial Oman Scouts, and the G.O.C. Persian Gulf
was known to be on a tour of inspection. "If there is trouble 'ere," he said, "then it mean only one thing—oil."
And suddenly, without warning, he said: "What about this
David Whitaker, eh?" He smiled at me. "Now you are
surprised. But that little girl knew him and you told her
your business is about this boy who is missing." He stared
at me. "But you don't want to talk about it, eh?"

"There's nothing to talk about," I said. "I'm his executor, that's all."

"An' you 'ave to see Sir Philip Gorde, who is four years
ago one of the most important men in the Gulf, but not
any more—who is also the life-long friend of Colonel
Whitaker, the boy's father. An' you 'ave nothing to tell
me, eh?" He shook his head sadly. "Per'aps you do not
know it, my friend—but I think maybe you are sitting on
the story I want." He stared at me a moment, and then
very seriously: "You will think I am being very stupid
now, but walk with care. I like you. I like men who 'ave a
sense of duty. That is why I am warning you."

"You sound very serious." I wanted to laugh it off. But
he said: "I am very serious. Oil is big money. And in a
country like this it is also political dynamite." Probably he
misread the shock his choice of words gave me, for he
added quickly: "You don't believe that, eh? Well, I will

take a bet with you. You will not get to Abu Dhabi or to
Sharjah. Saraifa is closed anyway. You will, in fact, not be
allowed out of Bahrain. And you will be got out of 'ere
somehow before Sir Philip Gorde returns. Have you got
your visas yet?"

"I have to go back to Jufair this afternoon."

"Okay," he said. "You can come with me. But you will
not get any visa."

He was right there. They were very apologetic about it
down at Jufair, but the only man who could deal with
my application had unfortunately been called away on urgent business. Perhaps if I came back tomorrow. There was
no point in arguing. The brick wall of officialdom can't
be battered down unless you have the right contacts, and
I'd no contacts at all. I went for a walk along the naval
jetty. There was a wind blowing off the anchorage, but it
was a hot wind and did nothing to refresh me.

Half an hour later Ruffini joined me. "Do you get your
visas?" He gave me a wicked smile. He knew I hadn't got
them.

"Did you get the low-down on the political situation?"
I asked him.

He gave a fat chuckle and shook his head. "The same
thing. Nobody is saying anything. What is more," he
added, "you and me, we are in the same boat. No visas for
Ruffini also. He is to stay 'ere and mind his bloody business." He hoisted himself on to the sea wall. "Officials can
be very stupid. If I have to stay on in Bahrain and write
my story from 'ere, then I have to guess at what goes on,
and maybe I guess wrong." He was staring out across the
anchorage, his eyes screwed up against the dazzle of the
water. "That gunboat, for instance . . ." He nodded towards the frigate, which was slowly fetching up to her anchor, the clatter of her winch coming to us very clear across
the water. "An exercise, they tell me. Routine. Maybe
that is all it is and they are speaking the truth. But 'ow do
I know?"

We stayed and watched her steam out of the anchorage, and then Ruffini heaved himself down off the wall. "Do you ever 'ear of the Emir of Hadd?" he asked as we walked back to the taxi. "The Emir Abdul-Zaid bin Sultan? Well, no matter." He wiped the perspiration from his face. "But try shooting that name at the political people 'ere and see 'ow their faces go blank. I tell you," he added, "this country is worse than a Sicilian village, full of old vendettas and not a clear boundary anywhere to mark the finish of one sheikh's piece of sand and the beginning of the next."

He took me back to the hotel and I lay and sweated on my bed till dinner-time, wondering how I was to contact Gorde and thinking about Ruffini. Was there really trouble brewing? But it all seemed remote—as remote as Colonel Whitaker out there in Saraifa and utterly inaccessible. And next day, after a full morning's work, I was no nearer either of my objectives.

I rang the Passport Office, but nothing had been decided. And when I checked on transportation I found that even if I were willing to charter a plane, there was none available with sufficient range to fly direct to Saraifa, and in any case flights there were prohibited. I went to the bank then and settled David's affairs as far as I was able. It was the same bank that his father dealt with, and the manager was helpful. He confirmed that Colonel Whitaker was living in Saraifa, this contrary to his very strict instructions. But he could tell me little else, and I went back to the hotel and had a drink with two RAF officers and a civilian pilot, a Canadian named Otto Smith. After lunch we all went down to the Sailing Club for a bathe.

Half the English colony was there, for it was Saturday, and amongst them was the girl from the GODCO reception desk sprawled half naked on the cement of the old seaplane jetty. "So you're off to Sharjah, Mr. Grant?" And when I told her I was having visa trouble, she smiled and said: "I think you'll find it's all right."

"How do you know?"

"Oh, I know everything." She laughed. "No, I happened to see your name on the flight list for tomorrow's plane."

She was perfectly right. When I got back to the hotel that evening I found my passport waiting for me, stamped with visas for Sharjah and Dubai. There was also a message, signed by Erkhard's secretary, informing me that "owing to the Company's desire to help you in every possible way" free passage was being granted to me in a Company plane leaving for Sharjah at 1030 hours the following morning, Sunday. The message added that accommodation would be available at the Fort and it was not anticipated that I should have to wait long before Sir Philip arrived from Abu Dhabi.

There was no doubt in my mind that Erkhard had intervened to get me the necessary visas. But why? The day before, he had made it clear that he didn't intend to help me. And after the way I had cross-examined him I hadn't expected it. And yet here he was giving me a free ride on a Company plane. I sat on my bed and smoked a cigarette whilst the hot evening breeze blew in through the open window, and the only conclusion I came to was that they had sent my note to Gorde and he had given the necessary instructions. Whatever the reasons, it was a great relief to me, and I got up and started to pack.

I had just closed the larger of my two suitcases when there was a knock at the door. It was one of the house-boys to say there was a young Arab asking for me at the desk. "It is a boy from the bazaar, sir. From the al-Menza Club." And he grinned at me.

I had a wash and then dressed. The boy was still there when I got down quarter of an hour later. He was little more than an urchin and none too clean, and when he realized I didn't speak Arabic, he seized hold of my wrist, pulling at me and hissing the words "al-Menza" and "girl-want." Girl-want seemed to be the sum total of his English, and I told him to go to hell. He understood that, for he grinned and shook his head. "Girl-spik. Spik, sahib."

I got hold of the house-boy then and he said the boy had been sent by one of the girls at the al-Menza Club. "She wishes to speak with you, sir." This time he didn't grin. And he added with a puzzled frown: "It is a personal request. This boy is from the house where she lives."

I didn't like it. "Tell him no," I said and I went over to an empty table and ordered a beer. It took two house-boys and a lot of argument to get rid of the boy. I drank my beer and then went in to dinner, a solitary, dreary meal. I had just finished when the waiter came to tell me a taxi-driver was waiting outside for me. It was Mahommed Ali. "There is a boy in my taxi," he said. "Is wishing you to go to the al-Menza to meet a girl."

"I've already told him I'm not interested."

"You should go, sir. She 'as something to tell you."

I hesitated. But, after all, the man was a taxi-driver attached to the hotel. "You'll drive me there, will you?"

"Okay, sir."

It wasn't far to the bazaar area and we finished up in a side-street that was barely wide enough for the car. The al-Menza was sandwiched between a cobbler's shop and a narrow alley, the door guarded by a turbaned Sudanese. I told the driver to wait, and the boy took me by the hand and hurried me down the alley and through the black gap of a doorway into a dark passage. He left me there and a moment later footsteps sounded, high-heeled and sharp, and then a girl's voice, low, with a peculiarly resonant quality, almost husky. *"Monsieur."* She took my hand, her fingers hard, not caressing. "Through 'ere, pleez."

A door was pushed open and there were soft lights and the faint beat of Western music, a jive record playing somewhere in the building. A beaded curtain rattled back and we were in a little room no bigger than a cell. The floor was bare earth with a rug and a few cushions. A naked light-bulb dangling from the ceiling showed me my companion.

I don't know quite how to describe that girl. She certainly wasn't beautiful, though I suppose that is a matter of taste, for she was obviously Arab; Arab mixed with something else—European, I thought, with a touch of the real African. She stood very straight with a lithe, almost animal grace. She was the sort of girl you could picture at the well drawing water and striding away across the sand with a pitcher on her head. She was that, and she was the other sort, too; the husky voice—dropped a shade, it would be totally erotic, a vicious invitation. No point in dramatizing; she was just a Middle Eastern tart, but I'd never met one before and it made an impression.

We sat cross-legged on the cushions, facing each other. She wore a queer sort of dress and I had a feeling that at the touch of a secret button she'd come gliding out of it like a butterfly out of a chrysalis. Her hands were pressed tight together and she leaned forward, her eyes, her lips devoid of invitation, hard almost and urgent.

"You know why I ask you to come 'ere?"

I shook my head.

"You do not guess?" There was the ghost of a smile on her half-open lips. But when I said "No," she snapped them shut. "If you are not the man," she blazed; "if you 'ave come 'ere because it is the sort of place . . ." At that moment she didn't look at all nice. "All right," she said, biting on her teeth. "You tell me now—is it because of David you come to Bahrain or not?"

David! I stared at her, beginning to understand. "Did David come here, then?"

"Of course. He was an oil man and this place is for oil men. They 'ave the same devil in them as other men where the sun is 'ot—but David was nice, a vair nice boy." She smiled then and the hardness went out of her face, leaving it for a moment like a picture of Madonna-with-child, despite the slightly flattened nose, the thickened lips. It was a queer face, changeable as a child's.

"How did you know I was here on account of David

Whitaker?" I asked her. "It is David Whitaker you're talking about?"

She nodded. "One of the men from the GODCO office is 'ere las' night. He tol' me about you." She didn't say anything after that, but sat staring at me with her big, dark eyes as though trying to make up her mind about me. "You like some coffee?" she asked at length.

"Please." I needed time, and I think she'd guessed that. She was gone only a few moments, but it gave me a chance to collect myself and to realize that she was perhaps the one person in Bahrain who could tell me what sort of man David had become in the four years since I'd seen him. She put the coffee down between us, two small cups, black and sweet. I gave her a cigarette and sat smoking and drinking my coffee, waiting for her to start talking. I had that much sense. If I'd rushed her, she'd have closed up on me.

"Have you seen his sister?" she asked finally.

"Not yet." It wasn't the question I'd expected.

"But you 'ave 'eard from her, no? Does she think he is dead?"

I sat there, quite still, staring at her. "What else could she think?" I said quietly.

"And you? Do you think he is dead?"

I hesitated, wondering what it was leading up to. "His truck was found abandoned in the desert. There was a ground and air search." I left it at that.

"I ask you whether you think he is dead."

"What else am I supposed to think?"

"I don' know." She shook her head. "I jus' don' know. He is not the sort of boy to die. He believe too much, want too much of life."

"What, for instance?"

She shook her head slowly. "I don' know what he want. Is a vair strange boy, David. He have moods; sometimes he sit for hours without saying nothing, without moving even. At such times he have a great sense of—of *tranquillité*. You understand? I have known him sit all night, cross-

legged and in silence, without moving almost a muscle. At
other times he talk and the words pour out of him and
his eyes shine like there is a fever in him."

"What did he talk about?"

She shrugged her shoulders. "So many words. I don' understand half of what he say. About the desert mostly, and
the Bedou. Water, too; he loved water—much more than
oil, I think. And the *falajes;* he often talk about the *falajes*
and about Saraifa—how the desert is moving into the
oasis."

I asked her what the word *falaj* meant, but she couldn't
explain it. "Is something to do with water; tunnels, I think,
under the ground because he say it is vair hot there, like
in a Turkish bath, and there are fishes. And when you look
up you can see the stars." She frowned. "I don' know what
it is, but he say once it is like the wind-towers at Dubai—
something brought from Persia. But I have never seen the
wind-towers at Dubai," she added.

"And this was in Saraifa?" I asked.

"*Oui.* Saraifa. With David it is always Saraifa. He has a
—a *folie* for that place." She said it almost sadly, and she
added: "He wish to prove something there, but what I do
not know—'imself per'aps." For a while she sat quite still
and silent, and then she said very softly: "He was a man
with a dream." She looked up at me suddenly. "And
dreams don' die, do they? Or are men's dreams like the
seed in a place like this—all barren?"

I didn't know what to answer. "You loved him, did you?"
I asked gently.

"Loved?" She shrugged. "You want everything black and
white. What is love between man and woman—and in a
place like this?" Her shoulders moved again, slight and impatient. "Per'aps. But sometimes he could be cruel. He
had a vein of cruelty in him—like the Arab. At other
times . . ." She smiled. "He showed me a glimpse of what
life could be. And when he talked about his dreams, then
he is near to God. You see," she added, her voice suddenly

tense, "he is important to me. The most important thing in my whole life. That is why I cannot believe he is dead."

I asked her when she had last seen him and she laughed in my face. "You don' see a man when is lying in your arms. You feel—feel . . . if you are a woman." She stared at me and then she giggled like a girl. "You look so shocked. Have you never been with a woman like me before? But no, of course, you are English. I forget. You see, I am Algérienne, from Afrique Nord. All my life I am accustomed to Frenchmen—and Arabs." She spat the word "Arabs" out as though she hated them. "I should have been still in Algérie, but when the Indo-China war is on, they send us out to Saigon, a whole planeful of women like me. We come down at Sharjah because of engine trouble and we are there in the Fort for two weeks. There I met a merchant from Bahrain, so I don' go to Saigon, but come 'ere to Bahrain, and later I am put into the al-Menza Club as hostess. That is 'ow I come to meet David."

"Yes, but when did you last see him?" I asked again.

"In July of las' year. And it was not 'ere, but at the place where I live."

"That was just before he sailed for Dubai?"

"*Oui.*" Her eyes were searching my face. "He was—how you say?" She hesitated, searching for a word. But then she shrugged. "Vair sad, I think. He say that there is only one man in the 'ole world that 'e can really trust and that this friend is in England."

"Didn't he trust his father?" I asked.

"*Le Colonel?*" She moved her shoulders, an expressive shrug that seemed to indicate doubt. "When I see him that las' time he trust nobody out here—only this friend in England. You are from England and yesterday you are at the Company's offices enquiring about David." She leaned forward so that the deep line between her full breasts was a black shadow. "Tell me now, are you this friend?"

"Didn't he tell you his friend's name?"

"No, he don' say his name—or if he do, I 'ave forgot."

"Well, I'm his lawyer. Does that help?"

"A man of business?"

"Yes. His executor, in fact. That means that I carry out his instructions when he is dead."

"And now you carry them out? That is why you are 'ere in Bahrain?"

"Yes."

"Are you never his friend—before?"

"Once," I said. "Four years ago." And I told her how I'd helped him to get away in the *Emerald Isle*. Evidently she knew this story, for she nodded her head several times and her eyes were bright with the memory of his telling of it.

"Yes," she said when I had finished. "Now I know you are the man." And then she leaned forward and gripped my hand. "Where you go now—after Bahrain?" she asked. "You go to find him, yes?" And she added: "You will give him a message, pleez? It is important."

I stared at her. Her dark face was so intense, her belief in his immunity from death so tragic.

"Pleez." Her voice was urgent, pleading. "It is vair important."

"He's dead," I reminded her gently.

She dropped my hand as though she had hold of a snake. "His truck is found abandoned in the desert. That is all." She glared at me as though challenging me to destroy her belief. "That is all, you 'ear me? Pleez." She touched my hand again, a gesture of supplication. "Find 'im for me, *monsieur*. There is trouble coming in the desert and he is in danger. Warn him, pleez."

There was no point in telling her again that he was dead. "What sort of trouble?" I asked.

She shrugged. "War. Fighting. What other trouble do men make?" And when I asked her where the fighting was going to break out, she said: "In Saraifa, I think. That is the rumour in the bazaar. And that boy who bring you 'ere, Akhmed; he is the son of a famous pearl-diver. He know the *naukhudas* of all the dhows, and there is talk of *sam-*

buqs with arms coming across the sea from Persia. I don'
know whether it is true or not, but that is the talk. And 'ere
in Bahrain we hear all the talk. That is why I ask to see you,
to tell you that you must warn him. He is in great danger
because of 'is father."

"What's Colonel Whitaker got to do with it?" I asked.

"He is drilling an oil well in Saraifa. Oh," she said angrily, "the greed of you men! Money, money, money—you
think of nothing else and you must cut each other's throats
to get more and more. But with David it is different. He
don' want money. He want something . . . I don' know.
I don' know what he want. But not money. He don' care
about money."

It was extraordinary, this girl telling me what Colonel
Whitaker was doing, confirming what I had already
guessed. "How do you know Colonel Whitaker is drilling
for oil?" I asked.

"How? I tell you, this place is for oil men. They 'ave
their intelligence, and because they are 'omesick and half
dead with ennui, they talk." She gave a little laugh. "There
is so much talk in this 'ouse that I can almost tell you what
each oil man eat for breakfast from Doha right down the
Gulf to Ras al Khaima."

I sat for a moment thinking about the rumours she'd
heard, remembering what Ruffini had said out there on the
Jufair jetty.

"You will tell him what I say. You will warn him?"

"Of course." What else could I say?

"Do you go to Saraifa? If you go there, pleez, you should
talk with Khalid. He is the sheikh's eldest son. He and David hunted together when he is first in the desert. They
are like brothers, he always say."

I gave a little shrug. How would Khalid know? How
would anybody know what had happened? The boy was
dead. "I'll see his father," I said. "If I can."

"Non, non." There was urgency, a sense almost of fear,
in her voice.

I stared at her hard. "Why not?" But if she knew anything, she wasn't saying. And because I didn't like the way
my thoughts were running, I asked her where David had
been going that last time she had seen him."

"To Dubai," she answered. "By ship."

"The *Emerald Isle?*"

She nodded.

"And after that—after Dubai?"

Again that slight, impatient movement of the shoulders.
"He don' say. He don' tell me where he go."

"Was it Saraifa?"

"Perhaps. I don' know."

"There's some suggestion that he was on loan to his father, that he was doing a survey for Colonel—"

"*Non, non.*" Again the urgency, the leap of something
stark in the wide dark eyes. "*C'est impossible.*" She shook
her head emphatically.

"Why is it impossible?"

"Because . . ." She shook her head again. "He cannot go
to work with him. I know that now." And she added under
her breath: "*Que le bon Dieu le protège!*" I felt I had to
know the reason, but when I pressed her for it, she shied
away from the subject. "I must go now." She got to her feet
in one easy, balanced motion. It was as though my questions had started an ugly train of thought—as though to
admit that he'd gone to Saraifa to join his father was to
admit the fact of his death. And as I stood up I was remembering again the nagging suspicion that had been in
my mind that day Griffiths had come to see me in Cardiff.

"*Au revoir.*" She held out her hand and I was conscious
again of the steel grip of those thin fingers. "You are his
friend. I know that now. And when you find him you will
warn him?" I nodded, not saying anything. "And you can
give him my love also," she said with a sudden flash of
gaiety. And then serious again: "The boy Akhmed will be
waiting each morning for you at the 'otel. I have arranged
it. He knows many people and he can help you if you wish.

And remember, please," she added, "this is an island very close to the great deserts of Arabia—much closer than Algérie is to the Sahara. And the desert is Arab. Your Eenglish officials and the oil men, they know only what 'appen on the surface. They can see the bees swarm, but they do not know when the old queen die. You understand?" And with that she pulled back the bead curtain and I was out in the passage again, where the dance music sounded faintly. She took me as far as the alleyway, where the boy was waiting, and then with a final touch of those fingers, a flash of white teeth, she was gone.

It was only after I was back in the car that I realized I didn't know her name. I got it from the boy—Tessa; a very European name for a girl of her mixed parentage. Later I learned that it was a shortened form of Tebessa, the town on the Algerian-Tunisian border where she had been born.

I lay awake a long time that night wondering about David, about what had really happened. Three women—his mother, his sister, and now this girl Tessa—all convinced he was alive. And the picture she had sketched of him, the warning of trouble brewing . . . I went to sleep with the unpleasant feeling that I was being caught up in the march of events. And in the morning Mahommed Ali drove me to the airport.

III

The Empty Quarter

We took off
shortly after ten, skimming low over sand flats that ran out
into the shallows where fish stakes stood in broad arrows.
The white coral buildings of Muharraq vanished behind
us, and after that the waters of the Gulf stretched away on
either side, a flat sea mirror shimmering in the heat, and
the colours were all pastel shades.

The plane was piloted by the Canadian I had swum with
the previous day—Otto Smith. He had joined me on the
apron just before take-off and, realizing that I'd never seen
what he called "this Godforsaken country" before, he had
offered to make it a low-level flight. We flew, in fact, at
less than a thousand feet. A white-winged dhow swam like
a child's toy on the sheet-steel surface below, and where
the water shallowed to islands banked with sand it was
translucent green, the sand-banks sugar white.

We crossed the Qattar Peninsula: a glimpse of an oil
camp, the airstrip marked out with oil drums, the camp
a wheel of concentric buildings and the rig a single lonely
tower. A sheikh's palace standing on an empty beach,
square like a military fort, the mud of its walls barely discernible against desert sand. The palm-frond shacks of a
barasti fishing village, and then the sea again, until the
white of gypsum appeared on the starboard side and minia-

ture buttes of sand standing out of the water marked the mainland coast of Arabia.

The plane was full of equipment and stores bound for an oil camp along the coast towards Ras al Khaima, beyond Sharjah. There were only three passengers besides myself —an officer of the Trucial Oman Scouts and two oil men who were straight out from England and could tell me nothing. I sat in silence, in a mood of strange elation, for the sight of the desert so close below the plane gave me the illusion at least that Saraifa was within my reach.

We followed the coast all the way. Shallow sand dunes replaced the glare of gypsum flats, the coast became dotted with palms, and here and there a pattern of nets spread out on the shore to dry marked a fishing village. About an hour and a half out Otto Smith called me for'ard to look at Dubai. "The Venice of Arabia," he shouted to me above the roar of the engines. A broad estuary dog-legged through the sand-banks, dwindling amongst the town's buildings, which crowded down to the waterfront, capped by innumerable towers, slender like *campanili*—the wind-towers that Tessa had talked of, a simple system of air-conditioning brought from Persia by the pirates and smugglers of the past.

Ten minutes later we reached Sharjah: another estuary, but smaller and with a sand-bar across the entrance, and the mud town crumbling to ruin. We came in low over a camel train headed south into the desert, the glint of silver on guns, the flash of white teeth in dark faces, and a woman, black like a crow, with a black mask covering her face, riding the last camel. Watch-towers stood lone sentinels against the dunes, and far away to the east and southeast the mountains of the Jebel were a hazy, dust-red wall. We came to rest close by the white glare of the Fort, and behind it lay the camp of the Trucial Oman Scouts.

Sharjah Fort was like any desert fort, only now it was an airlines transit hotel. Two rusty iron cannon lay in the sand on either side of the arched entrance, and all the interior was an open rectangular space with rooms built against the walls. Otto took me to the lounge and bought me a beer. The room was large, the walls enlivened with maps and coloured posters, the tiled floor gritty with blown sand. "How long are you going to stay here?" he asked me. And when I said I was waiting for Gorde, he looked surprised. "Well, you're going to have a darn long wait," he said.

"How do you mean?"

"Didn't they tell you? He sent a radio message through yesterday to say he'd changed his plans. He's being flown back to Bahrain tomorrow."

So that was it . . . that was why Erkhard had changed his mind. A free ride in a Company plane and I'd be in Sharjah by the time Gorde got back to Bahrain. "Thank God you told me in time," I said.

"In time? Oh, you mean you want to ride back with me." He shook his head. "Sorry, fellow. I got a full load from Ras al Khaima. And not to Bahrain either—to one of the off-shore islands." And he added: "It's too bad. They should have told you."

I sat, staring at my beer, momentarily at a loss. "Is there any way I can get to Abu Dhabi from here?"

"Today?" He shook his head. "Anyway, you haven't a visa, have you?"

That was no good, then. "When's the next flight back to Bahrain, do you know?"

"Civil? Oh, there'll be one through in a day or two. The manager will have the flight schedules."

I asked him then who would be flying Gorde back to Bahrain, but he didn't know. "Might be Bill Adams, might be me." He took a long pull at his beer. "Probably me, I guess. He likes to have me fly him. Reminds him of the old days when he was boss out here and we flew everywhere together." And he began telling me about an old Walrus they'd flown in the early days just before the war. "One of those push-prop amphibians. Boy! We had fun with that old kite. And Gorde didn't give a damn; he'd let me slam it down any old place."

"Could you give him a message?" I asked, for I was quite certain now that the note I'd left with Erkhard's secretary would never be delivered.

"Sure, what is it?"

I hesitated. "Perhaps I'd better write it."

"Okay. You write it. Then whoever picks him up tomorrow can give it to him." His freckled face crinkled in a grin. "You might've been waiting here for weeks. Not that there aren't worse places than Sharjah to be marooned in. This time of year the bathing is wizard. Know what I think? I think that in a few years' time this coast will be one of the world's great winter playgrounds." I finished my note whilst he was extolling the tourist attractions of the Persian Gulf, and then he began talking about the strange places he had landed in.

"Have you ever been to Saraifa Oasis?" I asked him.

"Saraifa? Sure I have. We had a concession there once."

I asked him how far it was to Saraifa and he said something over two hundred miles. A long way across the desert, but less than two hours by plane. "Has it got an airfield?"

"Sure. You don't think I walked, do you? But that was four years ago," he added. "I'm told the sand has moved in since then. Funny thing." He glanced at me quickly. "You're out here on account of young Whitaker; his lawyer—that right?"

I nodded.

"Well, that last time I flew Gorde into Saraifa, it was the day David Whitaker arrived there. It was about the last thing Gorde did before he handed over to Erkhard and went home on sick leave. We flew in to Saraifa to break it to Sheikh Makhmud that the Company wasn't going to renew the concession. They were arguing about it all evening, with that one-eyed devil *Haj* Whitaker sitting there

like an Arab and swearing by the Koran that he'd get even
with Erkhard. Has anybody mentioned the Whitaker Theory to you?"

I nodded.

"Oh, well, you'll know what it meant to the old Bedouin, then. Saraifa was his baby. He'd negotiated the concession, and if it hadn't been for Erkhard they might have
been drilling there now. But Erkhard was the new broom,
and if Whitaker could have got at him that night I swear
he'd have killed him with his bare hands. It was as elemental as that. Now, of course," he added, "it's a different story.
Erkhard's under pressure, and *Haj* Whitaker . . ." His
navigator called him from the doorway. "Okay, Eddie. Be
right with you." He swallowed the rest of his beer and got
to his feet.

"You were saying you were there in Saraifa when David
Whitaker arrived?" I said.

"Oh, yes. Well . . . I was just there, that's all. He was
dressed in Bedouin clothes; he was very young and he
looked scared stiff. Couldn't blame the poor kid. He'd
never been in Arabia before, never met his father before,
and that black-hearted bastard just stared at him as though
he wished the floor would open up and swallow him. He
even introduced the boy to us as David Thomas. It seemed
like he didn't want to acknowledge him as his own son,
which wasn't very clever of him, for the boy had the same
cast of features—the nose, the jaw, the heavy eyebrows.
Well, I must go now." He held out his hand for the envelope. "Don't worry. I'll see Gorde gets it. And I'll come
and rescue you sometime during the week if you haven't
flown out by Gulf Airways." A wave of the hand and he
was gone, out through the screen door. I was alone then
with the posters and the lazy circling flies and the old magazines.

It was siesta-time and after the departure of the plane the
Fort went back to sleep. I was allotted a room, and after
I'd had a shower, I went up on to the terrace that ran like a

broad firing-step round the inside of the walls and sat there in a pair of shorts and sun-glasses staring at the shimmering line of the mountains. Down there to the south, where the high volcanic peaks disappeared below the sand horizon, lay Saraifa. Two hundred-odd miles, Otto had said. I remembered Griffiths's description of conditions in summer: *hot enough to burn the tires off a truck and the soles off your boots.* The heat came up at me with a furnace fierceness, and the flat expanse of the airfield lay in mirage-pools of water.

But if I'd been manoeuvred clear of Gorde, and Whitaker was inaccessible, there was at least one person available to me here. And as the sun sank and the breeze came up, damp off the sea, I dressed and made enquiries about getting to Dubai. A lieutenant of the Trucial Oman Scouts, who was in the lounge having a drink, offered to take me in after the evening meal.

It was just over twelve miles to Dubai, out past the sheikh's palace with its string of fairy lights and the hum of its generator, and along a winding road beaten out of the *sabkhat*. The road was as black and hard as macadam, and all to the right of us were salt flats running out into the sea—a thin, baked crust, treacherously overlying a slough of mud that was as lifeless as the surface of the moon. To the left the desert sand was humped like the waves of a petrified sea, and far in the distance the mountains of the Jebel, purple and remote, stood sharp-etched on the earth's rim.

As we drove through this empty world I asked the lieutenant whether his outfit was expecting trouble in the interior. He laughed. "We're always ready for trouble. That's what we're for." And when I mentioned the rumours circulating in the bazaars of Bahrain, he said: "Oh, you don't want to worry about them. Bahrain's always buzzing with rumours." He had a soldier's contempt for civilians, and I think he thought I was scared.

The hospital was a mile or two outside Dubai, a solitary

building sprawled over a sand hill. The last glow of the
sun had gone, the sky fading to darkness, and the building
stood black against the sand. Night was falling fast. "Give
Doc Logan my salaams and tell him I'll come over tomorrow and help him drink his Scotch," my lieutenant said
and roared off in his Land Rover towards the distant wind-
towers of Dubai.

The hospital was a ramshackle building, part mud, part
wood—a strange place to meet a girl I hadn't seen for four
years. She came to the little waiting-room dressed in apron
and cap, and at the sight of me she stopped and stared in
surprise, for nobody had bothered to enquire my name.

"Mr. Grant! I—I can't believe it." She came forward
and shook my hand.

"Well, you're not the only one," I said. "I can hardly believe it myself."

Her hand was smooth and dry and firm. Her face looked
thinner, and the fat of youth had been worked out of her
body; her blond hair was bleached almost white by the sun,
her skin tanned. She looked fit, and the shine of youth was
still in her eyes. It was a strange meeting, and for me—and
I think also for her—it brought a feeling of relief, for there
was that bond between us, and from that moment neither
of us could feel entirely alone any more. It was also to have
the effect of making me determined, somehow, to get to
Saraifa.

"We can't talk here," she said. "I'll be b-back in a minute." Still that slight attractive hesitation in her speech.

When she returned she had removed her cap and apron
and wore a light coat. We left the hospital and strolled
north whilst the sand turned from brown to silver and the
stars came out. I held her arm because I felt her need and
mine for the touch of companionship, and the wind was
warm on my face.

She had received my letter, but she hadn't been to Bahrain, hadn't even written to Erkhard. "What was the use?"
She seemed at first to have accepted the fact of her broth-

er's death and she was quite willing to talk about him. And as she talked, the picture that emerged was of a man I had only just begun to guess at.

She had come to Dubai two years ago, not so much to be near him—she had had the sense to realize that she would very rarely see him—but because of his fascination for Arabia, which he had somehow managed to convey to her. "I was here almost three months before I saw him, and then he came without warning. He was straight out of the desert, from a survey down by the Liwa Oasis, and I didn't recognize him at first. He was dressed as an Arab, you see. But it wasn't that," she added. "And he hadn't changed, not really."

She paused there, as though collecting the details of that meeting from the recesses of her memory. "I can't explain it," she said finally. "He was just different, that's all. He had become a man, and there was a remoteness about him. Do you read the Bible, Mr. Grant? Those descriptions of the prophets. There was something of that about him. He always had enthusiasm, a sort of inner fire, but now it seemed to have depth and purpose."

She had only seen him four times in the two years she had been out there, but each time her reaction had been the same. "It was as though he had become dedicated."

"Dedicated to what?" I asked. But she couldn't tell me, not in so many words. "To a way of life," she said, and went on to talk about the influence his father had had on him. The relationship hadn't been at all easy at first. "They started off on the wrong foot, you see. When David arrived at Saraifa, Sir Philip Gorde was there with his pilot. The driver should have taken David to his father's house; instead he was brought straight to Sheikh Makhmud's palace. It meant, of course, that his arrival was immediately known to two Europeans. It complicated the whole thing, particularly as David was virtually smuggled into Arabia. His father thought it due to wilful disobedience, and he was furious." She smiled at me. "I think they

hated each other at first. They were too much alike, you
see."

I asked her whether she'd met Colonel Whitaker, and she
nodded. "Once, just over a year ago." He'd come to the hospital to see her. "It was just curiosity," she said. "There's
no feeling between us—not like there is between him and
David. David's got much more of his father in him than I
have. And anyway," she added, "after being so long in
Arabia he has the native attitude to girls—necessary for
the procreation of the race, but useless otherwise. Being a
nurse, I know. They'll go to any lengths to get a sick boy
to the hospital, but a girl child—she can die or not, just as
she pleases."

I asked her then what impression she had got of her father, and she gave a slight shrug. "There's no love lost between us, if that's what you mean."

"Yes, but what's he like?" And I explained that I was
looking after his financial affairs and had come out partly
in the hope of meeting him.

She didn't answer for a moment, as though she had to
think about it. "It's odd," she said at length. "He's my own
father. I know that. I think we could both feel that in our
bones. But it meant nothing." She hesitated. Finally she
said: "My only impression is one of hardness, almost of
cruelty. It's the desert, I think; the desert and the Moslem
faith and the Arabs he's lived with so long. He's a little terrifying—tall, one-eyed, imperious. He's like an Arab, but
the sheikhs I've met are much softer, gentler men, more
guileful. He has a strange quality of command, the sort of
quality I imagine some of our kings once had when they
believed implicitly in the Divine Right. You could never
be easy in his company. His whole personality, it radi-
ates . . ." She paused, at a loss for words. "I can't explain
it, but he frightens me."

"What about David?" I asked. "Did he feel the same
way?"

"At first. Later he came under his spell, so that he

looked upon him as something akin to God." He had been, she said, under the spell of his father when he had first come to see her. He had had six months at Saraifa, living the life of an Arab, and a year at an oil school, learning to become a geophysicist. He had come to her straight from his first experience of field work and was then going on leave to Saraifa. "He talked a lot about Saraifa—about the way the desert was moving in on the oasis, slowly obliterating the date-gardens. He could be very emotional about it." She smiled gently. "He was like a woman at times, the way he wanted to defend Saraifa."

"Defend it?" I thought for a moment she was referring to the rumours of trouble.

"From the Rub al Khali," she said. "From the sand. He dreamed of taking a seismological outfit there and proving his father's theory. Oil, he said, was the only hope. If he could prove there was oil there, then the concession would be renewed and there would be money to rebuild the *falajes*."

That word again. I asked her what it meant, but all she said was: "It's some system for bringing water to Saraifa, and it has largely been destroyed." She sighed and sat down on the sand, her hands clasped about her knees. I gave her a cigarette and she sat there smoking, remembering, I suppose, the last time they had been together.

"Did he ever take a seismological truck into Saraifa?" I asked her.

She looked at me quickly, her eyes big and round in the starlight. I think she had forgotten for the moment that I was there. "I don't know," she said. And after a long silence she added softly: "I know so little about him, really. I don't know what he was doing, or why he was so depressed; and the truck abandoned like that. I know so little." And then she looked at me again and said with great emphasis: "But I know he was a man—a real man; and also that he would endeavour to the limit for something he believed in."

"Saraifa?"

She nodded. "Perhaps—for Saraifa."

"Because of his father?"

She didn't answer for a while. At length, she said: "No. Not because of his father."

"What, then?"

"The people, his friend Khalid—the sand killing the place. I don't know. The sand, probably. That was something physical. He was always fascinated by physical things. He likes action."

"But he was a dreamer, too?"

She nodded. "Yes, he was a dreamer, too. He was always a rebel in the world he knew. When we were kids . . . he'd escape into a world of his own. A m-mental world, you see. It was always much larger than life. He'd invent games— just for the two of us. And then, later—well, the gang life attracted him for the same reason. It was a form of escape."

"And you think his father's world—Saraifa—was an escape?"

She shrugged. "Escape or reality—what does it matter? It was real to him. I remember the second time he came to see me. He took me to dinner at the Fort at Sharjah and he was full of plans, bubbling over with them. He was going to take over from a man called Entwhistle, who was sick. And after that he was going on a month's leave—to Saraifa. A busman's holiday; he was going to run a survey for his father. He was so full of it," she said a little sadly. "And so bloody optimistic," she added, almost savagely.

"Where exactly in Saraifa was he going to try for oil?"

"I don't know. What does it matter?"

"Was this in July of last year?"

She nodded, a glance of surprise. "He had his own ideas —something he'd unearthed in some old geological report. I couldn't follow it all. When he's excited he talks nineteen to the dozen and I'm never certain what is fact and what he's made up. He seemed to think he could do in a month

what GODCO had failed to do the whole time they'd had
the concession. He was always like that. He could build a
whole kingdom in five minutes—in his mind." She gave a
little laugh. "Once, you know, he ran a tramp shipping line
out of Cardiff. It got so big that every ship that came into
the docks belonged to him. That was the first time he got
into trouble. He beat up a night watchman for telling him
to get off the bridge of an old laid-up Victory ship." She
sighed. "That was the sort of boy he was."

"And after he'd been to Saraifa?" I asked. "Did he come
and see you?"

"No, he flew straight back to Bahrain. I didn't see him
until December."

She didn't seem to want to talk about it, for I had to
drag it out of her. Yes, he had been going to Saraifa again.
She admitted it reluctantly. He'd been loaned to his father.

"Are you sure?" I asked.

"I can't be sure about anything, but that's what I understood."

So the *Times* correspondent had been right. And I remembered how Erkhard had skated round the question.

"It was all so strange," she murmured. "I thought it was
what he'd been wanting all along. Instead he seemed—I
don't know how to put it—almost appalled at the prospect.
He was in a most extraordinary state of nervous tension. . . ."

"Had he seen Erkhard?" I asked. "Was it Erkhard who
had loaned him to his father?"

"I don't know. He wouldn't talk about it. He just came
to tell me where he was going and what he was doing. He
didn't stay long. In fact," she added, "it was a rather awkward meeting and I had the feeling he'd only come because
he'd felt it was his duty."

But I was barely listening to her, my mind on Erkhard
and this extraordinary arrangement. If it was true, then it
could only mean one thing—that Erkhard and Whitaker

had some sort of an arrangement . . . an improbable combination, if Otto was to be believed. "And this was in December?"

She nodded.

"You said you'd seen him four times," I said. "When was
the fourth?"

"The fourth?" She stared at me and her face looked very
pale. "It was in February." She couldn't remember the
date, but it was early in February. I knew then that he'd
come to her after he had boarded the *Emerald Isle*, probably that same night, because she said she was called out
well after midnight by an Arab boy and had found him sitting alone on the sand. "Somewhere near here," she said,
looking about her.

"Did he talk about his father?"

"No," she said. "Though . . ." She hesitated. "I think
they'd had a row. I can't be sure. It wasn't anything he
said." And she added: "He wasn't very communicative,
you see."

I asked her how he'd behaved. "Was he scared at all?
Did he behave as though he was in fear of his life?"

She looked at me quickly, her eyes searching my face.
"No," she said slowly. "No, I don't think he was scared.
More . . ." She shook her head. "I can't explain. He just
behaved strangely, that's all—very strangely." In fact, most
of the time he'd been with her he'd sat in absolute silence.
"David could do that. As a kid I got used to those silences.
But . . . I don't know. This seemed deeper, somehow, as
though . . ." But she couldn't put it into words. "He
didn't talk much," she reiterated. "There was a moon, and
I remember his eyes riveted on my face. It was as though he
couldn't look at me enough. I felt . . . it was as though
he wanted to capture an impression, take a sort of mental
picture with him. It was a very strange, uncomfortable feeling—and he looked so like his father in the Arab clothes he
was wearing."

"Did he tell you what he was doing?"

"No. He wouldn't tell me anything, but I had the feeling that it was dangerous. He was terribly thin, nothing but skin and bone, and his eyes, staring at me, looked enormous and very pale in the moonlight. When he left he kissed me, not with warmth, but as though he were kissing a priestess who held the key to the future in her hands. And just before he left me, he said a strange thing. He said: 'Whatever you hear of me, Sue, don't believe it.' And he added that if anything happened to him, I was to write to you. And then he left me, walking quickly across the sand without looking back."

We were sitting on a little rise and the sand fell away from us, sloping gently to a *barasti* settlement, the dark shapes of the palm-frond huts barely visible, for the moon was new and only just risen. Nothing stirred and the only sound was the bleat of a goat. "I can't believe he's dead," she said. "I won't believe it."

And because it was what she wanted to believe I told her about the girl in Bahrain and about her mother's reaction. "Yes," she said. "Mum did everything she could to discourage his interest in Arabia. But too late. When we were small she shared her thoughts with us, and her thoughts were of the man she called our 'Uncle Charles.' That album of press-cuttings—they were almost the first pictures I ever remember looking at. And now here we are, the two of us, in Arabia."

"And your father?" I asked. "Did he talk to you about Saraifa?"

"To me?" She smiled and shook her head. "I'm only a girl. He wouldn't talk to me about what he was doing."

"You say David was loaned to him by GODCO," I prompted.

She nodded, and when I pressed her for the reason, she said almost sharply: "Oh, his father is doing what he's always done out here—dabbling in oil." And then almost gently: "It's rather sad, really. One by one the concessions he negotiated for GODCO have been abandoned. He was

once a great figure out here—a sort of Lawrence." She had
pity for him, even if she had no love.

"And now?" I asked.

"Now?" She shook her head. "I don't know. David
wouldn't talk about him, not that last time. But there are
all these rumours. He had this theory, you know. Some say
it's crazy, but I've met others who believed he was right."

I asked her whether she'd met Entwhistle. I thought perhaps he might have been to see her. But she shook her
head.

"What about these rumours?" I said.

"They're just rumours." She shrugged. "I don't know
whether they're true or not. Nobody I've met has ever
been to Saraifa. With the border in dispute, nobody is allowed to go there. It's just . . . well, the desert is like the
sea used to be, you know—exaggerated stories are passed
on by word of mouth."

I pressed her then to tell me what the stories were, and
she said: "He's supposed to be drilling on his own account
—with an old broken-down rig operated entirely by Bedouin. The oil boys I've talked to all say that's nonsense,
that uneducated desert Arabs couldn't possibly operate an
oil rig. But I don't know. Though I'm scared of him and
have no feeling for him, I know he's a remarkable man,
and you've only got to talk to the officers here to realize
that the Bedouin are very quick to pick up a working
knowledge of machinery."

She threw the stub of her cigarette away and got to her
feet. "I wish to God I knew what had happened." Her voice
trembled; she was very near to tears. There was a lot more
I suppose she could have told me about him, but I didn't
press her. I thought there was plenty of time and that I'd
see her again. For her sake I steered the talk to other things.
We passed a watch-tower, standing like a lonely border
keep, and she told me they were still manned, the guard
climbing in through the hole halfway up the tower's side
every night and pulling the ladder up after him.

"It looks so peaceful here," I said.

She laughed. "It is—on the surface. But who knows what is going on underneath? Certainly not our people. Some of these young English boys who are sent out here to advise . . ." She shook her head. "Sometimes I wonder. What must the sheikhs think? This desert way of life, it goes right back to Hagar and Ishmael, racially and culturally hardly changed. They know human nature the way these youngsters out from England will never know it. They're full of guile and intrigue; the Pax Britannica, even the oil, is just an incident in time. It's only a few years back, you know, that the Sheikh of Dubai fell upon an Abu Dhabi raiding force, killing over fifty of them. It wasn't very far from here."

Back at the hospital, she asked me whether I had arranged transport to get me back to Sharjah. "I can walk," I said. But she wouldn't hear of it. "You'd lose your way in the dark. You'd either wander into the desert or else into the *sabkhat*. Step through the crust of that and nobody would ever see you again." She insisted that I stay at the hospital.

They had a small guest room, and I spent the night there, and in the morning she arranged a lift for me in a TOS truck going back to Sharjah. She looked cool and very matter-of-fact as she said goodbye to me. "Come and see me again before you leave. And if you have any news . . ." She left it at that, and I sat and watched her from the back of the truck as we drove away, a solitary figure in white standing motionless outside the hospital. She hadn't moved when I lost sight of her behind a shoulder of sand.

It was that lack of movement; I became suddenly, instinctively aware of a loneliness that matched my own, and my heart went out to her. And as the truck roared along the packed mud surface of the Sharjah track, it wasn't of the girl who had walked with me in the moonlight on my first night on the edge of the Arabian desert that I was thinking, but of that other girl—the girl who had come to my shabby office in Cardiff to plead for help for her brother. She was a woman now, and though she might not like her father, I felt he had given her something of himself that made her, like him, an unusual person. She had courage, loyalty, and a strange aura of calm, an acceptance of life as it was. They were qualities both restful and disturbing, and, remembering every detail of that walk in the sands, the watch-tower and her perceptive comments on the desert world, I knew I didn't want to lose her, knew that somehow I must discover what had happened to David and set her mind at rest. I was half in love with her. I knew that before ever the truck reached Sharjah, and all that morning I walked, filled with a restlessness that was the restlessness of frustration. But you could walk for a day and still have no sense of progress in the merciless emptiness of the sea of sand that stretched away to the south.

I had my lunch in the company of a German commercial traveller and two American tourists staying the night on their way to India. The German could talk of nothing but the fact that his product had been copied in Karachi and was on sale in almost the identical wrapping in the bazaars of Dubai. The Americans were from Detroit, plaintive and unable to see any attraction in the untamed beauty of the desert, faintly disturbed by the condition of the Arabs, nostalgic for a hotel that would give them the built-in sense of security of a Statler.

The sound of aircraft coming in low interrupted the desultory conversation. Ten minutes later the screen door was flung open and Otto came in with his navigator. "Hi!" He waved his hand and came over to me. "Fairy godfather, that's me. Anything you want, Otto produces it. The Old Man's in the manager's office right now."

"Gorde?"

He nodded. "But watch out. He's hopping mad about something."

"Thanks," I said and went across to my room and got my briefcase.

The manager's office was by the arched entrance, and seated opposite him in one of the big leather armchairs was a much older man with a yellowish face that was shrivelled like a nut. He had a tall glass in his hand, and on the floor at his side lay a rubber-ferruled stick. Small bloodshot blue eyes stared at me over deep pouches as I introduced myself. He didn't say anything, but just sat there summing me up.

I was conscious at once that this was a very different man from Erkhard. He looked as though he belonged in the desert, a man who had had all the red blood baked out of him by the heat. He wore an old pair of desert boots, khaki trousers, and a freshly laundered cream shirt with a silk square knotted round his throat like a sweat rag. A battered brown trilby, the band stained black by the perspiration of years, was tipped to the back of his grizzled head.

"You got my message," I said.

He nodded. "Yes. I got your message. But that wasn't what brought me." His voice was dry, rasping, the words staccato as though life were too short for conversation. "Should be in Bahrain now." He gave the manager a brusque nod of dismissal, and when we were alone he said: "There's a newspaper on the desk there. That's why I'm here. Read it. I've marked the passage."

It was the airmail edition of a leading London daily. The marked passage was on the foreign-news page. It was headed: NEW OIL DISCOVERY IN ARABIA?—*Desert Death of Ex-Borstal Boy Starts Rumours*. It was written "by a Special Correspondent," and besides giving a full and graphic account of David Whitaker's disappearance and the search that had followed, it included his background; everything was there, everything that I knew about the boy myself— his escape from the police in Cardiff, the fact that he was Colonel Whitaker's son, even the details of how he'd been smuggled into Arabia on a native dhow. The story ran to

almost a column with a double-column head, and about the
only thing it didn't give was the location he'd been surveying immediately prior to his death.

"Well?" Gorde rasped. "Are you responsible for that?"

"No."

"Then who is?"

That was what I was wondering. Whoever had written it
had access to all the information that I had. "I don't know,"
I said.

"You're David Whitaker's solicitor. His executor, in fact,
Otto tells me."

"Yes."

"And just over two days ago you were in London."

"Nevertheless, I'm not responsible for it."

"A young kid just out of oil school and operating in an
area he'd no business in . . . A criminal, to boot." He
glared at me, his fingers drumming at the leather arm of
the chair. "The Political Resident had that paper specially
flown down to me at Abu Dhabi. The Foreign Office has
teleprinted him that half the London press have taken the
story up. He's furious."

"The facts are correct," I said.

"The facts!" But he wasn't thinking of the boy's background. "You know where his truck was found abandoned?
Inside the borders of Saudi Arabia," he almost snarled. "A
story like that—it could spark off another Buraimi, only
worse, much worse." He paused then, staring at me curiously. "Your note said you wanted to see me. You said it
was urgent, something about this boy—a communication."

I didn't answer at once, for I'd read through to the end
of the newspaper story, to the editorial footnote that had
been added at the bottom: *The London Office of the Gulfoman Oilfields Development Company issued a statement
yesterday denying that there was any truth in rumours that
the Company had made an important new oil strike. Asked
whether David Whitaker had made a confidential report
prior to his death, an official of the Company stated cate-*

gorically that nothing was known in London about any such report. Despite the Company's denials, GODCO shares went ahead yesterday in active dealings on the London Stock Exchange.

"Well?"

"Suppose there's something in it?"

"Suppose pigs had wings," he snarled. "Well, come on, man. What was it you wanted to see me about?"

For answer I opened my briefcase and handed over the envelope David had addressed to him. "Have you seen Colonel Whitaker since you've been out here?" I asked.

"What's that got to do with it?" He was staring down at the envelope, and when I started to explain, he cut me short. "Oh, I've heard the talk, if that's what you mean. But it's nothing to do with the Company. If Charles Whitaker likes to waste his money trying to prove a theory . . ." He grunted. "It's just damned awkward, that's all. The boy's death makes a colourful story, and coming on top of his father's activities . . ." He gave a little shrug and slit open the flap of the envelope with his finger. "Erkhard was trying to keep it quiet—and rightly. Saraifa is a trouble spot. Always has been. And the political chaps are touchy about it."

"That doesn't explain why he should try to prevent me seeing you."

He had taken out a letter and two wads of foolscap. "What's that? What are you talking about?" He reached into his pocket for his glasses.

I told him then how I'd been given facilities for Sharjah as soon as it was known that he had changed his plans and was flying back to Bahrain.

"What are you suggesting?" he demanded.

"That Erkhard didn't intend us to meet."

"Nonsense. What difference could it make to him?" He put on his glasses, and after that he didn't talk as he read steadily through the contents. Finally he said: "Do you know what this is, Mr. Grant?" He tapped one of the foolscap sheets. "Do you know what he's trying to get me to do?"

"Sign some sort of undertaking, but I don't know exactly—"

"Undertaking!" he rasped. "If I sign this—" He waved the sheet of paper at me. "It would commit the Company to drilling four test wells at locations to be supplied by you." He took his glasses off and stared at me. "Is that right? You hold the locations?"

"Yes," I said. "They're in a separate envelope. If you sign that document, then I'm instructed to hand it across to you."

"But not otherwise?"

"No."

"And you've got it with you?"

I nodded. "It's here in my briefcase."

"And if I don't sign . . . What do you do then?"

"In that case I imagine my actions wouldn't concern you."

"No?" He laughed. And then he was looking down at the document again. "I see here that you will be acting as agent for Sheikh Makhmud and his son Khalid in this matter. Have you ever met Sheikh Makhmud?"

I shook my head.

"And you know nothing about the Middle East." He was staring at me and his eyes had the suggestion of a twinkle. "It has its humorous side, you know. The boy must have thought you a most remarkable lawyer." He went back to the document again. "Further, it commits the Company to the payment of an advance of a hundred thousand pounds in respect of oil royalties of fifty per cent, provided always that Sheikh Makhmud and his son agree to grant to the Company the sole concession from date of signature to the year two thousand. Well," he said, "there's your undertaking. The boy must have had a touch of the sun when he typed that." And he tossed it across to me. "Read it yourself and tell me what you think of it—as a lawyer."

I glanced through it quickly, wondering what he expected me to see in it. "It looks perfectly legal," I said.

"Exactly. That's what makes it so damned odd. He'd taken the trouble to look up all the legal jargon for that sort of a document." He leaned suddenly forward. "He couldn't have got that in the desert, could he? It means he looked it up before ever he went out there, before he'd even run his survey."

"What are you suggesting?"

"That his report's a phony. I'm not a fool, Grant. That boy's been got at, and I can guess who's got at him. Here. Take a look at the survey report." He thrust it at me. "He used his own typewriter for that. The other's different, probably an office machine. He typed that document and then went out into the desert—"

"David lost his life as the result of that survey," I reminded him.

"Did he? How do you know what caused his death?" He glared at me. "You don't, and nor do I. Nobody knows— or even what's happened to him. Has any one mentioned the Whitaker Theory to you?"

"I know about it," I said. "Is that why you think he's been got at?"

He nodded. "Way back in the thirties Charles Whitaker began claiming that we'd find the oilfields continuing down from the Gulf here between the sand seas of the Empty Quarter and the coastal mountain ranges to the east. It seemed a possibility, and, remembering how Holmes's theory had finally been proved right in Bahrain, I took a chance on it and moved some of my development teams in from the coast. It was an expensive business, and Buraimi was about the limit, from the practical point of view. I was operating partly in the Sharjah sheikhdom and partly in Muscat territory, and after I'd burned my fingers, even the big companies like Shell and ARAMCO wouldn't look at his theory."

"That was a long time ago now," I said.

"Yes, before the war."

"What about Saraifa? Did you do any development work there?"

"No, it was too far from the coast. I sent a geological party in in 1939, but the initial reports weren't very encouraging, and then the war came and the chap in charge of the survey was killed. We didn't try again, though Charles was always pressing us to do so. He had a political appointment for a short time after the end of the war, but when he rejoined the Company in 1949 he was still just as convinced that he'd be proved right in the end." He shook his head. "Poor fellow! It had become an obsession—Saraifa in particular; he wanted us to try again there. The wartime development of desert transport made it a practical proposition, but the political situation between Saraifa and Hadd was worsening, and anyway I'd lost faith in his theory by then." He stared at the foolscap sheets in my hand. "If that survey report had been turned in by one of our most experienced geophysicists, I wouldn't touch it."

"Because of the political factor?"

"No. Not just because of the political factor."

"What, then?"

He hesitated. "Because it doesn't fit in with the reasons I'm out here." He stared at me then, his eyes narrowed above the tired pouches of flesh. "The fact is," he said, "the Company's been spending too much money in the Gulf area and getting too little in return. Nobody is supposed to know this yet—not even Erkhard, though I think he's guessed. My instructions are to carry out a thorough investigation of all our development projects in the Gulf with a view to cutting down our commitments. It amounts to a reassessment of the value of each project, and those that show no real promise of yielding results are to be abandoned. So you see . . ." He gave a little shrug, his hands spread out. "This is hardly the moment for me or anybody else to involve the Company in new commitments."

"I see." There was really nothing more to be said, and I folded the papers and put them in my briefcase.

"It's a funny thing." He was leaning back in his chair, his eyes half closed, chuckling to himself. "The Company did this once before. They sent Alex Erkhard out, and because I was sick and hadn't the energy to fight him, he got my job. And now, four years later, I'm back with the same powers he had and the knowledge that he's made more mistakes than I did and lost the Company a lot of friends." Again that dry, rasping chuckle, and then his eyelids flicked back. "What I've told you is in the strictest confidence, you understand. You've been put to a lot of trouble to contact me. I thought it only fair to explain the situation to you. If it's any satisfaction to you, I'd add that a report like that isn't conclusive. Seismology never is; it's simply an indication. The only way to be sure you're sitting on an oilfield is to drill down and find out."

"And suppose Whitaker's doing just that?"

"Hmm. To know the answer to that, we'd have to know the locations the boy was surveying and where his father's drilling." He stared at me. "Well, there it is. You've got your instructions. . . ."

I nodded. There was no point in continuing the discussion. "You're going back to Bahrain, I take it, Sir Philip?"

"Bahrain? Oh, you'd like a lift in my plane, is that it?"

I nodded. "Please."

He seemed to hesitate. But then he said: "All right." He picked up his drink. "You know my pilot—Otto Smith? Perhaps you'd be good enough to get him for me." He tapped his leg. "Can't move about like I used to."

"I'll get him," I said. And I went out and left him there, leaning back in the chair with his eyes half closed as though exhausted.

I had some difficulty in finding Otto, but eventually I ran him to earth in the showers, sitting naked, smoking a cigarette and gossiping with his navigator. I waited whilst he dressed and then went back with him to the manager's office.

Gorde was in the same position, but now he had my briefcase open on his lap and he was peering down at a sheet of paper he held in his hand.

I can't remember what I said to him—I was too angry. I think I called him some pretty unpleasant names, but all he said was: "What did you expect me to do?" His tone was mild. Almost he seemed amused. "If I'd asked you to let me see the locations, you'd have refused. Quite rightly." And he added: "I just wanted to check them against the position where his truck was found."

"But you'd no right—"

"Of course I'd no right," he said. "But yelling at me and getting yourself into a muck sweat won't alter the fact that I now have them. Do you know where they are?" he asked, peering up at me.

"No," I said. "I haven't had an opportunity—"

"On the Saraifa-Hadd border. Right bang on the bloody border." He glared at me. "I suppose you'll tell me you didn't know that the border was in dispute?" The way he said it implied that I'd tried to put something over on him.

Angrily I told him that I didn't have the advantage of his lack of scruples. "I kept strictly to my instructions and refrained from opening the envelope until I'd seen you."

"All right," he said. "We'll talk about it in a moment." He levered himself round in his chair. "Is the plane re-fuelled yet, Otto?"

"I don't know, sir. I'll check, if you like. Are you wanting to leave right away?"

"Yes, right away. But first I want you to check that your tanks are full. A personal check, please. You've got to have enough fuel on board to fly to the Saraifa border and back."

"I'm afraid we have to have authority to fly to Saraifa, Sir Philip."

"Since when?"

Otto hesitated. "I don't know exactly. Since the trouble there, I guess. It was just after you left; a border clash between Saraifa and Hadd. They had to send the Trucial Oman Scouts in, and since then nobody has been allowed to go to Saraifa."

Gorde gave a little sigh. "Let's not argue about it, Otto. I intend to have a quick look at these locations. Now then, how do we go about it without some little clerk reporting my movements to the PRPG, eh?"

Otto thought for a moment. "I think the best thing would be to say we're doing a recce of certain areas, taking a look at a seismological outfit we've got operating at the foot of the Jebel, possibly landing at Ras al Khaima if we've time, otherwise returning here. If we make it vague like that, I guess it'll be all right. That is, so long as you don't want to land at Saraifa."

"I don't know what I want to do," Gorde grumbled. "Haven't had time to think about it yet." He poked around in my briefcase until he found a sheet of plain paper. "Communications here still functions for civilian messages, doesn't it?" And when the other nodded, he pulled a gold pencil from his pocket and began to write. I watched him as he signed his name and read it through. I was more curious than angry now; he'd taken matters out of my hands, and for the moment my only concern was to get on this flight.

"Have Communications send that off right away." He held out the message. "Then check your fuel. Oh, and Otto," he added as the pilot was leaving. "We'll be flying on to Bahrain tonight." The door closed and he turned to me. "I suppose you think I owe you an apology, hm?" He handed me back my briefcase. "Well, maybe I do. But I spent a lot of my time in Saraifa, and anyway I'm an oil man. We've no built-in moral code like you boys when it comes to things like locations." He folded the foolscap sheet and put it back in its envelope and sat there tapping it against his thumbnail, lost in thought. "It's just possible, I suppose. . . ." He said it softly, speaking to himself.

"That Colonel Whitaker's drilling in one of these locations?"

But he shook his head. "In that area? He wouldn't be such a fool." Silence again, and the rhythmic tapping of that envelope. "However . . ." The small, bloodshot eyes peered at me curiously, and then he began to chuckle. "A provincial lawyer—and it's just possible you might have got hold of the thing the Company has been searching the Gulf for during almost thirty years." The rasp of that chuckle seemed to threaten to choke him. "You and Charles Whitaker. God Almighty!" he gasped. "And that boy . . . he'd never have dared operate on that border on his own."

"You think they were together, then?"

"How the hell do I know?" He handed me the envelope. "I don't know where Charles is drilling any more than you do. I'm not even certain he is drilling. It's just rumours." He reached for his stick and dragged himself to his feet. "But I mean to find out," he said. "If Charles is drilling on these locations . . ." He let it go at that, and since he seemed to take it for granted that I was going with him, I stuffed the envelope into my pocket, picked up my brief-case, and followed him to the door. As he pulled it open, he said to me over his shoulder: "Prove Whitaker's theory correct, and on that border, and you'll be in politics so deep, my friend, that you'll wish you'd never been born. But I can't believe it," he added, limping out into the bright sunshine. "Pig-headed, proud, revengeful . . . He still couldn't be such a bloody fool." And he stumped off across the courtyard, shaking his head and muttering to himself.

We took off ten minutes later, and by then I'd had an opportunity to glance at the contents of that envelope. There were several foolscap sheets headed: REPORT OF SURVEYS CARRIED OUT ON SARAIFA TERRI-

TORY; and it was sub-headed: *Basis on which an Immediate Program of Test Drilling is Recommended at Points A,
B, C, & D.* Pinned to it were four sheets of graph paper
covered with figures and diagrams. There was also a sketch
map giving his survey points, a whole series of them, each
with the position pin-pointed in latitude and longitude.
A number of Arab names were given, but none that I
could recall from my brief examination of the map in Erkhard's office. Points A, B, C, and D were marked in red ink;
they were very close to each other, in a little huddle at the
eastern end of the line of his survey. There was no covering
letter. Just the report and the sketch map.

I read the report through carefully as we flew south into
the desert. It was typewritten, highly technical—quite beyond my comprehension. For this reason I do not intend
to give the details. But there were several references to the
"Whitaker Theory," and right at the beginning there was
a paragraph that read: *It should not be imagined that I
stumbled on this by accident. If anything comes of it, the
credit must go to Henry Farr. He surveyed the area in the
very early days of the war. The Saraifa Concession was
fairly new then and Farr's outfit was the only survey team
in the area. Moreover, he made his report at a time of crisis
in the Middle East; it was pigeonholed away in the Company's headquarters and shortly afterwards he died fighting
in Abyssinia. I was fortunate enough to come upon this
report when searching old surveys for anything that had a
bearing on Saraifa. . . .*

I leaned back in my seat, thinking about the war and
how that old report had got lost in the files. Colonel Whitaker had fought in Eritrea. The same area. I wondered
whether he and Farr had ever met. I was thinking about
that when Gorde leaned across to me. "Well?" he said.
"What are you going to do about that report when you get
back to Bahrain?" He was smiling, tight-lipped. "The
boy's like his father," he grunted. "A dreamer. The same
dream, too."

"The dreams of youth sometimes come true," I said. I was remembering how Sue had talked of him.

His eyes clouded and he looked away from me, staring out of his window towards the mountains. "Ah, yes, the dreams of youth." He gave a little sigh. "But the boy's dead and Charles isn't a young man any more."

"And what about Farr?" I asked.

He shrugged. "He's dead, too."

"You don't think they could be right?"

"The Whitaker Theory?" He gave a snort. "Charles had a nose for oil, a sort of instinct for it, like Holmes. But he didn't know a damn thing about geology. That nose of his cost the Company a lot of money. We struck oil, but never in large enough quantities. I should know," he almost snarled. "I backed him, and it cost me my job out here. And I loved it," he added quietly. "I loved this country. Look at it!"

He leaned across, pointing to the desert that lay below the wing-tip, a corrugated dune sea stretching to the mountains that lay all along the horizon. "Clean and hard and cruel. I had twenty years of it. I know it better than I know my own country, and it calls to me the way the sea calls to a sailor—and I'm stuck in a damned office in London; I haven't been out here for almost four years." And he relapsed into silence, staring out of his window.

But a moment later he touched my arm and pointed downward. A great sweep of dunes thrust eastward, narrowing like a finger till the tip of the yellow sand touched the red rock wall of the mountains. Right below us a black line wound like a thread across the dunes—a camel caravan going south and leaving a faded snail-like smudge behind it in the sand. "The Ramlah Anej," he said in my ear. "We're crossing the eastern edge of the Rub al Khali." And he added with a sort of boyish delight: "I'm one of the very few men who've crossed the Empty Quarter by camel. Charles and I did it together. We said we were looking for oil, but that was just an excuse." He was smiling and his eyes were alight with the memory of it, so that through age and illness I got a glimpse of the young man he'd once been.

After that he fell silent and left me alone with my thoughts as the aircraft roared steadily south, the mountains always away to the left, always marching with us, a moon-mad landscape of volcanic peaks, sometimes near, sometimes receding to the lip of the earth's surface. And below us the sun marked the desert floor with the imprint of our plane, a minute shadow dogging our course.

It was just after four when the navigator came aft and woke Gorde, who had fallen asleep with the curtain drawn across his window and his battered hat tipped to shade his eyes. "Jebel al-Akhbar coming up now, sir. Otto wants to know whether you'd like to fly over Hadd or make a detour."

"May as well have a look at the Emir's hide-out," Gorde murmured, rubbing the sleep out of his eyes. "Long time since I last saw it." He got to his feet and motioned me to follow him.

The view from the flight deck was a blinding glare made bearable only by the green shade above the pilot's head. All away to the right of us was sand as far as the eye could strain, a petrified sea corrugated by the action of the wind. But from the left, mountains were closing in, bare, black, lava-ash mountains marked by patches of a livid, chemical green. They swept round ahead of us in a long curve, terminating abruptly at the sand sea's edge in a bold headland topped by a pinnacle of bare rock. "Jebel al-Akhbar," Gorde said, nodding towards it over the pilot's head. "There's an old stone fort on the top of it, and the town of Hadd is right underneath. Remarkable place. There's a saying amongst the Arabs of this part: 'Who holds al-Akhbar holds Hadd.' You'll see in a minute."

Otto was pushing the control column forward, and as we lost height the headland began to come up fast. "See the fort?" Gorde's hand gripped my arm. "I got a gazelle there once. The Emir invited us hunting and a seluki bitch named Adilla cornered it for me right under the walls there. My first visit to Saraifa," he added. "The time we signed the original concession."

I could see the fort clearly now, a biggish place, crumbling into ruin, with an outer ring of mud-and-rock walls and in the centre a single watch-tower perched high on a pinnacle of rock. We skimmed it with about a hundred feet to spare, and on the farther side the hill dropped sheer to a valley shaped like a crescent moon and half ringed with mountains.

The valley floor was flat, a patchwork quilt of cultivation; date-palms, grey with dust, stood thick as Indian corn in mud-walled enclosures, and there were fields of millet green with new growth. In the further reaches of the valley, where cultivation dwindled into grey, volcanic ash, a solitary sand-devil swirled a spiral of dust high into the air.

"Hadd." Gorde stabbed downward with his thumb, and, peering over his shoulder, I caught a glimpse of a mud town that seemed built into the rock below the fort. Right below us a *mêlée* of men and goats and camels stood transfixed beside a well. Mud walls towered above them, and, looking back, I saw the town of Hadd climbing into its rocky cleft, with a great fortified palace built on many levels facing towards the desert. A green flag fluttered from a flagpole. "Always reminds me of the Hadhramaut," Gorde shouted in my ear. "They build like that in the Wadi Duan. Well-sited, isn't it?" He might have been a soldier, his interest was so professional.

Otto half turned in his seat. "I'm setting course now for the position given in the search report, that okay?" And when Gorde nodded he banked the plane so that I had a last glimpse of the Wadi Hadd al-Akhbar, a little oasis of green set against a nightmare backdrop of volcanic rock. And then it was gone and the arid, lifeless desert stretched out ahead of us.

Gorde produced the slip of paper he'd used for making

notes and handed it to the navigator. "Those are the fixes for the Saraifa-Hadd border locations. Plot them now. We'll be flying over them as soon as we've had a look at the spot where he abandoned his truck."

We flew on in silence then, and gradually the gravel plain gave place to sand, the dunes getting higher, their shadows longer, until they were towering crescent-shaped downlands stretching into infinity. The navigator passed Otto an alteration of course and the shadow of the plane came ahead of us, growing imperceptibly bigger, as we lost height.

"Have we crossed the border?"

The navigator nodded. "Just crossing it now."

Gorde's hand gripped my elbow. "That's the trouble with this damned country," he said. "The borders are nothing but map references. Nobody cared so long as it was just a waste of desert sand. But you try explaining map references to an Arab sheikh once he's dazzled by the prospect of oil."

The navigator leaned across and made a circling movement with his hand. Otto tipped the plane over on the port wing-tip and we searched the glaring dunes below us. We circled like that, slowly, for several minutes, and then suddenly we straightened out, swooping down towards the humped back of a dune, and there, halfway up it, was the truck, almost obliterated by sand. I never saw such a desperately lonely-looking object in my life, a piece of dead machinery lying there like a wrecked boat in the midst of an ocean of sand.

We slid down on to it like a hawk stooping to its prey. It was a big closed-in truck, old and battered-looking and patched with rust. There were no markings on it, and as it rushed away beneath us Gorde echoed my own thoughts. "What was the fool doing, driving that truck alone into these dunes?" he demanded. "Do you know?" He was glaring at me, and when I shook my head, he grunted as though he didn't believe me. "A good twenty miles west of the survey locations," he growled. "He must have had some reason."

Otto banked steeply so that the truck was there, just beyond the port wing for us to stare at. But looking at it couldn't explain its presence on the slope of that dune, and in the end Gorde gave instructions for us to proceed to the locations David had surveyed and motioned me to follow him back into the relative quiet of the passenger cabin.

"Well," he said, dropping into his seat, "what do you make of it, eh?" But I could see he didn't expect an answer. He was slumped in his seat, an old man lost in thought. "Doesn't make sense, does it?" he grumbled. "The boy dead somewhere down there below us and his father not caring a damn and busy drilling a well . . ." He turned to me. "How did they get on, those two, do you know? What were their relations just prior to the boy's death?" And when I didn't say anything, he snapped: "Come on, man. You must know something. You've come all the way out from England; you wouldn't have done that unless you knew a little more than you've told me." He stared at me angrily. "Have you seen his sister?"

I nodded.

"Well, what does she say about it? He must have talked to her."

"She'd like to think he's still alive."

"What, in this country—and the truck lying there on that dune for almost two months?"

"She's never been into the desert."

"No, of course not." He asked me again what she had said about him, and whilst I was telling him the desert below gradually changed, the dunes altering shape until they were long ridges like waves with gravel flats in the troughs.

I was just telling him about the last visit David had made to his sister when the plane gave a lurch, the port wing tipped down, and over Gorde's shoulder I caught a glimpse of tire marks running straight, like the line of a railway,

along the length of a flat stretch between two dunes. A pile
of rusted tins, the black trace of a fire, the remains of a dug
latrine—they were there for an instant and then the plane
straightened up and we flew on, following the tire marks
that had scored a straight line wherever the sand was
soft.

Gorde got up then and I followed him forward. Indica-
tions of another camp came up at us, swept by beneath the
plane. We were flying very low, the line of the dunes on
either side closing us in. And then, straight ahead, the black
shadow of a truck. It was stationary and we came up on it
fast, belly to the gravel flat, roaring over it so close that I
could read the black lettering on its side—G-O-D-C-O—
and could see the drill at its rear turning.

It was the same sort of truck as the one we had seen
abandoned a short while back, and as we turned and came
down on it again, a figure in khaki shorts and an Australian
bush hat waved to us. There were Arabs moving about by
the drill, and close by the truck was a Land Rover with
G-O-D-C-O painted across its bonnet.

Gorde swung round on me. "What the devil's a seismological truck doing here? Did you know it was here?"

"Of course not." For one wild moment I thought those
three women might be right, and I almost tore the glasses
from Gorde's hand. But the khaki figure was broad and
thick-set, the round, brick-red face covered with ginger
hair.

Gorde tapped Otto on the shoulder. "Can you land
here?" he demanded. "I want to talk to that man. Who is
it? Do you know?"

"Looks like Jack Entwhistle," Otto answered, and he
swung the plane over again, circling back with the wing-
tip almost scraping the top of the dunes. He was flying with
his eyes glued to his side window, searching the ground.
"Looks okay," he said. "No big stones, no wadis that I can
see. I guess I can get down. Don't know how it will be
taking off again."

Gorde didn't even hesitate. "Then put her down," he said. His face had gone a sickly yellow. He was furious.

"Hold tight, then." The plane banked again, came in level over the flat gravel pan, and I felt the drag as the flaps and undercarriage went down. He flew about half a mile with the ground so close that we might have been in a car, then he gave her full throttle, lifted her up and round in a turn that left my stomach behind me. We came back on to the line of the gravel, slow and dropping this time with the truck standing bang in our path. The wheels touched, bounced once on a rough patch, and next time we stayed down, bumping heavily over the rough surface, stones rattling against the outside of the fuselage, until the brakes came on and we slowed to a halt.

We were about three hundred yards from the truck, and the man who had waved to us was already in the Land Rover coming towards us. By the time the navigator had got the fuselage door open the Land Rover was drawing up alongside. The air that came in through the open door was hot with the glare of sun on sand. There was no wind, and the heat seemed trapped between the dunes. Gorde moved awkwardly down the fuselage, supporting himself with his hands on the backs of the seats. He looked tired and old and very grim as he faced the man who came in from the desert.

"Entwhistle, isn't it?"

"That's right, Sir Philip." The man was North Country, square and stocky, the eyes grey in the red, dust-filmed face. He looked pleased. "It's grand to see you out here again, sir. How are you?" He wiped his hand on the seat of his shorts and held it out.

Gorde ignored the hand, ignored the warmth and friendliness of the other's tone. "Who gave you orders to run a survey here?"

Entwhistle hesitated, dropped his hand. He looked momentarily off balance, uncertain of himself.

"Was it Erkhard?"

"No, sir. To be honest, Sir Philip, nobody gave me orders."

"Then what the hell are you doing here? You're a hundred miles from your survey area."

"Aye, I know that." He ran his hand a little nervously over his face. "It isn't easy to explain. You see . . ." He hesitated. "I was the chap who carried out the ground search for David Whitaker. You know about that, do you?"

Gorde nodded. "Go on," he said, his voice flat. "And make it short. I haven't any time to waste."

But Entwhistle wasn't the sort of man to be brow-beaten. "If it comes to that, Sir Philip, I don't have any time to waste myself. I want to run this survey and get the hell out of here as fast as I can." His tone was obstinate. "This isn't what you'd call a healthy place. I got here two days ago and we hadn't been camped twenty-four hours before we had a visit from a bunch of Bedou. They didn't behave like nomads; more like the Emir's men. Though we're still in Saraifa here."

"The Saraifa concession was abandoned four years ago," Gorde said sharply. "You've no right here. None whatever."

"I'm well aware of that, Sir Philip."

"Then why are you here?"

Entwhistle hesitated, rubbing gently at a desert sore that showed red and ugly beneath the sweat stain of his right armpit. "You never met David Whitaker, did you, sir?"

"What's that got to do with it?"

"Oh, well . . ." He hesitated, and then, unable apparently to put it into words, he sought refuge in facts. "I couldn't exactly say it in my report of the search. It would have put the Company on the spot, if you see what I mean. But there was something fishy about that truck stuck there on a sand dune across the border into Saudi. There was nought wrong with it mechanically, you know. It was just

out of fuel, as though he'd driven it straight into the
Empty Quarter until he'd no more petrol. And if you'd
known David . . ." Again the hesitation, and then a quick
shrug. "He knew the desert—knew it a damn sight better
than I'll ever know it. What was he doing there, that's what
I'd like to know? If he'd been scared out of here by the
Emir's men, why didn't he head for Saraifa?"

"Come to the point," Gorde said impatiently. "I want to
know why you're here."

"Aye. Well, I went over every inch of that truck. I
thought if there'd been foul play or anything like that, he'd
have left some clue, something that a chap like myself, a
fellow geophysicist, would understand. The only thing I
found was an old attaché case full of correspondence and
copies of survey reports. One of those reports concerned
this area."

"I don't seem to remember reading that in the account
you sent to Erkhard."

"No."

"You thought you'd keep it to yourself, eh? Thought
you'd check on his findings on the quiet?"

Entwhistle scratched uncomfortably at the sore. "He
was on loan to his father, you see. It didn't concern the
Company, exactly. And he seemed so sure he'd—"

"It never occurred to you, I suppose, that there's a political factor?"

Entwhistle's grey eyes stared at Gorde without flinching.
"David Whitaker was a good bloke. I don't know whether
he sent a copy of that survey report to the Bahrain office
or not; and I don't care. Nobody had done anything about
it. Not even his father. He was out on his own and he
thought he was on to something. I spent the better part of
a week searching the desert for his body, and it seemed to
me if I couldn't give him a headstone, I might at least see
if he was right and we could name an oilfield after him.
Maybe it sounds a little crazy to you, Sir Philip," he added
almost belligerently, "but I just felt it was up to me to do

something. I don't like to see a good chap's life thrown away for nothing. And if Erkhard kicks me off the Company's pay-roll as a result, I shan't cry my eyes out."

Gorde didn't say anything for a moment. He seemed lost in thought. "How far have you got with the check?" he asked at length.

"There are four locations given as probable anti-clines in the report. I've done a check on the most southeasterly— Location D, he called it. Now I've just begun drilling the first shot-hole on Location C. If you care to come to the truck, I can show you David Whitaker's report. Or has Mr. Erkhard already shown it to you?"

"No, he hasn't. Nevertheless," Gorde added, "I've seen a copy. Grant here was kind enough to show it to me." This on a note of irony, and he introduced me then. "A lawyer. Like you, he wants to know what young Whitaker was doing across the border into Saudi." He turned to me. "I don't suppose you've ever seen a seismological truck, have you?" And when I shook my head, he said: "Well, if you want to see the sort of work David Whitaker was engaged on, I'm sure Entwhistle would show you over his vehicle." He turned back to Entwhistle. "No point in stopping you in the middle of drilling a shot-hole. You can finish the check on your Location C. Then you're to pull out. Understand?"

"Yes, sir." Relief and something akin to affection showed for an instant on Entwhistle's face.

"Results to be sent direct to me. And now take Grant to your truck and show him how it works. Meanwhile, I'll write a letter for you to Sheikh Makhmud, just in case. I don't doubt he knows you're here." He stood back from the door. "Ten minutes," he said to me. "All right? And then I want to find Charles Whitaker's rig; find out why he isn't drilling here if his son was so damn sure."

I nodded. I didn't even hesitate. I was being given the opportunity of ten minutes alone with Entwhistle. I jumped out of the plane and it was like jumping into the full glare of an open-hearth furnace. Entwhistle remained a moment talking to Gorde, and when he joined me in the Land Rover he glanced at me curiously, so that I wondered what Gorde had told him about me. Stones rattled against the rusted mudguards as we batted over the gravel towards the truck, which seemed to be standing in a pool of water. The mirage only lifted when we were within a hundred yards of it.

I was more interested in Entwhistle than in the mechanics of his seismological equipment, and as soon as we were in the shade of the truck's interior I asked him what he thought had happened to David. "I suppose there's no chance that he's still alive?"

It didn't seem to surprise him that I'd made the suggestion. "Did you see my personal report to Erkhard, or was it some sort of a composite thing rehashed by the Bahrain office?" he asked.

"It was a general report," I told him.

"Aye, I thought so. They'll be letting the dust collect on mine in some pigeonhole. Can't blame them. I made it pretty plain what I thought." He hesitated, rubbing his hand across the ginger stubble on his chin. "A rum do, and no mistake. There was that truck half buried in sand and about forty miles from the nearest water-hole. And nothing wrong with the damned thing but lack of petrol. Even the spare jerry cans were empty.

"What are you suggesting?" I asked.

He hesitated. "I don't rightly know," he muttered, eying me cautiously. "But I know this," he added with sudden violence; "a chap like David doesn't drive into waterless desert with empty fuel cans. And to run out of juice just there . . . Except for the centre of the Empty Quarter, he couldn't have picked a spot that was much further from water." He stared at me and I think we were both thinking the same thing, for he said: "I'd like to know what his father thinks about it. In fact, when I've finished here I intend to drive over to Saraifa and see if the old Bedou knows . . ." He stopped and cocked his head on one side, listening. Faint through the noise of the drill came the distant sound of an engine. I didn't understand at first, but then it grew louder, overtopping the noise of the drill, and in a sudden panic of realization I dived for the door, just in time to see the plane become airborne.

It passed so low over the top of the truck that I instinctively ducked, and as I straightened up I was cursing myself for a fool. I should have known. I should have realized Gorde might want to get me out of the way. I turned furiously on Entwhistle, who was standing in the doorway of the truck looking slightly uncomfortable. "You knew about this?"

"Aye, he told me." He smiled a little doubtfully. "He asked me to give you his apologies for any inconvenience."

"God rot the old man!" I muttered savagely. To be caught like that, to be fooled into thinking he was just trying to be helpful, and all the time . . .

I stared at the plane, which was rapidly dwindling to a speck, feeling suddenly helpless, isolated out here in an oven-hot world that I didn't understand.

"A day or two, he said," Entwhistle murmured apologetically. "That's all. I'll try and make it as pleasant as possible."

The plane had altered course. I saw it circle once and then it was heading back towards us, and for a wild moment I thought perhaps he'd changed his mind. It came in low, flying slowly with the flaps down. But the undercarriage remained up. As it bumbled close over our heads something white fluttered down from the pilot's window. And then it turned and disappeared low over the dunes, and the sound of it was lost again in the noise of the drill.

Entwhistle was already running to retrieve the object they had dropped to us. He came back with a cigarette packet and a crumpled sheet of paper. "All right. You can stop drilling," he shouted. He repeated the order in Arabic, and as the drill slowed to an abrupt silence he handed me the paper. On it was written in pencil: *Stop drilling and proceed at once to Saraifa. Concentration of armed tribesmen camped in the dunes two miles north of you. Warn Sheikh Makhmud and give him my salaams. Philip Gorde.* A chill feeling crept up my spine as I read that message, and Entwhistle's comment did nothing to restore my morale. "Bit of luck, the Old Man flying down here." He flipped the coin that Otto had used to weight the packet. "Mightn't have seen the sun rise tomorrow otherwise."

It came as a shock to me to realize that he was perfectly serious. "They would have attacked you?" I asked.

"Slit our throats, probably." He sounded quite cheerful.

"But—" I looked about me, at the dunes asleep in the heat of the day, the furnace-hot world of the desert all around me, quiet and peaceful. It was hard to believe. "But you're still on Saraifa territory," I said.

He shrugged. "The Emir would dispute that. And the political boys, all those bloody old Etonians—they don't want any trouble. My name's going to be mud." He stared down at the coin in his hand. And then he put it in his pocket and set about organizing the packing up of the outfit, leaving me standing there, feeling slightly lost, a stranger in a strange world.

IV

The Doomed Oasis

His crew were all Arab
and they went about the business of breaking camp noisily
but efficiently. They had done it many times. In fact, it
seemed a natural process out there amongst the dunes.
They were mostly young men, a colourful mixture of race
and dress, their teeth flashing white in their dark faces as
they fooled around, making light of the work. They were
fit and full of life and laughter; they had a football, which
they kicked at each other periodically, the guttural Arab
tongue coming in staccato bursts from their lips.

There was nothing for me to do and I sat perched on the
Land Rover's mudguard, watching them and looking
around me at the surrounding country. There was a dune,
I remember, that ran away into the distance like the Pres-
celly Hills north of St. David's. I was looking at it, thinking
of holidays I had spent in that part of Wales, and suddenly
my eyes became riveted on a dark speck that showed for an
instant on its back. It vanished almost immediately, so that
I thought my eyes had played me a trick. In that shimmering heat it was difficult to be sure. And then it showed
again, nearer this time. I could have sworn it was a man
moving below the crest of the dune. I was just on the point
of telling Entwhistle that he had a visitor when I was jolted
off my seat; the clang of metal against metal was followed
instantly by the crack of a rifle, and I was looking down at

a hole the size of my fist in the side of the Land Rover's hood.

For an instant everything was still. There was no sound, no movement; Entwhistle and his Arabs just stood there, shocked into immobility, staring at that hole in the side of the Land Rover. Then Entwhistle shouted something. Rifles cracked from the top of the dune, little spurts of sand were kicked up round us. A bullet ricocheted off the truck's drill and went whining past my head. Entwhistle flung himself at the Land Rover. "Jump in!" he shouted. His crew were running for the truck. Another bullet smacked into the Land Rover, so close that the wind of it fanned my trouser legs, and then I heard shouts, saw men running towards us from the line of the dunes. The engines burst into life, drowning all other sounds. I dived for the seat beside Entwhistle as he slammed the Land Rover into gear. Two Arabs landed almost on top of me as the vehicle jerked forward. Behind us the truck was moving, too, and beyond its lumbering shape I caught a glimpse of long-haired tribesmen dropping on to their knees, aiming their rifles. But I never heard the shots. All I could hear was the revving of the engine as Entwhistle ran through the gears.

A moment later and we were clear, out of their range. The two Arabs sorted themselves out and I turned to Entwhistle. His foot was hard down on the accelerator and his lips were moving. "The bastards!" he was saying. "The bloody bastards!" And then he looked at me. "Dum-dum bullets." His face was white under the sunburn. "They cut them across to make them soft-nosed. Blow a hole in you the size of a barn door." It was this rather than the attack that seemed to outrage him.

"Who were they?" I asked and was shocked to find that I hadn't proper control over my voice.

"The Emir's men. They must have seen the plane turn back and realized we were being warned of their presence." He turned to make certain that the truck was following. "Fine introduction you've had to desert life." He grinned, but not very certainly. He shouted something in Arabic to the two men perched on the baggage behind and they answered him with a flood of words. Shortly afterwards he pulled up. The truck drew up beside us, its engine throbbing, excited Arab faces looking down at us, all talking at once.

He got out then and spoke to the driver, walked all round the truck, and then came back and lifted the hood of the Land Rover. "Look at that," he said. I got out and my legs felt weak as I stared at the hole that first bullet had made. Little bits of lead were spattered all over the engine. "Bastards!" he said and slammed the hood shut. "Well, it might have been worse, I suppose. Nobody's hurt and the vehicles are all right."

It was only after we'd got moving again that I realized the windscreen in front of me was shattered. Little bits of glass were falling into my lap. I kept my eyes half closed until I had picked out all the bits. "How far is it to Saraifa?" I asked him.

"Not much more than forty miles by air." I gathered it was a good deal more the way we'd have to go, for the dunes ran southeast and we had to get east. "Might make it shortly after dark if we don't get bogged down too often."

It was just after four thirty then. We kept to the gravel flats between the dunes, travelling at almost thirty miles an hour. The air that came rushing in through the shattered windscreen was a hot, searing blast that scorched the face. The ground was hard as iron, criss-crossed with innumerable ridges, over which the Land Rover rattled in an endless series of back-breaking jolts.

In these circumstances conversation wasn't easy; the wind of our movement, the noise of the engine, the rattle of stones—we had to shout to make ourselves heard. And Entwhistle wasn't a talkative man. He'd lived on his own too much. Besides, he had a North Countryman's lack of imagination. He even used the word "humdrum" when I asked him about his job. And yet I got the impression that he loved it. But it was the job, not Arabia, he loved. He'd no feeling for the country or its people. More than once he used the contemptuous term "wogs" when speaking of the Arabs. But though he wouldn't talk about himself much, he was quite prepared to talk about David.

He had met him three times in all, once in Bahrain and then later when he was sick and David had relieved him. "Queer chap," he said. "Fact is, I didn't like him much when he came out to take over my outfit. But then," he added, "you don't like anybody very much when you're suffering from jaundice."

"But you felt differently about him later?" I prompted.

"Aye. Got to know him a bit better then. We were two days together whilst we moved to a new location. Then he went off to Saraifa. He'd got some leave due and he was going to spend it mucking around with an old seismological truck his father had got hold of." I asked him what had made him change his mind about David, and he said: "Oh, the way he talked. He was a great talker. Mind you," he added, "he was still too chummy with the wogs for my liking, but you couldn't help admiring the chap. Wanted to make the desert blossom and all that."

"Water?" I asked.

He nodded. "That's it. He'd got a bee in his bonnet about it. Talked about Saraifa being doomed. Well, of course, it is. I've only been there once, but—well, you'll see for yourself. A few more years . . ." He didn't talk for a while after that, for we had come to soft sand; he took it fast, his foot pressed hard down on the accelerator, and we bucketed through it like a small boat in a seaway.

We came off the sand on to a hard gravel pan that scintillated with a myriad diamond gleams. "Mica," he shouted. The glare of it was dazzling. "You interested in geology?"

I shook my head.

"Pity." He seemed genuinely sorry. "Damned interesting country." For him there was nothing else of interest in Arabia. We bucked another stretch of sand ridged into

shallow waves, and then he told me what had decided him
to check David's survey report. Amongst the papers in that
attaché case he had found Farr's report. "Didn't tell the
Old Man. Thought I'd keep it in reserve. God knows where
David dug it up. It was twenty years old, the paper all
faded; the typing, too. Could hardly read the damned
thing."

"Have you got it with you?" I asked.

"Aye." He nodded. "I wasn't going to leave that behind.
I'll show it to you later. Can't think why the Company
didn't do something about it."

"There was a war on," I said. "And Farr was killed in
Abyssinia."

"You know about it, then?" He seemed surprised.

"David referred to it in his report."

"Oh, yes, of course."

We hit another patch of sand, a solid vista of it that
stretched interminably ahead of us. We didn't talk much
after that. It was soft sand and the going was tough. Twice
the seismological truck got bogged down and we had to lay
sand-mats. The sun sank slowly down into the desert behind us as we ploughed on, engines roaring, radiators
steaming. We were in big-dune country that was like a
huge, petrified sea, the waves coming up one after the
other, yet never moving, always motionless, and the shadows lengthening behind them. It had an eerie, still quality;
and it left me with a sense of awe, for it had a certain majesty, a cruel, lost quality that was unnerving. Once I
shouted: "Is it like this all the way to Saraifa?"

"Christ! I hope not," he yelled back.

"But don't you know?" I asked.

"How the hell should I? Never been here before."

The sun set, a brick-red ball of fire hazed, it seemed,
with dust. Here and there we came upon the derelict remains of trees, gnarled and twisted in a life-long struggle
against crippling odds. Dusk descended swiftly and the
light faded out of the dunes. Behind us they stood like

downlands etched sharp against the sky's last light. Above us the stars suddenly appeared. Again the truck behind us became bogged and we dug the sand-mats down in front of the wheels and pushed and strained to gain a few yards. And when at last we got it moving there was no light left and it was dark.

"Will you be able to find Saraifa in the dark?" I asked Entwhistle.

"*Inshallah*," he said, and we pushed on.

How he did it I don't know, but about an hour later the dunes became smaller, the stunted tree-growth more noticeable, and then suddenly we ran out on to hard gravel again. And shortly after that the headlights picked up the first of the date-gardens, a sad relic of a once fertile place, the walls no longer visible, just the starved tops of the palms sticking up out of the sand.

We passed between two of these ruined gardens and then we joined a well-worn track where the sand had been ground to a fine powder; there were the marks of tires, the droppings of camels. The headlights picked out the round bulk of a watch-tower with men running from it, their guns gleaming with silver furnishings. Entwhistle slowed as they stood barring our path. They wore turbans and long white robes, and strapped across their shoulders was a sort of harness of leather studded with the brass of cartridges; stuffed into their belts were the broad, curved-bladed *khan-jar* knives, the hilts of silver glinting wickedly. As we stopped they came swarming over us, enveloping us with their harsh guttural speech, all talking at once, white teeth flashing in villainous dark faces.

"What do they want?" A black-bearded ruffian had the muzzle of his gun jammed against the side of my neck, and though I tried to keep my voice under control, I don't think I was very successful.

"All right, all right," Entwhistle was shouting at them. "One at a time, for God's sake." He didn't seem the least bit scared. Finally, after a long conversation with my

bearded friend, he said: "It looks like trouble. We're more
or less under arrest." He spoke to the bearded Arab again
and then he was ordering men on to the Land Rover and
others to the truck behind. "It seems," he said as we moved
off, "that Sheikh Makhmud sent a party out in two Land
Rovers this afternoon to arrest my outfit and bring me back
to Saraifa for questioning." And he added: "This could be
the sort of thing David came up against. They're scared
stiff of the Emir and frightened to death of any activity on
the Hadd border."

"Didn't you know that before you decided to run a survey there?" I asked.

"Of course I did. But I was reckoning to run the survey
and get out before any one discovered I was there." He
crashed the gears savagely. "I took a chance and it didn't
come off, that's all."

We skirted the crumbling wall of a date-garden. The
palms were green here, the gardens uninvaded by the desert
sand. And then suddenly we were in the open, driving on
hard gravel, and straight ahead of us, a black bulk against
the stars, was the shadowy shape of the Sheikh's palace
standing like a fortress on its hill. The wooden gate of the
arched entrance was closed, but it opened to the cries of
our guards, and then we were inside, in a great courtyard
packed with men and camels and lit by the flames of cooking-fires. In an instant we were surrounded, lapped round
by a tide of men, all shouting and brandishing their
weapons.

A big, portly man appeared, his face black as a Sudanese.
"The Sheikh's secretary," Entwhistle said to me. He looked
like a eunuch, fat and soft, his manner almost feminine.
He gave orders for the care of the men and then escorted
us into the palace, along dark corridors sparsely lit by
smoking lamps made out of old cans, to a small room that
looked out on to a central courtyard. Here the earthen floor
was carpeted with rugs, the walls lined with cushions; an
Arab rose to greet us. He was a compact, stocky man with

almost black eyes and a proudly curved nose. The *khanjar* knife stuck in the girdle of his finely woven robe was a beautiful example of the silversmith's craft. "Sheikh Makhmud," Entwhistle whispered.

I found my hand held in a firm grip. "You are welcome to Saraifa," the Sheikh said in halting English. "My house is your house." He had an air of command, yet his voice was gentle. But the thing that surprised me most was the fact that he wore glasses. They were silver-rimmed glasses and they drew attention to the blackness of his eyes. His clean-shaven face was long and tired-looking. He was a man about Gorde's age, I suppose. The other occupant of the room had also risen, a thin man with a greying moustache and a little pointed beard, his eyes heavily made up with kohl. He was Makhmud's brother, Sultan.

We sat cross-legged on the cushions and there was nothing in the Sheikh's manner to indicate that we were anything but honoured guests. Polite conversation was made, partly in the Arab language, partly in English. Slaves came with a silver jug and a silver ewer. We washed our hands, and then they brought in a simple dish of rice and mutton. "You eat with your right hand," Entwhistle whispered to me, and I tried to copy his practised movements.

I was hungry enough not to care that the meat was stringy and over-fat. We ate almost in silence, and when we had finished, the hand-washing was repeated and then coffee was served in little handleless cups, poured by a slave from a silver pot of intricate native design. And with the coffee came the questions. Sheikh Makhmud's voice was no longer gentle. It had a harsh, imperious quality, and Entwhistle was soon in difficulties with the language, lapsing periodically into English as he tried to explain his presence on the Saraifa-Hadd border. In the end he passed Sheikh Makhmud the note Gorde had written.

Entwhistle had just launched into an account of the attack that had been made on us when a young man entered.

He was short, well-built, and beneath his brown cloak he wore an old tweed jacket. But it was the features that caught the eye; they were delicate, almost classic features, the nose straight, the eyes set wide apart, with high cheek-bones and the full lips framed by a neatly trimmed moustache that flowed round the corners and down into a little pointed beard. He looked as though he had just come in from the desert, and I knew instinctively that this was Khalid, the Sheikh's son; he had an air about him that showed he was born to command.

He greeted his father and his uncle, waved us to remain seated, and folded himself up on a cushion against the wall. The brass of cartridge belt, the silver of *khanjar* knife gleamed beneath the jacket. He sat in silence, listening intently, his body so still that I was given the impression of great muscular control—a hard-sinewed body below the Arab robes.

There was a long silence when Entwhistle had finished. And then Sheikh Makhmud made what sounded like a pronouncement, and Entwhistle exclaimed: "Good God! I'm not going to do that." He turned to me. "He wants us to go to the Emir and explain that we were on the border without authority."

"You go freely," Sheikh Makhmud said in English. "Or you go with escort. Which you prefer?"

Entwhistle didn't say anything. His face was set and pale.

"Is very difficult, this situation," the Sheikh said almost apologetically. "Very dangerous also. You must make the Emir understand, please."

"Very dangerous for us, too," Entwhistle muttered angrily.

"I don't want any trouble."

"You want oil, don't you?"

"Colonel Whitaker is already drilling for oil."

"Then what was his son doing on the Hadd border?" Entwhistle demanded. "He ran a survey there. He wrote a

report. And then he vanished." There was no answer. "Khalid. You were his friend. What happened to
him?"

But Khalid was staring out into the courtyard.

In the silence I heard myself say: "He got a letter
through to me just before he disappeared. He knew he was
going to die." I felt them stiffen, the silence suddenly intense. I looked at Khalid. "Did he die a natural death?" His
eyes met mine for a moment and then fell away. "Somebody here must know how he died—and why."

Nobody answered, and the stillness of those three Arabs
scared me. It was the stillness of unease. "Where's Colonel
Whitaker?" I asked.

The Sheikh stirred uncomfortably. "You are full of
questions. Who are you?"

Briefly I explained. I was still explaining when there
was a sudden uproar in the passage outside and a man burst
into the room, followed closely by the Sheikh's secretary. A
staccato burst of Arabic and they were all suddenly on
their feet. I heard the word *falaj* run from mouth to mouth,
saw Khalid rush out, quick as a cat on his feet. His father
followed more slowly, the others crowding behind him.

"What is it?" I asked Entwhistle. "What's happened?"

"One of the *falajes*. I don't know exactly, but for some
reason the water has stopped."

We were alone now. Everybody had forgotten about us.
It was as though that word had some sort of magic in it.
"What exactly is a *falaj*?" He didn't seem to hear me, and
I repeated the question.

"*Falaj*?" He seemed to drag his mind back. "Oh, it's the
water system on which the date-gardens depend. The water
comes from the mountains of the Jebel anything up to
thirty miles away and it's piped into Saraifa by underground channels."

"And the underground channels are the *falajes*?"

"Yes, that's it. They're centuries old—a Persian irrigation system. In fact, they're the same as the Persian *qanats*."

He went to the passage and stood listening. "Bit of luck," he said, dropping his voice to a whisper. "If we can get hold of the Land Rover . . ." He grabbed hold of my arm. "Come on."

I followed him down the dimly lit mud corridors and out into the courtyard. The cooking-fires still smoked. The camels still crouched in a shapeless, belching huddle under the walls. But in the whole courtyard there wasn't a single Arab to be seen.

"Look! Even the guard on the gate has gone."

"But why?" I asked. "Why should that word—"

"Water. Don't you understand?" He sounded impatient. "Water is life here in the desert."

"But they can't depend on one channel. There must be many to irrigate a place like this."

"Five or six, that's all." He was searching the courtyard. "There used to be more than a hundred once. But tribal wars . . ." He gripped my arm. "There's the Land Rover. Over by the wall there." He pointed. "Come on! There's just a chance. . . ."

"What's the idea?" I asked.

"Get out whilst the going's good. Hurry, man!" His voice was high-pitched, urgent. "I'm not risking my neck on a mission of explanation to that bloody Emir." He had seized hold of my arm again. "Quick!"

I started to follow him, but then I stopped. "I'm staying," I said.

"Christ, man! Do you want to get killed?"

"No, but I want to find out why that boy was killed."

He stared at me. "You think it was like that—that he was murdered?"

"I don't know," I said. I didn't know anything for certain. "But I'm not leaving here until I've seen Colonel Whitaker."

He hesitated. But then he shrugged his shoulders. "Okay. It's your funeral, as you might say. But watch your step," he added. "He's a tricky bastard, by all accounts. And if what you're suggesting is true and David was murdered, then your life wouldn't be worth much, would it?"

"I'll be all right," I said.

"Aye, I hope so. But just remember you're right on the edge of Saudi Arabia here and the British Raj is worn a bit thin in these parts." He hesitated, looking at me, and then he started towards the Land Rover.

I stood and watched him, certain I was being a fool, but equally certain that I wasn't leaving. I saw him jump into the driving-seat, heard the whine of the starter, the roar of the engine. And then the Land Rover was moving and he swung it round and came tearing towards me. "Jump in, Grant," he shouted as he pulled up beside me. "Hurry, man! Hurry!"

"No," I said. "I'm not leaving." My voice was like the voice of a stranger to me. "You get out whilst you can. I'll be all right." And I added: "I'll make your excuses to the Sheikh for you." I meant it to be a jocular, carefree remark, but my voice sounded hollow. He was still hesitating and I said quickly: "Good luck to you!"

He stared at me hard and then he gave a little nod. "Okay. I expect you'll be all right. I'll notify the authorities, of course." And he slammed in the gear and went roaring across the courtyard and out through the empty gateway. The cloud of dust he'd raised gradually settled, and I walked to the gate and stood there watching his headlights threading a luminous trail through the date-gardens. And when they finally disappeared in the open desert beyond, I went slowly down the hill, heading for the murmur of voices, the glimmer of lights amongst the palms beyond the village.

I was alone then—more alone than I'd ever been in my life before.

The moon was just risen, and with the stars the village was lit by a soft translucence. The mud buildings were pale and empty, the open square deserted save for the hens nested in the dust and a solitary sad-looking donkey. Beyond the village I followed the crumbling wall of a date-garden until I came out into the open again. All Saraifa seemed gathered there, the men bunched together like a crowd at a cock-fight, the women dark bundles flitting on the edge of the crowd or squatting like hens in the sand. Everybody was talking at once, a thick hubbub of sound that seemed to lose itself instantly in the great solitude of the desert that stretched away to the east, to the dim-seen line of the mountains.

Nobody took any notice of me as I skirted the crowd. It was thickest close by the date-garden. Out towards the desert it thinned, and here I found a raised water channel built of rock and spanning a hollow aqueduct that might have been built by the Romans. It was my first sight of a *falaj,* and it was empty. I leaned over it, touched the inside with my fingers. It was still damp, and in a little puddle of water at the bottom tiny fish flashed silver in the starlight as they gasped for breath. Clearly, the water had only recently ceased to flow, turned off as though by a tap.

Fascinated, I crossed the hollow to the far side. For perhaps twenty yards the *falaj* was open, a neat, vertical-sided trench running a black shadow line across the sand. It was about two feet across and the same deep. I walked along it to the point where it was roofed over. For a hundred yards or so I could trace the outline of it, but after that the sand swallowed it up entirely. From a slight rise I looked towards the mountains. Anything up to thirty miles, Entwhistle had said, and they were the source of the water.

I walked slowly back along the line of the *falaj* to the point where it broke surface, and at the sight of the empty trough with the little fish gasping out their lives I could understand the calamity of it, the sense of disaster that had seized upon the people of this channel-fed oasis. A dry *falaj* meant a ruined date-garden, the beginnings of famine. Only five or six left out of more than a hundred, tribal wars . . . The place was as vulnerable as an oil refinery fed by a desert pipeline. Cut the *falaj* and Saraifa ceased to exist.

The sound of male voices died away, leaving only the high-pitched chatter of the women; there was a stillness of decision as I approached the crowd gathered about the *falaj* channel where it entered the date-garden. In the centre stood Sheikh Makhmud and his brother Sultan. Khalid was facing them, arguing fiercely. His features had no trace of effeminacy in them now. From the skirts of the crowd I saw Sheikh Makhmud turn impatiently away from his son. He called a man forth by name—Mahommed bin Rashid, a fierce, hawk-faced man with a black beard, the one who had stopped us as we entered Saraifa. He gave him an order, and a long *"A-a-agh"* of satisfaction issued from the throats of the crowd. Instantly all was confusion. Men brandished their weapons, calling on Allah, as a dozen or more of them were singled out and went hurrying back to the palace. Sheikh Makhmud turned and with his brother and his secretary followed them slowly.

It was the signal for the crowd to break up, and as they straggled away from the empty *falaj* Khalid was left standing there alone. A few men only remained, a little, compact group of silent followers ranged behind him. They were different from the rest in that their arms were without any silver trappings; they carried British service-pattern rifles.

He stood for a long time without moving, staring after his father and the crowd that followed him, noisy now with the excitement of action. And when they had disappeared from sight he turned to his men with a gesture of dismissal and they, too, moved away, but still silent, still in a compact group. He was completely alone then, staring down at the empty water channel, lost in his own thoughts. Even when I approached him he didn't stir. I don't think he knew I was there, for when I asked him whether he spoke English, he turned to me with a start of surprise.

"A little English—yess." His speech was slightly sibilant, his features marred when he opened his mouth by long, widely spaced teeth. "I am at Bombay University, my education." He was staring up the hill towards the palace, his mind still on what had happened. "They think they are being brave and that I am afraid. They don't understand." His tone was bitter and angry. "Their guns are very much old, and the men of Hadd will be waiting for them."

I asked whether it was Hadd who had stopped the water supply, and he said: "Yess. They perpetrate it once before. Then the British help us. Your people send soldiers with automatic guns and mortars. But not now. This time we are alone." He turned and I saw his dark eyes, sad in the starlight. "The *falajes*, you understand, sir, are very much vulnerable." He had acquired the Indian penchant for long words. And he added with great determination, speaking slowly as though stating something to himself: "We must fight for them now. But not like this. This way is to die." He began to walk slowly towards the palace.

There were many things I wanted to ask him, but this didn't seem the moment, and I walked beside him in silence, conscious of his preoccupation. His head was bent and he moved slowly, his sandals dragging in the sand. He was only two years older than David. I learned that later. Yet his manner was that of a man upon whom the whole responsibility for this desert community rested.

"Do you know Arabia much, sir?" he asked suddenly. And when I told him this was my first visit and that I'd only arrived a few days ago, he nodded and said: "You are from a town called Car-diff, yess? David speak of you sometimes."

That mention of Cardiff, the knowledge that this young Arab knew who I was . . . Saraifa seemed suddenly less remote, my position here less solitary.

"When David first come here, he is like you; he speak Arabic a little, but he don't understand our customs or the way we live here in the desert. The *falajes* mean nothing to him and he has never seen the big dunes when the *shamal* is blowing." He had stopped and he was smiling at me. Despite the wide-spaced, fang-like teeth, it was a gentle smile. "I am glad you come now." He offered me his hand and I found my wrist gripped and held in a strong clasp. "You are David's friend, and I will see that no harm come to you."

I thanked him, conscious that he had given me the opening I needed. But already I was becoming vaguely aware of the subtlety of the Arab mind, and this time I was determined not to make the mistake of asking direct questions. Sue's words came unconsciously into my mind: *David wanted to defend Saraifa, too.* I saw his face soften as he nodded, and I asked: "What was it about this place that so captured his imagination? His sister said he could be very emotional about it."

"His sister?" He smiled. "I have seen his sister once, when I am taking a plane at Sharjah. She is with the doctor, and I do not speak. A very fine person, I think."

I knew then that David had spoken of Sue to Khalid. "What is there about Saraifa," I said, "that he fell in love with it the way other men do with a woman?"

He shrugged. "He came here for refuge and we made him welcome. Also his father live here. It became his home."

But that didn't explain it entirely. "It was something more than that," I said.

"Yess." He nodded. "Is a very strange chap. A *Nasrani*— a Christian. He live very much by your Book, the Bible." That surprised me, but before I could make any comment, he added: "I should hate him because he is an infidel. Instead, I love him like my own brother." He shook his head with a puzzled frown. "Perhaps it is because I have to teach him everything. When he first come here, he knows nothing—he has never hunted, never owned a hawk; he does not know how to ride a camel or how to make a camp in the desert. For six months we are living together, here in

Saraifa, in the desert hunting, up in the mountains shooting wild hare and gazelle. But he is very good with machines, and later, when he is on leave from the oil company and we are working for the reconstruction of one of the old *falajes,* then he spend all his time down in the underground channels with the family who specialize in that work. You see, sir, this oasis is one time very much bigger, with very many *falajes* bringing water to the date-gardens. Then Saraifa is rich. Richer than Buraimi to the north. Richer perhaps even than the Wadi Hadhramaut to the south. It is, I think, the richest place in all Arabia. But nobody can remember that time. Now it is . . ." He stopped abruptly, his head on one side, listening.

And then I heard it, too—the soft pad-pad of camels' feet on gravel. Down the slope towards us came a bunch of camels moving with that awkward, lumbering gait. A dozen dark shapes swayed past us, the riders kneeling in the saddles, their robes flying, their rifles held in their hands. For an instant they were like paper cut-outs painted black against the stars, beautiful, balanced silhouettes. Then they were gone and the pad of their camels' feet faded away into the sand as they headed towards the mountains.

"Wallahi, qalilet-el-mukh!" Khalid muttered as he stared after them. And then to me: "That man, Mahommed bin Rashid. You heard him when my father give the order. *Inshallah,* he said, we will kill every harlot's son of them. But he is more like to die himself, I think." And he turned away, adding as he strode angrily up the hill: "Allah give him more brain in the world hereafter."

The sight of that handful of men riding east into the desert along the line of the *falaj* had changed his mood. He was preoccupied, and though I tried to resume our conversation, he didn't speak to me again until we reached the gates of the palace. Abruptly he asked me what sleeping quarters I had been allotted. And when I told him none, he said: "Then I arrange it. Excuse my father, please. He is very much occupied." He asked about Entwhistle. "Good," he said when I told him he'd gone. "He is not a fool, that man. He knows when it is dangerous." And he added: "It would have been better perhaps if you had gone with him."

"I'm not leaving here," I said, "until I know what happened to David."

There was a moment then when he hesitated as though about to tell me something. But all he said was: "Is best you talk to his father—*Haj* Whitaker."

"I intend to," I said. And when I asked him whether Colonel Whitaker was in Saraifa, he replied: "I don't know. He has his house here, but is most times at the place of drilling."

"And where's that?"

"To the south of 'ere, about ten miles towards Sheikh Hassa's village of Dhaid."

We had entered the great courtyard. A man sidled up to us, made his salaams to Khalid. He was dark and toothy, with a ragged wisp of a turban on his head, and his eyes watched me curiously as the two men talked together. My name was mentioned, and finally Khalid turned to me. "Now all is arranged. Yousif speak a little English. He will show you where you sleep." His hand gripped my arm. "Ask *Haj* Whitaker why he goes to see the Emir of Hadd almost two moons past. Ask him that, Meester Grant." It was whispered to me, his lips close against my ear and a hard, angry glint in his eyes.

But before I could question him he had drawn back. He said something to Yousif and with a quick *salaam alaikum* he left me, moving quickly through the camp-fires, the only man in all that throng who wore a European jacket.

"Come!" Yousif seized hold of my hand. Heads were turned now in my direction, and here and there a man got up from the fireside and began to move towards us. I had no desire to stay there, an object of curiosity. Yousif guided me through dark passages and up to a turret room by a winding staircase where the plaster steps were worn

smooth as polished marble by the tread of many feet. The
floor was bare earth, the roof beamed with palm-tree boles.
A slit of a window no bigger than a firing-embrasure
looked out on to the flat, beaten expanse of the village
square. I was in one of the mud towers of the outer wall,
and here he left me with no light but the glimmer of moonlight filtering in through the embrasure.

Strange, disembodied sounds drifted up to me on the
warm night air: the murmur of Arab voices, the grunt of
camels, a child crying—and in the distance the weird
chuckle of a hyena. I knelt on the firing-step, peering
down. Beyond the mud houses I could see the darker mass
of the palms. Bare feet sounded on the turret stairs and
the yellow light of a hurricane lamp appeared; the room
was suddenly full of armed men bearing bedding, which
they laid on the floor—a carpet, some blankets, an oryx
skin, and a silken cushion. "May Allah guard you," Yousif
said, "and may your sleep be as the sleep of a little child."

He was halfway through the door before I realized what
that long speech in English must mean. "You're Colonel
Whitaker's man, aren't you?"

He checked and turned. "Yes, sahib. Me driver for Coll-
onel." He was staring at me, his eyes very wide so that the
whites showed yellow in the lamplight. "I tell Coll-onel
you are here in Sheikh's palace." He was gone then.

There was no doubt in my mind that he'd been sent to
find me. Whitaker was in Saraifa, and Khalid had known
it as soon as Yousif had sidled up to us. I sat down on the
silken cushion, staring blindly at that cell-like room. There
was nothing to do now but wait. I felt tired; dirty, too.
But I'd no water with which to wash. No soap, no clothes
—nothing but what I was wearing. Yousif had left me the
hurricane lamp, and its light reached dimly to the palm-
wood rafters. A large desert spider moved among them
with deliberation. I watched it for a long time as it went
about its unpleasant business, and finally I killed it, over-

come with a fellow-feeling for the flies caught in its web. And then I put out the lamp and rolled myself up in a blanket.

It was hot, but I must have fallen asleep, for I didn't hear Yousif return; he was suddenly there, his torch stabbing the darkness, almost blinding me.

"Coll-onel say you come."

I sat up, glancing at my watch. It was past eleven thirty. "Now?"

"Yes, now."

Down in the courtyard the fires were almost out, the Sheikh's retainers lying like corpses wrapped in their robes. A few stirred as we crossed to the gate, now barred and guarded; a brief argument and then I was in a battered Land Rover being driven at reckless speed across the deserted village square, down into the date-gardens. Behind us the palace fort stood bone-white in the moonlight, and then the palms closed round us.

Whitaker's house was an old mud fort on the far side of the oasis. Most of it seemed to be in ruins, the courtyard empty, the mud walls cracked and crumbling. There was sand everywhere as we hurried through a maze of passages and empty rooms. The place seemed dead, and I wondered that a man could live alone like this and retain his sanity, for he seemed to have no servants but Yousif and to live in Spartan simplicity in one corner of this vast, rambling building.

We came at last to a room where old portmanteaus and tin boxes stood ranged against the walls, and then I was out on a rooftop that looked out upon the desert. He was standing against the parapet, a tall, robed figure in silhouette, for there was no light there, only the moon and the stars. Yousif coughed and announced my presence.

Whitaker turned then and came towards me. His face was in shadow, but I could see the black patch over the eye. No word of greeting, no attempt to shake my hand. "Sit down," he said and waved imperiously to a carpet and some cushions spread on the floor. "Yousif. *Gahwa.*" His servant disappeared, and as I sat down I was conscious of the stillness all about us—no sound of Arab voices, none of the tumult of the Sheikh's palace, no murmur of the village below the walls. The place was as isolated, as deserted as though we were the only people in the whole oasis.

He folded himself up, cross-legged on the carpet facing me, and I could see his face then, the beard thinning and grey, the cheeks hollowed and lined by the desert years, that single imperious eye deep-sunken above the great nose. "You had a good journey, I trust." His voice was oddly pitched, hard but unusually high, and he spoke the words slowly, as though English were no longer a familiar language.

"It was interesting," I said.

"No doubt. But quite unnecessary. It was clearly understood between us that you would make no attempt to contact me direct. And though I admit the financial situation must have seemed—"

"I came about your son," I said.

"My son?" He looked surprised. "Your letter merely said you were worried about the amount of money I was spending."

"Your son appointed me his executor."

He moved his head slightly, the eye glinting in the moonlight, bright and watchful. He didn't say anything. Behind him the low parapet hid the desert, so that all I could see was the great vault of the night studded with stars. The air was deathly still, impregnated with the day's heat.

"I'm not convinced your son died a natural death." I hadn't meant to put it like that. It was his stillness, the overpowering silence that had forced it out of me.

He made no comment and I knew that this was going to be more difficult than my interview with Erkhard, more difficult even than my meeting with Gorde, and some sixth sense warned me that this man was much more unpredictable. The clatter of cups came as a distinct relief. Yousif moved, silent as a shadow, on to the rooftop and poured us coffee from a battered silver pot. The cups were handleless, the Mocha coffee black and bitter.

"Does his mother know he's dead?" It surprised me that Whitaker should think of her; and when I told him that I'd broken the news to her myself, he asked: "How did she take it?"

"She didn't believe it at first." And because I had an overwhelming desire to break through his strange aura of calm, I added: "In fact, she seemed to think it was your own death I was reporting."

"Why? Why did she think I was dead?"

"The stars," I said. "She believes in astrology."

He sighed. "Yes, I remember now. I used to talk to her about the stars." And he added: "It's a long time ago. A long time."

"Do you believe in astrology, then?" I asked.

He shrugged, sipping noisily at his coffee. "Here in the desert we live a great deal by the stars. It is very difficult not to believe that they have some influence." And then, abruptly changing the conversation: "How did you get here? It's not easy to get to Saraifa." I started to tell him, but as soon as I mentioned Gorde, he said: "Philip Gorde? I didn't know he was out here." It seemed to upset him. "Did he tell you why he was here?" He mistook my silence. "No, of course not. He'd hardly tell you that." He shook his cup at Yousif to indicate that he'd had enough, and when I did the same the man departed as silently as he had come, leaving a dish of some sticky sweetmeat between us. "*Halwa*. Do you like it?" Whitaker made a vague gesture of invitation.

"I've never tried it."

We were alone again now and the silence between us hung heavy as the thick night air, a blanket through which each tried to gauge the other. I let it drag out, and it was Whitaker who finally broke it. "You were telling me about your journey." He stared at me, waiting for me to continue.

I broke off a piece of the *halwa*. It was cloying on the tongue and it had a sickly-sweet taste. "You arri ed here with Entwhistle, one of the Company's geologis s. What was he doing on the Hadd border, do you know Th ellow had no business there."

"He was checking your son's survey," I said.

There was a sudden stillness. "I see." He said it quietly. And then, in a voice that was suddenly trembling with anger: "On whose orders? Not Philip Gorde's, surely?"

"No."

"Erkhard?"

"You seem very worried about this."

"Worried!" The word seemed forced out of him. "Don't you understand what's happened here tonight? The thing I've been dreading . . . The thing I've been trying to avoid ever since I knew . . ." He checked himself. And then in a quieter voice: "No, you're new out here. You wouldn't understand. One of the *falajes* has been stopped. And all because of this blundering fool Entwhistle running a survey on the Hadd border." His voice had risen again, trembling with anger.

"He was doing what David was doing at the time he disappeared," I said quietly.

But it didn't seem to register. He had withdrawn into his own thoughts. "Twenty years . . ." His voice sounded tired. And then his eye was staring at me again. "How would you feel if the thing you'd worked for over a period of twenty years was in danger of being ruined by young fools too impatient to understand the politics of the desert?" He turned his head and stared for a moment into the night. "The air is heavy. There'll be a storm soon." He gathered his robes about him and rose to his feet, crossing to the parapet and leaning against it, staring out into the desert like some Biblical figure from the distant past. "Come here, Grant." And when I joined him, he stretched out his arm. "Look, do you see those dunes?" He gripped my arm, pointing west into the desert.

Standing on that rooftop was like standing on the bridge of a ship lying anchored off a low-lying island. To the left lay the dark-treed expanse of the oasis, and beyond the date-gardens I could see the village and the squat bulk of the Sheikh's palace standing on its gravel rise. But to the right, where his arm pointed, was nothing but desert. Dim in the moonlight the dunes stretched away into infinity, a ridged sea of sand, pale as milk.

"When you've seen a storm here you'll understand. Then all the desert seems in motion, like the sea beating against the shore of the oasis, flooding into the date-gardens. The dunes smoke. They stream with sand. They're like waves breaking; the whole great desert of the Empty Quarter thundering in, the sand flowing like water." He turned to me and his grip on my arm tightened. "The only thing that stands between Saraifa and destruction is the camel thorn. Out there—do you see? Those trees. They're like a breakwater holding the sand sea back, and they're dying for lack of water."

"The *falajes?*" I asked, and he nodded. "Entwhistle said there used to be around a hundred of them."

"Yes. We've traced them from aerial photographs."

"Your son was very much concerned about—"

"Oh, yes, concerned . . . But he lacked patience. He was like a young bull. No subtlety. No subtlety at all." And he added: "What's been done tonight can be quickly repaired. There's an open well every mile or so along the length of the underground channel of the *falaj*. They've blocked one of these wells with sand and stone. It can be unblocked almost as quickly. But the old *falajes* . . ." He shook his head. "The wells are fallen in, the underground channels collapsed. Restoring them is a lengthy and costly business. Sheikh Makhmud has managed to restore just one in the fourteen years he's been Sheikh of Saraifa. It took two years and cost more than twenty thousand pounds. If Saraifa is to survive . . . " He gave a little shrug. "We need a dozen new *falajes,* not one."

"And only oil will pay for them?"

He nodded. "Yes."

"David took the same view," I said. "That's why he was prospecting on the Hadd border." And I added: "What happened, Colonel Whitaker? What happened to your son?"

He turned and looked at me. "You think I should know?"

"I've come a long way," I said, "in the certainty that you must know."

His eyebrows lifted, the single eye stared at me, not blinking. "The certainty?"

"Yes," I said. "The certainty." And I added: "He was on loan to you at the time he disappeared. It was the seismological truck you purchased in Basra last June that he left abandoned on the side of a dune twenty miles inside the borders of Saudi Arabia. And just before he disappeared, you visited the Emir of Hadd. You must know what happened."

"Well, I don't." He said it flatly, and it was difficult not to accept it.

"Then why did you visit Hadd?"

"Who else could do it?" And he added: "David was on the Hadd border against my orders—against Sheikh Makhmud's orders, too. Somebody had to try and convince the Emir there wasn't any oil there."

"Because the border's in dispute."

"Yes. There's been trouble there ever since the Company was first granted a concession to prospect in Saraifa. As you probably know, Saraifa is an independent sheikhdom. Unlike the Trucial States, it's not even in treaty relation with the British Crown, though it's generally considered to be a part of the British sphere of influence. Hadd is different again. It's independent in theory and in fact, and during the last few years it has strengthened its ties with Arab countries. Some years back we were finally driven to sending troops in, to keep the peace, and they occupied the fort of Jebel al-Akhbar overlooking the town of Hadd. But we couldn't do that now. It would be much too dangerous." He hesitated, and then he added: "The risk would only be justified if vital interests of our own were involved."

"What sort of vital interests?" I asked. But I knew the answer before he gave it.

"Oil," he said. "From a Western point of view—as you'd know if you'd been out here any length of time—everything in Arabia comes back to oil."

"Your son's death, too?" I asked. He looked at me, but didn't say anything. "When did you first hear he was missing?"

"Towards the end of February."

"Could you give me a date?"

He frowned and for a moment I thought he wasn't going to answer that. But then he said: "I can't be certain. Your calendar doesn't mean very much to us out here in the desert. But by the moon it would be about the beginning of the last week in February."

Almost a week before the abandoned truck had been found by the Bedouin, more than three weeks before his disappearance had been reported to the Company. "You didn't notify Erkhard."

"No."

"Why not? David was in the Company's employ, even if he was on loan to you."

He didn't say anything. He seemed suddenly to have withdrawn inside himself. I think perhaps he was waiting for my next question, knowing it was coming.

"The truck was discovered abandoned on February twenty-eight," I said. "Yet you say you knew he was missing almost a week before that. How did you know?"

There was a long pause. At length he said: "Some askari were dispatched from Saraifa. When they reached his camp they found it deserted, not a soul there; the truck and the Land Rover had gone, too."

"Askari?"

"Members of Sheikh Makhmud's bodyguard. Their orders were to arrest him and bring him back to Saraifa."

"Alive?"

"Of course." He stared at me angrily. "What other instructions do you imagine they would be given? They were dispatched by Sheikh Makhmud—at my request. That was immediately after my return from Hadd." And he added: "It was done for his own good—and because it was necessary. The Emir was in a very dangerous mood."

So that was how it had been. "And you didn't want Erkhard to know that he'd been operating on the Hadd border?"

"I didn't want Erkhard to know and I didn't want the political boys to know. As I've said, David was there against my express orders. God Almighty!" he breathed. "The impatience of youth! They want the moon for breakfast and the sun for lunch." He leaned on the parapet, staring down to the white sand below. "I blame myself," he said quietly. "I should have packed him off back to Cardiff. Instead, I let him stay. More, I tried to think of him as my son, as God's gift from my loins, a prodigal given back into my hands." He shook his head. "I should have known it wouldn't work."

He paused there and I didn't say anything, for I felt his isolation here might trap him into some self-revelation if I didn't try to force it. He looked at me again, the desert lines deep-etched by the moon, a long, sad, solitary face. "As you know, I'm a Muslim. I wanted him to become a Muslim, too. I wanted him to make the desert his home and to carry on where I left off in due course." He sighed softly. "I forgot the boy was already nineteen, and only half mine . . . and that half as obstinate as the devil." He smiled. In that harsh face it was a smile of extraordinary tenderness. "I turned him into a Christian instead." He said it with bitterness, adding: "In the end I think he came to hate me."

"Why?"

The question was out before I could stop myself, and I saw him freeze and close up on me. "People get at cross-purposes, you know." His tone was casual now. "It's one of the sad things about human relationships. But there . . . No point in talking about it now. The boy's dead, and that's that."

"You can't be sure of that," I said.

He stared at me, his eye blazing in the darkness. "What do you mean? I had all the chaps I could spare out looking for him. Khalid was searching, too, and Makhmud had men hunting for him all over Saraifa. The one place we never thought of searching was west into the Empty Quarter." And he said, with gentleness, softly to himself: "The desert is like the sea. No man can disappear into it for two months and come out alive."

"All right," I said. "He's dead. But if you haven't discovered what happened to him, what do you think happened to him?"

His eye looked into mine. "Have you ever been frightened?"

"Yes, once," I said. "In Tanganyika."

He nodded. "Then you'll understand me when I say no man knows how he'll react to fear until he's faced with it. Especially when he's alone. And David was alone. His Arab crew had deserted him. We found that out later. They panicked."

"And you think David did the same?"

He shrugged. "It's a cruel place, the desert. And solitary as hell. Empty, too. Even in company the Bedou sing to keep their spirits up." It was much what Griffiths had said, and it seemed plausible enough. He took my arm and led me back to the carpet. "You were telling me about your journey. . . ."

I told him as much as I thought he'd a right to know—about the package Griffiths had brought me and my meet-

ing with Erkhard. But it was Gorde he was really interested
in—Gorde and Entwhistle and the fact that the two of
them had been together at the locations David had been
surveying. It seemed to worry him, and he questioned me
closely about Gorde's reactions—what had he said, where
was he going when he'd left me there with Entwhistle?
And then he asked me what it was that had decided Entwhistle to check David's survey. "He must have known he
was risking his life there on that border. What made him
think it was so important?"

I hesitated. He was sitting there, watching me, very still,
very tense, and I knew suddenly that this was what the
whole interview had been leading up to and that he was
deeply concerned. "When Entwhistle searched the abandoned truck," I said, "he found all David's papers. They
included his own survey report and also the report of a
much older survey run just before the war. I think it was
that report—"

"Whose report?" The question was shot at me out of the
dark. "Was it Henry Farr's report?"

I stared at him. "You know about that?"

"Of course. Henry sent me a copy of it. He was well
aware of my interest in the area. Later we had a talk about
it—just before he went into Abyssinia."

"But if you knew about it . . ." It seemed so incredible. "In his letter to me David said he found it in the
Company's files. You never told him about it?"

"No."

"Why ever not? You must have known how he felt about
Saraifa, his desperate urge to—"

"He was employed by the Company—by Erkhard." His
voice was taut and hard, a note almost of hostility.

"But . . . I don't understand," I said. "All these years
. . . And Khalid says you're drilling to the south of the
oasis. That's at least forty miles from David's locations."

"Exactly. Just about as far from the Hadd border as it's

possible to get and still be in Saraifa." He got to his feet
and began pacing up and down, seeking relief in movement from the nervous tension that I now realized had
existed inside him from the first moment of our meeting.
"It's not easy to explain. You don't understand the situation." He stopped suddenly and faced me. "For twenty
years I've had to sit on this, convinced that my theory was
right, that the oil-bearing strata continued from the Gulf
down into Saraifa, between the Empty Quarter and the
mountains you can see there to the east." His voice was
sharp and bitter with frustration. "I had to find some
way. . . ." He paused, standing there over me, and he was
silent a long time, as though reaching for a decision. Finally
he said: "You know so much. . . . You may as well know
the rest. Erkhard's coming here tomorrow, flying down from
Sharjah. He's under pressure, as I think you'll have guessed
from your conversation with Philip Gorde. With God's
help I'll get him to sign the concession, and once the Company's involved . . ." He turned and resumed his pacing.
"There was no other way. No company would sign a concession with Saraifa if they knew it involved drilling on
the Hadd-Saraifa border. No company would dare. But
once they're committed . . . " He beat his fist against the
palm of his hand. "I've seen it happen before. The technical men come in. They're not concerned with politics.
They ride roughshod over everything, and in the end the
Government is forced to support them."

"So there isn't any oil where you're drilling?"

"No, not as far as I know."

It was a strange business. He'd spent all that money,
almost a year of desperate effort to lure the Company into
becoming involved again in Saraifa. It was clever, but . . .
"And you think Erkhard will sign the concession agreement?"

"I think so, yes. In the four years he's been General Manager he hasn't been very successful. His position isn't as
strong as it was when he came out here."

"But why didn't you tell David what you were doing?"

"How could I? He was Erkhard's man." And he added: "I still have contacts in the Bahrain office. According to them, he was under orders to report on everything I was doing."

"And he agreed?"

"They knew his background. After that, of course, I couldn't trust him."

"Then why was he on loan to you?"

"Erkhard offered him to me. I'd had him here before; I couldn't very well refuse." And then sadly: "I didn't dare tell him. Besides, he lacked patience. He always approached things head-on, wanting to force the issue. If I'd thought he'd have been guided by me . . ." He shrugged. "Well, it can't be helped now."

He turned to me, his manner suddenly matter-of-fact. "You must be tired, and I've a long day ahead of me. You're fixed up all right, I take it, at the Sheikh's palace?"

I nodded and got to my feet. "But I still don't understand why you did nothing about the Farr report—after the war when the Company had the concession."

"Various reasons," he answered. "Most of them political. All the time the Company had the concession there was spasmodic fighting on the border. The Emir, you see, was determined to grab any oil there was for himself. And when we finally sent in troops to keep the peace, it was too late for me to do anything about it. The concession had lapsed, Philip Gorde had gone home sick, and Erkhard had taken over. Erkhard would have dealt with the Emir or anybody else. He'd no feeling for Saraifa, the way Philip had." He turned abruptly and shouted for Yousif. And then, looking at me very hard, he said: "You've come at a strange moment, Grant, and I've told you things I've told no other man. I've had to, or you'd have caused more trouble. By the mere fact of coming out here . . ." He hesitated and I knew he was thinking of Gorde. "What did

Philip say? Was he surprised when he discovered where
I was drilling?"

"I don't think he knows," I said. "He wasn't even sure
you were drilling."

"Oh, he knows. A plane passed over the rig this afternoon. I thought for a moment it must be Erkhard arriving
a day early, but when it circled and turned away I began
to wonder." He was looking out into the desert again and
his face showed the strain he was under. "I could have
wished it had been anyone but Philip Gorde. He's the only
man in the whole Company who knows enough to guess
what I'm up to. But there's nothing I can do about it now."

Yousif had appeared, and Whitaker held out his hand to
me. "You're a lawyer, Grant. You've been involved in our
affairs for a long time. I rely on you not to talk." He held
my hand gripped in his. "We have two enemies here in
Saraifa—the Emir and the sands." He gestured towards
the white expanse of the dunes and added softly: "Tomorrow, with God's help, I'll lay the foundations of victory
over them both." It was said with great intensity, his eye
fixed on my face.

I left him then, standing alone as I had found him on
that rooftop, a strange, almost fanatical figure against the
backcloth of endless desert. Even when I got back to my
turret room, the memory of him was so clear in my mind
that I felt he was still with me. But I was too exhausted to
think clearly about that extraordinary meeting. I fell asleep
and dreamed instead of women crying over children dead
of thirst.

I woke in the small hours to the reality of their cries, a
queer, keening sound coming up from the square below.
The palace, too, was alive with voices, and though they
were muffled by distance and the thickness of the walls, I
caught the vibrant note of disaster.

It was quite chill as I flung off my blanket and went to
the embrasure. The village square was ghostly pale in
moonlight, empty save for a little group immediately be-

low me, a dozen women and some children huddled like rags around the dead body of a man. He had been shot in the face and he wasn't a pretty sight there in the moonlight. Nearby a camel lay in a pool of blood.

It was just after four by my watch and already the sky was paling in the east. I put on my shoes and went down into the courtyard. The place was in an uproar, fires smoking and men standing in little groups, all talking at once. The nearest fell silent as they saw me and the word *"Nasrani"* passed from mouth to mouth, a whisper of fear, perhaps of hate. I beat a hasty retreat to the seclusion of my turret cell.

Sleep was impossible after that, and I sat huddled in my blanket and watched the dawn break over the Jebel Mountains, the grey light of it creeping across the palm tops, heralded by the brazen sound of an ass braying. The keening ceased, and when I went to the window embrasure there was no sign of the dead man and the camel's carcass had gone. It might have been a bad dream, for as daylight flooded the square it was full of the sound of children and their carefree laughter.

There was a *shireeya*, or open water-hole, a short distance from the tower, and young Arab girls were driving goats towards it. There were boys there, too, with their asses, filling goat-skin bags and dripping a dark trail of the precious fluid as they took it to houses in the village. Skinny, undersized fowl pecked in the dirt; a shapeless bundle of womanhood passed, her face hideously concealed by the black mask of the *burqa*. And when the sun lifted its glaring face above the distant line of the mountains, the palms, the sand, the mud houses were all miraculously suffused with colour, as though I were looking at the scene through rose-tinted glasses. Exhausted, I lay down again and was instantly asleep.

I woke to the cry of *"Gahwa"* and a barefoot attendant pouring coffee for me, his gun slung across his back, the brass of his cartridge belt gleaming in the light from the embrasure. It was eight thirty, and the flies crawled over the dates he left for my breakfast.

I ate the dates slowly, for time hung heavy on my hands and I didn't dare venture out alone after what had happened. My eyes felt tired, my body lethargic. My mind wandered in weary circles as the heat of the desert grew in intensity, invading the room. It was almost eleven when Khalid came for me. A brief salaam, a polite hope that I'd slept well, and then he said: "My father holds a *majlis*. He desires your presence, sir." His face looked grave, and the eyes, deep-sunk and shadowed, spoke of a sleepless night. "The Emir of Hadd has sent one of his sheikhs to make demand for a new border." His voice sounded weary, too.

"What happened last night?" I asked. "There were women crying and a dead body in the square."

"They waited in ambush by the fourteenth well. Mahommed bin Rashid is dead and two of his men also. Three are wounded. Come! My father waits for you."

I asked him if I could wash first, but he said there was no time. "You must explain now, please, to the Emir's representative why you and Meester Entwhistle are on the border." And then urgently: "Tell Sheikh Abdullah there is no oil there."

"I'm not a geologist."

"He don't know that. He thinks you work for the oil company."

"Well, I don't." I spoke sharply, irritable with lack of sleep. "I'm a lawyer, and all I'm interested in is what happened to David Whitaker."

His dark eyes stared at me hard. "Is better you don't talk about David at this meeting," he said quietly.

"Why?" Angry and tired, I didn't stop to think what I was saying. "Because your father sent some of his bodyguard to arrest him?"

"You saw *Haj* Whitaker last night. You know why they were sent. He was on the Hadd border against my father's orders."

"Against Whitaker's orders, too, I gather."

"Yes. If he had been a Muslim instead of a *Nasrani*
. . ." He gave a little shrug. "The Prophet has taught
us that the word of the father is as a law and that the son
must obey." And he added: "My father is wishing to avoid
trouble. He does not believe that a few miles of desert sand
is worth fighting for."

"And you do?"

Again the little shrug. "My father is an old man and he
has known *Haj* Whitaker many years now. He is guided
by him in these matters. And I—I also am not a geologist."

"Who did your father send with the soldiers?" I asked.
"Was it you?"

"No. Mahommed bin Rashid." He turned abruptly.
"Come, please. My father is waiting." And as I followed
him down the turret stairs, he said over his shoulder:
"Please. You will not speak of David." He said it fiercely,
with great urgency.

He led me through passages that were cool in semi-
darkness and up to a rooftop by another staircase. The
majlis, or audience, was being held in an open room with
arches that looked out across the rooftop to the oasis.
Sheikh Makhmud didn't rise to greet me. His face looked
tired and strained, sullen with anger. He was also, I think,
a little frightened. Beside him sat the representative of
Hadd, a bearded, sly-eyed, powerfully built man with an
elaborately embroidered cloak and a headdress that was
like a turban of many colours.

Sheikh Makhmud motioned me to sit facing him. I was
thus in the position of the accused facing a Court, for all
the notables were there, seated cross-legged and grave on
silken cushions ranged round the inner walls of that airy
room. On a carpet in the centre were bowls of camel milk
and tinned pears. Nobody touched them except the flies.
The atmosphere was tense, almost electric.

The situation was distinctly unpleasant, for it was obvious as soon as Sheikh Makhmud began to question me

in halting English that he regarded me as responsible for
the situation that had developed. Entwhistle's absence
didn't help, and though I answered the questions truth-
fully, I could see from Sheikh Abdullah's manner that he
didn't believe me. He listened to the translation with a lack
of interest that he didn't bother to conceal.

In the end I lost my temper with him. I scrambled to my
feet, and, standing over the man, delivered myself of the
sort of broadside I occasionally indulged in in the Courts.
My action might have been dictated by expediency, for
attack was undoubtedly the best method of defence. But,
in fact, my nerves were on edge. "Your men attacked us
without warning and without cause!" I shouted at him.
And I described how the soft-nosed bullet had slammed
into the hood of the Land Rover, how the fusillade of
shots had raised spurts of sand all around us. He looked
suddenly uncomfortable. "Only a few years ago," I said,
"my country had to send troops here to keep the peace.
Now you break it again. Why? What explanation do you
wish me to give when I return to Bahrain?"

My words translated, the crafty eyes slid from my face to
the assembled men and he licked his lips as though suddenly uncertain of himself. "You have no answer," I said,
and with that I gave Sheikh Makhmud a quick bow and
made my exit. I couldn't go far, for armed retainers barred
the staircase leading down from the roof. But I had made
my point and felt better for it, even though I was now
forced to remain out in the full glare of the sun. I sat myself down on the oven-lid heat of the mud parapet and pre-
tended to be absorbed in watching a camel caravan being
loaded at a huddle of *barastis* close by the date-gardens.
Behind me I could hear the guttural sound of the men's
talk as they continued to deliberate.

Coffee was served and Khalid came over and joined me.
"Is no good," he said. "The Emir listens to Cairo Radio
and he believes he has powerful friends. It has made him
bold. Also he has many new rifles. They have come up

from the Yemen, I think. From the coast also." And he
added: "Only if we have oil here in Saraifa will your people
give us their full support. We know that."

"Mr. Erkhard is seeing Colonel Whitaker today," I said.

He nodded. "My father will not make a decision until he
hears from *Haj* Whitaker. He is full of hope."

"And you?" I asked, for the way he said it suggested he
didn't share his father's optimism.

He shrugged. "I also hope, but *Haj* Whitaker is old, and
he is tired and sick."

"Sick?"

"Sick here." And he touched his heart.

I asked him then what exactly Sheikh Abdullah was
demanding. "A new border," he said and drew it for me
in the sand of the rooftop floor with the toe of his sandalled
foot. It meant that all the area David had surveyed would
belong to Hadd.

"And if your father refuses?"

Again that fatalistic shrug. "Then Sheikh Abdullah say
they will destroy another *falaj,* and another and another,
until we have no water for the dates, no water for our
beasts, none for ourselves even. We die then of thirst and
starvation." He was staring out across the oasis. "I am
young yet. I had thought to rebuild the *falajes,* one by one,
until Saraifa is like a garden again and the desert at bay.
That is my dream."

"And David's, too."

"Yes, it is the dream we share since we first hunt the
gazelle together." His eyes had a far-away look, his voice
sad with the loss of that dream. His father called to him
and he finished his coffee and went back to his place. The
conference was resumed, and, looking at the faces of the
men gathered in that room, I knew he was right. They
were in no mood to fight, and if Whitaker didn't save
them, then they would accept it as the will of Allah and
agree to the Emir's demands.

The camel caravan down by the palm-tree fringe fin-

ished loading. I watched the heavily laden beasts move off
through the date-gardens, headed north into the desert.
The whole oasis shimmered in the heat, and beyond it
stretched the sands, a golden sea thrusting yellow drifts
amongst the palms. The sun climbed the sky. The heat
became unbearable, the talk spasmodic, and Sheikh Abdullah sat there, his heavy eyelids drooping, not saying anything, just waiting.

I was half asleep when I saw the dust trail of the vehicle.
It was coming through the date-gardens from the south,
driven fast, and when it emerged into the open I saw it was
a Land Rover packed with Arabs, all shouting and waving
their guns in a frenzy of excitement. And as it reached the
outskirts of the village they began firing into the air.

A few minutes later Yousif burst through the retainers
standing at the head of the stairs. He went straight up to
Sheikh Makhmud, interrupting the deliberations with that
extraordinary lack of respect that seems a contradiction
almost of the feudalism of the Bedou world. He was excited, and Arabic words poured from him in a flood as he
handed the Sheikh a folded slip of paper.

As soon as Sheikh Makhmud had read it his whole manner changed. His eyes lit up. He became revitalized, a man
suddenly in command of the situation. He said a few
words, speaking softly and with great control. The name
of Allah was repeatedly mentioned, presumably in praise.
And then he rose to his feet. The effect was remarkable.
The place was suddenly in an uproar, everybody on his
feet and all talking at once. There was a general movement
towards the stairs, and Sheikh Makhmud swept out ahead
of his elders, moving fast and with a light, soundless tread,
so that he seemed to flow like water from the rooftop.

Khalid followed him, the others crowding after them,
and in a moment there were only myself and the Emir's
representative left. He looked unhappy, his arrogance un-
dermined by this development which had clearly affected
his embassy. I smiled at him, waving him to the staircase

ahead of me, and was amused at the childish way he turned his back on me in a huff.

From the rooftop I could see men running. The news seemed to have spread round the oasis in a flash. And south, beyond the palms, another dust trail moved across the desert. By the time I had found my way down to the great courtyard the whole male population of Saraifa seemed gathered there. And when the Land Rover, driven by Colonel Whitaker himself, turned slowly through the gateway, forcing a passage through the crush to where Sheikh Makhmud stood waiting, a great shout went up: "*Haji! Haji!*" In the passenger seat beside Whitaker sat Erkhard, as cool and neat and spotless as when I had seen him last.

The greetings over, the Company's General Manager was taken into the palace. I had a glimpse of Whitaker's face as he walked beside Sheikh Makhmud, towering over him and all the Arabs around him. He wasn't smiling and yet it expressed his elation—a secret, almost violent emotion. Twenty years was a long time, and this the culmination of his life, the moment of victory. It seemed a pity David couldn't be here to share it.

Nobody took any notice of me now. I walked out through the main gate, down into the shade of the palms, and sat by the steaming waters of the *shireeya*. Gorde, Whitaker, Erkhard, Entwhistle . . . those three women . . . My brain reeled with the heat. Unable to fix any pattern to my thoughts, I returned finally to my turret room. It was cooler there, the shadowed interior peaceful, and I took my siesta to the lazy buzzing of flies, the distant murmur of people wild with joy.

I must have slept heavily, for when I woke the sun was low and there was a little pile of freshly laundered clothes beside me—a tropical suit, shirt, tie, pants, socks. There was also a note from Whitaker: *The concession is signed and there is a feast to celebrate. I thought you might like a change of clothes. Yousif will call for you at sunset.*

As soon as I started to put them on I knew the clothes
weren't his, for he was much taller and these fitted me
reasonably well. They were obviously David's, and it
seemed to me strange that I should be attending this feast
in his clothes.

The acrid smell of wood smoke permeated the room,
and the hubbub of sound from the village square drew me
to the embrasure. The whole beaten expanse was full of
people and cooking-fires. The carcasses of sheep and goats
hung by their hind legs, their slashed throats dripping
blood into bowls. Chickens were being prepared, and
blackened pots of rice simmered over the fires. Half
Saraifa was in the square, and there was a great coming and
going of the Sheikh's armed retainers, who carried the
cooked dishes into the palace. The sun sank and the sky
blazed red for an instant and then died to purples and light
greens.

"You come now, sir, please."

Yousif stood at the head of the stairway, almost unrecognizable in clean clothes and spotless turban, a curved
khanjar knife gleaming silver at his waist. He took me
down to a central courtyard that I hadn't seen before. It
was packed with retainers, the silver and brass of guns and
cartridges gleaming in the shadows. The Sheikh and his
guests were already gathered in the long, colonnaded room
on the far side, and dishes lay in lines in the dust.

Khalid came forward to greet me. He was beautifully
clad in long robes of finest cashmere, a brown cloak gold-
embroidered, and his eyes, newly made-up with *kohl*, looking enormous, his beard shining and silky with some
scented lotion. Whitaker was seated on one side of Sheikh
Makhmud, Erkhard on the other. And next to Whitaker
sat Sheikh Abdullah of Hadd. "You sit with me," Khalid
said.

As I passed Erkhard, he looked up. "Grant!" I couldn't
help being amused at his surprise. "They told me in
Sharjah that you'd left with Gorde, but I didn't expect

to see you here." He frowned. "Where is Gorde, do you know?"

"I think he flew back to Bahrain."

He nodded. "Good."

As I took my place beside Khalid, retainers were already moving amongst the guests with ewers of water. We rinsed our hands, and the first great platters were moved forward on to the rugs. The occasion was very formal. Nobody talked unless the Sheikh himself was talking. The result was that conversation went in disconcerting leaps—one moment bedlam, the next a silence in which the only sound was the coming and going of the retainers in the courtyard.

The feast was a monstrous, gargantuan affair—mutton, goat's flesh, young camel, chicken, gazelle. The platters came on and on and kept on coming, the meat nestled on piled-up heaps of rice, eggs floating in a spiced gravy like little yellow balls, omelettes piled in tiers, flat and leathery like griddle cakes, flat disks of bread, liquid butter and cheese. Half the dishes never got beyond the colonnades, but remained outside in the dust, enough to feed an army. Like all Bedouin feasts, it was intended as a meal for the Sheikh's bodyguard, who were waiting on us, for all the palace retainers, and finally for the people of Saraifa themselves so that they would all feel they had shared in the event.

The cooking was rough desert cooking, the meat over-done and swimming in fat, the dishes lukewarm at best. But I was so damned hungry I scarcely thought about what I was eating. Khalid kept plying me with delicacies—the tongue of gazelle, I remember, and something that I popped into my mouth and swallowed whole, hoping it wasn't what I thought it was. An old man sat in a corner playing intermittently on what I can only describe as a lute. The palace poet, I was told. Later he would unburden himself of a poem in praise of the guests and of the occasion. "It will be a long poem," Khalid said and his eyes

smiled whilst his face remained quite serious. There was
a sudden silence and into it the man next to me tossed a
belch of impressive loudness. There was a great deal of
belching. It was a mark of appreciation, and before we
were halfway through the meal I found myself doing the
same, so quickly and easily does one fall into other people's conventions. Also my stomach was by then very
full.

Outside in the courtyard Sheikh Makhmud's falconers
paraded their birds. He was very proud of his falcons, and,
seeing them, talons gripped around wooden perches spiked
into the sand or around the leather-gauntleted arms of their
keepers, I found myself glancing at Whitaker, noticing the
same quick, predatory look, the same sharp, beaky features.
Our eyes met for a moment and it seemed to me that the
mood of exhilaration had drained out of him, as though
success had a sour taste; or perhaps it was the clothes I was
wearing, reminding him of his son.

The main dishes had all been removed now. Lights were
brought, for the sun had set and it was growing dark. They
were modern, chromium-plated pressure lamps, and they
were hung on nails in the walls, where they hissed and
glared and had to be constantly pumped to maintain the
pressure. And with the lamps came dishes of every sort of
tinned fruit. There was *halwa,* too. Coffee followed, and at
a sign from Sheikh Makhmud the poet moved into the
centre. He sat facing the guests and began plucking at his
lute, chanting a ballad—the story, Khalid said, of Saraifa's
need of water and *Haj* Whitaker's long search for oil. It
had the effect of intensifying the mood of excitement that
gripped all the Arabs . . . all except Sheikh Abdullah,
who sat staring stonily into space.

And then suddenly the stillness was shattered by the
noise of an aircraft flying low. The ballad-singer faltered,
the sound of the lute ceased; the story came abruptly to a
halt, unfinished.

The sound swept in a roar over the palms. I thought I

caught a glimpse of a dark shape against the stars, and then the engine died. It was coming in to land. Sheikh Makhmud called to his secretary, and a guard was dispatched to escort the visitors. Everybody was talking at once, and Erkhard leaned across to me and hissed: "Who is it? Do you know?"

I didn't answer, but I think he must have guessed, for his eyes were coldly bleak and there was a tightness about his mouth. I looked past him to where Whitaker sat. His face was expressionless, but his body had a stillness that was without repose.

After what seemed a very long wait Gorde and Otto were escorted into the courtyard.

It was a strange moment, for Gorde walked straight in on the feast, limping and leaning on his stick, the sweat-stained trilby jammed firmly on his grizzled head, his battered features set in grim lines. He didn't greet Sheikh Makhmud. He didn't greet any one. He stopped in the middle of the centre archway and stared in silence at the gathering, my briefcase tucked under his arm. It was an effective entrance, and I knew by his aggressive manner that he had intended it to be. Impressive, too, for he was dressed exactly as I had last seen him, and behind him crowded the bodyguard, all armed to the teeth. It was impressive because of the contrast: the man so small, so completely at the mercy of the armed men behind him, and yet so dynamic, so completely in command of the situation.

He ignored Sheikh Makhmud's greeting. "What's the feast for?" That harsh voice seemed to cut through the room.

Nobody moved. Nobody spoke. Even Sheikh Makhmud seemed stunned into silence.

"Mister Erkhard." The "Mister" was a calculated slap in the face. "I take it you've signed a concession agreement? There's nothing else for Saraifa to celebrate at this moment." And then, without giving Erkhard a chance to reply, he turned to Sheikh Makhmud. "I hope you're not a party to this—that you signed in ignorance of the true situation."

"I don't understand." Sheikh Makhmud's hands fluttered in a way that suggested dark moths endeavouring to cope with the intrusion of unwelcome thoughts. Slipping into Arabic, he began a speech of welcome.

Rudely, Gorde cut him short. "Have you got the concession agreement on you? I'd like to see it, please." He held out his hand, and such was the driving force of the man's personality, the absolute conviction that men would obey him, that Sheikh Makhmud slipped his hand into the folds of his robe and brought out the document. Meekly he handed it over. "I think you find everything is all right." The soft words, the gentle voice gave no sign of doubt or tension.

Gorde called to one of the bodyguard to bring him a light. A stillness hung over the scene as he unfolded the document and glanced quickly through it. Then he raised his head and looked directly at Erkhard. "And you signed this on behalf of the Company."

The note of censure brought an immediate reaction from Erkhard. "As General Manager, I'm entitled to sign concession agreements." His voice was thin, a little venomous as he added: "You should know that. You signed enough of them in your day."

"But never one like this." And, slapping the document with his hand, he added: "This isn't our normal agreement. Our normal form of agreement simply gives the Company the right to prospect. This makes it a legal charge upon the Company to do so. Moreover—" and his gaze fastened on Whitaker—"it doesn't limit it to the area south of here where your rig is. It covers the whole of Saraifa, including the area in dispute on the Hadd border."

"Philip." Whitaker had risen to his feet. "I'd like a word with you."

"And I'd like a word with you," Gorde said sharply. "In private."

"No. We'll settle this thing here and now. I just want a straight answer to a straight question. Is there or is there not oil where you're drilling?"

"We're only down to three thousand-odd feet."

"That doesn't answer my question." Gorde stared at him coldly. "There isn't any oil, is there? There never was any oil there, and there never will be."

"I don't believe it." Erkhard, too, was on his feet.

"It doesn't matter whether you believe it or not, Alex," Gorde rapped back. "It's the truth."

"But he's drilling with his own money. He's invested every penny he's got. Ask Grant. He handles his financial affairs, and Whitaker admits he's out here partly because his money is almost exhausted. A man doesn't put all his savings first into a thorough seismological survey and then into a drilling program . . ."

"Bait." The tone of Gorde's voice brought Erkhard up short. "He was baiting the trap."

"I don't understand."

"Of course you don't. You'd never in a thousand years understand a man like Charles Whitaker. You ride him out of the Company and it never occurs to you that he'll get his own back some day. If you hadn't been so intent on trying at the last minute to rectify your position . . . And you thought you were getting an oilfield on the cheap, for the price of his development costs plus fifty per cent on royalties. Well, you ask him. You just ask him whether there's any oil there."

But it wasn't necessary. One glance at Whitaker's face told Erkhard all he needed to know. It was drawn and haggard, the colour of putty, and though the mouth moved, no words came. Erkhard crossed to Gorde, took the document from his hand, and tore it across and across and dropped the pieces in the dust.

There was a deathly hush. All eyes were turned on Sheikh Makhmud, waiting for his reaction. His face was the colour of clay, a shocked, almost old-womanish face, and his hands were trembling in the wide sleeves of his robe. "Sir Philip." He had some difficulty in controlling his voice. "Your Company has signed an agreement. To tear up the paper is not to say the agreement does not exist."

"You can take us to Court," Erkhard said. "But if Gorde's right, you'll lose your case."

Sheikh Makhmud waved his hands to signify that he had no intention of taking the Company to Court. He ignored Erkhard, addressing himself to Gorde. "I have always trusted the British. And you also; you have been my friend."

"I am still your friend," Gorde said.

"Then, please, you will honour the agreement."

"There is no agreement." His voice held a note of pity now. "Mr. Erkhard has done the only thing possible in the circumstances." He turned to Whitaker. "For God's sake, Charles, did you have to raise their hopes like this?" It was clear from his words that he didn't like the role he was being forced to play. "The truth was bound to come out in the end."

"What is the truth?" The pale eyes were fastened on Gorde in an aloof stare. "Do you know it? Are you so sure there's no oil in Saraifa? For twenty years now I have searched . . ."

"To hell with your theory," Gorde snapped. "Just answer me this, a simple yes or no. Is there oil where you're drilling?"

"I've told you, we're only down to just over three thousand feet. Erkhard could have waited—"

"You know damn well he couldn't wait. You're not such a fool that you haven't guessed why I'm out here risking my health on another tour of the Gulf."

"You thought my theory sound enough at one time. Remember?"

"And I backed you," Gorde rasped. "I backed you because you'd got faith in yourself. But now I wonder. Now

I think you've lost that faith. I don't think you believe in your theory any more."

"What makes you say that?" Whitaker's voice was sharp, unnaturally high, and his face looked shocked.

Gorde leaned his squat body forward. "Because," he said, "if you'd any faith in your theory, you'd have backed your son. Instead, you left him to die out there on his own—alone, deserted." Each word punched home in that rasping voice. It was a terrible indictment. And he added: "Didn't you understand that he was attempting to do what you'd no longer the guts to even try and do—to find oil, real oil? Not this sham, this clever, crooked dodge to trap us into signing—"

"Philip!" It came from Whitaker's mouth as a strangled cry. "I want to talk to you—alone."

It was an appeal, the call of past friendship. But Gorde ignored it. "I've nothing to say to you, Charles." The words came bleak and cold. "Except perhaps this: if there is any oil in Saraifa, then my guess is that it's right there on the border where your son was prospecting. But," he added, turning to Sheikh Makhmud, "I have to tell you that there's absolutely no question of our Company—or any other company, for that matter—undertaking exploratory work there at the present time. I was with the Political Resident for two hours this morning. He made the Government's attitude very clear. And now that I know what happened here last night, simply because one of our geologists was inadvertently on that border, I think he's right."

There was silence then, and for a moment Colonel Whitaker continued to stand there as though shocked into immobility. Knowing what I did, I felt sorry for him. Gorde had misinterpreted his motives, but there was nothing he could do about it at that moment. Whitaker knew that. Abruptly he gathered his dark, embroidered cloak about him. "I'm sorry you had to come when you did, Philip." His tone was bitter; his manner arrogant, unbending, aloof. "You'll live, I hope, to regret the words you've said and your hasty judgement. I did what I thought best for Saraifa, and Makhmud knows it." He walked past Gorde then, his one eye staring straight ahead of him as though on parade; a beaten, proud old man. The ranks of the bodyguard parted and he walked through them, magnificent and solitary.

With his departure the whole place became a babel of sound. It was as though Whitaker alone had held down the safety-valve of the crowd's temper. Violence quivered on the sultry air, and I got up quickly and went over to Gorde. "I think you ought to see Whitaker," I said. "As soon as possible. Tonight."

"Why?"

But the place had suddenly become quiet. Sheikh Makhmud was on his feet making a speech, presumably of explanation. "I can't tell you here. But I think it's important you should see him."

"It's true, is it—you look after his financial affairs?" He stared at me, his face tired now, leaning heavily on his stick. "Where's Entwhistle?" I told him and he nodded. "Sensible fellow. This is no place to be just now." He glanced at the sea of faces that packed the courtyard beyond. "It all looks very feudal, doesn't it? But there's an element of democracy in these desert states. The sheikhs rule by consent, not by right. Just bear that in mind." He was turning away, but then he checked. "Here's your briefcase." He handed it to me. "You'll find all the papers there."

Again I pressed him to see Whitaker, but he shook his head. "It wouldn't serve any purpose after what I've said. And anyway I don't intend to. He's the pride of the devil, has Charles."

"Go and see him," I said. "And take these papers with you." I held the briefcase out to him.

He looked at the case and then at me. "I took them along with me when I went to see the PRPG this morning. I thought I might persuade him . . ." He gave that little

shrug of his. "If he could have given us the All Clear po-
litically, I think I might have taken a chance on that boy's
survey and backed Erkhard. But he didn't. More, he gave
me a direct order that the Company was to keep clear of
the area."

It was final, and as though to emphasize the point, he
said: "I'll be leaving tomorrow morning as soon as it's light.
No doubt Charles will take care of you, but if you want a
lift out . . ." Sheikh Makhmud stopped talking and the
courtyard was in an uproar again. Gorde's hand gripped
my arm. "Hope turned to despair makes men dangerous,"
he said, his small, bloodshot eyes looking into mine.
"There's going to be trouble here, and these people are in
an ugly mood."

He turned abruptly away from me, and in the midst of
the noise and confusion I heard him saying casually to
Sheikh Makhmud: "Mind if we have something to eat?
I'm damned hungry."

Immediately Sheikh Makhmud was the solicitous host,
courteous and hospitable. *"Faddal! Faddal!"* He waved
Gorde to the place vacated by Whitaker, found room for
Otto, called for food to be brought. Khalid was in the courtyard now, pacifying the tribesmen, shepherding them out.
He was quick, decisive, a born leader, but they went sullenly.

I returned to my place, feeling nervous and ill at ease. I
didn't need to be told that they were in an ugly mood. I
could feel it all around me. It was like an electric charge.
And the uproar had spread from the feasting-place into the
great courtyard beyond and out into the village of Saraifa.
The sound of their voices murmured on the night air, a
continual angry buzzing as the whole population swarmed
about the palace. Men came in and out to stand and stare,
and it seemed to me that their eyes in the lamplight blazed
with a wild, fanatical hate. Erkhard felt it, too, for he
leaned across to me and said: "It's all very well for Gorde
to say he'll leave at daybreak. He's got his plane here. Mine

is ten miles away beside that rig." And he added: "Damn the man! A Moslem. I should have guessed he'd be up to every sort of trickery."

"Did you have to turn him against his son?" I said angrily.

But it didn't register with him. "Greed," he said. "It's an Arab failing."

I thought that was good, coming from an oil man with his reputation. But I didn't have a chance to reply, for Yousif was suddenly bending over me. "Coll-onel want you come," he whispered. "Very important, sahib."

I hesitated, unwilling to leave the protection of Sheikh Makhmud's presence or to lose contact with Gorde and his promise of a lift out. But I couldn't very well refuse. "All right," I said and got to my feet. Courtesy demanded that I pay my respects to Sheikh Makhmud before leaving. He didn't rise, and his eyes regarded me coldly from behind their glasses. No doubt he held me partly responsible for what had happened. His face looked haggard, the line of his mouth bitter beneath the grey wisp of his beard. I turned to Gorde. "I'm going to see Whitaker now," I said. "But I'd like to accept your offer of a lift."

He had just taken a piece of meat from the dish in front of him and he looked up, licking the grease from his fingers. "First light," he said. "And watch it, Grant. Charles has lost face, and anything can happen to a man that's been hit as hard as he has."

Yousif's hand was on my arm, and as I turned I saw Sheikh Abdullah's dark eyes fixed on me. The men in the courtyard fell back from me, suddenly silent, as we made our way out. Their eyes followed me, gleaming in the lamplight, and once again I caught the whisper of that word: *"Nasrani."* There was no mistaking the significance of it this time. They were hating us all that night.

V

The Quicksands of the Umm al Samim

Whitaker was waiting

for me on that same rooftop overlooking the desert, but this time he was pacing up and down it. His movements were caged and restless. He checked only momentarily as I entered. "Will Philip Gorde come and see me, do you think?" he asked, and when I told him no, he resumed his pacing. "After all these years, to talk to me like that!"

It was too dark for me to see his face, but I could tell from the stooped outline of his shoulders, the lowered head, above all, the nervous quickness of his movements, the way he spoke, that his mood was one of desperation. "All my life I've had to use subtlety. It's been part of my job out here. Always the need to find my way through the maze of Arab politics. Never a straight course. Always the devious approach. These oil men out from England—stupid men like Erkhard who don't understand the Arab mentality—they don't realize the problems of these Bedou sheikhs, the feuds, the vague boundaries that didn't matter so long as it was desert sand and nothing more. History, culture, race—they go back three thousand years and more, virtually without change, untouched by Western civilization. It's a culture in which the individual is still dominant, personality and human emotions the overriding factors governing men's actions. And over all this are the outside factors—international politics, the Foreign Office. Even Philip doesn't really know the Arab—though he likes to think he does."

It was the fact of having somebody with him of his own race. The words came out of him in a pent-up torrent. But what he said was said for his own benefit, not for mine; an attempt to justify his actions. But when he'd said it all, he turned and faced me, suddenly almost humble: "Suppose I go to Philip myself?"

There was no point in raising his hopes. "I don't think it would do any good." And I told him about Gorde's visit to the PRPG.

His head came up. "In other words, I was right. The Company's not allowed to enter into any agreement involving the Hadd border." There was relief in his voice, but it was overlaid by the bitterness of frustration. And he added acidly: "Nice of the Political Resident to confirm my own assessment of the situation so exactly." His shoulders sagged; he turned his face towards the desert. "Then I've no alternative now. . . ." He said it to himself, not to me, standing very still, looking out to where the stars met the hard line of the sands. "Over thirty years I've been out here, Grant. I'm practically a Bedou. I think like them, act like them. . . . I'm over sixty now and I know more about the Arab and Arabia . . ." He stopped there, and in the stillness I could hear the breeze rattling the palms. He turned slowly and stared at me. "All those years out here, and a boy of twenty-four sees it clearer than I do." His voice was harsh, his face grim, the lines cut by sand and sun so deep they might have been scored by a knife.

"It's a pity you didn't reach that conclusion earlier," I said.

He took a step forward, the eye bulging, his body taut, gripped in a sudden blaze of anger. But all he said was: "Yes, it's a pity." He turned and resumed his pacing, the

shoulders stooped again. "Heredity is a strange thing," he
murmured. "If we'd been less alike . . ." He shrugged and
added: "In that case, I don't suppose he'd have gone back
to the locations against my orders." He fell silent again
then. The breeze was from the east and it brought with it
the murmur of Saraifa, like the beat of the surf on a distant shore.

"You wanted to see me," I reminded him. The sound of
that distant crowd made me anxious to get back to Gorde.

"Yes, about finances." He kicked a cushion towards me
and told me to sit down. "Just what have I got left?" he
demanded, folding himself up on the floor beside me.

I was glad Gorde had returned my briefcase then. I could
have told him the position more or less from memory, but
all the papers were there and it made it easier. He shouted
for Yousif to bring a light, and for the next ten minutes I
went over the figures with him. He hadn't much left. But
there were some shares I hadn't sold and they'd appreciated quite considerably, and, after repaying bank loans, I
thought he'd have just enough if he lived quietly. I thought
he'd decided to go home, you see—to leave Arabia and retire. It seemed reasonable for a man of his age. "I'm sorry
it's not more," I said, putting the papers back in their
folder.

He nodded. "I'll have to borrow, then."

"It would be better," I said, returning the file to my
briefcase, "if you could arrange to live within your means."

He stared at me, and then he burst out laughing. But the
laughter was without humour. "So you think I'm beaten,
do you? You think I'm turning tail and heading for home
like a village cur. . . ." The fury building up in him
seemed to get hold of his throat, so that the words became
blurred. "That's what they'll all be thinking, I don't doubt
—Gorde, Makhmud, that man Erkhard." And then in a
voice that was suddenly matter-of-fact: "I take it you'll be
going back in one of the Company planes?"

"Gorde has offered me a lift."

"Good. I'll have letters for you to various merchants in Bahrain. A list of things to order, too. Would you like to wait here whilst I write them or shall I send Yousif up with them later? When is Philip leaving, by the way?"

"First light." And because I wanted to make certain I didn't miss the flight I asked him to have the letters sent after me.

He nodded. "That gives me the night in which to think this thing over." He summoned Yousif and gave him instructions to take me back to the palace. "By the way," he said, as I got to my feet, "you mentioned a package Griffiths had brought you, something David took to him on board the *Emerald Isle*. Was that his survey report?"

I nodded.

"Based on Henry Farr's old report?"

"Yes."

"I take it Entwhistle was running a check on David's locations. You don't know with what result, I suppose?"

"No. He didn't say."

He had risen to his feet and, standing close to me, he seemed to tower over me. "I'd like to see my son's survey report. Have you got it with you in your briefcase?"

I realized then why he'd considered his finances inadequate. "Good God!" I said. "You're surely not going to start drilling operations on that border. . . ." I was staring at him, remembering what Gorde had said. But there was nothing wild-eyed about him. He was bitter, yes. He'd been humiliated, deeply shocked by the behaviour of a man he'd always regarded as his friend, but the eye that met mine was level and unflinching, and I knew that he hadn't yet crossed the borderline into madness. "You haven't a hope of succeeding now," I said. "The Emir will be watching that border, and the instant you start drilling . . ."

He smiled thinly. "I'm not afraid of death, you know. Being a Muslim makes one fatalistic." He turned away, leaning his body on the parapet and staring out across the

dunes, grey now with the first light of the risen moon. "I
don't know what I'm going to do yet. I haven't made up my
mind." He hesitated and then turned to me. "But if I
should decide to go ahead, then I'd like to have David's report. He gives the locations, I take it?" And when I nodded,
he said: "Do they coincide with Henry Farr's?"

"I don't know."

"No, of course not. I ran a check survey myself, you
know. That was a long time ago now, when I had a bodyguard of more than a dozen men, all on the Company's pay-
roll, and the use of the Company's equipment. In those days
—quite soon after the war—I reckoned my chaps could
hold the Emir off if it came to a showdown long enough
for me to pull out with my equipment. But it never came
to that. I got away with it without the Emir knowing. But
I knew I couldn't do that with a drilling-rig."

"Then how do you expect to get away with it now?" I
demanded.

He shrugged. "I don't know that I can." He was smiling
softly to himself. "But I've been out here a long time,
Grant. I know that little Emir inside out. I've had spies in
Hadd sending me back reports, and I think I know enough
now. . . ." He gave a little shrug and the smile was no
longer soft; it was hard, almost cruel. "I'm outside the
Company now. It makes a difference. And it's just possible
I could get away with it where the Company couldn't." He
staightened up. "Well, what about it? Are you going to
let me have David's report?"

It wasn't ethical, of course. He hadn't been mentioned in
his son's will. But then I'd failed with Gorde and I could
now regard myself as free to take what action I liked.
Also I thought that, had David known what I now knew,
he would have wanted his father to have the locations. I
gave him a copy of the survey report and, after writing the
location fixes out on a slip of paper, I gave him that, too.

He glanced at it and then slipped it into the folds of his

cloak. "Thank you." He held out his hand. "You've come
a long journey. I'm sorry it didn't have a pleasanter ending.
I'll send Yousif with the letters in a few hours."

I hesitated. But I knew he wasn't a man to take advice.
"In that case, you'd better let me know what I'm to tell
Gorde."

"Nothing," he said. "Nothing at all."

I left him then, standing alone on that rooftop with the
desert clean and white behind him, and followed Yousif
out to the battered Land Rover. It was cooler now and I felt
almost relaxed. In a few hours I should be able to have a
bath and a change and sit back with a long, cool drink. And
yet, riding down the palm-shadowed track between the
date-gardens, I found myself filled with a strange nostalgia
for the place. It had an appeal I found difficult to define, a
sort of poetry, and the dim-remembered lines of a poem
came into my mind, something about being "crazed with
the spell of far Arabia" and stealing his wits away. I was beginning to understand what this place had meant to David,
to a boy who'd never had a real home before and who was
wide open to the strange beauty of it and as impressionable
as any Celt.

I was still thinking about this when we ran out from the
shadow of the palms and saw the square, black with the
mass of men standing there. The roar of their voices came
at us in a wall of sound. Yousif eased his foot off the accelerator, hesitating, uncertain whether to drive straight to
the main gate or not. And then three figures rose from beside the *shireeya* and stood blocking our path.

"Sheikh Khalid's men," Yousif said, and there was relief in his voice as he braked to a stop. They clambered on
to the mud-guards, talking urgently in the hard, guttural
tongue that is always associated in my mind with flies and
sand. "We go a different way. Is much better." Yousif
swung the Land Rover round, circling the gravel rise and
approaching the palace from the rear through a litter of
barastis, all apparently deserted. We stopped finally at a

small door with an iron-barred grille set in an otherwise
blank wall.

Khalid's three men closed round me as I got out, and
when I told Yousif I wanted to be taken straight to Gorde,
he said: "You go with them now, sahib. Sheikh Khalid's orders." And he drove off, leaving me there.

Eyes peered at us through the grille. The door opened
and I was hustled through the dark passages of the palace
and up to my turret room. There my three guards left
me, and, standing at the embrasure, I looked down on what
was obviously a very explosive situation. The crowd was being harangued by a man on a rooftop opposite, and another
was shouting to them from the back of a camel. The whole
square was packed solid. Every man and boy in the oasis
must have been gathered there, and many of them were
armed.

Camels were being brought into the square and men
were mounting on the outskirts of the crowd. And all the
time the agitators shouting and the crowd roaring and the
tension growing. The air was thick with menace, and then
somebody fired a rifle.

The bullet smacked into the mud wall not far from my
embrasure. It was all that was needed to set that crowd
alight. Other guns were fired, little sparks of flame, a noise
like firecrackers, and a great shout; the crowd became fluid,
flowing like water, moving with the sudden purpose of a
river in spate. Men leaped to their camels, mounting on the
arches of their lowered necks, driving them with the flood
tide down the slope to the dark fringe of the date-gardens.

In a moment the square was deserted, and with the murmur of the crowd dying to silence, the dark walls of my
room closed in on me. I had a sudden, overwhelming need
then to find Gorde and the others, and I picked up my briefcase and felt my way down the black curve of the stairs. A
light showed faint in the passage at the bottom. A figure
stirred in the shadows. Thick Arabic words and the thrust
of a gun muzzle in my stomach halted me. It was one of

Khalid's men, and he was nervous, his finger on the trigger. There was nothing for it but to retreat to my room again. In the mood prevailing in the oasis, it was some comfort to know that I had a guard. I lay down and tried to get some rest. The sound of the crowd was still faintly audible. It came to me through the embrasure, soft as a breeze whispering through the palm trees. And then it died and there was an unnatural quiet.

It didn't last long, for the shouting started again. Shots, too. It was a long way away. I got up and went to the embrasure, peering out at the empty square and the dark line of the palms shadowed by the moon. A glow lit the night sky to the east. It grew and blossomed. Then suddenly an explosion, a great waft of flame and smoke beyond the date-gardens. And after that, silence, the flame abruptly gone and the palms a dark shadow-line again in the moon's light.

Voices called within the palace, the sound muffled by the thickness of mud walls, and then for a while it was quiet. But soon the crowd was ebbing back into the square, flowing into it in little groups, silent now and strangely subdued. I was sure that it was Gorde's plane I'd seen go up in smoke and flame, and I stayed by the embrasure, watching the tide of humanity as it filled the square, wondering what they'd do now—hoping to God their passions were spent.

Bare feet sounded on the stairs. I turned, uncertain what to expect, my mouth suddenly dry. The beam of a torch probed the room, blinding me as it fastened on my face. But it was only my three guards back again, jabbering Arabic at me and gesturing for me to accompany them. I was hurried along dark passages, past gaping doorways where men sat huddled in dim-lit rooms, arguing fiercely. The whole palace was in a ferment.

We came finally to a low-ceilinged room lit by a pressure lamp, and in its harsh glare I saw Khalid sitting surrounded by robed figures. They were mostly young men and they had their guns resting across their knees or leaning close at hand against the walls. He rose to greet me, his face unsmiling, the bones sharp-etched in the lamplight. "I am sorry, sir, for the disturbance you have been given." A gesture of dismissal and the room quietly emptied, the conference broken up. "Please to sit." He waved me to a cushion on the carpeted floor and sat down opposite me, folding his legs neatly under him with the ease of a man who has never known a chair.

"What happened?" I asked. "Did they set fire to Gorde's plane?"

"Is a mistake. They are angry and they fire some bullets into it." He was very tense, coiled up like a spring too tightly wound. Somewhere a child was crying and I heard women's voices, soft and comforting. "You 'ave been to see *Haj* Whitaker, is not so?" And when I nodded, he said: "I understand you are concerned in the management of his affairs?"

"His financial affairs." I didn't want him to think I was responsible for anything that had happened out here. His manner, his whole bearing had changed, the surface layer of a university education gone entirely. I glanced over my shoulder. My three guards were still there, squatting in the open doorway.

Khalid was staring at me out of his dark eyes. The *kohl* had worn off. Lacking that artificial lustre, his eyes looked sad and sombre. "I have spoken with my father. I understand now what it is *Haj* Whitaker try to do for Saraifa. Unfortunately, I am not before tonight in my father's confidence." And he added with a trace of bitterness: "Better if he had told me. Better also if *Haj* Whitaker explain to David what he is doing." He paused there and I was conscious again of the strain he was under, of the tension building up in him. He leaned suddenly forward. "What will he do now?" he asked me. "Now that Meester Erk-hard don't honour the concession he sign. What will *Haj* Whitaker do?"

"That's his affair," I said. I didn't want to become involved in this.

"Please, Meester Grant. I must know."

"I don't think he's made up his mind yet."

He stared at me. "Do you think he may leave Saraifa?" And when I didn't answer, his eyes clouded and he seemed to sag. "We have very much need of him now," he said quietly. "He has the ear of many sheikhs, of some of his own people also." And he added: "Since ever I am a small boy I have known about this great man *Haj* Whitaker. I can remember the feast to celebrate the original concession. He is young then and full of fire. But always, always the people here—my father and myself also—we have looked to *Haj* Whitaker. He is known from the Persian Gulf to the Hadhramaut, from Muscat on the Indian Sea to the water-holes of the Rub al Khali and the Liwa Oasis, as a great man and the friend of all the Bedou. Particularly he is known as the friend of Sheikh Makhmud. If he desert us now . . ."

"I'm sure he's no intention of deserting you."

But he didn't seem to hear me. "There must be some reconciliation. It is altogether vital." He leaned suddenly forward, staring at me hard. "Meester Grant. There is something I must know. It is if I can trust you."

"That's up to you," I said, wondering what was coming. And I added: "I've been virtually a prisoner since I returned from seeing Colonel Whitaker."

He gave me a quick, impatient shrug. "Is for your own safety."

But I wondered. "Where's Sir Philip Gorde?" I didn't want to be involved in this any further. "I'd like to be taken to him now."

"First you will listen, please, to what I have to tell you." He seemed to consider, his dark eyes fixed on me, searching my face. "I think you are a friend to David before you work for his father, is not so?"

"It was because I befriended David that Colonel Whitaker asked me to look after his financial affairs."

"Yess. Yess, I believe that." But his eyes still searched my face as though he wasn't sure.

"What is it you want to tell me?" I wanted to get this over. Presumably Gorde and Otto would be leaving with Erkhard, and I wanted to be on that plane, away from the dark feuds of this desert world.

He didn't answer at once. But then he suddenly seemed to make up his mind. He leaned forward. "David is alive," he said.

I stared at him, too astounded for the moment to utter a word. "Alive?" Those three women . . . but, remembering their attitude, I remembered Whitaker's too. "What do you mean?" I was suddenly extremely angry with Khalid. "How can he be alive?" And when he didn't say anything, I added: "It's more than six weeks since your father sent an armed guard to arrest him and they found his camp deserted."

"I know. But is alive." He said it very seriously.

"Where is he, then?" I still didn't believe him. I thought it was a damned stupid lie he'd thought up to try and keep Whitaker in Saraifa. As if Whitaker, with all his experience of the desert, would believe it. "You tell me where he is and—"

"No." His voice was flat and decisive. "No, I don't tell you—not yet. But is alive. That I promise, Meester Grant." I suppose he realized that just stating it wouldn't convince me, for he went on quickly: "When *Haj* Whitaker is gone to visit the Emir, I am much disturbed for David's life. He is already on that border almost two moons with the truck that was brought by his father across the Jebel Mountains from Muscat. He is altogether alone, and his father I believe to be hating him for things he has said."

"What sort of things?"

He shrugged. "He don't tell me. But he is very much unhappy, I know that. He come here to this room to see me before he leave, and he warn me there is no oil where *Haj* Whitaker is drilling, that the only place there is any prob-

ability of oil is on that border. He says also that his father
is an old man now and has lost faith in himself and that he
is drilling to cheat the Company, for revenge against this
Meester Erk-hard and nothing more."

"And you believed him?"

"He is as my brother. He don't lie to me." And then he
told me how he'd taken two of his men and a spare camel
and had ridden to the border as soon as he knew David was
to be arrested. He'd found David alone, deserted by his
crew. After emptying the spare cans from the seismological
truck, David had driven it into the Rub al Khali desert until it had run out of petrol on the side of that dune. "Then
he leaves the truck and rides on with us. It is all as we arrange it together."

"You mean you planned it in advance?"

"Yess. It is all arranged between us because I am afraid
for this emergency."

The details fitted. They fitted so well that I was forced to
accept what he'd told me as the truth. But he wouldn't reveal where David was hidden. "He is with my two men—
Hamid and a boy called Ali. They are of the Wahiba and
altogether to be trusted."

"Why have you told me this?" I asked.

"Because everything is gone wrong, everything David
planned—and now I need your help. You are David's
friend, and also you work for his father. I think per'aps
only you can bring reconciliation between them. And without reconciliation . . ." But he seemed reluctant to put his
fears into words. "What do you think now, sir?" he asked
abruptly. "Is reconciliation possible? How will *Haj* Whitaker act when he finds David is alive?"

"How would you react if you thought your son were
dead?" But I realized I'd no idea what Whitaker's reaction
would be. I didn't know enough about their relationship,
how he'd come to regard his son in those last months. If Sue
were right and they really had been close at one time . . .
"It'll come as a hell of a shock to him."

"Yess, but is it possible—a reconciliation?"

"Of course. Particularly now that Colonel Whitaker . . ." I hesitated, wondering whether I ought to tell him what was in Whitaker's mind. But I thought he'd a right to know that Whitaker was considering drilling on his son's locations. After all, it was what David had wanted. They'd be able to work on it together now.

With this thought in mind, I was quite unprepared for the violence of Khalid's reaction when I told him. "Is imbecility!" he cried, jumping to his feet. "He cannot do that now. Is altogether too late." He was pacing up and down, very agitated and waving his arms about. "Sheikh Abdullah has already left to return to Hadd. He will report to the Emir all that has occurred here. If then *Haj* Whitaker remove his oil rig to the border . . ." He turned to me, still in great agitation, and said: "It will mean war between us and Hadd. War, do you understand? For my father is guided by *Haj* Whitaker. The Emir knows that. And if *Haj* Whitaker himself is on that border, then the Emir will know there is oil there and that my father will concede no revision of the boundaries between Hadd and Saraifa. You understand? You will help me?" He didn't give me time to answer, but summoned my escort. "We leave at once, for there is little time. Excuse, please. I go to my father now."

He left then and I was alone with my three Arab guards. The child had stopped crying. There was no sound of women's voices. The palace slept, and, sitting there, thinking about David, convinced now that he was still alive, I gradually became resigned to the fact that I wasn't going to get away in the plane that morning.

Khalid was gone about ten minutes. When he came back his face was pale, his manner subdued. "I tell my father I am going to Dhaid to gather more men."

"Did you tell him about Whitaker?"

"No. I don't tell him. And I don't tell him about David either—not yet. Is very much disturbed already. Come!"

"Is David at Dhaid?" I asked.

"No. But Sheikh Hassa holds that village for us. He will give us camels, and perhaps Salim bin Gharuf is there. I don't know. We have to hurry." He gave an order to my escort and I was hustled out of the palace into the great courtyard where his Land Rover stood. The escort piled in behind us, and as we drove down into the date-gardens it was difficult to believe that the people of this peaceful place were threatened with extinction, that they had been so roused that night that they'd set fire to an oil-company plane. The breeze had died and the whole world was still. Nothing moved. And when we ran out into the desert beyond the palms, it was into a dead, white world, for the moon was high now. We headed south, Khalid driving the Land Rover flat out, bucking the soft sand patches, eating up the flat gravel stretches at a tearing speed.

We were held up for a time by a choked petrol feed, and the first grey light of dawn was taking the brightness from the moon when a needle-tip of latticed steel showed above the grey whale-back of a dune. It was Whitaker's oil rig, a mobile outfit—the sort they call an "A" rig, truck and drill combined. It stood up out of the desert floor like a steel spear planted in the sand as a challenge to the vast wastes of emptiness that surrounded it. Beside it was a *barasti*, two Bedou tents and some tattered wisps of black cloth that acted as windbreaks.

As we neared it we heard the sound of the diesel, could see the Arab drilling-crew busy drawing pipe. Other Arabs were loading a second truck with lengths of pipe. Early though it was, the place was humming with activity, and when Khalid stopped and questioned them, he learned that Yousif had arrived just over an hour before with orders for them to prepare to move.

Whitaker had made his decision. He was moving his rig to the Hadd border, and up in my empty turret room there were doubtless letters waiting for me to take to Bahrain. "Is crazy!" Khalid cried, jumping back into the driving-seat. "Why does he do this now? He should do it before or not at all." He drove on then, passing close below the derrick. It looked old and battered, the metal bare of paint and burnished bright in places by the drifting sands. The derrick man was up aloft stacking pipe, his loin-cloth smeared with oil, his turbaned head a bundle of cloth against the paling sky.

Dawn was coming swiftly now, and beyond the shallow slope of a dune I saw the tinsel-gleam of Erkhard's aircraft. It stood at the far end of a cleared stretch of gravel, and the sight of it brought back to me my urge to escape from the desert. But when I demanded to be taken to it, Khalid took no notice except to give an order to the Arabs in the back. I reached for the ignition key. A brown hand seized my arm, another gripped my shoulders, and I was held pinned to my seat whilst we plunged at more than thirty miles an hour into a world of small dunes, and the plane vanished beyond my reach.

After that the going was very bad for mile after weary mile. And when finally we came out of the little-dune country, it was on to a gravel plain ribbed by crumbling limestone outcrops. A few dried-up herbs, brittle as dead twigs, bore witness to the fact that it had rained there once, many years ago. The land was dry and dead, flat as a pan, and as dawn broke and the sun came up, I lost all sense of horizon, for the whitish surface reflected the glare in an endless mirage.

All the way from the rig the going was bad. We had more trouble with the petrol feed, and it was past midday before we caught sight of the low hill on which Dhaid stood. It throbbed in the heat haze, looking like the back of a stranded whale surrounded by pools of water. The crumbling mud walls of the village were merged in colour and substance with the crumbling rock on which they were built, so that it wasn't until we stopped at the foot of a well-worn camel track that I could make out the shape of the buildings. There was a single arched gateway, and we had barely started up the track on foot when the villagers poured out of it and rushed upon us, leaping from rock to rock, shouting and brandishing their weapons.

Khalid showed no alarm, walking steadily forward, his gait, his whole bearing suddenly full of dignity. And then they were upon us, engulfing us: a wild, ragamuffin lot, teeth and eyes flashing, dark sinewy hands stretched out to us in the clasp of friendship. They were dirty, dusty-looking men, some with no more than a loin-cloth, and they looked dangerous with their black hair and bearded faces and their animal exuberance; and yet the warmth of that unexpected welcome was such after that empty, gruelling drive that I greeted them like brothers, their horny, calloused hands gripped around my wrists. It was the beginning of my acceptance of desert life.

Sheikh Hassa followed behind the rest of the villagers, picking his way sedately over the rock, his gun-bearer just ahead of him carrying his new BSA rifle, which was his pride and joy. He was a short, tough-looking man with a shaggy black beard that gave him an almost piratical appearance. He greeted Khalid with deference, touching his hand with his fingers, carrying them to his lips and to his heart. "*Faddal.*" And we went up the track and through the gateway into the village. A crowded square pulsating in the heat, a cool, darkened room spread with a rug, camel milk in bowls still warm from the beast's udder, and talk—endless, endless talk. I leaned back on the cushions, my eyelids falling, my head nodding. The buzz of flies. The buzz of talk. Not even coffee could keep me awake.

And then Khalid called to me and introduced me to a sinewy old man who stood half naked in the gloom, a filthy loin-cloth round his waist and his head-cloth wound in a great pile above his greying locks so that he looked top-heavy. This was Salim bin Gharuf. "He is of the Duru," Khalid said, "and he knows the place." I asked him what place, but he ignored that. "Is better now that you wear these, please." He produced a bundle of Bedou clothing, holding it out to me.

They were cast-off clothes and none too clean. "Is this really necessary?" I demanded.

He nodded emphatically. "Is better you look like one of us now."

"Why? Where are we going?"

"I tell you later. Not here. You will change, please." He helped me off with my European clothes and wound the loin-cloth round my waist; the long, dusty robe, the length of cloth twisted about my head, sandals, too, and an old brass-hilted knife for my belt. Sheikh Hassa watched me critically. I think the clothes were his. Men came and peered, and the crowded room resounded with their mirth. Khalid sensed my annoyance. "They don't mean any disrespect, sir. And you are going where no *faranji* has been before—save David."

It was meant to mollify, but all it did was rouse my curiosity again. "Well, if you won't tell me where he is," I said, "at least tell me how long it will take us to reach him."

"A day and then half a day if we travel fast. Perhaps two days. I don't know. There is possibility of a storm."

I think perhaps he might have told me more, but at that moment a man burst into the room shouting something, and instantly all was confusion. The room emptied with a rush that carried me with it out on to the white glare of a rooftop. Below us a single camel climbed wearily up the track, urged on by its rider.

Khalid pushed past me. "Is one of my father's racing camels," he said.

Five minutes later he returned with the rider, a thick-set man with long hair twisted up in his head-cloth. Khalid talked for a moment with Sheikh Hassa and then with Salim. Finally he came to me. "The oil men have left, and at dawn this morning several large raiding parties from Hadd crossed our borders. My father orders me to return."

My surprise was occasioned less by the news than by the realization that the camel must have made the journey in less time than we had taken in the Land Rover. But Kha-

lid's next words jolted me into awareness of what it meant
to me personally. "You go now with Salim."

"But . . ."

"Please, Meester Grant." His face looked old now beyond his years, haggard after the long drive, the sleepless
night. His eyes, staring at me, burned with an inner fire.
"Is altogether important now. Tell David what has happened, that his plan has failed and that there is no hope
now of the oil concession. He must go to his father immediately."

But my mind was on the practicalities. "That's all very
well," I said, glancing uneasily at the old man. "But Salim
doesn't speak any English. And I don't know the country."
I looked about me quickly. Khalid's bodyguard was behind
him, Sheikh Hassa right beside me. There was no escape.
"Where am I supposed to go, anyway? Where is David?"

"You go to the Umm al Samim."

Sheikh Hassa leaned his black beard forward, and his
harsh voice repeated the words "Umm al Samim" on a note
of surprise. And then he looked at me and rolled his eyes
up into his head and laughed and made a strangling sound.

"What's he mean by that?" I demanded. "What's he trying to tell me?"

Khalid's hand gripped my arm. "The Umm al Samim is
quicksands. But there is a way," he added quickly, and I
glanced at Hassa and knew that he'd been telling me that
I was going to my death. "I tell you there is a way," Khalid
said fiercely. "Salim knows it as far as the first good ground.
He will guide you as he guided us when we make original
exploration two seasons past."

"And what about the rest?"

"You will find by testing with a stick. Perhaps when you
call, David or the Wahiba will hear you." His grip on my
arm tightened. "You will go?"

"Suppose I refuse?"

"Then I take you with me back to Saraifa." He was looking me straight in the face. "This is what you want, isn't it

correct—to find David? Now you find him." And he added, staring at me hard: "Are you afraid to go?"

"No, I'm not afraid." I saw him smile. He knew after that I'd hardly refuse. "All right, Khalid," I said. "I'll go. But what do you want me to do? A boy hiding out in some quicksands isn't going to help you now."

"He must help us—he and his father. We are at point of desperation now, and it is his fault." He said it without rancour, a statement of fact, and he added: "It was a good plan, the way he visualize it—to go into hiding and, by making appearance he is dead, to draw attention to his survey. He think you will succeed to obtain the signature of Sir Gorde to a concession and that then per'aps we have oil, at least the support of the Company and so of your people. But instead all is turned to disaster. Because he is working on that border the raiders of Hadd are in our territory and the concession *Haj* Whitaker arrange is torn up. We have no Arab friends like the Emir has. We are alone, and everything is in conspiracy now to destroy us."

His words, the intensity with which he spoke, showed me the tragedy of it—father and son working for the same ends, but against each other. "Yes, but what can he do?"

"He must ride to a meeting with his father. Salim has good camels. You and David together—you must persuade *Haj* Whitaker to stop drilling on the Hadd border and to go to Bahrain, to the Political Resident. If they don't send soldiers, then please to send us modern weapons and automatic guns so that we can fight."

"Very well," I said. "I'll do what you say. I only hope it works out."

"Tell David also . . ." He hesitated. "Tell him it is possible I do not see him again. And if that is happening, then say to him that he is my brother, and the Emir Abdul-Zaid bin Sultan my enemy into death."

"What do you mean?" I asked.

"He will understand."

"But you're not going to your death."

"*Inshallah!* I do not know that." His tone was fatalistic.
"This is an old feud, Meester Grant. As old as Saraifa is old,
or Hadd. It goes back many centuries to the days when all
the *falajes* are running with water, a hundred channels
making irrigation for the palms. Then Saraifa is a great garden extenuating many miles, and the dates go by camel
north, to the sea and to India, across the mountains to the
Batina coast, and south to the Hadhramaut—even, some
say, to Mukalla and the olden port of Cana to be carried by
dhow to the far places of the world. But we are always too
much occupied with our gardens, and the people of Hadd
are very much envying us for our riches. They are men of
the hills, cruel and hard and altogether without goodness.
So." He gave a helpless little shrug. "So it is that we are
always fighting for our date-gardens and one after another
the *falaj* channels are being destroyed until Saraifa is as you
see it now, open to the desert and soon to die if the *falajes*
are not rebuilt. Do you know, Meester Grant, there is not
one man who can tell me, even when I am a little boy—
even by the hearsay of others, his father or his grandfather
—what it is like when there are more than six *falajes* working. Always wars . . . always, until the British come a hundred years ago. And now—" he spread his hands in a little
gesture of helplessness—"now another war perhaps, and if
we do not have a victory, then it is finish and in a few
months the *shamal* will have blown the sands of the Rub al
Khali over our walls and our houses and we shall be like
those old lost cities in India. . . . There will be nothing
to show that we ever exist in this place." He stopped there,
a little breathless because he had put so much of himself
and his emotions into foreign words. "You tell him that,
please." He turned then and spoke rapidly to Salim. The
tattered figure moved towards me. "You go now," Khalid
said. "*Fi aman allah!* In the peace of God."

"And you also," I said. The skinny hand of my guide was
on my arm, a steel grip propelling me down mud steps out
into the shadowed cool of an alley. In a little open space

beyond there were camels couched, and at his cries three tall beasts lumbered to their feet. They had provisions already loaded and dark skin bags bulging with water. A boy brought two more camels, and Salim chattered a gap-toothed protest as he realized that I didn't even know how to mount my beast. They brought it to its knees and put me on it, and at a word it hoisted me violently into the air. The old man put his foot on the lowered neck of the other and stepped lightly into the saddle, tucking his legs behind him.

We left Dhaid by a small gateway facing south, just the two of us and the three pack-beasts tied nose to tail. The boy ran beside us as far as the base of the limestone hill and then we were out on the gravel flat and travelling fast, a peculiar, swaying gait. It required all my concentration just to remain in the saddle. Perhaps it was as well, for it left me no time to consider my predicament. Our shadows lumbered beside us, for the sun was slanting towards the west, and Salim began to sing a high-pitched, monotonous song. It was a small sound in the solitude that surrounded us, but though I couldn't understand the words, I found it comforting.

The sun vanished before it reached the horizon, hazed and purple as a mulberry. We camped at dusk where the dusty green of new vegetation spattered the sand between ribs of limestone. The camels were let graze, and Salim built a fire of furze and cooked a mess of rice and meat. One of the pack-beasts was in milk, and we drank it warm from the same bowl. And when he'd looked to his ancient rifle, oiling it carefully, we mounted and went on again.

We travelled all that night without a break. The moon turned the desert to a bleak bone white, and in the early hours a mist came up and it was cold. By then I was too tired to care where I was going, and only the pain of the saddle chafing the insides of my thighs, the ache of unaccustomed muscles kept me awake. The dawn brought a searing wind that whipped the mist aside and flung a mov-

ing cloud of sand in our faces. Lightning flashed in the
gloom behind us, but no rain fell—just the wind and the
driving sand particles.

We stopped again for food, lukewarm and gritty with
sand, and then on again until the heat and the moving sand
drove us into camp. I laid my head on my briefcase, covering my face with my head-cloth, and slept like the dead,
only to be wakened again and told to mount. My nose and
mouth were dry with sand, and we went on and on at a
walking pace that was relentless in the demands it made on
my endurance. Dawn broke and the sun lipped the mountains that poked their rugged tops above the horizon to
the east. Salim didn't sing that day, and as the wind died
and the sand became still, the heat increased until my head
reeled and dark specks swam before my eyes.

By midday we were walking our camels along the edge of
a dead, flat world that stretched away into the west, to disappear without horizon in a blur of haze. There was no
dune nor any outcrop of rock, no tree, no bush, nothing to
break the flat monotony of it. Salim turned in his saddle.
"Umm al Samim," he said with a sweep of his hand, the
palm held downward and quivering. I remembered the
strangled sound Sheikh Hassa had made at the mention of
that name, and yet it looked quite innocent: only that unnatural flatness and the dark discolouration of water seep-
age revealed the quagmire that lay concealed below the
crust of wind-blown sand.

We followed the shore of the sands for about an hour
whilst the sun beat down on us and the dull expanse shimmered with humidity. And then, by the gnarled remains of
some camel thorn, we dismounted and started into the
quicksands, leading our camels.

Close inshore there were patches of solid ground, but further out there was nothing that seemed to have any substance, the ground and air both quivering as we struggled
forward. I can't remember any sense of fear. Fear is a lux-

ury requiring energy, and I had none to spare. I can, however, remember every physical detail.

It was a *sabkhat* on the grand scale, and beneath the hard-baked crust my feet touched slime. At times it was difficult to stand at all, at others I broke through to the black filth below, and at every step I could feel the quiver of the mud. The camels slithered, bellowing in their fear, in constant danger of losing their legs and falling straddled. We had to drag the wretched beasts, even beat them, to keep them moving. This and the need to be ready to give them some support when they slipped did much to keep my mind from the filthy death that threatened at every step. And whenever I had a moment to look ahead, there was the Umm al Samim stretched out pulsating in the humid glare, innocent-seeming under its crust of sand, yet deadly-looking because it was so flat and level—as level as a lake.

And it seemed to have no end. It was like the sea when visibility is cut by haze. But here there were no buoys, no markers that I could see, nothing from which Salim could get his bearings. Yet once I saw the old tracks of camels, the round holes half filled with sand, and whenever I broke through to the mud below, my feet found solid ground before I was in further than my knees; in some way that was not apparent to me Salim was following a rib of rock hidden below the surface of the sand.

Time had no meaning in the pitiless heat, and the sweat rolled dripping down my back. I had a moment of panic when I would have turned and run if it had been possible. But then a camel slipped, and a moment later Salim seized my arm and pointed ahead with his rifle. Little tufts of withered herbs lay limp in isolated clumps, and on the edge of visibility a gnarled thorn tree shimmered like a witch, its gaunt arms crooked and beckoning.

With the first of the withered herbs I felt the ground under my feet. It was hard and firm, and when I set my foot down nothing quaked, there was no gurgling sound, no sound of imminent break-up of the crust. Where the camel thorn stood there was naked rock, and I flung myself down, revelling in the scorched hardness of it.

We were on a little island, raised imperceptibly above the flat level of the quicksands, and it was as far as Salim had ever penetrated. I watched him as he searched for Khalid's tracks, stopping every now and then to call, a high-pitched, carrying sound made with his hands cupped round his mouth. But the steaming heat absorbed his cries like a damp blanket, and there was no answer.

In the end he gave it up and began prodding with his camel stick along the edge of the sands. Twice I had to pull him out, but finally he found firm ground beneath the crust, and, leaving the camels, we started forward again, moving a step at a time, watching the quiver of the crust and prodding with the stick.

Behind us our tracks vanished into nothing. The rock island vanished, too, the white glare swallowing even the bulk of our camels. We were alone then, just the old man and myself in a little circle of flat sand that quaked and gurgled and sucked at our feet.

I don't know how long we were feeling our way like that. Once we saw the faint outline of a camel's pad, but only once. And then suddenly thorn trees throbbed in the haze ahead, looking huge, but dwindling as we approached the firm ground on which they stood. They were no more than waist height, and, standing beside them, Salim cupped his hands and called again.

This time his cry was answered—a human voice calling to us, away to our left where the sands ran flat. I thought it was imagination, perhaps an unnatural echo of Salim's voice, for there was nothing there: an empty void throbbing in the heat, and the air so intensely pale it hurt the eyes.

And then suddenly the void was no longer empty. A man had materialized like a genie out of the heart of a furnace, his face burned black by the pitiless heat, his lips cracked, his ragged beard bleached by the sun, his hair, too, under the filthy head-cloth.

He came forward and then stopped, suddenly suspicious, reaching for the gun slung at his shoulder.

"Salim!" Recognition brought a quick flash of teeth, white in the burnt dark face. *"Wellah! Salaam alaikum."* He came forward and gripped Salim's wrist in a Bedou handclasp whilst the old man talked, his words coming fast and high-pitched with excitement. And then the man turned to stare at me, pale eyes widening in startled disbelief. It was only when he finally spoke my name that I realized this strange nomadic-looking figure was David Whitaker.

"It's a long time," I said. "I didn't recognize you."

He laughed and said: "Yes, a hell of a long time." He reached out his hand, and his grip was hard on mine. Not content with that, he took hold of both my shoulders and held them as though overwhelmed by the need for physical human contact. "I can't believe it," he said. And again: "I can't believe it."

I could hardly believe it myself. He was greatly changed. As Sue had said, he'd become a man. But even in that first glimpse of him I recognized again the quality of eagerness that had first attracted me to him. "So you really are alive." I don't think I'd fully accepted the fact until that moment.

"Yes, I'm alive—just." His dark face cracked in a boyish grin. "Christ!" he said. "It never occurred to me you'd come out here to look for me. Hell of a bloody journey. How did you know where I was?" But I suppose he saw I was exhausted, for he added quickly: "Come up to the camp. You can stretch out and I'll have Ali brew some coffee." He called to two men who had materialized out of the weird glare and were hovering on the edge of visibility. "My companions," he said.

They came forward warily, like dogs suspicious of a new scent, and they both had service rifles gripped in their hands. The elder he introduced as Hamid—a big man with

long hair to his shoulders, bearded and impressive like a
prophet. The other was little more than a boy, his face
full-lipped and smooth, almost a girl's face, and he moved
with the same natural grace. His name was Ali bin Mak-
tum.

"Now let's have coffee and we'll talk." David took my
arm and led me to where the ground was higher and tattered pieces of black Bedou cloth had been erected as windbreaks, stretched on the bleached wood of camel thorn
over holes they had scraped in the soft limestone. *"Faddal!"*
It was said with Bedou courtesy, but with an ironical little
smile touching the corners of his mouth.

He sent Hamid off to look to our camels, and whilst the
boy Ali brewed coffee over a desert fire of sand and petrol,
he sat beside me talking hard about the heat and the humidity and the loneliness he had been suffering in this
Godforsaken place. I let him run on, for I was tired and he
needed to talk. He was desperate for the company of his
own kind. He'd been there six weeks, and in that time
Khalid had made the journey twice to bring them food and
water. "I wouldn't trust any one else. They might have
talked." He was tracing patterns in the sand then, his head
bent, shadowed by the head-cloth. Flies buzzed in the sudden silence. "Why are you here?" His voice came taut with
the anxiety of a question too long delayed. "Who told you
where to find me—Khalid?"

"Yes," I said. "Khalid." And I added: "There's a lot to
tell you."

He misunderstood me, for his head came up, his eyes
bright with sudden excitement. "It's all right then, is it?
You saw Sir Philip Gorde and he signed that concession
agreement I typed out?" The words came breathless, his
eyes alight with hope. But the hope faded as he saw my
face. "You did see Sir Philip, didn't you?"

"Yes," I said. "I gave him the envelope."

"Well, then . . ."

"He didn't sign the agreement."

The effect of my words was to knock all the youth right out of him. His face looked suddenly old and strained; lines showed so that he seemed more like his father, and his shoulders sagged. "So it didn't work." He said it flatly as though he hadn't the spirit left for any display of emotion, and I realized that all the weeks he'd been waiting here alone he'd been buoyed up by this one hope. "I thought if I disappeared completely, so completely that everyone thought I was dead . . . They did think I was dead, didn't they?"

"Yes," I said. "Everyone, including your father, presumed you were dead." And I added, a little irritably because I was so tired: "You've caused a lot of people a great deal of trouble; and your mother and sister a lot of needless grief."

I thought for a moment he hadn't heard me. But then he said: "Yes, indeed, I realize that. But Sue at least would understand." His face softened. "How is she? Did you see her?"

"Yes," I said. "I saw her." And that, too, seemed a long time ago now. "I don't think she ever quite accepted the idea that you were dead. Nor did your mother or that girl in Bahrain."

"Tessa?" The lines of strain were momentarily smoothed out. "You saw her, too?" He seemed surprised, and he added: "I'm sorry. I'm afraid I've put you to a great deal of trouble." He was staring down at the sand patterns between his feet. Abruptly he rubbed them out. "I was so convinced it was the only way. I had to get past Erkhard somehow. I thought if I could get my report to Sir Philip Gorde. He was the one man. . . ." His voice faded. And then, still talking to himself: "But I couldn't just send it to him. It had to be done in some way that would enable him to override the political objections. I thought all the publicity connected with my disappearance . . . I'd planned it all very carefully. I had a lucky break, too. That night I visited Captain Griffiths on the *Emerald Isle,* there was an agency correspondent in transit to India stopping the night at the Fort in Sharjah. I saw him, told him the whole story—my background, how I'd escaped from Borstal and got myself out to Arabia, everything. I thought a story like that . . ." He darted a quick glance at me. "Didn't he print it?"

"After you were reported missing, when the search had failed and you were presumed dead."

"Yes, I made him promise he wouldn't use it unless something happened to me. But didn't it have any effect?"

"It seemed to cause quite a stir in the Foreign Office."

"But what about the Company?"

"It put the shares up," I said, trying to lighten it for him.

"Hell! Is that all?" He gave a bitter little laugh. "And I've been sitting here . . . waiting, hoping . . ." His shoulders had sagged again, and he stared out into the throbbing glare, his eyes narrowed angrily. "All these weeks, wasted—utterly wasted." His voice was bleak. He looked weary—weary and depressed beyond words. "I suppose you think now I've behaved like a fool—disappearing like that, pretending I was dead. But please try and understand." He was leaning towards me, his face young and defenceless, his voice urgent now. "I was on my own and I knew there wasn't any oil where my father was drilling. I ran a check survey without his knowledge; it was an anticline all right, but badly faulted. It couldn't hold any oil." His voice had dropped to weariness again. He'd been over all this many times in his mind. "I don't know whether he was kidding himself or trying to cheat the Company or just doing it to get his own back on Erkhard. But I wanted the Company to drill on my locations, not his. I wanted oil. I wanted it for Saraifa, and I wanted it to be the real thing."

"Your father wanted it, too," I said gently. "And he, too, was convinced there was oil where you did your survey."

"That's not true. He refused to believe me. Told me I

was inexperienced, that I'd no business to be on that border, and forbade me ever to go near it again."

"I think," I said, "you'd better listen to what I have to tell you."

The coffee was ready then, and I waited until Ali had poured it for us from the battered silver pot. It was Mocha coffee, bitter and wonderfully refreshing, and as I sipped the scalding liquid I told him the whole story of my journey and all that had happened. Once whilst I was telling it, he said: "I'm sorry. I didn't realize." And later, when I came to the point where Gorde had left me with Entwhistle and we'd been fired on, he apologized again. "I'm afraid you've had a hell of a time, sir, and all my fault." That "sir" took me back, for it still didn't come easily from him.

But it was my account of that first interview with his father that really shook him. When I had explained to him what his father had been trying to do, he was appalled. "But, Christ! Why didn't he tell me? I'd no idea. None at all. And when Khalid told me he'd been to see the Emir of Hadd . . ." He stared at me, his face fine-drawn, his voice trembling as he repeated: "Why the hell didn't he tell me what he was trying to do?"

"I think you know why," I said. "You were employed by the Company, and the Company to him meant Erkhard." And I added: "Erkhard knew your background, didn't he? He used that as a lever to get you to spy on your father."

It was a shot in the dark, but it went home. "He tried to." His tone was almost sullen; he looked uncomfortable.

"And you agreed?" I'd no wish to conduct a cross-examination, but I thought it essential he should see it from his father's point of view if I were to succeed in bringing them together again.

"I hadn't any choice," he said, stung to anger by my question. "Erkhard threatened to turn me over to the Cardiff police."

"And your father knew about that?"

"It didn't mean I was going to do what Erkhard wanted."

"But you'd agreed to do it," I insisted, "and your father knew you'd agreed."

"I suppose so." He admitted it reluctantly. "He's still got his friends inside the Company."

So there it was at last, the basic cause of the rift between them—the thing that girl Tessa had hinted at, that Sue had felt but hadn't been able to explain.

"Christ!" he said. "What a bloody stupid mess! And all because we didn't trust each other like we should have done. How could I guess what he was up to? Though it's just the sort of twisted, devious approach . . ." His voice faded and once more he was staring out into the void. "I got very close to him at one time, but even then I was always conscious of a gulf, of something hidden that I couldn't fathom. He's very unpredictable, you know, Mr. Grant. More Arab than the Arabs, if you see what I mean." He was very much on the defensive then. "After four years I can't say I really understood him. Switching races like that, and his religion, too—it left a sort of gulf that couldn't be bridged. And when Khalid told me he'd been to see the Emir, it made me wonder . . ." He hesitated. "Well, as I say, he's unpredictable, so I decided it was time I put my plan into action and disappeared. Khalid thought so, too. He'd brought Hamid and Ali, two of his most trusted men, and a spare camel. So . . ." He shrugged. "I knew it was hard on Sue. Hard on Tessa, too —and on my mother. But I was alone, you see. I'd nobody to turn to, except Khalid. He was the only man in the world who had faith in me. And I couldn't look to the Company for help. Erkhard had made that very plain. And, anyway, oil companies are in business for themselves, not for the Arabs. They've been known to sit on an oilfield for years for political or commercial reasons. . . ." The sweat was pouring off him and he wiped his hand across his brow. "Well, go on," he said. "What happened when Erkhard came to Saraifa—did my father succeed in getting a concession signed?"

But I think he'd guessed that I shouldn't have come here alone if it were all settled. He listened, silent, not saying a word, as I told him the rest of my story. Once his eyes came alight with sudden excitement; that was when I told him of my second talk with Whitaker and how Khalid and I had seen the drilling-rig being dismantled for the move up to the Hadd border. The thought that his father was at last doing what he'd been wanting him to do for so long gave him a momentary sense of hope. But it was only momentary, for I went straight on to tell him of the scene at Dhaid and how the lone rider had brought the news that Gorde and Erkhard had left and Hadd forces had crossed the border into Saraifa. "So it's come to that, has it? Open war between Hadd and Saraifa." His body was suddenly trembling as though with fever and his voice was bitter. "And Khalid sent you to me. What did he say before you left? What message did he give you?"

"He said he thought this time Saraifa had reached the point of desperation." And I gave him the gist of what Khalid had said to me. When I had finished he didn't say anything for a long time, sitting there lost in thought, staring out across the flat misery of the Umm al Samim. "The only home I ever had," he whispered. "Did you see it when the *shamal* was blowing, with the Rub al Khali like a sea, the dunes all smoking and the sands pouring into the date-gardens? It's like a flood then." His father's words—his father's voice almost. "The oasis is doomed, you see. Doomed to extinction by the desert. But that's a natural process, something to be fought with the natural resources of the country. Khalid and I, we were going to rebuild the old *falaj* channels with the money from oil royalties. That was our dream. But this . . ." He stared at me hard, his eyes wide. "You're sure it's war, are you? It's not just a border raid?"

I gave him Khalid's speech then, as near as I could remember it word for word.

"So it's my fault, is it?" He said it with deep bitterness,

and after that he was silent for a long time. Finally, he looked at me. "Unto death, you said. Khalid used those exact words, did he?" And when I nodded: "So it's not just a raid—it's the real thing this time." He was almost in tears, he was so deeply moved. And then sadly: "My father's fault, too—he's made his decision too late." And he began cursing softly to himself. "Those dung-eating bastards from Hadd, they'll smash down the last of the *falaj* channels. What would have taken twenty years by natural means will take less than that number of months. The desert will roll in. Christ Almighty! The bastards!" It was a cry from the heart, and I was conscious of desperation here, too—a desperation that matched Khalid's. "They can't fight a war against Hadd. They've nothing to fight it with—only antiquated guns."

He began questioning me then, pressing me for details, many of which I couldn't give him, for he wasn't interested in his father now, or Gorde or the Company; his attention was fixed on Hadd and the way Sheikh Abdullah, the Emir's representative, had behaved, and what had passed between him and Sheikh Makhmud that morning before Whitaker and Erkhard had arrived. The sun sank in a blood-red haze and the air became dank. My head nodded, my body suddenly drained of warmth and shivering with fatigue. "You'd better get some rest now," he said finally. "We'll be leaving as soon as the moon's up and it's light enough to see our way through the quicksands." He seemed to have reached some decision, for his voice was firmer, his manner less depressed. He brought me a tattered blanket musty with sand. "I've kept you talking when you should have been getting some sleep."

"What do you plan to do?" I asked him. "You'll go to your father, I take it?"

"Yes. He's still got a few of his bodyguard left. A dozen men and I could create a diversion that would keep the Emir busy until my father has time to make his influence felt in Bahrain. Khalid's right. We must work together now—my father and I." The mention of Khalid's name seemed to bring his mind back to his friend. "He said he was my brother, didn't he? Unto death?"

"Your brother, yes," I said. "But as I remember it, he used the words 'into death' in connection with the Emir— 'my enemy into death.' "

"Well, pray God it doesn't come to that." There were tears in his eyes, and, standing there, staring straight into the flaming sunset, he quoted from the Bible: *" 'The Lord be between me and thee, and between my seed and thy seed for ever.' "*

Dimly I recognized the quotation as the oath sworn by his namesake; I didn't realize it then, but this was the covenant, sworn in the midst of the quicksands of the Umm al Samim, that was to take him to that fort on top of Jebel al-Akhbar and to the terrible final tragedy.

I saw the sun set and the quicksands turn to blood, and then the sky faded to the palest pastel green and the stars came out. Lying there, it was like being stranded on a coral reef in the midst of a flat lagoon. Sometime in the small hours the wind woke me, blowing a drift of sand in my face. The moon was up, but its face was hidden in a cloud of moving sand. There was no question of our leaving, and I lay till dawn, unable to sleep, my eyeballs gritty, my nose and mouth clogged with sand, and when the sun rose all it showed was a sepia haze. We ate in extreme discomfort, the sand whistling like driven spume across the flat surface of the Umm al Samim.

The storm lasted until almost midday, and then it ceased as abruptly as it had started. We cooked a meal of rice and dried meat, and then we started back, collecting our camels on the way and struggling through the quicksands to the solid desert shore. We mounted then and, keeping the Umm al Samim on our left, rode till dusk, when we camped. A meal and a short two-hour rest and then on again, with Salim arguing sullenly.

"The old fool thinks the beasts will founder." David's

face was grim. He was in a hurry and he had no sympathy
for men or beasts. "Like all the Bedou, he loves his camels
more than he loves himself."

We marched all night and there were times when I
hoped the camels would founder. My muscles were stiff
and aching, and where the wooden saddle chafed my legs,
I was in agony. The starlight faded, swamped by the
brighter light of the risen moon, and in the grey of the
dawning day we reached the big well at Ain. Salim went
forward alone to water the camels, for, early as it was, there
were others at the well before us. "Men of the Duru tribe,
I expect," David said as we sat on the ground with the
loads stacked round us, brewing coffee. "Salim will bring
us the news."

I dozed, and woke to the sound of the old man's voice.
"What's happened?" I asked, for his face was lit by the
excitement of some great event. "What's he saying?"

"He's talked with some men of the Rashid, back from
selling camels at Saraifa." David's face was grey in the
dawn. "They say there's been fighting already—a battle."

"Between Hadd and Saraifa?"

"It's hearsay, that's all. They don't know anything." He
didn't want to believe it, but his voice was urgent as he
gave the order to mount.

We loaded the camels in a hurry, and as we started out
again, I saw that our direction had changed. I asked him
where we were going, and he said: "Dhaid. We'll get the
news there." And after that he didn't talk. His mood was
sullen and withdrawn, his temper short, and he answered
Salim angrily whenever the old man protested at the pace
of our march.

We rode all day and far into the night, and in the morning the camels were almost done, their pace painfully slow.
We reached Dhaid a little after midday. Nobody came out
to meet us. Camels dotted the limestone slopes of the hill,
and men lay listless under the walls of the village. Inside
the arched entrance, the little open place was packed with

people; whole families with their beasts and chattels were crowded there in the oven heat that beat back from the walls.

They were all from Saraifa—refugees; the atmosphere was heavy with disaster, the news bad. Two more *falajes*, they said, had been destroyed and a battle fought, out by one of the wells. Khalid was reported dead, his father's soldiers routed.

"Old-fashioned rifles against automatic weapons." David's tone was bitter. "For months the Emir has been receiving a steady trickle of arms. And we've done nothing about it. Nothing at all."

"They're independent states," I reminded him.

"That's what the political boys said when I told them arms were being smuggled in dhows to the Batina coast and brought by camel across the mountains. A perfect excuse for doing nothing. And now, if Khalid is dead . . ." His voice shook. His face looked ghastly, the skin burned black, yet deathly pale. "Sheikh Makhmud's an old man. He can't fight this sort of a war. And the Emir has only to block two more *falajes* and his men can just sit and wait for the end."

We left Salim with the camels and fought our way through the crowd to Sheikh Hassa's house. We found him in the room where I had left Khalid a few days before. He was sitting surrounded by a crush of men all talking at once. The new rifle lay forgotten on the floor. Beside him sat a young man with long features that were tense and pale. "Mahommed," David whispered. "Khalid's half-brother." He'd fled from the battlefield, but he'd seen enough to confirm the rumours we'd heard in the market place. The battle had been fought by the ninth well out along the line of the Mahdah *falaj*, and the casualties had been heavy. Sheikh Makhmud himself had been wounded, and the latest reports of survivors indicated that he had retired to the oasis with the remnant of his forces and was shut up in his palace and preparing to surrender.

David talked to the two of them for about ten minutes, and then we left. "Sheikh Hassa's scared," he said as we pushed our way out into the shade of the alleyway. "All these frightened people flooding into his village . . . It's knocked the fight right out of him. And Mahommed's only a boy. Hassa will hand over Dhaid without firing a shot." He said it angrily, with deep bitterness. And he added: "Fifty resolute men could defend this place for a month— long enough to preserve its independence from Hadd."

"What about Khalid?" I asked. "Did his brother say what had happened to him?"

"No. He doesn't know." His face was grey and haggard. "All this killing and destroying—it's so bloody futile, a lust for oil. Can't they understand the oil won't last? It's just a phase, and when it's past they'll be faced with the desert again; and the only thing that will matter then is what they've built with the oil against the future." And he added angrily: "The Emir didn't care a damn about that border until my father got Gorde to sign a concession. It was just sand, and nothing grew there. And then to cancel it . . . I can still remember the look on Sheikh Makhmud's face that night. God!" he exclaimed. "The callousness of men like Erkhard—Gorde, too. They don't care. These people are human beings, and they're being buggered around by hard-faced men who think only in terms of commerce and money."

We were out of the alley, back in the glare of the crowded market place. He spoke to Salim and gave him money, a handful of Maria Theresa silver dollars poured from a leather bag, and then we settled ourselves in the dust by the entrance gate, leaning our backs against the crumbling mud walls amongst a crowd of listless refugees who watched us curiously. "I've sent Salim to buy fresh camels," David said. "We'll leave as soon as he returns."

"How long will it take us to reach the Hadd border?" I was feeling very tired.

But his mind was on Khalid. "I must find out what's

happened to him." He was silent a long time then, tracing patterns in the sand with his camel stick. And then abruptly he rubbed them out with the flat of his palm. "If he's dead . . ." His emotions seemed to grip him by the throat, so that the sentence was cut off abruptly. And then, his voice suddenly practical: "In that case, there are his men. He had more than a score of them, a paid personal bodyguard. Wahiba mostly and some Rashid; all good fighters." He was staring hungrily out into the burning distance of the desert. "I need men," he whispered, his teeth clenched. "Men who'll fight. Not these—" He gestured with contempt at the listless figures around us. "A score of men properly armed and I could put the fear of God into that bloody little Emir."

I didn't bother to ask him how, for I thought it was just wishful thinking and all in his imagination. My eyes were closing with the heat and the weariness of my aching muscles. I heard him say something about getting me to Sharjah as soon as he could, and then I was asleep.

I woke to the voices of Salim and the two Wahiba; they were arguing loudly whilst David sat listening, a tattered Bible propped on the rifle across his knees. Two camels stood disdainfully in front of us. "They've become infected with the mood of this place, blast them!" David closed the Book and got to his feet. A crowd was beginning to collect. He said something to Hamid and the man looked suddenly like a dog that's been beaten. And then David took his rifle from him and handed it to me. "Come on!" he said. "Let's get going." He spoke angrily to the two Wahiba and then we mounted.

The camels were thoroughbred Oman racing camels. I could feel the difference immediately. The crowd parted, letting us through, and we picked our way daintily down the rocks. Out on the flat gravel of the desert below, we moved into an ungainly canter, circling the hill on which Dhaid rested and heading northeast again.

"These people," David said, "they're so damned uncer-

tain—full of guts one minute, craven the next. Salim I
didn't expect to come. But Hamid and Ali . . ." He
sounded depressed. "My father now, he can handle them
the way I'll never be able to." There was admiration, a
note of envy in his voice. "They'd never have left him in
the lurch." We rode in silence then and at a gruelling
pace, the heat very great, so that I was thankful for the
water we had got at Dhaid.

We camped at dusk and David had just lighted a fire
when he turned suddenly and grabbed his rifle. I heard the
pad of camels' feet and then the riders emerged out of the
gathering darkness. There were three of them, and David
relaxed. "Salim, too," he whispered. He didn't give them
any greeting, and they slunk to the fire like dogs. I gave
Hamid back his rifle. He took it as though it were a gift
and made me a long speech of thanks. "They're like children," David said. His voice sounded happy.

We had a handful of dates each and some coffee, that
was all. And then we rode on.

In the early hours of the morning, with the moon high
and a white miasma of mist lying over the desert, we approached the ninth well of the Mahdah *falaj*. Hamid and
Ali were scouting ahead on either flank. David and Salim
rode close together, their rifles ready-to-hand across their
knees. The tension had been mounting all through that
night ride, for we'd no idea what we were going to find
at the end of it.

For the first time I rode my camel without conscious
thought of what I was doing, my whole being concentrated
in my eyes, searching the mist ahead. The desert was very
still and, half concealed under that white veil, it had a
strange, almost eerie quality. From far ahead came a
weird banshee howl. It rose to a high note and then
dropped to an ugly cough. "Hyena," David said and there
was loathing in his voice. The sound, repeated much
nearer and to our flank, checked my camel in its stride. It
was an eerie, disgusting sound. A little later Salim stopped

to stare at some camel tracks. There were droppings, too, and he dismounted, sifted them through his fingers, smelt them, and then delivered his verdict: men of the Bait Kathir, and they had come south the night before with two camels belonging to Saraifa.

"Loot," David said, and we rode on in silence until about ten minutes later Hamid signalled to us. He had sighted the first corpse. It had been stripped of its clothes and there wasn't much meat left on the bones, which stared white through the torn flesh. The teeth, bared in the remains of a beard, had fastened in agony upon a tuft of dried-up herb.

It wasn't a pretty sight with the sand all trampled round about and stained black with blood, and after that the bodies lay thick. They had been caught in ambush and slaughtered as they rushed a small gravel rise where the enemy had lain in wait. There were camels, too, their carcasses bared to the bones and white and brittle-looking like the withered remains of dwarf trees dead of drought. The whole place smelt of death, and things moved on the edge of visibility. Two men slunk away like ghouls, mounted their camels, and disappeared into the mist.

We let them go, for David's only interest was to discover whether Khalid had been killed. Methodically he and Salim checked every corpse, whilst the two Wahiba scouted the edges of the battlefield. David could put names to most of the bodies, despite decomposition and the mutilations of scavengers, and one I recognized myself: the leader of Khalid's escort. He lay face down in the tire marks of a Land Rover, and close beside him were the bodies of three more of Khalid's men, stripped of their clothes and arms.

We hadn't far to go after that. The tire marks lipped a rise, and a little beyond, the burnt-out remains of the Land Rover itself loomed out of the mist. They had sought cover behind it, and their bodies had been ripped to pieces by a murderous fire. Khalid lay with eyeless sockets and half his face torn away. The near-naked body was already disintegrating, and where the stomach had been torn open the rotten flesh crawled with maggots and the blood was dry and black like powder. Four of his men lay near him in much the same state of putrefaction.

"The waste!" David breathed. He was standing, staring down at the remains of his friend, and there were tears in his eyes. "The bloody, senseless waste!" There was a shovel still clipped to the Land Rover, its handle burnt away. He seized it and attacked the ground with violent energy, digging a shallow grave. And when we'd laid what was left of Khalid to rest and covered it with sand, David stood back with bowed head. "He might have saved Saraifa. He was the only one of them who had the vision and the drive and energy to do it." He wiped his face with his head-cloth. "May he rest in peace, and may Allah guide him to the world beyond." He turned his back abruptly on the grave and strode blindly off across the sand towards the gravel rise that had been the scene of the ambush.

Along the back of it ran a ridge of bare rock. Behind it the ground was scattered with the brass of empty cartridges. "War surplus." He tossed one of them to me. "Governments sell that stuff. They never think of the loss of life their bloody auctions will ultimately cause. A pity the little bureaucrat . . ." But he let it go at that, wandering on along the ridge. At four places we came upon the empty magazines of automatic guns; in each case they lay beside the tire marks of vehicles. "They hadn't a chance," he said bitterly and started back to where Salim waited with the camels.

Before we reached them, Ali came hurrying back. He had been scouting to the east, along the line of the *falaj*, and had almost stumbled into a small Hadd force camped by the next well. He said the walls of the well had been thrown down, the whole thing filled with sand and rock. We waited for Hamid. He was a long time coming, and when he did arrive his manner was strange, his eyes rolling in his head as words poured out of him. "He's just buried his father," David said. "The old man's body had a dozen bullets in it." Grimly he gave the order to mount.

I was glad to go. Dawn was breaking and a hot wind beginning to blow from the northwest. I was sick of the sight of so much death. So was David. This, after the lonely weeks he'd spent in that filthy area of quicksands . . . I didn't need the set, withdrawn look of his face, the occasional mumbling of the lips to tell me that he was mentally very near the end of his tether. "Where are we going?" I asked as we rode towards the next well, the wall of which was just visible on the horizon, a little rock turret above the drifting, moving sands.

"Saraifa," he said. "I'll know the worst then." I think he could already picture the misery that awaited us.

Halfway there we met with a family of the Junuba heading towards the mountains with a long string of camels loaded with dates for the coast. They gave us the news. The last *falaj* had ceased to flow that morning. Sheikh Makhmud was said to have died during the night. His brother, Sheikh Sultan, ruled in his place. We purchased some dates from them—we had been unable to buy any supplies in Dhaid—and hurried on.

All the way to Saraifa the traces of disaster were with us: the carcass of a camel, a body sprawled in the sand, discarded arms. But, according to the Junuba, the Emir's men were not in the oasis. "They don't need to attack now," David said. "They can sit on the *falajes* they've destroyed and just wait for the end, like vultures waiting for a man to die." And he added: "Sheikh Sultan will make peace. He's a gutless, effeminate old man, and they know it."

The wind increased in force until it was blowing a strong *shamal* and we never saw Saraifa until the crumbling walls of a date-garden appeared abruptly out of the miasma clouds of wind-blown sand. The palms thrashed in the blinding air as they closed around us.

We passed a patch of cultivation, the green crop already wilted and turning sear. And when we reached the first *shireeya*, we found it dry, the mud bottom hard as concrete, split with innumerable cracks. The *falaj* channel that supplied it was empty. The skeletal shape of little fish lay in the sand at the bottom of it.

Only when we came to the outskirts of Saraifa itself was there any sign of human activity. Camels were being loaded, household possessions picked over. But most of the *barastis* were already empty, the human life gone from them. Men stopped to talk to us, but only momentarily. They were bent on flight.

It was the same when we reached the mud buildings in the centre of Saraifa. Everywhere there were beasts being loaded. But it was the tail end of the exodus; most of the houses were already deserted. And in the great square under the palace walls the watering-place no longer delivered its precious fluid to a noisy crowd of boys with their asses; the ground round it was caked hard, and the only persons there were an old man and a child of about two.

We circled the walls and came to the main gate. The great wooden portals were closed. No retainers stood guard on the bastions above. The palace had the look of a place shut against the plague and given over to despair. David sat for a moment on his camel, looking down on the date-gardens half hidden beneath the weight of driven sand, and tears were streaming down his face. He turned to me suddenly and swore an oath, demanding that the Almighty should be his witness—and the oath was the destruction of Hadd. "Khalid is dead," he added, and his eyes burned in their sockets. "Now I must do what he'd have done, and I'll not rest till the *falajes* are running again—not only the five they've destroyed, but the others, too. That I swear, before Almighty God, or my life is worth nothing."

We rode out of Saraifa then, leaving behind us the pitiful sight of a people driven from their homes by thirst, heading into the desert, our heads bent against the wind, our mouths covered. Once David paused, his arm flung out, pointing. "Now you see it. Now you see the Rub al Khali rolling in like the sea." And indeed it did look like the sea, for through gaps in the flying curtain of sand I could see the dunes smoking like waves in the gusts, the sand blowing off their tops in streamers. "That's what Khalid was fighting. Like water, isn't it? Like water flooding in over a low-lying land." And, riding on, he said: "With the people gone, the wells all dry . . . this place won't last long." His words came in snatches on the wind. "How long will they survive, do you think—those families hurrying to go? They're not nomads. They can't live in the sands. They'll die by slow degrees, turned away by sheikh after sheikh who fears they and their beasts will drink his own people out of water. And what can they live on when their camels are gone?"

He was riding close beside me then. "Sometimes I hate the human race . . . hate myself, too, for being human and as cruel as the rest." And then quietly, his teeth clenched, his eyes blazing: "There'll be men die in Hadd for what I've seen today."

It was the strange choice of words, the way he was trembling, and the violence of his manner—I thought he'd been driven half out of his mind by Khalid's death and the tragic things we'd seen.

"All I need is a few men," he whispered to me. "Khalid's are all dead. Half a dozen men, that's all I need."

The sun's heat increased and the wind gradually died. I suffered badly from thirst, for we hadn't much water left and we were riding fast. Towards midday, in a flat gravel pan between high dunes, we came upon the tracks of heavy vehicles. We followed them and shortly afterwards heard the roar of diesels. It was the drilling-rig, both trucks floundering in a patch of soft sand. The big eight-wheeler was out in front, the rig folded down across its back, and it was winching the second truck, loaded with pipe and fuel drums, across the soft patch.

They were working with furious energy, for they'd had
refugees from Saraifa through their camp just before
they'd pulled out, and they were scared. We stopped with
them long enough to brew coffee and give our beasts a rest,
and when we rode on, David said to me: "Why's he want
to bring that rig here now? What good will it do?" He
was haggard-eyed, his face pale under its tan. "They told
me he'd requisitioned Entwhistle's seismological outfit—
the men as well as the truck. He did that just after the
battle, when he knew what had happened. I don't understand it. He must realize it's too late now. . . ."

The shadows of the dunes were lengthening, their crests
sharp-etched against the flaming sky. We were working our
way across them then, and as the sun finally sank, we came
to the top of a dune, out of the shadow into the lurid light
of the blood-red sunset, and in the gravel flat below we
saw the tracks of vehicles and the blackened circles of
camp-fires. "Location B," David said, and we rode down
into shadow again.

The camp had been abandoned that morning. So much
Salim was able to tell us from the ashes of the camp-fires,
and after that we kept just below the dune crests, riding
cautiously, with Ali scouting ahead.

We'd only just lost sight of the abandoned camp when
the thud of an explosion shook the ground and the sands
on the steep face of a dune opposite slid into motion with
a peculiar thrumming, singing sound. Our camels stood
halted, their bodies trembling, and the singing sound of
the sands went on for a long time. There was no further
explosion. But almost as soon as we started forward again,
Ali called to us and at the same moment there was the
crack of a rifle and a bullet sang uncomfortably close.

I don't remember dismounting. I was suddenly stretched
on the sand with Salim pulling my camel down beside me.
David and Hamid were crawling forward to the dune crest,
their guns ready. I thought for a moment we had been am-
bushed. But then Ali shouted a greeting. He had dropped

his rifle and was standing up, throwing sand into the air. It was the Bedou sign that we came in friendship, and in a moment we were dragging our camels down the steep face of the dune and three Arabs were running to meet us, brandishing their weapons and shouting.

We had reached Colonel Whitaker's camp at Location C.

The tents were huddled against the base of a dune, black shapes in the fading light, and out on the gravel flat Entwhistle's seismological truck stood, lit by the glow of cooking-fires. There were perhaps fifteen men in that camp, and they flitted towards us like bats in the dusk. As they crowded round us, one of them recognized David. All was confusion then, a babel of tongues asking questions, demanding news.

David didn't greet them. I doubt whether he even saw them. His eyes were fixed on his father, who had come out of one of the tents and was standing, waiting for us, a dark, robed figure in silhouette against the light of a pressure lamp. David handed his camel to Salim and went blindly forward. I think he still held his father in some awe, but as I followed him I began to realize how much the day had changed him. He had purpose now, a driving, overriding purpose that showed in the way he strode forward.

There wasn't light enough for me to see the expression on Colonel Whitaker's face when he realized who it was. And he didn't speak, even when David stood directly in front of him. Neither of them spoke. They just stood there, staring at each other. I was close enough then to see Whitaker's face. It was without expression. No surprise, no sign of any feeling.

"It's your son," I said. "He's alive."

"So I see." The voice was harsh, the single eye fixed on David. "You've decided to return from the dead. Why?"

"Khalid asked me to come here and talk to you. He wanted us to—"

"Khalid's dead."

"I know that. I buried his body this morning." David's

voice trembled with the effort to keep himself under control. "He died because his father hadn't the sense to avoid a pitched battle." And he added: "We passed that rig of yours a few miles back. It's too late now to start drilling on my locations."

"On your locations?"

"On Farr's, then—as checked by me."

"And by me," Whitaker snapped. "Since you've got Grant with you, I presume you now have some idea what I was trying to do. If you hadn't disappeared like that—"

"Don't, for God's sake, let's have another row." David's voice was strangely quiet. "And don't let's start raking over the past. Its too late for that now. Khalid was right. We've got to work together. I came because I need men."

"Men?" Colonel Whitaker stared at him with a puzzled frown. "What do you need men for?"

"I'll tell you in a moment. But first I'd like to know what you're planning to do with that rig. You can't, surely, intend to drill here—not now, after what's happened?"

"Why not?"

"But it's crazy. It'll take you months—"

"You call it crazy now, do you?" Whitaker's voice was hard and pitched suddenly very high. "Last time I saw you, you were raising hell because I wouldn't drill here. Well, now I'm going to try it your way."

"But don't you realize what's happened in Saraifa?"

"Of course I do. Sheikh Makhmud is dead and I've lost an old friend. His brother, Sultan, is Ruler in his place, and you know what that means. Saraifa is finished."

David stared at him in disbelief. "You mean you're going to do a deal with the Emir?" His tone was shocked.

Whitaker's face was without expression. "I've seen him, yes. We've reached a tentative agreement." And then as he saw the look of contempt on David's face, he exclaimed: "*Allah akhbar!* When are you going to grow up, boy?"

"You don't have to worry on that score, sir. I've grown up fast enough these past few months." David's voice was calmer, much quieter. He seemed suddenly sure of himself. "But there's no point in discussing what's gone. It's the future I'm concerned with—the future of Saraifa. Can I rely on you for support or not?"

Whitaker frowned. "Support for what?"

"For an attack on Hadd. I've worked it all out in my mind." David's voice came alive then, full of sudden enthusiasm. "For centuries they've been destroying other people's wells. They've never known what it is to be short of water themselves. I'm going to give them a taste of their own medicine. I'm going to destroy the wells in Hadd."

"Are you out of your mind?" Whitaker glared at him. "Even if you did blow up a well, what good would it do? In a day or at most two they would have repaired it."

"I don't think so," David said quietly. "Just let me have a few men."

"Men? You won't get men out of me for a crack-brained scheme like this." And then in a gentler voice: "See here, David. I realize you've probably been through a lot during the past two months. And if you've been out to the battlefield on the Mahdah *falaj,* as I rather suspect from your attitude, I don't imagine it was a pleasant sight."

"It wasn't a pleasant sight riding through Saraifa and seeing the people there without water and fleeing from the oasis," David answered hotly.

"No. But . . ." Colonel Whitaker hesitated. He'd seen the obstinate look on David's face. No doubt he sensed his mood, too, which was desperately determined. "Come into the tent," he said. "I refuse to continue this discussion out here." He glanced at me. "If you'll excuse us, Grant. I'd like to talk to my son alone for a moment." He pulled back the flap of the tent. *"Faddal."* It was said quite automatically. A carpet showed red in the glare of the lamplight, some cushions, a tin box, and the two of them were inside the tent and the flap fell.

The outline of the dunes, smooth and flowing like downlands, faded into darkness as I sat alone on the sand, a

centre of curiosity for the whole camp. The sky was
clouded over, so that there were no stars and it was very
dark.

It was about half an hour later that David suddenly
emerged out of the night and sat down beside me.

"What happened?" I asked him.

"Nothing," he replied tersely. And after that he sat for
a long time without saying a word, without moving. Finally he turned to me of his own accord. "I don't understand him," he said. "It was like talking to a complete
stranger." And he added: "I don't think Saraifa means
anything to him any more." The bitterness of his voice
was overlaid with frustration. "It's tragic," he whispered.
"Half a dozen men. That's all I asked him for. But he
thinks it's all a dream, that I don't know what I'm doing."

"You told him about Khalid—what he'd said to me?"

"Of course."

"And it made no difference?"

"None."

"What did you talk about, then?"

He laughed a little wildly. "About locations, geological
formations, a drilling program. He wasn't interested in
anything else." And then, speaking more to himself than
to me: "I couldn't get through to him. I just couldn't seem
to get through." He beat his fist against the ground. "What
do you do when a man's like that?" He stared at me
angrily. "I don't understand him. Do you know what he
said? He said I was forgiven. He said everything was to be
just as it was between us in the early days when I first
worked with him. I'm to stay here and help him drill a
well. He and I—together; we're going to drill the most
important well in Arabia." Again that slightly wild laugh.
"And when I mentioned Hadd, he said Hadd or Saraifa,
what did it matter now? He'll treat with the Emir, with
the Devil himself, so long as he's left in peace to drill his
well and prove his bloody theory to the damnation of
Philip Gorde and all the rest of the oil boys. God! I won-

der I didn't kill him." And he added: "The man's mad. He must be mad."

"Obsessed, perhaps . . ." I murmured.

"Mad." He glared at me. "How else do you explain his attitude, his fantastic assumption that I'd be content to sit here drilling a well after what's happened? For Khalid's sake I'd have agreed to anything. I'd have played the dutiful bastard sitting at the feet of the Great Bedouin. But when I asked him for men . . ." He shook his head. "He wouldn't give them to me. He wouldn't do a damned thing to help. Said I was crazy even to think of it. Me? And all he could talk about, with Makhmud dead and men he'd known for years lying by that well with their guts half eaten out—all he could talk about was his damned theory and how he'd known all along he was right. I tell you, the man's mad." His voice was sharp with frustration. "I wish to God," he said bitterly, "I'd never come out here, never set eyes on him. And to think I worshipped the man. Yes, worshipped him. I thought he was the greatest man living."

The bitterness in his voice . . . "What are you going to do?" I asked him.

"Take what men I can and get the hell out of here. Do what I planned to do—without his help." His voice had a bite to it, and he slid to his feet. "There's nothing else left for me to do—nothing that means anything, nothing useful." He left me then and hurried down to the dark shapes sitting around the cook-fires, calling to them in their own tongue, gathering them about him. And then he began to harangue them.

A little wind had sprung up, and it chilled the sweat on my body. But it wasn't the drop in temperature that made me shiver. I was caught up in a situation that was beyond my control, isolated here in the desert with two men equally obsessed—the one with oil, the other with an oasis. And then Whitaker's voice close behind me: "Grant. You've got to talk him out of it."

I got to my feet. He was standing there, a dark silhouette

against the dunes, staring down at where his son stood amongst the smoke of the fires. "His plan is madness."

But I'd been with David too long not to feel sympathy for him. "He's fighting for something he believes in," I said. "Why don't you help him?"

"By giving him men?" His harsh, beaked face was set and stony. "I've few enough for my purpose as it is." And then in a softer voice: "I had my loyalties, too. But now, with Makhmud dead, I'm free to do what perhaps I should have done in the first place. I've seen the Emir. I've sent Yousif to Sharjah with those letters to merchants there. I'm re-checking the earlier surveys. In a few days we'll spud in and start to drill. And when I've brought in the first discovery well, then all this trouble between Hadd and Saraifa will be seen in perspective, a small matter compared with the vast changes an oilfield will bring to the desert here."

"And your son?" I asked.

He shrugged. "As I told you before, when I thought he was dead, I'd hoped he'd follow me, a second Whitaker to carry on where I left off. Instead, I find myself cursed with an obstinate, stupid youth who's no respect for my judgement and opposes me at every turn." He put his hand on my arm, and in a surprisingly gentle voice he said: "Talk to him, Grant. Try and do for me what I know I can't do myself. His plan is suicidal."

He was looking straight at me and I was shocked to see there were tears running down his cheeks—not only from the one good eye, but welling out from beneath the black patch that concealed the other. "Do what you can," he said softly. And then he turned quickly away and went back to his tent.

Ten minutes later David was back at my side, looking tired and drained. "One man," he said in a bleak voice. "One man will come with me. That's all. Hamid's brother, bin Suleiman. And he's coming, not because he understands my plan, but simply because with him, as with Hamid, it's a blood feud now." He gave a shrug and a quick laugh. "Well, the fewer the better, perhaps. They'll drink less water, and water is going to be our trouble." He called to Hamid and gave the order to load the camels. "We'll leave as soon as I've got the things I need out of Entwhistle's truck."

I started to try and talk him out of it, but he brushed my words aside. "My mind's made up. Talking won't change it." And then he said: "What about you? Are you staying here or will you come with me?" He stared at me, a long, speculative look. "If you should decide to come with me, then I can promise to get you away to the coast with Salim as your guide." And he added: "If you don't come, then I think I may be throwing my life away for nothing. You're my only hope of contact with the outside world, and if the world doesn't know what I'm doing, then it's all wasted."

I asked him what exactly he planned to do, but he wouldn't tell me the details. "You'd have to know the ground or you might agree with my father and think it crazy. But I assure you," he added with great conviction, "that with any luck at all it will work. It's the last thing the Emir will be expecting, and the fact that we'll be a very small party . . ." He smiled. "It makes it easier, really—the first part, at any rate. And I promise you you'll not be involved in the rest. Think it over, will you, sir? I need your help in this—desperately." He left it like that and disappeared abruptly into the night.

I lay on the hard ground, listening to the movement of the camels, the sounds of preparation for another journey. A little wind came in puffs, sifting the sand, and it was dark. A stillness had enveloped the camp. I don't think I'm any more of a coward than the next man, but to seek out death, deliberately and in cold blood . . . You see, it never occurred to me he could succeed. I thought his father was right and that he was throwing away his life in a futile gesture. I remembered Gorde's description of Whitaker— an old man tilting at windmills. David was very like his father in some ways. I closed my eyes, thinking of Tanganyika and the hard life I'd led there, and then I felt a hand on my shoulder.

"Well?" David asked, and when I nodded almost without thinking, he passed me a rifle. "I take it you know how to use it?" He had another, which he handed to bin Suleiman, and a revolver with holster and belt, which he strapped to his own waist.

The stark reality of what I was doing came with the feel of the well-oiled breech under my hand. It took me back to days I thought I'd forgotten—to the deadly slopes of Monte Cassino, to Anzio and the Gothic Line. I rose quietly to my feet. Salim and Ali were loading cartons of explosive cartridges on to one of the camels. Hamid and his brother, a squat, hairy man with wild eyes and a low-browed head, were packing coils of fine wire and a contact plunger with its batteries into the saddle-bags of another beast.

The camels staggered to their feet, bulking suddenly large against the overcast, and we were on our way.

A lone figure standing by one of the tents watched us go. It was Colonel Whitaker. He made no move to stop us, nor did he call out. We left the camp in silence, and though they knew we were going, no man stirred from the camp-fires. It was as though they feared to have any contact with us; it was as though we had already passed beyond the shadows of death.

Clear of the camp, we turned east, working our way silently up the face of a dune in short zig-zags. At the crest we stopped to mount, and then we were riding, the dark desert all around us and the swaying shapes of our camels the only movement in the stillness of night.

The clouds thinned and gradually cleared, leaving us exposed in bright moonlight. But if the Emir had men watching Whitaker's camp, we never saw them. Dawn found us camped amongst sparse camel thorn on a flat gravel plain. Sharp-etched against the break of day stood the jagged tops of the mountains. Dates and coffee, and then sleep. "We start at dusk," David said and buried his face in his head-cloth.

The withered camel thorn gave little shelter, and as the sun climbed the burning vault of the sky, it became very hot. Flies worried us, clinging to the sweat of exposed flesh, and we suffered from thirst, for our water-bags were empty and all we had was the contents of two water-bottles. We took it in turns to keep watch, but the shimmering expanse of gravel that surrounded us remained empty of life.

As the sun sank we lit a fire and had a huge meal of rice and dried meat. A bowl of warm camel's milk passed from mouth to mouth. Our four Arabs talked excitedly amongst themselves and, the meal finished, they began to oil their guns, cleaning them with loving care. In contrast, David and I sat silent, doing nothing. The sun set and in an instant the sky had paled. The visibility was fantastic in the dry air, everything sharp and clear, as though magnified.

"You'd better tell me what you plan to do," I said, and my voice reflected the tension that had been growing in me all through that long, inactive day.

David was staring at the distant line of the mountains and for a moment I thought he hadn't heard my question. But then he said: "It isn't easy to explain to somebody who has never been to Hadd."

"I've flown over it," I said.

He looked at me then, a sudden quickening of interest. "Did you see the fort of Jebel al-Akhbar? Did you see how the town is backed right into the rock?" And when I explained how I'd passed close over it in Gorde's plane, he said: "Then you know the situation. That fort is the key to Hadd. Who holds that fort holds the people of Hadd in the hollow of his hand. It's as simple as that." He was suddenly excited, his eyes bright with the vision of what he planned to do. "When there was trouble here before, the Trucial Oman Scouts moved into the fort and that was the end of it."

"We're not the Trucial Oman Scouts." I thought it was time he faced up to the facts. "There are six of us, that's all. We're armed with rifles and nothing else. And our ammunition is limited."

"There's ammunition for us in the fort," he said. "Two boxes of it and a box of grenades." Apparently he and Khalid had found them left there by the TOS and half buried under a pile of rubble. They were out hunting as the Emir's guests and had taken refuge in the fort during a sandstorm. "It's a long time ago now," he added, "but I think we'll find the boxes still there. We buried them pretty deep. As for numbers . . ." He gave a little shrug. "One man, well armed and determined, could hold that tower for as long as his water held out." He smiled grimly. "Water. It always comes back to water in the desert, doesn't it?" And he slid to his feet and gave the order to move.

As we rode he pointed out the fort to me, small as a pinhead on top of a hill that miraculously detached itself from the line of the mountains, standing clear in the last of the daylight and much nearer than I had expected. "Dawn tomorrow," he said, "that's where we'll be." He looked very much like his father as he stared at me, his youthful features set in the grimmer mould of an older man. "God willing!" he breathed. "And when we're there you'll understand." He rode on then with his four Wahiba, talking with them urgently in their own tongue and leaving me to ride alone, prey to my own forebodings.

Dusk fell and merged imperceptibly into night. The stars lit our way, and in no time at all, it seemed, there was the Jebel al-Akhbar, a black hat of a hill bulked against the night sky. We rode slowly in a tight little bunch. The time was a little after ten. "We'll water our camels at the well on the outskirts, fill our water-bags. . . ." David's voice was taut.

"And if there's a guard?" I whispered.

"We're travellers from Buraimi on our way to the coast. Bin Suleiman will explain. He's known here."

"And after we've filled our water-bags?"

"Ssh!" The camels had stopped at a signal from Hamid. We sat still as death, listening. There were rock outcrops ahead and the dim shapes of buildings. A solitary light showed high up on the slope of the hill, which now towered above us, a dark mass against the stars. Somewhere a goat bleated. There was no other sound.

A whispered word from David and we moved forward again. The well-head appeared, a simple wooden structure topping a crumbling wall of mud and stone. We dismounted and the leathern bucket was dropped into the depths. The wooden roller creaked as it was drawn up. One by one the camels were watered; one by one, the skin bags filled. And all the time the wood creaked and we stood with our guns ready. But nobody came. The solitary light vanished from the slope of the hill, leaving the whole town dark as though it were a deserted ruin. Salim and Ali left with the camels and David went to work with cartridges of explosive and detonators. And when he'd mined the well, we went forward on foot, running the thin line of the wire out behind us.

The second well was close under the walls and there were camels couched near it. We could hear them stirring uneasily, could even see some of them, dark shapes against the lighter stone. A man coughed and sat up, dislodging a stone. The sound of it was magnified by the silence. And then I saw his figure coming towards us. Hamid and bin Suleiman moved to intercept. They talked together in whispers whilst David went on working and I helped him, glancing every now and then over my shoulder, expecting every moment to hear the man cry out and raise the alarm.

But nothing happened. The camels quietened down, the man went back to his interrupted sleep, and David was left to complete his work in peace. He worked fast and with absolute sureness, but it all took time. It was past midnight before he had finished, and a paler light above the mountains warned that the moon was rising.

As we trailed our wire towards a gap in the crumbling walls, two shots sounded far out in the desert behind us. We checked, standing there motionless and sweating. But there were no more shots. "Somebody out hunting gazelle," David whispered. "They do it at night by the lights of their Land Rovers." And we went on through the gap, which led to a narrow alley. There were no doors to the buildings on either side, only window openings high up. The alley led into the market place. More camels, some goats and figures asleep against the walls of the houses. The well was on the far side. There was a baby camel there, and a small boy lay curled up beside it. The camel, its coat fluffy as a kitten's, rose on straddling, spindly legs and gazed at us in amazed silence. The boy stirred, but didn't wake. A dog began to bark.

I caught hold of David's arm. "You've done enough, surely," I whispered.

"Scared?" He grinned in the darkness and shrugged me off. "We can't climb to the fort till the moon's up." And he squatted down in the dust and went to work. The boy suddenly sat up, staring at us, round-eyed. I thought: My God! If he kills that child . . . But David said something and the boy got slowly to his feet and came hesitantly forward, gazing in fascination. David gave him the wire to hold. A man moved in the shadows by an archway. The boy's father. As he came forward, other figures stirred. A little knot of men gathered round us. But the boy sitting there in the dust beside David, helping him, made it all seem innocent. They stood and watched for a while, talking with Hamid and bin Suleiman, and then they drifted back to their sleep.

The moon rose. The mud walls of the houses on the far side of the open place stood suddenly white, and moment by moment the dark shadow-line retreated until it touched the base of the buildings and began to creep across the ground towards us. At last David tied his mine to the well rope and lowered it. We left then, and the boy came with us, trailing the baby camel behind him. Other figures followed us, curious but not hostile. "They don't belong to Hadd," David whispered. "They're Bedou in from the desert to sell camels. Otherwise we'd never have got out of there alive."

"What did they think we were doing?"

"I said we were testing the wells before installing pumping-equipment. They know all about pumps. They've seen them in Buraimi and also in Saraifa." By the second well we picked up the line of our wire, clipped on another coil, and trailed it to the limit up the hill just outside the walls. There David fastened it to the terminals of the plunger, and then he handed it to the boy and told him what to do. "He'll tell the story of this moment till the end of his days." He patted the boy on the shoulder, smiling almost cheerfully as he turned and left him.

We climbed quickly, came out from the shadow of the wall on to the moonlit slope of the hill, and on a rock well above the rooftops of the highest houses we halted. The boy was squatting there beside the detonator, his face turned towards us. David raised his hand above his head and then let it fall. The boy turned away and his shoulders hunched as he thrust down on the plunger.

The silence ceased abruptly, the stillness of the night rent by three deep, rumbling explosions that were instantly muffled and snuffed out by the collapse of the earth walls of the wells. The sound nevertheless went on, travelling back through the mountains, reverberating from face after face and gradually fading.

The boy still hadn't moved when all sound had ceased. The baby camel stood beside him. It was as though the shattering effect of the explosion had turned them both to stone. Then suddenly he was jerked to life. For an instant his face was turned towards us, white and startled in the moonlight, and then he fled screaming down the hillside, the camel breaking away in ungainly puppet strides.

VI
Fort Jebel al-Akhbar

We turned then

and followed a zig-zag track that climbed by crumbling
outcrops, and below us the town came to life—the sound
of voices, the glimmer of lights. A shot stabbed the night,
but it wasn't directed at anything in particular and we
were close under the fort before the pursuit got under
way. We could see them clear on the moonlit slope below
us, zig-zagging up the path by which we had come. There
were about a dozen of them, climbing in single file and
moving fast with the agility of mountain goats.

The fort tower hung on the lip of the cliff above us, a
white stone keep crumbling to decay, and where the track
doubled back through a narrow defile in the rocks David
posted Hamid to guard our rear. "I hope to God we find
Salim there," he panted. The path had steepened, so that
we climbed with our hands as well as our feet, rocks slipping away from under us. And then we reached the walls
and the track led through a narrow opening.

We were inside the outer defences then, an open space
of half an acre or more that occupied all the top of the
hill. The walls had originally been about twenty feet high,
with a firing-step round the inside, but they were now in a
bad state of repair and there were few places where they
were higher than ten feet. They were horseshoe-shaped,
the two ends finishing abruptly at the cliff edge, the tower
between them. There was no sign of the camels.

"Damn the old fool! He should have been here by now."
David's sudden uneasiness made me wonder whether perhaps Salim had taken the opportunity to desert us. But when I suggested this, he shook his head. "Why do you think I sent Ali with him? That boy knew what those camels meant to us. No, something has happened to them."

A shot ripped the silence apart. Hamid had opened fire on our pursuers, and the sound of it echoed back from the naked rock faces that surrounded us. A scatter of shots sounded from lower down the slope and a bullet hit the wall close by us with a soft thud.

"Wait for me here. I'm going to see what's happened." David ran quickly across the open courtyard of the fort and out through the main gate on the north side, and when he was gone I climbed to the broken top of the wall and threw myself down beside bin Suleiman. From this vantage point we commanded the final approach to the fort.

Perched high on the edge of the sheer cliff face, I could see right down into the town of Hadd. The market square, where we'd mined the third well, was clearly visible, a white rectangle with people moving about or standing in little groups. It was not more than a thousand feet away, an easy rifle shot. And the wells outside the walls—I could see them, too. I began to understand then why David had been so sure those damaged wells would stay out of action.

Immediately below was the defile. I could see Hamid stretched out on top of one of the rock shoulders. His rifle gleamed as he raised it to his shoulder. A stab of flame, the crack of the shot, and then silence again. On the slope beyond there was now no sign of pursuit. The men who had started to follow us were pinned down amongst the rocks. It was an incredible position, impossible to take from that side so long as it was defended by men who knew how to shoot.

A bullet whined low over my head and I ducked automatically, poking my rifle forward and searching the steep slope beyond the defile. But there was nothing to fire at. The night was still and without movement.

We remained in that position for two solid hours whilst the stars moved sedately round the sky and all away to our right the desert stretched its white expanse. The sense of isolation, of a long wait for ultimate death, gradually took hold of me. It had a strange effect, a throw-back, I think, to the mood that had filled me as we lay pinned down like rats on the slopes of Monte Cassino . . . a mood compounded of fear and the desire to survive that expressed itself in the need to kill, so that when a figure moved on the slope below me, my whole being was concentrated in my trigger finger, and as he stumbled and fell my only feeling was one of elation, a deep, trembling satisfaction.

A little after three the first glimmer of dawn brought the mountains into sharp relief. A small wind whispered among the stones and it was quite chill. It was the time of night when the body is at the lowest ebb, and I began to worry about David, and about our rear. By now men from the village below could surely have circled Jebel al-Akhbar to climb by the camel track to the main gate. I called to bin Suleiman and made a motion with my hand to indicate what I was going to do, and then I abandoned my position and started on a tour of the walls.

The result was encouraging. They were built on sheer rock slopes. Only on the north side was there any means of reaching the fort. There the camel track climbed steeply from the desert below to enter by the only gateway. Old palm-tree timbers sagged from rusted iron hinges. This was the way attack must come if it were to succeed. Bastion towers flanked the gate on either side, and from the top of one of them I could see down the whole length of the track. It was empty. So, too, were the slopes of the hill. There was no cover, and nowhere could I see any sign of David or the camels.

I was turning away when my eye caught a movement on the white floor of the desert below: four shapes moving slowly, their shadows more sharply defined than the shapes themselves. They were camels moving towards the bottom of the track, and as they turned to start the climb, I made out the figure of a solitary rider on the leading camel.

I lay down then on the broken stone top of the bastion and pushed the safety-catch of my rifle forward. Our camels had numbered six, and with David there should have been three riders. They came on very slowly whilst the grey of dawn overlaid the moonlight and the whiteness faded out of the desert.

As the light improved and they came nearer, I saw the body of a man lying slumped over the saddle of the second camel. Skin bags bulging with water confirmed that the beasts were ours, and soon after that I was able to recognize David. I met him as he rode in through the broken gateway. He didn't say anything as he dismounted, but his face looked grey. "What happened?" I asked.

"Those shots we heard . . . They rode straight into a party of the Emir's men camped outside the town." He asked me then whether they'd tried to rush us yet.

"No," I said. "They're still pinned down less than a third of the way up the slope."

"Good. Give me a hand, will you?" He led the second camel to the foot of the tower and got it couched. The body tied with cord across its back was Ali's. "He's badly hurt." We laid him gently on the ground. He moaned softly, barely conscious. He'd a ghastly wound in the chest. I'd seen the effect of a soft-nosed Bedouin bullet on the metal of a Land Rover; now I was seeing its effect on human flesh, and the sight appalled me. He'd a knife wound in the shoulder, too, and he'd lost a lot of blood; the dark, broad-lipped, girlish face had taken on a sickly pallor.

David stood for a moment, staring down at him. "Poor kid," he murmured. "I found him lying in a pool of blood by the ashes of their camp-fire. I suppose they thought he was dead. Salim's body was close beside him. They'd slit his throat." His voice shook. "The murdering, dung-eating

bastards! Why did they have to do it? There were at least
twenty of them there, twenty of them against an old man
and a boy." Apparently he'd found the camp deserted, our
four camels wandering loose. "They must have been disturbed by the sound of the explosions," he said. "Otherwise, they wouldn't have left the camels. They only took
one. It was the other that led me to their camp; it was
wandering around on three legs, bellowing with pain. I
had to finish it off." He gave a quick, angry shrug as though
wanting to dismiss the whole thing from his mind. "Well,
let's get him up into the tower. He can't lie here."

He got the camel to its feet and stood it close by the wall
of the tower. Standing on its back, he was just able to
reach the hole halfway up the tower's side. He scrambled
in and from the dark interior produced a crude ladder
made of palm-wood. We dragged the boy up and laid him
on the dirt floor and David plugged and bound the
wounds again, using his head-cloth, which he tore in strips.
"A bloody lousy piece of luck," he said. "I'd planned to
get you away before daylight. With Salim to guide you,
you'd have been in Buraimi tomorrow, in Sharjah by the
next day. I'd got it all planned. Now . . ." He shrugged.
"We'll have to do some fresh thinking."

It was daylight now. It came filtering into the interior
of the tower through the entrance hole and through four
narrow slits in the thick walls. They were firing-embra-
sures, and they reminded me of the turret room I'd occupied in Saraifa. But the view was vastly different. Two of
them looked out east and west, each covering an arm of
the walls. The other two, close together, faced south; they
looked straight down on to Hadd itself.

"Well, that's all I can do for him." David got to his feet.
"You stay here. I must have a word with Hamid and bin
Suleiman. And then we must deal with the camels."

He left me sitting by one of the embrasures and I had
time to think then. The excitement of action that had sus-
tained me so far was gone now. The future stared me in

the face and I began to be afraid of it. However impregnable the fort's position, there were still only four of us, and right there below me was that Arab town teeming with life and utterly hostile. I could see men clustered thick in the open square and some of them were armed. It could only be a matter of time.

They had already started work on the well inside the walls. Men were being lowered into it and every now and then a bundle of stones and rubble was handed up. The sun was rising behind the mountains. The sky was crimson and all the desert flushed the colour of a rose. It looked very beautiful, so serene in the clear morning air, and the mountains standing like cut-outs painted purple.

It was just after the sun had lipped the mountain-tops that David climbed back into the tower. "They've started work on that well in the square, haven't they?"

I nodded. The little square was teeming like an ant-hill.

"What are they—townspeople or the Emir's bodyguard?" He had his rifle with him and he came straight over to where I was squatting on the floor beside the embrasure.

"Both," I said. The men working on the well were mostly stripped to the waist. But, standing about, watching them, were a number of armed men, their bodies strapped about with cartridges, bands of brass that glinted in the sun; their rifles, untrammelled with silver, had the dull gleam of modern weapons.

He pushed past me, kneeling in the embrasure, steadying himself with his elbows on the sill as he brought the rifle to his shoulder and fired. The sound of the shot was very loud in that dim, confined place. "That's one of them that won't go murdering old men and boys again." He was trembling slightly as he sat back on his heels.

The crowd in the square was scattering. A little knot gathered in one corner, and then that, too, melted away and the square was suddenly empty. "An occasional shot like that and they'll learn to leave it alone. In a day or two they'll begin to understand what it's like to have the sources of water cut off, the wells dry." He got up and set his gun against the wall. "Not that they'll die of thirst. They're better off than the people we saw in Saraifa." He went back down the ladder and left me staring at the empty rectangle of the sun-drenched square, littered with the balks of timber they'd brought in to shore up the inner walls of the well. Behind me the wounded boy moaned restlessly, muttering words I couldn't understand, and when I went to him, I found his dark eyes wide open and staring, his skin dry and parched. I gave him some water, and then David called to me.

He and Hamid had started unloading the camels. Bin Suleiman kept watch from the eastern wall. We worked fast, but the sun was high above the mountains before we'd humped all the stores and the last of the water-skins up into the tower. "What about the camels?" I asked as we lifted the saddles from their backs. It was already blisteringly hot, the bare rock acting as a fire-brick and throwing back the sun's heat. There was no vestige of vegetation inside the fort for them to feed on.

"I'll keep one for you. The other three will have to be slaughtered."

They were fine beasts in the prime of life and in beautiful condition. But when I started to remonstrate, he cut me short. "What did you imagine we were going to do with them? We've no other meat." He stared at me angrily. "Even the Bedou, who love camels a damn sight more than I do, don't hesitate to kill them when they're short of food. And we're going to be short of everything before we're through."

I stood and stared at him. Without camels, he'd have no means of retreat. He'd be trapped here. . . .

"Do you reckon you could get through to Buraimi on your own?"

I hesitated. But I knew now there was no alternative for me—only death here on this pitiless hilltop. "I could try."

"Good. We'll keep the one you've been riding, then, and get you away tonight as soon as it's dark."

Immediately after we'd breakfasted, bin Suleiman butchered the three camels, slitting their throats and letting the blood drain into a tin bowl. The carcasses were then disembowelled, and the meat cut into strips and hung to dry in the sun. Flies buzzed and the place smelt of blood, and yet it didn't seem unnatural. Sand and rock and the blazing sky, that boy lying in the dim interior of the tower, his breath gurgling in his throat and blood seeping on to the floor, and below us an Arab town ruled by a man consumed by a murderous greed. Death didn't seem so hateful when life itself was so cruel.

Action followed hard upon my thoughts. Hamid, from his lookout post on the very top of the tower, called down to us: men were circling the hill to the north. From the walls we watched them climb by the camel track. They were well spaced out, their guns ready in their hands. Others were coming up by the zig-zag path direct from Hadd. Lying prone on the blistering stones, we waited, holding our fire. The stillness seemed to break their nerve, for they began shooting at a range of almost three hundred yards.

The attack, when it came, was a senseless, ill-directed affair, men clawing their way up the last steep rock ascent to the walls without any supporting fire. We caught them in the open, unprotected, and the attack petered out almost before it had begun. They went back down the sides of the hill, taking their wounded with them and not leaving even a single sniper to harass us from the shelter of the rocks.

"It won't be as easy as that next time they come." David's eyes had a cold, dead look, untouched by the light of battle that I'd glimpsed for a moment on bin Suleiman's broad animal face.

We had used, I suppose, no more than two or three dozen rounds, but it was sufficient to make David anxious

about his ammunition. Whilst the two Wahiba kept watch,
David and I lowered the ladder through a hole in the mud
floor of the tower and climbed down into the black rub-
ble-filled pit below. It was slow work, searching in the
dark, for we'd nothing but our hands to dig with and after
so long David wasn't at all certain where he had buried
the boxes. We must have been down there at least an hour,
and all the time we were scrabbling at the rubble with our
hands, Ali lay delirious on the floor above. Twice Hamid's
rifle cracked as he carried out David's orders and kept the
wells in Hadd clear of people. Those sounds and the darkness and the feeling that at any moment we might be overwhelmed through lack of amunition gave a sense of desperate urgency to our work.

Finally we found the boxes and hauled them through
the hole to the floor above—more than a thousand rounds
of ammunition and two dozen grenades. We'd barely got
the boxes open when Hamid reported a Land Rover leaving the palace. We watched it from the embrasures, blaring
its horn as it snaked through Hadd's crooked alleys and
out through the main gates of the town. It headed south
towards Saraifa, and David let it go, not firing a shot.
"The sooner Sheikh Abdullah is informed of the situation
here," he said, "the sooner his raiding force will leave
Saraifa in peace." His eyes were shining now, for this
was what he'd intended. That little puff of dust trailing
across the desert was the visual proof of the success of his
plan.

"But what happens," I said, "when Sheikh Abdullah attacks us here with all his forces?"

He smiled, a flash of white teeth in the dark, lean face.
"We're not short of ammunition now."

"But we're short of men. There are only four of us.
How many do you think Sheikh Abdullah musters?" I
thought it was time he faced up to the situation.

"It's not numbers that count," he answered tersely. "Not
up here. Whoever built this fort designed it to be held by

a handful of men." And he added: "We're bloody good shots, you see. Hamid and bin Suleiman, they're like all the Bedou—they've had guns in their hands since they were kids. And me, I learned to shoot out hunting with Khalid." He was almost grinning then. "I tell you, man, I can hit a gazelle running with a rifle bullet—and a gazelle's a bloody sight smaller than a man. Anyway," he added, "no call for you to worry. With any luck we'll get you away under cover of darkness tonight."

"And what about you?" I asked. "You've no camels now."

"No." He stared at me, a strange, sad look in his eyes. And then he gave a little shrug. "There comes a moment in every man's life, I suppose, when his destiny catches up with him."

Again I was conscious of his strange choice of words, the sense of fatalism. "If you don't get out . . . if you stay here until Sheikh Abdullah's men have surrounded you . . ." What could I say to make him see sense? "You'll die here," I told him bluntly.

"Probably."

We stood there, staring at each other, and I knew there was nothing I could say that would make him change his mind. He didn't care. He was filled with a burning sense of mission. It showed in his eyes, and I was reminded of the word Sue had used to describe his mood—the word "dedicated." All the misdirected energy that had involved him in gang warfare in Cardiff docks—now it had found an outlet, a purpose, something he believed in. Death meant nothing.

"What about Hamid and bin Suleiman?" I asked. "Will they fight with you to the end?"

"Yes," he said. "They've a blood feud on their hands and they want to kill."

There was nothing more to be said, then. "If I reach Buraimi and get through to the coast, I'll inform the authorities of the situation at once."

"Of course." He said it with a bitter little smile, so that I was afraid he'd read my thoughts and knew I was thinking that help would arrive too late. But then he said: "It's no good talking to the authorities, you know. They won't do anything. Much better give the story to the newspapers. I wouldn't like to die without anybody knowing what I'd tried to do." Again that bitter little smile, and then he turned away. "Better get some sleep now. You've a long journey and you'll need to be fresh for it."

But sleep wasn't easy. The only place where there was any shade was the tower, and there Ali's agony of mind and body was a thin thread of sound piercing each moment of unconsciousness, so that I dreamed I was listening to David's death throes, at times to my own. He died as the sun sank—a brief rattle in the throat and silence. And at that same moment David scrambled in by the entrance hole to announce that there were vehicles coming from the direction of Saraifa.

"I think Ali is dead," I said.

He bent over the boy and then nodded. "I should have put him out of his misery," he said. "Without a doctor, he hadn't a hope, poor kid."

From the embrasures we watched a trail of dust moving in from the desert . . . three open Land Rovers packed with men, a machine-gun mounted in the back of each vehicle. David called down to Hamid, who was cooking rice over a fire, and he grabbed his gun and climbed the outer wall to lie prone beside bin Suleiman. David motioned me to the other embrasure. "Don't fire till I do. And, remember, every man you hit is one less for us to deal with later." He had dropped to his knees, his rifle ready in the slit of the embrasure.

The three Land Rovers reached the main gates and there they halted, stopped by the crowd of people who swarmed round them, all pointing and gesticulating towards us. An Arab askari in the leading Land Rover swung his machine-gun, and a long burst ripped the sunset stillness. Bullets splattered against the base of the tower. The guns of the other two Land Rovers followed suit—a sound like ripping calico. Several rifles were let off.

It was a demonstration designed to restore morale. My hand trembled as I set the sights of my rifle to 500. And then David fired and I was conscious of nothing but my finger on the trigger and the third Land Rover fastened like a toy to the V of my sights. The smell of cordite singed my nostrils. Fire blossomed like a yellow flower against the dun of desert sand. Men scattered. Some fell. And in a moment there was nothing to shoot at.

One Land Rover in flames, the other two deserted; some bodies lying in the dust. Tracer bullets exploded like fireworks from the back of the burning vehicle, and almost immediately a second Land Rover caught fire as the petrol tank went up.

"I'm afraid they won't give us an opportunity like that again." David sat back on his haunches and cleared his gun. "It will be night attacks from now on."

Hadd was deserted now. Not a soul to be seen anywhere, the alleyways and the square empty. The Emir's green flag hung limp above the palace; nothing stirred. Hamid went back to his cooking. The sun set and the excitement of action ebbed away, leaving a sense of nervous exhaustion. "You'd better leave as soon as it's dark," David said. Dusk had fallen and we were feeding in relays. He began to brief me on the route to follow, and as I listened to his instructions, the lonely desolate miles of desert stretched out ahead. The embers of the fire were warm. The dark shapes of the surrounding walls gave a sense of security. I was loath to go, and yet I knew the security of those walls false, the embers probably the last fire for which they would have fuel.

He gave me dates and a bottle filled with water, sufficient to take me to the first well, and then began to saddle the camel. "You'll be seeing Sue?"

I nodded.

"Give her my love; tell her I'll be thinking of her and of a day we spent on the Gower. She'll know what I mean."

"She thinks you're dead," I reminded him.

"Well, tell her I'm not—not yet, anyway." And he laughed and slung the heavy blanket over the wooden saddle.

Ten minutes and I'd have been away. Just ten minutes, that was all I needed. But then the sound of a rifle cut the stillness of the night and a man screamed and went on screaming—a thin, high-pitched sound that had in it all that any one could ever know of pain. Bin Suleiman shouted a warning from the east-facing wall, and David let go the camel and raced to meet the attack. "Get out now," he called to me over his shoulder. "Get out now before it's too late!" He called something to Hamid, who was posted on the far side of the fort by the main entrance gate, and then the darkness had swallowed him. A stab of flame showed high up on the wall, and the echo of the shot cut through the man's screams as though it had severed his vocal cords. A sudden silence followed, an unnatural stillness.

The camel, startled by the noise, had fled into the night. I found him close under the wall of the tower. Bewildered and obstinate, the wretched beast refused to move, and by the time I had coaxed him to the main gate it was too late. Firing had broken out all round us. A figure appeared at my side, gripped my arm, and shouted something in Arabic. It was Hamid, and he gestured towards the tower. Rocks thundered against the wooden timbers of the gate we had barricaded that afternoon. Hamid fired, working the bolt of his rifle furiously, the noise of his shots beating against my ear-drums.

And then he was gone, running for the tower. I let the camel go and followed him, my gun clutched in my hands. Bin Suleiman was at the ladder ahead of me. David followed close behind as I flung myself through the hole and into the darkness beyond. As soon as we were all inside, we drew the ladder up. Bullets splattered the wall—the soft, dull thud of lead, the whine of ricochets. "Didn't expect them to attack so soon," David panted.

We heard the wood splinter as they broke down the gate. They were inside the walls then, vague shadows in the starlight, and we fired down on them from the embrasures. The shouts, the screams, the din of firing . . . it went on for about ten minutes, and then suddenly they were gone and the inside of the fort was empty save for half a dozen robed figures lying still or dragging themselves laboriously towards the shelter of the walls.

From the top of those walls our attackers kept up a steady fire. Bullets whistled in through the entrance hole so often that the slap of lead on the opposite wall became a commonplace. They caused us no inconvenience, for they struck one particular spot only, and the convex curve of the wall prevented them from ricocheting. We kept a watch at one of the embrasures, but did not bother to return their fire. "Let them waste their ammunition," David said. "Our turn will come when the moon rises."

Once they misinterpreted our silence and left their positions along the outer walls. We waited until they were in the open, and as they hesitated, considering how to reach the entrance hole, we caught them in a withering fire. Our eyes, accustomed to the darkness of the tower's interior, picked them out with ease in the starlight. Very few got back to the safety of the walls or out through the gateway. And when the moon rose about an hour later we climbed the ladder to the very top of the tower, and from there we were able to pick them off as they lay exposed along the tops of the walls.

Below us Hadd lay white and clearly visible. There was great activity round all the wells. David fired one shot. That was all. The people scattered, activity ceased, and in an instant the whole town appeared deserted again.

We took it in turns to sleep then, but there was no futher attack, and sunrise found us in command of the whole area of the fort. With no cover from which they could command our position, the Hadd forces had retired. We took the guns and ammunition from the dead and dragged the bodies outside the walls. Nobody fired on us. The hilltop was ours, and the sun beat down and the rock walls became too hot to touch. We buried Ali and retired to the shade of the tower. The camel that was to have carried me to Buraimi had disappeared. There was nothing for me to do but resign myself to the inevitable.

"How long do you think you can hold out here?" I asked.

"Until our water's gone," David answered. "Or until we run out of ammunition."

"And Hadd?" I asked. "How desperate will they become?"

He shrugged. "There's a well in the Emir's palace, and they can always evacute the town and camp out in the date-gardens. There's plenty of water there. It's more a question of the Emir's pride. He can't afford to sit on his arse and do nothing."

And each night we'd be a little wearier, the hours of vigilance more deadly. I closed my eyes. The heat was suffocating, the floor on which we lay as hard as iron. Sleep was impossible. The flies crawled over my face, and my eyeballs felt gritty against the closed lids. The hours dragged slowly by. We'd nothing to do but lie there and keep watch in turns.

Shortly after midday a cloud of dust moved in from the desert—men on camels riding towards Hadd from the south. It was Sheikh Abdullah's main force. They halted well beyond the range of our rifles, and the smoke of their cooking-fires plumed up into the still air. There were more than a hundred of them, and at dusk they broke up into small groups and moved off to encircle our hill. They seemed well organized and under a central command.

It was that and the fact that they were mounted on camels that decided me. I went to where David was standing by one of the embrasures. "I'm going to try and get out tonight," I told him. "Whilst it's dark, I'll get out on to the hillside and lie up and wait for a chance to take one of their camels." And I added: "Why don't you do the same? A quick sortie. It's better than dying here like a rat in a trap."

"No." The word came sharp and hard and violent. His eyes burned in their shadowed sockets, staring at me angrily as though I'd tried to tempt him. "To be caught running away—that isn't what I want. And they'd give me a cruel death. This way . . ." Again I was conscious of that sense of mission blazing in his eyes. "This way I'll write a page of desert history that old men will tell their sons, and I'll teach the people of Hadd a lesson they'll never forget." And then in a quieter, less dramatic voice: "Think you can make it on your own?"

"I don't know," I said. "But it's dark and there's bound to be a certain amount of chaos when they put in their attack."

He nodded. "Okay, it's worth trying. But they're Bedou. They've eyes like cats, and they know the desert. And, remember, the moon rises in four hours' time. If you're not away by then . . ." He left it at that and stood for a moment, watching me, as I gathered together the few things I needed—a canvas bandolier of ammunition, my rifle, the water-bottle, a twist of rag containing a few dates and some pieces of dried meat. My matches and my last packet of cigarettes I left with him and also something I'd become very attached to—a little silver medallion of St. Christopher given me by a mission boy in Tanganyika after I'd saved his life. "You're travelling a longer road than I am," I said.

Ten minutes later I was saying goodbye to him by the splintered timbers of the main gate. When I told him I'd get help to him somehow, he laughed. It was a quiet, carefree, strangely assured sound. "Don't worry about me. Think about yourself." He gripped my hand. "Good luck, sir! And thank you. You've been a very big factor in my life—a man I could always trust." For a moment I saw his eyes, pale in the starlight, and bright now with the nervous tension that comes before a battle. And then with a quick last pressure of the hand, a muttered "God be with you," he pushed me gently out on to the camel track.

Behind me the timbers creaked as he closed the gate. I heard the two palm trunks with which we'd shored it up from the inside thud into position.

I started down the track then, and in an instant the walls had vanished, merged with the dark shapes of the surrounding rocks. Black night engulfed me, and I left the track, feeling my way down the slope, my feet stumbling amongst loose scree and broken rocks.

High overhead a thin film of cirrus cloud hid the stars. It was this that saved me, for I was lying out in the open not two hundred paces from them as they climbed to take up their positions on the north side of the fort. I kept my face down and my body glued tight to the rock against which I lay. My rifle, clutched ready in my hand, was covered by my cloak so that no gleam of metal showed, and the two grenades David had given me dug into my groin as I waited, tense and expectant, for the moment of discovery.

And then they were past and the scuff of their sandalled feet faded on the slope above me.

I lifted my head then, but all I could see was the dark hillside in my immediate vicinity. No sign of the men who had passed, no shadows moving on the edge of the darkness. I slid to my feet, found the track, and went quickly down the hill. And at the bottom I walked straight into a camel. I don't know which of us was the more surprised. It had been left to graze, and it stood with a tuft of withered herb hanging from its rubbery lips, staring at me in astonishment.

There were other camels; they seemed to be all round me, humped shapes in the dark, champing and belching. I seized the head-rope of the one facing me, forced it down, and, stepping on to its neck the way the Arabs did, I found myself sprawled across its back as it started into motion with a bellow of fear and rage. There was a guttural Arab cry. A shot rang out, the bullet whining close over my head. But the only thing I cared about at that moment was whether I could hang on, for the brute had gone straight into a gallop.

If it hadn't still been saddled I should undoubtedly have come off, but the saddle gave me something to hold on to, and after a while the crazy motion slowed and I was able to get my feet astride and, by means of the head-rope, obtain some control. And when I had finally brought the animal to a halt, there was no sound of pursuit. There was no sound of any sort. That wild, swaying gallop seemed to have carried me right out into a void.

And then, behind me, the sound of shots, carrying clear and hard on the still night air. The rip and blatter of a machine-gun. Twisting round in my saddle, I saw the fire-fly flicker of the attackers' guns high up on the black bulk of Jebel al-Akhbar. Distant shouts and cries came to me faintly. More firing, and the sharper crack of small explosions. Three of them. Grenades, by the sound of it. The cries faded, the fire slackened. Suddenly there was no longer any sound and I was alone again, riding across an endless dark plain, haunted by the thought of David, wondering what had happened.

The silence and the sense of space were overwhelming now, particularly when the curtain of cirrus moved away and the stars were uncovered. Then I could see the desert stretching away from me in every direction and I felt as lost as any solitary mariner floating alone in an empty sea. Far behind me the Jebel al-Akhbar lifted its dark shape above the desert's rim, for all the world like an island, and all around me were small petrified waves, an undulating dunescape that seemed to disappear into infinity.

In the darkness, without any stars to guide me, I had

trusted to luck and let the camel have its head. Now I saw it had carried me westward—towards the big dunes of the Empty Quarter and Whitaker's lonely camp. I kept going, not changing my direction. It was a dangerous decision. I knew that. I'd only the one bottle of water and there were no wells where I was heading, no caravan routes to guide me, nothing but empty desert. My decision was based on the fact that Whitaker's camp was much nearer than Buraimi—and, after all, he was the boy's father.

I had two chances, that was all—our own camel tracks and the tracks of Whitaker's trucks. If I missed both of these, or if they had become obliterated by wind-blown sand, then I knew I'd never get out of the desert alive. I rode through the night without a stop, guiding myself as best I could by the stars, and when the dawn came I turned so that the rising sun was behind my right shoulder. If my navigation was right, then I had placed myself to the south of the line between Jebel al-Akhbar and Whitaker's camp. Some time during the morning my new course should intersect the tracks made by our camels three nights back.

It was the first time I had ridden in the desert alone. The solitude was immense, the emptiness overpowering. The heat, too—it came at me in waves, so that time had no meaning. It seared my eyes and beat against the membranes of my brain. I drank sparingly from the water-bottle, rinsing the tepid liquid round my mouth. A wind sprang up and small grains of sand were lifted from the gravel floor and flung in my face, a fine-ground dust that clogged nose and throat and made the simple act of swallowing an agony without any saliva. To look the desert in the face, searching for our old tracks, was like pricking needles into my eyes.

By midday I'd finished the water and still no sign of our tracks. I was trembling then, but not with the heat. I had reached the sands, and the dunes were growing bigger, like an ocean's swell building up against the continental shelf. Dune followed dune, and the sense of space, the feeling that this petrified world of sand went on and on without end, appalled me.

A dirty scum formed in my mouth as I rode, and my tongue became a swollen, leathery mass. The camel's pace was slow and reluctant. We had passed no vegetation, no sign of anything growing, and as the sun slanted to the west fear took hold of me, for I knew I was headed into a desert that was four hundred miles across. Memory plagued me with the vision of a stream I knew in the Black Mountains of Wales where the water ran over rocks brown with peat and fell tinkling to a cool, translucent pool. The sun sank into a purple haze, and the sense of space, with the dark, shadowed dune crests stretched out in endless ridges ahead of me, was more terrifying than the close confinement that produces claustrophobia.

And then a chance turn of the head, a sudden glance, and there it was: a diagonal line ruled faintly across the back of a dune away to my left. I stared at it through slitted, grit-swollen eyes, afraid I was imagining it. But it was real enough—a single, scuffed-up thread scored by the feet of camels and half obliterated by sand. In the hard gravel at the foot of the dune I counted the tracks of six camels. I had actually crossed the line of our three-day-old march without knowing it. If the sun had been higher I should never have seen that faint shadow-line. I should have ridden on to certain death. I realized then why David had insisted on my making for Buraimi. I had been very fortunate indeed.

I headed into the sunset then, following the tracks, knowing they would lead me to Whitaker's camp. The camel seemed to know it, too, for its pace quickened.

The sun set and darkness came. I camped at the foot of a dune, not daring to go on for fear of losing the faint, inter-mittent line of those tracks. The desert lost its warmth immediately. I ate a few dates, but my mouth was too dry and sore to chew on the meat. Tired though I was, I couldn't sleep. The moon rose just before the dawn, and I went on. The tracks became more difficult to follow; at times I lost them and had to cast about until I came upon them again. A wind was blowing and the sifting sand was covering them moment by moment. The sun rose and it was suddenly very hot.

Long before I reached Whitaker's camp, the sound of the drilling-rig was borne to me on the wind. The steady hum of machinery was utterly incongruous in that empty, desolate world. One of his Bedouin guards brought me into the camp, and as I slid exhausted from my camel, I saw Whitaker himself coming towards me from the rig.

I must have passed out then, for the next I knew I was lying in his tent and he was bending over me, holding a mug of water to my cracked lips. The water was warm, but its wetness cleaned my mouth, eased the swollen dryness of my tongue, and as I began to swallow, I suddenly wanted to go on drinking and drinking, for my body was all dried up. But he took the mug away. "Are you alone?" he asked. And when I nodded, he said: "What happened? Is he dead?"

I sat up, staring at him. Something in the way he'd said it . . . But his face was in shadow and I thought I must have imagined it. "He was alive when I left him."

"I see. So he's still up there." And he added: "He'd made his gesture. He'd carried out a successful attack on the wells. Why couldn't he leave it at that?"

I started to explain about David's determination to keep the wells from being repaired, but he cut me short. "I know all about that. I got the news from Hadd yesterday. My chap said the streets of Hadd were deserted and no man dared venture out of his house for fear of being fired at. He also said that the inhabitants had made a daylight attack on the fort and had been driven off by heavy fire."

"There were just the four of us," I said. And I told him how Salim had been killed at the outset and Ali fatally wounded.

"And he's alone up there now with just Hamid and his brother, bin Suleiman?" He was silent for a moment, and then he said: "I gather the Emir sent to Saraifa for Sheikh Abdullah. Had his forces arrived before you left?" And when I nodded, he said: "What happened? Were you there when they attacked the fort?"

"No." And I explained how I'd got out just before the attack started. "I don't know what happened. But if David did manage to beat off that attack, there'll be others, or else they'll just snipe at him from the rocks until they've worn him down or his water runs out."

"So he's got himself trapped." And then almost irritably: "What's wrong with the boy? Does he want to die?"

"He will," I said angrily, "if you don't get help to him somehow."

"I've done what I can. Yousif was just back from Sharjah and I sent him straight off with letters to Colonel George, who commands the Trucial Oman Scouts, and to Gorde. It's up to the authorities now. Fortunately, I don't think the Emir has any idea yet who it is holding that fort."

It was something at least that he'd notified the authorities, and I lay back, exhausted. He gave me some more water and then left me, saying he'd arrange for some food to be brought. When it came, it was a half-cold dish of rice and camel meat. I ate it slowly, feeling my strength beginning to return, and then I slept. I hadn't intended to sleep, but the food and the heat in the tent . . . I couldn't keep my eyes open.

I woke to the sound of voices speaking in English. It was almost three in the afternoon. The camp was strangely quiet. The drilling-rig had stopped. I peered out of the tent. An Army officer in khaki shirt and shorts and a peaked cap was standing talking to Whitaker. There was an RAF officer there, too, and resting on the gravel beside the silent rig was a helicopter.

Whitaker saw me as I came out of the tent and called me over. "This is Colonel George of the TOS."

He was a short, thick-set man, bouncing with energy, of a type that a Frenchman in Zanzibar had once described to

me as a typical officer of the *bled*. Small, protruding eyes
stared at me curiously from beneath the peaked cap. "I was
in Buraimi when I got Whitaker's message. The RAF had
loaned me a helicopter, so I thought I'd fly down and see
what it was all about." His words were sharp and crisp.
"Understand young Whitaker's alive and that he's playing
merry hell with our aggressive little Emir. Correct?"

I didn't answer, for I was staring past him to a strange
figure walking towards us from the rig—a short, fat figure
in a powder-blue tropical suit that was now crumpled and
dirty and sweat-stained. "Ruffini!" I called.

He came almost running. "Mister Grant!" He seized my
hand. I think he would have liked to embrace me, he
seemed so pathetically glad to see somebody he knew. " 'Ow
are you? I 'ave been so concerned for you. When you don't
return with Gorde, I am asking questions, making a dam'
nuisance of myself, and nobody tell me nothing."

"What are you doing here?" I asked.

"What is a newspaper man ever doing? Looking for a
story. I go to Buraimi, by invitation of the sheikh and an
Italian oil man who is there also. Then this gentleman is
sent by the British authorities to remove me. They don't
wish for Ruffini to be in Buraimi or anywhere else in the
desert. So I am under arrest."

"No question of arrest," Colonel George snapped. "I've
explained to you . . ."

But Ruffini wasn't listening. "I tell you once before,
signore," he said to me, still holding on to my hand, "I
think you are sitting on the story I want. Now I talk to
some of the Bedouin 'ere and I know it is true. What is this
boy doing? They say you are with 'im in that fort, that you
come from Hadd this morning."

I could have wished it had been a British journalist. But
that wasn't so important as the fact that chance had put me
in touch with the outside world. Ruffini might be prevented from filing his copy immediately, but the knowledge

that sooner or later David's story would become known might stir the authorities to action.

But when I suggested this to Colonel George, he shook his head. "I don't think you quite understand the official view." We were back in the tent then and I'd been talking and answering questions for more than an hour. The TOS, he said, had been reinforced with Regular Army units some time back and had been standing by for more than a month, ready to move at short notice. The attack on Saraifa and the battle at the Mahdah *falaj* were just the sort of trouble their Intelligence had expected, and as soon as he'd received the news he'd given the order to prepare to move. "It was two nights ago. We'd everything lined up, the convoy spread out round the perimeter of Sharjah airfield and everybody ready to go. And then the Foreign Office clamped down, the Political Resident called the whole thing off."

"But why?" I asked.

"Why? Because of Cairo, Saudi, the Americans, the United Nations, world opinion." Cairo Radio, he said, had first referred to the Hadd-Saraifa border dispute two weeks back. There were reports from Riyadh that Saudi intended to raise the matter at the next meeting of the UN.

The Political Resident came under the Foreign Office, and to the Foreign Office this wasn't just a local problem, but a small facet in the pattern of world diplomacy. Until that moment I had seen the attack upon Saraifa as it appeared to David, a personal matter; now I was being forced to stand back mentally and look at the situation as a whole, from the viewpoint of authority.

"Twenty-four hours," Colonel George said. "That's all we needed. In twenty-four hours we could have put paid to the Emir's little game and saved a hell of a lot of lives. I know we've no treaty obligation so far as Saraifa is concerned, but it lies within the British sphere of influence and we've certainly a moral obligation to protect them against this sort of thing." He shrugged. "Well, there it is. I'm just a soldier, not a politician." He glanced at his watch and then at the RAF Pilot Officer. "Time we were moving, eh?" Outside the tent, he turned to Whitaker. "That boy of yours. He's going to get himself killed if somebody doesn't do something." The protruding eyeballs stared. "You've been out here a long time, Colonel. Couldn't you see the Emir? Talk to your son? You must have considerable influence still."

"A little. But not with my son, it seems." Whitaker was clearly disconcerted. "He's acting contrary to my advice—contrary to my express orders, in fact." He hesitated. "Of course, if the Political Resident authorized me to negotiate a settlement of the Hadd-Saraifa border dispute, I have some influence with the Emir. But," he added, "a just settlement for Saraifa would almost certainly require the backing of British military forces."

"That's out of the question at the moment."

"Then . . ." Whitaker gave an awkward little shrug.

Colonel George grunted, a small, peremptory sound. "Pity! That boy's got a lot of guts and he's going to die." He started towards the helicopter, but then he stopped and faced Whitaker again. "I've heard stories about you. . . . And if half of what I've heard is true, your son's doing just the sort of thing you'd have done yourself in your younger days, eh?" He paused, and then in a harder voice: "I'll tell you something, Whitaker: if that boy holds out for a week, he'll go down in desert history, his name remembered long after yours is forgotten." He stared at him hard for a moment and then marched off across the gravel towards the helicopter. "Sorry I can't give you a lift out, Grant. No room. We've got to deliver this damned journalist to Sharjah. But I've got one of my company commanders with a wireless truck up at Buraimi. I propose to send him down to patrol Hadd's northern border and keep tabs on the situation. I'll tell him to pick you up, if you like. Name's Berry. Sound chap. Understands the Bedou. That do you?"

I nodded, and behind me Whitaker said: "You might tell him to keep an eye out for my two vehicles. My fuel tanker and the supply truck should have been in two days ago."

The rotor blade of the helicopter began to turn. Ruffini gripped my hand. *"A rivederla.* I see the story of this David Whitaker reaches London. Don't worry. We 'ave an arrangement with one of your newspapers." He was sweating already as he ducked into the oven heat of the fuselage.

Colonel George paused in the open door. "Want to give me a message for his sister? I could send it straight down to the hospital. She'd get it this evening."

I hesitated. "Just tell her he's alive. That's all she needs to know at the moment."

"I should have thought something more personal was called for." He stared at me, playfully tapping my arm. "Probably you don't realize it, but she's been raising hell on your account. As soon as she knew you were missing, she came straight down to Sharjah. She caught that oil chap, Gorde, just as he was boarding his plane, and the story is she tore him off such a strip for abandoning you that he dropped his stick and took off without it. Since then she's been badgering the life out of me. I'll be damn glad to be able to tell her you're safe. Well?" He cocked his eyebrow at me and grinned. "I'll give her your love—will that do?" And without waiting for a reply he got into the helicopter and slammed the door.

Whitaker and I watched it take off, a mechanical dragon-fly whirring in the clean, bright air. I turned then, conscious of the quickened beat of my pulse, the sudden desire to be alone. It was strangely heart-warming to know that somebody had been concerned about whether I got back safely or not. I walked to the steep, shadowed edge of the dunes and lay there, longing for a cigarette. The drill, so useless now without its fuel, stood like a toy, dwarfed by the dunes, the Arab crew lying about, listless with nothing to do. Whitaker had gone to his tent. The shadows length-

ened and I wondered what was happening on that hilltop
forty miles to the east. Was David still alive?

The answer came next day, just after Whitaker's two
trucks had pulled in and the noise of their arrival had
wakened me from the first long, uninterrupted sleep I had
enjoyed in well over a week. Everything was confusion,
stores being unloaded, the rig started up, when a bullet-
scarred Land Rover appeared, flying the Emir's green flag.
Out of it stepped a big, portly man with very black features
under a large turban. "The Emir's secretary," Whitaker
said and went forward to greet him. A bodyguard of four
askari sat silent in the back of the vehicle—wild-eyed men
with greasy locks hanging to their shoulders, who fingered
their weapons nervously.

Whitaker took the secretary to his tent and they remained there over an hour, talking over tinned fruit and
coffee. Finally the man left, but before getting into the
Land Rover, he made a long, angry speech, a harangue that
was clearly intended for the whole camp.

"What did he want?" I asked as the dust of his departure
finally settled and the men returned to their jobs.

"If I don't go at once to Hadd and get David out of that
fort, the Emir will hold me responsible." Whitaker's face
was very pale, his whole body trembling. *"Allah akhbar!"*
he muttered. "Why did the idiot have to choose this moment, when I'd talked the Emir into agreement and had obtained the financial backing I needed? Why now?"

"He's still alive, then?"

He turned his eye on me, a fixed, glassy look. "Yes," he
said. "He's alive. The night you left him, he beat back the
attack, captured a prisoner, and sent him to the Emir next
day with a message. It announced who he was and the
terms on which he'd vacate the fort and leave them free to
repair the wells." The terms required the Emir to declare
publicly that he accepted the present borders between
Hadd and Saraifa for all time, and this declaration was to
be supported by a signed document to the same effect,

lodged with the United Nations. David also demanded an escort of the Trucial Oman Scouts to see him and his men safely out of Hadd territory."

But it wasn't the terms that upset Whitaker. It was the fact that David had disclosed his identity. "Did he have to involve me?" he demanded angrily, staring towards the rig.

"I don't suppose he meant to involve you," I said. "You're involved by the simple fact that you're his father."

"His father!" He turned on me. "I took a servant girl," he said harshly. "A moment in time, a passing need—but that was all. It ended there, and I made provision for her."

"You can't buy immunity from your actions."

He ignored that. "Twenty years, and the moment catches up with me and I'm faced with the brat; a raw, undisciplined boy with a vicious background." He glared at me. "And you sent him out here."

"He'd have come in any case," I said, "once he knew you were his father." I was angry myself then. "I don't think you realize what a shock it was to him to learn that he was illegitimate—to discover that his mother had been deserted in childbirth."

"She'd no claim on me," he said quickly. "And even if she had, it doesn't justify his coming out here with some idea at the back of his mind that he was going to kill me. Did you know about that? I had it all out of him shortly after he arrived—that and his criminal background and how he was wanted by the police for causing the death of that man Thomas." And he added: "I should have sent him packing. I should have realized the boy was bent on destroying me, on ruining all my plans."

"You know that's not true," I said.

"Then why did he pretend he was dead when he wasn't? And now, when the truth of my theory is within my grasp, when the thing I've been searching for all my life is here, he gets me involved in this stupid, useless demonstration of his." He was sweating, and there were little flecks of white at the corners of his mouth.

"What he's doing," I said, "he's doing because he's accepted the things you believed in; he made your world his own, Saraifa his home. And the background you complain of is the reason he's doing it so successfully. He's got the Emir to withdraw his forces from Saraifa. Now is the time, surely, when your influence—"

"My influence? What influence do you think I have now? Men have been killed, and that's something only blood can wipe out." And he added, staring into the distance: "If I'd gone with the Emir's secretary, I'd have been held hostage for David's submission—his life or mine. And when next the Emir sends an emissary, he'll come in force. That was made very plain."

He put his hand up to his head, covering his eye as though to shut out the desert and concentrate on what was in his mind. "It's madness," he breathed. "Madness. He can't achieve anything. . . ."

"How do you know?" I demanded angrily. "Ruffini has the whole story now, and—"

"That Italian?" He let his hand fall, staring at me in surprise. "How can he affect the situation? The authorities aren't going to take any notice of him." He said it as though to convince himself, and then in a voice so hoarse it seemed to be torn out of him: "He'll die up there, and that'll be the end of it." The look on his face was quite frightening. He turned and walked slowly to his tent. I didn't see him again that evening, and the next day his manner was still very strange. We hardly exchanged a word, and I was glad when Captain Berry arrived.

Looking back on it, I suppose I should have tried to understand his predicament. He hadn't enough men to get David out by force and he was probably right in saying the situation had gone beyond the reach of his influence with the Emir. What I didn't realize was that I was seeing a man in the grip of events, forced to a reassessment of his whole life and the values by which he had lived—and being driven half out of his mind in the process.

It was late afternoon when Berry got in. A lean, bony-looking Scot with fair hair and a face that was almost brick-red in the slanting sun, he brought a breath of sanity into that sultry camp, for he was from outside and not emotionally involved in what was happening forty miles to the east. He had a message for me from Colonel George picked up on his radio that morning. "I'm to tell you that your Italian friend got his story out in time and that you're not to worry. Everything possible is being done. The Colonel has been ordered to Bahrain to report to the Political Resident in person. Oh, and he said a Nurse Thomas sent you her love and is glad to know you're safe. Okay?"

I nodded, not trusting myself to speak. For the moment I could think of nothing but that message from Sue. Captain Berry was speaking to Whitaker, something about his son showing what one determined and resolute man could achieve. He was one of those soldiers that believe action is the solution to everything. "You must be very proud of him, sir."

Colonel Whitaker's face was without expression, but a nerve flickered along the line of his jaw, and he turned away.

Berry watched him for a moment, a puzzled look on his face. "That's a man I've always wanted to meet," he said. "But I'm surprised he left this to his son. After what's happened in Saraifa, I should have thought he'd have been busy raising the desert tribes. It would have solved our difficulty if he had. We might be allowed to support a desert rising against the Emir."

"I take it," I said, "you'll be leaving at once." It wasn't only that I wanted to know what had happened since I'd left Jebel-al-Akhbar. I wanted to get away from that camp.

But he told me it was out of the question. They'd been driving for over twenty hours. Both the wireless truck and the Land Rover had to be serviced, the men needed sleep. He had a wireless operator with him and five levies of the TOS under a corporal. "Leave at first light. Makes no difference, I'm afraid," he added, seeing my impatience. "I can't help Colonel Whitaker's son. Mine's only a watching brief. Anyway, it's no good bashing these dunes in the dark."

He'd brought spare kit for me, so that I had the luxury of a camp-bed that night. And in the morning I was able to discard my Arab clothes, which by then were very filthy, and put on clean khaki shirt and shorts. We breakfasted on bully-beef and tinned peaches, washed down with a brew of strong tea, and then we left.

Colonel Whitaker was there to see us go, and as he said goodbye to me he gave me instructions that were to have considerable significance later: "If anything happens to me, Grant, I leave you to look after my affairs. I think you know enough about me now to understand what I want done if they find oil here." We drove off then, and I remember thinking he looked a very lonely figure standing there with the clutter of the rig behind him. We went north, taking the shortest route across Hadd territory and driving fast. Keeping to the flat gravel stretches between the dunes, we were clear of Hadd's northern border by ten thirty. We turned east then, and the going became much slower, for we were crossing the lines of the dunes.

At set times we stopped to make radio contact with TOS HQ. The only news of any importance was that Colonel George, before he left for Bahrain, and therefore presumably acting on his own initiative, had ordered Berry's company south into the desert for exercises.

Shortly after midday the dunes began to get smaller, and in an area where it had rained quite recently we came upon the black tents of a Bedouin encampment, and there were camels browsing on untidy bushes of *abal*. Berry stopped and spoke with some of the men. "Well, your chap was alive yesterday," he said as we drove on. "I thought they were Al Bu Shamis, but they were of the Awamir and they came up past Jebel al-Akhbar yesterday. They say they heard intermittent firing. They also told me that the people of Saraifa are beginning to return to the oasis, that two *falajes* are running again and Khalid's half-brother, Mahommed, is calling men to arms."

It was the first indication I had that what David had done had not been done in vain.

Soon after that we became bogged down for several hours in an area of small dunes so confused that it looked like a petrified tidal race. As a result, we didn't sight Jebel al-Akhbar until late afternoon. We stopped at sunset. The hill looked deceptively close in the clear still air, the colour of the rock almost mauve, the sky behind quite green. "It's about six miles away," Berry said, handing me his glasses. I could see the fort quite distinctly then, the tower in silhouette against the fantastic sky. Nothing moved there. No sign of life.

I was tired after the long drive and I felt depressed. Darkness fell. We had our food, and after the meal Berry disappeared into the back of the truck. He wanted to hear the BBC news. It kept him in touch, he said; but what he meant was that it brought home nearer and made the desert seem less remote.

Nature's needs took me into the desert and when he called to me I didn't hear what it was he shouted, but only caught the excitement in his voice. Back at the truck I found him seated with the earphones pressed tight against his head. "It was in the summary," he said. And then after a while: "Your chap's made the headlines, apparently. A big story in one of the papers this morning." He removed the earphones and switched off. "They even got his name right and the name of the fort. . . . And the Foreign Secretary is to be asked a question about it in the House tonight." He rolled his long body over the tailboard and stood beside me. "Funny thing," he said, "if it had been a soldier up there on the Jebel al-Akhbar, they'd have taken it for granted, or more probably somebody would have raised hell because the fellow had disobeyed orders. But because he's a civilian . . ." He gave a quick, derisive laugh. "Not that it makes any difference. One newspaper story and a question in the House won't change my orders. We'll be left to sit here and watch him die. That is, if he isn't dead already."

We'd heard no sound since we'd gone into camp. The night was deathly still, not a breath of air. And Berry made it plain to me that he couldn't go any nearer. His orders were to stay in Trucial territory, and in front of us stretched the invisible barrier of the Hadd border. "You can be certain we're under observation. If I cross that border the political repercussions would be endless. As it is, my colonel's sticking his neck out sending me down here on his own authority."

We stayed up late to listen to the last news summary from home. The item we were waiting for came towards the end. *"Questioned in the House this evening about reports that a British civilian, David Whitaker, with two Arabs, was holding the fort of Jebel al-Akhbar in the Arabian Emirate of Hadd, the Foreign Secretary said that the newspaper report emanated from a foreign source and was almost certainly without foundation. He added that he was having enquiries made. . . . Cairo Radio this evening accused Britain of concentrating a large force on the Hadd border, including armoured cars and artillery. . . ."*

"Armoured cars and artillery!" Berry snapped the receiver off. "Why the hell do they repeat that sort of nonsense?" Like most soldiers who know what the situation is on the spot, he was contemptuous of the organs of publicity. "And you heard what the Foreign Secretary said. It's all going to be hushed up. Oil and politics—it's always the same out here in the Middle East. For the sake of peace and quiet a petty tyrant is going to be allowed to get away with murder." He jumped out of the truck and stood staring a moment towards the Jebel al-Akhbar. Finally he gave a little shrug. "Care for a drink? I've got a little Scotch left."

I shook my head. I was wondering whether any of the

other papers would take the story up, and, if so, whether they'd make enough of it to stir up public opinion. Only public opinion could force the Government to accept its responsibility for Saraifa and take action; and without that, David's sacrifice became pointless. "I think I'll turn in now," I said. "I'm still very tired."

I slept like the dead that night, and in the morning it wasn't the sun that woke me, but Berry shaking my arm. "Somebody's still in the fort. I heard shots just after dawn—very faint, but definitely rifle fire. I've reported it to HQ."

I scrambled up, sweaty from lying in my sleeping-bag in the blazing sun, but even through the glasses there was nothing to be seen: just the Jebel al-Akhbar shimmering in a heat haze.

Berry glanced at his watch. "You might like to listen to what the newspapers are saying back home."

We went into the back of the truck and switched on the radio. It was an overseas service of the BBC with a round-up of news and opinions from the national press. I don't know what I expected—what Berry expected. A few references, perhaps a leader. Instead, every newspaper had taken up the story. For almost ten minutes the thin voice of the announcer came to me through the earphones, speaking as though from another world, and giving variations on the theme of the story I had told Ruffini. David was headline news. One I particularly remember: BORSTAL BOY HOLDS FORT FOR FOREIGN OFFICE. And another popular paper was quoted as attacking the Foreign Secretary for trying to hoodwink the public.

But the press reaction seemed to have made no impression on the official attitude. The only indication of increased interest was that radio contact with TOS HQ was every hour now on the hour. Colonel George, we learned, was back in Sharjah. Ruffini was still there. Berry's company was in a position ten miles west of Buraimi and about a hundred miles to the north of us. The day dragged on.

The sun rose until the sky was a burnished bowl, a throbbing ache to the eyes, and the desert sand beneath our feet
as hot as the lid of a stove. Several times we heard the distant sound of shots, but though we took it in turns to keep
watch through the glasses, we saw no movement.

We dozed between watches, ate snacks out of tins, and
waited. Water was rationed and we became thirsty. Bore-
dom set in. We listened to the BBC, but David was no
longer in the news. Time was running out for him, and my
presence here seemed to serve no purpose. Those occasional, intermittent shots didn't tell me whether he was
alive or dead; they only indicated that the fort was still
held. Repeatedly I tried to persuade Berry to move forward
and recce under cover of darkness. But he was absolutely
adamant. "I cross that border with British military vehicles
and God knows where it would end."

By the end of the day we were beginning to get on each
other's nerves. The truth was that nothing would have
pleased Berry more than to be allowed to call up his company and go in and settle the whole business. In his quiet
Scots way he was so tensed-up over the situation that the
battle would have been a welcome relief. Instead of which
he was tied down within sight of the Emir's stronghold in
the company of a man who was becoming more and more
irritable at the delay.

It wasn't that I didn't understand his difficulty. If he
acted on his own initiative he might plunge the whole of
Arabia into war, involve his own country, and certainly
ruin his career. It was a diplomatic tight-rope that I
couldn't possibly expect him to walk. But understanding
his difficulty didn't help me to bear the inaction. To have
to sit there, doing nothing, whilst six miles away that boy
was dying by inches . . . The heat and frustration, they
nearly drove me mad.

I suppose it was the strain of the past fortnight. Berry
gave me salt tablets, a large whisky, and sent me to bed at
dusk. At midnight he woke me to say we'd be moving at

first light. "The Colonel's finally got Bahrain to agree to my making an attempt to get him out alive. I'm to try and arrange an audience with the Emir in the morning."

"And suppose he refuses to see you?" I asked.

"He won't. What's more, he'll accept my offer to mediate."

"You seem very confident."

"I am. I'm offering him a way out that'll save his face. If we do what the men of his bodyguard have failed to do and get young Whitaker out of the fort, then the Emir at least gets credit for being cunning. That's something to set against the laughter of the Bedou round their desert camp-fires. I take it you'd like to come with me?"

"Of course."

He hesitated. "I think I'd better make it clear that I could be wrong about the Emir. He hasn't a particularly savoury reputation, and if he did decide to turn nasty . . .' He gave a little shrug. "So long as you understand the position."

Six hours later we were on the move, motoring across the flat, stony plain with the Jebel al-Akhbar growing bigger every minute until it towered above us, a grey sugar-loaf mass against the rising sun. A Union Jack fluttered from the Land Rover's bonnet. There were just the two of us and Berry's driver, Ismail, a tall, dark-skinned man, very neat in his khaki uniform and coloured TOS head-cloth. No sound reached us above the noise of the engine. I could see no sign of movement on the hill above us.

We rounded the shoulder of Jebel al-Akhbar by a dusty track, and there suddenly was Hadd, yellow now in the sunshine, with the Emir's green flag hanging limp above the palace and the town silent and strangely empty, with the tower I had known so well perched above it on the lip of the limestone cliffs. We passed a camp of the Emir's men. Smoke spiralled blue from their cooking-fires in the still morning air, and they watched us curiously, wild, lank-haired men, their bodies strapped around with cartridges, their rifles slung across their shoulders. Several were wounded, the blood caked black on their bandages.

The well outside the town was as we had left it that night, the wall destroyed by the explosion and nothing done to repair it. We entered Hadd by the main gate. The streets were empty, the little square deserted. Balks of palm timber still lay where they had been thrown down in panic beside the damaged well. "Looks as though the population has moved out into the date-gardens," Berry said. "Three men, and they've stopped the life of this whole town dead. It's incredible."

But as we looked up, it wasn't quite so incredible. That tower hung right over the town. All the way to the gates of the palace we could see it perched there above us. The narrowness of the streets was no protection; it looked right down into them.

Berry's appreciation of the Emir's situation proved correct. After keeping us waiting for over an hour, he received us in a small room off one of the palace rooftops. There were armchairs in the Western style and a table on which stood an expensive German camera and some models of tanks and armoured cars. The walls were hung with finely silvered guns and pictures of the Emir driving through Hadd in a glossy American car.

The man himself was small and wiry, with a face that somehow managed to combine craftiness with great dignity; it was a long, rather cruel face, its length emphasized by the big nose and the little pointed beard glistening black with oil. His eyes were heavily made-up with *kohl*. Sheikh Abdullah was there, and several other notables, including the Emir's secretary, and though I couldn't follow what was said, I was conscious of the atmosphere, which was distinctly hostile.

The audience lasted a long time, with the Emir insisting at first that Berry storm the fort with his own troops, take David prisoner, and have him shot. When he refused, the

Emir launched into a harangue that was so violent that the spittle actually flew from his lips.

"I thought for a moment," Berry said afterwards, "that we were for it." Threatening us, however, didn't solve the Emir's problem, which was that he was being made to look a fool before his own people and all the desert world. After a long argument he finally agreed that if we were able to persuade the defenders to evacuate the fort they would be allowed to go unmolested.

We waited whilst Sheikh Abdullah gave one of his men orders to climb the slopes of Jebel al-Akhbar under a white flag and announce a cease-fire. Berry had guessed that there were snipers posted among the rocks below the fort walls, and he was taking no chances. "The extraordinary thing is," he said as we hurried out of the palace, "that they're convinced there are at least a dozen men up there in the fort."

We drove back through the silent town, out past the deserted wells and the askari encampment, and took the dusty track that led round the shoulder of the hill. We left the Land Rover at the foot of the camel track on the north side and started up on foot. The sun was high now and the heat throbbed back from the bare, scorched rock, beating up through the soles of our shoes. For a time the fort was lost behind ridges, but as we climbed higher the walls gradually came into view. There was no sign of Sheikh Abdullah's snipers, no movement on the hilltop. The air was very still, the silence and the heat appalling. It was just over five days since I had come down this very track in the dark. Five days—just over one hundred and thirty hours, to be exact, and under constant attack . . . It didn't seem possible that David or any of them could still be alive. And yet Hadd was deserted and the Emir had agreed to Berry's terms. We climbed fast, hoping for the best—fearing the worst. They must be out of water by now, wounded probably, perhaps only one of them left alive.

The timbers of the main gate sagged open, splintered by

the rocks that lay at the foot of the two crumbling bastions. As we climbed the last steep rise, the tower appeared, framed in the gateway, pale yellow in the sun, with the shadowed opening halfway up yawning like a mouth agape. No sign of life. No sound. I called out: "David! It's George Grant!" The rocks echoed back his name and nothing stirred. "David!"

And then, unbelievably, he answered—a hollow, croaking sound from the interior of the tower.

"I have Captain Berry of the Trucial Oman Scouts with me." My throat was parched, my voice hoarse. "The Emir offers you a safe-conduct." Even as I said it I wondered, the stillness and the heat beating at my nerves. Concealed amongst the rocks below us were men with rifles. How did we know they wouldn't open fire on us? The hairs at the back of my neck crawled; treachery seemed to hang in the hot air, and even as David told us to come in through the open gateway I knew we shouldn't have trusted the Emir. The open expanse of the fort's interior was a shambles. There were the remains of fires, the tattered remnants of camels' carcasses—those things I remembered. But now there were bodies of Arabs, too, lying where they had fallen, unburied and rotting, buzzing with flies. I counted nine of them; the place smelt of death, was littered with the debris of attacks beaten back. And the sun—the cauterizing, sterilizing sun—blazed down.

Something moved in the black mouth of the tower and the rickety ladder was thrust out of it. It fell the last few feet to the ground and David appeared, climbing stiffly and very slowly down it. At the bottom he paused as though to gather his strength together, and then he turned and faced us, standing very stiffly erect, a bloodstained strip of cloth round his right forearm and blood showing in a black patch below his left shoulder.

Berry took a tentative step forward. "We've just seen the Emir. If you leave with us now, he's agreed to allow you to cross the border into Trucial territory unmolested."

"And you believed him?" David started to move towards us, but then he stopped. He was swaying slightly, too weak to walk.

"He's ordered a cease-fire."

He nodded slowly. "That's true. I heard the order given. A man came up by the path from Hadd a little while back. He carried a white flag. But then he disappeared; went to earth amongst the rocks." His voice was thin and very weak. "I don't trust the bastards," he added, coming towards us very slowly.

Close to, he looked ghastly. His eyes had gone quite yellow, the skin of his face yellow, too, and all the flesh fined away so that the cheeks were sunken, the bones staring. His body seemed smaller, dried up and shrivelled. He looked about half his normal size, completely desiccated. The death's-head face, the yellow, burning eyes, the croaking voice . . . I thought he couldn't last much longer, and I pleaded with him to take this chance. But he was like a man in a trance. "Have the authorities decided to act? Will they support Saraifa?" And when we told him no, all he said was: "They will. They will. If I hold out long enough, they'll be forced to act." The eyes fastened on me. "Why didn't you go to Sharjah? Why come here? This isn't what I wanted." His voice sounded desperately tired, utterly dispirited. "Didn't you understand? I wanted the world to know. If people at home don't know what I'm trying to do . . ."

"The people at home do know," I said, and I told him about Ruffini and how the story had been taken up by the national press and a question asked in the House.

His eyes lit up, his whole bearing suddenly changed. "Wonderful!" he breathed. "Wonderful!" He was standing erect now, his head up, his voice much stronger. "Time," he said. "Time and a little luck. That's all I need now."

"Time is against you," Berry said. "This is your last chance to get out of here alive."

"Is it?" The dry, cracked lips produced a twisted smile.

"Do you really believe the Emir would let us get out of here alive—particularly when they see how few we are? He'd lose too much face. Anyway, I'm not going. I'll stay here till I die unless the Emir agrees to my terms or the authorities make some move to safeguard Saraifa."

"Surely to God you've done enough," I said, and I gave him the rumour we'd heard about the two *falajes* running again at Saraifa and the people returning to the oasis.

Berry, more practical, said: "How much water have you got left?"

"Not much. But it's cooler inside the tower. We're drinking very little."

"And your two men?" Berry asked. "Are they alive?"

"Yes, they're still alive. Hamid's very weak—a bullet through the shoulder and a splinter of rock from a ricochet in the back. Bin Suleiman's leg is smashed. But they'll both last as long as the water."

"So you won't leave with us?"

"No."

Berry nodded, accepting his decision as final. He seemed to understand David's attitude and he didn't attempt to reason with him. Instead, he unstrapped his web belt, slipping his water-bottle from it. "It's not much," he said, holding it out. "But one day could make the difference. I'll report your decision by radio to HQ as soon as I get back to my wireless truck."

David took the water-bottle, and though there couldn't possibly be any moisture left in that emaciated, dried-up hull of a body, his eyes glistened for a moment. "Thanks," he whispered. "I'll remember." His thin hands were gripped tight round the bottle. "One more day," he breathed. "You'll have that—I promise." He wasn't looking at Berry or at me. He was looking upwards, to the burning vault of the sky . . . a pact with God. And on this barren, burnt-rock hilltop where the air was heavy with the stink of rotting bodies, it would be an Old Testament God. "One more day," he whispered again in that croaking voice, and at that moment a rifle cracked.

The thud of the bullet, the scream of pain, the clatter of a gun barrel on rock—it was all on the instant, and I turned to see the body of an Arab writhing on the eastern wall. It reached the edge, paused, and then fell, and as it pitched, screaming, on its face, a second shot rang out.

The screams thinned to silence. The body on the ground arched, a series of violent jerks; something sounded in the throat and after that it lay still. I glanced at Berry. He hadn't moved. Nor had David. The click of metal on stone drew my eye to the top of the tower. The glint of a rifle, a thin wisp of smoke. Everything was still again; it was difficult to believe that in that instant a man had died.

"You see! That's all the treacherous bastard's safe-conduct is worth." David gave a dry little laugh. "You'd better get out of here whilst you still can."

Berry hesitated, and then he nodded. He reached into his pocket and produced some field dressings and a small first-aid kit. "Had an idea these might be required." He handed them over and then drew himself up and gave David a formal parade-ground salute. "Good luck!" he said, and turned quickly.

David looked at the first-aid tin and the dressings, his eyes quite blank, his face suddenly fallen-in, the flesh tight on the bones of the skull. I could only guess what he was thinking. A few more days and if he hadn't been killed by a bullet, he'd be dead of thirst. He looked up. "This is goodbye, sir." He held out his hand. "Tell my father, will you, that I hope it's a bloody good well . . . but if he lets the Emir get his hands on one penny of the royalties I'll haunt him to the grave and beyond."

His skin was dry, the bones of the hand like an old man's bones. I stared at him, not knowing what to say, for I was sure I wouldn't see him again. He was so damned young to die—and like this, in cold blood with his eyes open, trading life for the sake of a gesture. And yet, like Berry, I didn't try and argue with him. "Goodbye," I said, and turned quickly before my eyes betrayed me.

At the gateway I paused and looked back. He hadn't moved. He was still standing there, quite alone and swaying slightly, all his muscles slack with weariness. We stared at each other for a second and then I went out through the gateway, and I knew if the Emir attacked again that night, it would be the end. "What a waste!" I said to Berry, stumbling almost blindly down the track.

He looked at me. "I don't agree." His voice was hard and there was a ring to it, as though I'd struck a chord deep down. "If there weren't men like David Whitaker . . ." He shrugged. "It's a big question, isn't it? Why we're born; what we do with our lives." And he added after a pause: "I'd like to think, given his circumstances, that I'd behave the same way." He had loosened his pistol holster and his eyes searched the rocks as we hurried back down the track. But we saw nobody and the only sound was the heat throbbing at our temples. The Land Rover was still there with Ismail standing beside it. Treachery had gone back to its lair, and high up over the fort the black speck of some carrion bird planed on the still air.

Berry had seen it, too, and as we drove off he said: "I give him four days. In four days I reckon he'll be dead of thirst."

"He's weak," I said. "They've only got to make a determined attack now."

But Berry shook his head. "So long as there's one man left in that tower capable of firing a rifle or tossing a grenade they'll never take it, and Sheikh Abdullah knows it now. Only artillery or mortars could blast them out. I couldn't understand, even from your description, how three men could hold a fort against a hundred tribesmen, but now that I've seen the place . . ." He was staring back at it over his shoulder. "I am only surprised that a civilian should have appreciated the military possibilities of it."

"He was a gang leader in Cardiff docks before he came out to join his father in Saraifa," I said.

He laughed. "Well, I suppose that's as good a training as any." And after that we drove in silence.

When we got back to the wireless truck, Berry found a message ordering him to return to Sharjah immediately. "But why?" I said. "You're not on Hadd territory."

"They've got cold feet over the situation, by the sound of it. My company's been ordered back, too." He stood staring towards Jebel al-Akhbar and there was an obstinate look on his face. "I've given orders that we move at dawn and I've notified HQ that I'm held here the night with a damaged spring on the wireless truck. Twelve hours isn't much, but you never know. The situation could alter."

By this simple stratagem we were still there on the border when the slanting sun showed a cloud of dust moving across the desert from the direction of Hadd. Through the glasses we counted thirty-two camels, and the riders were all armed. Berry ordered his corporal to issue additional ammunition and personally sited both the Bren guns on a low ridge. But the raiding force kept to Hadd territory, heading due west towards the sands. "Their objective must be Whitaker's camp," Berry said. "There's nothing else out there." But he made no move to follow them. "Colonel Whitaker will have to look after himself."

I thought of the lone figure we'd left standing with the clutter of that drilling-rig behind him. This was what he had feared, the emissary returning in force. Whitaker would go with them this time. He'd have no alternative. I wondered what would happen when he met the Emir. Would he agree to go up to the fort? And if he did, how would David react?

But that was all in the future. I watched the dust cloud until it disappeared below the rim of the horizon, and then I fetched my briefcase and settled down to write a report. It was finished by the time the sun had set and darkness

was closing in. I gave it to Berry and he agreed to have his
wireless operator transmit it to Sharjah at the next contact
with HQ. The report was a long one, for it covered David's
situation, our visit to the fort, and the treacherous attempt
on his life, and I addressed it to Ruffini. We were both
civilians and I thought there was just a chance that it
might be passed across to him before any one in authority
stopped it.

"If he's still there," Berry said. The thing was sent now,
and we were sitting in the truck waiting for the BBC news.
More questions in the House, and the Opposition had attacked the Government for refusing to grant newspaper
correspondents visas for any Arabian territory except Bahrain. They were accused of trying to hush up an ugly
situation.

And then, in the morning, when we picked up the BBC
newspaper round-up, I was staggered to find that virtually
the whole national press had carried a story obviously
based on the report I had sent to Ruffini. Somehow he had
got it through uncensored, and the result was a fantastic
perversion of the facts, so colourful, so written up as to be
almost unrecognizable as the sad spectacle we had wit-
nessed; and yet it was all there, the heroic quality of
David's stand magnified a thousand-fold to give jaded
townspeople the best breakfast-table reading for weeks.
And the story had spread from the front pages right
through to the editorial columns, an angry, outraged demand for Government action.

And when the last editorial flag had been waved by the
BBC announcer and the last exhortation to the Government to act immediately had been read, Berry and I looked
at each other in astonishment. I think we were both of us
quite dazed by the violence of the reaction at home. It was
only twelve hours since Berry's wireless operator had laboriously tapped out in Morse my long report, and in that
short time David's situation had been put before the highest tribunal in the land—the British Public. Moreover,

something had obviously roused the press to anger—the
secretive attitude of Whitehall, presumably. As one paper
put it: *Up to a late hour last night, despite a barrage of
phone calls, nobody in authority appeared to be in a position to confirm or positively deny the story. The only comment was: "We regard the source as highly unreliable."
This is either stupendous arrogance, or stupendous ignorance. We suspect both, and we demand that the Foreign
Secretary take immediate action. The country is deeply disturbed.*

On the strength of that Berry cancelled his orders to
move, and within half an hour his action was confirmed.
Colonel George, acting on a hunch that political decisions
would now have to be reversed—and entirely on his own
initiative, I gathered later—had already turned Berry's
company round and ordered it to drive with all possible
speed to the Hadd border. "I'm to wait here until they
arrive," Berry said. "By then the Colonel hopes to be here
himself to take command."

"How long before they get here?" I asked.

"If they keep going without being stopped in the dunes
they'll arrive sometime after midnight, I imagine." He
started to go back to the wireless truck, but then he
stopped. "It might interest you to know that Signor Ruffini
was appointed Reuter's correspondent with the full knowledge of the Political Resident yesterday afternoon. But for
that very odd appointment, I imagine your report would
have been passed to Bahrain. In which case I've no doubt
it would now be rotting in some pigeonhole in the Resi-
dency instead of making the world's headlines."

The official attitude was obvious. By agreeing to Reuter's request—perhaps even instigating it—they could
justify their refusal to grant visas to correspondents by saying that the press already had coverage from an accredited
agency correspondent, and that the very man from whom
the story had originated. No doubt they took the view that,
as a foreigner, Ruffini would be more amenable to control

than a British correspondent and therefore unlikely to cause them further embarrassment. It was a little ironical that in their hurry to appoint him they had given me almost direct and immediate access to the whole of the British press.

"I am to tell you," Berry added with a thin smile, "that no further messages for Ruffini will be accepted through military channels. A matter of bolting the door after the horse has gone."

"What about that raiding party headed for Whitaker's camp?" I said. I hadn't mentioned it in my report to Ruffini the previous night. "Somebody ought to be told."

"Already done," he said. "It won't be passed on to Ruffini, but the PRPG will be notified and so will Sir Philip Gorde. He's in Sharjah now."

So that was that, and nothing to do now but wait. The day passed slowly. No sound from the direction of Jebel al-Akhbar. Not a single shot all day. The hill seemed suddenly dead. The heat was very bad. The wireless operator was on constant watch on the headquarters wave-band. We switched only once to the BBC news. A Foreign Office spokesman had stated that, whilst there was no official news, there was reason to believe that press reports were substantially correct and that a young Englishman had instigated some sort of guerrilla activity against the Emir of Hadd. The whole matter was under urgent review. There were rumours of reinforcements standing by in readiness to be flown to Bahrain, and two destroyers had left Aden, steaming north along the Arabian coast. Cairo Radio had stepped up its propaganda offensive.

Late in the afternoon I was wakened from a stifling sleep in the shadow of the W/T truck with the news that the Hadd raiding force was returning. "And there's been no sound from the fort at all." Berry passed me the glasses as I stood with slitted eyes gazing at a dust cloud right in the path of the sun. "Thirty-three of them now," he said. The dust made it difficult, but as they passed to the south of us and I could see them more clearly, I confirmed his count. "They must have been travelling all night and moving very fast." The figures flickered indistinctly in the heat. "The Emir will have picked up the Arab news," he added. "He'll know he hasn't much time. Had Whitaker a radio, do you know?"

"I don't think so."

"Then he probably doesn't know what's happening at home—that the Government's being forced to take action. Oh, well," he added. "If he goes up to the fort and his son's still alive, Colonel Whitaker will learn from him what we were able to tell him yesterday. It might make some difference."

I thought of that scene: father and son facing each other in the shambles of that fort. Watching the Emir's force move past us, men and camels all lifted bodily off the ground by a mirage and turned into strange, distorted shapes by the heat rising from that sea of sand, I felt once again the cruelty of this desert world. It was so hard, so empty, so casual of human life—a crucible to transmute the flesh to skin and bone, the mind to something as distorted as those shapes dancing in a mirage. I had a premonition of disaster then; but not, I think, of tragedy—certainly not a tragedy quite so grim.

I watched them until they disappeared beyond the shoulder of Jebel al-Akhbar, and shortly afterwards the sun set. One more night. But there was still no news, no certainty of action. "Better turn in and get some sleep," Berry suggested. "I haven't even got an ETA from the Colonel yet."

"Will we move in the morning, do you think? David can't last out much longer." And in the morning he might be faced with his father's desperate situation. "For God's sake! It's got to be tomorrow."

"You'd better pray, then," he snapped back irritably. "For only God and the Foreign Office know what action will be taken and when." And he added angrily: "I don't

even know whether the Colonel's order to my company has
been officially confirmed."

I took his advice then and went to my camp-bed. But
sleep was out of the question. The night was hot and very
still, the stars bright. Time dragged and I dozed, to be
jerked awake by the distant sound of engines. It was 0155
hours and Berry's company was motoring in, dark shapes
moving in convoy across the desert without lights. An officer reported all present and correct, but warned that the
only orders he'd received were to wait for the Colonel and
not to cross the border.

Orders whispered in the night, the dark trucks spewing
men out on to the sand; the area of our camp was suddenly
full of movement, an ant-heap settling to sleep, and a voice
at my elbow said: " 'Ullo, Mister Grant. Is Ruffini." His
pudgy hand gripped my arm, patted my shoulder; words
tumbled out of him. They had rushed him up to this company to get him out of the way. He'd been made fabulous
offers by several newspapers. "I am lucky, eh—lucky to be
a journalist and out 'ere at this minute?" But I think he
was a little scared. He was certainly lonely. His knowledge
of the Arabs was based on Mussolini's short-lived em-
pire.

A bare two hours' sleep and then the dawn breaking . . . Another day, and the ant-heap stirred and came
to life, little groups of men forming and re-forming, an
ever-changing pattern against the blistering yellow of sand
and gravel. And standing there on the rim of the desert to
the southeast, the Jebel al-Akhbar—black at first against
the rising sun, but soon dun-coloured and bare. No sound,
no movement to be seen through the glasses. And the desert all around us—that was empty and silent, too.

And then that solitary shot. We were sitting under a
canvas awning, rigged from the side of the headquarters
truck, and drinking tea. We all heard it, a sharp, faint
sound from the direction of Jebel al-Akhbar. But when we
looked through the glasses there was nothing to see, and

there was no further sound; just that one isolated shot. The time was 10.34.

We had no reason to regard it as any different from the other shots we had heard, though afterwards we realized the sound had been slighter. We settled down again and finished our tea, an island of men camped in a void, waiting whilst the sun climbed the brassy sky and the oven-lid of the day's heat clamped down on us, stifling all talk.

Only Ruffini was active, trotting sweating from one to the other of us, tirelessly questioning, endlessly scribbling, staring through creased-up eyes at the Jebel al-Akhbar, and then finally badgering Berry until he had given orders for his copy to be transmitted over the radio to Sharjah.

And then, just before midday, the dead stillness of the desert was torn apart by the buzz-saw sound of a helicopter. It came sidling in from the north, a strange aerial insect painted for desert war, and in the instant of its settling the whole camp was suddenly changed to a single organism full of purpose. With Ruffini I stood apart on the edge of this ordered turmoil and watched the man responsible for it, surrounded by his officers, standing with legs straddled, head thrown back—a man conscious of the dramatic quality of the moment.

Ruffini noticed it, too. "*Il Colonello*—'e is going to war."

But my attention had shifted from Colonel George. Coming towards me from the helicopter was the squat, battered figure of Philip Gorde. "Grant." He was leaning heavily on his stick as he faced me. "Where's Charles Whitaker? What's happened to him?" And when I told him what we feared, he said: "Christ Almighty, man, couldn't you do something?" But then he shrugged. "No, of course not. Bloody politicians!" he growled. "Always too late making up their minds. Hope we're in time, that's all." He was staring at me out of his bloodshot eyes. "I gather he'd moved his rig up to the border. He'd started to drill, had he?"

"Yes."

"I wish I'd known that earlier." He looked tired, his face liverish. "Not that I could have done anything to help him," he added heavily. "It's a hell of a situation. And that boy of his a bloody little hero. Doesn't he realize what he's doing to his father—or doesn't he care? God!" He was jabbing at the ground with his stick. "Well, we'll just have to hope we get there in time," he said again, and he stumped off to talk to Colonel George.

The cluster of officers was breaking up now; voices shouting orders, men running, the whir of starter motors, the roar of engines, a Land Rover disappearing in a cloud of dust.

"Ah, there you are, Grant." The Colonel, neat and dapper, cool almost in the torrid heat, came towards me. "The boy's still alive, I gather."

"There was a shot fired. . . ."

"So Berry tells me. We'll just have to hope for the best. I'm sending a small force up to take over the fort. The rest of the outfit will move direct on Hadd. Berry's gone ahead to make contact with the Emir. You and Ruffini can ride in the headquarters truck."

The column was lining up now, and ten minutes later we were on the move. "If 'e is still alive, it is a great story, eh?" Ruffini said. "You think 'e is still alive?"

"How the hell do I know?" But Berry had given him four days. I was pinning my hopes to that.

"Well, it don't matter—alive or dead, 'e is a hero. And this is the biggest story I am ever writing."

That was all Ruffini saw in it—a newspaper story, nothing more. And Gorde hating David because I hadn't had time to explain his motives. I felt suddenly sad, depressed by the thought that David's action would be misunderstood. How could you explain to men like Gorde what Khalid's death had meant to him, how he'd felt when he'd seen the people of Saraifa forced to leave the oasis?

Half an hour later the column halted. We were close under the Jebel al-Akhbar. Time passed and nothing happened. The wait seemed endless. And then suddenly the Colonel's Land Rover came roaring down the column. He had Gorde in the seat beside him. "Jump in," he called to me. "Ruffini, too. The Emir has agreed to meet me at the first well." He was in a mood of boyish elation, a reaction from nervous tension. The column was moving again now and several vehicles had swung away and were headed for the camel track on the north side of Jebel al-Akhbar.

We reached the head of the column just as it breasted the shoulder of the Jebel. There once more was Hadd, jammed against the limestone cliffs, with the Emir's palace flying the limp green flag and the fort stark against the sky above it. "Hell!" Colonel George signalled his driver to stop, and Berry's Land Rover drew up alongside. The column ground to a halt behind us. "I don't like it," the Colonel said. "Too quiet."

Between us and the crumbling walls of Hadd there wasn't a living soul: no sign of Sheikh Abdullah's askari, no vestige of the camp we'd seen two days before. Even up by the date-gardens nothing moved. All the Wadi Hadd al-Akhbar, as far as the eye could strain through the glare and the mirages, was empty of human life.

"The blighter's up to something. What do you think, Berry?"

"I think we'd better be prepared for trouble, sir. I told you I didn't like the speed with which he saw me, the crafty look in his eye."

The Colonel nodded. "Go ahead, then."

The orders were signalled and the column fanned out across the level gravel plain, whilst we drove straight to the first well. Behind us the Bedouin Scouts leapt from their trucks and spread out over the sand—mortars and machine-guns, ammunition. And not a shot fired at us. We sat in the Land Rover, roasting by the shattered parapet of the well, and the tension mounted with the uncanny silence. Nothing stirred anywhere.

A full hour the Emir kept us waiting there in the blazing

sun. He judged it nicely. A little longer and Colonel George's patience would have been exhausted. And then at last life stirred in the mud-dun town, a scattering of figures moving towards us across the flat, shelved expanse of gravel that lay between the well and the walls: old men and children—not an armed man amongst them. "He's going to play the injured innocent," Gorde whispered in my ear.

The old men and the children had closed around us. Some had empty drinking-bowls, others goats' skins; they whined and begged for water as they had been told to do.

"My heart bleeds." Gorde snorted with contempt. "Ah, here he comes."

Through the arched entrance to the town came a figure riding a white camel, riding absolutely alone—not a single retainer. "He's clever," the Colonel muttered. "There isn't a desert ruler who wouldn't have regarded this as an occasion to parade his full power. And to ride a camel when he's got an almost brand-new Cadillac . . ." His eyes were fixed with a puzzled frown on the solitary figure, on the slow, stately gait of that lone camel. He turned abruptly to Gorde. "What's he got up his sleeve? Something. That Cadillac was a present from Saudi. He'd surely want to flaunt that in our faces."

Gorde didn't say anything, and we sat and waited. The crowd fell back, the clamouring ceased. The Emir rode his camel through them, and, sitting there in the Land Rover, I realized suddenly why he hadn't used his Cadillac. With set face and without any gesture of greeting, he rode his beast right up to us, and when he finally halted it, the supercilious head was right over us, the rubbery lips white with foam, dripping saliva on the Colonel's beret. The Emir himself towered above us, godlike against the burning sky.

It was extraordinarily effective. The man was simply dressed in spotless robes and looked much bigger, the features more impressive, the curve of the nose more marked.

He waited in silence for Colonel George to greet him.

Instead the Colonel barked an order and his driver backed the Land Rover, turning it so that the bonnet faced the Emir. But it was no good. Patiently, without expression, the camel moved, resumed the same dominating position.

And then the Emir began to speak. It was an address that lasted almost a quarter of an hour. The manner of delivery was cold and restrained, but underlying the restraint was the hate that filled the man. It was there in the thin, vibrant tone of his voice, in the black gaze of his eyes, in every gesture—a bitter fury of hatred. And that bloody camel, slavering over my head, seemed the very embodiment of his master's mood.

Gorde whispered the gist of the Emir's speech to me. It followed a familiar pattern. It ignored entirely the unprovoked attack on Saraifa, the cruel intention behind the blocking of the *falajes,* the murderous slaughter of men driven to desperate action to save life and home. Instead, it dwelt at length on Hadd's territorial claims. These the Emir based on a particular period in Hadd's history, a period that went back more than five hundred years. He conveniently brushed aside all that had happened in the area since that time. He attacked the oil companies for sucking Arabia's life-blood. The spittle flew from his mouth as he called them "*Nasrani* thieves, jackals of the West, imperialist blood-suckers." He ignored the fact that without the companies the oil would have remained beneath the sands, that the wealth of Arabia depended on them, that the very arms he'd been given had been bought with the royalties they paid. And in attacking the oil companies, he also attacked Britain and America. Imperialist murderers! he called us.

"He's coming to the point now," Gorde muttered. The camel belched, a deep, rumbling sound that blew a fleck of froth from its lips into my lap. The Emir leaned forward, the dark, cruel face bending down towards us. *Murderers!* he screamed. I thought he was going to spit in our faces.

"Start the engine," Colonel George ordered the driver. "I'm not standing for any more of this." He said something to the Emir. The man smiled. That smile—it was curiously excited. *I call you murderers because you come here armed to protect a murderer.* He gestured with his hands, pointing towards the fort. And when Colonel George tried to explain David's motives, the rough justice of his action in depriving Hadd of water, the Emir silenced him. *You do not think it is murder when an Arab man is killed. What do you say if he is the murderer of a white man— one of yourselves?*

He turned, raising his body in the saddle, shouting and signalling with his hand. A closed Land Rover emerged from Hadd. The crowd, which had drawn in a tight circle round us, scattered before it, and as it roared past us a figure in Arab clothes was thrust out of the back of it, a limp rag of a figure, battered and covered in blood.

It hit the sand beside us, rolled over once, and then lay sprawled face upwards in an undignified heap; and as the cloud of dust settled, I saw what it was that lay there: the dead body of Colonel Whitaker.

He had been shot in the face, and his head was badly battered, his arms broken. His clothes were black with blood. Flies settled in a swarm, and I felt suddenly sick.

You know this man? the Emir demanded. And when Colonel George nodded, the Emir explained that *Haj* Whitaker had that morning agreed to go up to the fort and reason with his son. What had happened up there he did not say. He merely gestured to the body. *This man's son has murdered my people. You say it is not murder. Look now at that which lies before you and tell me—is that murder?*

Colonel George sat there, his eyes hard, his face set. He had no answer. "His own father!" His voice was shocked, and he made no attempt to challenge the Emir's version of what had happened.

"You can't be sure," I said.

It was Gorde who answered. "Do you think it would have occurred to him to have the body flung at our feet like that if Charles had been killed by one of his men?" He was staring down at the bloody figure lying in the dust, his hands clenched. Then he looked up at the Emir and demanded to know where the body had been found, and when the Emir replied that his men had picked it up at the foot of the cliffs directly below the tower, he nodded his head slowly. As far as he was concerned, that settled it.

It was very hot there in the sun, yet a cold shiver ran through me. I was remembering the solitary shot we'd heard that morning, and into my mind came Mrs. Thomas's words: *It was never Dafydd that was going to die.*

Colonel George was the first to recover. Ignoring the body, he dealt with the terms on which the fort would be evacuated and his forces withdrawn. And when the Emir finally agreed, he made the prearranged signal to his troops waiting on the Jebel al-Akhbar and withdrew his force into the desert, taking Whitaker's body with him.

Back at our old encampment we found the helicopter gone and one of the trucks belonging to the Jebel al-Akhbar detachment already returned. After interviewing the driver, Colonel George announced: "David Whitaker is apparently still alive. The helicopter's gone up to bring him out." He said it flatly, and behind me I heard Gorde murmur: "God help him! He'd have been better dead."

The helicopter took off from the fort, and when it landed they carried David to the shade of the headquarters-truck awning. When I saw him, I thought for a moment it was all over. His face was relaxed, the eyes closed; the flesh, tight-drawn, was bloodless. It was a death's head, all skull and bone, and the skin like parchment. But then the eyes flicked open and he saw me. The cracked lips smiled and he tried to say something, but no words came. He was too dried up to speak. The eyes closed again and he went into a coma.

The helicopter had also brought bin Suleiman out. He

was badly wounded and very weak, but he was alive. Only
Hamid was dead. They brought his body down and buried
it beside Colonel Whitaker's within sight of the Jebel al-
Akhbar. Gorde stood with bared head and hard, frozen
eyes as they laid his old friend to rest in his shallow desert
grave, and Ruffini was there, sitting on the ground, his
pencil moving steadily across the pages of the notebook
held against his knee.

The burial over, I went to talk to him. I wanted to
persuade him to soft-pedal the fatal news. I was thinking
of Sue rather than David. The boy was a hero and the
newspapers were avid for news. And now the world was
going to be told that he'd killed his father. I was probably
the only person who could justify it, who understood the
provocation. The public's reaction would be one of revulsion. Sue would be torn to bits, her life made hell. I
touched Ruffini on the shoulder. "About Colonel Whitaker," I said.

He paused, his face creased against the sun's glare as he
glanced up at me. "We talk about 'im later," he said.
And he added: "It is fantastic, the most fantastic story I
ever write. There is this boy David, who by 'imself has
forced the British Government to take action. And now
this man they 'ave just buried—'is father, who is a great
figure in the desert, a sort of . . ." He clicked his fingers,
searching for a name. "It doesn't matter. What matter is
that 'e is dead, killed by a stupid tyrant, a sort of Arabian
condottiere, in a lousy little mud town in the desert."

"You mean you think the Emir . . ." I checked, staring
down at him.

"And for what?" he demanded, his mind concentrated
on assembling the English phrases he wanted. " 'E kill him
to blacken 'is son's name, a ridiculous attempt to destroy
this heroic young man. It is a tragedy, a great tragedy. And
with the death of Colonel Whitaker, it is the end of an
epoch in the desert, the last great Englishman in Arabia. . . ." He bent his head, his pencil flying again.

I stared at him in astonishment. He'd been there. He'd understood what the Emir had said. And he didn't believe him. His story would accuse the Emir of Colonel Whitaker's murder, and because he was the only journalist here, the press would carry his version. I could only hope that the authorities would leave it at that.

Colonel George took that story with him when he left shortly afterwards in the helicopter. He also took David, and because of that Gorde was left to travel by Land Rover. I was standing beside him as the helicopter took off. He turned to me, and I can still remember the rasp in his voice as he said: "If that little bastard of Whitaker's lives, you'll have a lot to answer for."

"How do you mean?" My mouth felt suddenly dry.

"You sent him out here, knowing he'd killed a man, knowing he was a self-dramatizing little gangster. Fellows like that don't change, and patricide is something every society abominates. He's a hero now. But when the public learns the truth . . ." He stared at me, his eyes cold and hard. "Charles Whitaker was a man in a thousand, probably the greatest Englishman who ever made the desert his home. I've known him since I first came out to Arabia, and you can rest assured I'll see to it that the truth is known." He turned abruptly, without giving me a chance to say anything, and I watched him as he limped across to where Berry was organizing his convoy.

Colonel George had placed a Land Rover at Gorde's disposal and he left immediately, so that I had no opportunity to talk to him. And when I finally reached Sharjah, he was on his way back to England and it was already too late. David had been placed under arrest and an official statement had been issued to the press.

Part Three

The Court
Stands Adjourned

I

It was the third day

of the trial and David Whitaker had gone into the witness
box immediately after the lunchtime recess. Counsel for
the Defence had taken him through the salient points aris-
ing from my evidence, with the object of showing his relationship with his father in the best possible light. Now,
late in the afternoon, he had arrived at the crucial point—
Colonel Whitaker's visit to Fort Jebel al-Akhbar. The
packed Court was very still, every eye on the fair-haired
boy standing, neat and tidy, in the box, his arm in a sling
and the sun-burnt face looking almost black in contrast
with his light tropical suit.

"I would like the Court to have a clear picture of your
situation on that particular morning." Counsel glanced
down at his papers, his hands resting lightly on the desk
in front of him. "By then you had been on the Jebel al-
Akhbar seven days. Is that right?"

"Yes."

"And there were only two of you left. Salim, Ali, and
Hamid were dead; Grant had gone. There was just yourself and bin Suleiman, and you were both wounded."

"Yes."

"Had you been attacked during the night?"

"No, it was some days since they'd made any attempt to
take the fort."

"But you were under fire?"

"They'd got men lying out in the rocks all round the
fort, but we were all right as long as we remained in the
tower. They'd fire a few shots once in a while just to re-

mind us they were there, and at night they'd move up to
the walls. But they didn't bother us much. We were
pretty used to them by then, you see." Just the trace of a
Welsh accent to remind the Court that this was the same
boy who had run wild in Cardiff docks.

The reporters were scribbling furiously. This was the
big moment, and when the Court adjourned there would
be a rush for the telephone to catch the daily papers before
they went to press.

"On the morning in question, were there any shots fired
—other than the shot that killed your father?"

"No, none."

"Did that strike you as unusual?"

"I can't remember that I thought about it. It was some
time since any shots had been fired. They were lying quiet,
you see, hoping we'd think there was nobody there and
get careless. But we knew the bastards were there, waiting
for us."

"So you remained inside the tower?"

"Of course. I hadn't been out of the tower since
Mr. Grant came up to talk to me. There wasn't any
point. It was cooler there and the walls were good protection."

"Was there any other reason you didn't leave it?"

"I tell you, man, they were lying out there waiting for
us. I wasn't risking being shot at when there wasn't any
point."

"Quite so. But what I'm getting at is this: wasn't it a fact
that you were too weak by then to attempt a descent from
the tower?"

"Well, yes, I suppose so. Anyway, there wasn't any reason for us to be wasting what little strength we had left to
no purpose."

"Were you weak because of lack of water or lack of
food—or was it because you were wounded that you hadn't
the strength to leave the tower?"

"I tell you, there wasn't any point." His tone was irritable; he didn't seem to understand what his Counsel was trying to establish.

"When had you last had any food?"

"I can't remember. We'd some dried camel meat left, but it wasn't any use to us. We couldn't swallow it. We did try and chew it, but it was very painful, and in the end we didn't bother."

"You couldn't chew because of lack of water?"

"Yes. We'd no saliva and our tongues were swollen and quite black. Our mouths were absolutely dry."

"Had you any water left?"

"Captain Berry had given me a water-bottle. We'd finished our own supplies and now that bottle was half empty."

"Your situation, then, was quite desperate."

"Pretty desperate."

"I want the Court to be absolutely clear about this." Counsel paused, glancing from the Judge to the crowded press desks. "In your opinion, how much longer do you think you could have held out? In other words—" and here he spoke slowly and with great emphasis—"how long before you were dead of thirst?"

David shook his head. "I can't be certain. We'd have finished the water-bottle that day. If we'd been left alone we might have stayed alive a few days more."

"You heard the evidence of Dr. Logan, who saw you when you arrived at Sharjah. He said you were in such a weak condition that he didn't believe you could have lasted more than another twenty-four hours."

David's head went up. "That all depends on how urgently you want to stay alive, doesn't it? I'd have lasted longer than that. But not if they'd attacked us."

Counsel seized on this. "You say, not if they'd attacked you. Do you mean you were too weak by then to defend yourselves?"

"That's about it."

"Could you stand?"

"I don't know. I didn't try."

"Could you have lifted a rifle to your shoulder and fired it?"

"If they'd attacked us, I expect I'd have managed somehow."

"But you were so weak that it would have required the urgency of an attack to give you the strength to lift even a rifle to your shoulder?"

David hesitated. "I suppose so," he murmured. And then in a clearer voice: "It's difficult to explain to you people here. But everything was an effort by then. Everything," he repeated.

"Quite so. And if you couldn't lift a rifle to your shoulder except in a moment of great urgency, then you'd hardly have had the strength to descend from the tower by that ladder and then climb back up again and pull the ladder—"

"Objection!" Counsel for the Prosecution was on his feet, facing the Judge. "The Defence is putting words into the witness's mouth."

But Counsel for the Defence had made his point. "I will rephrase the question, then." And, turning to the witness box again, he asked: "Did you at any time on the morning in question, and before the Trucial Oman Scouts arrived to take over the fort, leave the tower for any purpose whatsoever?"

"No, sir."

"Did you at any time attempt to lower the ladder?"

"No."

The Court breathed an audible sigh.

"One more question before we come to the moment of the meeting with your father: Did you know that the Trucial Oman Scouts would move into the Emirate of Hadd that day? In other words, had you any reason to suppose that your ordeal was nearing its end?"

"None at all."

"We have the evidence of Mr. Grant that from their position six miles away beyond the Hadd border they could see the fort quite clearly through field glasses. Could you see them? In other words, could you see that over a dozen vehicles had materialized at that position during the night?"

"No."

"As far as you were concerned, nothing had altered that morning—your situation remained as desperate?"

"Yes."

"All you knew of what was going on in the world outside was what Mr. Grant had told you two days before."

"That's right."

Counsel paused, again consulting his papers. "Now we come to the moment of your father's arrival at the fort. You'd no reason to expect him?"

"How could I?"

"Quite so. I suppose you've no idea what time it was when he arrived?"

David shook his head. "My watch had stopped. I'd forgotten to wind it a few days back. All I know is the sun had been up some time."

"Had you any warning that you were going to receive a visitor?"

"There was some shouting—an order in Arabic not to fire. It was given by a man holding a white flag. The last time that had happened was when Mr. Grant came with Captain Berry."

"That was the occasion on which a treacherous attempt had been made on your life?" And when David nodded, Counsel added: "And on that occasion you had taken the precaution of sending bin Suleiman to the top of the tower, just in case. Did you take the same precaution this time?"

"No."

"Why not?"

"He was unconscious."

"And you hadn't the strength to climb up there yourself?"

"No."

"Would you tell the Court, please, what happened when your father arrived?"

"Well . . ." David hesitated, his eyes glancing quickly round the courtroom. Finally he turned towards the Judge. "I thought it was an Arab at first—one of the Emir's men. He came in by the main gate, and he was dressed in Arab clothes, you see. I didn't recognize him—my eyes weren't too good. But then he stopped just inside the gate and called me by name and said who he was."

"Were you surprised to see him?"

David shrugged. "He was there. That was all there was to it." And he added: "No, I don't think I was surprised. When you're in the state I was, you just don't register anything."

"What happened then?"

"Well, he came to the foot of the tower and we talked."

"What about?"

"I don't remember."

"He wanted you to abandon the fort, didn't he?"

"At first."

"He changed his mind then?"

"Yes."

"What made him change his mind?"

An obstinate look had come into David's face. "He just changed it, that's all."

"Was that after you'd told your father that your defence of the fort had made headline news back home?"

"I don't remember."

"You did tell him that, didn't you? You did pass on to him this information which you had obtained from Mr. Grant?"

"I don't know. I expect so."

"Was your father surprised?" And when David didn't

answer, Counsel went on: "What I want the Court to know is whether or not Colonel Whitaker knew about the newspaper stories of your exploits and the fact that there had been questions in the House. The evidence at the moment points to the fact that he couldn't have known before you told him. Would you agree?"

"I really can't say."

"But he must have made some comment, shown some reaction?"

"I tell you, I don't remember. I wasn't in a fit state to remember details."

"You were talking to him from one of the embrasures of the tower or from the entrance hole?"

"From the embrasure. I should have been an easier target if I'd dragged myself to the entrance hole, and I was afraid of getting sniped at."

"And the whole interview was carried on with you in that same position. You didn't move at all?"

"No."

"Where was Colonel Whitaker?"

"Standing right below me."

"Could you see him?"

"Yes."

"And when the interview ended—where did he go then?"

"I think he moved nearer the tower, away to my right. I can't be sure, but I lost sight of him."

"Towards the cliff-top?"

"Yes."

"And what happened then?"

"Well, a little time passed, and then . . . then there was this shot."

"A rifle shot or a pistol shot?"

"It was a rifle shot."

"You're certain of that?"

"Yes."

"And after the shot, was there any other sound?"

"Yes, a sound of falling stones. That's when I knew he'd gone over the cliff."

"What did you do then?"

"I dragged myself to the southern embrasure, but I couldn't see directly down the cliff face, so I didn't know what had happened. I tried to call out to him, but I don't think my voice made any real sound."

Counsel leaned forward, his voice pitched low. "You've heard a ballistics expert give it as his opinion that your father was killed by a bullet from a pistol, not a rifle."

"It was a rifle."

Counsel stared at him, and the whole Court could see the quandary he was in. But the evidence that had gone before had to be disposed of. "You have also heard Dr. Logan's evidence. He has said that post-mortem examination strongly suggests that the shot that killed your father was fired at close range. He, too, thinks it was a pistol shot."

"How do they know?" David said almost belligerently. "They didn't find the bullet, did they? And they weren't there. I was, and I'm telling you it was a rifle shot."

The Judge leaned forward. "I would like to get this quite clear. You have said that your condition was such that you cannot remember what passed between you. You have, in fact, left the Court with the impression that your powers of perception at that time were at a very low ebb. Yet on this point of the shot, you are quite categorical. You say it was a rifle shot?"

"Yes, sir."

"Had you a rifle in your hand?"

"No, sir. I didn't fire the shot. It was fired by one of those treacherous—"

But the Judge stopped him. "You will kindly confine yourself to answering the questions put to you. Am I to take it that you're absolutely clear in your mind that the fatal shot was fired from a rifle and not from a pistol?"

"Yes."

The murmur of a sigh filled the courtroom. They didn't

like it. The Judge sat back, nodding to Counsel to continue. I glanced at Sue. Her face was white. She, too, felt
the change of mood in the room. It was obvious that David
was withholding vital evidence about what had passed between his father and himself, and he'd been altogether too
determined to put the blame for his father's death on the
Emir's men. I heard the man next to me whisper to his
companion: "He hasn't a hope if he goes on like this."

Counsel stood for a moment staring down at his papers,
undecided whether to pursue the matter further. Finally
he lifted his head and faced the witness box again. "Suppose we consider for a moment that you were in no fit state
to be certain on this point and that it was, in fact, a pistol
shot that killed your father. Had you a pistol?"

David stared at him, sullen and white-faced. "You know
I had. That ballistic chap's already given evidence that he
examined it."

"Quite. A six-chambered revolver with two rounds still
left in the chambers. And you had some spare rounds loose
in a leather bag. Exactly how many rounds had you fired
with that weapon?"

"Just the four. I didn't use any of the spare rounds."

"Why?"

"A rifle was more useful. I only used the revolver once.
That was on the night Mr. Grant left. They got pretty
close then, and when I'd emptied the magazine of my rifle,
I used the revolver."

"And you fired four rounds with it that night?"

"Yes."

"I see." Counsel paused. And then, speaking very slowly,
he said: "If we accept the medical evidence, based on
Dr. Logan's post-mortem following the exhumation of
your father's body, and the evidence of the ballistics expert, then the possibility of your father having been killed
by one of the Emir's men is ruled out entirely." He leaned
forward, staring at David. "I want you to be quite clear on
this point. There remain then only two possibilities. Ei-

ther you killed your father or he killed himself." A long pause this time. And then the question, put bluntly: "Did Colonel Whitaker kill himself?"

"He hadn't got a rifle. He wasn't armed."

"Are you sure? He might have had a pistol concealed under his robes." And then Counsel put the question again, trying for the way out, pressing the issue in an attempt to give David the one chance that might save him. "Did Colonel Whitaker shoot himself or did he not?"

David stared at him, his eyes unnaturally big in his dark face. And then his mouth opening slowly and the courtroom hushed, some sixth sense warning us all that he was about to close the door on this one hope of acquittal. And finally the words: "I've told you before—he was killed by a rifle shot fired by one of the Emir's men." And then, turning from Counsel towards the Court, he added in a firm, clear voice: "Does any one imagine my father was the sort of man who'd kill himself?"

That, more than anything else, settled it in the minds of the Court, for he was voicing what everyone there felt. And after that there was nothing Counsel could really do to help him. "The Defence rests." He sat down abruptly and the stillness in the courtroom was absolute.

The Judge spoke then, his thin, tired voice sounding remote and detached. "It is almost five thirty." He was leaning slightly forward. "And I gather there are certain gentlemen here who have deadlines to catch." The dry humour produced an easing of tension, a little whisper of relieved laughter. "I intend to adjourn now until tomorrow. But before I do so I think it is my duty to address a word to the prisoner. Your Counsel has advised you to go into the witness box, and you have elected so to do—rightly, in my view, since otherwise the Court would have no means of knowing what happened on the morning of your father's death." The voice was warmer now, almost fatherly. "Today you have been answering questions put to you by your own Counsel. When the Court resumes tomorrow, however, it will be the Prosecution's turn to cross-examine you, and I must warn you that he is likely to question you most closely on what passed between you and your father. The witness George Grant has shown in his evidence that there was a great deal of misunderstanding, not to say friction, between the two of you. I feel it my duty to warn you, therefore, that it will greatly prejudice your case if you refuse to tell the Court what passed between you, and I would ask you to take advantage of the adjournment to consider very carefully your attitude here. Justice is dependent on the evidence of witnesses. You are now a witness. You would be wise not to withhold, from whatever motive, vital evidence." For a moment he remained leaning forward, staring at the prisoner. Then he picked up his gavel and rapped. "The Court stands adjourned until ten o'clock tomorrow morning."

The Court rose, the Judge bowed, and the rush for the doors began. Still standing in the box, David glanced slowly round the courtroom. He was sweating and he looked tired. For a brief moment his gaze rested on his sister and he gave her an uncertain, almost apologetic smile; then police guards closed round him and he was lost to view beyond the milling heads of the crowd.

"I suppose the Judge meant it kindly." Sue's hand was on my arm and I could feel her trembling slightly. "But David won't change his mind, and tomorrow the Prosecution will make a strong case out of his silence, won't they?" She sounded nervously exhausted, her voice tired.

"It won't look good," I said.

"And it was a mistake, wasn't it—trying to blame it on one of the Emir's men?"

"Yes." No point in pretending it wasn't a mistake. "The medical evidence is against it; the ballistics expert, too. . . ." We passed out into the sunlight, and the humid heat of Bahrain engulfed us like a steam bath. The street was crowded with cars, packed with people, a solid mass of Bahrainis.

Gorde was waiting beside his car, and he called to me. "A word with you, Grant." He took me aside. "That boy's going to be convicted if somebody doesn't persuade him to talk."

"I thought you were behind this witch-hunt," I said angrily.

"I made a statement; but I hadn't all the facts, had I?" He stared at me accusingly as though I were to blame for that. "Now that I've heard your evidence, seen the way he's behaving in the witness box . . ." He hesitated and then turned abruptly towards the car. "Get in, Grant. You, too, Miss Thomas. I want to talk to you." And as the driver nosed the car through the crowds, he turned to Sue and said: "I think I could arrange for you to see your brother tonight."

She gave a hopeless little shrug. "It wouldn't do any good. I think he'd rather be convicted, you see, than have the world know that Colonel Whitaker, that legendary fig-ure of the desert, committed suicide." She was very near to tears, and she added with a hint of wildness in her voice: "Just because his father's dead, all David's feeling for him, the hero-worship my mother fed him when he was a kid, has returned, magnified a thousand times by the friction there was between them when he was alive. Nothing that I can say will make him change his mind. I know that."

"I see." Gorde didn't seem surprised. "Then we must think of something else. Nobody's happy about the situa-tion, least of all the authorities." He put his hand out, and his gnarled fingers rested for a moment on Sue's arm. "Miss Thomas. Your father was a strange man. And he'd been a long time in the desert. A hell of a long time, and alone." He spoke with surprising gentleness. "He was a great man in his way. You should be proud of him."

She stared at him, dry-eyed, her face white. "Well, I'm not. I don't care about him. To me it doesn't matter a damn whether he killed himself or was killed by somebody else. He's dead. All I care about is David."

Gorde sighed. "Would it help you to understand him if I told you that he tried to join David in that tower—that David either couldn't or wouldn't lower the ladder to him? He actually got as far as the entrance hole, but couldn't pull himself in."

"How do you know?"

"Bin Suleiman. After he left hospital, he disappeared. I've had men scouring the desert for him ever since. They brought him in two days ago. Your brother says he was unconscious. So he was, most of the time."

"You mean he regained consciousness?" I asked. And when Gorde nodded I thought he'd found the witness who could save David. "Why didn't you notify David's Counsel, then?"

"Because it wouldn't help. Bin Suleiman heard them talking, but he didn't know who it was David was talking to and he didn't know what they were saying. They were talking in English. And the fact that Charles climbed up to the entrance hole, which is the only material fact he can add to the evidence, would only operate against David. Bin Suleiman thought it was one of the Emir's men trying to get in, and he reached for his rifle. The effort, or more probably the pain of movement, caused him to lose consciousness again, so that he knows nothing of what happened after that."

"But it's sufficient to cause you to change your mind about David's guilt," I said. "Why?"

"Oh, it's not that. That's only a fragment of the picture that's been building up in my mind. One of the first things I did was to send Entwhistle down to take over at Charles's camp on the Hadd border. He reported the rig gutted, the seismological truck burnt out, the place deserted. He had the sense to go on to Saraifa, where he had a talk with some of Charles's men. That raiding party you saw heading into the desert towards the rig attacked the camp at dawn. They came in firing their guns, and when they'd got hold of Charles, the Emir's secretary had him bound to a camel and made him sit there whilst they set fire to everything. When they started back towards Hadd there wasn't a thing left that they hadn't destroyed."

Visualizing the scene, I began to understand how desperate Whitaker's mood must have been. "He said he had some sort of hold over the Emir," I murmured. "I can even remember his words. He said: 'I know that little Emir inside out.' "

"Probably he did—certainly well enough to know that the man was in a vicious mood and prepared to go to any lengths. I sent a couple of the best Bedouins we've got on the pay-roll into Hadd a month ago. They reported that when he reached Hadd the Emir gave Charles the choice— either he brought his son down from the fort, alive or dead, or he'd be taken out into the Empty Quarter and left there to die."

"Didn't it occur to him that Whitaker might throw in his lot with his son?" I asked.

"Oh, it was more subtle than that. The Emir also thought he knew his man. That was why he ordered the destruction of the rig. He offered to finance Charles's drilling operations once his son was out of the way and the Jebel al-Akhbar in his hands. That's the story, anyway."

"But surely the Defence had a right to know—"

"Rumours," Gorde growled. "It wasn't evidence. Besides, how could I be sure what had happened till I knew the facts? I wanted your evidence and David Whitaker's evidence. . . ." He shrugged. "Even now I can't be sure."

"But you think you know what happened?" Sue was leaning forward, staring at him.

"Yes, I think I know now. I think Charles realized, after talking to his son, that what he'd regarded as a useless demonstration had, in fact, a chance of succeeding. He wanted to join David then, but probably he hadn't told his son what the alternative was and David refused to lower the ladder. Charles tried to get into the tower and failed, and then he stood on the edge of that cliff looking down on to Hadd, knowing that if he went back to the Emir he'd be going to his death. It's a slow death to die of thirst, and it would serve no purpose. Whereas to die quickly, by a bullet . . . I suppose he'd been allowed to carry a pistol with him, and I've no doubt he thought that a dramatic end like that . . ." He sighed. "He'd nothing to live for any more—the rig destroyed, his son doing what he might have done himself. But he could still do something. He could still die. And like that, tumbling down from that cliff-top, the news of his death would be spread by camel men from water-hole to water-hole. He still had a great reputation amongst the Bedou, and his death would be attributed to the Emir's treachery. I suppose he thought it might provoke a desert rising against the tyrant." He hesitated, and then he gave a little shrug. "I'm just guessing, that's all. I knew Charles very well, and that, I think, was what was in his mind." He looked at Sue then. "That's why, Miss Thomas, I think you should be proud of your father. And he was right in a way. His death did influence the situation. If he hadn't died like that, the Emir might not have agreed to Colonel George's terms. There might have been fighting, and God knows where it would have ended."

"You must tell this to the Court," Sue said.

But he shook his head. "It's no good, Miss Thomas. The Judge trying this case has been brought out from England. He couldn't begin to understand the sort of man Charles was—the sweep of his vision, the almost Arab subtlety of his mind. And the only absolute proof—the pistol with one bullet fired—I don't possess. My men searched the ground where his body was picked up, but they couldn't find that or anything else that has a bearing on the case. Doubtless the Emir had it destroyed, since he wanted to show Charles as a defenceless man murdered by his son. No," he said quietly. "This is a matter for action now." He turned and ordered the driver to head for my hotel. "We'll drop Grant and then you'll come on with me, Miss Thomas. I'll arrange for you to see your brother tonight. When you do, give him this." He pulled his wallet out of his pocket and removed a thick wad of East African notes. "There'll be a message, too." He handed the notes to Sue.

She stared at him, too startled for a moment to say anything. And then she burst out: "I don't know what you're planning to do, Sir Philip. But, whatever it is, you're not doing it for David. You're doing it because you want him back in Saraifa. You're signing a concession, and you want to be sure you'll be drilling—"

"How do you know we're signing a concession?" Gorde barked in that peculiar rasping voice of his. "Alex Erkhard knows. A few other executives, but that's all. How the devil has it got to your ears?"

"It's true, then." She turned to me, her voice tired. "In Court, when you were giving evidence—I sat next to that girl-friend of David's. She told me. She'd got it from one of the oil men at the al-Menza Club, and she said she was telling me because, if things went badly for David, I might be able to make use of it." She glanced at Gorde and there was suddenly a glint of that irrepressible Celtic humour in her eyes. "She thought you'd need David—alive and free."

Gorde caught the glint, and the hard, battered features relaxed in a smile. "She sounds a clever girl. What's her name?"

"Tessa," I said.

"And she's a hostess at the al-Menza?" He nodded. "I'll remember that. But please understand this, Miss Thomas: free, your brother could be very useful to us. I admit that. Arabs respect force, particularly the force of a strong and fearless personality. The Emir is afraid of him, and in Saraifa he'd be worth more to us than a hundred armed men. We don't want any more trouble on that border. But I promise you this: anything I can do will be done for one reason only—because I'm satisfied now that he's innocent."

"Of course, Sir Philip." Sue's voice, the little smile on

her lips, were tinged with irony. But I noticed also that her eyes were alight with excitement.

The car slid to a stop. We had reached my hotel. "You get out here, Grant. I'm taking Miss Thomas on with me." Gorde's hand gripped my arm. "Don't try and get in touch with her tonight, and don't talk to anybody. What we've said here is between ourselves. Understand?"

I nodded and got out. The car drove off then and I went into the hotel. It was full of newspaper men; they crowded round me as soon as I entered. What did I think of David Whitaker's chances? Was he going to talk? I told them I'd no comment to make and escaped to my room. I had my dinner brought up to me, read the papers, which were full of the trial, and went to bed early.

To this day I don't know what part Gorde played in the events of that night. Sue saw David shortly after ten o'clock. She was allowed to see him alone, and she said afterwards that he looked tired at first, though he was quite cheerful. She gave him the money and also Gorde's message, and after that the tiredness seemed to drop from him. The message was simply: *Bin Suleiman is in Bahrain. He and another Bedouin will be waiting by the side entrance all night.* He asked her a lot of questions then, about Gorde's attitude to him and what he thought had happened up there in the fort. And when she had answered them all, he seemed anxious for her to go, his eyes very bright, his manner tense, almost nervous.

It was hot in my room, and I didn't sleep very well. My nerves were on edge and I kept worrying about Sue. And then just as it was beginning to get light I heard footsteps in the corridor outside and the door of the next room was flung open; muffled conversation and the movements of a man dressing in a hurry. I looked at my watch. It was just after four. I got dressed and went down. By then the hotel was in a ferment, reporters and camera men trying to telephone for cars, the word "escape" on everybody's lips. Within half an hour the hotel was deserted.

I got one of the house-boys to bring me some coffee and sat over it smoking endless cigarettes, waiting, and wondering what had happened. In less than an hour the first of the newspaper men were drifting back and it was official—David had escaped. I never got the details absolutely clear. I doubt whether any one did, for the thing was hushed up and there was no enquiry of any sort. There was a lot of talk about a force of Bedou from the desert, but that was clearly a story invented by his guards to cover themselves. The only Arab definitely implicated was bin Suleiman, and that only because a strolling reporter happened to recognize him loitering outside the walls. FAITHFUL COMPANION RESCUES AL-AKHBAR HERO ran the headlines of that particular newspaper. But it was more subtly managed than that, though whether David bribed his guards to unlock the doors or whether it was all arranged by some outside agency I don't know. The fact is that David was able to walk out of the place, and from that point it must have been very carefully organized, for when his guards raised the alarm at 0335 hours he had completely disappeared. There were rumours that he was being hidden in a rich merchant's house, that he was lying up, disguised as an Arab, in a house on Muharraq, that he had been got away in a dhow. The whole of Bahrain seethed with rumours, but nobody knew anything definite and neither Sue nor I dared go and see Tessa, who was the one person we both thought might know where he'd been taken.

The newspaper men stayed another twenty-four hours and then they were suddenly gone, like a cloud of locusts moving on, the story dead. And all Gorde would say when I went to see him was: "I don't know anything, and I wouldn't tell you if I did. But this way it's a lot easier for everybody." The heavy-lidded eyes stared at me. "Tell his sister not to worry. I expect she'll hear from him in due course."

. . .

We were married in a registry office in Cardiff four months later, and when we got back from our honeymoon there was a letter waiting for us. It came in a parcel containing a silver coffee pot, very intricately worked. The letter was headed Saraifa:

A mutual friend of ours in GODCO has sent me word that you two are getting married. Congratulations! I thought you'd both like something from Arabia as a wedding present. It should have been native work from Saraifa. But I came to the conclusion that only the best would do. The coffee pot comes from Riyadh, by courtesy of GODCO, and is as good as any Arab potentate possesses. Remember me sometimes when you use it.

The situation here has settled down. I have a small force under my command, composed mainly of men of the Wahiba and the Rashid, and the money for its upkeep is provided. All five falaj channels are running with water and we hope within about a month to have the first of the old channels back in use. The Concession agreement has provided the funds, and we are running the channel right through the oasis to irrigate the camel thorn we'll be planting as a break against the sands of the Empty Quarter.

As soon as you have time, I want you both to come out here for a holiday. I think I can promise you more comfort than you had last time, and there'll be plenty for you to see. Come next winter. The weather is perfect at that time of the year. We'll have struck oil by then. And if it's all that we hope, it will be called the Whitaker Oilfield.

Not much news, except that the Emir has invited Sheikh Mahommed and myself to go hawking. We shall go in force, exchange presents, and I hope live in peace thereafter. God bless you both!

> *Affectionately,*
> *"The Brother of Sheikh Khalid"*
> *(By which title I am now known)*

ATLANTIC FURY

As to the effect of a
mental or moral shock
on a common mind,
that is quite a legitimate subject
for study and description.

Joseph Conrad

FOR

Janet and Maurice

Who have painted and fished the Hebrides

Those who are familiar with the out-islands of the Hebrides will have no difficulty in recognizing Laerg, just as those who have served in the Western Isles will appreciate at once the extent to which I am in the Army's debt for their cooperation. However, in a work of fiction intended to give a picture of the conditions that face men serving in an unusual environment, certain liberties are inevitable. Because of this I should like to make it absolutely clear that, while I have naturally adhered to correct ranks and titles, the characters themselves, and the situation, are entirely imaginary.

Part One

Prelude to Disaster

I

Decision to Evacuate

(OCTOBER 12–13)

The decision to withdraw the Unit from Laerg was taken early in October. That it was a fatal decision is now obvious. It was taken too late in the year, and in the initial phases the operation was carried out with too little sense of urgency. Whether the disastrous consequences of that decision would have been avoided if the personalities involved had been different I cannot say. Certainly personality played a part in what happened. It always does. A decision that calls for action involves men, and men cannot escape their own natures: their upbringing, their training, their basic characters. Moreover, in this particular case, a series of mishaps, unimportant in isolation but cumulatively dangerous in combination with the colossal forces un leased against us, led inevitably to disaster. . . .

This was the opening paragraph of a statement I found among my brother's papers. It was written in his own hand, when his mind was still lucid. Intended as a refutation of the charges brought against him, the statement was never completed. Together with his notes and all his other papers, it lies before me now in the lamplight as I embark on the task of writing this account of the disaster. And the fact that I am writing of it in the solitariness of my winter isolation here on Laerg, with the same violent winds battering at the door, the same damp, salt-laden atmosphere blackening the night outside, and Sgeir Mhor standing like a battlement against the Atlantic, will I hope give it a clarity not otherwise possible; that, and the fact that I was involved in it, too.

Not directly, as my brother was; and not with his burden of responsibility. Laerg was a military establishment at the time, and I am an artist, not a soldier. But for both of us it held a fatal fascination. It was in our blood, and looking back on it, our paths crossing after so many years and in such circumstances, there seems to have been something inevitable about it, as though Laerg itself were an integral part of the pattern of our lives.

There is, of course, no mention in my brother's notes of his personal reasons for wanting the Army out of Laerg, no hint of the fearful thing that drew him back to the island. And the fact that he had been so many years in the Army inhibited him in his writing. For instance, he gives no account of his interviews with Standing. He merely states the facts and leaves it at that, so that there is no indication of his relations with his commanding officer. Fortunately I have my own notes from which to work. These last few months I have interviewed most of the men involved in the disaster. As a result I have been able to add considerably to my personal knowledge of what happened. I have also had access to the depositions taken at the Board of Inquiry and also to the transcripts covering the first two days of the abortive Court Martial. There are still gaps, of course. So many men were killed.

If I could have talked with Colonel Standing, for instance. . . .

However, the picture in my mind is as complete as it can ever be. And that picture is dominated, of course, by Laerg. Laerg—forbidding and mysterious, rising out of the Atlantic like the last peaks of a submerged land, its shaggy heights lost in cloud, its massive cliffs resounding to the snowflake swirl of millions of seabirds. Laerg dwarfs the men, the ships; it dominates the whole story.

Until that October I had never even seen Laerg. This may seem strange, considering that my father was born there and that I'd been half in love with it since I was a kid. But Laerg isn't the sort of place you can visit at will. It lies more than eighty miles west of the Outer Hebrides, a small island group composed of Laerg itself, which with Eileann nan Shoay and Sgeir Mhor constitutes the main island; the bare rock islet of Vallay; and Fladday with its attendant stacs of Hoe and Rudha. Eighty sea miles is no great distance, but this is the North Atlantic and the seven islands of the Laerg group are a lonely cluster standing on the march of the great depressions that sweep up towards Iceland and the Barents Sea. Not only are sea conditions bad throughout the greater part of the year, but the islands, rising sheer out of the waves to a height of almost 1,400 feet, breed their own peculiar brand of weather.

Oddly enough, it wasn't my father who'd made me long to go to Laerg. He seldom talked of the island. He'd gone to sea as a young man and then married a Glasgow girl and settled as a crofter on Ardnamurchan after losing his nerve in a typhoon. It was Grandfather Ross who'd filled our heads with talk of our island ancestors.

This gnarled old man with a craggy face and huge hands had been a powerful influence in both our lives. He'd come to live with us following the evacuation of the islanders in 1930. He'd been the only man to vote against it when the Island Parliament made its decision, and to the day he died in 1936 he'd resented living on the mainland. It wasn't only that he talked endlessly of Laerg; in those six years he taught my brother Iain, and myself, everything he knew about the way to live in a world of rock and towering heights where sheep and birds were the raw materials of existence.

I'd tried to get there once a long time ago, hiding away on a trawler anchored in the bay below our croft. But that trip they hadn't gone within a hundred miles of Laerg, and then the war came and I joined Iain, working in a Glasgow factory making shell cases. A year in the Navy and ten years at sea, tramping, mainly in old Liberty ships, and then I had embarked on the thing I had always wanted to do—I began to study as a painter. It was during a winter spent in the Aegean Isles that I suddenly realized Laerg was the subject that most attracted me. It had never been painted, not the way my grandfather had described it. I'd packed up at once and returned to England, but by then Laerg had become a tracking station for the new rocket range on Harris. It was a closed island, forbidden to unauthorized civilians, and neither the Army nor Nature Conservancy, who leased it from the National Trust for Scotland, would give me permission to visit it.

That was the position until October of the following year when a man called Lane came to my studio and I was caught up in my brother's strange story and the events that led to the disaster. But first I must give the background to the Army's decision to evacuate Laerg, for without that decision the disaster would never have happened.

The future of the tracking station was discussed at a conference held in the Permanent Under-Secretary's room at the War Office and the decision to close it was confirmed by the Director Royal Artillery at a meeting in his office four days later. In my reconstruction of the conference I am indebted to the frankness with which the

DRA described it to me. For the details of the subsequent meeting I have also had the benefit of talks with his Brigadier General Staff and with Brigadier Matthieson, the Brigadier Royal Artillery, Scottish Command. The latter, in addition, was able to recall for me in considerable detail his conversation with Braddock on the night train going north. These two senior officers both gave evidence at the Court Martial and my talks with them were supplementary to that evidence.

First then, the conference. This was held on October 7 and in addition to the Permanent Under-Secretary for War, there were present the Director of Finance, the Director Royal Artillery, and, during the vital discussion on the fate of Laerg, a member of the staff of the Ordnance Board. The object of the conference was to review Royal Artillery expenditure for the current financial year. This was one of a series of War Office conferences necessitated by the Prime Minister's refusal to face the House with supplementaries to the original estimates.

There were eleven items on the agenda for that afternoon, all affecting the Royal Artillery. Laerg was sixth on the list. It came up for discussion about half past three and I understand the Director of Finance had all the costings ready to hand, reading them out in a flat monotone that was barely audible above the roar of Whitehall traffic. It was a long list and when he'd finished he put it back in his brief-case and faced the DRA. "I think you'll agree," he said, "that the cost of maintaining the detachment on Laerg is quite disproportionate to the contribution it makes to our guided weapons tests." He then went on, I gather, to emphasize the point he wanted to make. "Your firing season finishes when?"

"Some time in August," the DRA replied.

"And it starts in May."

"In May—yes. But we begin the build-up in April."

"In other words, the station is dormant for at least

seven months of the year. And during those seven months it requires a detachment commander, usually a captain, a medical officer and two orderlies, cooks, drivers, a REME outfit, even seamen military, a total of anything from thirty to forty men. There are two LCT's Mark VIII involved in ferrying supplies and . . ."

"The tank landing craft don't function in the winter."

"Quite so. But they are nevertheless committed to this operation and are merely withdrawn to Squadron Headquarters at Portsmouth for refit. They are replaced by an RASC trawler. Not so costly perhaps, but still pretty expensive. In addition, a helicopter is periodically required to deliver mail."

Throughout this interchange the DRA explained to me that he was very much on the defensive. He knew the operation could not be justified on grounds of cost alone. "It's the men," he said. "They feel cut off if they don't get regular mail. In any case, we've already decided to dispense with the trawler this winter and rely on Army helicopters for mail and relief of personnel. An experiment recommended by Colonel Standing, the Range Commandant. We've yet to find out how it will work. Conditions for helicopter flying are not all that good, particularly after the end of October."

"That's merely a matter of detail," the Director of Finance said. "I have been into all this very carefully. Correct me if I'm wrong, but as I understand it the only maintenance required on the really vital equipment, the radar, is that it should be run once a day, mainly to warm it up. One man's work for a few hours each day. To keep him there you apparently require over thirty men. . . ."

"I've reported on this to the Secretary for War more than once," the DRA cut in. "The tracking station cost a lot to establish. It isn't only the radar that has to be maintained. There's the camp, the vehicles, the boats; to abandon Laerg for seven months in the year would result in

rapid deterioration through gales and the salt in the atmosphere. Moreover, trawlermen use Shelter Bay in the
winter—Norwegians, Belgians, French, Spanish, as well
as Scots. There wouldn't be much left of our installations
if there were nobody there to guard them."

At this point the Permanent Under-Secretary intervened. "I don't think we need query the number of men
involved, or the necessity for maintaining the station
throughout the year in present circumstances. Presumably
this was all gone into at the time and agreed as unavoid-
able. What we have to decide now is whether or not Laerg
has become redundant in view of this new equipment
we've been offered. You've had a report on it, I believe.
The results of the trials were very impressive, I thought."

The DRA didn't say anything. He was staring out of the
window at the cloudless blue of the sky. From where he
sat he looked across the pale stone outline of the Horse
Guards to the trees in St. James's Park. They were still in
summer leaf. It had been a mild autumn and so fine were
the yellow brush strokes of the early frosts that only a
painter's eye would have discerned the warning breath of
winter in that green canvas. The DRA was not a painter.
His hobby, he explained to me, was bird-watching and he
was wishing he had been able to find time to visit Laerg
during the nesting season. The room was hot and airless,
full of smoke, and the sun slanted golden bars of light
across the table.

"Before we finally make up our minds, perhaps we
should hear what Ordnance Board have to say about it."
The Permanent Under-Secretary reached for the phone
and asked for the Colonel who had conducted the trials to
be sent in. The discussion that followed was technical and
as the equipment concerned was secret the DRA did not
discuss it with me. He did, however, say that it was American equipment and that he had pointed out that it would
be costly to install. To this the Permanent Under-

Secretary had replied: "But as they are using the range themselves they are offering it to us on a long-term credit basis." That, the DRA told me, was the decisive factor. The matter was settled and what happened later stemmed from that moment, for the Permanent Under-Secretary was under considerable pressure. "I'd like to be able to report to the PM," he said, "that you'll have your men and equipment off the island and the station closed down, say by the end of the month. Would that be possible?"

"I suppose so. It depends on the weather."

"Naturally. But we're in for a fine spell now. I heard the forecast this morning."

"Laerg is over six hundred miles north of here and it's getting late in the season."

"All the more reason to hurry it."

The DRA was not disposed to argue. He had held his appointment for less than six months, and anyway he was wondering how to handle the next item on the agenda, which was of far more importance to the Artillery than Laerg. "I've no doubt we'll manage," he said and made a note on his pad to instruct his Brigadier General Staff.

The BGS, questioned by the President of the Court Martial about the DRA's acceptance of that time limit, made the point that some such limit was essential in an operation of this kind. If the evacuation were not completed before the winter gales set in, there would be little likelihood of getting the men and equipment off that winter. Even a partial failure to complete it would necessitate the maintenance of the station probably until the spring, with all the attendant problems of supply aggravated by the fact that essential stores would be lacking. "Without a time limit," he said, "the operation would have lacked the necessary atmosphere of urgency."

Unfortunately, all the items on the agenda could not be dealt with that afternoon and the conference was resumed again at ten the following morning. As a result, the Brigadier General Staff received his instructions about Laerg in the form of a hurriedly dictated memo that listed some half dozen other items for his immediate attention. The BGS was a keen yachtsman, and though he had never sailed in the Hebrides, he was able to appreciate better than most people in the War Office the difficulties that could arise in an evacuation involving landing craft operating across an open beach. With the weekend imminent he decided to shelve the matter until Monday when Brigadier Matthieson was due in London. He marked it in his diary for the morning of October 11, the final decision to be taken after discussion with the DRA. Meantime, he teleprinted Matthieson at Scottish Command ordering him to have a plan of operations prepared for the immediate withdrawal of all stores, equipment, and personnel.

Having established that there was a delay of four vital days between the DRA's original agreement to the principle of evacuation and the final decision to go ahead, I should perhaps add that only exceptional circumstances would have produced speedier action, and in this case the exceptional circumstances had not arisen. The pressure at this stage was from the Permanent Under-Secretary, not from the weather; a full two weeks was to elapse before that freak meteorological brew began to ferment in the sea areas Bailey, Hebrides, and Faeroes. There was, in any case, a good deal of preliminary work to be done. In particular, the agreement of the RASC to the use of the landing craft had to be obtained and the plan itself worked out. This last the BRA, Scottish Command, brought with him to London so that once it was agreed it only needed an executive order to start the thing moving.

After reading the plan and discussing it with Matthieson, the BGS took him in to see the General. It was then just after midday and again the weather was fine in London, the sun shining out of a clear sky. In describing this meeting to me, Matthieson made it clear that though the DRA was under considerable pressure at the time and obviously determined to proceed with the evacuation, he had, nevertheless, been at some pains to allay any fears his subordinates might have. "I suppose you're worrying about the weather," was his opening remark. "Naturally, I raised the point myself. The Permanent Under-Secretary was not impressed. The sun was shining and it was dam-nably hot in his room." He glanced towards the windows. "The sun is still shining. Did you listen to the shipping forecast this morning?" This to the BGS. And when he admitted he hadn't, the General said: "Well, I did. Made a special point of it. I know you sailing types. There's a high pressure system covering the British Isles and the nearest depression is down in the German Bight. As to the alternative we've been offered, the responsibility rests with Ordnance Board. I made that perfectly plain. If it doesn't work . . ."

"Oh, I expect it'll work, sir," the BGS said.

"Well, what's worrying you then?"

"Apart from the weather—Simon Standing."

"Standing? He's one of our best instructors."

"That's just the trouble. He's a wizard at ballistics, but this is his first independent command and if anything went wrong . . ."

"Have you any reason to suppose that anything is going to go wrong?"

"Of course not. All I'm saying is that this operation doesn't call for the qualities that make a brilliant In-structor-in-Gunnery. It calls for a man of action."

"Fine. It will give him some practical experience. Isn't that why you recommended him for the job? Practical experience is essential if he is to go on getting promotion at his present rate. How old is he?"

"Thirty-seven, thirty-eight."

"That makes him just about the youngest I.G. with the

rank of full colonel. And he's ambitious. He'll make out all right. I seem to remember he's got Hartley as his second-in-command. Met him at Larkhill. Excellent at administration and a sound tactician. Just the man Simon needs."

"Unfortunately he's in hospital—jaundice."

"I see. Well, there's an adjutant presumably."

"Young fellow by the name of Ferguson. He's not very experienced."

"And you're not happy about him?"

"I can't say that. I don't know anything much about him. He's only twenty-six, just promoted captain and filling in a vacancy."

"What's wrong with him then?"

"Well . . ." I don't think the BGS wanted to go into this, but it was essential to the point he was making. "His record shows that he volunteered for paratrooping and didn't complete the course."

"Funked his jumps?"

"Something like that. He was posted to BAOR."

"All right then. Get on to AG6. Have them post somebody up there temporarily just to hold Simon's hand— an older man with practical experience. The AAG ought to be able to rake up somebody to fill in for a few weeks. Anything else on your mind?"

"Only the timing. The operation has been planned on the basis of completion by the end of the month. But nobody can possibly guarantee that. Fortunately we'd agreed to Standing's idea of cutting the size of the wintering unit and maintaining contact by helicopter. As a result one of the huts has already been dismantled. Nevertheless, I must emphasize that the maintenance of a planning schedule as tight as this depends entirely on the continuance of the present fine weather."

"Of course. That's understood. Service Corps have already made it clear that they're not taking any chances with their landing craft. And rightly." He turned to Matthieson. "That satisfy you?"

Matthieson hesitated. He was well aware of the dangers. He told me he had tried to visit Laerg twice and each time had been turned back by bad weather. He had held his present post for almost two years and he knew the difficulties that must arise if conditions deteriorated and the operation became a protracted one. But this was only the second interview he had had with the DRA since the General's appointment. Doubtless he felt it wasn't the moment to voice his misgivings. My impression is that he decided to play his luck. At any rate, all he apparently said was: "Captain Pinney, the present Detachment Commander, is pretty experienced; so is the skipper of one of the landing craft—the other was a replacement halfway through the season. Still, I think the whole thing should go off quite smoothly." However, to cover himself, he added: "But Laerg can be the devil if it blows up and we're getting on towards winter in the north."

The DRA nodded. "Well, that settles it then. We pray for fine weather and get on with the job, eh? Signal them to go ahead with the operation right away."

And so the decision was finally agreed. Matthieson sent off the necessary signal and the BGS phoned about the temporary attachment of an officer to assist Standing.

He was immediately offered a Major George Braddock.

The reason given by the AAG for recommending this particular officer was that he wanted to be posted to the Hebrides. Not only had Braddock written twice from Cyprus, where he commanded a battery, but a few days before he had sought a personal interview with the AAG to press the matter. He had then just arrived in London on leave.

To the BGS it seemed the perfect answer to the problem. Braddock was about forty, his rank was right, and so was his record. He had an MC and two Mentions in Despatches, awarded during the last war, as well as an excellent record during the Malayan troubles. Moreover, he was in England and immediately available. Locating him took a little time. His wife, who with her two children lived at Hertford, had apparently been separated from him for a number of years and did not know where he was. All she could say was that he liked fishing and usually went to Wales for his leave. He was eventually traced to a country club near Brecon. By then it was late at night and Braddock didn't reach London until the following afternoon.

That was Tuesday and as far as I can gather that was the day Ed Lane arrived in Lyons. I suppose almost every disaster requires something to trigger it off—a catalyst, as it were. *A decision that calls for action involves men, and men cannot escape their own natures . . . their basic characters.* In writing that, I believe my brother was thinking of this Canadian business man from Vancouver. Lane wasn't, of course, involved in the operation. He was probing Braddock's background and to that extent he exerted a pressure on events and was, in a sense, the catalyst. He had seen Braddock in Cyprus a fortnight before and had then gone on to the Middle East on business for his firm. Now that business was finished and he was free to concentrate on his private affairs. While Braddock was travelling up to the War Office, Lane was interviewing one of the few people who could help him in his inquiries.

The BGS saw Braddock just after four. In his evidence, the Brigadier simply said that the interview strengthened the favourable impression already created by his record. He was satisfied that Major Braddock was the right man for the job. He was not asked for any details, only for confirmation that he had warned Braddock about weather conditions. As a result, the court was not aware that the

Brigadier was puzzled, even a little disturbed, by the answers Braddock gave to certain rather searching questions.

In the talk I had with him later the Brigadier admitted
that he had been curious to know why Braddock had applied for a posting to the Guided Weapons Establishment,
particularly as his record showed that he had been one of
the few survivors of the *Duart Castle,* sunk in those waters
during the war. "I should have thought your memories
of that area . . ."

"That's got nothing to do with it, sir. It's just that—well,
I guess it's because I spent part of my boyhood in Canada.
I like cold climates. The farther north the better. And I
like something to get my teeth into. Malaya was all right
for a bit. But Cyprus. . . ." And then with an intensity
that the Brigadier found disconcerting: "Is there any
particular reason why I'm being posted to the Hebrides
now—other than to deal with the problem of this evacuation of Laerg?"

"No, of course not. Why should there be?"

Braddock had seemed to relax then. "I just wondered.
I mean, when you apply for a posting and then suddenly
get it. . . ." The lined, leathery-hard face had cracked
in a charming smile. "Well, it makes you wonder what's
behind it."

"Nothing's behind it," the Brigadier told him. "I was
simply referring to what happened to you up there in
1944." He told me he was wishing then that he knew the
man better, feeling instinctively that there was more to it
than he'd admitted. "How many of you were on that raft
at the outset?" He watched the tough, poker face, saw
the nerve quiver at the corner of the mouth and the eyes
fixed wide in a flat, blank stare. "No, I thought not. It's
something you'd rather forget. Have you ever visited the
Hebrides since?"

"No."

"Then why do you want to be posted there now?"

But Braddock either couldn't or wouldn't answer that. "It's just that . . . well, as I said—it sort of calls to me. I can't explain exactly." And he'd smiled that engaging smile. "It's a bit like Canada, I suppose."

The Brigadier hesitated. But it was nothing to do with him and he'd let it go at that, staring down again at Braddock's record. The Normandy landings—anti-tank role—the M.C. for gallantry at Caen after holding a bridge with a single gun against repeated attacks by tanks—command of a troop two months later—promoted captain just before the dash for the Rhine—temporary rank of major at the end of the war. . . . "Now about this operation. Do you sail at all?"

"I've done a little."

"Good. Then you'll have some idea what the weather means to the LCT's, particularly in view of your previous experience. . . ." He had got up from his desk and turned towards the window. "However, that isn't why I wanted to see you personally." The sky was blue and the sun beat down on the stone ledge of the tight-shut window. "Ever met Simon Standing?" He turned as Braddock shook his head. "No, I didn't think your paths would have crossed. Can't imagine two people more entirely different —which may be a good thing, or again it may not. Colonel Standing is Commandant and Range Controller. He's a few years younger than you and it's his first independent command. Now this is what I want to make clear to you, and it's strictly between ourselves. Standing's up there primarily because he's an expert on ballistics and all that sort of thing. In fact, he's one of the best brains we've got in the field of guided weapons. But for a job like this . . ." He had hesitated then. "Well, his world is figures. He's not strictly an action man, if you see what I mean." And he went on quickly: "Officially, of course, it's his show and you come under him as acting second-in-

command. Unofficially, I want you to run the operation."
Faced with the blank stare of those black eyes he probably
felt it was all damnably awkward for he admitted to me
later that he thought Braddock should have been a half-
colonel at least. He had the experience and he had that
indefinable something, that air of confidence denoting a
born leader. He may even have wondered what had gone
wrong, but at the time all he said was: "Just keep Simon
Standing in the picture and get on with the job. If you
bear in mind that he's quite brilliant in his own field and
. . . well, use a little tact."

"I understand, sir."

"I hope you do." The Brigadier had hesitated then,
feeling instinctively that a clash of temperament was inevitable. Ever since Braddock had come into his office he
had been conscious of the strength of the man's personality, and something else—a tension, almost a sense of
urgency. But there was nothing he could do about that
now. Time was too short. "There's a sleeper reserved for
you on the night train. You'll be travelling up with the
BRA, Scottish Command. He'll give you all the details."
And with a murmured "Good luck" he had dismissed him.

He admitted later that Braddock should have been
given the opportunity to discuss the operation. But
throughout the interview he'd felt uncomfortable. The
large hands, the dark moustache, the lined, leathery face
with the heavy brows craggy above the black stare of the
eyes—somehow, he said, the man seemed to fill the office,
too big for it almost. So strong was this feeling that he'd
been glad when the door had shut behind him.

The train left Euston at nine thirty-five and ten minutes after it pulled out Braddock visited Brigadier Matthieson in his sleeper. I suspect that Matthieson was one
of those officers who joined the Royal Artillery for the
riding, back in the days when the guns were horse-drawn.
I don't think he had much of a brain, but he was cer-

tainly no fool and he was as good with men as he was with horses. He never forgot a face. "Met you somewhere before, haven't I?" he said and was surprised to find this overture rejected almost fiercely. "A long time ago, I think. Now where was it?"

"I think you've made a mistake, sir."

But Matthieson was quite sure he hadn't. "During the war." He saw Braddock's face tauten, and then he had it —a tall, hard-bitten youngster in a blood-stained battle-dress coming back with a single gun buckled by a direct hit. "Normandy. Autumn of forty-four. You'd been holding a bridge." The craggy face towering above him relaxed, broke into the same charming, rather tired-looking smile. "I remember now, sir. You were the major bivouacked in that wood. You gave us food—the few of us that were left. A tent, too. We were just about all in."

They'd talked about the war then, sitting on Matthieson's berth, finishing the bottle of Scotch he'd brought south with him. It was almost midnight and the bottle empty by the time they got around to discussing Laerg. Matthieson pulled out his brief-case and handed Braddock the Plan of Operations. "The schedule's a bit tight, but that's not my fault. About ten LCT loads should do the trick. Read it through tonight. Any points we can discuss in the morning. I've a car meeting me and I'll drive you out to Renfrew Airport."

Braddock, leafing quickly through the plan, immediately expressed concern about the schedule. "I have some experience of the weather up there. . . ."

"On an open raft. So the BGS told me. But you're not dealing with a raft this time. These LCT's can stand quite a lot."

"It's an open beach. If the wind's south-easterly . . ."

"You know the place, do you?"

He saw Braddock's face tighten. "I looked it up on a map," he said quickly, and Matthieson wondered how he'd got hold of a map with the shops closed. "If the weather goes against us . . ."

"It's the weather you're being posted up there to deal with. The weather and that fellow Standing." He was well aware that the schedule was too tight and he wanted to get Braddock off the subject. "Ever met Simon Standing? Do you know anything about him?" And when the other shook his head, he went on, "Give you a word of advice then. Don't fall out with him. War Office thinks he's wonderful. But I can tell you he's a queer fish and he's got no sense of humour." He was very frank about the words he'd used. "Bloody little prig, if you ask me." I imagine he smiled then, a flash of teeth that were too white and even to be his own. "Shouldn't be talking like this about your commanding officer, should I? But we've seen a war together. These adding-machine types haven't. Probably puke if they did. A real war, I mean—blood and the stink of rotting guts, the roar of a thousand guns blazing hell out of a dawn sky. They're push-button warriors; nothing but bloody electricians."

He was staring down at his glass then, memories of a long-dead war merging with the future. "Anyway, I'm getting out. In a few months' time I'll be running a stud farm near Melbourne. Australia, you know. Once I get out there they can push all the ruddy little buttons they like." It was the drink in him talking, and because he was aware of that he said: "Well, I'm off to bed now."

It was then that Braddock surprised him by asking a series of questions that seemed to have very little bearing on the operation. First, he'd wanted to know whether the men on Laerg were free to roam around the island or whether their duties kept them confined to the area of Shelter Bay. When told that off-duty they could go where they liked and that many of them became enthusiastic bird-watchers, Braddock asked if they'd reported any interesting finds. "I mean traces of . . . well, old dwellings, caves, things like that, with traces of human habitation?"

Matthieson wondered what he was getting at. "Are you a student of primitive man or are you thinking of the link between the Hebrides and Greenland? There was a link, I believe. The Vikings put the sheep on Eileann nan Shoay— *shoay* or *soay* is the old word for sheep, you know. They may well have been on their way west to the Greenland settlement."

"Yes, I've read about that, but . . . Well, I just thought something fresh might have been reported." And Braddock had stared at him with disconcerting directness, waiting for an answer.

"No, of course not," the Brigadier replied. "The boys are just amateurs."

"What about civilians—naturalists and so on? Are they allowed on the island?"

Matthieson admitted he was disturbed by the other's persistence. But all he said was: "Yes. There's usually a party of bird-watchers, a few naturalists. Students, some of them. They come in summer under the aegis of Nature Conservancy. A nuisance, but quite harmless."

"And they've reported nothing—nothing of exceptional interest?"

"If they have, we haven't been told about it." And he'd added: "Anyway, you won't have time to indulge your interest. Your job is to get our boys off, and it'll be a full-time job, believe you me. You'll understand when you've had time to study that Operations Plan." And he'd wished Braddock good night, wondering as the train rushed on into the night what Standing would make of his new second-in-command.

Two coaches back Braddock started going through the Operations Plan, sitting propped up in bed, the pages dancing to the sway and rattle of the train. And almost a thousand miles away another man in another sleeper was checking through the notes he'd made of his first interview with a non-Canadian survivor of the *Duart Castle*. Ed Lane was on the train to Paris, bound for London with a list of five possible names.

The night train to Glasgow got in at six-thirty in the morning. A staff car was waiting for Brigadier Matthieson at Central Station and while driving Braddock out to Renfrew Airport he discussed with him the details of the Operations Plan. In his evidence he made it clear that he'd allowed Major Braddock the widest possible interpretation of the evacuation orders. What in fact happened was that Braddock not only had a list of queries but seemed prepared to argue that the whole conception of the plan was at fault. It was the timing, of course, that chiefly worried him. "I agree it doesn't give you much room for manoeuvre," Matthieson had said. "But that's not my fault. It's the Government that's pushing the operation." And he'd added: "I'm a great believer in sound planning and the chaps who handled this are very good at it. If they say it can be done, then you can take it from me that it can."

But Braddock wasn't to be put off so easily. "LCT so-and-so to sail on such-and-such a date, arrive Laerg about twelve hours later, loading time six hours, leave at dusk, return to base at dawn. All very nice and neat if you're sitting on your backside in an office. But there's no allowance for weather or any of the hundred and one things that can go wrong on an amphibious operation. It's an open beach. The equipment is pretty valuable, I gather —some of it secret. What happens if a gale blows up? Do I risk a landing craft and the equipment simply to keep to a schedule I don't believe in?"

"Damn it, man. Use your initiative. That's why you're being posted there." And Matthieson had added, quoting, as no doubt he'd often done before, from the wartime leader he'd served under: "I never interfere in the detailed running of things. That's my speciality. I leave it to the experts. In this case, Braddock, you're the expert. Understood?"

By that time they had arrived at Renfrew. Matthieson left him then and after a leisurely breakfast Braddock caught the ten o'clock plane. At Stornoway there was an Army helicopter waiting for him. He landed at Northton on the west coast of Harris shortly after one. There he was met by the adjutant, Captain Ferguson, who informed him that Colonel Standing was waiting for him in his office. There is no record of what happened between the two men at that first meeting. But it lasted little more than ten minutes and when they came into the Mess for lunch the atmosphere between them was already strained.

The clearest impression of Braddock's impact on the operation is contained in the deposition made by Lieutenant Field, the Education Officer. This deposition, made at the Board of Inquiry, could have had considerable influence on the subsequent Court Martial. Not only was Field much older than the other officers, but his background and experience gave weight to his judgment. The first two paragraphs are the vital ones and I give them in full:—

Major Braddock arrived at Joint Services Guided Weapons Establishment, Northton, on October 13. I think it is right to say that his appointment came as a shock to most of the officers, not least to Colonel Standing, who had only been informed of it on the phone that morning. I say "shock" because that is how it seemed to officers accustomed to something in the nature of a winter hibernation in the Hebrides. Major Braddock was a driver. He had a very forceful personality. He was also a man of great nervous energy, great vitality. Whatever your findings, I would like to make it clear that I regard him as exactly the sort of man the operation needed at that time.

I have some knowledge of the leadership necessary in

an operation that is at the mercy of the elements, and from my own observations, and from what I heard from Captain Ferguson, who was a friend of my daughter's and often visited our croft of an evening, I may say that I already had certain very definite misgivings. Not until Major Braddock's arrival was there that thrust and pressuring of officers and men, that sense of being engaged with an enemy that is the essential prelude to exceptional human endeavour. He made them feel they were involved in a battle. Most of the youngsters got a kick out of it; the older ones, particularly some of the officers, resented it. Later, of course, they did all that any men could do in circumstances that became virtually impossible.

Before he left for London, Matthieson had had the foresight to arrange with RASC (Water Transport) for both LCT's to refuel, cancel all leave, and stand by to sail at short notice. As a result, the position on Braddock's arrival was not unsatisfactory. One landing craft had completed its first trip and was on its way back to Laerg; the other was just entering Leverburgh, a bare two hours behind schedule. And the weather was fine, cold, and clear with a light northerly wind.

But as Field pointed out, the fine weather could not be expected to last indefinitely, nor could the men. The strains were already beginning to show: at Leverburgh, where the quay was inadequate; on Laerg, where the bolts securing huts and equipment were rusted solid and the men, after only two days, were tiring, moving in a sleepless daze from dismantling to loading and back to dismantling again. And while Braddock threw himself into the work of ensuring a faster rate of turn-round for the landing craft, Ed Lane flew into London and began checking for relatives of Albert George Piper, one-time Master-at-Arms on the *Duart Castle*.

Piper's name was the first on his list. The second was my brother's.

II

My Brother, Iain

(OCTOBER 15)

It was two days later, just after ten on the morning of October 15, that my phone rang and a man's voice, rather soft, said: "Mr. Ross? My name's Ed Lane. Are you by any chance related to a Sergeant Iain Alasdair Ross reported lost when the *Duart Castle* was torpedoed in February 1944?"

"He was my brother."

"He was?" The voice had a vaguely American accent. "Well, that's fine. Didn't expect to strike it that fast— you're only the fifth Ross I've telephoned. I'll be with you inside of an hour. Okay?" And he'd rung off, leaving me wondering what in the world it was all about.

I was working on another book jacket for Alec Robinson, but after that phone call I found it impossible to go back to it. I went into the little kitchenette and brewed myself some coffee. And after that I stood drinking it at the window, looking out across the rooftops, an endless vista of chimney pots and TV aerials with a distant glimpse of Tower Bridge. I was thinking of my brother, of how I'd loved him and hated him, of how there had been nobody else in my life that had made up for the loss I'd felt at his going. And yet at the time I'd been almost glad. It had seemed better that he should die like that—in the sea, a casualty of war.

I turned away from the grubby window, glanced at the jacket design lying on the table among a litter of paints and brushes, and then fell to pacing my studio, wondering what this fellow Lane wanted, digging up the past that was dead these twenty years and more. Surely to God they weren't going to rake over the whole wretched business again. I could still remember the shock when the Military Police had come to interview me at the factory. Did I know where Iain was, had I seen him, had he visited me? Did I realize he'd deserted? Slinging questions at me until they'd discovered my father was dead and my mother alone and ill at Ardnamurchan. "We'll pick him up there then." And my bursting into tears and shouting at them that whatever my brother had done it was justified and why the hell did they pick on him and not the officer. And that M. P. sergeant with the big ears and the broken nose —I could have drawn his face even now—snapping back at me in a grating Glaswegian voice: "The officer was unconscious, laddie, with machine-gun bullets spraying him as he lay on the ground with a broken jaw. Aye and damn near twenty men dead who needn't have died. Justified? Christ, it was plain bluidy mur-rder."

The jacket design stared at me, the lettering of the book title already pencilled in—THE PEACE THAT FOLLOWED. I had read it, thought it good, but now I dropped a rag over it, remembering the wartime passages, the sense of futility the writer had invoked. Sounds from the street drifted up to me, the bustle of London's East End. My studio was just an attic over a butcher's shop. It was all I could afford. Bed, table, and easel took up most of the space, and the canvases stacked against the wall, all the work I'd done on Milos—there was hardly room to move. A cupboard in the corner held my clothes and above it was piled the camping equipment I'd bought from the proceeds of the only two pictures I'd sold—*Milos at Dawn Seen from a Caique* and *Greek Galley Under Water.* That was when I planned to paint on Laerg, before I'd been refused permission to go there.

I crossed to the window, thinking back over my life, back to the carefree days on Ardnamurchan and Iain in the glory of his youth fighting imaginary battles among the rocks below our croft, always in defence of Laerg with myself cast in the role of invader—a Viking, a pirate, a marauding trawler-man, anything that had recently captured his fancy. And in the evenings, sitting by the peat fire listening to the old man talking in that thick burr— tales of the Lovers' Stone, of cliff-crawling in search of puffins, of boat journeys to Fladday for the gannets that he called solan geese; wild tales of gales and ships being wrecked.

So long ago and yet so vivid, and Iain tall and handsome with his dark face, and his black hair blowing in the wind; a wild boy with a streak of melancholy and a temper that flared at a word. He could have done something with his life. I pushed up the window, leaning out to feel the warmth of the sun, thinking of my own life, stuck here in this dirty back street doing hack work for a living. I should be painting on Laerg, getting the lost world of my grandfather down on canvas. That would be something, a justification. Eleven years at sea, followed by the years learning to paint, and it all added up to this miserable little room and a few pounds in the bank.

A taxi drew up in the street below and a man got out. All I could see of him was his wide-brimmed hat and the pale sheen of his coat as he paid the driver. It crossed my mind that it was a good angle from which to paint a picture of a London street—but in the same instant I knew I wouldn't do it; nobody would buy it. He disappeared from sight and a few moments later I heard his footsteps labouring up the bare stairboards. I opened the door and ushered him in, a tubby, round-looking man with small eyes in a smooth face. His clothes were a business man's clothes, but not English. The small eyes took in the cluttered studio, scanning the walls as though in search of something. "I guess you're an artist, Mr. Ross. That right?"

"I kid myself sometimes."

But there was no answering smile. The small eyes stared at me, cold and humourless. "You got a picture of your brother?"

"Just why are you here?" I asked him.

He took his hat off then and sat down on the bed, a little out of breath. "It's a long story." Brown-stained fingers fumbled for his cigarettes. "Smoke?" I shook my head. He flipped one out of the pack and lit it. "It's about the *Duart Castle*. As I told you over the phone, my name's Lane. Ed Lane. I come from Vancouver. I'm over here on business—oil and gas; my company runs pipelines. I mention that just to show you I'm a man of some standing. The reason I've come to see you is a private one. I'm investigating something that concerns my wife's family. A matter of a will. There's quite a lot of money involved." He paused for breath, reached into the pocket of his light-coloured raincoat. "I've got some photographs here." He had come up with an envelope. But instead of producing the pictures, he sat dragging at his cigarette and staring round the room. "An artist," he breathed as though he'd just thought of something. "Do you do portraits?"

"No."

He frowned. "You mean you can't draw heads, faces, people's features."

"I don't paint portraits, that's all."

He looked at the table then, twisting his head round and reaching for the rag I'd dropped over the jacket design. Behind the lettering I had already painted in the first of a series of heads representing humanity in fear. "There you are. That's the sort of thing." The little button eyes stared at me as though I'd purposely misled him. "You remember your brother, do you? You haven't forgotten what he looked like?"

"Of course not. But I don't see . . ."

"You could draw me a portrait of him, couldn't you?"

"I could."

I think he saw I was getting annoyed, for he smiled and said, "Sure. You want to know what it's all about first."

"You mentioned some pictures," I said.

He nodded. "Later," he said. "Later. First, there are the press-cuttings." He pulled some clippings from the envelope, selected one and handed it to me. "You saw that at the time, I expect."

It was from the *Daily Telegraph*, dated February 24, 1944, the news of the sinking of the *Duart Castle* and the arrival at Donegal, Northern Ireland, of two boatloads of survivors, together with the list of their names, thirty-five in all. Pinned to it was a cutting dated March 2 giving the official account of the torpedoing and the names of those who were missing, presumed dead. Iain Alasdair Ross. There it was to bring back to me after all these years the sense of loss I'd felt at the time, the feeling of being alone in the world, all my family dead. "I read it in *The Scotsman*," I said and passed it back to him.

"Sure. It was in most of the papers." He was riffling through the bunch of cuttings. "That all you read about the *Duart Castle*?"

"That's all there was, as far as I know. Papers were small and a lot of ships were being sunk. They'd plenty of other news. . . ."

"Then you didn't see this?" He handed me another clipping. "It's from a Stornoway paper of March 14."

"Stornoway's in the Outer Hebrides," I pointed out. "I'd hardly be likely to see a copy of that."

"Sure, it's way up north and this is a local story. No other paper seems to have printed it. You read it. Then I'll tell you why I'm interested in your brother."

The cutting was headed: ORDEAL BY RAFT —Terrible Story of Lone Survivor. On Tuesday evening Colin McTavish, seventy-two-year-old lobster fisherman of Tobson on Great Bernera, while rowing out in his boat to visit his pots, came upon a Carley float lodged among the rocks of Geodha Cool. Two men lay on the raft, both apparently lifeless. The raft belonged to the *Duart Castle,* sunk by torpedoes some five hundred miles out in the North Atlantic on February 18. They had, therefore, been adrift on the raft for twenty-two days. Colin McTavish took the bodies into his boat and rowed back to Tobson. There it was discovered that despite the long time at sea one of the men was still alive. His name is George Henry Braddock, Second Lieutenant Royal Artillery, aged twenty. The terrible story of his ordeal cannot be told yet for a Merciful God has wiped it from his mind. He has been transferred to the hospital at Stornoway suffering from exposure and loss of memory. But we all know what he must have suffered out there in the open sea exposed to bitter cold and severe storms with no protection but the tattered remnants of a sail and his only companion dying before his eyes. The dead man is Private André Leroux, a French-Canadian from Montreal. He has been buried at the old cemetery above the bay at Bosta. Colin McTavish's rescue of Second Lieutenant Braddock brings the total of survivors of the *Duart Castle* to thirty-six and this doubtless writes *finis* to the tragic story of a ship that was transporting Canadian reinforcements to aid the fight for freedom.

"I didn't know about it," I said. "But I don't see what that's got to do with my brother—or with me."

"Your brother was on that raft when the ship sank."

"Well, he's dead," I said. "What difference does it make?" He didn't say anything; simply handed me one of the photographs from the envelope. It showed a man in a light suit walking along a street—tall, black-haired, with a dark moustache and what looked like a scar running down the centre of his forehead. It wasn't a very clear picture, just a snapshot taken in very bright sunlight. He passed me another. The same man getting out of a car. "And here's one taken with a telephoto lens." Head and shoulders this time, the face heavily shadowed by sunlight. "You don't recognize him?" He was watching me closely.

"Where were they taken?"

"Famagusta in Cyprus."

"I've never been to Famagusta," I said.

"I asked you whether you recognized him?"

"Well, I don't. Who is he?"

He sighed and took the photographs back, sitting there, staring down at them. "I guess they're not very clear. Not as clear as I would have liked. But . . ." He shook his head and tucked them away in the envelope together with the cuttings. "They're pictures I took of Braddock. Major Braddock." He looked up at me. "You're sure they didn't strike some chord in your memory?" And when I shook my head, he said: "They didn't remind you of your brother, for instance?"

"My brother?" I stared at him, trying to think back, remembering Iain's dark, handsome face. "How the hell could it be my brother?" The face in those photos, lined and scarred. "There's no resemblance at all. What are you getting at?"

"Think what he'd be like now." The small eyes stared at me, cold and with an obstinate look.

"He's dead," I said again, angry now, wondering what the hell this wretched little man was trying to dig up. "And the past, that's dead, too," I added.

"Okay, Mr. Ross. If that's the way you feel. But do something for me, will you. Draw me a picture of your brother —as you think he might look now."

"Damned if I do." I wasn't going to help him or anyone else rake up the past. "Why should I?"

"I'll tell you why." His voice had a sudden bite to it. "I don't believe the man I saw in Famagusta was Braddock." The eyes, staring at me, still had that obstinate look. "And if he wasn't Braddock, then who was he? That's what I want to know, and that's what I intend to find out." He dived into his breast pocket and came out with a diary. "I've got a list here of five names." He turned the pages quickly, spreading the diary open on his knee. "Five men definitely identified. That's in addition to Braddock and Leroux, the two who were still on the raft when it was washed ashore in the Outer Hebrides." He looked up at me then. "That makes seven we know for sure were on the raft at the time the *Duart Castle* went down. No doubt there were more, but those seven have been identified by witnesses I consider absolutely reliable. Your brother was one of them, Mr. Ross."

I didn't see what he was driving at. Whether Iain was on that raft or in the water didn't seem to make much difference. It didn't alter the fact that he was dead. "Who told you?" I asked. "Braddock, I suppose."

"No, it wasn't Braddock. Braddock says he doesn't remember. What you might call a mental blackout, I guess. Very convenient. No, your brother's name was given to me by a man I saw in Lyons on my way back from the Middle East—Tom Webster, an English textile buyer. He came ashore in one of the boats." He closed the diary. "I've seen altogether eight of the survivors, in addition to Braddock. The first seven were Canadians. I interviewed them before

I left for Europe. Only one of them remembered seeing the float. He gave me two possible names. Webster gave me a further three, and he was very positive about them because he was thrown into the water and clung to the float for a time before swimming to the boat." He stubbed out his cigarette. "The three men Webster was positive about were the Master-at-Arms, the second officer—and your brother. I've checked on the first two. Neither of them had any reason to change their identity. But your brother had. Did you know he was being brought back from Canada under escort to face a number of very serious charges?"

"Yes," I said. "I know that. But he's listed among those lost and it's over twenty years. . . ."

"He was presumed dead." His emphasis was on the word "presumed," his voice flat and hard and very determined. "There's a difference. His body was never recovered. He wasn't identified. And that brings me to the reason I'm here. The *Duart Castle* was a troopship. Most of the boys sailing in her were young Canadian conscripts. A hundred and thirty-six of them were officers, newly commissioned. Braddock was one of them." And he went on to tell me Braddock's story.

I wanted to throw the man out. This monstrous, fantastic suggestion of his. . . . But he went on talking—talking in that flat Canadian monotone. It was like a river in spate and I listened to it because I couldn't help myself, because the seed of doubt had been sown and curiosity is a universal failing.

Braddock had been born in London. His father was English, his mother Canadian. When he was two the family had moved to Vancouver. That was in 1927. In 1938 they had returned to England, the father having been appointed London representative of the Canadian firm he worked for. On the outbreak of war a year later, George Braddock, then a boy of fourteen and their only child, had been evacuated to Canada. For the next four years he'd

lived with his aunt, a Mrs. Evelyn Gage, on a ranch in
northern B.C. "A lonely sort of a place out on the old
Caribou Trail," Lane added. "And Evie had just lost her
husband. She was alone there except for the stockman.
She'd no children of her own and . . . well, I guess it's
the old story. She came to regard young George Braddock
more or less as her own son, particularly after his parents
were killed. They died in the bombing—a direct hit on
their flat. Now this is where I come into it. When the boy
went off to join the Army she made a will leaving everything to him 'in love and affection for the boy who was
like a son to me'—those are the actual words. She died
last year, at seventy-two, and that will still stands. She
never made another."

"And you're trying to break it?" Money, I thought—
this smooth-faced, hard-eyed little man's whole life was
money.

"Well, wouldn't you? Evie was my wife's aunt, too—by
marriage; and the ranch alone is worth a hundred thousand dollars. And the boy never wrote to her, you see. All
that time. It's taken lawyers six months just to trace the
guy. They thought at first he was dead."

So that was it. Because the fellow hadn't written. . . .
"It doesn't occur to you, I suppose, that Braddock might
not be interested in a ranch in Canada."

"There's more to it than the ranch—around a quarter
of a million dollars." He gave me a tight little smile. "You
show me the man who'll turn down that sort of money.
Unless there's some very good reason. And in Braddock's
case I'm convinced there is. He's scared of it." He got to
his feet. "Now then. You draw me a portrait of your
brother and then I'll leave you. Draw it as you think he'd
look now. Okay?"

I hesitated, my mind a confused mixture of thoughts.

"I'll pay you for it." He pulled out his pocket book.
"How much?"

I damn near hit him then. What with his suspicions, the stupid allegation he'd made, and then offering me a bribe. "Fifty dollars," I heard myself say and even then I didn't realize why I'd decided to take his money.

I thought for a moment he was going to haggle over it. But he stopped himself in time. "Okay, fifty it is." He counted five ten-dollar bills on to the table. "You're a professional. I guess you're entitled to your fee." It was as though he were excusing himself for being too open-handed.

But when I came to draw it, I found it wasn't so easy. I started the first rough in black with a brush, but it was too strong a medium; you need to have your subject clear in front of your eyes. And when I switched to pen and ink it required too much detail. In the end I used an ordinary pencil, and all the time he stood over me, breathing down my neck. He was a chain-smoker and his quick panting breath made it difficult to concentrate. I suppose he thought he'd be more likely to get his money's worth if he watched every pencil stroke, or maybe it just fascinated him to see the picture emerge. But my mind, going back, searching for the likeness I couldn't quite capture, resented it.

It didn't take me long to realize that time had coloured my memory. Iain's features had become blurred and in that first rough I was emphasizing what I wanted to remember, discarding what I didn't. I scrapped it and started again. And halfway through something happened —it began to take on a vague, shadowy likeness to the man in those photographs. I tore that sheet up, too. But when I tried again the same thing happened—something in the shape of the head, the way the hair grew down towards the forehead, the lines round mouth and eyes, the eyes themselves, particularly the eyes. A pity he'd shown me those photographs. But I knew it wasn't that. It had been quite unconscious. I screwed the sheet up into a ball and threw it

in the wastepaper basket. "I'm sorry," I said. "I thought
I could remember him. But I can't. Not clearly enough to
draw you a true likeness." And I picked up the fifty dollars
and thrust the notes back into his hand. "I can't help you,
I'm afraid."

"You mean you won't."

"Have it your own way," I said. I wanted to get rid of
him, to be alone with time to think, and I thrust my hands
in my pockets, for I knew they were shaking. *Donald my
Donald.* How Iain's voice came back to me down the years
—cruel and charming, gay and sombre, that queer Celtic
mixture. And Laerg, the Laerg of our imagination that
was like a Shangri-La, like a talisman—but still one thing
to him, another to me. *If I go to Laerg it will be to die.
Aye, Donald my Donald—death to me and life to you.* A
quarter of a century and I could remember the words, still
hear his voice slurred with drink in that dirty little pub.
And his face, lined already, sodden that night. . . . "I'm
sorry," I said again. "I can't do it." And I opened the door
for him, anxious to be rid of the man.

He paused, staring at me hard. "Okay," he said finally in
that flat voice of his. I thought he was going then, but he
paused in the doorway. "If you should want to contact
Braddock he's in this country."

"I thought you said he was in Cyprus."

"That's where I saw him on my way through to the Middle East. But he was due for leave. Now he's been posted to
the Hebrides." I didn't say anything and he added: "You'll
find him at the Guided Weapons Establishment on Harris.
Just thought you'd like to know." He was starting down
the stairs when I asked him how he'd found out. "Private
inquiry agent. They've been keeping an eye on him for
me." He smiled. "Odd, isn't it? Why should this guy Braddock get posted to the Hebrides now? And another thing,
Mr. Ross. I know why you wouldn't complete that drawing. I was watching your face." He pulled his hand out of

his pocket. "I guess I'll leave these here." He placed the dollar bills on the top step of the stairs. "Tear them up if you like. But before you do, remember they'll just about cover your fare to the Hebrides." And with that he left me, standing there listening to his footsteps descending the bare boards, staring down at those damned dollars.

And I thought I'd covered up. How many times in the past had I covered up for Iain when he'd acted on the spur of the moment without thought of the future? Father, the police, that poor little idiot Mavis . . . I reached down and picked up the dollar bills, feeling like Judas. But I had to know. A brother is still your brother—hate and love, the old hero-worship still there, dormant, but leaving a vacuum. And I'd no one else. No one in the world I'd really cared for. I had to know.

Part Two

Disaster

I

Guided Weapons HQ

(OCTOBER 16–19)

I left for the north the following day; the night train to Mallaig, the steamer to Rodil in the extreme south of Harris. And all the way there thinking of Iain—Iain and Braddock. The rattle of the wheels, the thump of the screws; their names pounding at my brain, till the two were one. And that Canadian . . . walking up the street to the bus stop there'd been a man in an old raincoat; he'd been on the bus with me and I'd seen him at King's Cross, just behind me waiting to get his ticket. Coincidence perhaps, but if I'd been Lane . . . I pictured him sitting by the telephone in some London hotel waiting for a report, smiling gently to himself when he was told I'd left for the north. Well, to hell with that. It was natural, wasn't it—that I should want to be sure?

I'd finished that jacket design in two hours flat and Alec Robinson had liked it sufficiently to pay me cash. Fifteen guineas. It had made all the difference. Camping out I could manage for a time and I had my return ticket. Something else I'd got from Robinson, too—an introduction to

Cliff Morgan, a meteorologist working at Northton five miles north of Rodil. I'd done the jacket for his book, *Airman's Weather*. It was a contact at any rate and Robinson had told me that Northton was where the Guided Weapons Establishment was.

I'd never been farther north than Ardnamurchan and all up through the islands, through the Sounds of Sleat and Raasay, I was conscious of a growing sense of familiarity, a feeling almost of contentment. The sea and the islands, and the great canopy of the sky—it called to me and my spirit sang with the smell of the salt sea air and the cold wind on my face. And then the mountains of Harris, rising abruptly from the rim of the sea, piled against a leaden sky, their tops blurred by a rainstorm. Rodil proved to be nothing but a hotel and a grass-grown quay falling into decay with an old stone church on the hill behind, built on the pattern of Iona. The boatman, ferrying us from the ship to the quay, looked at my tent and said: "If they've nae room up yonder, I could fix ye a bed maybe." His voice was soft as the rain that was beginning to fall and when I declined his offer he said: "Och weel, it's yer ain business. But it'll be a tur-rible wet night I'm thinking."

The night was both wet and cold and I went to sleep with the sound of the waves sloshing among the seaweed that clothed the rocks, and in the morning I started to walk to Northton. Just beyond the church a girl in a small estate car stopped and offered me a lift. She wore a faded green anarak with the hood pushed back and her face had the freshness of the islands; a dark, wind-browned face and bright blue eyes. "You must have had a very uncomfortable night," she said as we drove up the glen. Her voice was soft and that, too, belonged to the islands. "Why didn't you come to the hotel?" Something about the way she said it, the quick, almost hostile glance she gave me—it was almost as though she resented the presence of a stranger.

But my attention was concentrated on her features,

which were unusual; the dark colouring, the wide mouth below the strong, slightly beaky nose. I knew there were islands up here where Nordic blood had mixed with the Celt to produce blue eyes and dark hair and skin, and because it interested me, I said: "You're an islander, aren't you?"

"I live here."

"No, I meant you come from one of the islands up here."

"My father does." The blue eyes staring at me and again that sense of hostility. "I'm Marjorie Field." She said it defiantly, adding that she worked part-time at the hotel. She seemed to expect some reaction from me, and then she began asking me a lot of questions—my name, where I had come from, how long I intended to stay. At the time I put it down to the natural curiosity about strangers in an isolated community.

The fact that I was an artist seemed to surprise her. "You mean you paint—for a living?" We were at the top of the glen then and she concentrated on her driving until the road straightened out, running down to the flat desolation of buildings scattered round marsh and loch; ugly modern dwelling houses, impermanent-looking against the misted bulk of the hills beyond. "Artists don't come here at this time of the year," she said quite suddenly. "And they don't live in tents, Mr. Ross—not when it's cold and wet."

"D'you know many artists?" I asked.

"A few." She was tight-lipped now, her manner cold, and I had a feeling she didn't believe me. We drove through Leverburgh in silence. This, according to my guide book, had been the village of Obbe until Lord Leverhulme renamed it, as part of his grandiose scheme for making it the centre of the west coast trawler fleet. Beyond the village she turned to me and said: "You're a newspaper man, aren't you?" She said it flatly in a tone almost of resignation.

"What makes you think that?"

She hesitated, and then she said: "My father is Charles Field." She was watching me out of the corner of her eyes and again she seemed to expect some reaction. "He's the Education Officer at Northton." And then she slowed the car and turned her head. "Please. Won't you be frank? You haven't come up here to paint. It's something else—I can feel it."

Her reaction was disturbing, for this was something more than ordinary curiosity. We had reached the top of the next glen and there was the sea and a cloud-capped mountain, half-obscured by rain. To distract her I asked: "Is that Toe Head?"

She nodded. "The hill is called Chaipaval."

It seemed bedded on sand, for the tide was out and the bay to the north was a dull, flat gleam running out to dunes. Dunes, too, formed the neck of land that made Toe Head a peninsula. But much of the sand-bunkered area had been bulldozed flat to make a camp and a landing place for helicopters. Seaward of the camp was a wired-off enclosure with blast-protection walls. The whole effect— the tarmac apron, the tight-packed ranks of the hutted camp, the flat square of the launching pad—it was raw and violent, like a razor slash on an old oil-painting. "And that's the rocket range, I suppose?"

She nodded. "Surprised?" She gave me a quick, rather hesitant smile. "It always seems to surprise people. They've read about it in the papers, but when they actually see it. . . ." And she added: "Of course, being near the road, it's much more obvious than the old range down on South Uist."

In a few minutes now we should be at the camp. "Has a Major Braddock been posted up here?" I asked.

She nodded. "He arrived a few days ago." And after a moment she said: "Is that why you're going to Northton?"

"Yes," I said. "I'm hoping he'll be able to get me across to Laerg."

"Laerg? Then it isn't my father. . . . You really are a painter." She gave a quick, nervous little laugh—as though laughing at her own foolishness. "I'm sorry, but, you see, we get so few people at Rodil—only fishermen, a few tourists, the occasional bird-watcher. Why aren't you in the Mediterranean, somewhere warm and sunny? I never knew an artist come to the Hebrides, not for the winter." Her voice ran quickly on as though by talking she could conceal from me that the presence of an unexpected visitor had scared her.

"You're Scots, aren't you? Perhaps that explains it. But an artist wanting to go to Laerg—it's so unusual. And the birds will have flown. No gannets or puffins. They've all left now. What are you going to paint?"

"The island," I said. "Laerg as the islanders knew it at the worst time of the year."

She nodded. "I've never seen it. But Mike says it can be very beautiful, even in winter."

We were in Northton now and I could see what it had been before the Army came, a line of small crofts clinging to an old existence in a land as old as time. It was an anachronism now, pitiful-looking against the background of the camp with its fuel dump and its M.T. workshops and the barrack lines of its huts. "Where will I find Major Braddock?" I asked.

"His office is in the Admin. block. But he may not be there. He's supposed to be flying to Laerg today." She drew up at the main gate where the model of a rocket stood and a notice board read: Joint Services Guided Weapons Establishment. "The Admin. block is down there on the left," she said. I thanked her and the little estate car drove off along a concrete roadway drifted with sand that led to another part of the camp.

There was no guard on the gate. I simply walked straight in. The huts stretched in two straight lines on either side of a concrete road; sand everywhere and the

rain driving like a thick mist. A staff car and two Land
Rovers stood parked outside the Admin. block. There was
nobody about. I went in. Still nobody and a long passage
running the length of the hut with glass-panelled doors
to the offices leading off it. I walked slowly down it, feeling
oddly nervous, conscious of being an intruder in a completely alien world. Small wooden plaques announced the
contents of each closed box of an office: RSM—W. T.
Symes; Commanding Officer—Colonel S. T. Standing;
Second-in-Command—Major G. H. Braddock (this let-
tered in ink on a paper stick-on); Adjutant—Captain
M. L. Ferguson.

I stood for a moment outside Braddock's door, unwilling
now to face the awkwardness of this moment. Lane and his
snapshots seemed a whole world away and I felt suddenly
foolish to have come so far on such an errand. How could
the man possibly be my brother after all these years? But I
had an excuse all worked out, the excuse that I wanted to
visit Laerg. He could only refuse and at least I'd know for
certain then. I knocked on the door. There was no answer.
I pushed it open. There was nobody inside and I had a
feeling of relief at the sight of the empty desk.

There was a sliding hatch in the partition that separated
this office from the adjutant's and I could hear a voice
talking. But when I went into the next office Captain Ferguson was alone at his desk. He was speaking into the
telephone. He wore battledress, a ginger-haired youngster
with a square freckled face and a Scots accent that took
me back to my Glasgow days. ". . . I can see it is . . .
Aye, well, you check with the Met. Office. . . . Damned if
I do. You tell him yourself. He's down at Leverburgh, but
he'll be back soon. Eleven at the latest, he said, and he'll be
mad as hell when he hears . . . Laddie, you haven't met
the man. He'll be across to see you. . . . Okay, I'll tell
him." He put the phone down and looked at me. "Can I
help you?"

"My name's Ross," I said. "I wanted to see Major Brad-dock."

"He's out at the moment." He glanced at his watch. "Back in about twenty minutes. Is he expecting you?"

"No."

"Well, I don't know whether he'll have time. He's very busy at the moment. Could you tell me what it's about?"

"A private matter," I said. "I'd like to talk to him personally."

"Well, I don't know. . . ." His voice was doubtful. "Depends whether this flight's on or not." He reached for his pad. "Ross, you said? Ayea, I'll tell him." He made a note of it and that was that. Nothing else I could do for the moment.

"Could you tell me where I'll find Cliff Morgan?" I said. "He's a meteorologist at Northton."

"Either at the Met. Office or in the bachelor quarters." He picked up the phone. "I'll just check for you whether he's on duty this morning. Get me the Met. Office, will you." He cupped his hand over the mouthpiece. "There are two of them there and they work it in shifts. Hullo. That you Cliff? Well now look, laddie, drum up a decent forecast, will you. Ronnie Adams is on his way over to see you and he doesn't like the look of the weather. . . . Yes, Himself—and he'll raise hell if the flight's off. Okay. And there's a Mr. Ross in my office. Wants to see you. . . . Yes, Ross."

"Donald Ross," I said.

"Mr. Donald Ross. . . . Aye, I'll send him over." He put down the phone. "Yes, Cliff's on the morning shift. You'll find the Met. Office right opposite you as you go out of the main gate. It's below the Control Tower, facing the landing apron. And I'll tell Major Braddock you're here as soon as he gets back from Leverburgh."

I wished then that I hadn't given my name. But it couldn't be helped. I zipped up my windbreaker, buttoning it tight across my throat. It was raining harder now and I hurried out through the gate and along the road to the hangar. Pools of rain water lay on the parking apron where an Army helicopter stood like some pond insect, dripping moisture. The bulk of Chaipaval was blotted out by a squall. Rain lashed at the glistening surface of the tarmac. I ran for the shelter of the tower, a raw concrete structure, ugly as a gun emplacement. Inside it had the same damp, musty smell. The Met. Office was on the ground floor. I knocked and went in.

It was a bleak dug-out of a room. Two steps led up to a sort of dais and a long, sloped desk that filled all the window space. The vertical backboard had a clock in the centre, wind speed and direction indicators; flanking these were schedules and code tables, routine information. The dust-blown windows, streaked with rain, filtered a cold, grey light. They faced south-west and the view was impressive because of the enormous expanse of sky. On the wall to my right were the instruments for measuring atmospheric pressure—a barograph and two mercury barometers. A Baby Belling cooker stood on a table in the corner and from a small room leading off came the clack of teleprinters.

The place was stuffy, the atmosphere stale with cigarette smoke. Two men were at the desk, their heads bent over a weather report. They looked round as I entered. One of them wore battledress trousers and an old leather flying jacket. He was thin-faced, sad-looking. His helmet and gloves lay on the desk, which was littered with forms and pencils, unwashed cups and old tobacco tin tops full of the stubbed-out butts of cigarettes. The other was a smaller man, short and black-haired, dressed in an open-necked shirt and an old cardigan. He stared at me short-sightedly through thick-lensed glasses. "Mr. Ross?" He had a ruler in his hand, holding it with fingers stained brown with nicotine. "My publishers wrote me you would be coming." He smiled. "It was a good jacket design you did for my book."

I thanked him, glad that Robinson had taken the trouble to write. It made it easier. The clack of the teleprinter ceased abruptly. "No hurry." I said. "I'll wait till you've finished."

"Sit down then, man, and make yourself comfortable." He turned his back on me then, leaning on the tubular frame of his swivel seat to continue his briefing. ". . . Surface wind speed twenty to twenty-five knots. Gusting perhaps forty. Rain squalls. Seven-eighths cloud at five hundred. . . ." His voice droned on, touched with the lilt of his native valleys.

I was glad of the chance to study him, to check what I knew of Cliff Morgan against the man himself. If I hadn't read his book I shouldn't have known there was anything unusual about him. At first glance he looked just an ordinary man doing an ordinary routine job. He was a Welshman and he obviously took too little exercise. It showed in his flabby body and in the unhealthy pallor of his face. The shirt he wore was frayed and none too clean, the grey flannels shapeless and without crease, his shoes worn at the heels. And yet, concentrated now on his briefing, there was something about him that made my fingers itch to draw. The man, the setting, the pilot leaning beside him— it all came together, and I knew this would have made a better jacket for his book than the one I'd done.

The background of his book was a strange one. He had written it in prison, pouring into it all his enthusiasm for the unseen world of air currents and temperatures, of cold and warm fronts and the global movements of great masses of the earth's atmosphere. It had been an outlet for his frustration, filled with the excitement he felt for each new weather pattern, the sense of discovery as the first

pencilled circle—a fall in pressure of a single millibar
perhaps reported by a ship out in the Atlantic—indicated the birth of a new storm centre. His quick, vivid
turn of phrase had breathed life into the everyday meteorological reports and the fact that he was an amateur
radio operator, a "ham" in his spare time, had added to
the fascination of the book, for his contacts were the
weather ships, the wireless operators of distant steamers,
other meteorologists, and as a result the scope of his observations was much wider than that of the ordinary airport weather man taking all his information from teleprinted bulletins.

How such a man came to be stationed in a God-forsaken
little outpost like Northton needs some explanation.
Though I didn't know it at the time, there was already a
good deal of gossip about him. He had been up there over
six months, which was plenty of time for the facts to seep
through, even to that out-of-the-way place. The gossip I
don't intend to repeat, but since the facts are common
knowledge I will simply say this: there was apparently
something in his metabolism that made him sexually an
exhibitionist and attractive to women. He had become
mixed up in a complex affair involving two society
women. One of them was married and a rather sordid
divorce case had followed, as a result of which he had
faced a criminal charge, had been found guilty and sentenced to nine months' imprisonment. He had been a meteorologist at London Airport at the time. On his release
from prison the Air Ministry had posted him to Northton,
where I suppose it was presumed he could do little or no
harm. But a man's glands don't stop functioning because
he's posted to a cold climate. Nor, thank God, do his wits—
a whole ship's company were to owe their lives to the accuracy of his predictions, amounting almost to a sixth
sense where weather was concerned.

The pilot was leaving now. "Okay, Cliff, that settles it. No dice." He picked up his helmet and his gloves. "Pity they don't admit it's blowing like hell out there. No down-draughts, Shelter Bay calm as a mill-pond—that the report I had from Laerg earlier this morning."

"It's always the same when the boys are waiting for their mail."

"That's true. But this time I'm under pressure from both ends. The mail could just as well go by LCT, but then this fellow Braddock . . ." A rain squall lashed the windows. "Just listen to that. He should try his hand at landing a helicopter—that'd teach him to be so bloody enthusiastic. What's he want to do, commit suicide? When it's gusting forty it whams down off Tarsaval. . . ." He stared angrily at the blurred panes. "Thank God they're closing the place down. That idea of relying on a helicopter service through the winter months—who dreamed that one up?"

"Colonel Standing."

"Well, it was bloody crazy. They'd soon have discovered the LCT's were more reliable."

"The landing craft never operated in Scottish waters after the end of September. You know that."

"Well, the trawler then. What was wrong with that?"

"A question of cost; that's what I heard, anyway. And there was still the problem of trans-shipping men and stores from ship to beach. They lost a lot of dories smashed up on the rocks or overturned."

"Well, if it's a question of cost, dories are a damn sight cheaper than helicopters." He turned up the collar of his flight jacket, huddling down into it with a jerk of the shoulders. "Be seeing you, Cliff." But as he turned towards the door, it was flung open and Major Braddock entered. In place of the light suit he wore battledress, but it was the same face—the face of Lane's photographs, lined and leathery, dark-tanned by the Mediterranean sun, and that scar running in a vertical line down the crease of the forehead to the nose.

"What's all this about the flight being off?" Not a glance at me, yet he knew I was there. I could feel it. And that urgent vitality, the way he leaned forward, balanced like a runner on the balls of his feet. "Mike just told me. Is it definite?"

" 'Fraid so, sir," the pilot said. "You see . . ."

But he had turned to me. "You the guy that's wanting to see me?" The black eyes staring straight at me, not a flicker of recognition, only the twitch of a muscle to reveal the nervous tension.

"Yes," I said. "My name's Donald Ross."

He smiled. And in that instant I was sure. He couldn't change that smile; he'd relied too much on its charm all his life.

"A private matter," I said.

He nodded. "Okay, just let me deal with this. . . ." He swung round on the pilot then. "Now look here, Adams, it's all arranged. I'm staying the night there and coming back by LCT tomorrow. Just because it's a bit wet and windy . . . damn it, man, what do you expect in the Hebrides?"

"It's the down-draughts," the pilot said unhappily. "Being slammed down on the deck—well, you ask Cliff here. It just isn't on, not in this weather."

And Cliff Morgan agreed, nodding to the wind speed indicator. "Blowing twenty plus now, almost forty in the gusts. And beginning to veer already. It'll be worse out there." He shook his head. "The forecast's bad."

"The immediate forecast, d'you mean?"

"Well, no. That's bad enough. But I was thinking of the next forty-eight hours. I've an idea the wind's going to veer and go on veering halfway round the clock. We could have a polar air stream with a drop in temperature of perhaps ten degrees and wind speeds as high as fifty, sixty knots."

"When?"

"How do I know? It's just a feeling I have. It may not happen that way at all. He indicated the wall to our left, where the big weather maps hung. "The lower one shows the position when I came on duty at six o'clock; it relates to o-o-o-one hours this morning. The upper one is my forecast of what the pattern will look like twenty-four hours later." This map was perspex-framed and the isobars had been drawn in with chinograph pencil on the perspex. Here the High that had covered the British Isles for days, and which was still shown centred over Eastern Europe in the lower map, had disappeared completely, to be replaced by an intense depression moving in from the Atlantic. There was another, smaller depression behind it and a weak High over Greenland. "A south-westerly air stream now, you see—somewhere between twenty and forty knots. But the outlook is entirely dependent upon those two depressions and what happens to that High over Greenland. My feeling is this—those depressions are going to merge, the High is going to build up. The effect would be for that depression to intensify very rapidly. By tomorrow it could be a very deep one centred over Norway and if at the same time the High builds up . . ." He shrugged. "Wind would be north, you see, gale force at least— perhaps very strong indeed. But there's no certainty about it. Just my interpretation based on nothing more than a feeling I have."

Braddock stared at the map. "Well, whether you're right or wrong, the fine spell's over, eh?"

"Looks like it, Major."

"Still, if you're right—northerlies; we'd still be able to use Shelter Bay."

The phone rang and Cliff Morgan answered it. "For you," he said, handing it to Braddock.

I watched him as he took the call. The way the black

brows came down and the lines deepened. The years had greatly changed him. His voice, too, was harsher and more mature. ". . . Who? I see . . . badly hurt? . . . Okay, Mike, I'll tell Adams." His eyes met mine for a moment as he put the receiver down. I thought he smiled, but it was so fleeting a movement of the mouth below the dark moustache that I couldn't be sure. He got up, went over to the pilot, and stood facing him. "Well now, that gives you a fine little problem. McGregor, the driver of the Scammell, has got himself badly smashed up. A piece of radar equipment toppled on him after he'd got it stuck on one of the bends of the High Road. His leg's crushed right up to the thigh, abdominal injuries, too." And he stood over the wretched man, daring him to say that he still wouldn't go, just as he'd stood over me when we were kids. "Doc says he must be flown out immediately."

Adams licked his lips. "What about the LCT's?"

"No good. Four-four-Double-o left Laerg at eleven-thirty last night. She should be in the South Ford by now. And Eight-six-one-o left shortly after two this morning. She's due in Leverburgh any moment. To get her unloaded . . ." He shook his head. "It'd be almost twenty-four hours before we could get him ashore by LCT, and from what I gathered he wouldn't last that long. His life's in your hands. Either you fly him out . . ." He gave a little shrug and left it at that. And then he turned to me as though the matter were settled. "If you're around when I get back tomorrow, we'll have that chat, eh?" He said it with his eyes staring straight at me, still not the slightest flicker, and his voice so matter-of-fact I could easily have persuaded myself that he really was Braddock—just Braddock and nothing to do with me.

"I'll be here," I said.

He nodded and went towards the door, opening it and marching straight out, leaving Adams standing there.

Cliff Morgan glanced again at the wind speed and and direction indicators, pencilled a note or two on a piece of paper, and passed it to the pilot. Adams took it, but he didn't look at it, nor did he look at the meteorologist. He didn't seem conscious that we were both of us watching him. He was facing the window, his eyes turned inwards, his whole mind given to the decision. I knew the answer, just as Braddock had known it. Adams knew it, too. I watched him bow to the inevitable, turning up the collar of his flight jacket and walking out without a word, the decision to fly made against his better judgment.

It was the moment that things began to go wrong, but none of us could know that, though perhaps Cliff Morgan sensed it, or again perhaps he knew his weather better than the rest of us. "The poor bastard!" he murmured, and I knew he was referring to the pilot, not to the injured man.

He looked at me as the door shut behind Adams. "They vary, you know," he said. "In temperament." And he added: "If it had been Bill Harrison now, he wouldn't have hesitated. A reckless devil, Bill; but he knows his own mind. He'd never have let himself be forced into it like that." He sucked on the end of his pencil, hollowing his cheeks, and then with a quick, abrupt movement, he went into the back room, tore off the teleprint sheets, and came back reading them. "This bloody evacuation, that's what it is, man. Thinking God Almighty would arrange the weather for them while they got their men and equipment off the island. I warned them."

It was the first I'd heard about the evacuation, and realizing this he began to explain as we stood by the window, watching Braddock and Adams walk out to the helicopter and climb in. But I barely took in what he was saying for my mind had room only for one thought at that moment— the certainty that Braddock was my brother. This in itself was such a staggering revelation that it was only later that

I began to consider the other factors—why, for instance, he had applied for a posting to the Hebrides, why he should have been so set on Adams making the flight?

The engine started, the rotor blades began to turn, and the helicopter rose from the parking apron, drifting sideways in a gust and just clearing the hangar. Almost immediately its shape became blurred; then it vanished completely, lost in the low cloud and a squall of rain. For a moment longer the engine was faintly audible. Then that, too, was swallowed up as rain lashed at the windows.

The risk they ran in attempting that flight was something I couldn't assess; I had no experience then of the incredible malignant power of the down-draughts that come smashing down from Tarsaval and the other heights of Laerg, down into Shelter Bay. Nor was it possible for me to absorb the whole complex set-up of this military operation into the midst of which I had suddenly been pitchforked. Even when Cliff Morgan had explained to me the details of the evacuation, how Braddock had insisted on sending a detachment with towing vehicles down to the old rocket range on South Uist so that the LCT's could beach in the South Ford as an alternative to Leverburgh, the night-and-day drive to get Laerg cleared and the round-the-clock movement of landing craft, I still didn't appreciate how vulnerable the whole operation was to the weather. I had no experience of landing craft.

Nor for that matter had Cliff Morgan. But weather to him was a living thing, the atmosphere a battle-ground. He had, as I've said, a sixth sense where weather was concerned and he was very conscious of the changed pattern. "A polar air stream now." He said it to himself as though facing the implications for the first time. "Jesus, man!" He lit a cigarette, staring at me over the flame. "Know anything about weather?"

"A little," I said, but he didn't seem to hear.

"No imagination—-that's the Army for you. Look at

Braddock. Up into the air and not a clue what he faces at the other end. And Standing—you'd think Standing would try to understand. He's got brains. But no imagination, you see, none at all." He slid his bottom on to the swivel seat and drew a sheet of paper towards him. "Look you now, I'll draw it for you. As I see it—in here." And he tapped his forehead. "Not the wind on my face, but a map, a chart, a picture. Imagination! But *dammo di,* they're none of them Celts. Though Braddock—" He shook his head as though he weren't quite certain about Braddock, and then he reached for a blank sheet of paper and with his pen drew a map that included North America, Greenland, Norway—the whole North Atlantic. On this he pencilled in the existing pattern; the Azores High bulging north towards Ireland and the two Lows driving that other High, which had been over England, east towards Russia.

"Now, the area I'm watching is down here." His pencil stabbed the left-hand bottom edge of the map. "That's about seven hundred miles north-east of Bermuda. It's the place where our depressions are born—the place where the cold, dry air from the north, sweeping down the east of North America, meets up with the warm, damp air of the Gulf Stream. It's the breeding place for every sort of beastliness—hurricanes bound for the States, big depressions that move across the North Atlantic at tremendous speed to give Iceland, and sometimes the Hebrides and the north of Scotland, wind speeds almost as bad as the much-publicized Coras and Ethels and Janets and what-have-you's that cause such havoc in America. Now look at this."

He picked up a red pencil and with one curving sweep drew an arrow across to the area between Iceland and Norway. "There! That's your Low now." He drew it in, a deep depression centred over Norway, extending west as far as Iceland, east into Siberia. And then on the other side, over towards Greenland and Canada, more isobars drawn in with long, curving sweeps of hand and pencil. A high pressure area, and between the High and the Low, in ink, he marked in arrows pointing south and south-east. "That's a polar air stream for you. That's a real big polar air stream, with the wind roaring out of the Arctic and temperatures falling rapidly. Snow at first in the north. Then clear skies and bitter cold."

He stared at it for a moment, an artist regarding his handiwork. "I haven't seen that sort of weather pattern up here—not at this time of the year. But I experienced it once in Canada just after the war when I was working for the Department of Transport at Goose Bay. By Christ, man, that was something. A Low over Greenland, a High centred somewhere over the mouth of the Mackenzie River and a polar air stream pouring south across the Labrador." He drew it for me then on another sheet of paper, adding, as his red pencil circled in the pattern: "Have you any idea what a polar air stream means up there in the Canadian North in October—to the Eskimos, the prospectors, the ships in Hudson's Bay?" And when I shook my head he embarked on an explanation. I can't remember all he said; I found myself listening to the tone of his voice rather than to his actual words. It had become noticeably more Welsh, a distinct lilt that seemed to change his personality. It was his enthusiasm for the subject, I suppose, but all at once he was like a poet, painting with words on a canvas that was one quarter of the globe. I listened, fascinated; and as he talked the red pencil was constantly moving, filling in that old atmospheric battle picture until the high-pressure system over north-western Canada had become a great whorl of concentric lines.

Like an artist he couldn't resist the picture as a whole, but as his pencil flew over Greenland and down as far as the Azores, it was this big High he talked about; the effect it had had on people, animals, and crops—on transportation, particularly aircraft and ships. The High represented cold, heavy air; clean, crisp, dry-frozen stuff hugging the earth's surface, weighing down on thousands of square miles of ocean, thousands of square miles of pack ice. The winds around this cold mass had been clockwise and wherever they had touched the periphery of the low-pressure area to the east, the movement of the cold air stream had been accelerated to hurricane force. At first those gales had been blizzards, thick with driving snow as damp, humid masses of air were forced into the upper atmosphere and cooled to the point of precipitation. "When that High got really established," he said, "there was snow in many places that didn't expect it for another month. Blizzards in the Middle West of Canada reaching south across the border into the States, and that High was like a young giant. It went on drawing strength into itself —like a boxer in training and working himself up for the big fight."

"You make it sound very dramatic," I said.

"Weather is dramatic, man; indeed it is, when you've got something like that building up." He was entirely engrossed in the picture he had drawn from memory. "It's fluid, you see; always a shifting pattern, never still. It's a battlefield of pressures and temperatures and humidity; Highs versus Lows, with the cold fronts and the warm fronts the points of engagement. A break-through at one point can spell disaster a thousand, two thousand miles away—a ship overwhelmed, breakwaters demolished, the flooding of lowlands, the destruction of houses, death to men and livestock."

He was being carried away again on the tide of his imagination. But then he suddenly stopped. "It was a long time ago. But I can remember it—by God I can." He picked up the map he'd drawn, stared at it for a moment, then crumpled it up and threw it into the biscuit tin that acted as a wastepaper basket. "That's just one of dozens of maps I could draw you—weather I've known. . . . Some

of it I covered in my book. And when this High disinte-
grates or that Low fills in it's something different again."
He turned with a quick movement of his head to stare at
the map framed on the wall, the chinagraph bright on the
perspex. "Those two Lows coming in. . . . Look at them.
I'm already getting figures that complicate the whole picture. They may behave normally. They may remain separate entities. But somehow, I don't know why exactly, they
worry me. That's something you learn in this game, you
see—it's ninety per cent science, a matter of filling in
figures, but there's the other ten per cent . . . your instinct comes into it then, instinct based on experience." He
gave a little laugh and shook his head. "Make yourself comfortable," he said, "while I catch up on my homework."
He glanced at the clock. "Another fifteen minutes and
then we'll go over to the Mess for lunch. I expect you
could do with a drink. I certainly could."

I sat and watched him checking his instruments, going
through the teleprinter sheets, flying a balloon to check
ceiling height, marking up his meteorological forms, phoning his report through to Pitreavie, and all the time I was
thinking of Iain, trying to remember him as I had last seen
him, nineteen years old and wearing battledress, the sergeant's stripes white-new on his arm. He's been drunk that
night and within the week he'd sailed with his unit out
of the Clyde, bound for North Africa—Operation "Torch."
"Can I have a piece of paper?" I said, and when Morgan
passed me a scribbling pad, I began pencilling a sketch
from memory. The result was the same as when I had
tried it in my studio with that bloody little Canadian business man breathing down my neck. I wondered what
Lane was doing now—would he come up here to bust Braddock's identity wide open?

I didn't like the thought of that. The wild streak in Iain
had always bordered on violence. That poor devil of a

lieutenant, his jaw smashed—and there had been other in-
cidents, before that; Big Neil McNeill knocked senseless
with an oar after he'd shot a seal. My fault that time. I
hadn't wanted the seal killed and when it was done I'd
flown at Big Neil, blubbering with anger, and got a
kick in the groin that sprawled me screaming in the bottom of the boat. And in Glasgow, at that factory—they'd
called him Black Iain—black because of his temper and
his dark features and his arrogance. They'd picked him
up drunk one night and he'd knocked out three policemen
and got away. That was the night he joined the Army.

"That's Braddock." I looked up to find Morgan standing
over me with a puzzled look. "Yes, Braddock," I said. I'd
have to call him Braddock now. I'd have to think of him as
Braddock. I tore the sheet from the pad, crumpled it, and
tossed it into the biscuit tin.

"You made him look much younger."

"I was just passing the time."

He gave me a sharp, inquiring look, nodded and went
back to the desk. It was a warning. I'd have to be careful.
And if Lane came north. . . .

Cliff Morgan was at the barograph now. He went back to
his work at the desk, and watching him again, I was conscious of a tenseness. It showed in the way he paused every
now and then to stare out of the window, the quick glances
at the wind-speed indicator. And then the phone rang.
"All right, Mike—as soon as I'm relieved." He slammed
the receiver down. "Can I give Colonel Standing a weather
briefing? No interest in this office so long as the sun's shining, but now it's wet and blowing half a gale. . . ." He
shrugged. "Have you met Colonel Standing?" And when I
told him No, he added: "I'll introduce you then. Alec
Robinson said something about your wanting to get to
Laerg and for that you need Standing's permission."

Prompt at twelve Cliff Morgan's junior came dripping

in out of the rain, a quiet, reserved man who gave me a fleeting smile as we were introduced. His name was Ted Sykes. "I hear Ronnie took off. What's his ETA?"

"About twelve-thirty. Wind speed's twenty-five knots—almost a dead-noser." Cliff Morgan pulled his jacket on and took a tie from the pocket.

"Rather him than me," Sykes said, at the desk now, riffling through the teleprint sheets. "Braddock with him?"

"Yes."

"Well, I hope it keeps fine for them." He said it sourly. It was obvious neither of them liked it. Cliff Morgan was standing at the desk, tying his tie, staring at the grey misery of the sky. Rain dribbled down the panes.

"There's a casualty to be lifted out."

"So I heard."

"Keep your fingers crossed then." He turned abruptly and got his raincoat, and then we were out in the wind and the rain, hurrying through pools of water to the camp. "Better not ask for a flight out to Laerg. It means a blood chit, you see, and they don't like it. Landing craft's all right. I think Standing would agree to that." His voice came to me, staccato fragments blown on the wind. "Perhaps tomorrow. But it'll be rough. You a good sailor?" And when I told him I'd had almost eleven years at sea, he nodded. "That's all right then. At least you'll see Laerg as it really is. Funny thing. I've never been there. Wanted to ever since I came up here. No time, and now it's being evacuated. . . ." We had reached the Admin. block. "You might offer to do some sketches of the evacuation. Standing, you see, is not a man who's very easy with strangers, but he's artistic. Paints a bit himself and I'm told he has some interesting pictures up at his house. Nudes mostly, but not sexy—the real thing."

Standing was waiting for us in his office, tall and slightly stooped, with a thin, serious face and glasses, a tight, unsmiling mouth. He looked a cold, moody man and his long-fingered hands were seldom still, nervously shifting the papers on his desk, toying with the slide-rule, or gently tapping. Cliff Morgan introduced me as an artist who wanted to visit Laerg, but all I got was a nod and a cold stare. He had Ferguson with him and he was only interested in one thing, the weather. He listened to what Morgan had to say, his eyes on the window, which was tight-shut against the wind. The view was depressing—the brown creosoted back of a hut, a grey waste of sky, and the rain driving.

"Can Adams get the man out? That's all I want to know." Even then he didn't look at Cliff Morgan, but sat staring at the window, drumming with his fingers.

"Only Ronnie could tell you that," Cliff answered and I sensed his antagonism.

"Adams isn't here. I'm asking you, Mr. Morgan."

"I'm a meteorologist. I feed the pilot information. He makes his own decisions."

"I know that. I'm asking your opinion."

Cliff shrugged. "It's dicey—but then that's to be expected when you're flying to a place like Laerg." The native lilt was stronger now.

"The decision was made in your office, I believe. Did Major Braddock order Adams to fly?"

"How could he? It's the pilot's decision—always. You know that."

"Very well. I will put it another way. Would Captain Adams have flown if there hadn't been an injured man to bring out?"

"No."

Colonel Standing sighed and reached for his slide-rule, running it back and forth in his hands. "Two men's lives and an expensive machine. . . ." He was staring at the slide-rule as though calculating the risk in terms of a mathematical equation. "Captain Fairweather has all he needs, hasn't he?" This with a quick glance at his adjutant. "I mean the hospital is still functioning, isn't it?"

"Aye, but it's little better than a first-aid post now, sir. And Fairweather's not a surgeon."

"He's still a member of the medical profession. If he has to operate, then he's got the means and we can link him up with Scottish Command and give him a surgeon's guidance." He dropped the slide-rule. "Have them contact Adams. He's to cancel the flight and return immediately. Now what's the landing craft position? Stratton is the more experienced of the two. Where's Eight-six-one-o?"

"She passed through the Sound of Harris about nine-thirty this morning. If the tide's right, she should be beaching any moment now."

"In the South Ford."

"Aye. They're double-banked, you see. If you remember, sir, it was to cope with just this eventuality that Major Braddock arranged for a stand-by detachment based on the old range. Four-four-Double-o cleared from Laerg on the same tide, about three hours after Stratton. She'd have been in Leverburgh by now if it hadn't been for a wee bit of trouble with one of the oil pumps. It slowed her down for a while."

"How far out is she—an hour, two hours?"

"Two I should think. I'll check if you like."

"No, there's no time." Standing's fingers were drumming gently on the desk again. "It makes no difference anyway. She's the nearest. A pity it's Kelvedon and not Stratton. But it can't be helped. Have Signals contact him: Double-four-Double-o to turn round and make back to Laerg at full speed to pick up a casualty."

"It'll be eight, maybe nine hours before she gets there. A falling tide then and it'll be dark."

"They should be able to run their bows in, pick the

man up, and winch off again. There won't be much of a sea running in the Bay. He'll just have to do the best he can. See if you can speak to Kelvedon yourself, explain the urgency."

Ferguson hesitated. "You wouldn't have a word with Bob Fairweather first? Maybe the man's condition . . ."

"No, Ferguson. Captain Fairweather's concern is with the injured man. I have to consider what the position will be if Major Braddock and Captain Adams are injured, perhaps killed, and their machine written off. All right?"

"Yes, sir."

"Contact Adams first. Then have a word with Kelvedon and get Four-four-Double-o turned round as soon as you can."

"She'll still be loaded."

"Of course she will. That can't be helped. Now get moving. Every minute counts." He watched his adjutant leave. Then when the door was shut he turned to me. "You've come at an awkward time." His voice shook slightly, so did his hands; his nerves were strung taut by the decision he'd had to make.

"I didn't realize you were evacuating the island," I said.

He was staring down at the desk. Behind him on the wall hung a six-inch to the mile map of Laerg and beside it were graphs, presumably of the past season's shooting; part of the skin of a rocket, a jagged, crumpled piece of light alloy, lay on the floor beside his chair. "There's always somebody wanting to go to Laerg—naturalists, birdwatchers, archaeologists. They're a darned nuisance."

"My father was born on Laerg."

It made no impression. He wasn't interested in the island as such. Later I learned that in the year he'd been in the Hebrides, he'd only visited Laerg once—a quick trip by helicopter on a fine day. "You're an artist, you say. Professional?"

"Yes."

He nodded to the wall behind me. "What do you think of that?"

It was a landscape, the mountains of Harris by the look of it, in sunlight with a glimpse of the sea. The brush-work was technically quite good, but it lacked feeling. I didn't know what to say for I knew he'd done it himself, and presumably he liked it since he'd hung it in his office. "Well?"

I hesitated; but better to be honest. I told him it was nice but that I didn't think the artist was at home with his subject. To my surprise, he nodded agreement. "I hung it there just to remind me that the sun does shine up here sometimes. It was hot when I painted that. But you're right—I'm not at home with landscapes. If you're here for a time I'll show you some others. My wife models for me." The phone rang on his desk. "Standing here. . . . Thinks he can make it?" He glanced at the window as the rain beat against it in a gust of wind. "Tell Adams it's an order. . . . Yes, Ferguson, an order, do you hear?" He was trembling again as he put the phone down. For a moment he just sat there, drumming with his fingers at the desk. Then, as though suddenly conscious of my presence again, he said: "All right, Ross, we'll see what we can do. Are you any good at seascapes, ships, that sort of thing?"

"Sea and mountains and rock," I said; "that's what I like to paint."

"Good. A sketch or two of the evacuation—a painting perhaps; the DRA would like that, particularly if there are some birds in it." I pointed out that the birds wouldn't be back for another three months. "Well, there's such a thing as artists' license. The General likes birds." He hesitated. Finally he nodded. "All right. Have a word with Ferguson. He'll fix it with the Movements Officer and arrange with one of the landing craft skippers to take you out. You'll have about two days there, maybe three."

"It'll be something just to see the island," I said.

"So long as you don't get in Captain Pinney's way. They're under considerable pressure. Where are you staying?" And when I told him I was camping at Rodil, he said: "We can do better than that. I'll tell Ferguson to allocate you a room for the night. We've always plenty of space in the winter months."

I thanked him and followed Cliff Morgan out of the stuffy little office into the cold, driving rain. I was feeling in a daze. First Iain, and now Laerg . . . Laerg within reach at last. "I didn't think it would be as easy as that," I murmured.

"Well, they're not worried about security, you see. The place is a write-off and that makes it easier than when they were lobbing missiles into the water beside it. But you wouldn't have got there if you hadn't been an artist." And he added, "You never know where you are with Standing. And now that Braddock's here. . . ."

He left it at that. "What about Braddock?" I asked.

"Oh, he's all right, whatever anybody else may say. By God, he's woken this place up since he arrived. Yes indeed, and he'll have a drink with you, which is more than Standing will."

The bar was deserted when we reached the Mess. But as we stood there drinking our gin-and-tonic, the officers drifted in one by one. Major Rafferty, the Quartermaster, a big beefy man with a florid face and a Scots accent; the Movements Officer, Fred Flint—short and round, with a button nose and the face of a pug, all bulging eyes, and a way of dropping his aitches and watching with a glint of humour to see if it startled you; the Doc, also a captain but younger, with the air of a man nothing can surprise any more; several lieutenants, much younger still; and finally Field—Lieutenant Field, who was old enough to be their father. He had a strange hatchet face, grey hair, and a mouth that drooped at the corners. His eyes were deep-socketed, tired—blue eyes that had a nervous blink and didn't look straight at you but beyond, as though searching for some lost horizon. ". . . Our Education Officer," the ebullient Captain Flint added as he introduced us. "Now what y'aving, Professor?"

"Oh, that's very thoughtful of you, Flinty. Let me see now. The usual, I think—a gin-and-tonic without the gin." He smiled and the smile lit up his whole face so that it suddenly had a quality of great warmth. It was a striking face; moreover, it was a face that seemed vaguely familiar. But not in battledress; in some other rig. "I take it the LCT's are all at sea since Movements can take time off for a lunchtime drink."

"All at sea is just about right, Professor. Stratton's missed his tide and dropped his hook under the lee outside Loch Carnan. It'll be five hours at least before he can get her into the beaching position in the Ford, another three before the boys can start off-loading. Major B. will like that— I don't think."

"Braddock won't know anything about it. He's flown to Laerg."

"Oh yes, he will. I just met the Colonel. He's cancelled the flight. And he's turned Four-four-Double-o round fully loaded and sent her steaming back to Laerg to pick up a casualty. Proper box-up if you ask me."

"Well, why not switch Stratton's ship to Leverburgh?" Major Rafferty suggested. "Damn it, man, with Kelvedon turned back, the quay will be empty."

"Tim, my boy, you're a genius. I never thought of that." The quick grin faded. "I did mention it, but Stratton told me to go to hell. His men needed sleep, and so does he. If Major B. wants Eight-six-o-o at Leverburgh, then he'll have to give the order himself. I bet he gets the same answer, too. Those boys are just about out on their feet, and Stratton's his own master. He's not at the beck and call of anybody here—the Colonel or anybody else. I only hope," he added, "that Kelvedon gets there in time." He looked down at his glass and then at Field. "Did you know this bloke McGregor?" And when the other nodded, he said: "Poor beggar. First blood to the new drive." His voice sounded angry. "And if you ask me it won't be the last. When they're tired they get careless. I told Command it needed more time when they were planning this flipping operation. But they wouldn't listen. I'm only the bloke that loads the ships. I wouldn't know." Ferguson came in then, the freckles on his face showing up like spots in the electric light, a strained look about the eyes. "You look shagged, my boy. I prescribe a night out with the fattest trollop you can find between the Butt of Lewis and Barra Head."

"Aye, that'd do me fine."

"What's the matter? Caught between the upper and the nether millstone again?"

"If by that you mean what I think you mean, then the answer is Yes and it'll cost you a Scotch for stating the obvious. The Colonel ordered Major B to turn back."

"We know that. And he's bust the schedule wide open by converting Four-four-Double-o into a hospital ship."

"This is going to put everyone in a good temper for the rest of the day." Major Rafferty downed his drink and set his tankard on the bar top. "That poor laddie, Doc— how is he?"

"He's still alive." The M.O. ordered another Scotch.

"What are his chances?"

The dark eyebrows lifted. "Now? Nil, I should say. If they'd got him out by air. . . ." He shrugged. "But I told the Colonel that. So did Bob Fairweather. McGregor had the whole of that crushing weight on top of him for almost an hour before they were able to release him."

There was a hushed silence. "Oh, well," Flint said, "let's have some lunch." He stubbed out his cigarette and hitched up his trousers. "And after lunch," he added,

"I'm going to have a ziz. Four o'clock this morning, two
the night before, and stone the bloody crows it looks like
four again tomorrow morning." He glanced at me, his eyes
popping with that irrepressible glint of Cockney humour. "Four o'clock suit you—Captain Stratton driving
and an iron bathtub slamming into a head sea fit to knock
your block off?"

"For Laerg?" I asked.

"That's right—where the Jumblies live. The Colonel
mentioned it to me just now. I'll fix it with Stratton; he'll
give you the ride of your life . . . that is, if our weather
genius 'ere doesn't frighten him so as he loses his nerve."

"Water Transport take the shipping forecasts," Cliff
said. "They don't trust me."

"It isn't that, Cliff. It's just that Stratton believes in con-
tinuity—likes his forecasts all the time from the same
source. But shipping forecasts—hell! What I've seen of
the shipping forecasts up here, they only tell you what
you've got sitting on top of you, never what you're going to
get—which for my money is the only thing worth a
damn." He turned to me. "What's your view? I gather
you've put in a good deal of sea time?"

It was said out of politeness to include me in the conversation, and as I stood there, sipping my drink and
listening to their talk, I was conscious that this was a
tight-knit, closed little world, a community not unlike
a ship's company. They accepted me, as they accepted Cliff
Morgan—not as one of themselves, but as an interesting specimen of the outside world, to be tolerated and
treated kindly. I was even more conscious of this at lunch,
which was a good meal pleasantly served by a bright little
Hebridean waitress. The atmosphere was a strange mixture of democracy and paternal feudalism. It was the Navy
all over again, but with a subtle difference; and the
youngsters calling me "sir" to remind me how the years
had flown. "What do you think of modern art, sir?" Picasso,

Moore, Annigoni—a reproduction of Annigoni's picture of the Queen hung on the Mess wall; they knew the most publicized names and seemed eager for artistic information, so that for the moment they gave me the illusion of being a visiting genius, and I hoped to God I didn't sound pompous as I tried to answer their queries.

And then Braddock came in and the table fell suddenly silent. He sat down without a word to anyone, and I could see by the way his head was tucked down into his shoulders that he was in a blazing temper.

"Too bad you didn't make it," Major Rafferty murmured.

The black brows came down in a frown. "Too bad, you say?" His tone was clipped and angry. "If Adams had had any sense he'd have unplugged his radio. We'd have made it all right."

"Have you seen the Colonel?"

"He'd gone up to his house by the time we landed. Anyway, no point. He's made his decision." He started in on his soup. But after a moment he glanced at the Movements Officer. "Flint. What's the ETA for that landing craft?"

"At Laerg? Eight-thirty—nine o'clock. Maybe later. She's bucking a head sea. And that's presuming they don't have any more trouble with that oil pump."

"Which means embarking a stretcher case from a dory in the dark."

"Unless Kelvedon beaches her. The wind's westerly. Shelter Bay shouldn't be too . . ."

"He's not to beach her—do you understand? Stratton might do it. He's an old hand up here, but Kelvedon's new and if he gets his craft . . ." He gave a quick shrug. "I'll have a word with him." His eyes, shifting along the table, met mine for a moment. There was a hardness, an urgency about him. Maybe it was telepathy—I had always been able to sense his mood; I had the feeling that there was something he desperately wanted, something quite unconnected with the injured man. I was remembering the scene in the Met. Office, his determination to make that flight. And then from the files of my memory a sentence sprang: *It's the breath of life to you, isn't it, Donald? But I tell ye, man, it's death to me. That I know —deep down. Death, do ye hear, and I'll not be going there for you or anybody else.* So long ago now, but I could hear his voice still. He'd been talking of Laerg—just after that trawler had brought me back. Had he forgotten? For some reason I'd never been able to fathom, he'd been afraid of the place, as though it bore him some personal animosity; and yet at the same time he'd been fascinated— a fascination that was born of his instinctive, almost primitive fear of it. And now he was desperate to get there, had had himself posted up here to the Hebrides for that purpose; why?

The table had fallen silent, an awkward stillness. One by one the officers rose, put their napkins in the pigeonholes on the side-table, and went out into the lounge for coffee. I rose with Cliff Morgan, conscious that Braddock was watching me. "Mr. Ross." Strange that he could call me that. His dark eyes held no glimmer of a smile, his voice no trace of the old Highland accent. "We'll have our talk— later."

I nodded and went out. Surely to God I couldn't be mistaken. Field handed me my coffee. "Sugar?" I shook my head. The radio was playing softly—some jazzed-up singer mouthing of love. "You met my daughter, Marjorie, I think." I nodded, my mind still on Braddock. "I thought perhaps you'd care to drop in this evening. We're not far, just beyond the church at Rodil; one of the old black houses. As a painter it might interest you. About nine o'clock. Would that suit you?"

It was kind of him, almost as though he'd known what it was like to lie alone in a small tent on the shores of a loch with a gale tearing at the nylon canopy. I felt I was very near to remembering that face then, but still the connection evaded me. In a newspaper, or a magazine, perhaps. I thanked him and added: "But I believe I'm staying the night in the quarters here."

He turned to Ferguson. "Will you be along tonight, Mike? Marjorie's expecting you."

"Yes, of course—my lords and masters permitting."

"Then bring Mr. Ross with you."

It wasn't the sort of face you could forget, just like an axe-head, keen and sharp in the features and broadening out to the head. I was still thinking about this when Cliff Morgan said he was going over to his quarters and suggested I might like to see his radio equipment.

Outside, the rain had stopped and the overcast had lifted. "That's the warm front—it's passed over us, you see." The wind was still as strong, west now and colder. "Whatever Braddock says, Colonel Standing was right to recall Adams. This is no weather for a helicopter landing on Laerg." The quarters were only a step from the Mess. He led me down a long passage and stopped at Room 23. As he unlocked the door, he said: "I don't sleep here, except when I'm calling Canada or some place that means staying up half the night. I've billeted myself out with a widow and her daughter in one of the crofts in Northton. Very irregular, but I like my comfort, you see." He smiled and pushed open the door. There was a bed thrust close against one wall, a bureau and wardrobe huddled in a corner; all the rest of the room was taken up with his equipment. "Since I published that book I've been able to buy all the things I couldn't afford before. It's been produced in the States and translated into German, Italian, and Swedish. Now I have everything I need; very complete it is now." He switched on, seated himself at the keyboard with his earphones. "It's the weather I'm interested in. But you know that, of course. Now I want to find one or two ships who can tell me what it's like out to the west and north of here." His hands, delicate as a pianist's, were fingering the dials, deftly tuning. The tall cabinet full of valves began to hum gently. And then his right hand thumbed the key and the soft buzz of his call sign sounded in the room. He was lost to me now, silent in a world of his own.

I sat on the bed, smoking a cigarette and watching him. Time passed. I found some paper in the bureau and began to sketch him. Periodically he spoke, but to himself rather than to me: *"The Kincaid.* An old freighter that, six thousand tons. She's outward bound for the Saguenay to pick up a cargo of aluminium. Reports wind north-easterly, force four . . . *Bismuth*—that's one of the Hastings on air reconnaissance five hundred miles west of Ireland; reporting to Bracknell." He picked up two more ships out in the Atlantic, and then he was talking to a trawler south-east of Iceland. *"Arctic Ranger.* Wind veering northerly and a swell coming down past the east coast of Iceland. Getting quite cold up there. Temperature down to thirty-eight and flurries of snow. Wind increasing, around thirty-five knots." He took off his earphones. "I think I'll go up to the office now and see what Ted has on the teleprints." He switched off.

"Worried?" I asked. I had finished my sketch and was lounging back on the bed.

"No, not worried. Uneasy, though. And if it develops as I think it might . . ." He pushed his chair back and stood there a moment, running his hand through his thick dark hair, biting on the pencil clenched between his teeth. "It would be unusual—so early in the season. In January now . . ." He gave that quick little shrug of his that always seemed accompanied by a sideways movement of the head, and then he was pacing up and down; half a dozen steps and then about and retrace them, back and forth with his eyes on the ground, not seeing anything but what was in his mind. He could have got the habit from his time in prison, but I thought it more likely to be the loneliness of his job. He was a solitary. Why otherwise become a meteorologist and then take to operating a ham radio station as a hobby? There are countless men like Cliff Morgan—intelligent, sensitive, artists in their way. They get on all right with women, but escape from the competitive male world by burying themselves body and soul in work that is concerned with things rather than people—impersonal things. With Cliff it was the impersonal forces of the earth's atmosphere, his human contacts mostly made at one remove through the tenuous medium of the ether. I wondered what he'd do if he met opposition—direct opposition, man to man, on his own ground. I thought perhaps he could be very tricky then, perhaps behave with quite astonishing violence.

He had stopped his pacing and was standing over me, staring down at the sketch I'd drawn. "You work pretty fast."

"It's just a rough," I said. "Pencil sketch of a man who's made his work his life."

He laughed. "Oh, I can relax. Indeed I can—if she's pretty enough. But then there's not much difference, is there now; women and weather, they both have their moods, they can both destroy a man. That's why storms are given girls' names. Do you need that sketch? I mean, if you were just drawing to pass the time. . . ."

I saw he really wanted it. "It's your paper anyway," I said and I handed it to him. He stood for a moment looking down at it. Then he placed it carefully on the key board. "This trip to Laerg," he said. "Do you have to go —I mean now, tomorrow morning?"

"Of course I'm going," I told him. "It's what I've wanted ever since I returned to England."

He nodded. "Well, let's go over to the Met. Office and see what makes. But I'm telling you, man, you could have it very rough indeed."

"No good telling me," I said. "Better tell the skipper of the landing craft."

He didn't say anything, and when I glanced at him, his face was clouded, his mind concentrated on a world beyond the one in which we walked. Two big towing trucks went grinding past trundling red-painted trailers piled with stores. I don't think he even saw them, and in the Met. Office he went straight to the teleprint file and without a word to Sykes settled down at the desk to mark up a weather map.

Now that I knew something of the set-up, the Met. Office seemed somehow different—familiar ground like the bridge of a ship. The rain had stopped and it was lighter, the visibility much greater. To the left I could see the single hangar standing in the drifted sand like a stranded hulk. It was the only building in sight. Ahead, the wide windows looked out across the tarmac to a sea of dune grass rippling in the wind, humped and hollowed, as full of movement as the sea itself. And beyond the grass-grown dunes was the white blur of broken water, wind-blown waves moving in long regular lines towards the Sound of Harris.

Standing there, with the instruments of meteorology all around me, it wasn't difficult to slip into the mood of men like Cliff Morgan, to visualize the world they lived in, that great amorphous abstract world of atmosphere. I found myself thinking of Laerg, out there beyond the sea's dim horizon. I had seen photographs of it—etchings, too, by the Swedish artist, Roland Svensson. It was the etchings I was thinking of now, for I was sure Svensson had caught the mood of the wild wet world better than any photograph. Unconsciously I found my legs straddled as though to balance myself against the movement of a ship. A few hours and I should be on my way, steaming towards those sheer rock islands that for over thirty years had existed in my mind as the physical embodiment of an old man I had greatly loved.

Oddly, I felt no elation at the prospect; only a sense of awe. In my mind's eye I saw the cliffs rising sheer—black and dripping moisture. But because of my surroundings, the weather instruments, and the two men working at the desk, I had also a picture of that other world comprising the moving masses of the earth's outer skin. It was no more than the vague impression that a shipping forecast handed to the officer of the watch conjures in his mind, but it produced the same feeling of being at one with the elements, so that I found myself recapturing that sense of responsibility, of being a protagonist. The phone ringing cut across my thoughts. Sykes answered it. "Yes, he's here." He glanced at me. "Okay, I'll tell him." He put the phone down. "Major Braddock. He'll drive you down to Rodil to pick up your things."

"Now?"

"He'll be waiting for you outside the Admin. block."

I had known this moment would come, but I'd have been glad to postpone it. What did you say to a man who'd spent twenty years masquerading as somebody else, and that man your brother? "All right," I said, and went out into the wind, wishing at that moment I'd never come north to the Hebrides. Even Laerg couldn't compensate for this.

He was sitting at the wheel of a Land Rover waiting for me. "Jump in." He didn't say anything more and we drove out through the main gate and down the sand-blown road to Northton. Neither of us spoke and yet oddly enough there was nothing awkward about the silence. It helped to bridge the years, both of us accepting the situation and adjusting ourselves to it. Side-face, his true identity was more obvious—a question chiefly of the shape of the head and the way it sat on the shoulders. The profile, too;

he couldn't change that. And the hair, and the short, straight forehead, the shape of his hands gripping the wheel. "Why didn't you contact me?" I said.

"You were away at sea." He hunched his shoulders, an old, remembered gesture. "Anyway, what was the point? When you take another man's identity—well, you'd better damn well stick to it."

"Did you have to do that?"

"Do what?"

"Take Braddock's name?"

"I didn't have to, no. But I did." A muscle was moving at the corner of his mouth and his voice was taut as he added: "What would you have done? Given yourself up, I suppose. Well, I wasn't going to stand trial for busting the jaw of a man who hadn't the guts to lead his own men."

"What happened?" I asked. "What exactly happened out there in North Africa?"

"You really want to know?" He hesitated, frowning. "Well . . . It was after we'd landed. The French had us pinned down. They'd got a machine-gun nest in one of those walled villas. We were all right. We were in a dried-up wadi. But it was murder for the lads on our right. They were caught in the open, a whole company of them lying out there on the bare rocks, and we had the shelter of that gully right up to the villa's walls. Instead of attacking, Moore ordered the platoon to stay put and keep their heads down. He was frightened to death. In the end I knocked him out and took command myself. It was the only way. But by then the French had got a gun in position to cover the wadi and they opened up on us when we were halfway up it. "That's when I got this." He pointed to the scar on his forehead. "I lost eighteen men, but we took the villa. And when it was all over, I was under arrest. If I hadn't hit the little sod I'd have been all right, but that fixed me, so I got the hell out of it and back to the beach. Wasn't difficult; everything a bit chaotic. The fact that I was wounded made it dead easy. I was taken off to a troopship that was just leaving. She'd been damaged and when we were clear of the Straits she was ordered to proceed to Montreal for repairs. That was how I landed up in Canada." He glanced at me. "They didn't tell you that?"

"Some of it—not all."

"I had just over a year in Canada before they picked me up. It was conscription that fixed me. I hadn't any papers, you see. And then, when the *Duart Castle* went down . . ." He gave a quick shrug. "Well, I took a chance and it worked out."

But looking at the deep-etched lines of his face I wondered. He looked as though he'd been living on his nerves for a long time. There were lines running underneath the cheek-bones and down from the sides of the mouth, others puckering the scar on the forehead, radiating from the corners of the eyes; some of them so deep they might have been scored by a knife. Those lines and the harsh, almost leathery skin could simply be the marks of a hard life, but I had an uneasy feeling they were something more than that.

Through Northton he began to talk—about the Army and the life he'd led and where he'd been. It seemed to help, for he began to relax then and become more at ease; in no time at all the years had fallen away and we were on our old, easy footing, with him talking and myself listening. It had always been like that. And then suddenly he said: "You married Mavis, did you?"

"For my sins," I said. "It didn't work out."

"And the child?"

"It died."

I thought he didn't care, for he made no comment, driving in silence again. But as we came down the hill into Leverburgh, he said: "What was it—a boy?"

"Yes." And I added: "I had him christened Alasdair."

He nodded as though he'd expected that. We were passing ugly blocks of Swedish pre-fabs, and as we turned right past the loch, he murmured: "I'm sorry." But whether he was sorry for what he'd done to us or because the child had died I couldn't be sure. We were on a track now that led out to the quay. "I just want to check that they're moving the stuff fast enough," he said. "Then I'll drive you on to Rodil to collect your gear."

The quay looked a mess, the whole length of it littered with material brought from Laerg—piled-up sections of wooden huts, double-ended dories, trailers still loaded with stoves, radios, refrigerators, a deep-freeze, clothing, and crates full of foodstuffs, sacks of potatoes, fruit, coal; all the paraphernalia of an isolated unit being withdrawn in a hurry, and all of it soaked by the rain. One Scammell was trying to inch a trailer through the debris. Two three-ton trucks were being loaded, the men moving slowly, lethargically, as though they had been doing this a long time. A single mobile crane swung its gantry lazily against the leaden dullness of the sky, and beyond the quay skerries barred the way into the Sound of Harris with here and there a light mounted on iron legs to mark the channel through the rocks.

It was a depressing sight. I wandered along the concrete edge of the quay while Braddock spoke to the officer in charge. "A fine mess you'd be in," I heard him say, "if Four-four-Double-o had come in on schedule instead of being sent back to Laerg fully loaded." His voice, harsh now, had a whip-lash quality.

"We're shifting it as fast as we can," the youngster answered. "But the men are tired. They've been at it since early this morning, and we're short of vehicles."

"They're tired, are they? Then just think how Captain Pinney's men must be, working round the clock, crammed into only two huts, soaked to the skin. Now get moving, boy, and have this quay cleared to receive Kelvedon's ship when it comes in."

"When will that be?"

"Dawn, I should think, or a little after." I saw him grip the young man's shoulder. "Between now and the end of the operation this may be our one chance to catch up. See the men understand that. If Stratton's crew hadn't been dead beat you'd have had Eight-six-one-o up here by now. Make the most of this opportunity, Phipps."

"I'll do the best I can, sir."

"Better than the best; I want miracles." The hard face cracked in a smile. "Okay?" He patted the lieutenant's shoulder, instilling into him some of his own urgent drive. Then he turned. "Sergeant!" He had a word with the sergeant and then came back to the Land Rover. "Peace-time soldiering," he muttered as he climbed into the driving seat. "They don't know what it is to be beaten to their knees and still fight back. They haven't known a war. I was in Burma." He started the engine and yanked the wheel round. "That was after the Normandy landings. Half these guys would get shot to bits before they'd dug a slit trench. Just because they're technicians a lot of them, they think the Army's a branch of industry—a cosy factory with set hours and plenty of recreation."

We drove out of Leverburgh and up the glen with him talking about the evacuation and how he'd had his leave cut short to come up here and see the operation through. "If I'd known what I know now I'd never have accepted the posting. It's drive, drive, drive, and they hate my guts most of them. But what can you do with the weather on top of you and time so short? And now we're at the critical stage. The run-down of accommodation and stores on Laerg has reached the point where the operation has got to be completed. Pinney's detachment haven't enough food and fuel left on the island to last a fortnight, let alone see the winter through. And the weather chooses this moment to break. Goddammit, the War Office should have had more sense." He glanced at me quickly. "What did you think of Standing?"

I hesitated, not knowing what he expected. "I've only seen him for a few minutes."

"Long enough to fix yourself a trip to Laerg." There was a bite to his voice, a resentment almost, as though he disliked the thought of my going to the island. "You were there when he cancelled that flight. How did he seem?"

"A little nervous," I said. "But in the circumstances . . ."

"Nervous! He's scared. Scared he'll make a wrong decision. In fact, he's scared of making any decision. Scared, too, of leaving it all to me. He's a bloody old woman with a mind like an adding machine. And his wife's one of the most beautiful women I've ever met."

"Are you married?" I asked.

"Yes, but it didn't work out any better than yours. Lasted longer, that's all. And I'll never get shot of her. She's a Roman Catholic." We passed the church and a moment later drew up by the hotel. He came down to the loch-side with me and helped strike the tent and carry my stuff to the Land Rover. It only took ten minutes or so and then we were driving back. It was as we topped the rise and sighted Northton that he said: "D'you know a man called Lane—a Canadian?" He tried to make it casual, but the tightness in his voice betrayed him.

"I've met him," I said. "Once."

"And that's why you're here."

"Partly—yes."

He braked so suddenly that the engine stalled and I was flung forward in my seat. "Why do you want to go to Laerg?" The tension in his voice flared to a higher pitch. "What's behind it? What are you expecting to find there?"

"Peace. Subjects to paint." And I added: "I've always wanted to go to Laerg."

"But why now? You've managed very well for over twenty years. . . . Now, suddenly, you have to go there. Why? What did Lane tell you?"

"It's nothing to do with Lane."

"Then what the hell is it?" He had gripped hold of my arm and was almost shaking it. "As soon as I was away on that flight you went running to Standing and somehow persuaded him to ship you out on an LCT. What did you tell him?"

"Nothing about you," I said. "Just that my father came from Laerg and that I wanted to paint there."

"That all?" He was staring at me, the pupils of his eyes almost black and strangely dilated. And then he let go my arm. "You could have waited." His voice sounded suddenly tired. "I'd have got you to Laerg in time—if you'd asked me."

Was he hurt that I hadn't? "I was going to ask you," I said. "But you went off on that flight, and then, when I saw Colonel Standing . . ."

"Standing's not running this operation. I am. And I'm not having you or anyone else going out there and making a nuisance of themselves." He shifted in his seat, watching me, his mouth twitching and a gleam of perspiration on his forehead. "After all these years. Bit of a shock, isn't it?" He was smiling now, trying to recapture the old charm. But somehow the smile wasn't right. "Be frank with me. You always were—in the old days. We never hid anything from each other."

"I'm not hiding anything from you now."

But he didn't seem to hear. "What did Lane tell you? Come on now. He told you something that sent you scurrying up here with a sudden, urgent desire to get to Laerg."

"He guessed who you were. Suspected it, anyway. He's been interviewing survivors. . . ."

"I'm talking about Laerg. What did he say about Laerg?"

"Nothing," I said. "He's discovered you were on that raft and he's put two and two together. . . ."

"Then why are you so anxious to get out to Laerg?"

There it was again. Laerg—Laerg! Why did he keep harping on Laerg? "He never mentioned Laerg."

"No?"

"Just listen to me, Iain," I said. "I came up here with one object in mind—to find out whether you were still alive or not. Having done that, I thought it was a good opportunity to see the island. I've been wanting to go to Laerg for two years now, ever since I came back from the Aegean. I want to paint there. Just to paint, that's all. Nothing else."

But I don't think he believed me even then. His face had a stony look, as though he'd shut his mind to all reason, and I had a sudden feeling there was tragedy here, a deep, wasting wound that fed on his nerves. It was a moment of intuition, I think—blood calling to blood and the sense of his desperation very strong.

"Well, you're not going." He said it flatly, more to himself than to me. And then, as though suddenly aware of what he'd said and the need for some explanation: "This is a military operation. The landing craft are fully committed. It's no moment for shipping tourists out to the island."

"I'm not a tourist," I said, resenting the implication. "Not where Laerg is concerned."

"You are from the Army's point of view. I'll have a word with Standing." And he got the engine going again and we drove down into the camp, neither of us saying a word. He dropped me off at the officers' quarters. "Room forty-two," he said as I got my gear out of the back of the Land

Rover. "Maybe I'll have time for a drink with you before dinner." He was Major Braddock again and we were strangers. I watched him drive off, wishing now that I'd made more of an effort to discover what it was that was eating into his soul, for this wasn't the brother I'd known. This was quite a different man—a man driven and desperate. I had that feeling, and it scared me. Later, I said to myself. Later I'll find out.

I didn't know that there wasn't going to be a later, that time was running out and I'd missed the only chance I'd get of being alone with him before it was too late.

Room 42 was the same as Cliff Morgan's, a standard pattern with standard furniture—bed, bedside table, bureau, chair, wardrobe, all in natural oak, an armchair, wash basin, and the rusted steel windows looking out onto a drab patch of coarse dune grass. I dumped my things and went for a walk, heading north from the main gate, away from the camp and the landing apron. Ten minutes and I was among the dunes, alone in a world that hadn't changed since the first man set foot in the Outer Hebrides. To my left Chaipaval reared heather and grass-clad slopes to the clouds. To my right the mountains of Harris stood black and sombre, their storm-bound peaks shrouded in rain. I came to the last sanded bluff and ahead of me was a great stretch of sands, glistening wet, and a line of dunes standing like a breakwater between them and the sea. The island of Taransay rose misty-green beyond the dunes. There were sheep sheltering in the hollows they had worn along the edge of the bluff, and below, a river of water flowed towards the sea, fish marking the smooth surface with little whorls.

It was a wild wet world and I walked there until it was almost dusk, thinking of Laerg and my brother Iain, the wind on my face bringing back to me the salt taste of Ardnamurchan and my youth. The picture in my mind

was of a bare, wood-lined room and the two of us, sprawled
on the floor, gazing with rapt attention at the craggy,
bearded face of my grandfather softened by the peat-fire
glow—old Alasdair Ross at eighty-five or thereabouts telling two boys of the wonders of Laerg, describing the
strange remote island world that had been his life, and
speaking all the time the Laerg brand of Gaelic he'd
taught us to understand. It was a picture etched for all
time in my mind. It had stood between me and the fear
of death as I'd gazed down at the waxen face and the
pitifully shrunken body in the big bed; it had comforted
me that cold day when I stood shivering and crying bitterly
beside the open grave. I could hear the rattle of the first
frozen clods on the coffin lid still, but the face I remembered was the live face, vital and glowing in the firelight, the soft voice, the sea-grey eyes beneath the shaggy
tufted eyebrows.

And here I stood now at the threshold of his world. In
twenty-four hours I should be ashore on Laerg. Would
it match my dreams, or had the old man so coloured the
picture with his longing to return that he'd spoiled it for
me? I wondered; wondered, too, about Iain. Was the picture the old man had painted as vivid to him as it was to
me? Was that why he'd been so determined to make the
flight? Or was it something else—something to do with the
tension I'd sensed in him?

I had a drink with him that night in the Mess, but there
were others there and I couldn't probe. In any case, his
mood didn't encourage it—he had a black look on his
face and was barely civil to anyone. And after dinner, Mike
Ferguson drove me down to Rodil. By then the weather
had closed in again, the rain slanting in the beam of the
headlights. "The forecast's not too good," he said. "You
may be out of luck."

I thought for a moment he was breaking it to me that
permission for me to sail with the LCT had been with-

drawn. But then he added: "Stratton may decide not to go."

"But if he does . . . ?"

"Then Movements will get you on board in time. Colonel Standing's orders." And he added: "Major Braddock wanted him to cancel your trip. Said visitors were a damned nuisance. But the Old Man dug in his toes." He seemed preoccupied and I didn't like to ask him what had been said. In any case, it didn't matter. It wouldn't solve the mystery of my brother's extraordinary attitude. That was something deep-buried in his past, and I sat, puzzling over it, silent as the road unwound in the headlights, my interest in Laerg more urgent than ever.

The Field's croft was just below Rodil church. It was stone built with small windows and looked like a cow byre, the thatch curving in dim silhouette and roped against the wind, each rope-end weighted with a stone. Field met us at the door, dressed now in grey flannels and an open-necked bush shirt. "Come in, my dear fellow." The gentleness of his voice struck me again, strangely at odds with the hard lines of his extraordinary hatchet features. "Marjorie's seeing to the coffee," he told Ferguson. "You'll find her in the kitchen." He took me through into the living-room, which was Spartan and furnished only with the bare essentials. A peat fire smouldered in the grate. "We live very simply, as you can see." But they had electricity, and despite its bareness there was an intimacy, a cosiness about the room that made me feel instantly at home. "Marjorie usually makes coffee about this time. Would that be all right?" There was a note of apology in his voice as though he thought I might have preferred whisky. "I imagine this is the first time you've seen the inside of a black house?" And he went on quickly to explain that the word derived from the fact that the original Hebridean croft had virtually no windows and a peat fire in a central hearth that was never allowed to go out. "The chimney was just a hole in the roof and smoke blackened the interior." He smiled. "I should know. I was born in one—not far from here, on the west coast of Lewis." He was talking quickly, putting me at my ease, and all in the same soft, gentle voice.

He sat me down by the fire, gave me a cigarette, went on to talk about crofting, the subsidies, land disputes. The religion, too, and drunkenness, so that the impression left in my mind was one of a feckless, hard-drinking, lazy people. "It's the climate," he said. "The remoteness of the islands. It's as insidious as a disease." He smiled gently as though he himself were infected by it."

"It must be a pretty hard life," I murmured.

"Aye, and they're the salt of the ear-rth." There was a twinkle of humour in his eyes. "Being one of them my-self, I understand them. But I've been outside the islands most of my life. It makes a difference. And coming back . . ." He shrugged. "One would be more sympathetic if they made a greater effort to help themselves. Take this place; here's a dwelling ideally suited to the climate, the materials all ready to hand—but the status symbol up here is something constructed by a builder out of breeze-blocks. You try and paint the interior of any black house that's still occupied. They wouldn't let you across the threshold."

"Why not?" I asked.

"Because they're ashamed of them now." He was staring into the glowing peat, his long legs stretched half across the bearskin rug. "Islanders should never have contact with the mainland. It's destroying them here just as it's de-stroyed the people of the out-islands. Laerg would never have been evacuated if the island had remained in isola-tion. It had a perfectly sound economy until the outside world brought to their doorstep the illusion of an easier life. They had their sheep—the sheep the Vikings intro-duced a thousand years ago—and they had the birds. In its heyday Laerg supported a population of over two hundred. They salted away huge numbers of puffins each year, splitting them open like kippers and hanging them up to dry in the peat smoke. Puffins and Guga—that's the young of the solan goose. They had the down of the birds for bedding, the oil for lamps. They carded their own wool, weaved their own clothes. Peat was there for the digging and the wind dried it in the loose stone cleits that litter the slopes of Tarsaval. They didn't need money."

I knew all this—from my grandfather, from the books I'd read. What I wanted to know was how much the island had been changed by the Army. "Not a great deal," he said. "There's a concrete ramp built on the storm beach in Shelter Bay for the LCT's. There's the camp, of course. That's just below the village, near to the Factor's House. And there's the High Road. That's probably changed the island more than anything else. It starts at the camp, skirts the Bay just back of the storm beach, climbs Keava in three hairpins, then up the ridge to Creag Dubh where the radar station is. There's a spur, too, that runs out to the Butt of Keava overlooking Sgeir Mhor. I can show it to you on the Ordnance Survey, if you're interested."

The door opened and Marjorie Field came in; Ferguson followed with the coffee tray. "Talking about Laerg," her father said.

"Laerg?" She smiled. "Everybody's always talking about Laerg, and I'm not allowed to go there." She turned to me. "I owe you an apology, don't I? You are a painter. I checked."

"How?"

"With Cliff." She turned to her father. "Mr. Ross did the jacket for Cliff's book."

"Your daughter seemed under the impression I was a journalist." A shadow crossed his face and he didn't smile.

"You like it black or white?" she asked me.

"Black," I said, and she handed me my coffee and then switched the conversation by asking Ferguson if there was any more news of the Russian trawlers.

"Coastal Command had a Shackleton out yesterday. They didn't see anything."

Field shifted in his seat and reached for his coffee. "It's just a newspaper story, Mike."

"Not necessarily. Visibility was bad and with the cloud base down to between four and six hundred the search was very restricted. There is no doubt whatever that they do have trawlers operating in the area."

"So have the French, the Belgians, the Portuguese. Anyway, what information could they hope to get? It would be different if the range was operating. If they could check the accuracy of fire of the various units. . . ."

"That's not half so important, sir, as the fact that we're getting out of Laerg. It means we've developed some other method of pin-pointing the fall of shot—a long-range tracking service. Moscow would be very interested to know that."

"But, my dear fellow, they wouldn't need trawlers to tell them we're getting out. Any crofter in Harris . . ." The discussion didn't concern me and I took the opportunity to examine the room, which I found much more interesting. The walls were bare; no pictures, no photographs even, nothing to give a clue to Field's past. Only that bearskin rug. I wondered where that had come from. It was old, the head marked by burns. Had he shot it or was it something they'd picked up in a junk shop? The door to the kitchen had been left half open. His Service greatcoat hung there, the two pips a reminder of the incongruity of his age and rank. Below it hung a quilted jacket rather like a parka; green once, but now faded and worn and rather dirty.

My eyes turned to the daughter then; the nose, the blue eyes—I could see the likeness. But the mouth was softer, the skin darker. I wondered who her mother had been. She was perched on the arm of Mike Ferguson's chair and she looked strikingly beautiful, her face glowing in the lamplight, the skin almost nut-coloured and soft with the bloom of youth. I felt my blood stirring as it hadn't done since I'd left the Aegean. Her glance met mine and she smiled quickly, a wide-mouthed smile that had her father's warmth, lighting up her whole face. "So you've got your wish; you're going to Laerg."

"Yes."

It was then that Field gave me the clue to his identity. "Laerg," he said, and there was a wistfulness in his voice. "I shall miss it. One of the plums, being Education Officer here, was that I got out to Laerg once in a while. I should have been going next Saturday. . . ." He shrugged. "But I can't complain. I've had three tours." He smiled. "I'm envious, you see. It's an experience, particularly the first time. And, of course, the cliffs—there's some of the finest rock climbing . . ."

"It's the birds he's really interested in," his daughter said quickly.

But she was too late. That reference to climbing. I knew who he was then for his name had been in all the papers. Pictures of him, too. Some time in the early fifties it must have been for we were still on the Far East run and the papers had come aboard with the mail at Singapore. He'd been the leader of one of the Himalayan expeditions. I couldn't remember the details, or the name of the peak, only that he'd been brought down from somewhere near the summit just before the final assault. The official statement had simply announced that he'd been taken ill, but the newspapers had reported it in a way that made it obvious there was more to it than that. As though conscious of my thoughts, he turned away from me. "Any news of Mc-Gregor?" he asked Ferguson.

"An emergency operation. I fixed Bob up with a link

through to Command on the military line just before I left camp. He's doing it under instruction."

"How horrible for him."

He glanced up at the girl. "Aye, and the laddie could have been in hospital hours ago. As it is . . ." He shook his head. "Bob's not happy about it; nobody is."

"You think the man's going to die?" Field asked.

"Frankly, yes. I don't think he has a hope. When Bob's finished with him, the poor devil's got ten hours or more being bucketed about on a landing craft and then a flight to the mainland. If the Colonel had only left it to Ronnie Adams. . . ."

"The helicopter might have crashed."

"It might. But I doubt it. The worst the down-draughts have done to a helicopter so far is slam it on the deck so hard the rotor blades were shivered and split for about a yard from the tips. Anyway, it's for the pilot to assess the risk. That was Braddock's view, and for once I agreed with him. Not that either of them asked my views. They were too busy hammering away at each other."

"When was this?"

"Just before dinner."

"And you think Standing was wrong to cancel the flight?"

Mike Ferguson hesitated. "Yes. Yes, I do; considering what was at stake—a man's life."

Field sighed. "Every man makes his decisions in the light of his own experience, Mike. Did you know that Colonel Standing once saw a helicopter crash? It caught fire and the chaps inside it were burned alive, right before his eyes. It makes a difference, you see."

"And he told you about it?" Ferguson smiled. "You've become a sort of father confessor to us all, haven't you." There was affection as well as admiration in his voice.

"To some, yes. Not all."

"Meaning Braddock?"

"Perhaps." He leaned forward and poked at the fire. "Man is a complex mechanism, each individual a solitary unit afraid of loneliness. That's something you'll discover as the years pass. Most of them seek escape from loneliness by membership in a group. The herd instinct is very strong in all of us. But there are always a few rogues—some of them men of real stature, others forced by circumstances to live solitary lives." I thought he was speaking from experience then. The gentle voice sounded tired, weighted with weariness.

"They needn't be solitary if they're happily married," his daughter said. And she added: "I saw Laura this morning. She looked almost haggard."

"Laura could never look haggard." Her father smiled.

"Well, strained then. She knows what's going on. Ever since Major Braddock was posted up here. . . ."

"Braddock's only doing his job." Field glanced at me. "I'm afraid Mr. Ross must find this very boring." It was a signal to close the ranks in the face of the outside world, and after that the talk was general. We left just before ten, and Ferguson drove fast, anxious to contact Laerg and get news of the LCT.

He was reluctant to talk about Field at first, but when he realized I'd already guessed his background, he admitted I was right. "That business . . . it pretty well broke him up at the time. His whole life was climbing."

"What did he do—afterwards?"

"Took to drink. That's why there's no liquor in the house." And after a moment he added: "Maybe you can't understand it. But I can. I know how he must have felt—and it's not something you can control. It just takes charge. . . ." We were on the hill above Leverburgh then and he slammed into lower gear. "Damned shame. To escape it all he came up here, back to the islands where he was born. Then the Army arrived and that gave him the opportunity to do something useful again. He's all right now as long as Marjorie keeps an eye on him."

I asked him then why she was so worried about newspaper men bothering him after all this time.

"Oh, it's his wife," he said. "He's quite a story—wartime hero, then all through the Karakoram and up into Mongolia. Now she's found out he's buried himself in the Army and she's threatening to put the press on to him again if he doesn't go back to her. She's a bitch and no good to him—or to Marjorie."

I thought he was referring the the girl's mother. But he said: "No, this is his second wife I'm talking about. The first was an islander like himself. From Pabbay, I think, though he met her out in Egypt. She was a nurse in the hospital where he was sent after getting himself shot up in a Long-Range Desert Group foray. Unfortunately she was killed in a plane crash. If she'd lived it might have been different. They were very happy, I believe." And after that he was silent and we drove down into the camp.

Back in my room I found a note waiting for me. The trip to Laerg was off. *Owing to bad weather, L8610 will not be sailing on the morning tide.* It was scribbled on a sheet of paper torn from a notebook and was signed Fred Flint. I had seen a light in Cliff Morgan's quarters as we drove in, and I walked across.

He was seated at the keyboard and didn't look up as I entered. He had the earphones clamped to his head and his mind was concentrated on another world. I sat down on the bed and lit a cigarette. He didn't notice me until he looked up to change the tuning. He started to speak, but then held up his hand, listening. After a moment he pushed up one earphone. "You've heard the news, have you?"

"Captain Flint left a note in my quarters. Eight-six-one-o won't be sailing."

"I wasn't referring to that. I thought, as you were with Ferguson . . . He's calling him now."

"Who?"

"Four-four-Double-o—Captain Kelvedon. He's in trouble. I picked him up on Voice about half an hour ago asking for Major Braddock. He's got himself stuck on a falling tide. Went in to pick up McGregor. . . . Ah, here we are. Listen!" He switched in the loudspeaker and a metallic voice broke into the room. It was Ferguson: "*. . . ask him, but I'm quite sure he wouldn't agree to Adams attempting it in these conditions. I don't think Adams would go, anyway.*"

"*The Doc here says there isn't much time. . . .*"

"That's Kelvedon," Cliff whispered.

"*. . . and I can't get out of here for another five hours at least. We're grounded hard.*"

"*What happened?*"

"*It was the wind partly. We had it westerly, bang on the nose most of the way across. Then it suddenly backed. I'd never have attempted it, but Fairweather told me the man wouldn't live if they tried to bring him off in a dory. It was dark as hell and quite a sea running, but I thought I could edge in close enough to drop the ramp with the kedge well out astern. Maybe it was badly laid. And that sandbank. I think it must have been building up without our realizing it. The seas slewed us round and we touched the edge of it. Two hours after high water. When we came to winch off we found we were stuck fast.*"

"*I see. And what about McGregor?*"

"*He's back in his bed in the hospital hut. But Fairweather doesn't think he'll last long. The only hope is to get him out by helicopter.*"

"*Okay. I'll tell the Colonel. What about you now? Do you want me to have the Navy stand by?*"

"*Oh Lord, no. We're pounding a bit and it's not very comfortable. But the wind's veered now. Seems all over the bloody place. But if it stays where it is, north of west, we'll get off all right on the flood."*

"Fine. Call me again if there's anything fresh to report. Good Luck." And then he was calling Laerg. *"Are you there, Laerg? Base calling Laerg."*

"Laerg here," a Scot's voice answered. *"Go ahead, Base."*

"Captain Ferguson here. Keep your set manned through-out the night. I may want to contact Captain Fairweather later."

"Very good, sir."

"Is Captain Pinney there?"

There was a pause and then a new voice answered: *"Pinney here."*

"How does the landing craft look from the shore, John?"

"Slewed off about twenty degrees and grounded on that ridge of sand. Nowhere near the ramp."

"And the sea?"

"Moderate. Wind's getting round into the north-west, so the beach is sheltered, but there's still a biggish swell com-ing in. The old can's grinding a bit, but she'll be all right. It's this poor devil McGregor I'm worrying about. Just nothing but bad luck." The voice sounded tired. *"Do what you can, will you? Have a talk with Major Brad-dock."*

"He's down at Leverburgh trying to get the quay cleared."

"Well, send a car down for him, see if he can persuade the Colonel. This boy's going to die if somebody doesn't take a chance."

"Okay, John. Leave it with me."

Cliff Morgan switched off and the room was suddenly dead as he reached automatically for a cigarette. He lit it, gulping a mouthful of smoke deep into his lungs, breath-ing it out through his nostrils. "Not good, is it? And the wind playing tricks like that. . . ." He noticed his old cigarette still burning in the ash tray at his elbow and stubbed it out. "I don't like it when I feel like this. The number of times I've sat talking to some poor beggar riding the night sky with a load of trouble, or tapping out a message with the radio shack turning somersaults around him. I've been right too often, you see. There was that trawler, *Grampian Maid*. Nobody else could raise her and I was relaying messages until black ice turned her turtle. And a Boeing up over the Arctic—ice again and I was with him up to the moment when his messages ceased abruptly. I'm not like an ordinary ham, you see. I've got something to give them—the weather. Ships, aircraft, they live by the weather, and if you know as much about it as I do. . . ." He sighed and scratched himself under the arm, his hand burrowing inside his shirt. It was an unconscious, reflective gesture. "You'd better go and get some sleep. And have your things packed and ready." He was leaning forward, tuning the dials of the radio again.

"You think the LCT will sail?" I asked.

"I don't know. Anything could happen. . . ." He shifted in his seat, his body tense, his eyes fixed on the set as his fingers moved with the touch of a pianist, filling the room with the crackle of static. And behind the static, a man's voice, the words indecipherable. "There they are again. Two trawlers south-east of Iceland." He clamped both earphones tight to his head, leaning forward, his whole being concentrated in the tips of his fingers as they hovered over the dials. He'd left the loudspeaker on and a Scots voice came faintly, a voice so broad it might have been talking in a foreign tongue: *"A' dinna ken w-what it means ony mair thin ye du yersel', mon. Twa hoors ago the wind was fra the north. Noo it's roond into the sou'east an' blowing a bluidy gale."*

And another voice barely audible through the crackle: *"Aye, an' the glass ganging doon agin."*

"Did ye hear that noo? A bluidy great sea reecht o'er the bows, and the fish still coming in."

"Ye're on top of a shoal, are ye, Doug?"

"Aye, blast it. But this is no' the time to be trawling, whativer the bluidy fish. It's a hell of a night. You hove-to the noo, Jock?"

"Aye, hove-to and wishing to God I were in me bed with the wife and a wee dram inside o' me. Ha' ye got the forecast?"

"Bluidy lot o' good the forecast was . . ." The static overlaid the voices then and I couldn't decipher the rest.

After a moment Cliff Morgan pulled his earphones off. *"Arctic Ranger* talking to *Laird of Brora.* It's bad up there and I don't know quite what it means yet. There's no clear pattern, you see." He was staring down at his notebook, drawing without thinking deep concentric rings. "You go to bed," he said. "Get some sleep while you can." He ran his hand up over his face, rubbing at his eyes. He looked tired.

"Are you going to stay up all night?" I asked.

"Probably. Maybe when they've stopped getting in the nets I'll be able to contact their radio operators—get some facts out of them. A pair of skippers blethering at each other. Doesn't tell you anything. I don't want to know how they feel with all hell let loose. I want to know what the barometer reads and how it compares with the reading three, four hours ago, what the weight of the wind is, and whether the temperature is rising or falling." He leaned back. "Leave me to it, will you now. I want to see if I can raise some vessel further west. If not, I'll have a talk with the weather ships, see what they've got to say."

"You get their reports anyway, don't you?"

He nodded. "But it takes time. And talking to them is very different, you know, from reading the lists of figures they send in." He put the earphones on again, leaning closer to the set as he began to tune, his fingers light as a caress on the dials. "Those trawlers . . ." He was speaking to himself, not to me. "On the fringe of the High and now that first depression's starting to come through. Still two of them, but very close. That would account for what happened to Kelvedon—the sudden changes of wind. . . ." His voice died away, his expression suddenly intent. And then his thumb was on the key and the buzz of Morse, very rapid, filled the room as he made contact across miles of ocean.

I watched him for a moment longer, and then I left. Back in Room 42 I undressed, doing familiar things slowly, automatically, smoking a cigarette and mulling over the day. It had been a long one, so much packed into it, and London, my dismal attic of a studio, the years of hard work to become a painter—all seemed so far away. I was back now in a man's world of decisions and action, involving ships and weather, my movements governed by the sea, and I found I was glad, as though painting had been no more than an affair with a beautiful woman and this the real love of my life. I sat on the bed and lit a cigarette from the butt of the old and thought about that. Was I painter or sailor, or was this new mood that had my blood tingling the physical reaction to the prospect of a childhood dream becoming a reality? I didn't know. My mind was strangely confused. All I knew for certain was that the sea was calling.

I finished my cigarette, turned the thermostat of the central heating down to "low," and went to bed thinking of Laerg.

II

Forbidden Island

(OCTOBER 20)

I woke from a deep sleep with the ceiling lights blazing in my eyes and the duty driver standing over me, shaking me by the shoulder. "There's a cuppa' tea for you, sir. Captain Flint said to tell you he's leaving at four-ten."

"What's the time now?"

"Quarter to. I'll pick you up in twenty minutes. Okay? You are awake, aren't you, sir?"

"Yes, I'm awake, thanks." I sat up and rubbed my eyes. Even with the thermostat turned right down, the room was suffocatingly hot. I felt sweaty and drugged with sleep; the tea was black and thick and sweet. I got up, washed and shaved, and then dressed in my heaviest clothes, two sweaters and an anarak over the top. I packed my shoes and wore my gum boots; it was the easiest way to carry them. Outside, it was cold and windy; no sign of dawn yet, but the sky had cleared and there were stars. A half moon hung low over the camp, giving a frozen look to the unlighted huts. A long wheel-base Land Rover stood parked outside the Mess, torches glimmered, and the muffled shapes of men stood dark in the eerie light. "That you, Ross?" The Movements Officer took my bag and tossed it into the back of the vehicle. "Sorry there's no coffee laid on. No time for it anyway. Is that the lot, driver?"

"Yes, sir."

"McGregor's replacement?"

A voice from the back of the Land Rover said: "Here, sir. Patridge."

"Okay. Let's get cracking then."

We climbed in. A big, heavy-jowled man in a beret and a sheepskin jacket squeezed in beside me. Flint introduced him as Major McDermott. "You'll be brothers in misery for the next twelve hours—that is, if Stratton decides to go. But it's by no means certain yet. Things are in such a flipping mess this morning, nothing's certain." He sounded tired and irritable.

We drove out by the main gate and headed towards the hangar with the moon hanging over it. The helicopter was standing on the tarmac apron. The Land Rover drew up beside it. Adams was there waiting for us, dancing up and down on the balls of his feet to keep himself warm. The wind sifted sand in a light film across the surface of the apron. I hadn't expected to be travelling by helicopter. It seemed an odd way to be joining ship, but as we settled into our seats I realized that there was no other means of getting to the landing craft. The South Ford, I knew from the map, was the shallow channel between Benbecula and South Uist; it was more than thirty miles away to the south with no road link because of the Sound of Harris.

The door shut and the rotors turned, gathering speed until the whole fuselage shook. And then the ground was falling away and we were slipping sideways across the hangar like a gull blown by the wind. "Did you know

we've got an LCT grounded in Shelter Bay?" Flint
shouted in my ear. And when I nodded, he said: "Stratton's standing by just in case. If the ship gets off all right,
then Stratton will slip round into Carnan and land you
at the quay there. If she doesn't, then he'll probably have
a bash at it. Even then you may land up back at Leverburgh." He leaned across me, peering out through the
window. "Thank God I won't be with you if you do sail.
My stomach doesn't like the sea."

We were over the Sound now, the waves breaking white
in the moonlight a thousand feet below us. And beyond
the Sound we flew over a drowned land, all lakes, with the
sea lochs reaching long, wet fingers into it. There was
more water there than land. It looked wicked country in
that ghostly light, and it went on and on with only a single
sugarloaf hill to relieve the flat pan of its deadly monotony. At four-thirty we crossed the North Ford with the
first pale glimmer of daylight showing the Isle of Skye in
jagged relief on the eastern horizon. We were over Benbecula then and ten minutes later we saw the ship
grounded in the South Ford with the tide creeping in over
the sands; she wasn't quite afloat yet.

The helicopter dropped like a lift, turned head-to-wind,
and hovered just clear of her stern while the crew lowered
the boat. Flint got up and pulled the door open. A gale
of cold wind blew into the fuselage. We moved ahead
then, settling gently on to the water about two hundred
yards up-wind of the landing craft. As the rotors slowed
and stopped, a new sound invaded the cabin—the slap of
waves against the floats. The buzz of an outboard motor
came steadily nearer and then the dory was alongside and
we were piling into it. Small waves tossed spray over the
gunnel, wetting feet and baggage. A young man in a white
polo-necked sweater, his fair hair blowing in the wind,
jumped out onto the float. "Flinty. You want to come
aboard?"

"Not on your life. I'm going straight back to bed. Just came to see you boys were all right. What's the news?"

"Nothing yet. They're still grounded. But Captain Kelvedon was on the air about ten minutes ago to say he'd be starting to winch off any moment now."

"Hope he makes it."

"By God, so do I. It's going to be a dirty trip if we have to go out there in this. We're recording twenty-five knots, and we're under the lee here."

"Stratton's made up his mind to go, has he?"

"If Four-four-Double-o doesn't get off, yes. We've got to."

"Well, good luck, sonny."

"Thanks, we'll need it." He jumped off the float into the dory, balancing himself neatly. "Wouldn't like a trip round the island, would you, Flinty?"

"Not bloody . . ." The sound of the outboard motor drowned his voice. The dory swung away, running downwind with the steep little breaking waves. As the grey steel hull of the landing craft loomed over us, I saw the helicopter lift its dripping floats from the water and go whirling away northwards in the pale light.

There was coffee waiting for us in the wardroom. It was hot in there after the raw cold outside. "The Skipper will be along in a minute," the fair-haired youngster told us. "He's in the radio shack now, waiting to see what the form is. My name's Geoff Wentworth; I'm the Number One. If there's anything you want, just press the tit." He indicated the bell-push.

I thought I had everything I wanted; hot coffee and the feel of a ship under me again—the soft, continuous hum of dynamos, the smell that is always the same, a compound of salt dampness, hot oil and stale food, the slight suggestion of movement to give life to the hard steel of deck and bulkheads. "We're afloat, aren't we?"

"Just about," he said, and then he left us. McDermott

had removed his sheepskin jacket and I saw the insignia of the Army Medical Corps, the serpent of Aesculapius, on his battledress. He was a surgeon, he told me, and he'd left Edinburgh shortly after eleven, flown to Stornoway, and then been driven right across Lewis and Harris to Northton. "I'll be honest—I hope we don't have to go. I'm a damned bad sailor and from what I hear this boy's in a mess." He was puffing nervously at a cigarette.

Half an hour passed. Then a door slammed, a voice gave an order, somebody shouted, and rubbered feet pounded aft. The dynamos changed their note as the lights dimmed momentarily. Another piece of machinery had come into action. The door opened and Captain Stratton came in, small and dark, with premature streaks of grey in his black hair and a quiet air of command. Snatched hours of sleep had left his eyes red-rimmed. "Sorry I wasn't here to greet you. As you've probably gathered by the sounds of activity, we're getting under way."

"I take it," McDermott said, "this means the LCT is still stuck out there?"

"Yes. Kelvedon's made one attempt to winch himself off. Over-eager, by the sound of it. Anyway, she didn't budge. And now he's going to wait for the top of the tide before he tries again." And then he went on to explain his own plans. "As we're afloat now, I thought I'd get started. We'll be bucking a head-wind up to the Sound of Harris; may take us three hours. If he gets off all right, then we'll put into Leverburgh. If he doesn't, we'll be that much nearer Laerg." He turned to me. "I hear you have a lot of sea time. Master's ticket?" And when I nodded, he said: "I hope you're a good sailor then."

"I'm not seasick, if that's what you mean."

He smiled. "You may regret that statement. Have you ever been in a landing craft before?"

"No."

"You'll find the movement a little different." And he

added: "If you want to visit the bridge any time. . . ."
It was an invitation that accepted me as belonging to the
brotherhood of the sea. He went out and a moment later
the deck came alive under my feet as the main engines
began to turn.

I watched our departure from the open door on the starboard side of the bridge housing. Dawn was breaking and
the bulk of Mount Hecla sliding past was purple-brown
against the fading stars. A seal raised its head snake-like
from a rock, and then with a jerking movement reached
the weed growth at the edge and glissaded without a
splash into the water. A heron lifted itself from a grass-
grown islet, ungainly in flight as it retracted its head and
trailed its feet, grey wings flapping in the wild morning
air. Five cormorants stood on a ledge and watched us go,
curious and undisturbed. These were the only signs of
life, and though the door was on the leeward side and I
was sheltered from the wind, I could see it whipping at
the surface of the water.

One of the crew appeared at my side hooded in his duffel
coat. "Battening down now, sir." He pulled the steel door
to and fixed the clamps. "In a few minutes we'll be rounding Wiay Island. We'll begin to feel it then."

The visitors' quarters were immediately aft of the wardroom pantry, a clutter of two-tier bunks with clothing
scattered around and a desk littered with papers. Mc-
Dermott had already turned in, fully clothed. "Seems
steady enough," he murmured.

"We're still under the lee."

My bag had been dumped on the bunk immediately aft
of his. I stripped to my vest and pants and got into it,
pulling the blankets up over my head to shut out the grey
light from the portholes. The time was ten to six. I must
have slept, but it wasn't a deep sleep, for I was conscious
all the time of the movement of the ship, the sounds, the
pulsing of the engines. I knew when we turned the bottom

of Wiay Island for the bunk began to heave and every now and then there was a crash as though the bows had hit a concrete wall; at each blow the vessel staggered and a shiver ran through her. Vaguely I heard McDermott stumble out to the heads. Later he was sick in his bunk.

The steward woke me shortly after eight, a teen-age youngster in a khaki pullover, balancing a cup of tea. "I don't know whether you'd care for some breakfast, sir. The Skipper said to ask you."

I told him I would, though the battering was much worse now that I was awake. "Where are we?"

"Off Lochmaddy, sir. Half an hour and we'll be in the sound. It'll be quieter then."

The cabin reeked of vomit, sickly sweet and mixed with the smell of human sweat. I dressed quickly and breakfasted in solitary state, burnt sausage and fried bread, with the fiddles on the table, the blue settee cushions on the floor, and the framed photograph of L8610 banging at the wall. I smoked a cigarette thinking about Laerg and the ship stuck in Shelter Bay. Lucky for them the wind was in the north. If it had come in southerly during the night . . . I got up and went along the alleyway for'ard. A curtain was drawn across the open door to the Captain's cabin. There was the sound of gentle snoring, and behind the closed door opposite I heard the buzz of the radio operator's key. I slid back the door to the wheelhouse and went in.

The deck was almost steady now. A big, heavily built man stood at the wheel, dressed like the officers in a white polo-necked sweater. There was nobody else there, but the door to the port-side wing bridge stood open and almost immediately the Number One appeared framed in the gap. "Port ten."

"Port ten of wheel on, sir," the helmsman repeated.

"Steady now."

"Steady. Steering three-o-four, sir."

Wentworth went to the chart table, checked with his parallel rule against the compass rose. "Steer three-one-o."

"Three-one-o, sir."

He straightened from the chart table and looked across at me. "Skipper's got his head down. Did you manage to get some sleep?"

"A certain amount." And I asked him if there was any news.

"He didn't get off." And he added: "The wind apparently—or so he says. It was round into the north-east and a gust caught him. Personally I think he dragged his kedge anchor when he tried that first time. Anyway, he's right up against the beach now, almost broadside-on to it."

"You're going to Laerg then?"

He nodded. "Going to have a shot at it, anyway. They've despatched a Navy tug. But the Clyde's over two hundred miles away and she'll be butting straight into it. We're the only vessel that can reach Laerg by next high water." He glanced through the for'ard porthole and then went out on to the open wing bridge again. "Starboard five."

The needle of the indicator half right of the helmsman swung to five as he spun the wheel. I crossed to the port side where the chart table stood, a mahogany bank of drawers. Spread out on the top of it was Chart No. 2642; it showed the Sound littered with rocks and islands, the buoyed channel very narrow. "That's Pabbay straight ahead," Wentworth said, leaning his elbows on the table. "Steer two-nine-six."

"Steer two-nine-six."

Through the porthole I looked the length of the ship. The tank hold was an empty shell with vertical walls and a flat bottom that ended abruptly at a steel half gate. Beyond the gate was the black hole of the beaching exit, with the raised ramp acting as a bulkhead immediately behind the curved steel bow doors. Water sloshed in the open hold and sprung securing hooks banged in their racks.

The vertical walls were topped by steel decking that ran like twin alleyways the length of the ship to finish at a small winch platform. This platform was swinging now against a backcloth of sea and islands; it steadied as the helmsman reported: "Steering two-nine-six." Pabbay was on the starboard bow then, a smooth hump of an island, emerald-green in a drab grey world; while I had slept a thin film of cloud had covered the sky.

Wentworth swung himself up the ladder to the open bridge immediately above the wheelhouse. He was back in a moment with three compass bearings which he ruled in on the chart to produce a fix. Watching him, intent, alert, entirely concentrated, I thought how young he was; a soldier in charge of a ship. That was something new to me. Later I learned that he came from a seafaring family. Not his father, who kept a pub at Burnham Overy, but further back when every staithe along that North Norfolk coast was packed with sailing ships. He was very proud of the fact that one of his ancestors had sailed with Nelson, who'd been born at the neighbouring village of Burnham Thorpe. The sea was in his blood and the fact that he was driving a ship at her maximum speed of around ten knots through a tortuous channel in a rock-infested sound he accepted as no more than part of the day's work; accepted, too, the fact that beyond the sound the North Atlantic waited. He ordered a slight adjustment of course and then turned to me. "Another half hour and we'll be out of the lee of Harris. If you'd like to know what we're running into . . ." He reached across the chart table and removed a clipped sheaf of message forms from its hook. "The synopsis makes nice reading." His grin was friendly, unconcerned.

The top message, scribbled in pencil, read: *Weather forecast 0645. Gale warning: Warning of N gales in operation sea areas Rockall, Bailey, Faeroes, South-East Iceland: NW gales areas Cromarty, Forties, Viking. Synopsis for*

0600 GMT: a complex depression moving ENE towards Norway will affect all northern sea areas of the British Isles. This depression is likely to intensify over the next 24 hours. Another depression 500 miles W of Ireland is almost stationary and there is a belt of high pressure over Greenland. Forecast sea area Hebrides: Winds NW or N force 7, reaching gale force 8 later. Visibility moderate to good with some rain or sleet.

"Sounds like a pleasant trip," I said. "What's the barometer say?"

He pushed the chart aside and pointed to the log book. "Nine-eight-two. Falling." In fact, the log showed that it had dropped two points in the last hour, five since we'd sailed. Wind strength was recorded as northerly thirty-two knots, which is almost gale force eight on the Beaufort scale. My eyes went involuntarily to the porthole, to the vulnerable length of that open tank deck. It wasn't difficult to imagine what it would be like with big seas breaking over the flat sides of the ship, flooding the hold with water. As though he guessed what was in my mind, he said: "We've very powerful pumps. Last summer we were hove-to for nearly six hours in force ten with a destroyer standing by. It wasn't very comfortable, but we managed." The Army had apparently acquired the Navy's knack of embellishment by understatement.

The full force of the wind struck us as soon as we cleared the islands of Killegray and Ensay. There was a big swell coming in from the direction of Toe Head, now only a few miles away, and on top of the swell were steep, breaking waves. We were steaming north then, heading straight into it, and the movement was at times quite violent—a crash for'ard as we butted a wave, a shudder and then a lift and a twist as the comber went seething beneath us. Spray was whipped aft as far as the bridge. With Pabbay abeam, we altered course to almost due west, heading straight for Laerg. The motion was different then. We were no longer butting straight into it but steaming across the seas, rolling heavily with the wave crests breaking against the starboard bow. I could see the peak of Chaipaval clear of cloud and standing green against the darker Harris hills; even the camp was visible across a white waste of tumbled water.

It was while we were steaming out of the Sound of Harris that Colonel Standing was faced with the difficult choice of yielding to the views of his second-in-command or adhering to the Plan of Operations. Major Braddock saw him in his office shortly after nine and what he advised was the immediate withdrawal of all personnel from Laerg. He based his argument on the weather and he had Major Rafferty with him to support his case. That he had a personal motive for wishing to hasten completion of the evacuation was not, of course, apparent to either Rafferty or Standing.

Briefly his argument was this: The weather had broken and there was a landing craft in difficulties. Even presuming that L4400 was hauled off the beach undamaged, the Squadron Commander at Portsmouth would almost certainly insist on the withdrawal of both ships from Scottish waters. The Army would then have to fall back on the RASC trawler. This vessel was anchored in the Clyde and no longer in commission. It might be a month before it was on station. The alternative would be to charter. Either way it would be expensive, and meantime the detachment on Laerg would have to be supplied by air drop.

Rafferty confirmed that the run-down of supplies on the island had reached the point where the detachment had food and fuel for less than a fortnight at full strength. He also made the point that all but one of the vital radar installations had already been shipped out. There were still four huts standing and a fair amount of equipment, clothing, and stores, but the only other items of real value were the bulldozer, two towing vehicles, about a dozen trailers loaded with gear, and a Land Rover. All these could be driven straight on to the beached landing craft in a very short time.

Braddock had been up to the Met. Office that morning and he had with him a weather map drawn for him by Cliff Morgan. It was Cliff's forecast of what the situation would be at midnight. It showed the "complex depression" as an intense Low centred over Norway. It showed, too, the belt of high pressure over Greenland as having established itself, a massive High now extending from just west of Iceland to the Labrador coast with pressures of 1040 millibars or more at the centre. And between the High and the Low the isobars narrowed until, just east of Iceland, they were almost touching. Inked arrows indicated a strong northerly air stream.

"With northerly winds," Braddock said, "both landing craft could beach in safety. It may be our last chance." And Rafferty had agreed.

If Rafferty had put the case, Standing might have accepted it. At least he might have teleprinted Command for authority to act on it. Rafferty had an Irishman's gift for winning people over to his point of view. But faced with Braddock's virtual demand for immediate evacuation, Standing reacted strongly.

"I have my orders, and so have you, Major Braddock," he said. "Our job is to complete evacuation according to plan."

"But the weather. . . . You can't just ignore the weather." Braddock's voice was impatient, almost angry.

"All right. But there's no immediate hurry. We've got till this evening. We'll decide the matter then."

It is always easier to postpone decisions and let events dictate the course of action. But in fairness it must be said that Cliff Morgan, alone of the men immediately concerned at Northton, had the weather constantly under review. It was being drummed into him all the time by the teleprinters—sheet after sheet of pressure figures. By eleven o'clock the picture had clarified to the extent that he was convinced beyond any doubt that his hunch had been right—the Hebrides lay full in the path of a polar air stream of considerable force. The magnitude and intensity of that low-pressure area, combined with the Greenland High, would be drawing great masses of air south from the frozen wastes of the polar seas. This cold, dry air would be sliding in under the warmer, more humid air of the low-pressure area, cooling and condensing it. Snow at first in the far north, up in the Barents Sea; sleet and rain farther south; and in the Hebrides clear skies, or perhaps a film of cloud.

That would be the natural pattern. But before coming on duty that morning Cliff Morgan had re-established contact with *Arctic Ranger* and *Laird of Brora*. Both trawlers had reported a big swell still running from the north, but the wind backing westerly and the barometric pressure two to three millibars lower than the weather map indicated in that area. And now the Faeroes were reporting low cloud and rain squalls. What worried him was the original nature of that Low; the result of two depressions merging, it had the inherent weakness of all complex systems. He thought trough lines might be developing, perhaps even some more serious weakness.

Shortly after eleven o'clock he phoned the camp. Colonel Standing was not in his office. It was Mike Ferguson who took the call. He listened to what Cliff had to say and agreed to get Colonel Standing to ring him back. Meantime he passed the information to Major Braddock and it was Braddock who raised it with the Colonel immediately on his return. It is more than likely that he used Cliff Morgan's vague fears—and they were nothing more at that time—to reinforce his own argument. Almost certainly Standing rejected them. As an Air Ministry

man, Cliff had no connection with the Army. Standing
was under no obligation to accept the local Met. Officer's
advice or even to consult him. He may well have considered that Braddock was exaggerating. At any rate, he
didn't phone Cliff Morgan, deciding instead to wait for
the shipping forecast, which was by then due in less than
two hours.

Quite a number of officers were gathered round the Mess
radio at one-forty. The synopsis was much the same as before—gale warnings and the complex low-pressure area
intensifying to give a northerly air stream for much of the
British Isles. The forecast for the Hebrides was no worse
than it had been at six forty-five—winds northerly, gale
force eight increasing to nine later; visibility good but
chance of rain squalls.

As a result, Colonel Standing took no action. There was
not, in fact, much he could have done at that stage, but
another commander might have thought it worth walking
across to the Met. Office for a local weather briefing. There
may have been something personal in the fact that Standing didn't do this; he was a man of narrow moral outlook
and knowing Cliff's record he probably disliked him.

I missed the one-forty shipping forecast for I was lying in
my bunk at the time. I wasn't asleep. I was just lying there
because it was easier to lie down than to stand up, and
even flat on my back I had to hang on. The ship was lurching very violently and every now and then there was an
explosion like gunfire and the whole cabin shivered. Mc-
Dermott was groaning in the bunk ahead of me. The poor
devil had long since brought up everything but his guts;
twice he'd been thrown on to the floor.

About four in the afternoon I got up, paid a visit to the
heads, and had a wash. The heads were on the starboard
side and from the porthole I had a windward view; it was
an ugly-looking sea, made more ugly by the fact that we

were passing through a squall. Daylight was obscured by
the murk so that it was almost dark. Visibility was poor,
the seas very big with a rolling thrust to their broken tops,
and the spindrift whipped in long streamers by the wind.

I went down the alleyway to the wheelhouse. Stratton
had taken over. He stood braced against the chart table
staring out of the for'ard porthole. He was unshaven and
the stubble of his beard looked almost black in that
strange half light. A sudden lurch flung me across the
wheelhouse. He turned as I fetched up beside him. "Glad
to see you haven't succumbed." He smiled, but the smile
didn't reach his eyes, and his face was beginning to show
the strain. "My DR puts us about there." He pencilled a
small circle on the chart. Measuring the distance from
Laerg by eye against minutes of latitude shown on the
side of the chart, it looked as though we still had about
eighteen miles to go. But I knew his dead reckoning
couldn't be exact in these conditions.

"Will you make it before dark?" I asked.

He shrugged. "We're down to six knots. Glass falling,
wind backing and increasing. It came up like a line squall.
Some sort of trough, I imagine." He passed me the log.
Barometric pressure was down to 976, wind speed 40–45
knots—force 9. "Looks as though the weather boys have
slipped up." He gave me the one-forty shipping forecast.
"If the wind increases any more before we get under the
lee in Shelter Bay, we're going to have to turn and run
before it." He glanced at the radar. It was set to maximum
range—30 miles; but the sweep light showed only a
speckle of dots all round the screen. The probing eye was
obscured by the squall, confused by the breaking seas.
"We'll pick up Laerg soon." It was less of a statement than
an endeavour to convince himself, and I had a feeling he
was glad of my company. "Ever sailed in these waters?"
He switched the Decca to 15-mile range.

"No," I said. "But the Pacific can be quite as bad as the

North Atlantic and the Indian Ocean isn't all that pleasant during the monsoon."

"I've never commanded a proper ship," he said. "Always landing craft." And after a moment he added: "Considering what they're designed for, they're amazingly seaworthy. But they still have their limitations. They'll only take so much." As though to underline his point, a towering wall of water rose above the starboard bow, toppled and hit with a crash that staggered the ship. Water poured green over the sides, cascading like a waterfall into the well of the tank deck. I watched the pumps sucking it out through the gratings and wondered how long they would be able to cope with that sort of intake. The steward appeared with two mugs of tea. A cut on his forehead was oozing blood and there was blood on the mugs as he thrust them into our hands, balancing precariously to the surge and swoop as we plunged over that big sea.

"Everything all right below decks, Perkins?"

"Pretty fair, sir—considering." I saw his eyes dart to the porthole and away again as though he were scared by what he saw out there. "Will we be in Shelter Bay soon, sir?"

"Two or three hours." Stratton's voice was calm, matter-of-fact. "Bring coffee and sandwiches as soon as we get in. I'll be getting hungry by then."

"Very good, sir." And the boy fled, comforted but glad to leave the bridge with its view of the wildness of the elements.

The squall turned to sleet and then to hail, but the hail sounded no louder than the spray which spattered the walls of the wheelhouse with a noise like bullets. And then suddenly the squall was gone and it was lighter. The radar screen was no longer fuzzed. It still had a speckled look caused by the break of the waves, but right at the top a solid splodge of light came and went as the sweep light recorded the first emerging outline of Laerg·

It was about half an hour later that the helmsman relayed a report from the lookout on the open bridge immediately over the wheelhouse. "Land fine on the starb'd
bow, sir."

"Tell him to give the bearing."

The helmsman repeated the order into the voice pipe
close above his head. "Bearing Green o-five, or it may be
o-ten. He says there's too much movement for him to get
it more accurate than that."

Stratton glanced at the radar screen, then reached for
his duffel coat and went out by the port door, leaving it
open to fill the wheelhouse with violent blasts of cold air
and a whirling haze of spray. He was back within the
minute: "Laerg, all right—bearing o-three as far as I can
tell. There's a lot of movement up there and it's blowing
like hell."

But at least visual contact had been established. I leaned
against the chart table, watching as he entered it in the
log, hoping to God that Shelter Bay would give us the protection we needed. It was now only two hours' steaming
away. But even as my nerves were relaxing to the sense of
imminent relief from this constant battering, the helmsman announced: "Lookout reports something about
weather coming through on the radio."

Stratton glanced up quickly, but I didn't need the surprise on his face to tell me that there was something very
odd about this. I had had a talk with one of the radio
operators before I'd turned in and had discovered something of the set-up. There were two radio operators on
board working round the clock in twelve-hour watches.
Their main contact was the Coastal Command net—
either Rosyth or Londonderry. When not working the
CCN, they kept their set tuned to 2182 kcs., which is the
International Distress frequency, and any calls on this
frequency were relayed through a repeater loudspeaker to
the upper bridge. "Something about trawlers," the helms-

man reported. I think Stratton and I both had the same thought, that we were picking up a deep-sea trawler. Trawlers and some other small ships use 2182 kcs. on Voice. "Lookout says he couldn't get all of it. There's too much noise up there."

"Ask him whether it's a Mayday call."

"No, sir. Definitely not Mayday. And he was calling us."

Stratton knew better than to disturb his radio operator in the middle of receiving a message. We waited while the ship pounded and lurched and the outline of Laerg took clearer and more definite shape on the radar screen. At last the operator came in. "Special weather report for you." He steadied himself and then placed a pencilled message on the chart table. It was from Cliff Morgan. The message read: *GM3CMX to L8610. Advise weather conditions may deteriorate during night. Trawlers SE of Iceland report wind easterly now, force 9. At 0530 it was westerly their area. Suspect local disturbance. If interpretation correct could reach your area early hours tomorrow morning. This communication is unofficial. Good luck. Morgan.*

"And God help you, he might have added. A local disturbance on top of this lot. . . ." Stratton was staring down at the message, cracking the knuckles of his right hand. "How the hell can he have contacted trawlers southeast of Iceland?"

"Morgan's a ham operator," Sparks said.

"Oh yes, of course. You've mentioned him before." He straightened up. "Get on to Coastal Command. Check it with them." He had to shout to make himself heard above the thunder of a breaking sea. The ship lurched, sprawling us against the chart table. There was a noise like a load of bricks coming aboard and then the roar of a cataract as water poured into the tank deck. "A local disturbance. What the hell does he think this is?" Stratton glanced at his watch and then at the radar. The nearest point of

Laerg was just touching the ten-mile circle. "Two hours to go." And after that he didn't say anything.

Cliff Morgan's latest contact with the trawlers had been made at 15.37 hours. He took the information straight to Colonel Standing with the suggestion that L8610 be ordered to return to the shelter of the Hebrides until the weather pattern became clearer. This Standing refused to do. He had a landing craft in difficulties and an injured man to consider. Two factors were uppermost in his mind. The Navy tug, now in The Minch and headed for the Sound of Harris, had been forced to reduce speed. A message on his desk stated that it would be another twenty-four hours at least before she reached Laerg. The other factor was the position of our own ship, L8610. We were in H/F radio contact with the Movements Office at Base at two-hourly intervals and the three o'clock report had given our position as just over twenty miles from Laerg.

Cliff says he tried to get Standing to pass on the information. "I warned the bloody man," was the way he put it later. "I warned him that if he didn't pass it on he'd be responsible if anything happened." But Standing was undoubtedly feeling the weight of his responsibility for what had already happened. His attitude, rightly or wrongly, was that unofficial contacts such as this would only confuse Stratton. In fact, he was probably quite determined to do nothing to discourage L8610 from reaching Laerg. "I told him," Cliff said. "You are taking a terrible responsibility upon yourself. You are concealing vital information from a man who has every right to it." The fact is that Cliff lost his temper. He walked out of Standing's office and went straight to Major Braddock. My brother took the same line as Standing, though his reasons for doing so were entirely different. He wanted L8610 available in Shelter Bay to evacuate personnel. At least, that is my interpretation, based on his subsequent actions. He was determined to get the Army out of the island before the whole operation ground to a halt for lack of ships.

Having failed with both Standing and Braddock, Cliff decided to send the message himself. His broadcasting installation had an output of 200 watts, giving him a range on vh/f Voice of anything up to a thousand miles according to conditions. As a result, his message was picked up by another trawler, the *Viking Fisher,* then about sixty miles due south of Iceland. Her first contact with him, reporting a drop of two millibars in the barometric pressure in that locality, was made at 17.16.

Meantime, the Meteorological Office had begun to appreciate that the pattern developing in northern waters off the British Isles was becoming complicated by local troughs. The shipping forecast at 17.58 hours, however, did not reflect this. The gale warnings were all for northerly winds and the phrase "polar air stream" was used for the first time.

"So much for Morgan's forecast," Stratton said, returning the clip of forecasts to their hook above the chart table. "Maybe there'll be something about it on the midnight forecast. But a polar air stream. . . ." He shook his head. "If I'd known that at one-forty, I'd have turned back. Still, that means northerlies—we'll be all right when we reach Laerg." And he leaned his elbows on the chart table, his eyes fixed on the radar screen as though willing the blur of light that represented Laerg to hasten its slow, reluctant progress to the central dot.

As daylight began to fade, a rim of orange colour appeared low down along the western horizon, a lurid glow that emphasized the grey darkness of the clouds scurrying low overhead. I thought I caught a glimpse of Laerg then, a fleeting impression of black piles of rock thrust up out of the sea; then it was gone, the orange light that had momentarily revealed its silhouette snuffed out like a candle flame. Dusk descended on us, a creeping gloom that gradually hid the violence of that cold, tempestuous sea. And after that we had only the radar to guide us.

At 18.57 we passed close south of Fladday, the isolated island to the east of Laerg. The two stacs of Hoe and Rudha showed up clear on the radar screen. Ahead and slightly to starboard was the whole mass of Laerg itself. For the next quarter of an hour the sea was very bad, the waves broken and confused, the crests toppling onto our starboard bow, and the tank deck swilling water. The dim light from our masthead showed it cascading over the sides, torrents of water that continued to pour in almost without a break. The whole for'ard part of the ship seemed half submerged. And then, as we came under the lee of Malesgair, the eastern headland of Laerg, it became quieter, the wave crests smaller—still white beyond the steel sides, but not breaking inboard any more. The pumps sucked the tank deck dry and suddenly one could stand without clinging on to the chart table.

We had arrived. We were coming into Shelter Bay, and ahead of us were lights—the camp, the floodlights on the landing beach, and Four-four-Double-o lying there like a stranded whale. Low cloud hung like a blanket over Tarsaval and all the island heights, but below the cloud the bulk of Laerg showed dimly as a darker, more solid mass.

The home of my forebears, and to see it first at night, in a gale, coming in from the sea after a bad crossing. . . . I thought that this was how it should be, and I stood there, gazing out of the porthole, fixing it in my mind, a picture that somehow I must get on to canvas—a grim, frightening, beautiful picture. In that howling night, with the wind coming down off Tarsaval and flattening the sea in sizzling, spray-torn patches, I felt strangely at peace. All my life, it seemed, had been leading up to this moment.

And then suddenly my seaman's instinct came alive

and I was conscious that Stratton didn't intend to anchor. He had reduced speed, but the ship was going in, headed straight for the other landing craft. Wentworth was in the wheelhouse now. The Cox'n, too. And men were running out along the side decks, heading for the fo'c'stle platform. I caught the tail-end of Stratton's orders: ". . . heaving the lead and give the soundings in flashes on your torch. At two fathoms I'll go astern. Get the line across her then. Okay, Number One? Cox'n, you'll let go the kedge anchor when I give the word. And pay out on the hawser fast. I don't want that anchor to drag. Understand? We're almost at the top of the tide. We haven't much time."

They left and Stratton swung himself up the ladder to con the ship from the square, boxed-in platform of the upper bridge. I followed him. "Slow ahead both engines," he ordered down the voice pipe. Their beat slowed and the ship glided, moving steadily and irrevocably nearer the beach. The stranded LCT was growing larger all the time. A spotlight had been switched on and I could see the number on her bows—L4400 painted black on grey. Wentworth and his men on the fo'c'stle were picked out in the beam's glare.

Stratton lifted a phone from its hook. "All ready aft?" He stood, staring ahead, his eyes narrowed as he watched the approach of the shore. "Let her go." He replaced the phone on its hook and the ship went on with no check to show that the kedge anchor had been dropped astern. A torch stabbed five flashes from the fo'c'stle. "Stop both engines." The deck died under my feet. Four flashes. I could see the man heaving the lead, bracing himself against the fo'c'stle rail for the next throw. "Slow astern together."

Three flashes. Then two. "Full astern both. . . . Stop both." The ship hung motionless, heaving to the swell, staggering like a drunkard in the down-draughts. The howl of the wind came and went, a thousand demons

yelling murder. The sound of the rocket was thin and insubstantial, but I saw the line curve out and fall across the
stern of the other LCT. Men ran to grab it and a moment
later a hawser was being paid out over our bows.

Just two minutes, and as the hawser was made fast,
Stratton was on the phone again, giving the order to winch
in. For a moment nothing seemed to be happening. Up
for'ard the lead was dropped again, the torch flashed
twice. Then I felt the tug astern as the anchor bit to the
power of the winch hauling in. Our bows were swinging
towards the shore. From the compass platform I watched
the sagging line of the hawser come dripping out of the
sea, rise until suddenly it was bar-taut and shivering, all
the water shaken off it. Our bows stopped swinging then.
A ragged cheer came to us on the wind. Men in oilskins
lined the beach, standing watching just clear of the surf.
It was they who had cheered.

The bows swung back towards the other craft's stern.
The hawser slackened momentarily, then tightened again,
and I sensed that the ship was straightened out now, a
direct link between stern and bow hawsers. Stratton
sensed it, too. "Slow astern both engines." And as the
screws bit, he ordered full astern. And after that we
waited, tense for what would happen.

"Either she comes off now . . ." The phone buzzed
and Stratton picked it up. ". . . Well, let it labour. . . .
All right, Cox'n. But don't let the fuses blow. Just hold
her, that's all. Leave the rest to the main engines." He
put the phone down. "The stern winch—bloody useless
when you're in a jam." His teeth were clenched tight, his
face taut. "Something's going to give soon. Breaking strain
on that kedge hawser is only about forty-five tons. Not
much when you're trying to hold a thousand-ton vessel.
And right now the Cox'n's got to control both ships, and
on top of that there's the added weight of all that sand
piled up round Kelvedon's bottom."

Time seemed to stand still, with the whole ship trembling and vibrating with the effort. I left the compass platform and went aft to the port rail of the flag deck. It was dark on that side. No glimmer of light and the screws streaming a froth of water for'ard along the port side, toppling the waves so that all the surface of the water was ghostly white. I felt a sudden tremor. I thought for a moment one of the hawsers had parted. But up for'ard that single slender thread linking us to L4400 remained taut as before. A faint cheer sounded and then I saw the stern of the other ship was altering its position, swinging slowly out towards us.

Stratton joined me. "She's coming. She's coming, Ross—do you see?" His voice was pitched high, exhilaration overlaying nervous tension. The stern swung out, the ship's profile thinning till she lay like a box end-on to us, and there she hung for a moment, still held by her bows, until suddenly we plucked her off and Stratton ordered the engines stopped for fear of over-running the stern hawser.

Ten minutes later both ships were out in the bay with their bow anchors down, manoeuvring under power to let go a second anchor. Ashore, men waded waist-deep in the surf to launch a dory. It lifted to the break of a wave and the oars flashed glistening in the floodlights. Clear of the surf, it came bobbing towards us, driven by the wind. We were at rest, with both anchors down and the engines stopped, by the time it came alongside. An oilskin-clad figure swung himself up the rope ladder and came dripping into the wheelhouse, a shapeless mountain of a man with tired brown eyes and a stubble growth that was almost a beard. "Nice work," he said. "I was beginning to think we might be stuck here for the winter with a load of scrap iron on the beach." He glanced round the wheelhouse. "Where's Major McDermott? He's needed ashore."

"I'll get him for you." Stratton went out and the big

man stood there dripping a pool of water from his oilskins, his face lifeless, dead with weariness.

"Bad trip, eh?" His voice was hoarse and very deep.
The words seemed wrung out of him as though conversation were an effort.

"Pretty rough," I said.

He nodded, briefly and without interest, his mind on
something else. "The poor bastard's been screaming for
hours." And with that he relapsed into silence until
McDermott appeared, his face paper-white and walking
delicately as though not sure of his legs.

"Captain Pinney? I'm ready when you are." He looked
in no shape to save a man's life.

"Can you take Mr. Ross ashore this trip?" Stratton
asked.

"May as well, if he's ready." The tired eyes regarded me
without enthusiasm. "I've received instructions from Major Braddock about your visit. It's all right so long as you
don't stray beyond the camp area."

It took me only a moment to get my things. McDermott
was being helped down the rope ladder as I said goodbye
to Stratton. I dropped my bag to the men in the dory and
climbed down the steel side of the landing craft. Hands
clutched me as the boat rose to the slop of a wave and then
they shoved off and we were down in a trough with the
sea all round us, a wet world of broken water. The oars
swung and clear of the shelter of the ship the wind hit us,
driving spray in our faces.

It wasn't more than half a mile to the shore, but it took
us a long time even with the outboard motor. The wind
coming down off the invisible heights above was so violent
that it drove the breath back into one's throat. It came in
gusts, flattening the surface of the sea, flinging it in our
faces. And then we reached the surf line. A wave broke,
lifting the stern, flooding the dory with water. We drove in
to the beach in a seething mass of foam, were caught mo-

mentarily in the backwash, and then we touched and were out of the boat, knee-deep in water, dragging it up on to the concrete slope of the loading ramp.

That was how I came to Laerg that first time, in darkness, wet to the skin, with floodlights glistening on rain-soaked rock and nothing else visible—the roar of the surf in my ears and the wind screaming. It was a night I was to remember all my life; that and the following day.

We groped our way up to the road, staggering to the buffets of the wind. A Bailey bridge, rusted and gleaming with beads of water, spanned a burn, and then we were in the remains of the hutted camp. Everywhere the debris of evacuation, dismantled hut sections and piled-up heaps of stores, and the mud shining slippery in the glimmer of the lights. The putter of a generator sounded in the brief intervals between the gusts, and out in the darkness of the bay the landing craft were twin islands of light.

I was conscious then of a depressing sense of isolation, the elements pressing in on every hand—the sea, the wind, the heights above, grass and rock all streaming water. A lonely, remote island cut off from the outside world. And living conditions were bad. Already more than half the huts had been dismantled. Two more had been evacuated and officers and men were crowded together in the remaining three, with the cookhouse filled with stores and equipment that would deteriorate in the open. They were living little better than the original islanders and working much harder. Everywhere men in glistening oilskins toiled in the mud and the wet and the cold, grumbling and cursing, but still cheerful, still cracking the occasional joke as they man-handled hut sections down to the loading beach or loaded trailers with stores.

Pinney took us to his office, which was no more than a typewriter and a table beside his bed in the partitioned end of a hut that was crammed with other beds. The beds were mostly unmade, with clothing and odds and ends of personal effects scattered about; the whole place told a story of men too tired to care. Pinney's bed was no tidier than the rest, a heap of blankets thrown aside as he'd tumbled out of sleep to work. The two other officers' beds were the same and they shared the end of the hut with the radio operator and his equipment. "Cigarette?" Pinney produced a sodden packet and McDermott took one. His hands were trembling as he lit it. "If you'd like to get cleaned up. . . ." Pinney nodded vaguely to the washbasin. "Or perhaps you'd prefer a few minutes' rest. . . ."

McDermott shook his head. "Later perhaps—if I have to operate." His face looked shrunken, the bones staring, the skin grey and sweating. He seemed a much older man than when he'd come aboard. "I'll have a wor-rd with Captain Fairweather now, and then I'd like to have a look at the laddie."

"There's not much of him left to look at, and what's there is barely alive." Pinney glanced at me. "I'll be back shortly." They went out and I got my wet things off, towelled myself down, and put on some dry underclothes. The only sound in the hut was the faint hum from the radio, the occasional scrape of the operator's chair as he shifted in his seat. He had the earphones clamped to his head, his body slouched as he read a paperback. He alone in that camp was able to pierce the storm and leap the gap that separated Laerg from the outside world.

The sound of the work parties came to me faintly through the background noise of the generator and the rattle of a loose window frame. I lit a cigarette. The hut had a musty smell, redolent of damp and stale sweat. Despite the convector heating, everything I touched was damp; a pair of shoes under Pinney's bed was furred with mould, the paper peeling from his books. A draught blew cold on my neck from a broken pane stuffed with newspaper.

I was sitting on the bed then, thinking that this was a

strange homecoming to the island of my ancestors, and all
I'd seen of it so far was the camp litter of the Army in retreat. They were getting out and I thought perhaps old
Grandfather Ross was laughing in his grave, or was his
disembodied spirit roaming the heights above, scaling the
crags as he'd done in life, waiting for the island to be returned to him? Those eyes, sometimes blue and sometimes sea-grey, and the beard blowing in the wind—I
could see him as clearly as if I was seated again at his feet
by the peat fire. Only Iain was missing; somehow I
couldn't get Iain back into that picture. Every time I
thought of him it was Braddock I saw, with that twitch
at the corner of his mouth and the dark eyes turned inwards.

Laerg and Alasdair Ross—they went together; they
fitted this dark, wet, blustery night. But not Braddock.
Braddock was afraid of Laerg and I found myself thinking
of death and what Iain had once said. I got up from the
bed then, not liking the way my thoughts were running,
and went over to the radio operator. He was a sapper, a
sharp-faced youth with rabbity teeth. "Are you in touch
with Base all the time?" I asked him.

He looked up from his paperback, pushed one of the
earphones up. "Aye." He nodded. "I just sit on my backside and wait for them to call me."

"And if you want to call them?"

"Och weel, I just flick that switch to 'Send' and bawl into
the mike."

As simple as that. The radio was an old Army set, the
dials tuned to the net frequency. Contact with Base was
through the Movements Office. There a Signals operator
sat by another set of the same pattern. The only difference
was that it was linked to the camp switchboard. "You
mean you can talk direct to anybody in Northton?"

"Och, ye can do more than that, sir. Ye can talk to anybody in Scotland—or in England. Ye can get the bluidy

Prime Minister if you want." They were linked through the Military Line to the G.P.O. and could even ring up their families. "A've heer-rd me wife speaking to me fra a call box in Glasgie an' her voice as clear as a bell. It's no' as gude as tha' every time. A wee bit o' static sometimes, but it's no' verra often we canna get through at all."

A small metal box full of valves and coils and condensers, and like an Aladdin's lamp you could conjure the whole world out of the ether, summoning voices to speak to you out of the black, howling night. It was extraordinary how we took wireless for granted, how we accepted it now as part of our lives. Yet fifty, sixty years ago . . . I was thinking of the islanders, how absolutely cut off they had been in my grandfather's time. There had been the Laerg Post, and that was all, the only means of getting a message through to the mainland; a sheep's inflated stomach to act as a float, two pieces of wood nailed together to contain the message, and the Gulf Stream and the wind the only way by which it could reach its destination. It had worked three or four times out of ten. At least, that's what my grandfather had said. And now this raw little Glaswegian had only to flip a switch.

The door at the end of the hut banged and Pinney came in. "Clouds lifting. But it's still blowing like hell. Lucky for Stratton he's tucked into Shelter Bay." He reached into his locker and passed me a plate and the necessary implements. "Grub's up. We're calling it a day." And as we sloshed our way through the mud to join the queue at the cookhouse, he said: "Pity you're seeing it like this. Laerg can be very beautiful. On a still day with the sun shining and the air clean and crisp and full of birds. . . . The best posting I ever had."

The men had Mess tins; it was like being back on active service. A cook ladled stew and peas and potatoes on to my plate. Another handed me a hunk of bread and a mug of tea. We hurried back to the hut, trying to get inside be-

fore the wind had cooled our food. Another officer had
joined us, Lieutenant McBride. We ate quickly and in
silence. A sergeant came in, a small, tough-looking Irishman. "Is it true you're wanting the generator run all
through the night again, sor?"

"Not me," Pinney answered. "Captain Fairweather."

"It means refuelling."

"Then you'll have to refuel, that's all. They're going to
operate."

The sergeant sucked in his breath. "What, again? The
poor divil."

"Better see to it yourself, O'Hara. Make bloody sure no
rainwater gets into the tank."

"Very good, sor."

He went out and Pinney, lying flat on his bed, his eyes
closed, smoking a cigarette, said: "McDermott's as white
as a ghost and trembling like a leaf. He was ill coming
across, I suppose."

"Very ill," I said.

He nodded. "I thought so. He wouldn't have any food.
Bob gave him a couple of slugs out of the medicine chest.
Damned if I could operate on an empty stomach, but
still . . ." His eyes flicked open, staring up at the ceiling,
and he drew in a lungful of smoke. "What the hell am I
going to say to his mother? The police will locate her
sooner or later and then I'll have her on the R/T and
she'll be thinking it's my fault when it was his own bloody
carelessness. But you can't tell her that." He closed his
eyes again and relapsed into silence, and on the instant he
was asleep. I took the burning cigarette from between
his fingers and pulled a blanket over him.

McBride was already in bed, stripped to his vest and
pants. "You'll have to excuse us," he said with a sleepy,
boyish grin. "Not very sociable, but I don't seem able to
remember when we had more than four hours at a stretch.
We just sleep when we can." And he pulled the blanket up

over his head. A moment later he was snoring with a whistling intake of the breath and a gurgling quiver of the nostrils. "Och, he's awa'." The operator showed his long front teeth in a smile. "I mind the time when a' couldna hear a wor-rd they were saying at Base for Mr. McBride lying there snoring."

From beyond the partition the murmur of men's voices continued for perhaps five minutes, gradually dying away to silence. And after that there wasn't a sound except for the generator and the wind blasting the four corners of the hut and McBride snoring. But not everybody was asleep. Through the uncurtained window I could see a glow of light from the next hut. The shadow of a man's figure came and went against the drawn blinds, distorted and grotesque, and I knew it was McDermott . . . McDermott, who'd retched his guts out all the way across and was now trying to put together the broken pieces of another man's body.

I must have dozed off, but it could only have been for a moment. I jerked awake in my chair to see the operator shaking Pinney by the shoulder. "Captain Pinney, sir. Captain Pinney." There was a movement. His head came up and his eyes ungummed themselves.

"What is it, Boyd? Somebody want me?"

"Major Braddock, sir."

"Then it's not . . ." He glanced at his watch. "Oh well. . . ." He kicked the blanket aside and swung his legs off the bed. He was obviously relieved it wasn't the call he'd been expecting. "What's Major Braddock want?" he asked, rubbing at his eyes.

"It's urgent, sir. We're evacuating."

"Evacuating? Nonsense." He stared at the operator in disbelief.

"Aye, it's true, sir. We're leaving right away, tonight. I hear-rd him give the order to Captain Stratton. Eight-six-one-o is coming in to beach noo."

It was the moment of the fatal decision, the moment when the order was given that was to cost so many lives.

Pinney shook his head, forcing himself back to full consciousness. Then he was over at the set and had the earphones on, speaking into the mouthpiece. "Pinney here." He sat down in the chair the operator had vacated. "Well, yes. The wind's off the shore, northerly. There shouldn't be any risk. . . . What's that. . . . Yes, but what about the rest of the stores? According to the schedule the landing craft should be running six more trips. . . . Yes. Yes, I quite agree, but . . ." He laughed. "No, we shan't be sorry to go. Life isn't exactly a bed of roses here. It's just that my orders . . . Yes, I gathered it was a War Office appointment. But I should have thought Colonel Standing . . ." There was a long pause, and then he said: "All right, sir. So long as it's understood that I'm quite prepared to continue here until every piece of Army equipment has been shipped out. And so are my men. . . . Fine. We'll get cracking then." He got up and handed the earphones back to the operator. "Remain on the set, Boyd, until you're called for boarding." He stood there a moment looking round the room as though finding it difficult to adjust himself to the fact of leaving. Then he woke McBride and in an instant all was confusion, orders being shouted and men cursing and stumbling about as they sleep-walked into the clothes they'd only just taken off. Outside, the night was clearer, no stars, but the shadowed bulk of Tarsaval just visible. The wind was still very strong, coming in raging gusts that tore at the men's clothing, bending them double against the weight of it as they stumbled towards the beach.

An engine revved and a big six-wheeled Scammell lumbered past me. Seaward the lights of the two landing craft showed intermittently through the rain. One of them had its steaming lights on and the red and green of its navigation lights stared straight at the beach, coming steadily nearer. Orders shouted above the gale were whipped away by the wind. Pinney passed me, big in the lights of a truck stuck in the mud with its wheels spinning. "Better get straight on board." His voice was almost lost in a down-blast.

I was standing on the beach when Stratton brought his landing craft in towards the loading ramp. There was almost no surf now, the sea knocked flat by the wind. Bows-on, the landing craft was square like a box. He came in quite fast—two knots or more, and ground to a halt with an ugly sound of boulders grating on steel, the bows lifting slightly, towering over us. Lines were flung and grabbed, steel hawsers paid out and fastened to shore anchor points, and then the bow doors swung open and the ramp came down; a stranded monster opening its mouth to suck in anything it could devour.

The bulldozer came first, its caterpillar tracks churning sand and water. It found the edge of the ramp and lumbered, dripping, up the slope, clattering a hollow din against the double bottom as it manoeuvred to the far end of the tank hold. The Scammell followed, towing a loaded trailer, wallowing through the shallows and up the ramp where Wentworth and the Cox'n with half the crew waited to receive it. Men straggled in from the camp and they unhitched the trailer and man-handled it into position. The Scammell reversed out, and by the time it was back with the next trailer, the first had been parked and bowsed down with the sprung steel securing shackles.

This went on for almost two hours; more than thirty oilskin-clad figures sweating and cursing in the loading lights and the tank deck gradually filling up. By eleven the tempo was slackening, though Pinney was still loading equipment from the camp, sending down all the small, portable, last-minute stuff.

I was working on the tank deck until about eleven-thirty. By then the Cox'n had more men than he needed. I went up to the bridge housing, took over my old bunk and cleaned myself up, and then went into the wardroom, lured by the smell of coffee. Stratton and Wentworth were there and I knew at once that something was wrong. They barely looked up as I entered, drinking their coffee in silence, their faces blank and preoccupied. "Help yourself," Wentworth said. Beside the coffee a plateful of bully-beef sandwiches lay untouched. "Afraid you didn't get much of a run ashore."

I poured myself some coffee and sat down. "Cigarette?" I held the packet out to Stratton. He took one automatically and lit it without saying a word. Wentworth shook his head and I took one myself. A message form lay on the table close by Stratton's hand. He glanced at his watch. It was an unconscious gesture and I had the impression he knew the time already. "Another half hour yet before low water. If we off-load—sling all this heavy stuff ashore . . ." He left the sentence unfinished, the question hanging in the air.

"And suppose nothing happens—the wind remains in the north?" Wentworth's voice was hesitant.

"Then we'll look bloody silly. But I'd rather look a fool . . ." He shook his head angrily. "If he'd come through just two hours earlier, before we took the ground." He pushed his hand up wearily over his eyes and took a gulp of coffee. "Thank God there's only one of us on the beach anyway. If Kelvedon hadn't buckled a plate . . ." He lit his cigarette. "I'd give a lot to be anchored out there in the bay with Four-four-Double-o right now."

"It may not come to anything," Wentworth said. "The midnight forecast didn't say anything about it. Troughs, that's all. And the wind northerly. . . ."

"Of course it didn't. This is local. Something very local." Stratton shook his head. "Nothing for it, I'm afraid. We'll have to unload. Empty we'll be off—what? An hour sooner?"

"Three quarters anyway."

"Okay. Find Pinney. Tell him what the position is. And get them started on off-loading right away."

Wentworth gulped down the remainder of his coffee and hurried out. Stratton lay back against the cushions and closed his eyes with a sigh. The effort of reaching a decision seemed to have drained him of all energy. I was thinking of the wasted effort, all the trailers and vehicles to be got off with the men tired and exhausted. "You've met this fellow Morgan. How good is he?" His eyes had opened again and he was staring at me. "I think very good," I said. And I told him something about Cliff's background and about the book he'd written.

"Pity you didn't tell me that before. I might have taken him more seriously." And then angrily: "But it's all so damned unofficial. Coastal Command don't know anything about it. All they could give me was what we've got right now—wind northerly, force nine, maybe more. They're checking with Bracknell. But I bet they don't know anything about it. Read that." He reached out with his fingers and flipped the message form across to me: "A polar air depression. That's Morgan's interpretation. And all based on contact with a single trawler whose skipper may be blind drunk for all I know."

The message was impersonal, almost coldly factual considering the desperate information it contained: *GM3CMX to LCTs 8610 and 4400. Urgent. Suspect polar air depression Laerg area imminent. Advise you be prepared winds hurricane force within next few hours. Probable direction between south and west. Interpretation based on contact* Viking Fisher *23.47. Trawler about 60 miles S of Iceland reports wind speed 80 knots plus, southwesterly, mountainous seas, visibility virtually nil in heavy rain and sleet. Barometric pressure 963, still falling—a drop of 16 millibars in one hour. Endeavouring reestablish contact. Interpretation unofficial, repeat unoffi-*

cial, but I believe it to be correct. C. Morgan, Met. Officer,
Northton.

I didn't say anything for a moment. I had a mental picture of Cliff sitting in that room with his earphones glued
to his head and his thumb resting on the key, and that big
Icelandic trawler almost four hundred miles to the north
of us being tossed about like a toy. I thought there wouldn't
be much chance of re-establishing contact until the storm
centre had passed over, supposing there was anything left
to contact by then. A polar air depression. I'd heard of such
things, but never having sailed in these waters before, I'd
no experience of it. But I knew the theory. The theory was
very simple.

Here was a big mass of air being funnelled through the
gap between the big Low over Norway and the High over
Greenland, a great streaming weight of wind thrusting
southwards. And then suddenly a little weakness develops,
a slightly lower pressure. The winds are sucked into it,
curve right round it, are suddenly a vortex, forcing the
pressure down and down, increasing the speed and size of
this whirligig until it's like an enormous high-speed drill,
an aerial whirlpool of staggering intensity. And because it
would be a part of the bigger pattern of the polar air
stream itself, it was bound to come whirling its way south,
and the speed of its advance would be fast, fast as the winds
themselves.

"Well?" Stratton was staring at me.

"He had other contacts," I said. "Those two trawlers. . . ."

"But nothing on the forecast. Nothing official." He was
staring at me and I could read the strain in his eyes. No
fear. That might come later. But the strain. He knew what
the message meant—if Cliff's interpretation was correct;
knew what it would be like if that thing caught us while
we were still grounded. The wind might come from any
direction then. The northerly air stream from which we

were so nicely sheltered might be swung through 180°. And if that happened and the wind came in from the south . . . I felt my scalp move and an icy touch on my spine. My stomach was suddenly chill and there was sweat on my forehead as I said: "How long before you get off?"

He didn't give me an answer straight off. He worked it out for me so that I could check the timing myself. They had beached at nine forty-eight, two and three-quarter hours after high water. Next high water was at seventwenty. Deduct two and three-quarter hours, less say half an hour to allow for the amount the ship had ridden up the beach. . . . It couldn't be an exact calculation, but as far as he could estimate it we should be off shortly after five. I glanced at my watch. It was twenty minutes to one now. We still had nearly four and a half hours to wait. Four and a half solid bloody hours just sitting here, waiting for the wind to change—praying it wouldn't before we got off, knowing the ship was a dead duck if it did. "No way of getting out earlier, I suppose?"

He shook his head.

It was a silly question really, but I didn't know much about these craft. "There's a double bottom, isn't there? What's in between—fuel?"

"Water, too. And there are ballast tanks."

"How much difference would it make?"

"We'll see; I should think about eighteen inches up for'ard when we've pumped it out. Geoff's checking with the ballasting and flooding board now. About cancel out the amount we ran up the beach; give us a few extra minutes, maybe."

Sitting there in the warmth of that comfortable little wardroom with the ship quite still and solid as a rock, it was hard to imagine that in little more than four hours' time so few minutes could possibly make the difference between getting off and being battered to pieces.

"More coffee?"

I passed my cup and lit another cigarette. The radio operator came in and handed Stratton a message. "Coastal Command just came through with the supplementary forecast you asked for."

Stratton read it aloud. "Winds northerly, force nine, decreasing to seven or eight. Possibility local troughs with rain squalls. Otherwise fair visibility." He slapped the message form down on top of the others. "Same as the midnight forecast. Nothing at all about a polar air depression; no reference to winds of hurricane force." He turned to the radio operator. "Anything new from Morgan?"

The operator shook his head. "I heard him calling *Viking Fisher,* but I couldn't raise him myself."

"Did the trawler reply?"

"No."

"Well, see if you can get Morgan. Keep on trying, will you. I'd like to talk to him myself." He reached for a message pad lying on the shelf below the porthole. "And there's a message I want sent to Base. When's the next contact? One o'clock, isn't it?"

The operator nodded. "But I can get them any time. They're standing by on our frequency."

"Good. Give them a buzz then. Say I want to speak to Colonel Standing. And don't be fobbed off. Understand? If he's in bed, they're to get him out of it. I want to speak to him personally." As the operator left, he tossed the message pad back on the shelf. "Time these chaps who sit in their cosy offices issuing orders lost a little sleep on our account."

I started in on the corned-beef sandwiches then. I had a feeling this was going to be a long night. Stratton got up. "Think I'll go and see what the wind's doing. I'll be in the wheelhouse." Later Perkins brought some more coffee. I had a cup and then took one through to Stratton. But he wasn't there. The door was open on the port side and the wind came crowding through it in a gusty roar. The duty watch stood sheltering there, clad in sou'wester and oil-skins. "Where's Captain Stratton?" I asked him.

"On the R/T. Radio operator just called him."

"And the wind's still in the north, is it?"

"Aye, just aboot. Varies a wee bit, depending which side of Tarsaval it strikes."

I went over to the porthole and looked down on to the wet steel decks gleaming under the loading lights. They'd got about a third of the tank deck clear, but the men moved slowly now, all the life gone out of them. Stratton came in then. He didn't say anything but got his duffel coat. I handed him his coffee and he gulped it down. "Don't know what's going on at Base. Colonel Standing says he'd no idea we were evacuating. Sounded damned angry— what little I could hear. There was a lot of static." He pulled his coat on. "I'd better have a word with Pinney." He turned to the duty man. "If anybody wants me I'll be down on the loading beach."

After he'd gone I went over to the chart table and had a look at the log. Barometer reading at midnight was given as 978, a fall of one millibar since the previous reading at eleven. I leaned over and peered at the glass itself—977. I tapped it and the needle flickered, and when I read it again it was 976.

Time was running out; for the ship, for the men labouring on the tank deck to undo what they had done—for me, too. I could feel it in my bones, in the dryness of my tongue—a lassitude creeping through me, a feeling of indecision, of waiting. And all because a needle in a glass instrument like a clock had moved so fractionally that the movement was barely discernible. Long years at sea, standing watch on the bridges of ships, had taught me the value of that instrument, what those small changes of barometric pressure could mean translated into physical terms of weather. Somewhere in the bowels of the ship the cook would be sweating in his galley producing food to replace the energy those men on the tank deck had consumed. Deeper still, the engineers would be checking their oiled and shining diesels, preparing them for the battle to come. And out there beyond the lights, beyond the invisible peaks and sheer rock cliffs of Laerg, out across the sea's tumbled chaos, the enemy was coming relentlessly nearer, ten thousand demon horsemen riding the air in a great circle, scouring the sea, flailing it into toppling ranges of water, spilling violence as they charged round that vortex pot of depressed air. Fantasy? But the mind is full of fantasy on such a night. Science is for the laboratory. Other men, who stand alone and face the elemental forces of nature, know that science as a shining, world-conquering hero is a myth. Science lives in concrete structures full of bright factory toys, insulated from the earth's great forces. The priesthood of this new cult are seldom called upon to stand and face the onslaught.

The radio operator poked his head into the wheelhouse, interrupting my thoughts. "Seen the Skipper? I've got that chap Morgan on the air."

"He's doon to the beach to see Captain Pinney," the duty man said.

Between the wheelhouse and the beach was the littered tank deck, and Cliff Morgan wouldn't wait. "Can I have a word with him?" I suggested.

The operator hesitated. "Okay, I don't see why not—as one civilian to another." He gave me a tired smile.

I followed him into the box-like cubby-hole of the radio shack. He slipped his earphones on and reached for the mike. "L8610 calling GM3CMX. Calling GM3CMX. Do you hear me? Okay, GM3CMX. I have Mr. Ross for you." He passed me the earphones. Faint and metallic I heard Cliff's voice calling me. And when I answered him, he said: *"Now listen, man. You're on board Eight-six-one-o, are you?"* I told him I was. *"And you're beached—correct?"*

"Yes."

"Well, you've got to get off that beach just as soon as you can. This could be very bad."

"We're unloading now," I said. "To lighten the ship."

"Tell the Captain he's got to get off—fast. If this thing hits you before you're off . . ." I lost the rest in a crackle of static.

"How long have we got?" I asked. His voice came back, but too faint for me to hear. "How long have we got?" I repeated.

". . . barometric pressure?" And then his voice came in again loud and clear. *"Repeat, what is your barometric pressure reading now?"*

"Nine-seven-six," I told him. "A drop of three millibars within the last hour."

"Then it's not far away. You can expect an almost verti-cal fall in pressure, right down to around nine-six-o. Watch the wind. When it goes round . . ." His voice faded and I lost the rest. When I picked him up again he was saying something about seeking shelter.

"Have you made contact with that trawler again?" I asked.

"No. But somebody was calling Mayday a while ago—very faint. Now listen. I am going to try and raise the Faeroes or weather ship India. *It should be passing be-tween them, you see. And I'll phone Pitreavie. Tell the operator I'll call him on this frequency one hour from now. Good luck and Out."*

I passed the message to the operator and went back into the wheelhouse. Nothing had changed. The duty man was still sheltering in the doorway. The barometer still read 976. Another trailer had been unloaded, that was all. And the wind still northerly. It was ten past one. Four hours to go.

III

Storm

(OCTOBER 21–22)

A few minutes later Stratton came in, his duffel coat sodden. "Raining again." He went straight to the barometer, tapped it, and entered the reading in the log. "And McGregor's dead. They're bringing his body on board now." His face was pale and haggard-looking in the wheelhouse lights.

I passed Cliff's message to him, but all he said was: "We're dried out for two thirds the length of the ship and I can't change the tides." His mind was preoccupied, wound up like a clock, waiting for zero hour. He went to his room and shortly afterwards a macabre little procession came in through the open tunnel of the loading doors— McDermott and the camp doctor, and behind them two orderlies carrying a stretcher. All work stopped and the men stood silent. A few moved to help hand the stretcher up one of the vertical steel ladders on the port side. The body on the stretcher was wrapped in an oiled sheet. It glistened white in the lights. Once it slipped, sagging against the tapes that held it in place. The orderlies stopped to rearrange it and then the procession moved aft along the side decking. I could see their faces then, the two officers' white and shaken, the orderlies' wooden. They passed out of sight, moving slowly aft. They were taking the body to the tiller flat, but I only learned that later, when death was facing us, too.

I went back into the wardroom and ten minutes later McDermott came in, followed by Captain Fairweather. They looked old and beaten, grey-faced, and their hands were trembling. They didn't speak. They had a whisky each and then McDermott went to his bunk, Captain Fairweather back to the camp to get his kit.

By two-thirty the tank deck was clear, a wet steel expanse emptied of all vehicles. By three the incoming tide was spilling white surf as far as the loading ramp. The glass stood at 971, falling. No further contact with Cliff Morgan. Nothing from Coastal Command. And the wind still driving out of the north, straight over the beached bows. Pinney was arguing with Stratton in the wheelhouse. "Christ, man, what do you think we are? The men are dead beat. And so am I." The decks were deserted now, all the men swallowed up in the warmth of the ship, and Stratton wanted them ashore. "My orders were to embark my men and all the equipment I could. We got the stuff on board and then you order it to be taken off again. And when we've done that . . ."

"It's for their own good." Stratton's voice was weary, exhausted by tension.

"Like hell it is. What they want is some sleep."

"They won't get much sleep if this depression . . ."

"This depression! What the hell's got into you? For two hours now you've been worrying about it. The forecast doesn't mention it. You've no confirmation of it from Coastal Command, from anybody. All you've got is the word of one man, and he's guessing on the basis of a single contact with some trawler."

"I know. But the glass is falling—"

"What do you expect it to do in this sort of weather—go sailing up? All that matters is the wind direction. And the wind's north. In just over two hours now . . ."

It went on like that, the two of them arguing back and forth, Stratton's voice slow and uncertain, Pinney's no longer coming gruff out of his big frame, but high-pitched with weariness and frustration. He was a soldier and his men came first. Stratton's concern was his ship and he had a picture in his mind, a picture conjured by the falling glass and Cliff Morgan's warning and that information I had passed on about a faint voice calling Mayday on the International Distress frequency. But even in these circumstances possession is nine tenths of the law. Pinney's men were on board. They had their oilskins off and hammocks slung. They were dead beat and they'd take a lot of shifting. Stratton gave in. "On your own head then, John." And he gave the orders for the ramp to be raised and the bow doors shut.

Thirty-three men, who could have been safe ashore, were sealed into that coffin of a ship. The time was three-fourteen. Just over one and a half hours to go. Surely it would hold off for that short time. I watched figures in oilskins bent double as they forced their way for'ard and clambered down to the tank deck. The open gap, with its glimpse of the beach and the blurred shape of vehicles standing in the rain, gradually sealed itself. The clamps were checked. The half gate swung into place. Now nobody could leave the ship. And as if to underline the finality of those doors being closed, messages began to come through.

Coastal Command first: *Trawler* Viking Fisher *in distress. Anticipate possibility of very severe storm imminent your locality. Winds of high velocity can be expected from almost any direction. Report each hour until further notice.*

Then Cliff crashed net frequency to announce contact with Faeroes and weather ship *India. Faeroes report wind southerly force* 10. *Barometer* 968, *rising. W/S* India: *wind north-westerly force* 9 *or* 10. *Bar.* 969, *falling rapidly. Very big seas.*

CCN again with a supplementary forecast from the Met. Office: *Sea areas Hebrides, Bailey, Faeroes, South-East Iceland—Probability that small, very intense depression may have formed to give wind speeds of hurricane force locally for short duration. Storm area will move southwards with the main northerly airstream, gradually losing intensity.*

The outside world stirring in its sleep and taking an interest in us. Stratton passed the messages to Pinney without comment, standing at the chart table in the wheelhouse. Pinney read them and then placed them on top of the log book. He didn't say anything. There wasn't anything to say. The moment for getting the men ashore was gone half an hour ago. Waves were breaking up by the bows and occasionally a tremor ran through the ship, the first awakening as the stern responded to the buoyancy of water deep enough to float her. And in the wheelhouse there was an air of expectancy, a man at the wheel and the engine-room telegraph at stand-by.

The time was twelve minutes after four.

The radio operator again. Base asking for Captain Pinney on the R/T. Pinney went out and an unnatural quiet descended on the wheelhouse, a stillness of waiting. In moments like this, when a ship is grounded and you are waiting for her to float again, all sensitivity becomes concentrated on the soles of the feet, for they are in contact with the deck, the transmitters of movement, of any untoward shock. We didn't talk because our minds were on our feet. We were listening by touch. Perhaps that's why our ears failed to register how quiet it had become.

Through my feet, through the nerves that ran up my

legs, connecting them to my brain, I could feel the tremor, the faint lifting movement, the slight bump as she grounded again. It all came from the stern. But it was a movement that was changing all the time, growing stronger, so that in a moment a slight shock preceded the lift and there was a surge running the length of the ship. It was different. Definitely a change in the pattern and it puzzled me. I glanced at Stratton. He was frowning, watching a pencil on the chart table. It had begun to roll back and forth at each surge. The bumps as we grounded were more noticeable now, a definite shock.

Wentworth came in. "What is it? I told you to stay on the quarter-deck with the Bos'n." Stratton's voice was irritable, his nerves betraying him. "Well?"

"There's quite a swell building up." The youngster's face looked white. "You can see it breaking on the skerries of Sgeir Mhor. It's beginning to come into the bay. And the wind's gone round."

"Gone round?"

"Backed into the west."

Stratton went to the door on the port side and flung it open again. No wind came in. The air around the ship was strangely still. But we could hear it, roaring overhead. The first grey light of dawn showed broken masses of cloud pouring towards us across the high back of Keava. The moon shone through ragged gaps. It was a wild, grey-black sky, ugly and threatening. Stratton stood there for a moment, staring up at it, and then he came back into the wheelhouse, slamming the door behind him. "When did it start backing? When did you first notice it?"

"About ten minutes ago. I wasn't certain at first. Then the swell began to . . ."

"Well, get back to the after-deck, Number One. If it goes round into the south . . ." He hesitated. "If it does that, it'll come very quickly now. Another ten minutes, quarter of an hour. We'll know by then. And if it does—then the

Bos'n will have to play her on the kedge like a tunny fish. That hawser mustn't break. Understand? I'll back her off on the engines. It'll be too much for the winch. Your job is to see she doesn't slew. Slack off when you have to. But for Christ's sake don't let her stern swing towards the beach. That's what happened to Kelvedon."

"I'll do my best."

Stratton nodded. "This swell might just do the trick. If we can get her off before the wind goes right round. . . ."

But Wentworth was already gone. He didn't need to be told what would happen if the wind backed southerly—wind and waves and the breaking strain on that hawser a paltry forty-five tons. And as though to underline the point, Stratton said to me: "One of the weaknesses of these ships, that winch gear only rates about ten horse-power." He picked up the engine-room telephone. "Stevens? Oh, it's you, Turner. Captain here. Give me the Chief, will you."

He began giving instructions to the engine-room and I pushed past him, out on to the wing bridge and up the steel ladder to the open deck above. The lookout was standing on the compass platform staring aft, his face a pallid oval under his sou'wester. A ragged gap in the clouds showed stars, a diamond glitter with the outline of Tarsaval sharp and black like a cut-out; a glimpse of the moon's face, and the wind tramping overhead, driving a black curtain of cloud across it. I went aft down the flag deck where the tripod structure of the mainmast stood rooted like a pylon, and a moment later Stratton joined me. "Any change?"

"West sou'west, I think." I couldn't be sure, but there was a definite swell. We could see it coming in out of the half-darkness and growing in the ship's lights as it met the shallows. It slid under the stern and then broke seething along the length of the sides, lifting the stern and snapping the anchor hawser taut. Across the bay we could see spray bursting against the dim, jagged shape of the skerries. The wind was definitely south of west. I could feel it sometimes on my face, though the force of it and the true direction was masked by the bulk of Keava. Raindrops spattered on my face.

But it was the swell that held us riveted, the regular grind and bump as the ship was lifted. And then one came in higher, breaking earlier. It crashed against the stern. Spray flung a glittering curtain of water that hung an instant suspended and then fell on us, a drenching cascade. But it wasn't the water so much as the ship herself that alarmed us, the sudden shock of impact, the way she lifted and slewed, the appalling snap of the hawser as it took the full weight, the thudding crash as she grounded again, grinding her bottom in the backwash.

"I hope to God he remembers to slip the winch out of gear," Stratton murmured, speaking to himself rather than to me. "All that weight on it. . . . We've stripped the gears before now. I'd better remind him." He turned to go, but then he stopped, his gaze turned seaward. "Look!" He was pointing to the other LCT, a cluster of lights in the grey darkness of the bay. "Lucky beggar." She had her steaming lights on and was getting her anchor up; and I knew what Stratton was thinking—that he might have been out there, safe, with room to manoeuvre and freedom to do so.

A blast of air slapped rain in my face. South—south-west. Again I couldn't be sure. But into the bay; that was definite. Stratton had felt it, too. He went at once to the compass platform. I stayed an instant longer, watching the men on the after-deck immediately below me. Wentworth was standing facing the stern, with two men by the winch on the starboard quarter, their eyes fixed on him, waiting for his signal. The sea seethed back, white foam sliding away in the lights, and out of the greyness astern came a sloping heap of water that built rapidly to a sheer, curving breaker. The winch drum turned, the cable slackened; the wave broke and thudded, roaring against the stern. The men, the winch, the whole after-deck disappeared in a welter of white water. The ship lifted under me, swung, and then steadied to the snap of the hawser. The thud as we hit the bottom again jarred my whole body. I saw the mast tremble like a tree whose roots are being attacked, and when I looked over the rail again, the stern was clear of water, the men picking themselves up.

The wind was on my face now. It came in gusts, and each gust seemed stronger than the last. L4400 had got her anchor; she was turning head-to-sea, steaming out of the bay.

I went for'ard to the bridge wondering how long it would be before the hawser snapped or the men on the after-deck were swept overboard. The deck under my feet was alive now, the engine-room telegraph set to slow astern and the screws turning. Stratton was on the open side deck, trying to keep an eye on stern and bow at the same time. If only she could shake herself free. I could feel it when she lifted, the way she was held by the bows only; for just a moment, when the wave was right under her, you could almost believe she was afloat.

Pinney came up. I don't think anyone saw him come. He just seemed to materialize. "Would you believe it? The Old Man's countermanded Braddock's orders. Said we'd no business to be pulling out. . . ." There was more of it, but that's all I can remember—that, and the fact that he looked tired and shaken. Nobody said anything. Nobody was listening. We had other things on our minds. Pinney must have realized this, for he caught hold of my arm and said angrily: "What's happening? What's going on?"

"The wind," I said. "The wind's gone round."

I could see it now, blowing at Stratton's hair, whipping the tops off the combers and sending the spray hurtling shorewards in flat streamers of white spindrift. We were no longer sheltered by Keava. God, how quickly that wind had shifted, blowing right into the bay now—thirty, maybe forty knots. I went down to the wheelhouse. The barometer was at 969, down another two points. *Quick fall, quick rise*—that was the old saying. But how far would it fall before it started to rise? Cliff had mentioned 960, had talked of a near vertical fall of pressure. That was what we were getting now. I hadn't seen a glass fall like that since I'd sailed into a cyclone in the Indian Ocean. I tapped it and it fell to 968.

"Full astern both engines." Stratton's voice from the bridge above came to me over the helmsman's voice pipe. The telegraph rang and the beat of the engines increased as the stern lifted to slam down again with a deep, rending crash that jolted my body and set every movable thing in the wheelhouse rattling. "Stop both engines."

I was gripping hold of the chart table, every nerve taut. Gone was the silence, that brief stillness of waiting; all was noise and confusion now. "Full astern both." But he was too late, the stern already lifting before the screws could bite. Stop both and the jar as she grounded, the bows still held and the hawser straining. Spray hit me as I went back to the bridge. The wind was pitched high in the gusts, higher and higher until it became a scream.

The phone that linked us to the after-deck buzzed. There was nobody to answer it so I picked it up and Wentworth's voice, sounding slight and very far away, said: "We took in half a dozen turns on the winch that time. Either the anchor's dragging . . ." I lost the rest in the crash of a wave. And then his voice again, louder this time: "Three more turns, but we're getting badly knocked about." I passed the information to Stratton. "Tell him," he shouted back, "to take in the slack and use the brakes. I'm holding the engines at full astern. If we don't get off now . . ." A gust of wind blew the rest of his words away. The phone went dead as the ship heaved up. The crash as she grounded flung me against the conning platform.

I was clinging to the phone wondering what was happening to those poor devils aft and trying to think at the same time. The wind was south or perhaps sou'sou'west; it would be anti-clockwise, whirling round the centre of that air depression and being sucked into it at the same time. I was trying to figure out where that centre would be. If it was north of us. . . . But north of us should give us a westerly wind. It depended how much the air currents were being deflected in towards the centre. I was remembering Cliff's message: the Faeroes had reported barometric pressure 968, rising, with winds southerly, force ten. Our barometer was now showing 968. If the storm centre passed to the west of us, then this might be the worst of it. I decided not to go down and fiddle with the glass again.

"We made several yards." Wentworth's voice was shrill in the phone. "But the winch is smoking. The brakes. They may burn out any minute now. Keep those engines running, for God's sake."

I glanced at Stratton. But I didn't need to ask him. I could feel the vibration of the screws through my whole body. "Engines at full astern," I said. "Keep winching in."

I put the phone down and dived across the bridge to yell the information in Stratton's ear. The weight of the wind was something solid now. I felt the words sucked out of my mouth and blown away into the night. "Christ! If the winch packs up now. . . . Stay on the phone, will you." Stratton's face was white. I was lip-reading rather than hearing the words. Below him white water glistened, a seething welter of surf sucking back along the ship's side. A shaggy comber reared in the lights, curled, and broke. Spray went whipping past and ectoplasmic chunks of foam suds.

The ship moved. I could feel it, a sixth sense telling me that we were momentarily afloat. And then the shuddering, jarring crash. I was back at the phone and Wentworth's voice was yelling in my ears—something about the winch gears. But his voice abruptly ceased before I could get what it was he was trying to tell me. And then Stratton grabbed the phone from my hand. "Oil," he said. "There's an oil slick forming." He pressed the buzzer, the phone to his ear. "Hullo. Hullo there. Number One. Wentworth." He looked at me, his face frozen. "No answer." There was a shudder, a soundless scraping and grating that I couldn't hear but felt through the soles of my feet. And then it was gone and I felt the bows lift for the first time. "Winch in. Winch in." Stratton's voice was yelling into the phone as a wave lifted the stern, running buoyant under the ship. There was no grounding thud this time as we sank into the trough and glancing for'ard I saw the bows riding high, rearing to the break of the wave. "Wentworth. Do you hear me? Winch in. Wentworth." His hand fell slack to his side, still holding the phone. "There's no answer," he said. His face was crusted with salt, a drop of moisture at the end of his slightly up-turned nose. His eyes looked bleak.

"You look after the ship," I told him. "I'll go aft and see what's happened."

He nodded and I went out on to the flag deck. Clear of the bridge, the full weight of the wind hit me. It was less than half an hour since I'd stood there and felt that first blast of the storm wind in my face. Now, what a difference! I had to fight my way aft, clinging to the deck rail, my eyes blinded by salt spray, the wind driving the breath back into my lungs. Fifty, sixty knots—you can't judge wind speeds when they reach storm force and over. It shook me to think that this perhaps was only the beginning. But we'd be round Malesgair then, sheltered under its lee—I hoped. By God, I hoped as I fought my way to the after-rail and clung there, looking down at the tiny stern platform with its spare anchor and its winch gear.

Wentworth was there. He was bending over the winch. His sou'wester had gone and his fair hair was plastered to his head. He looked drowned and so did the two men with him. They were all of them bent over the winch and the

drum was stationary. A broken wave-top streaming spray
like smoke from its crest reared up in the lights, a shaggy,
wind-blown monster, all white teeth as it slammed rolling
against the stern. It buried everything, a welter of foam
that subsided to the lift of the ship, water cascading over
the sides, the men still gripping the winch like rocks awash.
I yelled to Wentworth, but my shout was blown back into
my mouth and he didn't hear me. The winch remained
motionless and the hawser, running through two steel pul-
leys and out over the stern, just hung there, limp.

I turned and went like a leaf blown by the wind back to
the open bridge and Stratton standing there, the phone in
his hand and the engines still pounding at full stern. I
grabbed his arm. "The hawser," I yelled. "You'll over-run
the hawser."

He nodded, calm now and in full control of himself.
"Gears jammed. I've told him to cut it." And then he said
something about taking her out on radar as he put the
phone down and went quickly, like a crab, down the steel
ladder to the wheelhouse. It was a relief just to be out of
the wind. The radar was switched on, set to the three-mile
range. The screen showed us half surrounded by the mass
of Laerg, the shore still very close. And when he did try to
turn—what then? Broadside to that sea with the weight of
the wind heeling her over, anything might happen.

But that was something else. What worried me was the
thought of that hawser. I could see it clear in my mind, a
great loop of wire running from the stern down through
the heaving waters and under the whole length of the ship
to the anchor dug into the sea bed somewhere beyond our
bows now. It had only to touch one of the propeller blades
—it would strip the propeller then or else it would wrap.
And that wasn't the only hazard. Driving astern like this,
backing into sea and wind, it might come taut at any moment. Then if it were fractionally off-centre our stern
would swing. Or was that what Stratton was trying to do? I

glanced quickly at his face. It was quite blank, his whole
mind given to the ship as he stood just behind the helmsman, watching the compass and at the same time keeping
an eye on the radar.

I thought I felt a jerk, a sort of shudder. "Stop port.
Half ahead port."

"Port engine stopped. Port engine half ahead, sir."

Slowly the bulk of Laerg shifted its position on the radar
screen. The bows were moving to starboard, swung by the
screws and the pull of the anchor against the stern. The
movement slowed. A wave crashed, breaking against the
starboard side. The ship rolled. "Helm hard a'starboard.
Stop starboard engine. Half ahead together."

The beat changed. The ship shuddered as she rolled.
The outline on the radar screen resumed its circling anti-
clockwise movement. The bows were coming round again.
A big sea crashed inboard, the tank deck awash. The ship
reeled, heeling over so steeply that Pinney was flung across
the wheelhouse. Slowly she righted, to be knocked down
again and yet again, the weight of the wind holding her
pinned at an angle, driving her shorewards. But the bows
kept on swinging, kept on coming round. The helmsman's
voice pipe whistled.

"Number One reporting anchor hawser cut," he said.
Stratton nodded.

"He's asking permission to come for'ard."

"Yes. Report to me in the wheelhouse." Stratton's whole
mind was fixed on the radar. Now the bulk of Laerg was
on the left-hand lower side of the screen, at about eight
o'clock. "Full ahead both engines." The telegraph rang.
The shuddering was replaced by a steadier beat.

And the helmsman confirmed: "Both at full ahead, sir."

"Helm amidships."

"Midships."

We were round with Laerg at the bottom of the radar
screen, the two sheltering arms running up each side, and

the top all blank—the open sea for which we were headed. Steaming into it, we felt the full force of the wind now. It came in great battering gusts that shook the wheelhouse. Spray beat against the steel plates, solid as shot, and the bows reared crazily, twisting as though in agony, the steel creaking and groaning. And when they plunged, the lights showed water pouring green over the sides, the tank deck filled like a swimming pool.

"Half ahead together. Ten-fifty revolutions."

God knows what it was blowing. And it had come up so fast. I'd never known anything like this—so sudden, so violent. The seas were shaggy hills, their tops beaten flat, yet still they contrived to curve and break as they found the shallower water of the bay. They showed as a blur beyond the bows in moments when the wind whipped the port-hole glass clean as polished crystal. The barometer at 965 was still falling. Hundreds of tons of water sloshed around in the tank deck and the ship was sluggish like an over-laden barge.

Wentworth staggered in. He had a jagged cut above his right eye; blood on his face and on his hands, bright crimson in the lights. Beads of water stood on his oilskins, giving them a mottled effect. "The tiller flat," he said.

Stratton glanced at him. "That cut—you all right?"

Wentworth dabbed it with his hand, staring at the blood as though he hadn't realized he was bleeding. "Nothing much. Fenwick has hurt his arm." And he added: "They didn't secure the hatch. There's a lot of water . . ."

"What hatch?"

"The tiller flat."

But Stratton had other things to worry about. The helmsman had been caught off balance, the wheel spinning. A figure moved and caught the spokes. "All right, sir. I've got her." It was the Quartermaster. A sea broke slamming on the starboard bow, but she was coming back again, swinging her bows back into the waves. God, what a sea!

And I heard Stratton say: "What's that on your oilskins—oil? It looks like oil."

"There was a lot of it in the sea," Wentworth answered. "Every time a wave broke . . ."

But Stratton had pushed past me and was staring alternately at the radar screen and out through the porthole.

It was just on five-thirty then and dawn had come; a cold, grey glimmer in the murk.

Darkness would have been preferable. I would rather not have seen that storm. It was enough to hear it, to feel it in the tortured motion of the ship. The picture then was imaginary, and imagination, lacking a basis of experience, fell short of actuality. But dawn added sight to the other senses and the full majesty of the appalling chaos that surrounded us was revealed.

I had seen pictures of storms where sea and rock seemed so exaggerated that not even artistic licence could justify such violent, fantastic use of paint. But no picture I had ever seen measured up to the reality of that morning. Fortunately, the full realization of what we faced came gradually—a slow exposure taking shape, the creeping dawn imprinting it on the retina of our eyes like a developing agent working on a black and white print. There was no colour; just black through all shades of grey to white, the white predominating, all the surface of the sea streaked with it. The waves, like heaped-up ranges, were beaten down at the top and streaming spray—not smoking as in an ordinary gale, but the water whipped from their shaggy crests in flat, horizontal sheets, thin layers like razor blades cutting down-wind with indescribable force. Above these layers foam flew thick as snow, lifted from the seething tops of the broken waves and flung pell-mell through the air, flakes as big as gulls, dirty white against the uniform grey of the overcast.

Close on the starboard bow the skerry rocks of Sgeir Mhor lifted grey molars streaming water, the waves exploding against them in plumes of white like an endless succession of depth charges. And beyond Sgeir Mhor, running away to our right, the sheer cliffs of Keava were a black wall disappearing into a tearing wrack of cloud, the whole base of this rampart cascading white as wave after wave attacked and then receded to meet the next and smash it to pieces, heaping masses of water hundreds of feet into the air. Not Milton even, describing Hell, has matched in words the frightful, chaotic spectacle my eyes recorded in the dawn; the Atlantic in the full fury of a storm that had lifted the wind right to the top of the Beaufort scale.

That the landing craft wasn't immediately overwhelmed was due to the almost unbelievable velocity of the wind. The waves were torn to shreds as they broke so that their force was dissipated, their height diminished. The odd thing was I felt no fear. I remember glancing at Stratton, surprised to find his face calm, almost relaxed. His eyes met mine for an instant, cool and steady. No fear there either. Fear would come later no doubt, as a reaction when the danger had lessened. Fear requires time to infect the system, and we had had no time; it had come upon us too quickly with too much to do. And panic is an instantaneous thing, a nerve storm. Men carrying out the duties for which they have been trained, straining every nerve to meet the situation, their minds entirely concentrated on the work in hand, are seldom liable to panic.

"Have the men put their life-jackets on." Stratton's voice was barely audible as he shouted the order to Wentworth. "Everyone. Understand?" He turned to Pinney. "Go with him. See that every one of your men has his life-jacket on."

"What about the tiller flat?" Wentworth asked.

"How much water got in?"

"I don't know. It was dark down there and I couldn't see. Quite a bit, I think."

"Did you fix the hatch?"

"Yes. But it may have got in through the rudder stock housings. It may still be . . ."

"All right, Number One. I'll have a word with Stevens. His engineers will get it pumped out." He picked up the engine-room phone. "And have that cut seen to."

It was after Wentworth had left that I found my bowels reacting and felt that sick void in my guts that is the beginning of fear. If I'd been in control I wouldn't have noticed it. I'd have been too busy. But I was a spectator and what I saw both on the radar screen and through the porthole was the tip of Sgeir Mhor coming closer, a gap-toothed rock half awash and the wicked white of the seas breaking across it. Stratton was keeping the bows head-on to the waves. He had no choice. To sheer away in that sea was impossible—the head of the ship would have been flung sideways by the combined thrust of wind and water and she'd have broached-to and been rolled over. But bows-on we were headed about one-ninety degrees, sometimes nearer two hundred, for the wind was just west of south. We were slowly being forced towards the rocks that formed the western arm of Shelter Bay. Sometime back Stratton had realized the danger and had ordered full ahead on both engines, but even at full ahead our progress was painfully slow, the ship labouring to make up against the almost solid wall of the elements. Yard by yard we closed Sgeir Mhor and we kept on closing it. There was no shelter behind those rocks—not enough in that force of wind; our only hope was the open sea beyond.

It was six-ten by the clock above the chart table when we came abreast of Sgeir Mhor and for a full six minutes we were butting our bows into a welter of foaming surf with the last rock showing naked in the backwash of each trough less than a hundred yards on our starboard side. Every moment I expected to feel the rending of her bottom plates as some submerged rock cut into her like a knife gutting a fish. But the echo-sounder clicking merrily away recorded nothing less than forty fathoms, and at six-sixteen we were clear, clawing our way seaward out of reach, I thought, at last.

North-westward of us now the sheer rock coast of Laerg was opening up, a rampart wall cascading water, its top vanishing into swirling masses of cloud. We were in deeper water then and Stratton was on the phone to the engine-room again, cutting the revolutions until the ship was stationary, just holding her own against the wind. "If the old girl can just stay in one piece," he yelled in my ear. I didn't need to be told what he planned to do; it was what I would have done in his shoes. He was reckoning that the storm centre would pass right over us and he was going to butt the wind until it did. Nothing else he could do, for he couldn't turn. When we were into the eye of the storm there would be a period of calm. He'd get the ship round then and tuck himself tight under those towering cliffs. We'd be all right then. As the centre passed, the wind would swing round into the east or north-east. We'd be under the lee of Laerg then. But how long before that happened—an hour, two hours? Out here in the deeper water the waves no longer built up in range upon range of moving hills; they lay flat, cowed by the wind, which seemed to be scooping the whole surface of the sea into the air. The noise was shattering, spray hitting the wheel-house in solid sheets. Visibility was nil, except for brief glimpses of the chaos when a gust died. And then a squall blotted everything out and the Quartermaster quietly announced that the wind had caught her and she wasn't answering.

"Full astern starboard."

The ring of the telegraph, faint and insubstantial, the judder of the screws, and the bows steadying. She'd have come back into the wind then, but a sea caught her and she heeled over. If we'd been in the shallow waters of the bay, she'd have rolled right over, but out here it was the wind more than the waves that menaced us; it held her canted at a steep angle and the man who brought Stratton his life-jacket had to crawl on his hands and knees. Stratton tossed it into the corner by the chart table. "Better get yours, too," he said to me. "Just in case." The bows were coming round now, sluggishly. "Full ahead both. Starboard wheel." And then she was round with her blunt nose bucking the seas, her screws racing as they were lifted clear in the troughs.

Even head-to-wind again it was a struggle to get down the alleyway to my quarters. McDermott lay on the floor. He had tied himself with a blanket to the bunk support and he'd been sick again, all over himself and the floor. The place was a shambles. "Was that the power steering packed in?" Wentworth asked me. He was clinging to the desk while Fairweather tried to stitch the cut in his head.

"We were blown off," I said.

But he didn't seem to take that in. "I tried to tell Stratton. They forgot to close the hatch. To the tiller flat. You remember? I told him. . . ."

I did remember and my first reaction was a mental picture of McGregor's corpse being sloshed around in that small compartment above the rudders. My mind must have been sluggish for it was a moment before I realized what was worrying him. If the electric motors shorted . . . The possibility brought the sweat to my palms, a sting to the armpits that I could have sworn I smelt despite the layers of clothing. And then I remembered that the hatch was closed now and the engineers would have disposed of the water. "They'll have pumped it out by now," I said.

He nodded. "Yes. Yes, of course. I remember now." He seemed dazed, staring at me wide-eyed. "But that oil. What do you think it was, Mr. Ross?" Staring at me like that, the whites of his eyes beginning to show, I began to wonder.

"What oil?" I said.

"It was all round the stern and every time a sea broke . . . Look at my hair?" He leaned his head forward, ignoring the Doc's warning. "See? It's oil. Diesel oil."

"Don't worry," I said. "Another couple of hours. . . ." I ducked out of the cabin. I wanted fresh air, the confidence that only men doing something to preserve themselves can inspire. Was Wentworth scared, or was it me? All I knew was that something like a contagious disease had touched me in that sour cabin full of the sick smell of vomit. That oil . . . I remembered when he'd first come up to the wheelhouse, how his oilskins had been mottled with it, and Stratton asking about it.

The wheelhouse steadied me. There Stratton smoking a cigarette, the Quartermaster at the wheel, everything going on as before and the bows headed slap into the wind. The radar screen showed Sgeir Mhor dead astern of us less than a mile away. I dropped my life-jacket beside Stratton's. Should I remind him about the oil, or just forget about it? I decided to keep silent. Nothing to be done about it. What was the point? And yet . . . I lit a cigarette and saw my hand was trembling. Hell! "What's under the tank deck?" I heard myself ask. "Water and fuel oil, I think you said."

"Yes, fuel oil." Stratton's voice had an edge to it and he added: "Something on your mind?" He was staring at me hard and I realized suddenly that he knew—knew we'd damaged the bottom plates getting off.

"No, nothing," I said, and I left it at that, happier now that the knowledge was shared. Perhaps he was, too, for he smiled. "Keep your fingers crossed," he said.

But keeping your fingers crossed doesn't mend steel plates, and it doesn't prevent fuel oil seeping out through the cracks and rents in those battered plates. I stayed with him until I'd finished my cigarette and then I made some excuse and slipped out. There was only one way of finding out. I went down the companion ladder to the deck below, unclamped the steel door leading to the side deck and leaning out grabbed hold of the rail. I was just in time, for the force of the wind swept my legs from under me. I was left clinging there, my body flattened along the deck and my lungs filled to bursting with the pressure of air forcing its way into mouth and nostrils.

The power of that wind was demoniac. It forced my eyeballs back against the membranes with a stabbing pain. It tore at my hair and clothing. And the sheet spray flung against my face had the cutting power of sand. Raw and shaken, I held on till there was a slight lull, and then I hurled myself back through the door. It took me quite a time to get it shut and the clamps in place. I was wet to the skin and panting with the effort, but I now knew— I had seen the surface of the water sheened with a film of oil, the surface spray held static by the viscosity of it.

When I got back to the wheelhouse Wentworth was there, clinging to the chart table, fresh plaster covering the cut on his forehead. Stratton glanced at me, a slight lift to his brows as he saw the state of my clothes. He knew where I'd been so I just gave a slight confirmatory nod. "Bad?" he asked.

"Impossible to tell."

He nodded.

"What's bad?" Wentworth asked. "Where've you been?" His voice was slightly slurred and the whites of his eyes . . . I didn't like that tendency for the whites to show.

"I've just been sick," I said.

He accepted that. "So've I." He said it quite cheerfully, the beginnings of a smile lighting up his face. He couldn't have been more than twenty-two; much too

young, I thought, to face a storm like this. It was the sort
of storm you only expect to face once in a lifetime, and
then only if you've been all your life at sea. I wondered
whether I could paint it. Could any artist get it down on
canvas—this soul-destroying, brain-numbing battering,
this violence that went beyond the limits of experience?

And the fact that we existed, that the ship still held
her blunt bows head-to-wind, battling against the driving
planes of water, made it somehow marvellous, the little
oasis of the wheelhouse a miracle. In the midst of chaos,
here within the tight frame of fragile steel walls, there was
the reassurance of familiar things—the radar, the charts,
the burly Quartermaster quite unperturbed, orders being given, messages coming in—particularly the messages.
L4400 signalling that she was under the lee of Malesgair
and riding it out, safe for the moment at any rate. Coastal
Command asking us whether we needed assistance, relaying to us the information that the Admiralty tug was now
waiting instructions in Lochmaddy. First Braddock and
then Standing asking for news of us—how many men had
we embarked, what stores and equipment, obviously quite
oblivious of the magnitude of the storm. The last contact
with Cliff before he went on duty had given the wind
locally as south, approximately fifty knots. Fifty knots,
when out here it was blowing eighty, ninety, a hundred—
God knows what force it was. And at six forty-five the shipping forecast: *A local depression of great intensity may
affect parts of sea areas Faeroes, Hebrides. . . . Winds
cyclonic and temporarily reaching hurricane force. . . .* I
think that was the most extraordinary part of it—the sense
of still being in contact with the outside world when all
our own world was being blown to bits by the wind, the
whole surface of the sea apparently disintegrating and being forced up into the atmosphere.

And then suddenly our little oasis of ordered security
crashed about our ears. The engine-room phone had prob-

ably been buzzing for some time. But nobody had heard it. The din was too great. It was the ring of the telegraph that informed us and the Quartermaster's voice: "Port engines losing power, sir." The spokes of the wheel were turning under his hand, turning until he had full starboard helm on. Again he reached for the brass handle of the port telegraph, gave it two sharp rings, and jammed it back at full ahead. Stratton leapt to the engine-room telephone. "It's all right now, sir." The Quartermaster was bringing the wheel back amidships. But I was watching Stratton. His face was white, his body rigid. ". . . Sea water, you say? . . . Yes, I knew about the leak. . . . Well, can't you drain it off? . . . I see. Well, that must have happened when we were broadside on in the bay. . . . All right, Stevens. Do what you can. . . . Yes, we'll try. But we can't hold her any steadier. There's quite a sea. . . . Well, give me warning when the other engines start cutting out." He put the phone back on its hook. His face looked bleak.

"What is it?" Wentworth demanded. "What's happened?"

"Main tank's leaking and we've been pumping sea water into the ready-use tank. Only the port engines affected so far, but . . ." He turned to the Quartermaster. "Think you can hold her on starboard engines alone?"

"I'll try, sir."

The Cox'n came in then. His flat, broad face was smeared with oil. "Port outer engine starting to cut out, sir. Chief asked me to tell you he's afraid . . ." Something in Stratton's face stopped the breathless rush of his words. In a quieter voice he added: "I was going round the Mess decks. I could feel there was something wrong so I slipped down to the engine-room. Chief said he couldn't get you on the phone."

"Thank you, Cox'n. I've just had a word with him. The starboard engines are all right, I gather?"

"For the moment, sir. But he's afraid the ready-use tank may be . . ."

"I've had his report on that." Stratton's voice, quiet and controlled, stilled the suggestion of panic that had hung for a moment over the wheelhouse.

"There's another thing, sir. The tiller flat. Bilge pumps not working. Chief thinks they're choked. Anyway, there's a lot of water. . . ."

"All right, Cox'n. Have some men closed up on the tiller flat, will you—just in case."

"Very good, sir." And as he went out Wentworth, close at my side, said: "I had a feeling about that tiller flat. Ever since I found the hatch unfastened. We must have taken a hell of a lot of water through it when we were getting off the beach." His manner was quite different now, almost calm, as though he'd braced himself against the urgency of the situation. He reached for the log book and began entering it up.

Everything normal again, the ship headed into the wind, the beat of the engines steady under our feet. But even with both engines at full ahead she was making little or no headway against the moving masses of air and water that seemed fused into a solid impenetrable wall. The shape of Laerg on the radar screen came and went, fuzzed by the thickness of the atmosphere. The quartermaster shifted his stance at the wheel, gripped the spokes tighter. And in the same instant I felt it through the soles of my feet, a change of beat, a raggedness. The wheel spun. Full starboard helm and the beat steadier again, but not so strong. "Port engines both stopped, sir."

Stratton was already at the phone. He held it to his ear, waiting. "Good. . . . Well, if you can drain off all the sea water. . . . Yes, we'll try and hold her bows-on. . . . All right. Now what about the tiller flat? . . . You've got a man working on it? Fine. . . . Yes, we'll just have to hope for the best." He put the phone down, glanced at the radar screen and then at me. His lips moved stiffly in a smile. "Hell of a time you picked to come for a sail with us." He glanced at the helm. The wheel was amidships again. "Answering all right, Quartermaster?" he asked.

"Pretty fair, sir."

But we weren't making headway any longer and Sgeir Mhor a bare mile away, directly down-wind of us. Stratton produced his packet of cigarettes and we stood there, braced against the violence of the movement, smoking and watching the radar screen. And then, suddenly, the Quartermaster's voice announced that the helm had gone dead. "Full starboard helm and not answering, sir."

Wentworth was already at one of the phones. "Cox'n reports steering motors shorted. There's a lot of water. . . ."

"Emergency steering." Stratton rapped the order out and I saw the Quartermaster lean down and throw across a lever at the base of the steering pedestal.

A sea broke thundering inboard. A solid sheet of spray crashed against the wheelhouse. And as the porthole cleared I saw the bows thrown off and sagging away to leeward. It had taken a bare ten seconds to engage the hand steering, but in those ten seconds the weight of sea and wind combined had caught hold of the bows and flung them off to port.

"Emergency steering not answering, sir."

The ship staggered to another blow and began to heel as the wind caught her on the starboard bow. She was starting to broach-to. And the Quartermaster's voice again, solid and unemotional: "Hand steering's all right, sir. But not enough power on the engines."

Only two engines out of four and the bows swinging fast now. Stratton was at the engine-room phone, but I could see by his face that no one was answering. "Keep your helm hard a'starboard. You may be able to bring her up in a lull."

But there wasn't a lull. The ship heeled further and further, and as she came broadside-on to wind and sea we were spilled like cattle down the sloping deck to fetch up half-lying along the port wall of the wheelhouse. "Any chance," I gasped, "of getting the other engines going?" And Stratton, looking at me, the sweat shining under the stubble of his beard: "How can they possibly—do any-thing—down there." I realized then what it must be like in the engine-room, cooped up with that mass of ma-chinery, hot oil spilling and their cased-in world turning on its side. "We're in God's hands now," he breathed. And a moment later, as though God himself had heard and was denying us even that faint hope, I felt the beat of those two remaining engines stagger, felt it through my whole body as I lay against the sloped steel of the wall.

I have said that panic is a nerve storm, an instinctive, un-controllable reaction of the nervous system. I had experi-enced fear before, but not panic. Now, with the pulse of the engines dying, something quite uncontrollable leapt in my throat, my limbs seemed to dissolve, and my whole body froze with apprehension. My mouth opened to scream a warning, but no sound came; and then, like a man fighting to stay sober after too much drink, I man-aged to get a grip on myself. It was a conscious effort of will and I had only just succeeded when the beat of the engines ceased altogether and I felt the ship dead under me. A glance at the radar showed the screen blank, half white, half black, as the sweep light continued to circle as if nothing had happened. We were heeled so far over that all the radar recorded was the sea below us, the sky above.

It was only the fact that we had such a weight of water on board that saved us. If the ship had been riding high, fully buoyant, she'd have turned right over. It was that and the terrific weight of the wind that held the seas flat.

The time was seven twenty-eight and Sgeir Mhor much

less than a mile away now, the wind blowing us broadside towards it. Engines and steering gone. There was nothing we could do now and I watched as Stratton fought his
way up the slope of the deck, struggling to reach the
radio shack. In less than two minutes the operator was
calling *Mayday*. But what the hell was the good of that?
In those two minutes the velocity of the wind had blown
us almost a quarter of a mile. And it wasn't a case of
the ship herself being blown—the whole surface of the sea
was moving down-wind, scooped up and flung north-
eastward by the pressure of the air.

Mayday, Mayday, Mayday.

I, too, had scrambled up the slope and into the alleyway. Through the open door of the radio shack I saw the
operator clinging to his equipment, could hear him saying that word over and over again into the mike. And then
he was in contact, reporting to the world at large that our
engines had packed up and we were being driven down on
to the southernmost tip of Laerg, on to the rocks of Sgeir
Mhor.

The nearest ship was L4400, lying hove-to on the far side
of Malesgair, a mere four miles away. But it might just
as well have been four hundred miles. She didn't dare
leave the shelter of those cliffs. In any case, she'd never
have reached us in time. Nothing could reach us. It was
pointless putting out a distress call. The ship lurched. I
slipped from the supporting wall and was pitched into
Stratton's cabin. I fetched up on the far side, half-sprawled
across his bunk. A girl's face in a cheap frame hung on the
wall at a crazy angle—dark hair and bare shoulders, calm
eyes in a pretty face. She looked a million miles away. I
don't know why, but I suddenly remembered Marjorie
Field's eyes, blue and serious, the wide mouth smiling.
And other girls in other lands. . . . Would it have made
any difference if there'd been only one? Did it make any
difference to Stratton that he was married? When it comes

to the point you're alone, aren't you, just yourself to make the passage across into the unknown?

It wasn't easy, sprawled on that bunk, to realize that in a few short minutes this cabin would be a shattered piece of wreckage tossed in the surf of breaking waves. I closed my eyes wearily. I could hear the wind and the sea, but the full blast of it was muffled, and I couldn't see it—that was the point. It made it difficult to visualize the end; flesh torn to pieces on the jagged rocks, the suffocation of drowning. And yet I knew that was the reality; disembowelment perhaps or going out quickly with the skull smashed to a pulp.

Hell! Lie here like a rat in a trap, that was no way to go. I forced myself to my feet, hauled my body up into the alleyway crowded now with men. They lay along the wall, big-chested with their life-jackets, their faces white. But no panic, just leaning there, waiting. It was all very ordinary, this moment of disaster. No orders, nobody screaming that they didn't want to die. And then it came to me that all these men saw were the steel walls of the ship. They were wrapped in ignorance. They hadn't seen the storm or the rocks. Exhausted, their senses dulled with sea-sickness, they waited for orders that would never come.

When we struck, the ship would roll over. That's what I figured, anyway. There was only one place to be then—out in the open. In the open there was just a chance. Wentworth had seen that, too. With two of the crew he was struggling to force the door to the deck open. I moved to help him, others with me, and under our combined efforts it fell back with a crash, and a blast of salt air, thick with spray, hit us. The Quartermaster was the first through. "You next." Wentworth pushed me through, calling to the men behind him.

Out on the side deck I saw at a glance that we were only just in time. Sgeir Mhor was very close now; grey heaps of rock with the sea slamming against them. Stratton was climbing out of the wheelhouse, the log book clutched in his hand. I shouted to him, and then I went down the ladder to the main deck, my body flattened against it by the wind. It was awkward going down that ladder, my body clumsy in the bulk of my life-jacket. I wondered when I'd put it on. I couldn't remember doing so. The Quartermaster followed me. "Out to the bows," he yelled in my ear, and hand over hand, clinging to the rail, we worked our way along the side of the ship. Clear of the bridge housing, there would be nothing to fall on us. A big sea struck the ship and burst right over us. It tore one man from the rail and I saw him sail through the air as though he were a gull. And then we went on, working our way out above the tank deck. Only two men followed us. The rest clung in a huddle against the bridge.

Another sea and then another; two in quick succession and all the breath knocked out of me. I remember clinging there, gasping for air. I was about halfway along the ship. I can see her still, lying right over with water streaming from her decks, the sea roaring in the tilted tank hold and all her port side submerged. And broadside to her canted hull, Sgeir Mhor looming jagged and black and wet, an island of broken rock in a sea of foam with the waves breaking, curved green backs that smoked spray and crashed like gunfire exploding salt water fragments high into the air.

And then she struck. It was a light blow, a mere slap, but deep down she shuddered. Another wave lifted her. She tilted, portside buried in foam, and Sgeir Mhor rushed towards us, lifted skywards, towering black.

I don't remember much after that—the detail is blurred in my mind. She hit with a bone-shaking impact, rolled, and butted her mast against vertical rock. Like a lance it broke. Half the bridge housing was concertinaed, men flung to the waves. And then from where I

clung I was looking down, not on water, but on bare rock
—a spine running out like the back of a dinosaur. It split
the ship across the middle; a hacksaw cutting metal
couldn't have done it neater. A gap opened within feet of
me, widening rapidly and separating us from all the after-
part of the ship. Rocks whirled by. White water opened up.
For a moment we hung in the break of the waves, grating
on half-submerged rocks. I thought that was the end, for
the bows were smashing themselves to pieces, the steel
plates beaten into fantastic shapes. But then the grating
and the pounding ceased. We were clear—clear of the submerged rocks, clear of the tip of Sgeir Mhor. We were in
open water, lying right over, half-submerged, but still
afloat. Buoyed up by the air trapped behind the bulkheads in her sides, she was being driven across Shelter Bay,
buried deep in a boiling scum of foam and spray. I didn't
think of this as the end, not consciously. My brain, my
body, the whole physical entity that was me, was too concentrated on the struggle to cling on. And yet something
else that was also me seemed to detach itself from the
rest, so that I have a picture that is still clear in my mind of
my body, bulky in clothes and life-jacket, lying drowned in
a turmoil of broken water, sprawled against the steel bulwarks, and of the front half of the shattered ship rolling
like a log, with the sea pouring over it.

People came and went in my mind, faces I had
known, the brief, ephemeral contacts of my life, giving me
temporary companionship at the moment of death. And
then we grounded in the shallows east of the camp, not far
from the ruined Factor's House. But by then I was half-
drowned, too dazed to care, mind and body beaten beyond
desire for life. I just clung on to the bulwark because
that was what I had been doing all the time. There was
no instinct of self-preservation about it. My hands seemed
locked on the cold, wet steel.

It was a long time before I realized that the wind had

died away; probably because the seas, no longer flattened by its weight, were bigger then. The remains of the bows lay just where the waves were breaking. They beat upon the hollow bottom like giant fists hammering at a steel drum. Boom . . . Boom . . . Boom—and the roar of the surf. Fifty thousand express trains in the confines of a tunnel couldn't have made so great a noise.

And then that, too, began to lessen. My senses struggled back to life. The wind had gone round. That was my first conscious thought. And when I opened my eyes it was to a lurid sun glow, an orange, near-scarlet gash, like the raw slash of a wound, low down behind Sgeir Mhor. The toppling waves stood etched in chaos against it and all the cloud above me was a smoke-black pall of unbelievable density. There was no daylight on the shore of Shelter Bay, no real daylight; only darkness lit by that unearthly glow. The crofts of the Old Village, the roofless church, the cleits dotting the slopes of Tarsaval high above me— none of it was real. The light, the scene, the crazy, beat-up sea—it was all weird, a demon world.

So my mind saw it, and myself a sodden piece of flotsam washed up on that shore, too battered and exhausted to realize I was alive. That knowledge came with the sight of a fellow creature moving slowly like a spider, feeling his way down the jagged edges of what had been the tank deck.

I watched him fall into the backwash of a wave, beating at the surf with his arms. I closed my eyes, and when I looked again, he was ashore, lying spread-eagled among the boulders.

That was when the instinct for self-preservation stirred in me at last.

I moved then, wearily, each movement a conscious effort, a desperate, aching struggle—down the jagged edges of deck plates twisted like tin-foil, down into the surf, falling into it as the other had done and fighting my way ashore, half-drowned, to lie panting and exhausted on the beach beside him.

It wasn't the Quartermaster; I don't know what had happened to him. This was a small man with a sandy moustache and tiny, frightened eyes that stared at me wildly. He'd broken his arm and every time he moved he screamed, a febrile rabbit sound that lost itself in the wind's howl. There was blood on his hair. Blood, too, on the stones where I lay, a thin bright trickle—my own blood, from a scalp wound.

"Shut up," I said as he screamed again. "You're alive. What more do you want?" I was thinking of all the others, the picture of the ship crushed against the rocks still vivid in my mind.

My watch had gone, torn from my wrist. How long had it been? I didn't know. Leaning up on one elbow, I stared out across the bay. The orange glow had vanished and Sgeir Mhor was a shadowy outline, a grey blur masked by a rain squall. I forced myself to my feet and was immediately knocked down, beaten flat by a violent down-draught. That was when I realized the wind had gone right round. It was blowing from the other side of the island now, whipping across the Saddle between Malesgair and Tarsaval and down into Shelter Bay, cutting great swathes across it, the water boiling in its wake, a flattened, seething cauldron.

I made the grass above the beach, half crawling, and staggered past the Factor's House, up towards the Old Village and the camp. Daylight was a mockery, drab as a witch, and the wind screamed hell out of the confused masses of cloud that billowed above my head. And when I finally reached the camp I barely recognized it, the whole place laid waste and everything weighing less than a ton whirled inland and scattered across the slopes of Tarsaval. And down on the beach, the trailers we'd off-loaded in haste all gone, the trucks, too—only the bulldozer remained lying in the surf like a half-submerged rock. Wreckage was everywhere. The roof of one of the huts was gone, blown clean away, the walls sagging outwards, and where the latrines had been there was nothing but a row of closets standing bare like porcelain pots.

Pinney's hut was still intact. I turned the handle and the wind flung the door open with a crash, the walls shaking to the blast. It took the last of my strength to get it shut and in the relative peace of the hut's interior I collapsed on to the nearest bed.

How long I lay there I do not know. Time is relative, a mental calculation that measures activity. I was inactive then, my brain numbed, my mind hardly functioning. It might have been only a minute. It might have been an hour, two hours. I didn't sleep. I'm certain of that. I was conscious all the time of the shaking of the hut, of the battering, ceaseless noise of the wind; conscious, too, that there was something I had to do, some urgent intention that had forced me to struggle up from the beach. I dragged myself to my feet, staggering vaguely through the hut until I came to the radio, drawn to it by some action of my subconscious.

I realized then why I'd made the effort. The outside world. Somebody must be told. Help alerted. I slumped into the operator's chair, wondering whether there was any point, still that picture in my mind of the bridge crushed against sheer rock and the waves pounding. Could any of the crew have survived, any of those men huddled like sheep awaiting slaughter in the narrow alleyway out of which I'd clawed my way? But the wind had changed and they'd be under the lee. There was just that chance and I reached out my hand, switching on the set. I didn't touch the tuning. I just sat there waiting for the hum that would tell me the set had warmed up. But nothing happened. It was dead and it took time for my brain to work that out—the generator silent and no current coming through. There were emergency batteries below the table and by following the cables back I was able to cut them in.

The set came alive then and a voice answered almost immediately. It was thin and faint. *"We've been calling and calling. If you're still on Laerg, why didn't you answer before?"* He didn't give me a chance to explain. *"I've got Glasgow on the line for you. They've found Mrs. McGregor. Hold on."* There was a click and then silence, and I sat there, helpless, the salt taste of sea water in my mouth. Fifty men battered to pieces on the rocks of Sgeir Mhor and they had to fling Mrs. McGregor at me. Why couldn't they have waited for me to tell them what had happened? *"You're through."* The police first, and then a woman's voice, soft and very Scots, asking for news of her son. I felt almost sick, remembering what had happened, the tiller flat flooded and the poor devil's body tombed up there. "I'm sorry, Mrs. McGregor. I can't tell you anything yet." And I cut her off, overcome by nausea, the sweat breaking out all over me and my head reeling.

When I got them again, my brother was there. Recognizing his voice, I felt a flood of instant relief. "Iain. Iain, thank God!" I was back on Ardnamurchan, crying to my older brother for help—a rock to cling to in moments of desperation.

But this was no rock. This was a man as sick and frightened as myself. *"Major Braddock here."* His voice, strained and uneasy, had the snap of panic in it. "Iain," I cried again. "For God's sake. It's Donald." But the appeal was wasted and his voice when it came was harsh and grating. *"Braddock here. Who's that? What's happened?"*

The time was then 08.35 and Braddock had been almost six hours in the Movements Office, waiting for news. God knows what he must have been feeling. Flint said he'd paced up and down, hour after hour, grey-faced and silent, while the periodic reports came through from our own radio operator and from the man on L4400. Up to the moment when disaster overtook us Movements had a fairly clear picture of what was happening. And then suddenly that Mayday call, and after that silence. "Get them," Braddock had shouted at the Signals operator. "Christ, man! Get them again." But all the operator could get was L4400 announcing flatly that they were in the storm centre steaming for the shelter of the other side of the island.

"It's Eight-six-one-o I want," Braddock had almost screamed. "Get them, man. Keep on trying."

He'd had far too little sleep that night and the interview he'd had with Standing at two-thirty in the morning cannot have been a pleasant one. Standing had been roused from his bed by a duty driver at twelve-forty, and Ferguson described him as literally shaking with rage when he realized what Braddock had done. The first thing he did was to speak to Stratton on the R/T and then he walked across to the quarters and saw Cliff Morgan. "White-faced he was, man," was the way Cliff put it. "Calling me all sorts of names for interfering. But when I'd explained the situation, he calmed down a bit. He even thanked me. And then he went out, saying it was all Braddock's fault and if anything went wrong he'd get the bloody man slung out of the Service."

Standing had gone straight to his office and sent for Braddock. There was nobody else present at that meeting so that there is no record of what passed between them. But immediately afterwards Braddock had teleprinted the BGS direct, giving his reasons for ordering an immediate evacuation on his own responsibility. And after that he'd remained in the Movements Office, waiting for news; and when our Mayday call went out, it was he, not Standing, who had alerted Scottish Command and set the whole emergency machinery in motion. At half

past eight he'd walked over to the Met. Office. He was with
Cliff Morgan for about ten minutes and it was during those
ten minutes that I called Base. A relief operator had just
taken over, which was why I was given the Glasgow call
instead of being put straight through either to Braddock at
the Met. Office or to Standing, who was waiting alone in
his office.

Probably if I'd got Standing his reaction would have been
as slow as my brother's, for neither of them could have
any idea of the appalling ferocity of that storm or the
magnitude of the disaster. He didn't seem able to understand at first. *"You and one other chap. . . . Is that all?
Are you certain?"*

I wasn't certain of anything except the memory of the
ship on her beam ends and the waves driving her against
the rocks. "If you'd seen the seas. . . . It was Sgeir Mhor
she hit."

"Jesus Christ, Donald!" It was the first time he'd used
my name and it made a deep impression. *"Jesus Christ!
There must be others. There've got to be others."*

But I didn't think there could be then. "I've told you,
the whole bridge deck was concertinaed in a matter of
seconds. They can't possibly . . ."

"Well, have a look. Go and find out."

"The wind," I said wearily. "Don't you realize? You
can't stand."

*"Then crawl, laddie—crawl. I must know. I must be cer-
tain. Surely to God it can't be as bad as you say."* He was
almost screaming at me. And then his voice dropped abruptly to a wheedling tone. *"For my sake, laddie—please.
Find out whether there are any other survivors."*

His voice. It was so strange—it was Iain's voice now,
my own brother's, and the accent Scots. The years fell
away . . . "All right, Iain. I'll try." It was Mavis all over
again—Mavis and all the other times. "I'll try," I said
again and switched the set off, going down the hut and out

into a blast that whipped the door from my hand and knocked me to the ground.

I met the other fellow coming up from the beach, crawling on his hands and knees and crying with the pain of his broken arm. He called to me, but I heard no sound, only his mouth wide open and his good arm pointing seaward. But there was nothing there, nothing but the seething waters of the bay churned by the wind; all the rest was blotted out by rain and Sgeir Mhor a vague blur. "What is it?" I yelled in his ear and I amost fell on top of him as the wind came down, a solid, breath-taking wall of air.

"The rocks, sir. Sgeir Mhor. I thought I saw . . ." I lost the rest. It was almost dark, a grey gloom with the clouds racing, and so low I could almost have reached up and touched them.

"Saw what?" I shouted. "What did you think you saw?"

"It was clear for a moment, and there were figures—men. I could have sworn. . . ." But he wasn't certain. You couldn't be certain of anything in those conditions. And your eyes played tricks.

I lay there beside him till the rain squall passed. But even then I couldn't see what he still swore he'd seen. Cloud, forced low by the down-draughts, obscured all the upper half of Sgeir Mhor. There was only one thing to do. I told him to go to the hut, and then I started out along the beach road alone. But it was impossible. The weight of the wind was too great. It caught me as I was crossing the Bailey bridge that spanned the burn and it threw me against the girders as though I were a piece of paper. The sheer weight of it was fantastic. If it hadn't been for the girders I think I should have been whirled into the air and flung into the bay. I turned back then, and when I reached the hut I collapsed on Pinney's bed and immediately lost consciousness.

How long I was out I don't know. My whole body ached and there was a pain in mv side. The cut in my head had opened again and the pillow was dark with blood. Lying there with my eyes open, slowly struggling back to life, I found myself staring at Pinney's locker. Either my eyes didn't focus immediately or else it took a long time for me to realize that a pair of binoculars might save me the long walk out to Keava and up its steep grass slopes. There they were, lying on a shelf, tucked in between some books and an old khaki jersey. It was much lighter in the hut; quite bright, in fact. And the noise of the wind was less.

I picked up the binoculars and staggered stiffly to the door. And when I opened it I was looking out on to a changed world. The clouds, torn to shreds by the wind, were ragged now. And they had lifted so that all the great spine of Keava was visible and I could see the sheer gap that separated it from Sgeir Mhor, could see all the rocks and caves and patches of grass on Sgeir Mhor itself. The air was clear, washed clean by the rain. Only Tarsaval and the very top of Creag Dubh remained shrouded in gloom, the clouds clinging to their drenched slopes, billowing and swirling among the crags. Seaward, shafts of brighter light showed white water tossed in frightful confusion. I slipped into the lee of the hut and with my back braced against its sodden wall I focused the glasses on Sgeir Mhor.

Seen suddenly at close vision, isolated like that from the rest of the island, it looked like some massive medieval fortress. All it lacked was a drawbridge spanning the narrow gut that separated it from the Butt of Keava. With the change of wind, the seas no longer exploded against it in plumes of white, but the foam of the waves that had wrecked us lay in banks like snow over all the piled-up battlements of rock. In that clean air I could see every detail and nothing moved. The place was dead; just a great heap of rock and not a living thing. How could there be? Like the cliffs of Keava, it had taken the full brunt of the storm.

I lowered the glasses. Just the two of us. All the rest dead; gone, buried, drowned under masses of water, battered to pulp, their bodies food for the fish, for the lobsters and crabs that scuttled in the holes and crevices of submarine rock terraces. Stratton, Wentworth, Pinney—all the faces I had known so very briefly on board that ship.

Can you will people alive? Was I God-given that I could stand there and pray so desperately, and then on the instant conjure movement? It seemed like that, for I looked again, hoping against hope, and there in the twin circles of magnification something stirred, a man stood for a moment etched against the luminosity of clouds thinning. Or was it my imagination? Flesh and blood among that waste of rock. It seemed impossible, and yet one knows the extraordinary indestructibility of the human body. Countless instances leapt to my mind—things I had read about, things I had been told, things I had actually seen during the war; all things that had really happened, and not so much the indestructibility of the human body as the unwillingness, almost the inability of the human spirit to accept defeat. And here, now, I was gazing at the impossible, and it was no figment of the imagination. This, too, was real; there was a man, off the sky-line now and crawling down the rocks, trying to reach sea level, and another following close behind him.

How many were still alive I didn't know. I didn't care. It was enough that there were survivors on Sgeir Mhor, and I rushed back into the hut and switched on the radio. Base answered my call immediately. *"Hold on."* And then a voice, not my brother's this time, asking urgently for news.

It was Colonel Standing, and when I told him I'd seen two figures moving on Sgeir Mhor, he said *"Thank God!"* in a voice that was like a beaten man grasping at the faint hope of recovery. *"If there are two, there may be more."* He wanted me to find out. But two or twenty—what dif-

ference did it make? The problem of rescuing them remained the same. Could I launch a boat? That was his first
suggestion and I found myself laughing inanely. I was
tired. God! I was tired. And he didn't understand. He'd
no idea of the weight of wind that had hit the island.
"There are no boats," I told him. "And if there were,
there's only myself and a chap with a broken arm." It
was like talking to a child. I found I had to explain in
simple terms what the storm had been like—all the trailers gone and a heavy thing like the bulldozer sucked into
the sea, the camp a wreck and everything movable shattered or whirled away, the slopes of Tarsaval littered
with the Army's debris. I described it all to him—the fight
seaward, the engines packing up, the way she'd struck
Sgeir Mhor and how the bows had stayed afloat and
been driven ashore in Shelter Bay. I talked until my voice
was hoarse, my mind too tired to think. Finally, I said:
"What we need is men and equipment—a boat with an
outboard motor or rocket rescue apparatus to bridge the
gut between Keava and Sgeir Mhor. Where's the other
LCT? She could come into the bay now the wind is
northerly again."

But L4400 was twenty miles south-west of Laerg, running before a huge sea, her bridge deck stove in and her
plates strained, a wreck of a boat that might or might not
get back to port. Weather ship *India* had left her station
and was steaming to intercept her. The nearest ship was
the Naval tug, but still twenty-four hours away in these
conditions. Something my grandfather had told us came
sluggishly to the surface of my mind, something about
landing on Sgeir Mhor, the sheerness of the rocks. "I
don't think a boat would help," I said. "The only landing
place on Sgeir Mhor is on the seaward side. And that's not
possible except in flat calm weather."

It took time for that to sink in. He didn't want to believe
it. How did I know? Was I absolutely certain? Surely

there must be rock ledges up which a skilful climber
. . . "Check with my . . . with Major Braddock," I said.
"Check with him." This man arguing, questioning. I
wished to God he'd get off the line and give me Iain again.
Iain would understand. "I'd like to have a word with
Major Braddock."

"I'm handling this." The voice was curt. *"Major Braddock's caused enough trouble already."*

"I'd still like to speak to him."

"Well, you can't."

"Why not?"

A pause. And then: *"Major Braddock is under arrest."*

God knows what I said then. I think I cursed—but
whether I cursed Standing or the circumstances, I don't
know. The futility of it! The one man who could help,
who had a grasp of the problem, and this stupid fool
had had him arrested. "For God's sake," I pleaded. "Give
me Braddock. He'll know what to do." And sharp and
high-pitched over the air came his reply—unbelievable in
the circumstances. *"You seem to forget, Mr. Ross, that I'm
the commanding officer here, and I'm perfectly capable of
handling the situation."*

"Then handle it," I shouted at him, "and get those men
off Sgeir Mhor." And I switched off, realizing that I was
too tired now to control my temper. I just sat there then,
thinking of Iain. Poor devil! It was bad enough—the loss
of life, the shipwreck, but to be under arrest, sitting inactive with no part in the rescue, with nothing to do but
mull over in his mind what had happened. Didn't Standing realize? Or was he a sadist? Whichever it was, the effect on Iain would be the same. The bloody, sodding
swine, I thought. The cruel, stupid bastard.

"Mr. Ross! Mr. Ross, sir—you're talking to yourself."

I opened my eyes, conscious of a hand shaking my shoulder. The fellow with the broken arm was standing there,
staring at me with a worried frown. He no longer looked

frightened. He even had a certain stature, standing there proffering me a steaming mug. "It's only Bovril," he said. "But I fort some'ing 'ot after our bathe. . . ." He was Cockney. False teeth smiled at me out of a funny little screwed-up face. "When you drunk it, you better change them clothes. Catch yer deaf if yer don't. Borrow off of Captain Pinney; 'e won't mind." This little runt of a man trying to mother me and his broken arm still hanging limp. My heart warmed to him. The lights were on and a new sound—the hum of the generator audible between the gusts.

"You've got the lights going."

He nodded. " 'Ad ter—all electric 'ere, yer see. Wiv'at the generator yer can't cook. I got some bangers on and there's bacon and eggs and fried bread. That do yer?" I asked him his name then and he said: "Alf Cooper. Come from Lunnon." He grinned. "Flippin' long way from Bow Bells, ain't I? Fort I 'eard 'em once or twice when we was in the flaming water, an' they weren't playin' 'ymn toons neither."

As soon as we'd had our meal I set his arm as best I could, and after that I showed him how to work the radio. I felt stronger now and perhaps because of that the wind seemed less appalling as I tried again to get a closer look at Sgeir Mhor. This time I was able to cross the bridge, but in the flat grassland below the old lazy beds the wind caught me and pinned me down. A bird went screaming close over my head. I crawled to the shelter of a cleit and with my back to the ruins of its dry-stone wall I focused the glasses on Sgeir Mhor.

Visibility was better now. I could see the rocks falling sheer to the turbulence of the sea, the cracks and gullies, and a figure moving like a seal high up on a bare ledge. There were others crouched there, sheltering from the swell that still beat against the further side, covering the whole mass with spray. I counted five men lying tucked into crevices, the way sheep huddle for protection against the elements.

Five men. Perhaps there were more. I couldn't see. Just five inert bodies and only one of them showing any signs of life, and now he lay still. I started back then, keeping to the edge of the beach, which rose steeply and gave me a little shelter. The burn forced me up on to the bridge and as I entered the camp a blast hit me, flung me down, and a piece of corrugated iron went scything through the air just above my head to hit the sea and go skimming across its flattened surface.

Back in the hut I called Base and was immediately put through to Colonel Standing.

IV

Rescue

(OCTOBER 22–24)

Long before my first contact with Base, before even our Mayday call had gone out, all Services had been alerted and the first moves made to deal with the emergency. Coastal Command at Ballykelly had flown off a Shackleton to search for the *Viking Fisher;* the Navy had dispatched a destroyer from the Gareloch. Weather ship *India* had left her station headed for Laerg, a fishery-protection vessel north-west of the Orkneys had been ordered to make for the Hebrides at full speed, and a fast mine-layer was getting steam up ready to sail if required. By nine o'clock the emergency operation was being concentrated on L4400, then a battered wreck running before the storm somewhere to the west of Laerg. The destroyer was ordered to close her with all possible speed and either stand by her to take off survivors or to escort her to Leverburgh or back to the Clyde if she could make it. A second Shackleton had taken off from the Coastal Command base in

Northern Ireland with orders to locate her and circle her until the destroyer arrived or until relieved by another aircraft.

That was the situation when I contacted Base with definite news of survivors from the wreck of L8610. Neither the Shackletons nor the destroyer could be of any help to the men on Sgeir Mhor. Both the fishery-protection vessel and the mine-layer were too far away to be effective and conditions made the use of Northern Air Sea Rescue's helicopters out of the question. The task was allocated to the Naval tug. Not only was she a more suitable vessel than a destroyer for working close inshore among rocks, she also happened to be much nearer. She sailed from Lochmaddy at 09.17 hours.

In these conditions and in these northern waters the Army was largely dependent on the other Services, and their resources were limited. Standing had to make use of what was available and in the circumstances improvisation was probably justified. When I spoke to him I think his mind was already made up. It's easy to be wise after the event and say that it was a panic decision, but considered from his point of view, he hadn't all that much choice. The tug couldn't possibly reach Laerg before nightfall. In those seas, even allowing for the fact that such a violent storm was bound to die down quickly, it would be good going if she were in Shelter Bay by dawn, and the forecast for dawn next day was not good. The depression, which had been stationary to the west of Ireland, was on the move again and expected to reach the Hebrides within twenty-four hours. Instead of a polar air stream there would then be southerly winds force six, veering later south-west and increasing to force seven, possibly gale force eight. He had checked with Ferguson and with Field, both officers who knew Laerg well and who had climbed over Sgeir Mhor. They confirmed what I had told him, that the rocks were sheer on the side facing Shelter Bay

and that the only possible landing place was on the seaward side. And since that was the side exposed to winds
between south and west it was obvious that the forecast
not only made it extremely unlikely that any landing could
be attempted the following day, but also that there was a
grave danger of the survivors being overwhelmed by the
force of the waves. That there were any survivors at all was
obviously due to the change of wind direction that had occurred almost immediately after the ship had struck, and
by dawn they might all be dead of exposure.

Time was, therefore, the vital factor. Moreover, both
Ferguson and Field agreed that the only practical way of
getting them off was to fire a line to them from the Butt of
Keava and bring them over the gut by breeches buoy. That
meant a rocket life-saving apparatus. The only equipment
of this sort possessed by Guided Weapons had been allocated to the Laerg detachment and nobody was certain
whether it had been shipped out or not. Rafferty thought
not, but the Movements Officer disagreed and a squad
was dispatched to search the stores heaped behind the
quay at Leverburgh. Meantime, Adams had been called in.
The wind at Northton was around 35 knots, gusting 40
plus. He refused point blank to fly his helicopter anywhere
near Laerg. He had come to Standing's office direct from
the Met. Office. He was well aware of the urgency of the
situation. He also knew that the turbulence of the air
around Laerg made it quite impossible for him to make
a landing there.

Time was wasted contacting the two main lifeboat stations. They were standing by, but though they had
breeches-buoy equipment available, they were even less
well placed than the tug for getting it there. There was
only one answer then, to parachute the life-saving gear in.
But no Shackleton would dare fly low over the island
and a high-level drop would almost certainly result in the
parachutes being blown out to sea.

It was Adams who suggested a possible solution. A small aircraft owned by one of the charter companies was waiting at Stornoway for weather clearance back to the mainland. He thought the pilot, a Canadian named Rocky Fellowes who'd done a lot of bush flying in the North West Territories, might have a shot at it. And at Stornoway there was the life-saving gear they needed.

It was then that Ferguson volunteered; if the first drop were successful and the gear landed in a place that was accessible, then he'd make the jump and organize the setting up of the breeches buoy. It faced Standing with a difficult choice. He had now received my second call. He knew there were at least five men marooned on Sgeir Mhor and only seven hours of daylight left. The risk of one man's life against the almost certain death of five; rightly or wrongly, he accepted Ferguson's offer. It was then eleven forty-five. Ten minutes later Ferguson was on his way. Field went with him: also a sergeant and two men, all of whom had completed a parachute course. And while the staff car started its forty-mile dash to Stornoway, Standing got through to the airport and asked them to find Fellowes and have him ring Northton immediately. He also asked them to arrange for the life-saving apparatus to be brought to the airfield and the parachutes to be got ready. Meantime, the tug was ordered to put into Leverburgh in the hopes that the Army's life-saving gear would be located.

This was the situation when I made my next contact with Base. I had found an alarm clock in the remains of the cookhouse and the time by this was 12.53. Standing was then able to tell me that Fellowes had agreed to attempt the drop. The wind speed at Stornoway was slightly less than the reading shown by Cliff Morgan's anemometer. It was beginning to fall off and he was optimistic. I suppose I should have warned Standing. The wind speed had fallen at Laerg, too. But there is a difference between a drop from around fifty knots and a drop from the fantastic wind speeds we had been experiencing. It was still coming down off the Saddle in gusts of considerable force. Whether it would have made any difference if I had warned him, I don't know. Probably not. Nobody sitting in his office almost a hundred miles away could possibly have any idea of the battering Laerg had received and was still receiving. In any case, I was thinking of those men out on Sgeir Mhor. If the pilot was willing to try it, then it wasn't for me to discourage him. The ETA Standing gave me for the plane's arrival was 14.15 approximate. In an hour's time the wind might have dropped right away. I had known it to happen with storms of this intensity. And if it did, then the whole situation would be changed, and a plane overhead could make the difference between life and death to the survivors. It was up to the pilot anyway.

Standing was still talking to me, explaining about the tug and that Adams was standing by in the hope that conditions might improve sufficiently for him to fly the helicopter. Suddenly he stopped in mid-sentence and I heard him say: *"Just a minute."* And then another voice—a voice I recognized, much fainter, but still quite audible: *"Please. I must see you. You can't do it. If you make Mike jump . . ."*

"I'm not making him. He volunteered."

"Then stop him. You've got to stop him. He'll kill himself. It's murder expecting him to jump in this wind, just to prove he can do it."

"For God's sake, Marjorie. Pull yourself together. He's not trying to prove anything."

"Of course he is. You're taking advantage of him." She was beside herself, her voice shaken with the violence of her emotions. *"It isn't fair. He'll be killed and . . ."*

I heard the clatter of the phone as he dropped it and his voice was suddenly farther away: *"Look, my dear. Try to understand. This isn't just a question of Mike*

Ferguson. *There are survivors out there and the one chance of getting them off . . ."*

"*I don't care. I'm thinking of Mike."*

"*Your father's with him. He'll see he doesn't do any- thing rash."*

But she didn't accept that. "*Daddy and Mike—they're both made the same way. You know that. They've both . . ."* She hesitated, adding: "*He'll jump whatever the con- ditions."* And then on a different note: "*Is it true Mr. Ross is one of the survivors? Major Rafferty said something about . . ."*

"*I'm just speaking to him now."* And then I heard him say: "*Marjorie!"* his voice sharp and angry. She must have grabbed hold of the phone for her voice was suddenly clear and very close to me, trembling uncontrollably so that I caught her mood, the desperate urgency of her fear. She might have been there in the hut with me. "*Mr. Ross. Help me—please. Mike mustn't jump. Do you hear? You've radio. You can contact the plane."* And then, al- most with a sob: "*No, let me finish."* But he'd got the phone away from her. "*Ross? I'll call you back at fourteen hundred hours."* There was a click, and after that silence.

Fellowes took off from Stornoway at 13.40 hours. Condi- tions had improved slightly, with the wind easterly about thirty knots. The overcast, however, had come down again and there were rain squalls. They were in cloud before they'd reached a thousand feet and they had to climb to more than six thousand before they were above it. Field was in the co-pilot's seat; Ferguson, the sergeant, and the two men back in the fuselage. The plane was an old Consul, the metal of the wings burnished bright by hail and rain, by subjection over many years to the abrasive forces of the elements. They flew for almost forty minutes in watery sunlight across a flat cotton-wool plain of cloud. Airspeed 120, the altimeter steady at 6.5, and towards the end the pilot searching for an orographical cloud, a bulge in the overcast that would pinpoint the position of Laerg. But there was no orographical cloud and at 14.20 they started down through the overcast.

Fellowes's dead reckoning was based on course and speed. He had corrected for drift, but he had no means of telling whether the wind had remained constant and he was doing his sums the way the early fliers did them, his navigational aids on his knee. And all the time he was having to fly his plane in strong winds. He had spoken to me on the radio. But I couldn't even make a guess at the wind speed, for it was broken by Tarsaval and Malesgair and came down from the direction of the Saddle in violent eddies. All I could tell him was that the ceiling was under a thousand. Creag Dubh was just over the thousand and Creag Dubh was blanketed.

Coming down like that through thick cloud couldn't have been very pleasant. Field told me later that he didn't dare look at the altimeter after it had unwound to two thousand. He would like to have been able to shut his eyes, but he couldn't; they remained fixed on the grey void ahead, his body tense and strained forward against the safety belt. The engines made hardly a sound, just a gentle whispering, the wing-tips fluttering in moments of turbulence. Fellowes, too, was strained forward, eyes peering through the windshield. They were both of them waiting for that sudden darkening in the opaque film ahead that would mean hard rock and the end. Theoretically, Fellowes had overshot by five miles and was coming down over empty, unobstructed sea. But he couldn't be certain. Tarsaval was 1,456 feet high.

Five minutes—one of the longest five minutes of his life, Field said. Finally, he tore his eyes away from the empty windshield and glanced at the altimeter. Eight hundred feet. The cloud darkened imperceptibly. His eyes, with nothing substantial to focus on, were playing tricks. He was on the high slopes of a great mountain again, the cloud swirling about him. And then suddenly there was a pattern—streaks of black and white, long foaming lines coming up towards them. The sea, and the long march of the waves had their tops torn from them by the wind.

The aircraft banked sharply, the wing-tip seeming almost to touch the crest of a roller that reared up, curling and then breaking in a great surge of thrusting water. They straightened out, skimming the surface, the black curtain of a rain squall ahead. Bank again to skirt it and then momentarily blinded as water beat against the windshield, driven by the force of the wind into long rivulets that were never still. And on the other side of the squall a dark wall coming to meet them, towering cliffs of black rock sliding back from the starboard wing, the glimpse of two stacs, their tops hidden in cloud. Fladday. Course 280° then and Shelter Bay opening out ahead. Fellowes came right into it, flying at just over five hundred feet, and when he turned the wind caught him and flung him like a wounded gull across the top of Sgeir Mhor.

They saw nothing that first run, but when he came in again, slower this time on a course of 020° headed straight into the wind, Field could see men standing among the rocks, waving to them. Through his glasses he counted eleven, and when they came in again, slightly lower this time, skimming the tops of the rocks, he made it fourteen. They stood off then, circling the open sea beyond the two arms of the bay while Fellowes reported to Base by radio.

Fourteen men still alive. Standing had no choice then. Nor had Ferguson. Nor had Fellowes. He yelled for the men back in the fuselage to get ready and headed back into Shelter Bay. The fuselage door was held open against the slip-stream, the two packages poised in the cold blast of the opening. Fellowes raised his hand. "Let go." They were flung out. The fuselage door slammed shut. The aircraft banked.

I had left the radio then and was standing in the lee of the hut. I saw the two packages fall—two black dots like bombs dropping from the side of the plane. Twin white canopies blossoming and the plane blown like a leaf towards Sgeir Mhor, losing height, its wings dipping like a bird in flight. It cleared the rocks and vanished into rain. The parachutes moved across the sky above my head, growing larger, but drifting very fast. And then first one and then the other were caught by down-draughts, the nylon canopies half-collapsed. They came down with a rush and then, just before they hit the beach, they each filled with a snap I could almost hear, were whirled upwards and then landed gently, almost graceful, halfway up the slopes of Keava.

I saw what happened to them, but Fellowes didn't. He was too busy fighting his plane clear of Sgeir Mhor. And Field had his eyes on the rocks, not on the parachutes. All they saw when they came out of the rain squall and circled the bay were two parachutes lying side by side like two white mushrooms close under the first scree slope on Keava. They didn't realize it was luck, not judgment, that had put them there. Field signalled back to Mike Ferguson, both thumbs up, and Fellowes took the plane in again. The drill was the same. The two men held the fuselage door open. The sergeant acted as dispatcher. But this time he was dispatching a man, not two inanimate packages. Again Fellowes judged his moment, raised his hand and shouted: "Jump!"

Whether Fellowes misjudged or whether Mike Ferguson hesitated, as the sergeant said he did, nobody will ever know. Field's impression was that he jumped immediately. But in moments like this, fractions of a second count and a pilot, tensed and in control of his machine, possesses a sensitivity and a speed of reaction that is much faster than that of the ordinary man. Fellowes thought it was a long time before the sergeant called out that Ferguson was away. In view of his parachute-course record, it seems more than likely that Ferguson did, in fact, hesitate. If he did, it was a fatal hesitation. He may have felt in those last few moments of the run-in that he was jumping to his death. The sergeant reported that his face was very white, his lips trembling as he moved to the door. But then again, in view of his previous experience, some nervous reaction was inevitable.

In a tragedy of this sort it is pointless to try and apportion the blame. Each man is doing his best according to his lights and in any case it was the wind that was the vital factor. My back was against the hut and at the moment the plane banked and that tiny bundle of human flesh launched itself from the fuselage I felt the whole structure tremble under the onslaught of the wind. It wasn't just a gust. It came in a steady roar and it kept on blowing. I saw the parachute open, his fall suddenly checked. He was then at about five hundred feet and right over my head; the plane, still banking, was being flung sideways across Sgeir Mhor.

If the wind had been a down-draught it might have collapsed his parachute momentarily. That was what had happened to the two previous parachutes. He might have landed heavily and been injured, but he would still have been alive. But it was a steady wind. It kept his parachute full. I saw him fighting the nylon cords to partially collapse it, but it was like a balloon, full to bursting and driving towards Keava at a great rate, trailing him behind it. For a moment it looked as though he would be all right. The sloped rock spine of Keava was a good seven hundred feet high at the point he was headed for, but as he neared it the steep slope facing Shelter Bay produced an updraught. The parachute lifted, soaring towards the clouds.

He cleared the top by several hundred feet. For a moment he was lost to sight, swallowed by the overcast.
Then I saw him again, the parachute half-collapsed and
falling rapidly. It was a glimpse, no more, for in the instant he was lost behind Keava.

Beyond the ridge was sheer cliff, and beyond the cliff
nothing but the Atlantic and the gale-torn waves. It was all
so remote that it seemed scarcely real; only imagination
could associate that brief glimpse of white nylon disappearing with a man dead, drowned in a wet, suffocating
world of tumbling water.

The plane stood off, circling by the entrance to the bay.
It didn't come in again and nobody else jumped. I went
slowly back into the hut and picked up Standing's voice
on the radio. It was so shaken that I barely recognized it.
He was ordering the pilot to return to Stornoway.

I was glad of that—glad that nobody else was going to be
ordered to jump, glad that I didn't have to stand again outside the hut and watch another parachute blown out into
the Atlantic. I found I was trembling, still with that picture in my mind of a man dangling and the white
envelope coming out of the clouds, half-collapsed, and the
poor fellow falling to a cold death in the Atlantic. I had
liked Mike Ferguson. He'd a lot of guts to face that jump.
And then I was thinking of Marjorie Field and of that
interview she'd had with Colonel Standing when I had
been an involuntary eavesdropper. Somebody would have
to tell her and I was glad I wasn't her father. The dead
have their moment of struggle, that brief moment of
shock which is worse than birth because the ties with this
world are stronger. But for the living, the pain does not
cease with death. It remains till memory is dulled and the
face that cased the loved one's personality has faded.

I was still thinking of Marjorie when Standing called me
demanding estimates of wind speed, force of down-
draughts, height of ceiling. I went to the door of the hut.

The wind's roar had momentarily died away. Nothing stronger now than forty knots, I thought. My eyes went involuntarily to the sloping back of Keava. If only Mike had waited. He would have had a chance now. But it was done. He'd jumped and he was gone. The sky to the south, by the bay entrance, was empty, the plane gone.

I went back and reported to Standing. He asked particularly about down-draughts and I told him they were intermittent, that at the moment they had lost much of their force. There was a long pause and then he said they'd try to make a helicopter landing. I didn't attempt to discourage him. Those men were still on Sgeir Mhor and I was tired. Anyway, it was quieter now. How long it would last I didn't know. I just wished to God they'd flown the helicopter instead of trying to parachute men in. I wondered whether it was really Adams who had refused to fly or whether Standing's cold mathematical mind had been influenced by the high cost of these machines. That was a thought that made me angry. When you consider how the Services waste the taxpayers' money, millions stupidly spent, and here perhaps a decent man had been sent to his death for fear of risking a few thousands. "About bloody time," I said angrily. "If you'd used the helicopter in the first place. . . ."

I let it go at that. The poor bastard! It wasn't his fault. Decisions have to be made by the men in command and sometimes, inevitably, they're the wrong decisions. It was something that he'd tried to get help to the survivors before nightfall. I wondered what my brother would have done. With all his faults, Iain was a man of action. His behaviour in an emergency was instinctive. "A pity you didn't leave it to Major Braddock." I'd said it before I could stop myself. I heard his quick intake of breath. And then, in a stiff, cold voice, he said: *"We'll be with you in under the hour."*

We! I remember thinking about that, sitting there, dazed

with fatigue. Was Standing coming himself? But it didn't seem to matter—not then. The life-saving gear was up there on the slopes of Keava and all we needed was the men to collect it and set it up. Men who were fresh and full of energy. I was tired. Too tired to move, my aching body barely reacting to the orders of my brain. Nerves, muscles, every part of my anatomy cried out for rest.

I woke Cooper, told him to keep radio watch and wake me in forty minutes' time. Then I fell on to Pinney's bed, not bothering to undress, and was instantly asleep.

"Mr. Ross. Wake up." The voice went on and on, a hand shaking my shoulder. I blinked my eyes and sat up. "Gawd Almighty! Yer didn't 'alf give me a turn. Thought you'd croaked. Honest I did." Cooper bending over me, staring at me anxiously. "You orl right, sir?" And then he said: "They're on the air now. Want ter know what conditions are like I told 'em: still blowing like 'ell, but it's clearer—only the top of Tarsaval's got cla'd on it now."

I got up and went to the radio. The time was twelve minutes to four. Adams's voice came faint and crackling. He wanted an estimate of the wind speed, its direction, the strength of the down-draughts. I went to the door of the hut. It was certainly much clearer now; quite bright, in fact. The overcast was breaking up, torn rags of clouds hurrying across a cold blue sky and the broken water seaward shining white in patches of slanting sunlight. Keava and Malesgair, the two arms that enclosed Shelter Bay, were clear of cloud. So was Creag Dubh. For the first time I could see the lookout where the tracking-station radar had been housed. Only the summit of Tarsaval was still obscured, a giant wearing a cloth cap made shapeless by the wind. It was blowing harder, I thought, and the down-draughts were irregular. Sometimes there was a long interval in which the wind just blew. Then suddenly it would wham down off the heights, two or three gusts in quick succession.

I went back to the radio and reported to Adams. He said he could see Laerg quite plainly and estimated that he had about seven miles to go. *I'll come in from the south at about four hundred,* he said. *You know where the landing ground is—down by the Factor's House. I'll watch for you there. I'm relying on you to signal me in. I'll need about sixty seconds clear of down-draughts. Okay?* I don't think he heard my protest. At any rate, he didn't answer, and I went out, cursing him for trying to put the onus on me. Did he think I could control the down-draughts? There was no pattern about them. They came and went; one minute I was walking quite easily, the next I was knocked flat and all the breath pushed back into my throat. Damn the man! If I signalled him in, it would be my responsibility if anything went wrong.

But there wasn't time to consider that. I'd barely reached the beach when I saw the helicopter, a speck low down over the water beyond the entrance to the bay. It came in fast and by the time I'd reached the Factor's House I could hear its engine, a buzz-saw drone above the suck and seeth of the surf. A down-draught hit, beating the grasses flat and whistling out over the bay, the surface boiling as though a million small fry were skittering there. It was gone almost as soon as it had come. Another and another hit the ground, flattening the long brown wisps of grass, whirling the dried seaweed into the air. They came like sand devils, spiralling down. The helicopter, caught in one, slammed down almost to sea level and then rocketed up. It was very close now and growing bigger every minute, the sound of its engine filling the air. In the sudden stillness that followed that last gust I thought I could hear the swish of its rotor blades.

No point in waiting, for every second he hovered there he was in mortal danger. I waved him in, praying to God that he'd plonk himself down in one quick rush before the next blast struck. But he didn't. He was a cautious man, which is a fine thing in a pilot; except that this was no moment for caution. He came in slowly, feeling his way, and the next gust caught him when he was still a hundred feet up. It came slam like the punch of a fist. The helicopter, flung sideways and downwards, hit the beach; the floats crumpled and at the same instant, with the rotor blades still turning, the whole machine was heaved up and flung seaward. It touched the water, tipped, foam flying from the dripping blades, and then it sank till it lay on its side, half-submerged, a broken float support sticking stiffly into the air like the leg of some bloated carcass.

Stillness then, the wind gone and everything momentarily quiet. A head bobbed up beside the floating wreck. Another and another. Three men swimming awkwardly, and then the tin carcass rolled its other splintered leg into the air and sank. Air came out of it, a single belch that lifted the surface of the water, and after that nothing; just the flat sea rippled by the wind and three dark heads floundering in to the beach.

Fortunately there was little surf. One by one they found their feet and waded ashore, drowned men gasping for air, flinging themselves down on the wet stones, suddenly exhausted as fear gripped them. I ran down to them, looking at each face. But they were men I didn't know. They were alive because they'd been in the fuselage within reach of the door. Standing had been sitting with Adams up by the controls. They'd both been trapped.

It was only minutes before, a few short minutes, that I'd been talking to Adams. It didn't seem possible. One moment the helicopter had been there, so close above my head that I'd ducked involuntarily—and now it was gone. I stood there with those three men moaning at my feet, staring unbelievingly at the waters of the bay. Nothing. Nothing but the steel-bright surface exploding into spray and beneath it Standing and Adams still strapped in their seats, eyes already sightless. . . . Was it my fault? I felt sick right through to my guts, utterly drained.

"Christ, man. What are you staring at?"

One of the figures, a sergeant, had staggered to his feet and was staring at me, wild-eyed, his hair plastered limp across his head.

"Nothing," I said. It was nothing that he could see. The two dead men were in my mind and he wasn't thinking of them, only of the fact that he was alive.

"Jesus! It was cold." He was shivering, moaning to himself. But then habit and training reasserted itself. He got his men to their feet and I took them up to the camp.

It was, I thought, the end of all hope for the survivors on Sgeir Mhor; three men killed and nothing achieved.

Standing's death had a numbing effect on the rescue operation. It was not so much the man himself as the command he represented. It left a vacuum and there was only one man in Northton with the experience to fill it; that man was lying on his bed, nursing a hatred that no longer had any point. In the midst of the flood of teleprints back and forth nobody thought of informing him that Standing was dead. He heard about it from his escorting officer, who had got it from the orderly who brought them their tea. It took time for the implications to sink in and it wasn't until almost five-fifteen that he finally stirred himself, got to his feet, and ordered Lieutenant Phipps to accompany him to the Movements Office. There he sent off a teleprint to Brigadier Matthieson: *In view of Colonel Standing's death presume I have your authority to take over command. Please confirm so that I can organize attempt to rescue survivors dawn tomorrow.* This was despatched at 17.23 hours.

Brigadier Matthieson, who admitted later that he considered Standing's action in placing his second-in-command under close arrest ill-advised, immediately signalled back: *Your temporary command Northton confirmed. Advise action planned for getting survivors off.*

Queen's Regulations are not very specific on the subject of an arrested officer assuming command and Matthieson's signal carefully avoided any reference to the matter. He had, in fact, very little alternative. There was no other officer at Northton competent to take control in a situation like this, and to fly a replacement C.O. in would take time. Moreover, Braddock had the confidence of his superiors at the War Office. There was another factor, too. The press were now alerted to what was happening up in the Outer Hebrides. The press officer at Scottish Command had, during the past hour or so, faced a barrage of demands for information from London as well as Scottish newspaper offices. They knew about the trawler that had disappeared. They knew that a landing craft was in difficulties to the west of Laerg. They also knew that another LCT had been shipwrecked on the island and that there were survivors. No doubt they had been briefed by amateur radio operators—either Scottish ham operators monitoring my radio contacts with Base or Irish radio enthusiasts picking up the signals passing between Coastal Command and their two Shackletons.

Whatever the source of their information, the effect was the same; it convinced Matthieson that this was no longer a strictly Army affair but had become something much bigger. Like a submarine disaster it had all the dramatic qualities to capture the imagination of the British public. From tomorrow morning onwards the whole country would be waiting for news of the survivors, and if the news were bad. . . . Well, he certainly didn't intend to be blamed for it, not with only a few months of his time to go. In confirming my brother as temporary Base Commander, he was clutching at a straw. If things went right then he could take some credit. And if things went wrong then he had his scapegoat. I'm convinced that that was the way his mind was working when he made the decision.

At approximately five-thirty when my brother officially took command the position was this: Two relief Shackletons had been flown off, one to continue the search for the missing trawler, the other to watch over L4400 until the destroyer, now little more than a hundred miles away, reached her. W/S *India* had been ordered back on to station. The Naval tug was still snug against the quay at Leverburgh.

Apart from shore-based aircraft, there was nothing else available in the area to assist in the rescue operation. True, the destroyer would pass quite close to Laerg, but L4400 urgently needed her. The landing craft was barely afloat. Almost half her crew were casualties, the bridge deck ripped to pieces, mast and funnel gone, the tank hold full of water and the pumps barely capable of holding in check the sea pouring in through her strained and buckled plates.

And since conditions made the use of aircraft impracticable, the tug remained the only hope.

In the uncertainty that followed immediately on Standing's death, nobody had apparently thought of informing the skipper of the changed situation. That his vessel was still tied up in Leverburgh was not due to any lack of initiative on his part. He was waiting for conditions to improve, knowing that he needn't sail until six at the earliest to reach Laerg by first light.

Braddock's immediate reaction to the situation was to send out three signals in quick succession—to Command, demanding the instant despatch of two helicopters; to Coastal Command requesting that a further Shackleton be held fuelled and ready for immediate take-off should he require it; to the destroyer urging her captain to close Sgeir Mhor on his way out to L4400 and endeavour to float off supplies to the survivors, or if that were not possible to signal them by lamp that help was on its way. Then he went to see Cliff Morgan.

Captain Flint, who was in Movements at the time, said he personally felt a great lift when Braddock took command. If any man could get the survivors off, he thought Braddock would.

Cliff Morgan's reaction, on the other hand, was very different. Like Standing, he regarded Braddock as responsible for what had happened. He was appalled when Braddock came into his quarters—"Bold as brass, man," was the way he put it. " 'Colonel Standing's dead and I've taken over command. Now, Morgan, let's have your ideas of the weather for the next twelve hours.' Just like that. And when I told him it was a pity it was Standing who'd gone and not him he laughed in my face; told me to mind my own bloody business and stick to the weather, which he thought perhaps I understood. I was in radio contact with a ham over in Tobermory at the time and when I started to finish the conversation he put his big hand over the key. 'You take your fat arse off that chair,' he told me, 'and come over to the Met. Office or I'll take you there by the scruff of your neck.' "

Over in the Met. Office Cliff had given him a forecast that he admitted was enough to daunt any man planning a rescue operation on an island a hundred miles out in the Atlantic. The effect of the local depression that had caused all the havoc would die out entirely within the next hour or so—probably it had died out already. For a time then the island would come again under the influence of the polar air stream with winds northerly between thirty and forty knots. Later those winds would decrease and perhaps die out for a while as the polar air stream was gradually dominated by the new depression moving in from the Atlantic. The period of relative calm would be followed by winds of rapidly increasing strength as the depression built up and spread over the area. Southerly at first, the winds would veer south-westerly, increasing to gale force.

"When?" Braddock had asked. "When will that happen?" And Cliff had shrugged.

"You're asking me how fast that depression is moving. I don't know."

"Then contact somebody who does. There are more than a dozen men on that bloody rock and when this depression hits . . ." Braddock checked himself. He even patted Cliff on the shoulder. "Just tell me when. Better still, tell me when that period of calm will be."

Cliff says he hesitated, unwilling to commit himself. He was staring at the map he'd drawn. Sykes came in with another sheet from the teleprinter, more barometric-pressure figures. He entered them, connected them up, scoring the isobars with a red pencil. One of those figures represented a report from the Shackleton circling L4400. It showed a drop of two millibars in the past hour. "The calm will be just about there; within the hour, at any rate."

"Goddammit!" Braddock said. "An hour. Are you certain?" And when Cliff nodded, he said: "How long will it last? Listen. In an hour and a half perhaps I could have helicopters here. Say three hours by the time they're refuelled and have reached Laerg. I need four hours. Can you give me four hours?"

"No." Cliff shook his head, quite definite now. "You can see for yourself." He was pointing to the red lines he'd drawn. The nearest was almost touching Laerg, coming down in a broad sweep from Iceland and running away westward just north of Ireland. "Two hours I'd give it; no more. Two hours from now and the wind will begin blowing from the south. It must do."

"Then God help them," was all Braddock said and he turned and went out, walking swiftly through the fading light. Cliff called after him that there was a warm front associated with the depression. There would probably be heavy rain accompanied by low ceiling and poor visibility. Braddock didn't answer. He made no acknowledgment that he'd heard, but walked straight on, shoulders very square, head held well back on the short, thick neck —a man bracing himself for a fight, Cliff thought. And overhead the clouds gathering again, aerial cavalry of a new enemy onslaught forming themselves into dark ranks, galloping eastward and rolling up the blue-green late-afternoon canopy that, though cold, had the bright promise of hope. Now hope was fallen victim to the gathering clouds and my brother, alone in the loneliness of command, had to decide what further lives, if any, should be risked to attempt to save men doomed to face a night of terror, exposed again to the fury of the elements.

Field was back when he reached the Movements Office —Charles Field, looking old and grey and stooped, the lines of his face etched deeper than ever and an uneasy, shifting light in his steel-blue eyes. He said what he had to say, adding: "It was nobody's fault. Nobody's fault at all. I'll write a full report, of course." He was edging towards the door. "Think I'll go over to the Mess now."

"The Mess?" Braddock stared at him, saw the lips twitching, the slight blink of the eyes, that shifting look. "For a drink?"

Field nodded unhappily. "I thought just one. Just a quick one, to steady me. A shock, you know. A most frightful shock." And he added, justifying himself: "I hope you realize, I don't normally drink. But on this occasion. You understand. . . ."

Braddock reached him in two quick strides, seized hold of him by the arm. "Sure. I understand. Just one, and that'll lead to another. You're the one man I want sober. So you stay here. Okay?" And he pushed him into a chair. "You're going back to Laerg—tonight."

"No." Field was up from the chair, his eyes overbright. "No. I absolutely refuse."

"Then I'll place you under arrest and have you escorted on board." He patted his arm as though comforting a child. "Don't worry. I'll be with you. We're going out there together." And he sent Phipps for the long wheel-base Land Rover and dictated a signal to Brigadier Matthieson: *Weather forecast suggests quite impracticable attempt lift survivors out by helicopter. Am proceeding to Laerg by Naval tug. Will personally direct rescue operations on arrival dawn tomorrow.* It was sent out signed: *Braddock, Commanding Officer Guided Weapons, Northton.*

In taking Field with him my brother was instinctively seeking the support of the one man whose experience and background could help. He also took the M.O., Lieutenant Phipps, a Sergeant Wetherby, and four men, all hand-picked for their toughness and their known ability in the water and on the Laerg crags. Flint went with them. It took almost half an hour to gather them and their kit and the necessary equipment—climbing ropes, inflatable dinghy, aqua-lung cylinders and frogmen's suits, everything that might possibly be of use. Meantime, radio contact had been established with the tug and the skipper requested to stand by to sail immediately they arrived on board.

They left the Base at ten to six. Unfortunately, the clothes Field needed were at his croft. It was only a few minutes' drive from Leverburgh, but Marjorie was there. For the past two hours she had been with Laura Standing. She knew what had happened. She was white-faced, on the verge of hysteria. "Why did you let him jump?" she demanded of her father. "Why in God's name did you let him?" And he stood there, not saying a word, because there was nothing to say, while his own daughter accused him of being responsible for Mike's death.

Braddock got out of the Land Rover. "Hurry up, Field. We've no time to waste."

Marjorie was still pouring out a flood of words, but she stopped then, staring at the Land Rover, the significance of it standing there full of men slowly dawning on her. She doesn't remember what she said or what she did, but Flint described it to me: "Moments like that, when you're headed for trouble an' you don't know how bad it's going to be, you don't want a girl around then, particularly a girl who's just lost somebody she cared about. One moment she was giving her father hell, saying it was all his fault, and then all of a sudden she switched her attention to Major B. That was when she realized he was taking her father out to Laerg. 'You can't do it,' she said. 'He's not a young man. He hasn't climbed in years.' She knew what it was all about. She'd broken the news of Standing's death to his wife. She knew what had happened. She knew the sort of man Braddock was—guessed he'd stop at nothing, risk anything to get those men off. She went for him like a bitch defending her last remaining puppy, screaming at him that it was all his fault, that he'd killed Mike, killed Simon Standing; it was plain bloody murder, she said, and she wasn't going to let him kill her father. Braddock tried soothing her with logic—her father was in the Army, there was a job to do, and that was that. But reasoning with a girl who's scared out of her wits, whose emotions are tearing her nerves to shreds is like pouring water on a high-voltage short—it just doesn't make a damn bit of difference. In the end he slapped her. Not hard. Just twice across the face and told her to pull herself together and not disgrace her father. It shut her up, and after that she just stood there, white an' trembling all over."

It was just after six-fifteen when they boarded the tug. The warps were let go immediately and she steamed out into the Sound of Harris, heading west. We were then experiencing the lull Cliff had forecast. It was so still in the

hut that I went out to see what was wrong. After hours of
battering, the sudden quiet seemed unnatural. Darkness
was closing down on Laerg, the clouds low overhead and
hanging motionless. I could see the outline of Sgeir
Mhor, the sloping spine of Keava disappearing into the
blanket of the overcast, but they were dim, blurred shapes.
The air was heavy with humidity, and not a breath of
wind.

I got a torch and signalled towards Sgeir Mhor. But there
was no answering flash. It meant nothing, for it was unlikely that any of the survivors had got ashore with a torch.
I tried to contact Base, but there was other traffic—Rafferty
talking to the destroyer, to the tug, finally to Coastal Command. And then the destroyer to me: ETA Laerg 01.25
hours. Would I please stand by the radio as from 01.00.
Base came through immediately afterwards: The tug's
ETA would be about 04.30 dependent on conditions. I was
requested to keep radio watch from four-thirty onwards.
Roger. I had six hours in which to get some rest. I arranged with Cooper for a hot meal at one o'clock, set the
alarm, undressed, and tumbled into bed.

I must have recovered some of my energy, for it wasn't
the alarm that woke me. I reached out and switched on
the light. There was a mouse by the edge of my empty
plate, sitting on its haunches on the bedside table cleaning
its whiskers with its forepaws. It was one of the breed
peculiar to Laerg, a throw-back to pre-glacial life, to before the last Ice Age that covered the British Isles anything up to ten thousand years ago. It was larger than the
ordinary British field-mouse, its ears were bigger, its
hind-legs longer, and the tail was as long as its body; the
brown of its coat had a distinctly reddish tinge brighten-
ing to dull orange on the underbelly. It sat quite still, two
shiny black pin-head eyes staring at me. It seemed possessed of curiosity rather than fear, and after a moment it
resumed its toilet, cleaning its whiskers with little stroking

movements of its paws. The time was eleven minutes past midnight. The wind was back, beating round the corners of the hut in a steady roar that drowned the sound of the generator. And behind the wind was another, more sinister sound—one that I hadn't heard for some time; the crash and suck of waves breaking on the beach. I thought it was this sound rather than the mouse that had woken me.

There was something about that little morsel of animal life that was infinitely comforting; a sign perhaps of the indestructibility of life. The mouse in that moment meant a lot to me and I lay there watching it until it had finished its toilet and quietly disappeared. Then I got up and dressed and went to the door of the hut. It was a black night, the two lights Cooper had left on in the camp shining in isolation. The wind was from the south, about force seven. The waves, coming straight into the bay, broke with an earth-shaking thud. The sound of the surf was louder than the wind, and as my eyes became accustomed to the darkness, I could see the ghostly glimmer of white water ringing the beach; just the glimmer of it, nothing else. It was a wild, ugly night, the air much warmer so that I thought I could smell rain again, the warm front moving in.

At one o'clock I contacted the destroyer. She had Laerg clear on the radar at thirteen miles' range. ETA approximately one-thirty. Alf Cooper appeared at my side, a khaki gnome, his head encased in a woollen balaclava. "Grub up." He put the tray down on the table beside the radio—a thermos flask of oxtail soup and two mess tins full of corned beef and potato hash all steaming hot. "A night for the flippin' bears, ain't it. 'Ibernation, that's my idea o' paradise this time of the year. You reck'n that destroyer'll be able to do any good?"

"No," I said.

He nodded, sucking at his soup. "That's wot I fort. Ruddy waves must be breaking right over the poor bastards." I asked him about the men from the helicopter. "Sleepin' their ruddy 'eads orf," he said. "Orl right for them. They got full bellies. Me, I'm fair famished." He reached for one of the mess tins. " 'Ope yer don't mind bully. Easy ter make, yer see. Fillin' too."

At one-thirty we went out of the hut and stood in the teeth of the wind staring into the black darkness that hid Sgeir Mhor. It was drizzling, a wet, driving mist. Suddenly light blazed, the pencil stab of a searchlight that threw the blurred shape of Sgeir Mhor into black relief. It probed the mist, producing strange halos of light in the damp air. A gun flashed, a small sound against the thunder of breaking waves. The overcast glimmered with light as the star shell burst. It was a minute or two before it floated clear of the clouds over Keava; for a moment the bay and the surrounding rocks were bathed in its incandescent glare. It was an unearthly sight; the waves marching into the bay, building up till their tops curled and broke, roaring up the beach in a welter of foam, and all around the horseshoe curve of breaking water, the rocks standing piled in ghostly brilliance. Rock and cliff and sodden grass slope all looked more hellish in that macabre light. I saw the spume of waves breaking over the lower bastions of Sgeir Mhor. Then the flare touched the sea and was instantly extinguished, and after that the night was blacker, more frightening than before.

A signal lamp stabbed its pinpoint of light just beyond the tip of Sgeir Mhor: *Help arriving first light. Stick it out four more hours and . . .* That was all I read, for the destroyer was steaming slowly westward and the stab of her signal lamp was obscured by the rocks. The searchlight probed again, searching the far side of the rock promontory as though trying to count the survivors. And then that too went out and after that there was nothing but the pitch-black night.

I reset the alarm and lay down again on Pinney's bed,

not bothering this time to undress. Time passed slowly
and I couldn't sleep. The mouse came back. I could hear
its claws scratching at the aluminium of the mess tins, but
I didn't switch the light on. I lay there with my eyes
closed waiting for the alarm, thinking of those men out
on the rocks drenched by the mist and the spray, wondering whether it would be possible to get them off.

At four-thirty I was at the radio and the tug came
through prompt on schedule, my brother's voice requesting information about sea and landing conditions. I was
able to tell him that the wind was now west of south. But
it had also increased in strength. It was definitely blowing
a gale now and it was raining heavily. However, if the
wind veered further, as seemed likely, there was a chance
that a landing could be made in the western curve of the
bay, close under Keava where there would be some shelter.
"Okay," he said. *"We'll recce the lee side of Sgeir Mhor
first, and if that's no good, we'll anchor and attempt to
make the beach on inflatable rafts."*

It was still dark when they came into the bay and all I
saw of the tug was the two steaming lights, one above
the other, swinging and dipping. She came right into the
bay, almost to the break of the waves, and then the lights
moved apart and the distance between them increased as
she turned westward. The green of her starboard navigation light showed for a while, still half-obscured by rain.
And then that vanished, together with the steaming
lights, and I caught glimpses of her stern light as she
browsed along the western arm of the bay, a will-o'-the-
wisp bounced from wave-top to wave-top. A searchlight
stabbed a brilliant beam, iridescent with moisture, and
the rocks of Sgeir Mhor showed ghostly grey across
tumbled acres of sea; columns of spray like ostrich-feather
plumes waved behind it, sinking and rising with the surge
of the Atlantic.

Dawn came slowly and with reluctance, a sheathed pallor

stealing into the curve below the encircling hills. The tug lay close under Keava, just clear of the narrow, surf-filled gut that separated it from Sgeir Mhor. She didn't anchor, but stayed head-to-wind under power, and they came ashore in rubber dinghies where the surf was least.

I was coming along the foreshore when my brother staggered dripping out of the suck of the waves, dragging a rubber dinghy after him. He was dressed like the others in a frogman's suit and I can see him still, standing there in that twilit world that was the dawn, finned feet straddled at the surf's edge, not looking at that moment at his companions, but staring up at the cloud-hidden heights. There was a stillness about him, an immobility—he seemed for an instant petrified, a part of the landscape, his body turned to stone, statuesque like a rock.

Then the others piled in through the surf and he was a man again, moving to help them, going back into the waves to pull two more rubber dinghies ashore.

I met them on the beach. "Thank God you made it," I yelled to him above the wind.

He stared at me. His face looked haggard, his eyes wild. I swear he didn't recognize me.

"Iain. Are you all right, Iain?"

For a moment his face stayed blank. Then his eyes snapped. "Ross." He glanced quickly at Field standing at the surf's edge. Then he came towards me, gripped my shoulder. "The name's Braddock, damn you," he hissed, his fingers digging a warning into my flesh. His mouth had hardened and his eyes blazed black. He'd have seen me dead and drowned before he'd have admitted to his real name.

Field wiped a smear of phlegm from below his nose. "We saw several men clinging to the rocks." His eyes looked dead and tired, bloodshot with the salt. "Where are the parachutes—the life-saving gear you dropped?" Braddock asked.

"Up there." Field nodded to the heights of Keava, the long slope leading to the spine.

"Yes, up there." I agreed. But the rain-dimmed dawn showed nothing on the slopes—only the clouds writhing in white pillars.

Their clothes, tied in plastic bundles in the dinghies, were safe and dry. They changed in the bird-oil stench of an old cleit, and then we climbed, strung out across the slopes, climbed until we met the clouds, gasping wet air. The daylight had strengthened by then and ragged gaps in the overcast showed the slopes of Keava bare to its spine and to the cliffs beyond. The parachutes had gone. Some time during the night, I suppose, a gust had filled the nylon canopies and carried them over the top and far out into the sea beyond.

Braddock shook Field's arm. "Are you sure that's where you dropped them?"

Field nodded.

"Then they're gone."

Field's face was set in a wooden look as he agreed they'd gone. Up there in the wind and the driving clouds, with the thunder of the waves breaking at the foot of the cliffs, we could both recall the solitary parachute lifting and sailing out into the Atlantic. "Wasted. All wasted." There were tears in his eyes, but it may have been the wind.

"Okay. Well, there's only one way to get a line across."

Field nodded absently.

"We'll have to take it ourselves. Swim it across the gut, and then climb with it."

Easy to say; not so easy to do. The drop from the Butt of Keava was possible, the 350-foot cliff went down in a series of ledges. It was the gut between and the sheer cliff beyond. The gut was fifty yards at its narrowest and the seas were breaking there in a welter of foam; the cliffs of Sgeir Mhor were black volcanic gabbro, hard as granite, smooth and unbroken for long stretches.

"Well?" Braddock stared at Field. "I swim it, you climb it, eh?" And his face cracked in a grin. It was a dare. This was the sort of thing he loved—physical action spiced with danger. And if the other man cracked. . . . Poor Field's face was ashen, his eyes staring at the smooth black panels of wet rock beyond the maelstrom of the chasm.

I think my brother had watched quite a few men crack. I don't say it gave him pleasure, but it may well have been something he needed, a bolster to his own morale. His world had always been a physical one. Mentally and emotionally he was something of a child; or that was how he had often seemed to me; which was why, I suppose, our relationship, so inimical at times, had been at others so strangely close; we had each supplied what the other lacked.

Now, he didn't hesitate. He didn't even watch for Field's reaction. He caught the man's fear at a glance and overlaid it with his own determination, the quick, positiveness of his orders. He led us pell-mell back down the slope, back to the beach and the dinghies laden with rope and all the things he'd feared they might need. And then, in his frogman's kit again, up the sloping shoulders of the rocks to the wet thunder of the surf breaking through the gut.

The sergeant and I, with two men, were ordered to the top of the cliff with one end of the nylon climbing rope. Down at the bottom he and Field, together with Lieutenant Phipps and the two other men, manoeuvred one of the rubber dinghies.

Flat on my stomach at the cliff's edge I watched Iain working his way along the ledges westward through the gut. He was alone and his thick, powerful body in its black rubber suit looked like a seal's as it flattened itself against the rocks to meet each wave as it broke foaming across the ledges—a baby seal from that height, the rope around his waist and trailing white behind him like an umbilical cord. And then from the farthest point west that he could fight his way, he suddenly stood on a sheer-edged shelf of rock and dived.

He dived into the back-surge of a big wave and went deep, his fins beating furiously, drumming at the surf. It looked so easy. One moment he was diving and the next he had bobbed up on the back of a breaker on the far side, a black head with black arms paddling. A quick look round, then down again as the next comber broke, and as it spent its energy, he rode its back on to a long, sloped ledge, and pulled himself up.

Now, with the dawn light stronger, I could see two figures prone among the rocks on the far side, peering down. I thought I recognized Wentworth, but I couldn't be sure. The face was a dim blur in the rain and the flying spray.

Iain was clear of the water now, clear of the surge of even the biggest waves, curled up at the farthest end of that sloped ledge and pulling on the rope. Below me I saw Field hesitate. The rope came taut on the rush of a wave. The rubber dinghy shifted on the rocks. And then it was in the water, and he was in it, head down, hands gripping the gunnels as it was pulled across. Once I thought he was lost. The dinghy reared on a curling crest, turned half over as it broke. But then it righted itself, lifted on the backwash from the far side, and in one buoyant rush came to rest on the ledge where Iain crouched.

I saw arms wave on the cliff opposite. There were three bodies there now, all waving in the excitement of imminent rescue. But there was still that sheer cliff, and the men on the top could do nothing to help. It was up to Field now. Field alone could lift the end of that rope the three hundred feet that would transform it from just the tail-end of a line into a connecting link, a bridge between the two masses of rock—a bridge that could act as a means of escape.

Field had crossed the gut barefooted, but in his battle-dress. Now, soaked to the skin, he leaned against the vertical rock and put on his climbing boots. That done, he fastened a belt round his waist that was stuffed with rock pitons like steel dogs' teeth. An ice hammer looped by its thong to his wrist, the rope fastened around his waist, and he was ready. But then he stood for a long time with his head thrown back, gazing up at the cliff above him.

He stood like that for so long that I thought he was held fast by the sheer impossibility of it. Perhaps by fear, too. And I for one wouldn't have blamed him. Those shining panels of rock, trickling water—a spider would have its work cut out to find a footing. There were ledges and crevices, it was true. There are in almost any rock. But they were so minute and spaced so far apart. And all the time the sea swirled about his legs. The din of it was incessant, the gut streaming with wind-blown spray, gusts of spume, spongy masses of it flying through the air.

At last he moved; a flick of the hand holding the rope. Iain squatted tighter into his niche, waiting, both hands on the rope. The three men on the cliff-top opposite me leaned out and waved. Field saw them, for he lifted his hand. And then at last he began to climb, traversing out along a toe-hold crack that was a fractured continuation of the ledge on which he had stood.

It was fascinating to watch him. He must have been over fifty and out of practice, yet he balanced himself like an acrobat, hanging in space and moving steadily upwards, his feet doing the work, the rest of his body still and quiet. To the left at first, a long traverse, and then a quick gain of perhaps fifty or sixty feet up toe and finger holds I couldn't see; a short traverse right and then a pause. The pause lengthened out, his hands reaching occasionally and drawing back. Then for a long time he hung there quite motionless.

Had his nerve gone? I don't know. I asked him once,

but he only smiled and said: "It was an ugly place. I thought it better to start again."

I didn't see him jump. One moment he was there, and the next he was in the sea, and Iain was hauling him back to the ledge where he lay for a while getting his breath. Then he started up again.

The same route, but a left traverse at the top and then he was hammering a piton into a crevice, snapping on a hook for the rope, and up again using pitons from the clanking string of them around his waist, one after another. He must have hammered in about two dozen of them before he reached the overhang, and there he stuck with less than fifty feet to go—a fly on wet slate with the spume curling up like smoke from the cauldron below him.

He got round it eventually by going down about half the distance he'd climbed and working another crevice line to the right. This brought him almost opposite me, and right below him then was a deadly mass of rocks awash. He looked down once and I could imagine how he felt with only the rope running now through three pitons to hold him. The last fifty feet seemed to take him almost as many minutes. The crevices were too shallow for the pitons and he was white with cold, his clothes heavy with water. But he did it.

His head came level with the cliff-top. Hands reached down and he went over the top on his belly. Then he suddenly passed out, lying there, limp. But the rope was there and that was life to those who'd survived. The tail-end, passed back down the cliff to Iain, was made fast to a heavier line, and so, with many goings back and forth to the camp, we rigged up a makeshift breeches-buoy.

It took us all morning in the teeth of the gale with five of the tug's crew and the Doc and the men who had survived the helicopter crash. Baulks of timber had to be brought up, heavy hawsers, block and tackle, and everything rigged by trial and error. Just after midday we managed to get food and clothing across to them. But it wasn't until almost 2 p.m. that we got the first man over the gut and safe on to Keava. And after that it was slow, back-breaking work, for many of them were stretcher cases who, when they reached Keava, had to be carried down the slopes and along the beach to the camp. There was no vehicle, no means of transporting them other than by hand.

We took altogether twenty-three men off Sgeir Mhor, five of them unconscious and several badly injured. All were suffering from exposure, their skin a leprous white from constant immersion in salt water. Wentworth was the last to come across, a different man now, burned up by the twenty-four hours he'd been in command. Stratton was dead—with the Cox'n he'd been getting the men out of the Mess deck when the whole bridge structure had been crushed like a biscuit tin; and Pinney, who'd thought Laerg the best posting he'd had. Four men had died during the night, including the young steward, Perkins, whose rib-cage had been stove-in by the slam of the water-tight doors. Field said there was no sign of the landing craft, only bits and pieces of metal scattered among the rocks.

The wind went round that night into the north-west and the tug came close inshore. By midnight everybody had been embarked. Everybody except my brother. It was the Doc who discovered he wasn't on board. He'd had a list made and a roll called, for the confusion on the tug was indescribable—thirty-five extra men, many of them casualties.

"Where's Major Braddock?" I heard the question passed along the deck. "Anybody seen Major Braddock?" Voices calling in the darkness of the decks. And then the Skipper giving orders, Sergeant Wetherby piling into the boat again, the outboard motor bursting into life. I jumped in beside him and we shot away from the tug's side, slapping through the shallows over the low-tide sand-bar.

The outboard died as the bows grated and the boat came to a sudden halt. We scrambled out into a foot or more of water and ploughed over the sands to the beach. Wetherby thought he might have gone to check the remains of the transport that lay, battered and derelict, among the rocks behind the loading beach. He was an MT sergeant. While he went towards the dim shape of the bulldozer, now standing high and dry on the sands, I hurried to the camp. Every now and then the wind brought me the sound of his voice calling: "Major Braddock! Major Braddock!"

The lights were out in the camp now, the generator still. I stumbled about in the darkness, calling. At first I called his Army name, but then, because it didn't seem to matter here alone, I called: "Iain! Iain—where are you?" I reached the hut and fumbling in the dark found the torch I'd used. The place was empty; the radio still there and all the mess and litter of its temporary use as a casualty-clearing station. I went outside then, probing and calling.

I'd never have found him without the torch. He was standing in the lee of the cookhouse, quite still, his back turned towards me as though afraid his face might catch the light. "What the hell are you playing at?" I demanded. "Why didn't you answer?"

He stared at me, but didn't say anything for a moment. There was a twitch at the corner of his mouth and his face was deathly pale. "Are you ill?" I asked.

He moved then, came closer to me and reached for my arm. "Donald." His voice was hoarse, little more than a whisper against the blatter of the wind. "Go back. Go back to the ship. You haven't seen me. Understand?" The urgency of his request was almost as startling as the request itself. He jerked at my arm. "Go—back." Behind the hoarseness of his voice, I caught the tremor of his mood, something deep that he couldn't control. "As you love me, Donald, go back."

"But why? What's wrong? Is it Lane?" I asked. "Has he been worrying you?"

"He's been on to me—twice from the mainland. But it isn't that." His grip tightened on my arm. "Leave me now, will you."

"But why?"

"Damn you, Donald! Can't you do what I ask?" And then, his voice more controlled: "Something I have to do. We left in a hurry—the tide and a change of wind. No time . . . and Leroux half dead, too weak to do anything. It was either that or be trapped." His voice had died to a whisper.

"You mean you were here?" I asked. "After the *Duart Castle* . . ."

"Try to understand, can't you? Just leave me here and no questions."

I hesitated. The torch on his face showed his mouth tight-set, his eyes urgent. "All right," I said. "If that's what you want. . . ."

But I was too late. As I switched off the torch and turned to go, a voice spoke out of the darkness behind me: "You've found him then?" It was Sergeant Wetherby. His jacketed figure loomed bulky from the direction of the generator. And to Iain, he said: "Major Braddock, sir. The tug's all ready to go—everybody on board. Only yourself, sir. They're waiting for you."

I heard Iain's muttered curse. And then in a flat voice: "Very good, Sergeant. Sorry if I held things up—just a last check round." He came with us then. There was nothing else he could do, for he couldn't hope to persuade the sergeant to let him stay. And so we embarked, and at 01.15 hours on the morning of October 24, the tug steamed out of Shelter Bay with the last remnant of the Army detachment.

The evacuation was complete at a cost of fifty-three lives, the loss of one landing craft, a helicopter, and a great deal of equipment.

Part Three

Aftermath of Disaster

I

Witch-hunt

(OCTOBER 24–FEBRUARY 28)

Press reaction to the news of the disaster was immediate. The first scattered fragments had begun coming through within hours of our landing craft being wrecked. Radio and TV put it out in their newscasts as it filtered through and during the day the story moved from the Stop Press of the evening papers to the front page. The main body of the press, however, had almost twelve hours in which to build the story up; and because it involved the out-islands, ships, the sea, the weather, they knew the impact it would have on the public. All that day telephones rang continuously in the press offices of the three Services and in the Meteorological Office in Kingsway. The Admiralty and the Air Ministry were helpful; the Army less so for they were inhibited by the knowledge that a commanding officer had ordered the arrest of his second-in-command. In an attempt to avoid this becoming known to the press, they clamped down on all comment, closed the military line to Northton to all but official calls, and confined their press releases to the facts of the situation. The effect was to make the press suspicious.

An enterprising reporter on the local Stornoway paper got hold of Fellowes. His story of the flight to Laerg and Mike Ferguson's death was scooped by a popular daily. A Reuter's man, who had flown north from Glasgow that morning, reached Northton in time to get the news of Standing's death and watch the tug leave from Leverburgh quay. His despatches went out on the Reuter teleprint service to all newspaper offices.

By that night the full extent of the disaster was known, the presses of the national dailies were rolling out the story, and reporters and photographers were hurrying north. So many took the night train to Glasgow that BEA, who had cancelled the morning flight to Stornoway, had second thoughts. The newspaper men had a rough flight, but by midday they were piling into Northton and Leverburgh. Others, mainly photographers with specially chartered planes, stood by at Stornoway from dawn onwards waiting for the weather to lift and give them an opportunity to take pictures of Laerg. Fellowes found his plane in great demand.

The fact that there were survivors gave a dramatic quality to the news and most of Britain had the story on their breakfast tables, front-paged under flaring headlines—a story of storm and disaster, of a colonel and his adjutant killed in attempts to rescue men trapped on a gale-torn rock in the North Atlantic. And to add to the drama was the suggestion that the Army had something to hide. Editors' instructions were to get at the truth.

Two reporters in search of a drink landed at the hotel at Rodil. They got hold of Marjorie. She was in a highly emotional state and prepared to talk. If Standing had been alive, she might have blamed him on account of Mike Ferguson's death. But Standing was dead, and because she was frightened for her father, she put the blame for every-thing on Major Braddock, and in attacking him, she re-vealed that he had been placed under arrest for ordering the LCT in to the beach. For those two reporters she was worth her weight in gold.

Other reporters, casing the Northton HQ and getting no change out of the Army personnel, who had all been instructed to have no contact with the press, transferred their attention to the Met. Office. They, too, struck gold. Cliff was a story in himself and nothing would have stopped that little Welshman from talking. He gave it to them, blow by blow, as seen from the weather man's point of view. One correspondent, reporting him from a tape-recorded interview, gave his words verbatim: "I tell you, the man must have been off his bloody nut, ordering a landing craft into the beach on a night like that. Oh yes, the wind was north then and they were under the lee of the island in Shelter Bay. But aground like that, she was at the mercy of the elements, you see, and when the wind swung into the south . . ."

There was more in the same vein and it all went south by wire and phone to the waiting presses in London. And by the following morning the public was convinced that the man responsible for this appalling loss of life was Major Braddock. They weren't told that in so many words, but it was implied, and this before he had had a chance to defend himself, when he was, in fact, still out on Laerg organizing the rescue operations.

Once the survivors had been reported safe, the excite-ment of the story dwindled and news-hungry reporters, looking for a fresh angle, began delving into the relations between Braddock and his commanding officer. What had happened at that interview in Standing's office in the early hours of the morning of October 22? Why had he placed Braddock under arrest? Cliff was interviewed on TV and radio. So was Marjorie. Laura Standing, too, and Fellowes.

The evidence piled up and all this canned material was being rushed down to London while the tug was still battling its way through the aftermath of the gale.

We steamed into Leverburgh just after four-thirty in the afternoon. We had been hove-to twice for the M.O. to carry out minor operations. The rest of the time we had managed little more than seven knots. The tug's internal accommodation was sufficient only for the serious casualties. The rest—men suffering from exposure and extreme exhaustion—had to be left out on the open deck. Anything over seven knots and the tug would have been shipping water in the heavy seas. As a result the voyage took almost sixteen hours and during all that time the men were exposed to wind and spray. One man died during the night and several showed symptoms of pneumonia by the time we docked.

The quay was packed as we came alongside, packed solid with men whose dress proclaimed them foreigners to the Hebrides. Army personnel in charge of the vehicles to take the survivors to Northton tried to hold them back, but as the tug's sides touched the quay they swarmed on board. They were all after one man. "Where's Braddock? Which is Major Braddock?" A man in a bow tie and thick horn-rimmed glasses seized hold of my arm. "I want Major Braddock. Where is he—in the Captain's cabin?"

In fact, Iain had been sleeping in the scuppers on the port side. "I don't think he'll see anybody. He's very tired."

"I can't help that. He's news." He told me the paper he represented and thrust a note into my hand. "Here's a fiver. Just point him out to me, that's all." And when I told him to go to hell, he tried to make it a tenner.

They found him in the end, of course. They brought him to bay like a pack of hounds in a corner under the bridge housing and he stood there, facing them, his battered face grey with fatigue, his voice hoarse with shouting

above the wind. They were all round him, their notebooks out, firing questions. And all he said was: "No comment."

He didn't realize that this was his one opportunity to defend himself—that he'd never get another. He stuck to
the letter of QR's and refused to make a statement, relying on his superiors to back him up. Relying, too, on the
fact that without his efforts the survivors would never have
been got off Sgeir Mhor alive. He didn't know then that
his superiors were going to throw him to the wolves, that
he was to be the scapegoat. How could he? For the last
thirty-six hours he'd been involved in physical action,
body and mind devoted to one thing alone—getting those
men off. He didn't understand that these reporters
couldn't visualize the circumstances. He was dead tired
and his own mind was incapable at that moment of making
the leap from individual effort to the broader aspects of
the affair. No comment! A statement will be issued in
due course. His Army training overlaid whatever personal
inclination he had. He behaved, in fact, with perfect cor-
rectness and in doing so he damned himself before that
most violent and blind of all judges—the public.

I saw the faces of the reporters harden. Frustration developed into anger. One man, snapping his notebook shut,
seemed to speak for the rest: "Okay, Major, have it your
own way. But don't blame us if the public forms its own
opinion of your evacuation order."

Other notebooks snapped. The circle broke up and
Iain stood there, tight-lipped and with a baffled look on
his face, as they suddenly abandoned him to move among
the survivors in search of personal, human-interest stories.
There was no shortage of these. The struggle to get the
landing craft off the beach, the fight to get her out of
Shelter Bay and clear of the rocks of Sgeir Mhor in the
teeth of the hurricane, the failure of the engines, the
scene of utter confusion as she struck with the bridge deck

concertinaed against the fortress mass of Sgeir Mhor; how
for a short while the up-lifted stern section had acted as a
sort of ramp, enabling those that were still alive to scramble ashore, the desperate hours of waiting through that
ghastly night and the rising seas and the new storm breaking over them.

There was so much of human interest. In particular,
there was Field. They got the story of his climb from
Sergeant Wetherby and a bunch of them crowded round
him. "Tell me, Mr. Field—how did you feel? Were you
scared?" He tried to tell them about Braddock's crossing
of the gut between Butt of Keava and Sgeir Mhor, but
they weren't interested in that now. Reporters in London,
working on the background of the officers involved, had
interviewed Field's wife. As a result they knew who he
was. "Could you give us your reactions please? . . . How
did it feel climbing that sheer cliff face? . . . Was it as
stiff as the climbs you faced in the Himalayas?" Cameras
clicked, the TV men closed in.

And all the time Captain Flint with a squad of men were
trying to get the injured off the ship and into the waiting
vehicles. "Get the hell out of it, you bloody blood-sucking
bastards." His Cockney humour had deserted him. The
essential warmth of his nature was revolted by this spectacle of news-hungry men milling among injured and exhausted survivors, fighting to get to grips with their stories.
I saw him take a camera out of a photographer's hand and
throw it over the side. The man had been trying to get a
close-up of some poor devil with his face smashed in. "The
next one of you ghouls that tries that, I'll 'eave the beggar
over the side, camera an' all."

I found Marjorie struggling to get near her father—shut
out by the ring of men surrounding him. "Oh, thank
God!" she said when she saw me. "What happened? Why
are they all crowding round him?" The bloom was gone
from her face, all the vitality knocked out of her. "I can't

get near him." The pupils of those strangely blue eyes were dilated and the words came in a panic rush, almost a sob.

Briefly I told her what her father had done, and all the time she had hold of my hand, clinging to it as though I were the one stable thing left to her. But as I talked I saw a change come over her. She seemed gradually to come alive. "Then perhaps it's all right," she breathed. "Perhaps this is the end of it then." It was extraordinary—the recuperative power of youth. Her eyes were suddenly shining, bright with hope, and then she kissed me full on the mouth for no apparent reason that I could see except that she needed to express her joy, her sense of relief that her father was safe and she didn't have to worry about him any longer. "And what about you? All those hours alone on Laerg. You must be exhausted." And she suggested that I come up to the croft with her father. "It'll be better than going to the camp." And with an understanding that surprised me because I'd never had anybody who'd cared a damn how I felt, she said: "You'll need to unwind—slowly."

I knew she was right. I was still extraordinarily keyed up. And yet at the same time I was utterly exhausted—a state of complete nervous fatigue. I did need to unwind, and I was grateful to her.

"If you'll just try and extricate my father. . . ."

And so I left with them in the little estate car and I didn't see my brother again for a long time.

The next day's papers were full of the story of the disaster, pages of it—eyewitness accounts and personal stories, timetables of the events leading up to the rescue and Field's climb. Charles Field was suddenly a hero again. There were pictures of him. Pictures of the survivors. But reading the papers with the whole story written up like a thrilling serial, the blow-by-blow account of a great storm with human courage surmounting disaster,

I detected an ominous note. There were leaders implying that men had died unnecessarily. There were feature articles that showed the whole course of that intense local depression—some gave the wind speed as high as 150 knots, though they had no means of knowing since there were no anemometers to record it—and here the implication was that if the officer in charge (meaning my brother) had taken the advice of the local Met. Officer, no lives need have been lost. They completely ignored the fact that Cliff's warning had come too late, almost three hours after the order to evacuate had been given.

Throughout every paper there was the same searching, angry note of inquiry. Somebody was responsible, and with Standing dead that man could only be Braddock. The order to evacuate, taken on his own responsibility, and his subsequent arrest, damned him utterly. There were questions asked about it in the House. The Secretary of State for War promised a full-scale inquiry.

It was a witch-hunt, nothing less, and my brother was the man they were all gunning for. The people responsible for his appointment to the Hebrides did nothing to demonstrate their confidence in him. The reverse, in fact. They relieved him of his temporary command and sent him on indefinite leave pending the results of the Inquiry. No doubt this action was intended to relieve him of the pressure of phone calls, but its effect, inevitably, was to confirm the press in their condemnation of his conduct.

I only heard that he'd been ordered away on leave two days later, when I felt sufficiently recovered to visit Northton. Marjorie drove me to the camp. With her father and myself to look after, the croft to run, and reporters to keep at bay, she was out of touch with camp affairs. I went straight to the Admin. block. There was a new adjutant, a Captain Davidson, short and dapper with a little moustache. "Major Braddock? I'm sorry, he's away on leave. Colonel Webb's in command here now." And he added:

"I'm afraid I can't give you Braddock's address. I don't think we've been notified where he's staying."

And that was that. I saw Rafferty and Flint. Nobody had Iain's address. The slate had been wiped clean, my brother expunged as though he'd never existed. Whether they acted under orders, I don't know. The effect, at any rate, was the same. He was gone and nobody would, or could, tell me where. I returned to Marjorie waiting in the car and all the way back to Rodil I was thinking of Iain, somewhere in the British Isles, a man condemned without a hearing. They hadn't even been able to tell me when the Inquiry would be held. "You'll be notified in due course, Mr. Ross," the dapper little adjutant had said. "At least, I imagine you will, since I gather you're a vital witness."

A witness! I hadn't thought of that. A witness against my own brother. And Iain wandering lost and alone with nobody to turn to. If he hadn't been separated from his wife, if he'd been able to draw on the strength of his family. . . . But life had kicked even that support from under him.

"He's alone," I said, not realizing I was speaking aloud. "Absolutely alone."

Marjorie braked, glancing at me quickly. "Who? Major Braddock?" And then, in a quiet voice, she said: "Donald. I've been wondering—we've both been wondering. . . . What is your connection with Major Braddock?" She was staring straight ahead of her then, her eyes fixed on the road. "There is a connection, isn't there?"

So they'd noticed. I didn't say anything for a moment. "If you don't want to talk about it. . . . But I thought perhaps it might help."

I had to think about this, about whether it was fair to Iain. But I, too, was alone. And they'd been kind to me. Friendship, understanding . . . I suppose even then I was aware of the attraction of this girl, a growing closeness between us that wasn't only physical. And to share my fears. . . .

But remembering the haunted look on his face, I shook my head. "Not now," I said. "Later perhaps. . . ."

She touched my hand, a gesture of sympathy. "If I'd known . . ." But then she shook her head. "No, I'd still have felt the same. He did give the order, you know." And she added: "Why? Why was he so determined to get them away on that last LCT?"

Why indeed? With a woman's intuition she had hit on the real point, the basic fact that made my brother guilty. But I couldn't see it then. I was thinking only of the disaster, not of what might have gone before, when he cloaked himself in another man's identity, and I said: "It was because he knew if he didn't get them off then, they'd have been stuck there for the winter with insufficient supplies." I was quoting Field, who'd had it from Rafferty, and all the time the thing was there, staring me in the face.

But Lane, his mind concentrated on his own monetary affairs, unclouded by all the details of the disaster, had seen it. I had a phone call from him within an hour of my return to London. "That you, Ross? Glad to know you're back at last. Where's your brother?" I tried to deny that he was my brother, but he ignored that. "I want a word with that guy. Now you just tell me where he is or I'm going to pass this whole story over to the press. After what's happened, they'll just lap it up."

"I don't think so," I said.

"And why not?"

"In this country the law of libel is still very . . ."

"Libel!" His soft voice was suddenly tough. "You talk about libel when the man may prove to be a murderer. Yeah, a murderer." I thought he was referring to the men who'd been drowned. But it wasn't that. His one-track mind was making a much more specific charge. "Have you considered, Mr. Ross, what happened to the original

Braddock—the young George Braddock, aged twenty and just commissioned, afloat on that life-raft with this monster of a brother of yours? Have you considered that?"

It came as a shock. And yet it had been at the back of my mind ever since I'd seen Iain standing with his finned feet in the surf, staring up at the hidden heights of Laerg; ever since that moment when I'd come ashore to find him waiting up in the camp, desperate to be left alone there. "I think," I said, trying to keep control of my voice, "you'd better not repeat that. Major Braddock may be facing an Inquiry, but that doesn't mean you can make wild accusations . . ."

"Major Braddock!" There was anger and contempt in his voice. "His name's Iain Ross. It's Iain Ross we're talking about, and you know it. Why else did you go north to the Hebrides? How else could you have managed to get on that landing craft and finish up in Laerg? Both of you, there on your own island together. Now you just tell me where I'll find the son-of-a-bitch. That's all I want from you—for the moment." And when I told him I didn't know he said: "All right, Ross. You stick by him. Very admirable of you—very fraternal. But you won't fob me off as easily as that. I'll just stay on here in England. I can wait. They'll produce him when the Board of Inquiry sits. And then I'll get him. I'll get the truth out of him then, so help me God, and if it's what I think it is, I'll brand him for the Goddammed murdering bastard he is. Goo'bye." And he slammed the phone down.

I didn't see my brother again until the Board of Inquiry, which was held at Scottish Command on November 2. He had, however, been in touch with me once, very briefly, during the intervening ten days. It was a phone call late at night, about eleven-fifteen. I recognized his voice at once, for he made no pretence of concealing his natural accent. "Donald? Is that you, Donald?"

"Where are you?" I said. "In London?"

"Aye, in some bluidy night club—I forget the name. I must ha' a wee talk wi' you, Donald. Can you come down here? Right away. I must ha' a talk wi' ye."

"Of course." And I added: "Are you all right, Iain?" His voice sounded thick and slurred. I thought he'd been drinking.

"Yes, I'm all right, laddie. It's just that I've made up my mind. I must talk to somebody. I'm all alone, you see. An' I thought maybe if you'd nothing better to do . . ."

"Whereabouts are you?" I said. I didn't want to lose him. "I'll come right down. Just tell me where to meet you."

"Aye, weel—I'm somewhere doon Curzon Street way." The accent was very broad and getting more slurred. "What aboot Cooks now, meet me outside Cooks in Berkeley Street."

"Okay, I'll be there at midnight," I said.

"Fine, fine, that'll do fine. We'll ha' a wee drink together, eh? Like old times. Only hurry. I canna stand my own company much longer." And he'd hung up.

I'd just gone to bed, so that I had to dress, and then there was the problem of transport. Fortunately I had enough money in the studio for a taxi and I found one on the rank outside Aldgate East Station. I was at Cooks by five to twelve. But he wasn't there, and though I hung around until 2 a.m., he never showed up.

He didn't ring me again and that was my only contact with him until I saw him in Service dress walking out of the Conference Room where the Board of Inquiry was being held. I was shocked at the change in him. The twitch at the corner of his mouth had become much more marked, the lines of his face deeper. There were bags under his eyes, and above them the eyes themselves stared weary and lack-lustre out of darkened sockets. He'd obviously been drinking heavily. His hands were trembling. He passed me without a flicker of recognition.

Shortly afterwards I was called to give evidence. The Inquiry was being conducted by a colonel. He sat at a mahogany table with a major on one side and a captain on the other. None of these officers were connected with Northton. They were taking depositions and by the way they questioned me I was certain it was merely the prelude to a Court Martial.

They took my evidence under oath. To some extent it was a cross-examination, with the Major making notes of my replies. They went over the whole sequence of events and my part in them. And when I had told them all I knew, the Major laboriously wrote out a summarized version in longhand. Then he read it through to me, and when I had agreed that it was a fair statement of what I'd told them, I was asked to sign it.

I thought that was the end of it and was just getting up to leave when the Colonel said: "One moment, Mr. Ross." He searched through the folder in front of him and produced a letter. "D'you know anything about a Mr. Edward William Lane of Vancouver, a Canadian business man?" I'd been expecting this and I was prepared for it. "Yes," I said. "He visited me in London on October 15. My brother Iain was among those missing when the *Duart Castle* was torpedoed in 1944. Lane had a theory that he was still alive."

"In fact, he thought Major Braddock might be your brother. Correct?"

I nodded.

"A day later you left London for the Outer Hebrides. You landed at Rodil in the Island of Harris on October 18 and I understand you saw Major Braddock the following day."

"Yes."

"Had you ever visited the Outer Hebrides before?" And when I admitted I hadn't, he said: "I take it then that you went up there for the express purpose of checking on

Major Braddock's identity? In other words, you thought there was a possibility that he might be your missing brother?"

"It was partly that," I agreed. "Lane had convinced me that my brother could have been with Braddock on that life-raft and I thought he might be able to tell me what had happened. Also," I added, "there seemed a possibility that I might be able to get out to Laerg." I started to explain to him then about my connection with the island and my desire to paint the scenes that my grandfather had described, but he cut me short.

"We are only concerned here with your visit as it affected Major Braddock. Now then, is there any truth in Lane's suggestion?"

I didn't give him a direct answer. Instead I said: "I understand that you've already taken evidence from the Senior Meteorological Officer at Northton. My first meeting with Major Braddock took place in the Met. Office. I imagine you have already asked Cliff Morgan whether Braddock and I recognized each other."

He nodded.

"What did he say?" I asked.

"That as far as he can remember there was no indication that you had ever met each other before."

It was a great weight off my mind to know that. "Then that surely is your answer, sir," I said. "If Braddock had, in fact, been my brother, then I would hardly be a reliable witness. At the same time, it would have shown in our reaction to each other at that first meeting. You can have my word for it, if you like, but I think you will agree that the best evidence you have that there is no connection between us is Morgan's." And I added: "Perhaps you haven't appreciated this point. I don't know whether Lane explains it in that letter, but he's over here in an attempt to prove that Major Braddock is not entitled to a fortune of some quarter of a million dollars left him by his aunt.

From what Lane told me, I got the impression that he was prepared to go to almost any lengths to upset the will and get the money for his wife's family."

"I see. No, he doesn't mention that here." The Colonel hesitated. Finally he said: "It puts rather a different complexion on the whole business."

For Iain's sake I'd been prepared to lie, but after that it wasn't necessary. The Colonel was faced with an unpleasant enough task as it was. He'd no wish to become involved with something that had happened more than twenty years ago. "Very well, I agree. That settles it. And I'm glad, for if there'd been any truth in it, then it would have raised the question of what had happened to the real George Braddock." He gave a little sigh and pushed the letter back into the folder. "Extraordinary what people will do for money. I'm sorry I've had to raise the matter . . . most unpleasant for you." And he smiled his relief and said: "That's all, Mr. Ross. Thank you for coming to give evidence. I am also asked by my superiors to thank you for all you did on Laerg to assist in the rescue of the survivors."

"I didn't do much," I said. "Braddock's the man to whom the survivors owe their lives. Field would never have made that climb if it hadn't been for Braddock. He organized the whole thing."

The Colonel's sharp little eyes stared at me hard and I wondered for a moment if I'd said too much. But it was true and I was damned if I was going to leave the Inquiry without making the point. If they were going to blame him for what had happened, at least they ought to realize that without the driving force of his personality nobody would have been saved and the loss of life would have been that much greater.

Probably they knew that already. But it made no difference.

After hearing over two dozen witnesses they passed the

depositions to the Director of Army Legal Services and in due course the next step towards Court Martial proceedings was taken. This was a Summary of Evidence and again I was called. Iain was present throughout the examination of witnesses, and this, more than anything else, seemed to emphasize the seriousness of his situation.

I understand he had the right to question witnesses. Whether he availed himself of this right I do not know; in my case he certainly did not, sitting tense and very still, his eyes never raised to my face. I was in the room almost two hours and all the time I was conscious of the nervous tension in him, could literally feel it. And he looked desperately ill.

I thought perhaps he would contact me afterwards, but he didn't, and though I stayed the night in Edinburgh just in case, I had no word from him. Perhaps he thought it would be unwise. In any case there was nothing I could have done—only given him moral support. Back in London I wrote him a carefully worded letter beginning *Dear Major Braddock* and inquiring whether there was anything I could do to help. I received no reply.

The waiting I knew would be hard on him, a nervous strain. The loneliness, too. This worried me as much as anything else, and in desperation I went to see his wife.

I'd kept a newspaper cutting that gave her address and I found her living in one of the back streets of Hertford, a small woman with doe-like eyes and a will that was hard as iron. I went in the evening with the story that I was a welfare worker for SAAFA, but nothing I could say would induce her to visit her husband. She got the Army allowance, and that was all she wanted of him. And the only clue she gave as to why they had parted was when she said: "I had five years of it." And added: "Nerves are one thing, but nerves and drink. . . . No, I don't want to see him again."

Yet she still had his photograph in a silver frame standing on a table beside the TV set—aged about thirty, I thought, and much as I remembered him in the Glasgow days, the lines of his face barely showing, but still that scar above the bridge of the nose. "If it's any comfort to him in his present circumstances," she said as she showed me to the door, "you can tell him both the girls are well and pray for him nightly." And she added, her lips tight and no tenderness in her eyes: "I told them he'd been killed—and then this business with reporters coming here and the news of it on the telly, you can imagine the shock it was—how I felt."

Christmas came and went; the New Year. Marjorie wrote from Rodil that Iain was in hospital. "My father says they think Major Braddock is suffering from some sort of nervous breakdown. It's not serious apparently, but I thought you'd like to know. It's the waiting, of course. And now I can't help feeling sorry for him."

There was nothing I could do about it. I couldn't very well write to him again, and if I tried to visit him the authorities would wonder at my interest. I was working all the time and so January slipped into February, with news from Marjorie that he was out of hospital. The rest of her letter was about the fishing and how the solan geese were starting to come back. "Soon there'll be all manner of birds and it'll be warmer with clear skies. Come back then and paint. It's so beautiful in the spring. . . ."

And then at last the official letter notifying me that Major Braddock's Court Martial would be held in Edinburgh on February 24, starting at 10 a.m.: *You are, pursuant to Section 103 of the Army Act, 1955, and Rule 91 of the Rules of Procedure (Army), 1956, made thereunder, hereby summoned and required to attend at the sitting of the said court . . . and so to attend from day to day until you shall be duly discharged; whereof you shall fail at your peril.*

Four days later I got an airmail letter from Lane in

Vancouver. Obviously he was paying somebody to keep
him posted. "Tell your brother that I'm flying over immediately and will be in Edinburgh on the twenty-
fourth. Tell him also that I have some fresh evidence. My
agents have located one of the military policemen who
acted as his escort on the *Duart Castle*. This man survived
on one of the boats that reached Ireland and he is prepared to swear that Sergeant Iain Alasdair Ross was on
that life-raft. He also saw Second Lieutenant George Braddock clinging to it. Furthermore, he says he would recognize your brother . . ."

The Court Martial was held at the Dreghorn Camp
just outside Edinburgh. It opened prompt at ten o'clock
with the swearing-in of the court. For this ceremony the
witnesses were present, all of us standing at the back of
the court. It was a bare, rather bleak room, but the arrangement of the desks and tables and the grouping of the
officers transformed it, and the colour of the uniforms
made it impressive so that I was conscious of the atmosphere, the sense of being caught up in the military legal
machine. Instead of a judge with his wig and scarlet robes,
five officers sat in judgment. And in the body of the court
—the accused, the officer defending him, the prosecuting
officer, all the various officials, even to the NCO's on duty,
in full dress. The effect was overpowering and I wondered
how my brother felt as the doors closed and quiet descended. The judge advocate, seated on the president's
right hand, read the convening order.

From where I stood I could see only the back of Iain's
head, hunched down into his shoulders, which sagged
slightly as he sat slumped in his seat, staring down at the
table in front of him. He seemed quite passive, almost
dazed, and when he was asked if he objected to being
tried by the president or any of the other members of the
court his reply was inaudible. And then the judge advocate's voice, clear and crisp: "Everybody will stand un-

covered while the court is sworn." A shuffle of chairs and
the court-room rose to its feet as he faced the president.
"Please repeat after me——" The Brigadier spoke the
words he knew by heart in a clipped, very clear voice: "I
swear by Almighty God that I will well and truly try the
accused before the court according to the evidence and
that I will duly administer justice according to the Army
Act, 1955, without partiality, favour or affection . . ."

The four other officers who constituted the court were
sworn and then the president swore in the judge advocate
himself. After that the witnesses were ushered out into an
adjoining room. There were altogether twenty-seven
witnesses. Most of them were from Northton—Field, Rafferty, Flint, the M.O., Phipps, Sergeant Wetherby, and
several other ranks I'd never seen before, including the
Signals NCO who'd been on duty when the fatal order
was given. Cliff was there and another civilian who turned
out to be Fellowes, the pilot who had flown the plane
from which Mike Ferguson had jumped to his death.
Wentworth, too, and a young captain who Field told me
was the Commander of L4400. Both Brigadier Matthieson
and the BGS from the War Office had also been called, but
their rank enabled them to avoid the tedium of waiting
in the confines of that small room.

There was a military policeman on the door to see that
we didn't discuss the case, nothing to do but sit and smoke,
and I had ample opportunity to consider what my brother
must be going through in the next room. Occasionally we
could hear the murmur of voices, the stamp of boots as
some NCO moved, the scrape of chairs, the sound of
coughing.

The preliminaries took just over an hour—the reading
of the charges and the prosecuting officer's speech in which
he put his case. We could just hear the murmur of his
voice. The first witness was called shortly after eleven-
thirty. This was the Signals NCO. He was followed by

the duty driver, then Flint, then Wentworth. Wentworth was still giving evidence when the court adjourned for lunch. The order in which the witnesses had been called was our only indication of the course the case was taking. Clearly the prosecuting officer was establishing the fact that the order to evacuate had been given.

Field was called during the afternoon, and when the court finally rose, he was waiting for me outside. "Marjorie asked me to give you her love." He smiled. He was looking younger, more buoyant, and his eyes had lost that nervous blink.

"How was Braddock?" I asked.

He hesitated, then shook his head. "Not good, I'm afraid. Very nervy-looking; at times I wondered whether he understood what was going on. He's still a sick man, I'm afraid."

I asked him about the nervous breakdown, but he didn't know the details. "The strain of waiting, I imagine. Three months almost. It's a long time. Too long. But once it's over, probably he'll be all right then."

"What are the chances?" I asked.

He shrugged. "Hard to say. He's got a good man defending him, good enough at any rate to handle the two brigadiers. But even if he gets them to say they had every confidence in the accused, it won't outweigh the fact that Standing had him arrested. If Standing were here to be cross-examined . . ." Again that little shrug. "But he isn't, you see, and dying like that, he's something of a hero. That counts for a lot in a case like this. And there's all the publicity. The judge advocate may tell them what the law is, but the court is human; they can't help being influenced by it. And the size of the disaster. Fifty-three men dead. Who's to be blamed if Braddock is acquitted? The press will say the Army is covering up and there'll be more questions in the House."

"So you don't think he's got a chance?"

He hesitated. And then he said: "No. Frankly, I don't."

I was called the following afternoon, immediately after Cliff Morgan had given evidence. When I took my place at the witness table I was shocked to see how ill Iain looked, his eyes wandering vacantly, his big, powerful hands never still—plucking at the buttons of his uniform, toying with his pencil, sometimes brushing over his face and up through his hair with a quick, nervous gesture. I don't think he once looked directly at me all the time I was being questioned. As Field had said, he still seemed a sick man—all his intense nervous energy beaten down, as though something had destroyed his will to fight back. I had that feeling very strongly, that his strength was being sapped from within, and I wondered to what extent he had been affected by the fact that Lane was in Edinburgh. I had seen Lane that morning, just a glimpse of him as I was entering the main gate of the camp. He was sitting there in a car with another man.

"Will the witness please answer the question." The president's voice, kindly but firm, brought me back to the stillness of the court-room and the rather bland-looking major who was defending Iain standing facing me, waiting patiently for my answer.

"I'm sorry," I said. "Perhaps you would repeat the question."

"I asked you, Mr. Ross, whether you could recall the time at which Major Braddock gave the order to evacuate the island?"

"Yes," I said. "Or rather, I can remember when the landing craft came into the beach. She grounded at nine forty-eight."

"And Major Braddock's order?"

"About ten minutes earlier. The landing craft was coming into the beach as we left the hut. Say, nine-thirty."

"Now I want the court to understand the circumstances in which that order was given. What was the direction of the wind at that time?"

"Northerly. It had been northerly all day."

"And no indication of a change?"

"No."

"After the landing craft beached, you went on board?"

"Yes."

"Where were you then?"

"I was helping on the tank deck until nearly midnight. After that I went to the wardroom."

"Where you found Lieutenant Wentworth talking to Captain Stratton?"

"Yes."

"What were they discussing?"

"A radio message they had received from the Met. Officer at Northton."

"Do you know when that message was received?"

"It had just come in so it would have been shortly after midnight."

"Two and a half hours after Major Braddock had given the order."

"Yes."

"And the wind at Laerg was still northerly then?"

"Yes." I saw the point he was trying to establish and I added: "It remained northerly for another four and a half hours."

The Major reached for his glasses and glanced at his notes. "Mr. Morgan in his evidence said that he was in contact with the *Viking Fisher* at twenty-three forty-seven. That's the trawler that was finally lost with all hands. Thirteen minutes to midnight. In your opinion was there any way in which Major Braddock could have foreseen how circumstances were going to change?"

"No," I said. "Definitely not." I glanced at Iain as his defending officer said: "Thank you, Mr. Ross," in a satisfied tone. I was surprised to see him running his pencil back and forth across the table in front of him, apparently taking no interest in the proceedings.

The defending officer turned to the president of the court. "That is the point I wish to establish." And then to me: "You have some experience of the sea, I believe. A year in the Navy and ten in the Merchant Service as a deck officer. Correct?"

"Yes."

"You were on the bridge with Captain Stratton part of the time during the crossing to Laerg and throughout the events that led up to the loss of the ship. Would you say he was a capable seaman?"

"Very capable."

"So that in coming in to the beach you would say, would you not, that it was the action of a capable seaman?"

"Yes," I said. "I'm certain Captain Stratton would never have brought his landing craft into the beach if he had thought there was any danger."

"And he was in a much better position than Major Braddock to assess the local weather situation?"

"I think you have made your point, Major Selkirk," the president said.

The Major gave a nod and a quick smile. "I just wanted to make it quite clear, sir." He glanced down at the papers on his desk. "Lieutenant Wentworth in his evidence has said that after the ship was unloaded Captain Pinney refused to take his men ashore. Can you confirm that?"

"Yes. I was in the wheelhouse at the time."

"When was this?"

"Between two-thirty and three, I should say."

"Can you recall the conversation?"

"It was hardly a conversation," I said.

"A row?"

"No, not a row." Briefly I told them what Pinney's attitude had been.

"So even then, somewhere between two-thirty and three, there was doubt about the wind shifting from the north?"

"Yes."

"Not only in Pinney's mind, but in Stratton's as well?"

I nodded.

"Thank you." He shifted his stance, glanced at my brother, who was still fiddling around with that damned pencil, and then his gaze came back to me. "You remember that Captain Stratton asked his radio operator to contact Colonel Standing. About what time would that have been?"

"Around twelve-thirty. We were in the wardroom then. He wanted to talk to Colonel Standing personally and he told the operator that the Colonel was to be got out of bed if necessary." And I added: "He said something about it being time the men who gave the orders lost a little sleep on our account."

Quick as a flash he said: "Are you implying that he knew Colonel Standing had gone up to his house, which was a mile from the camp—that he had in fact retired to . . ."

But the president interrupted him. "Major Selkirk. I must remind you again that Colonel Standing is dead. References to him should be confined to facts. You must not include vague statements about him or expressions of opinion or the comments of other officers."

"I quite understand, sir." The defending officer's face was wooden and he rustled the papers in his hand as he faced the court. "I will endeavour to follow your ruling, but I must point out that the officer I am defending faces very serious charges and my case rests to some extent on the clash of personalities that, I submit, was the direct and inevitable result of this somewhat, shall I say, unusual appointment. You have heard the evidence this morning of two brigadiers, both of whom briefed the accused following his appointment. Both have admitted that their instructions could be interpreted as making Major Braddock directly responsible for the success of the operation. However, if Colonel Standing's behaviour is not to be referred to. . . ." He flung his papers on to the desk. "Mr. Ross, you will now tell the court what Captain Stratton said after he'd spoken to Colonel Standing."

I hesitated, for I didn't see how this could help Iain. But the court was waiting and I said: "He didn't say very much—just that Colonel Standing hadn't known about the order and was angry."

"Angry? Because he'd been got out of bed in the middle of the night?" I saw the president lean forward, but Selkirk was too quick for him. "Or was it because he didn't know, at that time, that there was a landing craft grounded on the beach in Shelter Bay?"

"I think it was because he didn't know about the evacuation."

"Did he know there was a landing craft on the beach or not?"

"He couldn't have known."

"Did he know about the Met. Officer's latest forecast?"

"I don't think so."

"In other words, he was completely out of touch with the situation and it was Major Braddock . . ."

The prosecuting officer was on his feet, but the president forestalled him: "I must insist that you confine yourself to questions of fact and refrain from putting opinions of your own into the witness's mouth."

"Very well, sir. But I would ask the court's indulgence. It is a little difficult to know who exactly was in command." Again he adjusted his glasses, leaning down to check his notes. "Now, about radio contact. In your deposition, which I have here, you say you spoke to Mr. Morgan yourself on R/T. What was the reception like?"

"Very poor," I told him. "And Stratton said it was bad when he was talking to Colonel Standing."

"Was that the reason, do you think, that Captain Pinney wasn't given a direct order by his superiors to get his men off the ship?" And before I could reply, he went on: "Or would you say, from your own experience, that in a situation like this Major Braddock would be fully justified in leaving any decision like that to the men on the spot?"

"I think by then," I said, "the situation was beyond the control of anybody at Base."

He nodded, and after that he stood for a moment reading through his notes. I saw my brother's attention wander to the door at the back of the court. He had done that several times. Major Selkirk had stepped back from his desk, head thrown up and his eyes fixed on me again. "Now we come to the loss of L8610 . . . the cause, or rather the twin causes, for there were two, weren't there?" And when I nodded, he went on: "These were covered very fully by Lieutenant Wentworth in his evidence, but I would like to confirm one point with you—the failure of the steering. Do you remember Lieutenant Wentworth making a comment about the tiller flat? He says he told Captain Stratton that it was being flooded. Do you recall him making that report?"

"Yes."

"And did he give a reason?"

I told them then how the stretcher party had taken McGregor's body to the tiller flat and had failed to secure the hatch on leaving. "That was what caused the flooding."

"And it was the failure of the steering, was it not, that threw the ship on her beam ends and made it impossible to deal with the sea water in the ready-use tank?"

"Yes."

"And that again was something that Captain Stratton couldn't have foreseen?"

"Nobody could have foreseen it," I said.

"And certainly not Major Braddock, back at Base?"

"No."

And on that he sat down. There was a moment of shuffling relaxation in the court-room, and then the prosecuting officer rose to cross-examine me. He was a large, quiet man with a soft voice and a manner that was easy, almost friendly. "One or two small points, Mr. Ross. We know that Captain Pinney virtually refused to take his men off the ship. But later, just before you got off the beach, I think I'm right in saying that Colonel Standing spoke to him on the R/T. Am I also right in saying that the result of that talk was a direct order from his Colonel to get his men disembarked?"

"I believe so, but by then it was quite impossible." I knew what he was after. He wanted to show that Standing had not only countermanded the order, but had come very near to saving the situation. He was going to try and show Standing as a decisive man whose subordinate had let him down and who was making a last-minute effort to rectify the damage that had been done. I glanced at my brother, but his head was again turned towards the door, which was half open. A sergeant had come in and was just closing it. I turned to the president, determined not to have this point twisted to the advantage of the prosecution. "The first contact Colonel Standing had with the ship was when he spoke to Captain Stratton. My impression is that he had already taken personal command; yet he gave no order for the disembarkation of the Laerg detachment. I agree he did eventually give the order to Pinney, but by then it was at least two hours too late."

The president nodded. "And in your view the accused officer was not responsible at that time?"

"That's my impression—that Colonel Standing was in control."

The prosecuting officer continued: "You mentioned that radio conditions were bad. . . ." He was shifting his ground, but at that moment the sergeant came down the room, his footsteps loud on the bare boards. He handed the president a note. When he had read it, the president glanced quickly at me, and from me to Iain. He didn't say anything, but after consultation with the judge advocate he cleared the court.

Nobody has ever told me what was in that note. But I can guess. Lane made a statement to the court and this was supported by the man he had brought with him. After we had been kept waiting about half an hour, it was announced that the court was adjourned until the following day.

Knowing what Lane would have told the court, I was expecting every moment to be called to an interview. But nothing happened. Instead a rumour circulated that Major Braddock had collapsed and had been rushed unconscious to the Medical Reception Station. This proved correct. A statement was issued to the press that night and the following morning my newspaper carried the story under the headline: ACCUSED MAJOR BREAKS DOWN—LAERG COURT MARTIAL POSTPONED.

I read it over my breakfast and I was still drinking my coffee and wondering about it when the hotel receptionist came in to tell me that there was an Army officer waiting to see me. He was a young second lieutenant and he had orders to take me to the hospital. It is not clear to me even now whether the Army had accepted the fact that Major Braddock and I were brothers. I think probably they had —privately. But the Army, like any other large organization, is a community in itself with its own code of behaviour. As such it closes its ranks and throws a protective cloak over its members when they are attacked by the outside world. I suspect that Lane's accusation was not accepted by the court—officially, at any rate. In any case, it was quite outside the scope of their proceedings.

To Lane it must have seemed nothing less than a conspiracy of silence. First the Army, and then the press. I know he approached several newspapers, for they dug up the *Duart Castle* story, and in addition they wrote up Lane himself—not very kindly. But none of them referred to his accusations, other than obliquely. The law of libel made that too hot a story. There was another factor, too. Braddock's collapse had to some extent swung public feeling. The disaster was now past history. It had happened more than three months ago and here was this man being hounded into a nervous breakdown.

An RAMC colonel and a psychiatrist were waiting for me at the M.R. Station. Possibly they thought my presence might jerk Braddock's mind back into an awareness of the world around him. In fact, he stared at me without a flicker of recognition or even interest, face and eyes quite blank. He had a room to himself and was lying in bed, propped up on pillows. The lines of his face seemed smoothed out so that he looked much younger, almost like the youth I had known. He could talk quite lucidly, but only about the things going on around him. He appeared to remember nothing of the Court Martial or of the events on Laerg. At least he didn't refer to them. "Do I know you?" he asked me innocently. "We've met before, I suppose, but I'm afraid I don't remember. They say I've lost my memory, you see."

"Talk to him about Laerg," the psychiatrist whispered to me.

But Laerg meant nothing to him. "You were there," I said. "You saved the lives of twenty-three men."

He frowned as though making an effort to remember. And then he smiled and shook his head. There was a vacant quality about that smile. "I'll take your word for it," he said. "I don't remember. I don't remember a damn thing."

I was there nearly an hour and all the time, at the back of my mind, was the question—was his loss of memory genuine, or was he pretending? There was that smoothed-out quite untroubled face, the vacant, puzzled look in his eyes. And in a case of this sort, where is the borderline between genuine mental illness and the need to seek refuge from the strain of events? One leads to the other, and by the time I left I was convinced that even if he had deliberately sought this refuge, there was now no doubt that he had willed himself into a state of mental blackout.

"Kind of you to come to see me," he said as I was leaving. He spoke quite cheerfully, but his voice sounded tired as though talking to me had been a strain.

Outside, the psychiatrist said: "Afraid it didn't work. Perhaps in a few weeks' time, when his mind's rested, eh?" No reference to the possibility that we might be related. But it was there all the same, implicit in his assumption that I'd be prepared to come all the way up from London at my own expense to visit him again.

This I did about two weeks later at their request. By then my brother had been moved to a civilian institution and he was up and dressed. On this occasion they left us alone together. But it made no difference. His mind was a blank, or it appeared to be—blank of everything he didn't want to remember. And if he recognized me, he didn't show it. "They've got microphones in the walls," he said. But whether they had, I don't know. The psychiatrist said no. They'd been giving him treatment, electric-shock treatment. "This place is like a brain-washing establishment. Refinements of mental cruelty. They think I'm somebody else. They keep trying to tell me I'm somebody else. If I'll admit it, then I needn't have shock treatment. And when I say I know who I am, they put the clamps on my head and turn up their rheostats full blast. Ever had shock treatment?" And when I shook my head, he grinned and said: "Lucky fellow! Take my advice. Don't ever let them get their hands on you. Resist and you're in a strait-jacket and down to the torture chamber."

There was a lot more that I can't remember and all of it

with a thread of truth running through the fantasy. "They think they'll break me." He said that several times, and then words tumbling out of his mouth again as though he were afraid I'd leave him if he didn't go on talking—as though he were desperate for my company. "They want me to admit that I'm responsible for the death of a lot of men. Well, old man, I'll tell you. They can flay me alive with their damned machines, but I'll admit nothing. Nothing, you get me? I've even had a lawyer here. Wanted to give me some money—ten thousand dollars if I'd say I'm not George Braddock. But they won't catch me that way." He had fixed me with his eyes and now he grabbed hold of my arm and drew me down. "You know they've got a court sitting, waiting to try me."

"All right," I said. My face was so close to his nobody could possibly overhear. "Then why not tell them? Why not tell them what happened out there in the Atlantic? Get it over with." All the way up in the train I'd been thinking about it, certain that this was the root of the trouble.

But all he said was: "Somewhere in the basement I think it is. And if I admit anything . . ."

"It's a long time ago," I said. "If you just tell them what happened."

But it didn't seem to get through to him. ". . . then they're waiting for me, and I'll be down there, facing a lot of filthy accusations. I tell you, there's nothing they won't do." And so it went on, the words pouring out to reveal a mental kaleidoscope, truth and fantasy inextricably mixed.

Mad? Or just clever simulation? I wondered, and so apparently did the psychiatrist. "What do you think?" he asked me as I was leaving. It was the same man, thick tortoise-shell glasses and the earnest, humourless air of one who believes that the mystery of his profession elevates him to a sort of priesthood. "If we let him out, then he's fit and the Court Martial will have to sit again. He's not fit—

or is he?" He stared at me, searchingly. "No, of course—not your department. And you wouldn't admit anything yourself, would you?"

Veiled allusions like that. And the devil of it was there was nothing I could do to help Iain.

A week later they had another attempt at shock treatment—mental, not electrical this time. They brought Lane in to see him, and before the wretched man had been in there five minutes, they had to rush in and rescue him. Iain had him by the throat and was choking the life out of him.

After that they left him alone.

Two days later the police came to my studio. It was just after lunch and I was working on a canvas that I was doing entirely for my own benefit—a portrait of Marjorie, painted from memory. I hadn't even a photograph of her at that time. I heard their footsteps on the bare stairboards, and when I went to the door a sergeant and a constable were standing there. "Mr. Ross?" The sergeant came in, a big man with a flattened nose and small, inquisitive eyes. "I understand you're acquainted with a certain Major Braddock who is undergoing treatment in the James Craig Institute, Edinburgh?" And when I nodded, he said: "Well now, would it surprise you, sir, to know that he's escaped?"

"Escaped—when?" I asked.

"Last night. He was discovered missing this morning. I've been instructed to check whether he's been seen in this neighbourhood and in particular whether he's visited you."

"No," I said. "Why should he?"

"I'm given to understand you're related. They seemed to think he might try to contact you." He stood staring at me, waiting for me to answer. "Well, has he?"

"I'm afraid I can't help you. He certainly hasn't been here."

I saw his eyes searching the studio as though he wasn't prepared to take my word for it. Finally he said: "Very good, Mr. Ross. I'll tell them. And if he does contact you, telephone us immediately. I should warn you that he may be dangerous." He gave me the number of the police station and then with a jerk of his head at the constable, who had been quietly sniffing round the studio like a terrier after a bone, he left.

Their footsteps faded away down the stairs and I stood there without moving, thinking of Iain on the run with the police as well as the Army after him. Where would he go? But I knew where he'd go—knew in the same instant that I'd have to go there, too. Everything that had happened, his every action . . . all led inevitably back to Laerg.

I lit a cigarette, my hands trembling, all my fears brought suddenly to a head. Twenty-two days on a raft in the North Atlantic. Sooner or later they'd guess—guess that no man could have lasted that long, not in midwinter; and Laerg on his direct route. They'd work it out, just as I had worked it out, and then. . . . I turned to the window; drab vistas of grey slates, the mist hanging over the river, and my mind far away, wondering how to get there —how to reach Laerg on my own without anybody knowing? I hadn't the money to buy a boat, and to charter meant involving other people. But I could afford a rubber dinghy, and given twenty-four hours' calm weather . . . I thought Cliff Morgan could help me there. A radio to pick up his forecasts, a compass, an outboard motor—it ought to be possible.

I was up half the night working it out, making lists. And in the morning I drew all my cash out of the bank, booked a seat on the night train for Mallaig, and began a hectic six hours, shopping for the equipment I needed.

II

Lone Voyage

(MARCH 1–6)

There was news of Iain in the papers that night. It was in
the Stop Press—MISSING MAJOR SEEN AT STIRLING. A mo-
torist had given him a lift to Killin at the head of Loch
Tay. And in the morning when the train pulled into Glasgow I found the Scottish papers full of it, his picture all
over the front pages. He'd been seen on the railway station
at Crianlarich and again at Fort William. A police watch
was being kept on the quay at Mallaig in case he tried to
board the steamer for the Western Isles and all the villages
along the coast had been alerted. The net was closing in
on him and in that sparsely populated district I didn't
think he had a chance.

A man who boarded the train at Arisaig told me a
stranger had been seen walking the coast towards Loch
Moidart, and with Ardnamurchan so close, I toyed with
the idea that he might be making for our old croft. But at
Mallaig there was more definite news, a lobster boat stolen

during the night from a cove in Loch Nevin. The whole town was talking about it and an old man on the quay told it was an open boat, thirty feet long, with a single screw and a diesel engine. "An oldish boat, ye ken, but sound, and the bluidy man will wreck her for sure." I was certain he was wrong there; just as I was certain now that Iain was making for Laerg. He'd push across to Eigg or Rhum or one of the smaller islands and lie up in the lee. But to cross The Minch and cover the eighty-odd miles of Atlantic beyond he'd need better weather than this; he'd also need fuel. By taking the steamer I'd be in the Outer Hebrides before he'd even left the mainland coast.

It was late in the afternoon of the following day, March 3, that I reached Rodil. The passage across The Minch had been bad—the steel-grey of the sea ribbed with the white of breaking waves, the sky a pale, almost greenish-blue with mares' tails feathering across it like vapour trails. Later the black outline of the Western Isles had become blurred by rain.

I had planned to pitch my tent at the head of Loch Rodil, well away from the hotel, but the boatman refused to attempt it and landed me at the jetty instead, along with my gear and two other passengers. "Will you be staying long this time, Mr. Ross?" He eyed me doubtfully. "Last time you were here . . ." He shook his head. "That was a tur-rible storm." The two passengers, Army officers in civilian clothes, regarded me with interest.

I dumped my gear and got hold of Marjorie. I was in too much of a hurry to consider how she would react to my sudden unexpected appearance. All I wanted was to contact Cliff and get away from Rodil before the Army discovered I was there.

As she drove me in to Northton, she said: "It's true, then, that Major Braddock has stolen a Mallaig boat. That's why you're here, isn't it?"

I didn't want to be questioned and when I didn't answer

she gave me a wry grin. "For one wild moment I thought you might have come to see me."

"I'm sorry." I ought to have managed this meeting better, but it couldn't be helped. She was wearing the faded anarak she'd had on when I'd first seen her. Wisps of her black hair escaped the hood, glistening with moisture. She looked very attractive and any other time . . .

"That rubber dinghy, the outboard, all that gear on the jetty—it's yours I take it." And when I nodded, she said: "I'm afraid you haven't chosen a very good time. It's been like this for almost a fortnight, nothing but rain and wind." She meant it as a warning. And she added: "It's Laerg, isn't it? You're going to Laerg."

"Yes," I said. "I'm going to Laerg." No point in denying it when she'd known it instinctively. "But please don't tell anybody. I'm hoping Cliff will give me the local forecasts and then I'll get away from here just as soon as I can."

We were driving into the camp then and she stopped at the main gate. "I'll wait for you here. I have to pick my father up anyway."

My luck was in. Cliff was on the afternoon shift and he was still there, standing by the sloped desk, checking through a teleprint sheet. "Ross." He put down the teleprint sheets. "Damn it, man, what are you doing here?" He hadn't changed—still the same old cardigan, the open-necked shirt, the quick, volatile manner.

"I want your help," I said. And I told him about my plan to go to Laerg.

"Good God! I should have thought you'd have had enough of the place after what you went through there." The quick brown eyes stared at me curiously from behind their thick-lensed glasses. "What makes you want to go back?"

"You forget I'm an artist," I said. "And my father was born on Laerg. Now that the Army's evacuated, it's an opportunity to be there alone. The birds will be back now. I want to paint."

He nodded and I thought he'd accepted my explanation. But he was still looking at me curiously. "Have you got the Army's permission?"

"No."

"What about Nature Conservancy then?"

"I haven't got anybody's permission," I said. "I'm just going to go there." And I explained what I wanted from him; a weather clearance at the first possible moment, the certainty of at least twenty-four hours of light winds; and one, preferably two, personal weather forecasts during the voyage. "I want to sail as soon as possible and it's essential that I have calm conditions on arrival at Laerg."

He asked then about the sort of boat I'd got, and when I told him, he reached for his cigarettes. "You know what you're doing, I suppose." He didn't expect an answer to that, but went on to inquire about my radio. Could I take Morse? What speed?

"Fast enough," I said.

"And you'll be on your own?"

"Yes."

He lit his cigarette, staring thoughtfully out of the window.

"Well," I said. "Will you do it?"

"And you need calm weather at the other end." He seemed to be thinking aloud. "That means you're not planning to land in Shelter Bay." I thought he was much too shrewd where weather was concerned. But instead of pursuing the matter, he turned abruptly to the maps on the wall. "Well, there's the situation." The lower one showed a low-pressure area south-east of Iceland and another Low coming in from the Atlantic. But it was the upper one that interested me, the one that gave his forecast for midnight. It showed that second Low just west of the Hebrides. "A southerly air stream, you see, with the

wind veering south-westerly some time during the night."
Behind the depression with its wedge-shaped lines marking the warm and cold fronts was a shallow ridge of high
pressure. Beyond that, farther out in the Atlantic, another
Low.

"It doesn't look very promising," I said.

He had walked over to the map and was standing there,
staring up at it. "No. Fine tomorrow with the wind falling fairly light, and after that high winds again. But it's
not quite as bad as it looks. The Azores High is strengthen-
ing—I was just looking at the figures when you came in.
Maybe in a couple of days . . ." And then without a
change in his voice: "You know Braddock's been seen
on the mainland." He turned abruptly and faced me.
"There's talk in the Mess that he's stolen a boat—one of
those lobster boats. He could reach Laerg in a boat like
that." He was staring at me, his gaze fixed on my face.
"The last time you were in this office, Braddock came in.
Remember? They questioned me about that at the Inquiry. They asked me whether you'd recognized each
other. Did you know that?" And when I nodded, he
added: "I told them no." He hesitated. "You're not being
quite frank with me now, are you? It's because of Braddock you're going to Laerg."

It was no good denying it. I needed his help. "Yes," I
said. "But I'd rather not talk about it now."

To my relief he seemed to accept that. "Well, it's your
own business, nothing to do with me. I don't give a bloody
damn about Braddock. He cost a lot of men their lives and
if he'd bothered to consult me first . . . However—" He
shrugged. "It's done now and I don't like to see a man
hounded out of his wits. Did you know they'd got an aircraft up looking for him?" He stood there a moment,
thinking it out. "Suppose I refuse to give you the local
forecast—what then, would you still go?"

"Yes. I'd have to rely on the B.B.C. shipping forecasts,

and that wouldn't be the same as having the local weather from you. But I'd still go."

He nodded. "Okay. That's what I thought." And he added: "I don't know what your connection with Braddock is or what you hope to achieve by going to Laerg, but nobody would undertake a trip like that unless they had very strong reasons for doing so. I accept that, and I'll do what I can to help you." He stubbed out his cigarette. "The weather's been bloody awful these last few weeks and that Low that's coming in from the Atlantic—" he nodded to the weather map—"it's still intensifying. The new figures just came in over the teleprinter. Pressure at the centre is nine-seven-two falling and unless the ridge of high pressure in front of it builds up—and I don't think it will—that next Low will start coming through some time tomorrow night. After that . . . well, this is just guesswork, but we might get a fine spell. It's about time, you know." He went back to the desk. "I'll give you my call sign and the frequency you have to listen on." He wrote it down for me and suggested I tune in to his net at 22.00 hours. "Just to check that you're picking me up all right. Phone me at nine o'clock tomorrow morning here. I usually look in about that time if I'm not on the morning shift."

I thanked him, but as I turned to go he stopped me. "Take my advice, Ross, and keep clear of the military. It's not only Braddock they're worried about. There's a report of a Russian trawler in the area, and this new chap, Colonel Webb—very cautious he is. Can't blame him, after what's happened. And a fellow alone in a rubber dinghy, you see . . . thought I'd better warn you."

I left him then. It was just after six-thirty. The car was waiting for me at the main gate and there was an officer leaning against it, talking to Field. It was the dapper little captain who had replaced Mike Ferguson as adjutant. He watched as I climbed into the back of the car and I thought he recognized me.

"Marjorie tells me you're going to Laerg," Field said as we drove off. "Alone?"

"Yes."

"Well, I hope Cliff Morgan was able to offer you the prospect of some better weather." He didn't ask me why I was going.

But later that evening, sitting by the peat fire in their croft, it was obvious he had guessed. "The air search is being stepped up tomorrow—two helicopters and a Shackleton. They'll be concentrating on The Minch and the Inner Hebrides, and every fishing vessel will be on the lookout for him."

"He hasn't been seen then?"

"No. But it's just a matter of time." And he added: "I gather he was under treatment. It's possible he said things . . ." He didn't look at me, but sat staring into the fire, his long, beaked face in silhouette against the lamplight. "These truth drugs, they quite often work, you know." And then he gave me the same advice that Cliff had given me. "If you don't want the Army bothering you, I should get away from here just as soon as you can. The North Ford, between North Uist and Benbecula, is as good a jumping-off place as any. Nobody will bother you there, and when you do sail you'd have the Monach Isles to land on if the wind got up." He turned his head suddenly and looked at me. "I wonder what makes you so certain Braddock is headed for Laerg?" And when I didn't say anything, he added: "That night when we were leaving, he wanted the tug to go without him, didn't he?" I hadn't expected him to have guessed that. His gaze returned to the fire. "A strange man. Quite ruthless. But a great deal of courage. And with a drive . . . I think that's what one most admired, that driving energy of his." And after a moment he added: "For your sake, I hope the end of it all isn't—" he hesitated—"some ghastly tragedy."

Marjorie came in then with supper on a tray. We ate it

there by the fire. It was a cosy, pleasant meal, and for a while I was able to forget the weather and the sense of loneliness, almost of isolation, that had been growing in me ever since I'd returned to the Hebrides.

I had to leave at nine-thirty in order to be back in time to pick up Cliff's transmission and test reception. "I'll walk down with you," Field said. Marjorie came to the door with us. "I'll see you in the morning," she said. "I hope you don't have too unpleasant a night."

Outside the rain had ceased, but it was blowing harder than ever. Field didn't say anything until we had passed the church. "I wanted to have a word with you alone." His voice was hesitant. "About Marjorie. You realize she's in love with you." And he went on quickly. "She's Celt—both sides. She's the sort of girl who'd break her heart over somebody." He stopped and faced me. "I wouldn't be talking to you like this if you were an ordinary fellow. But you're not. You're an artist. I don't know why that makes a difference, but it does."

I didn't know what to say, for I hadn't given much thought to the way the relationship between us had been developing, and now . . . "Probably it's just the reaction . . . I mean, she was fond of Ferguson."

"Fond, yes. But nothing more. You're an older man . . ." He hesitated. "Not married, are you?"

"I was—for a few months. But that finished years ago."

"I see. Well . . ." He sounded awkward about it now. "We're very close, Marjorie and I—always have been since her mother died. And now she's grown up . . ." He started walking again, his head down. "Not your fault perhaps, but don't make a fool of her. I couldn't bear that—nor could she." And he added: "Well, there it is . . . just so that you understand." He didn't give me a chance to say anything, but switched abruptly to the subject of my voyage to Laerg. "I don't like it," he said. "The weather up here can change very quickly. Right now there are half a dozen lobster fishermen marooned on the Monachs. Been there almost a fortnight."

"I'll be all right," I said. "Cliff's giving me the local forecasts."

"If I weren't tied up here, I'd offer to come with you. I don't like the idea of your doing it alone. Nor does Marjorie." We had reached the dip in the road that led down to the hotel and he stopped. "Well, you know what you're doing, I suppose." And he added: "I'll let you know if there's any further news of Braddock." He left me then, going back up the road, the darkness swallowing him almost at once.

I had pitched my tent on the same grass slope just beyond the small boat harbour and I got back to it just in time to pick up Cliff's transmission. He gave me his call sign first —GM3CMX, repeated several times; then the weather forecast keyed much slower than he would normally send. Reception was good, loud and clear with no interruption. He followed the forecast with a brief message: *Your arrival commented on. Remember my advice and clear out tomorrow.* He ended his message with the letters *CL,* which meant that he was closing down his station.

I lit the pressure lamp and got out my charts, starting with 2508, which covered the whole hundred miles of the Outer Hebrides chain and included all the out-islands. Laerg stood solitary and alone on the very edge of the chart, a tiny speck surrounded by the blank white of ocean, with only scattered soundings. The shortest line from Laerg to the Hebrides touched North Uist at its westernmost point, Air-an-Runair. The distance was eighty-three nautical miles.

But now that I had disembarked my gear and contacted Cliff, I was no longer tied to Rodil and could shorten the voyage by crossing the Sound of Harris. The west coast of North Uist was too exposed, but remembering what Field had said, my eyes were drawn to the North Ford and to a straggle of islands shaped like the wings of a butterfly that lay barely a dozen miles to the west. These were marked on the chart—Heisker (The Monach Islands).

I lit a cigarette, got out chart No. 3168, and began to examine the North Ford in detail. It would be low water before I got there and I saw at a glance that the narrow channels through the sand would make it possible for me to pass, whatever the tide. And at the western end, beyond the causeway that joined North Uist to Benbecula, the island of Baleshare stretched a great dune tongue down from the north, a bare waste devoid of any croft. I pencilled a circle round it, let the pressure out of the lamp, and lay down with a sense of satisfaction. From Baleshare to the Monachs was about nine miles. From the Monachs to Laerg, seventy-six miles. This way I should reduce the open-sea passage by at least thirteen miles.

I left the following morning immediately after phoning Cliff. A cold, clear day with the wind fallen light and the clouds lifted to a thin grey film of cirrostratus high in the sky. And late that afternoon I pitched my tent against a background so utterly different that I might have been in another country. Gone were the lofty hills of Harris, the sense of being shut in, pressed against the sea's edge by sodden heights. Gone, too, was the brown of the seaweed, the sombre dark of rocks. Here all was sand, great vistas of it, golden bright and stretching flat to the distant hump of a solitary, purpling peak. My camp faced east and the tide was out. The peak was Eaval. Behind me were the dunes of Baleshare. All the rest was sky, thin mackerel scales of cloud, silver grey and full of light. And not another soul to be seen, only the distant outline of solitary crofts, remote on islands in the Ford.

From the top of the dunes I could see the channelled entrance to the Ford, marked out for me by the white of waves breaking on the sand bars. A mile or more of

broken water, and beyond that, low on the western horizon, the outline of the Monachs, the pointed finger of the
disused lighthouse just visible.

The sun set and the heavens flared, a fantastic, fiery red.
From horizon to horizon the sky blazed, a lurid canopy
shot through with flaming wisps of cloud. It was a blood-
bath of colour, and as I watched it, the red gradually
darkening to purple, the whole vast expanse of sky was
like a wound slowly clotting. Darkness fell and the tide
rose; the dinghy floated closer until it rested just below
my tent.

Cliff came through prompt at ten o'clock. The weather
pattern was unchanged. I had some food then and went
to bed and lay in the dark, thinking of Laerg—out there
to the westward, beyond the break of the sand-bar surf,
beyond the dim-seen shape of the Monachs, hidden below
the horizon.

If, when I had left Rodil that morning, the engine had
failed to start, or I had found an air leak in the dinghy,
or anything had gone wrong, then I think I should have
regarded it as an omen. But across the Sound of Harris,
and all the way down the coast of North Uist, the engine
had run without faltering. The speed, measured between
identified islands, had been just over three and a half
knots. Even in the North Ford, where it was wind against
tide and quite a lop on the water, I hadn't experienced a
moment's uneasiness. The craft was buoyant, despite her
heavy load. She had shot the rapids under the Causeway
bridge without taking any water, and though the tide was
falling then and the channel tortuous, she had only twice
grounded, and each time I had been able to float her off.

I was sure, lying in my tent that night, that I could
make Laerg. But confidence is not easily maintained
against such an elemental force as the sea. The break of
the waves on the bar had been no more than a murmur
in my ears when I had gone to sleep. When I woke it was

a pounding roar that shook the dunes and the air was thick with the slaver of the gale; great gobs of spume, like froth, blown on the wind. Rain drove in grey sheets up the Ford and to stand on the dunes and look seaward was to face layer upon layer of rollers piling in, their creaming tops whipped landward by the wind.

It lasted a few hours, that was all, but the speed with which it had arrived and the suddenness of those big seas was disturbing.

The synopsis at the beginning of the one-forty forecast confirmed the pattern transmitted to me by Cliff the previous night; the depression centred over Scotland, moving away north-eastward, and a high-pressure system building up behind it and covering the Eastern Atlantic from the Azores to approximately latitude 60° north. Outlook for sea area Hebrides was wind force six, veering north-westerly and decreasing to light variable; sea moderating, becoming calm; visibility moderate to good, but chance of fog patches locally.

I moved fast after that. The gale had lost me half the day and now the tide was falling. Where I was camped on the southern tip of Baleshare, the deep water channel swung close in to the dunes, but on the other side, towards Gramisdale, the sands were already beginning to dry. My most urgent need was petrol. I had used over eight gallons coming down. I filled up the tank of the outboard, slid my ungainly craft into the water, and pushed off with the two empty jerricans, following the channel north-east past the tufted grass island of Stromay towards the village of Carinish.

Beyond Stromay the deep-water channel forked. I took the right fork. It was still blowing quite hard and by keeping to the roughest water I avoided the shallows. I beached just south of the village, tied the painter to a stone and hurried up the track, carrying the jerricans. There was no petrol pump at Carinish, but the chart indicated a post office and as I had expected it was the centre of village information. There were about half a dozen women gossiping in the little room, and when I explained what I'd come for, one of them immediately said: "There's Roddie McNeil now. He runs a car. D'ye ken the hoose?" And when I shook my head, she said: "Och weel, I'll get it for you myself." And she went off with my jerricans.

I asked if I could telephone then and the postmistress pushed the phone across the counter to me. "You'll be the pairson that's camped in the dunes across the water to Eachkamish," she said. Eachkamish was the name of the southern part of Baleshare. "Would you be expecting somebody now?"

"No," I said, thinking immediately of the Army.

"A lassie, maybe?" Her eyes stared at me, roguish and full of curiosity. "Weel noo, it'll be a pleasant surprise for ye. She came in by the bus from Newton Ferry and now she's away to the Morrisons to inquire aboot a boat."

"Was it a Miss Field?"

She shook her head, smiling at me. "I dinna ken the name. But she was in a turrible hurry to get to ye." And she turned to a young woman standing there and told her to go down to the Morrisons and bring the lassie back.

I picked up the phone and gave the exchange the number of the Met. Office at Northton. It couldn't be anyone else but Marjorie and I wondered why she'd come, for it wasn't an easy journey from Rodil. There was a click and a voice said: "Sykes, Met. Office Northton, here." Apparently Cliff had been called down to the camp. "Will you give him a message for me," I said. "Tell him I'll be leaving first light tomorrow. If there's any change in the weather pattern he must let me know tonight." He asked my name then and I said: "He'll know who it is," and hung up.

Five minutes later Marjorie arrived, flushed and out of

breath. "We'd almost got the boat down to the water when
I saw the dinghy there. If I hadn't gone in for a cup of
tea with the Morrisons I'd have seen you coming across."

"How did you know where I was?"

"Daddy was sure you'd be somewhere in the North Ford
and this seemed the most likely place." She glanced
round at the faces all eagerly watching us. "Walk down
the road with me, will you. We can't talk here. What with
that odd craft of yours and me coming here asking for a
man camped in the dunes—it'll be all over North Uist
by this evening." She gave me a quick little nervous smile.
"I didn't give your name." And then, when we were
clear of the post office, she said: "The boat's been seen at
Eriskay, on the east side. Colonel Webb was notified this
morning and Daddy rang the hotel. He thought you'd
want to know." And she added: "A crofter saw it there
last night. They're not sure it's the one Major Braddock
took, but it's a lobster boat and it doesn't belong to any
of the local fishermen."

So he's crossed The Minch and was waiting like me
for the expected break in the weather. I was quite sure it
was Iain. The island of Eriskay was immediately below
South Uist and right opposite Mallaig. "What are they
doing about it?" I asked.

"They've sent out a plane to investigate."

"A helicopter?"

"No. A plane, Daddy said."

A wild coast and no place to land. A plane wouldn't
stop Iain. And for me to try and intercept him was out of
the question. He'd shift to the little islands in the Sound
of Barra and by tomorrow he'd be gone.

"It's what you were expecting, isn't it?" She had stopped
and was standing, facing me, the wind on her face.

"Yes." And I added: "It was good of you. To come all
this way."

"I suppose you'll go now."

"Tomorrow morning."

"He's got a much bigger boat than you. If anything happened . . . I mean, you ought to have somebody with you—just in case."

"In case I fall overboard?" I smiled. "I wouldn't have far to fall—a few inches, that's all."

"It's nearly a hundred miles to Laerg, and that wretched little dinghy . . ." She was staring at me, her eyes wide. "I realize you can't take anyone—anyone who wouldn't understand. But—" she hesitated, her gaze, level and direct, fixed on me. "I've brought cold weather clothing and oilskins. I thought if you wouldn't take anyone else . . ." Her hand touched my arm. "Please. I want to come with you."

I didn't know what to say, for she wasn't a fool; she knew the danger. And she meant it, of course. "Don't be silly," I said. "Imagine what your father would say."

"Oh, Daddy knows." She said it quite gaily and I knew she really had settled it with him. And when I said: "You know it's out of the question," her temper flared immediately. "I don't know anything of the sort. You can't go alone. . . ."

"I've got to," I said.

She started to argue then, but I cut her short. "It's no good, Marjorie. You can't help me. Nobody can. In any case, there isn't room. When the stores are in it, that rubber dinghy is full—there's barely space for me."

"That's just an excuse."

I took her by the shoulders, but she flung me off. She was angry now and her eyes blazed. "You're so bloody pigheaded. Just because I'm a girl. . . ."

"If you'd been a man," I told her, "The answer would have been the same. There's no room for anybody else. And to be perfectly honest, I don't want anyone. This is something I've got to do alone."

"But why? Why do you have to?"

"He's my brother," I said. No point in concealing it from her now.

"Your brother?" She stared at me, and I could see her thinking it out and going over it in her mind.

"Now do you understand? This is something I've got to work out for myself. Perhaps for Iain, too." I took her by the shoulders and this time she didn't draw away.

"It's settled then. You're going—tomorrow."

"Yes."

She didn't argue any more, and when I drew her to me, she let me kiss her. "Thank you," I said. "Thank you for coming, for offering to go with me." Her lips were cool with the wind. "That's something I'll always remember. And when I get back . . ." I felt her body come against me, the softness of it and her arms round my neck, her mouth on mine; and then she had drawn away. "I'll see you off, anyway." She was suddenly practical and we walked back in silence.

The woman who had gone off with the jerricans was waiting for me outside the post office. "Ye'll find Roddie McNeil wi' your petrol doon by the landing place." I thanked her. "It's nae bother. And there's nae call for ye to be thanking Roddie. He'll be charging ye for his time as well as the petrol, ye ken."

McNeil was waiting for me on the sands, a small, dour man with sandy hair. "There's a wee bit extra for the cartage," he said. I paid him and he helped me launch the dinghy and stow the jerricans. "Is it long ye'll be camped over to Baleshare?" And when I told him I'd be gone in the morning if the weather were fine, he said: "Aye, weel . . ." And he sniffed at the breeze like a sheltie. "It'll be fine weather the noo, I'm thinking."

He held the boat while I started the engine, and then I looked back at Marjorie. There was something almost boyish about her, standing there alone on the sands, the faded anarak and the green cord trousers tucked into gum

boots, her head bare and her hair blown across her face.
And yet not boyish; more like an island woman, I thought,
her body slim and erect, her face clouded—and she'd been
quite prepared to come to sea. The noise of the engine
drowned all possibility of speech. I waved and she waved
back, and that was that, and a feeling of sadness enveloped
me as I motored down the channel. I didn't look back
and in less than twenty minutes I had beached the dinghy
below my tent. I was on my own again, with the surface of
the dune sand dried now and the wind sifting it through
the wiry grass stems.

I began loading the dinghy ready for the morning.
Reed's Nautical Almanac gave time of sunrise as o6.43.
There was no moon. I thought I should have sufficient
light to cross the bar just before five. And once out beyond the bar I should be stuck at the helm hour after hour
with no chance to change the stowage or search for things.
Everything I needed had to be ready to hand.

There was another problem, too. At five o'clock in the
morning the tide would be almost low. If I left the dinghy
where it was, moored to the shore, it would be high and
dry when I wanted to leave, and loaded it would be much
too heavy to drag into the water. The only alternative was
to anchor off in deep water and sleep aboard.

I stowed everything in its place except the tent and the
radio set, and by the time I had finished the sun was shining, the wind no more than a rustle in the grasses. It was
a calm, clear evening with Eaval standing out brown and
smiling against the black storm clouds still piled against
the mainland hills. I climbed to the top of the dunes, and
all to the west the sky was clear, a pale pastel shade of
blue, with the seas white on the bar, but breaking lazily
now and without much force.

There was nothing more I could do and I got my sketch-
book out. The two drawings I did show the loaded dinghy
lying like a basking shark stranded at the water's edge,

the tent snugged in its hollow against the dunes, and that flat world of sand and water stretching away to the sunken hulks of the distant hills. They set the scene, but they miss the bright calm of that suddenly cloudless sky, the curlews piping to the more anxious note of the oyster-catchers, the flight of the grey plover and the laboured strokes of a heron. The sun set, an orange ball that turned the Monachs black like a ship hull-down, and as twilight fell, the darkening world seemed hushed to a sort of sanctity so that I felt I understood what it was that had drawn the early Christians to these islands.

Cliff Morgan's transmission came through very sharp that night, with almost no interference. *Message received. Weather set fair for twenty-four hours at least, possibly forty-eight. Fog your chief hazard. Future transmissions twice daily at 13.30 and 01.00 continuing for three days. Thereafter 22.00 as before for four days. If no message received by March 10 will presume you are in trouble and take appropriate action.* He repeated the message, the speed of his key steadily increasing. Finally: *Bon voyage CL.*

I marked the times of his transmissions on the chart and checked once again the course I should have to steer. He had given me seven clear days in which to get a message through to him. Time enough to worry how I was going to do that when I reached Laerg. I wished Iain could have heard that forecast. Fog was just what he wanted now.

I checked the tides given on the chart for every hour before and after high water Stornoway, pencilling in the direction and speed for the twenty-four hours commencing 05.00. I also made a note of the magnetic variation —13° west—and my compass deviation, which I found to be a farther 4° west with all my gear stowed. Taking these factors into account, the compass course I should have to steer after clearing the Monachs was 282°.

Having satisfied myself that all the navigational information I required was entered on the chart, and having checked through again for accuracy, I folded it and slipped it into its spray-proof case. Together with the radio, I stowed it in the dinghy within reach of the helm. Then I struck the tent and when that was loaded and the camp entirely cleared, I waded into the water, pushed off and clambered in. I moored out in the channel, a stone tied to the painter, and went to sleep under the stars, clad in my oilskins, lying crossways, my feet stuck out over the side and my head cushioned on the fat curve of the tight-blown fabric.

It was cold that night and I slept fitfully, conscious of the yawing of the dinghy, the ripple of the tide tugging at the mooring. I had no alarm clock, but it wasn't necessary. Seabirds woke me as the first glimmering of dawn showed grey in the east, silhouetting the dark outline of Eaval. I dipped my face in salt water, conscious now of a feeling of tension; eyes and head were sluggish with the night and the cold had cramped my bones. I drank the tea I had left hot in the thermos, ate some digestive biscuits and cheese, and then I pulled up the mooring, untying the stone and letting it fall back into the water. The outboard engine started at the second pull and I was on my way, circling in the tide run and heading down the centre of the pale ribbon of water that ran between the sands towards the open sea.

The light in the east was pale and cold as steel; the stars overhead still bright. The speed of my passage made a little wind, and that too was cold, so that I shivered under my oilskins. All ahead was black darkness. I had a moment of panic that I should lose the channel and get stranded among the breakers on the bar. Passing through the narrows between Eachkamish and the northern tip of Benbecula—the channel marked on the chart as Beul an Toim—the broken water of the bar showed in a ghostly semicircle beyond the piled-up bulk of my stores.

Even when I could see the breaking waves, I could not hear them. All I heard was the powerful roar of the outboard. I steered a compass course, running the engine slow, and as the dunes slid away behind me, my craft came suddenly alive to the movement of the waves.

Breaking water right ahead and no gap visible. The light was growing steadily and I jilled around for a moment, searching the line of breakers. A darker patch, farther south than I had expected . . . I felt my way towards it, conscious of the tug of the tide under the boat, noting the sideways drift. And then suddenly my eyes, grown accustomed to the light, picked out the channel, a narrow highway of dark water, growing wider as I entered it. The swell was bad out here on the bar, the waves steep but only occasionally breaking. The dinghy pitched wildly, the engine racing as the prop was lifted clear of the water.

There was a moment when I thought I'd missed the channel, the waves higher than my head and starting to curl at the top. I wanted to turn back then, but I didn't dare for fear the dinghy would overturn. The jerricans were shifting despite their lashings and I had to grip hold of the wooden slats at my feet to prevent myself from being thrown out. This lasted for perhaps a minute. Then suddenly the waves were less steep. A moment later, I was motoring in calm water and the sea's only movement was a long, flat, oily swell. I was over the bar, and looking back I could scarcely believe that I had found a way through from landward, for all behind me was an unbroken line of white water, the confusion of the waves showing as toppling masses against the dawn sky, the low land surrounding the Ford already lost in the haze of spray that hung above the bar. I set my course by the compass, took a small nip from the flask I had kept handy, and settled down to the long business of steering and keeping the engine going.

Shortly before seven the sun rose. It was broad daylight
then and the Monachs clearly visible on the port bow. At
06.45 I had tuned in to the B.B.C. on 1500 metres. There
was no change in the weather pattern and the forecast for
sea area Hebrides was wind force one to two variable, good
visibility, but fog locally. Shortly after nine the Monachs
were abeam to port about two miles. They were flat as a
table and at that distance the grass of the *machair* looked
like a lawn. My compass was one of those which could be
taken out of its holder and used as a hand-bearing compass.
I took a bearing on the disused lighthouse, and another on
Haskeir Island away to the north. These, together with a
stern-bearing on the top of Clettraval on North Uist, gave
me a three-point fix. I marked my position on the chart
and checked it against my dead reckoning, which was based
on course and speed, making due allowance for tide. The
difference was one and four-tenths miles at 275°. That fix
was very important to me, for thereafter I was able to base
my dead reckoning on a speed of three and eight-tenths
knots.

The sun was warm now, shimmering on the water, a
blinding glare that made me drowsy. The one thing I
hadn't thought of was dark glasses. I had taken my oilskin jacket off some miles back. Now I removed the first
of my sweaters and refilled the tank with the engine
running slow. In doing so I nearly missed the only ship I
was to sight that day—a trawler, hull-down on the horizon,
trailing a smudge of smoke.

Every hour I wrote up my log and entered my DR position on the chart, just as I had always done back in the
old days on the bridge of a freighter. The engine was my
main concern, and I was sensitive to every change of note,
real or imagined. All around me the sea was alive: the
movement of the swell, the flight of birds; and whenever
I felt the need, there was always the radio with the light
programme churning out endless music.

Just after eleven I ran into a school of porpoise. I thought at first it was a tidal swirl, mistaking their curving backs for the shadow cast by the lip of a small wave breaking. And then I saw one not fifty yards away, a dark body glinting in the sun and curved like the top of a wheel revolving. The pack must have numbered more than a dozen. They came out of the water three times, almost in unison and gaining momentum with each re-entry. At the final voracious plunge, the whole surface of the sea ahead of me seethed; from flat calm it was suddenly a boiling cauldron as millions of small fry skittered in panic across the surface. For an instant I seemed to be headed for a sheet of molten silver, and then the sea was oily smooth again, so that I stared, wondering whether I had imagined it.

A flash of white from the sky, the sudden splash of a projectile hitting the water . . . this new phenomenon thrilled me as something dimly remembered but not seen in a long while. The gannets had arrived.

There were a dozen or more of them, wheeling low and then hurling themselves into the sea with closed wings and out-thrust head, a spear-beaked missile diving headlong for the herring on which the porpoise were feeding and which in turn were attacking the small fry. I could remember my grandfather's words before I had ever seen a gannet dive: "Aye," he'd said, his thick, guttural voice burring at us, "ye'll no' see a finer sight this side of heaven, for there's nae muckle fowl (he pronounced it the Norwegian way—*fugl*) can dive like a solan goose."

Where the gannets came from I don't know, for until that moment I had seen none. They appeared as though by magic, coming in from all angles and all heights, and the little bomb-plumes of their dives spouted in the sea all round me. My presence didn't seem to disturb them at all. Perhaps it was because the dinghy was so different in shape and appearance to any boat they had encountered before. Three of them dived in quick succession, hitting the water so close that I could almost reach out and touch the plumes of spray. They surfaced practically together, each with a herring gripped in its long beak. A vigorous washing, a quick twist to turn the fish head first, and then it was swallowed and they took off again, taxiing clumsily in a long run, wings and feet labouring at the surface of the water. Other birds were there—big herring gulls and black-backs; shearwaters and razorbills, too, I think, but at that time I was not so practised at bird recognition. The smooth-moving hillocks of the sea became littered with the debris of the massacre; littered, too, with porpoise excreta—small, brown aerated lumps floating light as corks.

It was over as suddenly as it had started. All at once the birds were gone and I was left alone with the noise of the engine, only then realizing how the scream of the gulls had pierced that sound. I looked at the Monachs and was surprised to find they had scarcely moved. There was nothing else in sight, not even a fishing boat, and the only aircraft I saw was the BEA flight coming into Benbecula, a silver flash of wings against the blue of the sky.

Though less than four miles long from Stockay to the lighthouse, the Monachs were with me a long time. It was not until almost midday that they began to drop out of sight astern. Visibility was still very good then. The stone of the lighthouse stood out clear and white, and though the North Ford and all the low-lying country of Benbecula and the Uists had long since disappeared, the high ground remained clearly visible; particularly the massive brown bulk of the Harris hills.

It was about this time that I thought I saw, peeping up at me over the horizon ahead, the faint outline of what looked like a solitary rock. The peak of Tarsaval on Laerg? I couldn't be certain, for though I stared and stared and blinked repeatedly to refocus my eyes, it remained indefinite as a mirage, an ephemeral shape that might just as easily have been a reflection of my own desire; for what I wanted most to see—what any seaman wants to see—was my objective coming up right over the bows to confirm me in my navigation.

But I never had that satisfaction. It was there, I thought, for a while; then I couldn't be certain. Finally I was sure it wasn't, for by that time even the Harris hills had become blurred and indistinct.

I was conscious then of a drop in temperature. The sun had lost its warmth, the sky its brilliance, and where sky met sea, the pale, watery blue was shaded to the sepia of haze. Where I thought I had glimpsed Laerg there was soon no clear-cut horizon, only a pale blurring of the light like refraction from a shallow cloud lying on the surface of the sea.

Fog! I could feel it in my bones, and it wasn't long before I could see it. And at 13.30 Cliff Morgan confirmed my fears. After giving me a weather forecast that was much the same as before, he added: *Your greatest menace now is fog. Weather ship* India *reports visibility at eleven hundred hours fifty yards.* The B.B.C. forecast at 13.40 merely referred to *Chance of fog patches.*

I had already put on my sweaters again; now I put on my oilskin jacket. Within minutes the atmosphere had chilled and thickened. A little wind sprang up, cats' paws rippling the oily surface of the swell. One moment the hills of Harris were still there, just visible, then they were gone and the only thing in sight, besides the sea, was the tower of the Monachs lighthouse iridescent in a gleam of sun. Then that, too, vanished, and I was alone in a world where the sky seemed a sponge, the air so full of moisture that the sun scarcely percolated through it.

Half an hour later I entered the fog bank proper. It

came up on me imperceptibly at first, a slow darkening of
the atmosphere ahead, a gradual lessening of visibility.
Then, suddenly, wreathing veils of white curled smoky
tendrils round me. The cats' paws merged, became a
steady chilling breeze; little waves began to break against
the bows, throwing spray in my face, Abruptly my world
was reduced to a fifty-yard stretch of sea, a dank prison
with water-vapour walls that moved with me as I advanced, an insubstantial, yet impenetrable enclosure.

After that I had no sense of progress, and not even the
sound of the engine or the burble of the propeller's wake
astern could convince me that I was moving, for I took my
grey prison with me, captive to the inability of my eyes to
penetrate the veil of moisture that enclosed me.

Time had no meaning for me then. I nursed the engine,
watched the compass, stared into the fog, and thought of
Laerg, wondering how I was to find the entrance to the
geo—wondering, too, whether I should be able even to
locate the island in this thick wet blanket of misery that
shut out all sight. It would be night then, and the slightest
error in navigation . . .

I checked and rechecked my course constantly, the moisture dripping from my face and hands, running down the
sleeves of my oilskin jacket on to the celluloid surface of
the chart case. Tired now and cold, my limbs cramped, I
crouched listless at the helm, hearing again my grandfather's voice; stories of Laerg and his prowess on the
crags. He had claimed he was fleeter than anyone else.
Even at sixty, he said he'd been able to reach ledges no
youngster dare visit. Probably he was justified in his
claims. At the time the islanders left Laerg there were
only five men left between the ages of fifteen and twenty-
five, and remembering those long, almost ape-like arms,
those huge hands and the enormous breadth of his shoulders, I could well imagine the old devil swinging down

the face of a thousand-foot cliff, his grizzled beard glistening with the vapour that swirled about him as he sought some almost invisible ledge where the guillemots or solan geese were nesting.

In just such a fog as this he had gone down the face of the sheer cliffs on the north side of the island, below Tarsaval, lowering himself on the old horse-hair rope that had been part of his wife's dowry when they married at the turn of the century. Those cliffs were over thirteen hundred feet high, the most spectacular volcanic wall in the British Isles. He was on his own and he had missed his footing. His hands had slipped on the wet rope and he had fallen fifty feet, his foot catching in the loop at the end. They had found him hanging there head-downwards in the morning. He had been like that most of the night, a total of five hours, but though he was frozen stiff as a board and his joints had seized solid, he nevertheless managed to walk down to his cottage. He had been fifty-two years old then.

These and other stories came flooding back into my mind; how when he had married my grandmother he had had to undergo the ordeal of the Lovers' Stone. That sloped crag, jutting out high over the sea where it boiled against the base of the cliffs, had made an indelible impression on my young mind. He had told us that all bridegrooms had had to pass this test, walking out along the tilted stone to stand on the knife-edge, balanced on the balls of their feet and reaching down to touch their toes. It was a test to prove that they were competent cragsmen, men enough to support a woman on an island where the ability to collect eggs and birds from their nesting places could make the difference between a full belly and starvation in winter. "Aye, and I was fool enough to stand first on one foot and then on the other, and then put my head down and stand on my hands—just to prove I wasna scared of anything at all in the whole wide wor-rld." The old man's voice seemed to come to me again through the roar of the engine.

I was tired by then, of course, and I had the illusion that if only I could penetrate the grey curtain ahead of me, I should see the towering cliffs of Laerg rising out of the sea. At moments I even imagined there was a sudden darkening in the fog. But then I reached for the chart and a glance at it confirmed that my imagination was playing me tricks. At five o'clock the island was still almost thirty miles away. I had most of the night ahead of me before I reached it. Then, if the fog held, the first indication would not be anything seen, but the pounding of the swell at the base of the cliffs, perhaps a glint of white water.

And that was presuming my navigation was accurate.

It was just after the six o'clock weather forecast, in which the B.B.C. admitted for the first time that the whole Eastern Atlantic was enveloped in fog, that the thing I had most feared happened. There was a change in the engine note. The revolutions fell off and it began to labour. I tried it with full throttle, but it made no difference. I adjusted the choke, giving it a richer mixture, but it still continued to labour. The water-cooling outlet thinned to a trickle and finally ceased. The engine was beginning to pound as it ran hot. In the end it stopped altogether.

The sudden silence was frightening. For more than twelve hours I had had the roar of the engine in my ears to the exclusion of all other sounds. Now I could hear the slap of the waves against the flat rubberized gunnels. I could hear the little rushing hisses they made as they broke all round me. There wasn't anything of a sea running, but the swell was broken by small cross-seas. The wind was about force three, northerly, and in the stillness I could almost hear it. Other sounds were audible, too— the slop of petrol in a half-empty jerrican, the drip of moisture from my oilskins, the rattle of tins badly stowed as the dinghy wallowed with a quick, unpredictable movement.

My first thought was that the engine had run out of fuel, but I had refilled the tank less than half an hour ago, and when I checked, it was still more than half full. I thought then that it must be water in the petrol, particularly when I discovered that the jerrican I had last used was one of those that had been filled by the crofter at Carinish. Rather than empty the tank, I disconnected the fuel lead, drained the carburettor and refilled it from another jerrican; a difficult and laborious business, cramped as I was and the motion at times quite violent.

The engine started first pull and for a moment I thought I had put my finger on the trouble. But no water came out of the cooling outlet, and though it ran for a moment quite normally, the revolutions gradually fell off again, and for fear of permanent damage due to overheating, I stopped it.

I knew then that something must have gone wrong with the cooling system. The outlook was grim. I was not a mechanic and I had few spares. Moreover, the light was already failing. It would soon be dark, and to strip the engine down by the light of a torch was to ask for trouble, with the dinghy tossing about and all available space taken up with stores. The wind seemed to be rising, too; but perhaps that was my imagination.

I sat there for a long time wondering what to do—whether to start work on it now or to wait until morning. But to wait for morning was to risk a change in the weather conditions, and at least there was still light enough for me to make a start on the job. First, I had to get the engine off its bracket and into the boat. It was a big outboard, and heavy. For safety, I tied the painter round it, and then kneeling in the stern I undid the clamp and with a back-breaking twist managed to heave it on to the floor at my feet.

It was immensely heavy—far heavier than I had expected. But it wasn't until it was lying on the floor at my feet that the reasons became apparent. The propeller and all the lower part of the shaft, including the water-cooling inlet and the exhaust, was wrapped and choked with seaweed. I almost laughed aloud with relief. "You silly, bloody fool." I had begun talking to myself by then. I kept repeating: "You bloody fool!" for I remembered now that as I had sat with the earphones on, listening to the forecast, I had motored through a patch of sea that was littered with the wrack of the recent gale—dark patches of weed that produced their own calm where the sea did not break.

Cleared of weed and refastened to its bracket, the engine resumed its purposeful note and the sound of the sea was lost again. Lost, too, was that sense of fear which for a moment had made me wish Cliff Morgan had allowed less than seven days before presuming I was in trouble.

I switched on the compass light and immediately it became the focus of my eyes, a little oasis of brightness that revealed the fog as a stifling blanket composed of millions upon millions of tiny beads of moisture. All else was black darkness.

It became intensely cold. Surprisingly, I suffered from thirst. But the little water I had brought with me was stowed for'ard against an emergency—and in any case, relieving myself was a problem. I suffered from cramp, too. Both feet had gone dead long ago due to constriction of the blood circulation.

My eyes, mesmerized by the compass light, became droop-lidded and I began to nod. I was steering in a daze then, my thoughts wandering. "You'll go to Laerg, and I'll go to my grave fighting for the mucking Sassenachs." That was Iain, ages and ages ago, in a pub in Sauchiehall Street. What had made him say that, standing at that

crowded bar in his new battledress? I couldn't remember
now. But I could see him still, his dark hair tousled, a
black look on his face. He was a little drunk and swaying
slightly. Something else he'd said . . . "That bloody old
fool." And I'd known whom he meant, for the old man
had both fascinated and repelled him. "Dying of a broken
heart. If he'd had any guts he'd have stuck it out alone on
the island instead of blethering about it to the two of us."
But that wasn't what I was trying to remember. It was
something he'd said after that. He'd repeated it, as though
it were a great truth, slurring his words. "Why die where
you don't belong?" And then he'd clapped me on the back
and ordered another drink. "You're lucky," he'd said.
"You're too young." And I'd hated him, as I often did.

Or was that the next time, when he'd come swaggering
back, on leave after Dieppe? Too young! Always too
young where he was concerned! If I hadn't been too
young, I'd have taken Mavis. . . .

The engine coughed, warning that the tank was running
dry. I refilled it, still seeing Iain as I had seen him then,
cocksure and getting crazy drunk. Another pub that time,
his black eyes wild and lines already showing on his face,
boasting of the girls he'd ploughed, and me saying: "She's
going to have a baby."

"Yours or mine?" said with a jeering, friendly grin.

I came near to hitting him then. "You known damn well
whose it is."

"Och well, there's a war on and there's plenty of lassies
with bairns and no father to call them after." And he'd
laughed in my face and raised his glass. "Well, here's to
them. The country needs all they can produce the way
this bloody war is going." That was Iain, living for the moment, grabbing all he could and to hell with the consequences. He'd had quite a reputation even in that Glasgow factory, and God knows that was a tough place to get

a reputation in. Wild, they called him—wild as a young stallion with the girls rubbing round him and the drink in him talking big and angry.

And then that last evening we'd had together . . . he'd forgotten I was growing up. It had ended in a row, with him breaking a glass and threatening to cut my face to ribbons with the jagged edge of it if I didn't have another drink with him—"One for the road," he'd said. "But not the bloody road to the Isles." And he'd laughed drunkenly: "Donald, my Donald, my wee brother Donald." I'd always hated him when he'd called me that. "You've no spunk in your belly, but you'll drink with me this once to show you love me and would hate to see me die."

I'd had that last drink with him and walked with him back to his barracks. Standing there, with the sentry looking on, he'd taken hold of me by the shoulders. "I'll make a bargain wi' ye, Donald my Donald. If ye die first, which I know bloody well ye'll never do, I'll take your body to Laerg and dump it there in a cleit to be pickled by the winds. You do the same for me, eh? Then the old bastard can lie in peace, knowing there's one of the family for ever staring with sightless eyes, watching the birds copulate and produce their young and migrate and come again each year." I had promised because he was tight and because I wanted to get away and forget about not being old enough to be a soldier.

Damn him, I thought, knowing he was out there somewhere in the fog. He wouldn't be thinking of me. He'd be thinking of the last time he was in these waters—a Carley float instead of a lobster boat and men dying of exposure. All those years ago and the memory of it like a worm eating into him. Had Lane been right, making that wild accusation? Quite ruthless, Field had said. I shivered. Alone out here in the darkness, he seemed very close.

III

Island of My Ancestors

(MARCH 7)

Thinking of him, remembering moments that I'd thought obliterated from my mind, the time passed, not quickly, but unnoticed. I got the weather forecast just after midnight—wind north-westerly, force three, backing westerly and increasing to four. Fog. Cliff Morgan at 01.00 was more specific: *Fog belt very extensive, but chance of clearance your area midmorning.* The wind was westerly, force four already, and my problem remained—how to locate the island.

Between two and three in the morning I became very sleepy. I had been at the helm then for over twenty hours and it was almost impossible for me to keep my eyes open. The engine noise seemed to have a brain-deadening quality, the compass light a hypnotic, sleep-inducing effect. Every few moments I'd catch my head falling and jerk awake to find the compass card swinging. This happened so many times that I lost all confidence in my ability to steer a course, and as a result began to doubt my exact position.

It was a dangerous thing to do, but I took a pull at the

flask then. The smell of it and the raw taste of it on my
dried-up tongue, the trickle of warmth seeping down into
my bowels—I was suddenly wide awake. The time was
02.48. Was it my imagination, or was the movement less?

I picked up the chart, marked in my DR position for
03.00, and then measured off the distance still to go with a
pair of dividers. It was four and eight-tenth miles—about
an hour and a half.

I hadn't noticed it while I had been dozing, but the wind
had definitely dropped. I could, of course, already be under the lee of Laerg if my speed had been better than I'd
reckoned. But I'd no means of knowing. The fog remained
impenetrable. I switched off the compass light for a moment, but it made no difference—I was simply faced with
darkness then, a darkness so absolute that I might have
been struck blind.

With my ETA confirmed now as approximately 04.30,
I no longer seemed to have the slightest inclination to
sleep. I could easily be an hour, an hour and a half out in
my reckoning. At that very moment I might be heading
straight for a wall of rock—or straight past the island, out
into the Atlantic.

I topped up the tank so that there would be no danger of
the engine stopping at the very moment when I needed it
most, and after that I kept going. There was nothing else
I could do—just sit there, staring at the compass.

Four o'clock. Four-fifteen. And nothing to be seen,
nothing at all. If this had been a night like the last, the
bulk of Tarsaval would be standing black against the stars.
There would have been no difficulty at all then.

At four-thirty I switched off the engine and turned out
the compass light. Black darkness and the boat rocking,
and not a sound but the slop and movement of the sea.
No bird called, no beat of waves on rock. I might have
been a thousand miles from land.

I had only to sit there, of course, until the fog cleared.

But a man doesn't think that rationally when he's bobbing about in a rubber dinghy, alone in utter darkness and virtually sitting in the sea. My grandfather's voice again, telling us of fogs that had lasted a week and more. I switched on the torch and worked over my figures again, staring at the chart. Was it the tide, or an error in navigation, or just that, dozing, I had steered in circles? But even a combination of all three wouldn't produce an error of more than a few miles, and Laerg was a group of islands; it covered quite a wide area. The only answer was to cast about until I found it. The search pattern I worked out was a simple rectangular box. Fifteen minutes on my original course, then south for half an hour, east for fifteen minutes, north for an hour. At four forty-five I started the engine again, holding my course until five o'clock. Stop and listen again. Steering south then, with the grey light of dawn filtering through and the sea taking shape around me, a lumpy, confused sea, with the white of waves beginning to break.

The wind was freshening now. I could feel it on my face. At five-fifteen I stopped again to listen. The waves made little rushing sounds, and away to my left, to port, I thought I heard the surge of the swell on some obstruction—thought, too, I could discern a movement in the fog.

It was getting lighter all the time, and I sat there, the minutes ticking by, straining to listen, straining to see. My eyes played tricks, pricking with fatigue. I could have sworn the clammy curtain of the mist moved; and then I was certain as a lane opened out to starboard and the fog swirled, wreathing a pattern over the broken surface of the sea. Somewhere a gull screamed, but it was a distant, insubstantial sound—impossible to tell the direction of it.

I continued then, searching all the time the shifting, wraith-like movements of the fog. A gust of wind hit me, blattering at the surface of the sea. A down-draught? I was given no time to think that out. A sudden darkness loomed ahead. A swirling uplift of the fog, and there was rock, wet, black rock ahead of me and to port.

I pulled the helm over, feeling the undertow at the same instant that I saw the waves lazily lifting and falling against a towering crag that rose vertically like a wall to disappear in white, moving tendrils of mist. Laerg, or Fladday, or one of the stacs—or was it the western outpost reef of Vallay? In the moment of discovery I didn't care. I had made my landfall, reached my destination.

I celebrated with a drink from my flask and ate some chocolate as I motored south-west, keeping the cliff-face just in sight.

It wasn't one of the stacs, that was obvious immediately. That darkening in the fog remained too long. And then it faded suddenly, as though swallowed by the mist. I steered to port, closing it again on a course that was almost due south. The wind was in front of me, behind me, all around me; the sea very confused. Then I saw waves breaking on the top of a rock close ahead. I turned to starboard. More rock. To starboard again with rocks close to port.

A glance at the compass told me that I was in a bay, for I was steering now north-west with rock close to port. The rocks became cliffs again. Four minutes on north-west and then I had to turn west to keep those cliffs in sight. I knew where I was then. There was only one bay that would give me the courses I had steered—Strath Bay, on the north side of Laerg itself.

I checked with the survey map, just to be certain. There was nowhere else I could be. Confirmation came almost immediately with a ninety-degree turn to port as I rounded the headland that marked the northern end of Aird Mullaichean. Course south-west now and the sea steep and breaking. I hugged the cliffs just clear of the backwash and ten minutes later the movement became more violent.

I was in a tide-rip, the sound of the engine beating back

at me from hidden rock surfaces. An islet loomed, white with the stain of guano, and as I skirted it, the wind came funnelling down from the hidden heights above, strong enough to flatten the sea; and then the down-draught turned to an up-draught, sucking the fog with it, and for an instant I glimpsed a staggering sight—two rock cliffs hemming me in and towering up on either side like the walls of a canyon.

They rose stupendous to lose themselves in vapour; dark volcanic masses of gabbro rock, high as the gates of hell, reaching up into infinity. *Sheer adamantine rock.* Wasn't that how Milton had described it? But before I could re-call the exact words, I was through, spewed out by the tide, and Eileann nan Shoay had vanished astern, mist-engulfed as the fog closed in again.

I had marked the geo on the survey map, guessing at the position from the stories my grandfather told of how he had stumbled on it by accident and as a result had some-times been able to bring in lobster when the waves were so big in Shelter Bay that nobody dared put to sea. "I didna tell them, ye ken. A tur-rible thing that, in a com-munity as close as ours." And his eyes had twinkled under his shaggy brows. "Forken it was a secret and I'm telling it to ye the noo so it willna die wi' me. There'll come a day mebbe when ye'll need to know aboot that geo."

For me, that day was now. I closed in to the cliffs, the engine ticking over just fast enough to give me steerage way. South of Eileann nan Shoay, he'd said, about as far as it is from the Factor's House to the old graveyard. Meas-ured on the map, that was just over six hundred yards. The middle one of the three—he had described the other two as full of rock and very dangerous to enter.

I saw the first of the gaping holes, black with the waves slopping in the entrance. It was a huge yawning cavity. The other two were smaller and close together, like two mine adits driven into the base of the cliffs.

Geo na Cleigeann, the old man had called it. "And a tur-rible wee place it looks from the water wi' a muckle great slab hanging over it." I could hear his words still and there was the slab jutting out from the cliff face and the black gap below about as inviting as a rat hole with the sea slopping about in the mouth of it. It took me a moment to make up my mind, remembering the old devil's dour sense of humour. But this was no place to hang about with the wind whistling down off the crags above and the tide sweeping along the base of those fog-bound cliffs.

I picked up the torch, put the helm hard down and headed for the opening. A gull shied away from me and was whirled screaming up the face of the cliffs like a piece of wind-blown paper. The fog, torn by an up-draught, revealed crag upon crag towering over me. I had a fleet-ing impression of the whole great mass toppling forward; then the overhanging slab blotted it out and I was faced with the wet mouth of the cave itself, a grey gloom of rock spreading back into black darkness and reverberating to the noise of the engine.

The hole was bigger than I had first thought—about fifteen feet wide and twenty high. The westerly swell, broken on the skerries of Shoay Sgeir that jutted south from Eileann nan Shoay, caused only a mild surge. Be-hind me the geo was like a tunnel blasted in the rock, the entrance a grey glimmer of daylight.

I probed ahead with the beam of my torch, expecting every moment to see the shape of the lobster boat. I was so certain Iain must be ahead of me, and if I'd been him I thought I'd make for the geo rather than Shelter Bay. The surface of the water was black and still, lifting and falling gently; rock ahead and I cut the engine. The roof was higher here, the sides farther away. I was in a huge cavern, a sort of expansion chamber. No daylight ahead, no indication that there was a way out. The bows touched the rock and I reached out to it, gripping the wet surface with my fingers and hauling myself along.

In a westerly, with the waves rolling clean across the reef of Shoay Sgeir, this place would be a death trap. The rock round which I hauled myself had been torn from the roof, now so high that my torch could barely locate it. I probed with an oar. The water was still deep. Beyond the rock I paddled gently. The walls closed in again. The roof came down. And then the bows grounded on a steep-sloped beach, all boulders. I was ashore in the dark womb of those gabbro cliffs, and no sign of Iain.

In the tension of the last hour I had forgotten how stiff and cramped I was. When I tried to clamber out I found I couldn't move. I drank a little whisky and then began to massage my limbs. The enforced wait made me increasingly conscious of the eeriness of the place, the slop of the sea in the entrance magnified, and everywhere the drip, drip of moisture from the roof. The place reeked of the sea's salt dampness and above me God knows how many hundred feet of rock pressed down on the geo.

As soon as I was sure my legs would support me, I eased myself over the side and into the water. It was knee-deep and bitterly cold; ashore I tied the painter to a rock, and then went on up, probing with my torch, urgent now to discover the outlet to this subterranean world. It was over thirty years since my grandfather had been here; there might have been a fall, anything.

The beach sloped up at an angle of about twenty degrees, narrowing to a point where the roof seemed split by a fault. It was a rock cleft about six feet wide. The boulders were smaller here, the slope steeper. I seemed to cross a divide with mud underfoot and I slithered down into another cave to find the bottom littered with the same big rounded boulders.

It took me a little time to find the continuation of the fault, and it wasn't the fault I found first, but a rock ledge with the remains of some old lobster pots resting on a litter of rotted feathers. On the ground below the ledge was a length of flaking chain half-buried among the skeletal remains of fish. All the evidence of the old man's secret fishing, all except the boat he'd built himself and had abandoned here when he'd left with the rest of the islanders. And then, probing the farther recesses of the cavern, I saw a blackened circle of stones and the traces of a long-dead fire. Though the planking had all gone, the half-burnt remains of the stem and part of the keel were still identifiable, rotting now among a litter of charred bones.

I was too tired then, too anxious to locate the exit to the geo to concern myself about the wanton destruction of the boat, vaguely wondering who had made that fire and when, as I scrambled up the last steep slope to see a gleam of sunlight high above me. The slope was almost vertical here and slabs of stone had been let into the walls to form a primitive staircase, presumably the work of some long-dead generation of islanders.

The cleft at the top was wet and grass-choked, the crevices filled with tiny ferns; a small brown bird, a wren, went burring past me. And then I was out on a steep grass slope, out in the sunlight with the fog below me. It lay like a milk-white sea, lapping at the slopes of Strath Mhurain, writhing along the cliff-line to the north of Tarsaval, and all above was the blue of the sky—a cold, translucent blue without a single cloud. The sun had warmth and the air was scented with the smell of grass. Sheep moved, grazing on the slopes of Creag Dubh, and behind me white trails of vapour rose and fell in strange convoluted billows above the cliff-edge, where fulmars wheeled in constant flight, soaring, still-winged, on the up-draughts.

I stood there a moment filling my lungs with the freshness of the air, letting the magnificence of the scene wash over me—thanking God that my grandfather hadn't lied, that the exit from the geo had remained intact. I thought it likely now that Iain had landed in Shelter Bay, and because I was afraid the fog might clamp down at any moment, I stripped off my oilskins and started out across the island. I crossed the top of Strath Mhurain, skirting black edges of peat bog, and climbed to the Druim Ridge with the sun-warm hills standing islanded in fog and the only sound the incessant wailing of the birds.

From the Druim Ridge I looked down into the great horseshoe of Shelter Bay. The Military High Road was just below me, snaking down into the fog. To my left Creag Dubh, with the pill-box shape of the Army's lookout, rising to Tarsaval; dark scree slopes falling to the dotted shapes of cleits and, beyond, the long ridge of Malesgair vanishing into the milk-white void. To my right the High Road spur running out towards the Butt or Keava, the rocky spine of the hills piercing the fog bank like a jagged reef. It was a strange, eerie scene, with the surge of the swell on the storm beach coming faint on puffs of air; something else, too—the sound of an engine, I thought. But then it was gone and I couldn't be sure.

I hurried on then, following the road down into the fog, iridescent at first but thickening as I descended until it was a grey blanket choked with moisture. Without the road to follow, the descent would have been dangerous, for the fog was banked thick in the confines of the hills and visibility reduced to a few yards. It lifted a little as the road flattened out behind the beach. I could see the swell breaking and beyond the lazy beds the outline of the first ruined cottage, everything vague, blurred by the dankness of the atmosphere. And then a voice calling stopped me in my tracks. It came again, disembodied, weird and insubstantial. Other voices answered, the words unintelligible.

I stood listening, all my senses alert, intent on piercing the barrier of the fog. Silence and the only sounds the surge of the waves, the cries of the gulls. Somewhere a

raven croaked, but I couldn't see it. Ahead of me was the
dim outline of the bridge. And then voices again, talking
quietly, the sound oddly magnified. The fog swirled to a
movement of air from the heights. I glimpsed the ruins
of the old jetty and a boat drawn up on the beach. Two
figures stood beside it, two men talking in a foreign
tongue, and out beyond the break of the waves I thought
I saw the dark shape of a ship; a trawler by the look of it.
Two more figures joined the men by the boat. The fog
came down again and I was left with only the sound of
their voices. I went back then, for I was cold and tired
and I'd no desire to make contact with the crew of a foreign trawler. Looting probably, and if Iain had landed
in Shelter Bay he'd have hidden himself away in one of
the cleits or among the ruins of the Old Village. Wearily
I climbed the hairpin bends, back up to the Druim Ridge
and the sunlight, nothing to do now but go back down
into the bowels of that geo and bring up my gear. My
mouth was dry and I drank from a trickle of peat water at
the head of Strath Mhurain.

And then I was back on the slopes of Aird Mullaichean,
walking in a daze, my mind facing again the mystery of
that fire, conscious of a growing sense of uneasiness as I
approached the rock outcrop that marked the entrance to
that dark, subterranean fault. Had the crew of some
trawler rowed into the geo and made a fire of the boat just
for the hell of it? But that didn't explain the bones, unless they'd killed a sheep and roasted it. And to burn the
boat. . . . On Laerg itself and all through the islands of
the Hebrides boats were sacrosanct. No man would borrow so much as an oar without permission.

I picked up my torch and started back down the slabbed
stairway. Darkness closed me in. The dank cold of it
chilled the sweat on my body. I tried to tell myself it was
only the strangeness of the place, my solitary stumbling in
the black darkness, and the cavernous sound of the sea

that made me so uneasy. But who would come into that geo if he hadn't been told about it? Who would have known there was a boat there, firewood to burn? I was shivering then, and coming to the cave where the boat had been, I was suddenly reluctant, filled with a dreadful certainty. Twenty-two days. I'd had only a night at sea, a single cold night with little wind. But I knew what it was like now—knew that he couldn't possibly have survived . . . And then I was into the cave, my gaze half-fascinated, half-appalled, following the beam of my torch, knowing what I was going to find.

Down on my knees, I reached out my hand to the bones, touched one, plucked it from the blackened heap with a feeling of sick revulsion as I recognized what it was. The end of the bone disintegrated into dust, leaving me with a knee joint in my hand. I poked around—a hip bone, femurs, pieces of the spinal column, the knuckles of human fingers. It was all there, all except the head, and that I found tucked away under a slab of rock—a human skull untouched by the fire and with traces of hair still attached.

I put it back and sat for a moment, feeling numbed; but not shocked or even disgusted, now that I knew. It had to be something like this. I was thinking how it must have been for him, his life soured by what had happened here, the prospect of discovery always hanging over him. And then automatically, almost without thinking, I stripped my anarak off and began to pile the grim relics of that wartime voyage on to it. There was more than the bones—buttons like rusted coins, the melted bronze of a Unit badge, a wrist watch barely recognizable, all the durable bits and pieces that made up a soldier's personal belongings. And among it all an identity disc—the number and the name still visible; ROSS, I. A.—Presb.

A pebble rattled in the darkness behind me and I turned. But there was nothing, only the swell sloshing about in the great cavern of the geo, a faint, hollow sound coming to me from beyond the narrow defile of the fault. The last thing I did was to scatter the blackened stones about the cave, flinging them from me. Then, the pieces of wood bundled into my anarak, the last traces removed, I scrambled to my feet and picking up my burden started for the faulted exit that led to the geo.

I was halfway up the slope to it when the beam of my torch found him. He was standing by the exit, quite still, watching me. His face was grey, grey like the rock against which he leaned. His dark eyes gleamed in the torch beam. I stopped and we stood facing each other, neither saying a word. I remember looking to see if he were armed, thinking that if he'd killed Braddock . . . But he'd no weapon of any kind; he was empty-handed, wearing an old raincoat and shivering uncontrollably. The sound of water in the geo was louder here, but even so I could hear his teeth chattering. "Are you all right?" I said.

"Cold, that's all." He took a stiff step forward, reaching down with his hand. "Give me that. I'll do my own dirty work, thank you." He took the bundled anarak from me.

"Who was it?" I asked. "Braddock?" My voice came in a whisper, unnatural in that place.

"Give me the torch, will you."

But I'd stepped back. "Who was it?" I repeated.

"Man named Piper, if you must know."

"Then it wasn't Braddock?"

"Braddock? No—why?" He laughed; or rather he made a noise that sounded like a laugh. "Did you think I'd killed him? Is that it?" His voice was hoarse, coming jerky through the chattering of his teeth. "Braddock died two days before we sighted Laerg." And he added: "You bloody fool, Donald. You should know me better than that." And then, his voice still matter-of-fact: "If you won't give me the torch, just shine it through here."

I did as he asked and he went through the narrow defile

in the rock, down the slope beyond into the geo, hugging the bundle to him. The falling tide had left my dinghy high and dry. The bows of his boat were grounded just astern of it. There were sails, mast, and oars in it, two rusted fuel cans, some old lobster pots; but no clothing, not even oilskins. "Got anything to drink with you?" he asked as he dumped the bundle.

I gave him my flask. His hands were shaking as he un-screwed the cap, and then he tipped his head back, suck-ing the liquor down. "How long had you been there?" I asked.

"Not long." He finished the whisky, screwed the cap back in place, and handed me the empty flask. "Thanks. I needed that."

"Were you watching me all the time?"

"Yes. I was coming through the fault when I saw the light of your torch. Luckily it shone on your face; other-wise . . ." Again that laugh that had no vestige of hu-mour in it. "You reach a certain point . . . You don't care then." He waded into the water, swung a leg over the side of the boat, and clambered wearily in. "You wait there. I'll be back in a moment. Deep water . . . if I'd been able to do this at the time . . ." He swung the engine and it started at once, the soft beat of it pulsing against the walls. He pushed the gear lever into reverse. The engine revved and the bows grated and then he was off the beach and reversing slowly, back down that geo towards the grey light of the entrance. He backed right out and then dis-appeared, and I stood there in the half-darkness of the cavern's gloom, wondering whether he'd come back and if he did what would happen then. Did he trust me? Or did he think I was like the rest of the world—against him? My own brother, and I wasn't sure; wasn't sure what he'd do, what was going on in that strange, confused mind of his—wasn't even sure whether he was sane or mad.

And all the time the drip, drip of moisture from the

roof, the slop of water never still as the swell moved gently against the rock walls.

The beat of the engine again and then the boat's bows nosing into the gap below that hanging slab. It came in, black against the daylight, with him standing in the stern, a dark silhouette, his hand on the tiller. The bows grated astern of my dinghy and he clambered out, bringing the painter with him. "Is the tide still falling?" he asked.

"For another two hours."

He nodded, tying the rope to a rock. "No tide table, no charts, nothing in the lockers, and bloody cold." He straightened up, looking down at the rubber dinghy. "How did you make out in that thing—all right?" And then he was moving towards me, his eyes fixed on my face. "Why?" he demanded hoarsely. "Why did you come here?"

"I knew you were headed for Laerg." I had backed away from him.

"Did you know why?"

"No."

"But you guessed, is that it?" He had stopped, standing motionless, his eyes still on me.

"How could I?" I was feeling uneasy now, a little scared, conscious of the strength of that thick-set body, the long arms. Standing like that, dark in silhouette, he reminded me of my grandfather—and the same crazy recklessness, the same ruthless determination. "I just knew there was something, knew you had to come back." And I added: "Twenty-two days is a long time. . . ."

"Yes, too long." He seemed to relax then. He was looking about the cavern now and I could see his mind was back in the past. "Thirteen days it took us. And then in the dawn I saw Tarsaval. God! I thought I'd never seen anything more beautiful." He glanced about him, moving his head slowly from side to side, savouring the familiarity. "This place—brings it back to me. We were five days . . . Yes, five, I think."

"In here?"

He nodded, handing me back by anarak, empty now.

"How many of you?"

"Just the two of us—Leroux and myself. Alive. The other—he died during the night. We were grounded, you see. On one of the rocks of Eileann nan Shoay, out there. Hadn't the strength to get her off. It was heavy, that raft. The tide did that, sometime during the night, and when the dawn came we were right under the cliffs. That dawn —there was a little breeze from the nor'east. Cold as ice, and the stars frozen like icicles fading to the dawn sky— pale blue and full of mares' tails. We paddled along the cliffs. Just got in here in time. The wind came out of the north. I'd never have stood that wind. We were frozen as it was, frozen stiff as boards, no heat in us—none at all. We hadn't fed for six days, a week maybe—I don't know. I'd lost count by then." He turned his head. "What made you come?" he asked again.

I shrugged. I didn't really know myself. "You were in trouble. . . ."

He laughed. But again there was no humour in that laugh. "Been in trouble all my life, it seems. And now I'm too old," he added, "to start again. But I had to come back. I didn't want anybody to know—about that." And he added: "Not even you, Donald. I'd rather you hadn't known."

I stared at him, wondering how much was remorse, how much pride and the fear of discovery. "Did you have to do it?" I shouldn't have asked that, but it was out before I could stop myself, and he turned on me then in a blaze of fury.

"Have to? What would you have done? Died like Leroux, I suppose? Poor little sod. He was a Catholic. I suppose if

you're a Catholic . . ." He shook his head. "Christ, man
—the chance of life and the man dead. What did it matter?
Lie down and die. I'm a fighter. Always have been. To die
when there was a chance. . . . That isn't right. Not right
at all. If everybody lay down and died when things got
tough—that isn't the way man conquered his world. I did
what any man with guts would have done—any man not
hide-bound by convention; I had no scruples about it. Why
the hell should I? And there was the boat—fuel for a fire
ready to hand. I'll be honest. I couldn't have done it otherwise. But life, man—life beckoning. . . . And that poor
fellow Leroux. We argued about it all through the night,
there in the cave with the wind whistling through that
fault. God in heaven, it was cold—until I lit that fire." He
stopped then, shivering under that thin raincoat. "Colder
than last night. Colder than anything you can imagine.
Cold as hell itself. Why do they always picture hell as flaming with heat? To me it's a cold place. Cold as this godforsaken geo." He moved, came a step nearer. "Was the old
man right? Is there a way out of here?"

"Yes," I said. "If you'd only tried. . . ." I was thinking of the sheep that roamed the island wild. "Didn't you
try?"

"How could I? We only just had strength to crawl
through to that cave. We were dead, man—both of us as
near dead as makes no odds. You don't understand. When
the ship went down . . . I wasn't going to have anything
to do with the boats, I'd an escort. Did you know that? I was
being brought back under escort. I saw those two damned
policemen make bloody sure they got into a boat. They
weren't worrying about me then. They were thinking of
their own skins. I saw this Carley float hanging there, nobody doing anything about it. So I cut it adrift and jumped.
Others joined me just before she sank. It was late afternoon and the sun setting, a great ball. And then she went,
very suddenly, the boilers bursting in great bubbles. There

were seven besides myself." He paused then, and I didn't say anything. I didn't want to interrupt him. Nobody to confide in, nobody to share the horror of it with him; it had been bottled up inside him too long. But he was looking about the place again and I had a feeling that he had slipped away from me, his mind gone back to his memories. And then suddenly: "You say the way out is still there —you've been up to the top, have you?"

"Yes."

"Well, let's get out of here. Up into the fresh air." He started to move up the beach towards the fault, and then he paused. "What's it like up there? Fog, I suppose."

"No, it's above the fog. The sun's shining."

"The sun?" He was staring at me as though he didn't believe me. "The sun. Yes, I'd like to see the sun . . . for a little longer." I can't describe the tone in which he said that, but it was sad, full of a strange sadness. And I had a feeling then—that he'd reached the end of the road. I had that feeling very strongly as I followed him up the slope and through the fault, as though he were a man condemned. "Give me the torch a minute." His hand was on it and I let him have it. For a moment he stood there, playing the beam of it on that recess, standing quite still and searching the spot with his eyes. "Thanks," he said. "I couldn't bear to go, you see, with the thought that somebody would find that. It wouldn't have mattered—not so much—if I hadn't changed my identity. But taking Braddock's name . . . They'd think I'd killed the poor bastard. Whereas, in fact, I saved his life. Pulled him out of the water with his right arm ripped to pieces. Managed to fix a tourniquet. He was tough, that boy. Lasted longer than most of the others despite the blood he'd lost. Do you know, Donald—I hadn't thought of it. But when he was dying, that last night—he was in my arms, like a child, and I was trying to keep him warm. Though God knows there wasn't much warmth in me by then. The other two, they

were lying frozen in a coma, and young Braddock, whispering to me—using up the last of his breath. You're about
my build, Iain, he said. And his good arm fumbling at his
pockets, he gave me his pay book, all his personal things,
and the identity disc from round his neck, and all the time
whispering to me the story of his life—everything I'd need
to know." The beam of the torch was still fastened on the
recess and after a moment he said: "When a man does that
—gives you a fresh start; and he'd got such guts, never com-
plaining, not like some of the others, and none of them
with so much as a scratch. Hell! You can't just pack it in.
Not after that." And then he turned to me suddenly.
"Here. Take the torch. You lead the way and let's go up
into the light of day." But instead of moving aside, he
reached out and gripped my shoulders. "So long as you
understand. Do you understand?" But then he released
me and stepped back. "Never mind. It doesn't matter. It's
finished now." And he gave me a gentle, almost affection-
ate push towards the cave's exit. "We'll sit in the sun and
listen to the birds. Forget the years that are gone. Just
think of the old man and the way it was before he died.
The island hasn't changed, has it? It still looks the way he
described it to us?"

"Yes," I said. "It looks very beautiful." And I climbed
up through the continuation of the fault, up the slabbed
stairway and out through the final cleft into the sunlight.
The fog had thinned, so that it no longer looked like a sea
below us but more like the smoke of some great bush fire.
It was in long streamers now, its tendrils lying against the
lower slopes, fingering the rock outcrops, turning the
whole world below us a dazzling white. Iain stood quite still
for a moment, drinking it in, savouring the beauty of the
scene just as I had done. But his eyes were questing all the
time, searching the slopes of the hills and seaward where
the rents in the fog were opening up to give a glimpse of
the Atlantic heaving gently to the endless swell. The sun-

light accentuated the greyness of his face, the lines cut deep by fatigue. He looked old beyond his years, the black hair greying and his shoulders stooped. As though conscious of my gaze, he pulled himself erect. "We'll walk," he said gruffly. "Some exercise—do us good." And he started off towards the head of Strath Mhurain, not looking back to see if I were following him. He didn't talk and he kept just ahead of me as though he didn't want me to see the look on his face.

At the top of the Druim Ridge he paused, looking down into Shelter Bay, where the fog was still thick. And when I joined him, he turned and started up the High Road, heading for the lookout. He went fast, his head bent forward, and he didn't stop until he'd reached the top of Creag Dubh. Then he flung himself down on the grass, choosing the south-facing slope, so that when the fog cleared he'd be able to see down into Shelter Bay. "Got a cigarette on you?" he asked.

I gave him one and he lit it, his hands steadier now. He smoked in silence for a while, drawing the smoke deep into his lungs, his head turned to feel the warmth of the sun, his eyes half-closed. "Do you think they'll have guessed where I was going in that boat?" he asked suddenly.

"I don't know," I said. "Probably."

He nodded. "Well, if they have, they'll send a helicopter as soon as the fog clears. Or will they come in a ship?" I didn't answer and he said: "It doesn't matter. From here you'll be able to watch them arrive."

"And then?" I asked.

"Then . . ." He left the future hanging in the air. He was watching two sheep that had suddenly materialized on an outcrop below us. They were small and neatly balanced, with shaggy fleece and long, curved horns. "It would be nice, wouldn't it," he said, lying back with his eyes closed, "if one could transform oneself—into a sheep, for instance, or better still, a bird." Startled by his voice, the sheep moved with incredible speed and agility, leaping sure-footed down the ledges of that outcrop and disappearing from view.

"You've nothing to worry about—now," I said.

"No?" He raised himself on one elbow, staring at me. "You think I should go back, do you? Tell them I'm not Braddock at all, but Sergeant Ross who deserted in North Africa. Christ! Go through all that." He smiled, a sad, weary smile that didn't touch his eyes. "Funny, isn't it—how the pattern repeats itself? Lieutenant Moore, Colonel Standing. . . . I wonder if that little bastard Moore is still alive. Ten to one, he is and ready to swear he gave the only order he could. Probably believes it by now. No," he said, "I'm not going back to face that."

He was silent then, lying there, smoking his cigarette—smoking it slowly, his face, his whole body relaxed now. I thought how strange the human mind is, blank one moment and now remembering every detail. The sun, shining down into the horseshoe curve of Shelter Bay, was eating up the fog. The whole world below us was a blinding glare. And high in the brilliant sky above, an eagle rode, a towering speck turning in quiet circles. "Well . . ." He shifted and sat up. "I'll leave you now." He looked around him, turning his head slowly, taking in the whole panorama of the heights. "God! It's so beautiful." He said it softly, to himself. Then, with a quick, decisive movement, he got to his feet. I started to rise, but he placed his hand on my shoulder, holding me there. "No. You stay here. Stay here till they come, and then tell them . . . tell them what you damn well like." He dropped his cigarette and put his heel on it. "You needn't worry about me any more."

"Where are you going?" I asked.

But he didn't answer. He was staring down into the bay where the fog had thinned to white streamers with glimpses of the sea between. "What's that? I thought I saw a ship down there."

"I think it's a trawler," I said.

"Are you sure it isn't . . ."

"No," I said. "It's a foreign trawler." And I told him how I'd been down into the bay and heard the crew talking in a language I couldn't recognize.

He stood for a moment, staring down into the bay. The streamers of the fog were moving to a sea breeze and through a gap I caught a glimpse of the vessel lying at anchor with a boat alongside.

"Yes. A foreigner by the look of her." Another rent and the view clearer. I could see men moving about her decks and a lot of radar gear on her upper works. And then his hand gripped my shoulder. "Donald my Donald," he said, and the way he said it took me back. "Thanks for coming —for all your help. Something to take with me. I'd rather be Iain Ross, you know, and have a brother like you, than stay friendless as George Braddock." And with a final pat he turned and left me, walking quickly down the Druim Ridge.

I watched him until he disappeared below the ridge, not moving from my seat because there wasn't any point. A little later he came into sight again crossing the top of Strath Mhurain, walking along the slopes of Aird Mullai-chean until he reached the outcrop. He paused for a moment, a small, distant figure standing motionless. And then he was gone, and I sat there, seeing him still in my mind going down that subterranean fault, back to the geo and the waiting lobster boat. The bright sunlight and the warm scent of the grass, the distant clamour of the birds and that eagle still wheeling high in the vaulted blue; the whole world around me full of the breath of life, and I just sat there wishing I could have done something, and knowing in my heart there was nothing I could have done.

I watched the fog clear and the trawler lift her boat into its davits. She got her anchor up then and steamed out of the bay. She was flying a red flag, and as it streamed to the

wind of her passage, I thought I could make out the hammer and sickle on it. She rounded Sgeir Mhor, turned westward, and disappeared behind the brown bulk of Keava.
And later, perhaps an hour later—I had lost all track of
time—a helicopter came in and landed on the flat green-
sward near the Factor's House. Men in khaki tumbled out,
spread into a line, and moved towards the camp. I got up
then and started down to meet them, sad now and walking
slowly, for I'd nothing to tell them—only that my brother
was dead.

They found the lobster boat two days later. A trawler
picked her up, empty and abandoned, about eight miles
north-east of Laerg. Nobody doubted what had happened.
And in reporting it, there was no reference to my brother.
It was Major George Braddock who was dead, and I think
it was the story I told them of what had really happened in
North Africa that caused the various officers concerned,
right up to the DRA, to be so frank in their answers to my
questions. And now it is March again here on Laerg, the
winter over and the birds back, my solitary vigil almost
ended. Tomorrow the boat comes to take me back to Rodil.

I finished writing my brother's story almost a week ago.
Every day since then I have been out painting, chiefly on
Keava. And sitting up there all alone, the sun shining and
spring in the air, the nesting season just begun—everything so like it was that last day when we were together on
Creag Dubh—I have been wondering. A man like that, so
full of a restless, boundless energy, and that trawler lying
in the bay. Was he really too old to start his life again—in
another country, among different people?

A Note about the Author

Hammond Innes, born in England in 1913, wrote his first book at the age of nineteen. A journalist before the Second World War and an army officer during it, he has become an increasingly success- ful novelist since the publication in 1952 of Air Bridge, *a novel that dealt with the Berlin airlift. Next came* Campbell's Kingdom, *with a background of the oil boom in Canada.* The Naked Land *was set in French Morocco. A return to England, France, and the seas between in- spired* The Wreck of the Mary Deare, *probably Innes's most widely read book thus far. Follow- ing this came* The Land God Gave to Cain, *the result of two trips he made to Labrador. Readers of his next book, the non-fiction narrative of his travels entitled* Harvest of Journeys, *will recall the vivid section on Arabia and the Persian Gulf. These provide the setting for* The Doomed Oasis, *which followed.*

A Note on the Type

The text of this book has been set on the Lino-type in a type face called Baskerville. The face is a facsimile reproduction of types cast from molds made for John Baskerville (1706–75) from his designs. The punches for the revised Linotype Baskerville were cut under the super-vision of the English printer George W. Jones. John Baskerville's original face was one of the forerunners of the type-style known as "modern face" to printers—a "modern" of the period A.D. *1800.*

This book was printed and bound by
The Haddon Craftsmen, Inc., Scranton, Pa.